THE TRICKSTER

MURIEL GRAY

The Trickster

HarperCollins*Publishers*

HarperCollins*Publishers*
77–85 Fulham Palace Road,
Hammersmith, London w6 8jb

Published by HarperCollins*Publishers* 1994
1 3 5 7 9 8 6 4 2

A catalogue record for this book is
available from the British Library

ISBN 0 00 224326 1

Set in Baskerville by
Rowland Phototypesetting Ltd
Bury St Edmunds, Suffolk

Printed in Great Britain by
HarperCollinsManufacturing Glasgow

For
Hamish MacVinish Barbour
and Hector Adam Barbour.
With love.

Acknowledgements

My thanks are due to these:

Hamish – the ideas bank that is constantly robbed, yet never calls the police. Jane Anne Purdy for her uncomplaining research. Michael Fishwick, Jane Johnson, and Bruce Hyman for their support. Paul Morris. Co-Co Powderface. The Banff detachment of the Royal Canadian Mounted Police. The 'snakes' at the Canadian Pacific freight yard; Golden, for the ride up front. Nora Webber, Rocky Mountaineer, for the trip through some tunnels. Dr Isabelle Cullen for being pedantic. M & J Barbour for Grianan. And Betty, Adam and Fraser Gray for lots.

1

Alberta 1907
Siding Twenty-three

When he screamed, his lips slid so far up his teeth that the rarely exposed gum looked like shiny, flayed meat. Hunting Wolf's eyes flicked open and stared. There was a semi-circle of faces above him. Silent. Watching.

For a moment he stayed perfectly still, allowing himself to regain the feeling of being inside his body, that dull ache of reality after the lightness of the spirit's escape. Then the numbing cold of the snow beneath his naked back stabbed at his skin, and mocked him with the knowledge that he was firmly back in the realm of the flesh.

Sweat was still trickling down his breast, beads of moisture clinging to his brown nipples like decoration, and he stared up at the grey, snow-laden sky in hot despair.

The faces looked on. They would not step forward to touch him or help him in this state. The shaman's trance was sacred and they had no way of knowing when it would be over.

But it was over, now. He had looked into the thing's face. Oh, Great Spirit, he had. And the filthy darkness, the bottomless malice he had seen there, had been nearly impossible to bear.

The white men gathered by the mountain were insane. He had seen that, too. Their madness, their folly.

And what could he do?

The shaman got up from the ground with a swiftness that surprised his audience of watchers, and walked away. The faces regarded him for a moment, and then, one by one, followed.

2

'The living rock.'

If Wesley Martell had caught the look his engineer threw him, he might have regretted the remark. As it was, he shifted his huge bulk in the conductor's chair, leant a flabby arm, its hand dimpled like a baby's, on the sill of the cab window and said it again.

'Yes indeed. Liiiviiing rock.'

Joshua Tennent, to whom the remark was principally addressed, returned his gaze to the track in front of them, his forefinger caressing the throttle handle as though it could make toast of his corpulent colleague. As the mouth of the first tunnel slid into view from behind a cliff crusted by aquamarine ice, Joshua felt panic mash his guts again.

How many times had he done this, for Christ's sake? He'd pulled freight back and forwards through the Corkscrew Tunnel for nearly three years, and just because of one foolish, possibly imagined incident, he found himself nearly caking his shorts like a toddler every time that black arch yawned in front of him.

He'd guessed Martell would have a go, could tell by the way he had shifted eagerly in his seat as they'd climbed up the approach to Wolf Mountain. Joshua had hoped the lump of lard would doze illegally until they reached Silver, but he'd been alert and beady-eyed for miles. Those two serpentine tubes of blackness lay between them and town, and the conductor wasn't in the mood for regulation-breaking sleep.

Joshua thought it best to ignore the bastard. Martell wasn't the first to twist the knife and he wouldn't be the last. Concentrating on smothering his fear was labour enough for now.

3

The conductor peeked across at his white-faced engineer, as he slapped the shoulder of the third occupant of the cab, a sullen brakeman called Henry. He gesticulated grandly towards Joshua, his two rodent-like eyes narrowing into slits of mirth.

'Look, Henry. Hoghead's got the jimmy-shits again 'bout goin' through the Corkscrews.'

The brakeman disregarded both the slap and the remark, answering only with a barely perceptible upward movement of his head, the reverse of a nod. Martell was undeterred. This shift had bored the balls off him, with the brakeman sitting motionless and silent in front of him, his big ears sticking out like one of those Easter Island heads Martell had seen in a magazine once. And this damn engineer had no conversation either. Wasn't much to ask that a man could expect a bit of parley at his work, instead of watching speechless as three hundred miles of Canadian Pacific track snaked beneath them in the snow.

There was nearly a mile of train behind them. Being in charge of a hundred cars of coal rumbling slowly across Canada meant big-time responsibility to Wesley Martell. He often pictured how his train looked from the air, a giant metal caterpillar picking its way through the mountains, the engine like the insect's head, and himself, C.P. conductor, Martell, the brains in that head. This mile of hardware stopped, started or stayed at his say-so, and that made him feel good; made him more of a man than those jockeys braying into portable phones you saw on the sidewalks in Vancouver. No kid was ever going to look at those guys with big, wide, jealous eyes when they went about their business, least not the way they looked up at him in his cab, when he hi-balled his monster load through a station waving down at them like an oily Father Christmas.

But Martell didn't get to be conductor, the big cheese on this buggy, without expecting a crumb of respect from his crew. Part of that respect was the civility to pass the time, jaw a little.

Seemed like this crew didn't know the meaning of the word respect, sitting there like two dumb fucks, lost in their own dumb thoughts.

Wesley Martell didn't much like to be left alone with his thoughts: too much track gazing and those thoughts had the habit of chucking up things he'd rather not meet again, thanks. Especially on a night haul, when the lights of the train illuminated a few yards of the track ahead, making it dance and gyrate on the edge of darkness like

4

something alive. No, he'd rather talk. Talk was life. Silence was a kind of death, and he'd had enough silence on this journey.

Ten miles back Henry had said something to Joshua that Martell didn't catch, and apart from that, nothing. Not a sound except the clacking of the wheels on the track and the throaty roar of the engine. So when the Corkscrew Tunnel rolled round, Martell took his shot.

Back at the depot, Joshua and his tunnels were the butt of an endless running joke amongst the local crews, and Martell was damned if he wasn't going to use anything he could to get a little spark into this seven-hour bitch of a shift.

Joshua was still, quiet, and white. He had it coming.

'Best keep a hand on that throttle, engineer. Think I saw something movin' in there.' He threw his head back and wheezed out a guffaw.

He laughed alone, but Henry turned his head slightly towards Martell before returning to gaze vacantly out of the window.

Joshua could feel his hands turning clammy. It wasn't hard to ignore the fat guy. Ever since he'd confided in some brakemen from Toronto what had happened to him that day in the Tunnel, he'd taken a ribbing that was now so obligatory it had practically entered the Canadian Railway Operating Rules Book.

What was hard, and getting harder every time they came through, was trying to resist jamming the dynamic brake handle on and jumping out of the train cab into the snow, before the three men and those hundred cars of grade one coal were launched into the gaping black mouth.

Funny to think that right now, on the wooden viewing platform up on the highway, tourists would be yelping to each other like excited coyotes, at spotting a freight train about to go through the famous tunnels. It was a Kodak-moment, all right: with a train as long as this one, the onlookers would see the engine disappear into the first tunnel, then double back on itself, only to appear to be travelling in the opposite direction to its freight before entering the second tunnel. There was a big painted illustration up on that platform for the real dumb tourists, the ones who stumbled out of a Winnebago and couldn't figure out where they were, never mind what they were seeing.

Joshua had stopped on the highway once to look at the sign. It told him in kiddie-speak letters that they had blasted into the mountain ninety years ago, using the spiral design to avoid a wicked

5

gradient through Wolf Pass. There were shitty pencil drawings of pioneers with big hats and moustaches, and a lot of bull about the early days of railway, but at least there was a diagram of how the tunnels worked inside the mountain. That was neat. You could see exactly how the Corkscrew worked, how it quartered the gradient with those two curly holes in the hill. Joshua had never thought about it much before then, and he didn't think about it much after either. That is, until he had his fright.

It didn't matter how many times he went over it in his head. He'd lain awake at nights in the C.P. bunkhouses and at home in Stoke, trying to figure out why he'd gotten scared. Worst thing was, it was a whole year ago, almost exactly this time last winter, and the scare hadn't worn off.

Martell could go shaft himself. Joshua would tolerate all the fat fingers in the world poking him in the ribs, if he could just shake free of this paralyzing, childish fear. He began to run through it again, the way he did every time they passed this way, trying to flush the memory away, make it safe.

The way he remembered it, they'd come through the lower tunnel, the engine just entering the second, when the End-to-Train unit had gone apeshit. There was a hot box back there and nothing for it but to stop. With the gradient they had to negotiate coming up before the higher tunnel, the last thing they needed was a car with screaming white-hot axles dragging behind them. Joshua recalled whistling through his teeth with exasperation as the whole damn hulk screeched to a halt and conductor and brakeman got up from their chairs and stretched their legs.

The boxes had stopped out there in the gorge, sitting in the thin wintry sunlight, leaving the cab of the engine about fifty yards into the tunnel, and Joshua knew he had to get back there and investigate. Barney the brakeman handed Joshua a thick black rubber torch with one hand and put the kettle on the hot plate with the other, saying clearly without words that the engineer would have their assistance when they were good and ready.

It was the delay that had pissed off Joshua. Just the time it was going to take to check it all out and put it right. It had been his homeward shift, taking him back to Beat River and Mary's bed, a heavenly prospect after five nights in the bunkhouses, lying beside guys in their pits, snoring like they were sawing logs. He remembered thinking two things. The first was that at least it was lucky the cars had stopped outside the tunnel, and the second thought, like it had come from nowhere, was 'the living rock'. Three innocent words, just sitting there doing nothing, going nowhere, meaning little. But there.

He took the torch and saluted sarcastically to Barney as he opened the cab door and left.

As he climbed down out of the huge red DRF30, Joshua touched the hand rail with an ungloved hand. Cold metal that has just rolled through the passes between the Alberta Rockies in minus twenty is not welcoming to naked flesh, and Joshua's fingers stuck fast, forcing him to breathe on them to release his hand. It stung like crazy as it relinquished his grip and he sheathed it with a curse in a leather work gauntlet.

It was the only time he'd ever stopped in the tunnels, and yes, compared to the cement-lined tunnels that ran under the highways on the east coast, the rock was alive all right. So much for "a feat of grand engineering". Seemed like the guys had just blasted the sucker and left. The walls and ceiling surprised him with their unhewn crudity, something he had never perceived by the weak light of the cab as they'd passed through here a hundred times. Ice hung from every crack in thin savage spikes and sporadically coated the rock-face with vast, glistening bulbous sheets.

And everything was dark ahead of the engine. Really dark. The curve of the tunnel meant that you could only ever see one entrance at a time. In fact, there was a point, right in the middle of the tunnel's arc, where you couldn't see any light at all; but he didn't care to think of that right now. His breath billowed up in front of his face like steam, partially obscuring his view of the sunlit opening ahead each time he exhaled.

He should have been thinking about how they were going to get to the maintenance yard forty kilometres away without too much damage or time loss: he should have been thinking like an engineer. But he wasn't. All he could hear, echoing in his head as though his skull were a tunnel, were the words, *the living rock, the living rock.*

He hadn't needed the torch for the first few yards, the walls being lit by the cab interior, but by the time he drew level with the first car, Joshua had to use it, picking his way along the track trying not to pratfall over the sleepers half-buried in gravel. The arch of sunlight was clear ahead, its illumination extending barely a few feet into the dark, and already he was starting to regret he hadn't insisted that Barney come with him. He touched the walkie-talkie hanging on his hip, annoyed that it hadn't crackled into life. Clearly his two crew companions were treating this like a break instead of a breakdown. He was tempted to press 'talk' and shout *horse's ass* at them as he passed the second car just to remind them he was there, but realized grimly that it wasn't irritation making him keen to summon them, but apprehension. His hand left the radio, unclipped the ear flaps on his cap and let them fall. Joshua Tennent was suddenly very cold.

It wasn't so much a noise he heard, more the feeling of a noise. That is, he sensed there was something scraping in the rock above him. Not scraping on the surface, like a bat or a chipmunk, but scraping inside the rock as if the stone itself was shifting, turning in its sleep.

But he didn't hear it. He felt it. The tunnel was not silent: the idling engine hissed and clanked, dripped and cracked at random as he progressed along its metal flanks. Any rustling in the tunnel would have to work hard to make itself heard above the cacophony.

Even now, he still couldn't say which sense was being alerted, but the memory of the feeling was pungent.

At first he ignored it. How could you feel a noise? Walking on, he realized that he hadn't breathed for about six or seven seconds and corrected the oversight with a cloud of vapour. He struggled to free his body from that atavistic state of standby every child adopts in the darkened bedroom when they hear a creak from a floorboard; breath held, eyes wide open, body still and ready to flee. But why was he on red alert? There was nothing to fear in this situation, except the diminishing drinking time in Stoke, and the wrath of Mary, who even now would be soaking in a bath reeking of something made from coconut or peach.

He felt it again. It was above him, he was sure of that. Something stirring in the rock above the ceiling. But no, that wasn't right. It was the rock in the ceiling itself that was stirring, moving above him like iron filings attracted to his magnet.

Joshua wanted to run then. He wanted to run very badly indeed. But from what? There was no sound, for God's sake, nothing to hear but the train. If he gave in to his instincts, how would he explain to Barney or the conductor why he ran flailing along the track, stumbling into the sunlight like a fool? He kept that picture close as he walked more quickly towards the tunnel mouth, making himself visualize Barney's face as he described how a sound 'felt'.

'You bin drinkin' meths?' he would say for sure. Barney's favourite joke. A joke he used on anything he didn't agree with, understand or like.

(Union official tells him there's an overtime ban.

'You bin' drinkin' meths?'

Wife tells him it's time he got up off his fat fanny and put the trash out . . .

'You bin drinkin' meths?')

You see Barney, you couldn't hear it exactly, you could only feel it . . .

'You bin drinkin . . .'

Enough. He would walk on like an adult and fix that fucking car. The sooner it was done, the sooner he'd be downing a cold one in The Deerbrush, with Mary perched beside him on a stool. He was only three cars away from the sun, and whatever else his heart was saying, his head was saying *there* is *no noise*. He had looked back then and been surprised by how far away the lights of the cab seemed.

All the way back into the tunnel Barney would be standing looking at the kettle with his hands in his pocket. All the way back there the conductor would be fishing down the back of his chair for his dog-eared novel. All the way back there the rock was still living. Joshua stopped breathing again and stood still. The noise, the feeling, halted with him. He waited. It waited. Then, it happened.

Like a released pinball, the noise, the feeling, concealed in its ceiling of rock, shot away from Joshua with a velocity that made him dizzy. He knew it was something alive, and he knew it was travelling the whole length of the tunnel's arc to the other entrance. There was a fraction of a pause, the fraction of a pause you expect when something thrown very hard is bouncing off its wall. The pause before it starts to come right back at you.

It was darkness, and it was rushing up the tunnel towards him like water forced through a pipe. Again he felt it first, reeling from its shock-waves as they pushed him back towards the entrance. But when he saw it, the natural black of the tunnel's sunlessness being obscured by a deeper blackness impossible to comprehend, he remembered to breathe. As the black tide swallowed up the cab of the train, breaking over it like a wave, he turned and ran, his legs buckling and floundering beneath him. He had to make the entrance. There was no doubt about that at all. Instinct had told his logic to shut the fuck up and run, and instinct was telling him that if that wall of rushing blackness reached him before he reached the light, he would never feel the sun on his face again.

He ran like a child, making involuntary grunting sounds as his feet gouged the gravel, chin high, eyes rolling in their sockets.

When he fell out of the tunnel gulping for breath, the last thing he remembered was the darkness slamming into the entrance, as though the man-made arch described an invisible prison door. He was sure the darkness screamed with fury. No sound again, just a visceral reading of a ripping, hungry, scream.

Joshua was sure he had just preserved his sanity. The brakeman and conductor were not so sure. When they found Joshua, he was lying in the snow jabbering, and the best they could get out of him was *the living rock.*

He was taken home by road and was back at work in a fortnight. The conductor and brakeman filed a report, recalling that there had been a short power cut in the cab at the time that engineer Tennent ran. Yes, they had experienced temporary darkness, and yes, that's probably what spooked him so bad. No harm done. Everybody safe, and a whole new joke to pass around the bunkhouses now that the one about Joe's bear encounter had worn thin.

But even now, a whole year on, and after a hundred nudges and grins when Joshua walked into the canteen, each time the Corkscrews loomed he toyed with trading his railway pension for steady work in a hamburger joint.

Martell was still chuckling as the cab entered the tunnel. 'Rock still livin', Tennent? Can't hear no breathin'.'

He wheezed some more in Joshua's direction, until he realized that neither his brakeman or engineer were going to respond. Martell was starting to get mad. A man making a joke deserves some kind of answer, even if the joke's an old one. He'd put up with this silence too long.

The dark engulfed them, the yellow light from the cab flickering on the irregular shapes of the rough rock walls, but the entrance to the tunnel was clearly visible ahead.

Martell leant forward in his chair.

'Guess you're keepin' it shut 'cause you know that whole livin' rock thing was a crock of shit, Tennent. That right?'

Joshua kept his eyes on the growing arch of light.

'Guess so, Wesley.'

It was shaking a stick at a steer, a hoghead calling Martell by his first name.

'Well let's us just stop in the upper tunnel and check it out. Clear it up for good.'

Joshua dared not look at him. He sat motionless, his throat dry.

'You heard. Hit the brakes. Now.'

He heard all right. Why not? Joshua knew it would get him one day. Every time he dreamed of that rushing, hungry darkness, he knew it would get him. Why not now? Now was as good a time as any.

Turning slowly to look at Martell, he pulled back the brake and watched the conductor's florid face as the train began its laborious process of halting.

Forty five seconds later, they stopped just inside the mouth of the upper tunnel.

Joshua Tennent held his conductor's eyes in a gaze like a mongoose holding a snake. Martell twitched. Maybe the engineer was really crazy. Maybe this was where he went Charlie Manson and they'd all end up being stencils for a cop's chalk outline. But then again maybe not. There was face to be saved here, and when all was said and done he was the guy in charge, and crazy or not, Tennent had better understand that, and understand it good.

Henry was open-mouthed, looking from Joshua to Martell and back again, as though the secret of why a substantial portion of B.C.'s coal supply came to be stationary in the mouth of the upper Corkscrew Tunnel, lay in the air somewhere between them.

'Want to get out and say hi to the rock?' The conductor spat the words.

A pause.

'Sure. After you, Wesley.'

The delay in the reply was deliberate, the tone of voice imitating Joshua. 'After you, son.'

Joshua stood. It would get him. Of course it would. He would face it now, it would get him, and the thing would be done. Over.

It would be okay. Better than all those bad dreams, and the feeling in those dreams that someday the sunlit arch might not be enough to stop it. His eyes never leaving those of the conductor, he walked to the cab door behind his seat, pushed down the thin aluminium handle, and opened it. Cold air poured in like syrup.

'Coming? Or are you scared, Wesley?'

Funny thing though, Wesley Martell *was* scared. He kept thinking about the rock. *The living rock.* Even though he knew the whole thing was bullshit, his stomach turned a loop at having to walk out that cab door and stand three feet from the craggy wall. But he was still more mad than scared, and if that crazy shit-for-brains hoghead thought he was going to back down now, then he ate loony flakes for breakfast.

'Oh sure, Tennent. It's tricklin' down my legs and fillin' my boots. But I'm right at your heels, boy.'

Joshua inhaled a lungful of warm cab air and stepped out onto the metal platform to face the rock. Martell was at his side immediately.

Joshua waited. The two men stood silently, their backs to the light of the window, staring at the icy stone. Nothing happened. Joshua closed his eyes. Nothing. The only sound was that of the massive diesel engine chugging beneath a sheath of steel. Martell felt the cold settle on him like a silk cloak.

Joshua opened his eyes, his breast heaving with a mixture of relief and dismay. Did he really imagine it last time? Was he crazy? He'd dreamed of this so many times in the last year, tossing and sweating in his bed as the nightmare darkness swept him away, and yet he knew there was nothing here but rock. He couldn't 'feel' any sound at all.

He looked at Martell with naked contempt. 'Happy?'

'Pleased as a baby at the tit. I guess the livin' rock ain't home today.'

He squeezed another laugh out of that box of phlegm he stored somewhere under his shirt and kept laughing as they re-entered the cab, closed the door and returned to their chairs.

The throttle opened and the train made a series of metallic screeches of protest as it inched away. It was the deafening noise of the engine that prevented the three men hearing the other sound.

The sound of two six-foot-long icicles shattering as they splintered onto the metal platform where the conductor and engineer had stood.

3

Billy broke the laws of physics every time he yelled. How a holler that loud came to be emitted from such a tiny frame would have given Einstein pause to pull his moustache in thought.

'It's coming!'

Sam Hunt made a mock ear-trumpet with his hand and leant towards his son. 'Sorry? Didn't get that.'

Billy's small oval face looked up at Sam and broke into a grin. 'Sure you did. Feel. It's coming now.'

Sam bent into a crouch and laid a palm on the freezing rail. He could feel nothing, but Billy, they both knew, was the expert here.

'Okay then. Bird or Queen this time?'

Billy was thoughtful. He turned the pale yellow dollar coin over in his mittened hand and made a decision. 'I'm gonna go for the duck. You put yours Queen-up.'

He leant forward and placed the dollar on top of the rail track as carefully as if he were handling a rod of plutonium. Sam, smiling, positioned his dollar a yard further up the track, the profile of the Queen of England facing the direction of the oncoming train like she knew what she was in for.

From here on the edge of town you could just make out the entrance of the tunnel, looming above the pines about three miles off, but Sam was damned if he knew how Billy could feel the vibrations of a train that far away. But he did, and here it came, the head-light emerging from the dark hole right on cue.

'Stand back, Billy.' Sam stretched a hand out for the boy's.

'Aw get real, Dad. That's not gonna be here for at least five minutes.'

13

Sam stood up and looked towards the tunnel mouth, his hand still extended to his son. 'No you're right, Billy boy. Why don't you just lie with your head on the rail, and if it gets cut off at the neck your Mom and I see what we can get for your bike at a rumble sale?'

Billy sighed and rolled his eyes. He stood up and took the large offered hand, and together they moved back from the track. Still holding hands, they squatted on the snowy embankment ten feet away to wait.

From behind the forest came the deep, long, discordant hoot of the train's horn, filling Silver Valley with a sound so thick it resonated in the spine as well as in the ears. Sam lifted his head like a cat smelling fish.

'You like that sound Dad, don't you?'

'Yeah.'

'I like it too.'

Sam looked down at the face of the boy, framed now in his blue anorak hood, his black eyes glittering in a brown face. 'What's it make you think of Billy?'

The boy looked solemn. 'You.'

Sam was silent. He tightened his grip on the mitten containing his son's small hand and resumed gazing up the track.

Billy smiled up at him. 'Don't you want to know why?'

'Do I have a choice here?'

The boy giggled, a sound so sweet that Sam thought it might make primroses poke through the snow at their feet. 'It just sounds like you, that's all. I don't know why.'

'So I sound like a freight train horn, is that what you're saying? Remind me of that if I'm ever tempted into a Karaoke Bar.'

But he'd lost his son's attention. Billy had his timing wrong for once. The train was already in sight on the long straight leading into town, and it would be on top of their dollars in about a minute.

Billy yelped like a rodeo MC and jumped to his feet.

'How big, Dad? How big? What's the record?' He was jumping on the spot.

'Two and a half inches. I think.'

'Metric, Dad. What's that in centimetres?'

Sam, legs drawn up to his armpits, his arms flopping lazily over the knees, looked down into the snow and laughed. 'Got me there,

Billy boy. Guess I'm not doing so hot today. Sound like a horn and can't count modern.'

The rails were singing now as fourteen thousand tons of iron tested their rivets, and when the horn sounded again, father and son nearly felt it blow their hair.

Billy was right. Sam loved that sound. He remembered seeing a small ad in the *Silver Valley Weekly* that read 'Superior condo to let near ski slopes. Off highway and no train noise' and thinking he wouldn't much care for that, not if you couldn't hear the trains. He also knew the advertiser was lying. There was nowhere in Silver, or anywhere in the whole valley for that matter, where you could insulate yourself from that melancholy trumpeting. Not even the grazing elk looked up when it sounded. As far as Sam figured, it was part of the mountains, a sound as natural as the woodpecker or the squirrel, and anyone who wanted a condo where you couldn't hear it deserved a dunce cap.

The train was on them. They could see the men in the cab, sitting high in the dirty red-and-white-striped metal box. The engine looked like a face, the crew peering out of small windows that made eyes at either side of a huge snout housing the horsepower.

Billy waved up at the big metal face, yelling hopelessly, his voice lost in the roar of the thundering diesel engine, unaware that Sam held the hem at the back of his anorak protectively.

From one of the eyes in the iron face, the flesh and blood face of a fat man scowled down at them as the engine rumbled past. No one was going to wave at Billy today. Sam watched his son's expression turn from excitement to disappointment as the cab slipped away and they faced nothing but a mile of coal cars, shedding ice as the sun got to work on them.

'He didn't see us, Dad.'

Sam knew they'd been seen all right. In fact he knew exactly what that fat face had been thinking, as it looked lazily out of its window and fixed its beady eyes on them. But he would do everything in his power to protect Billy from that thought.

'Guess not. How're the dollars doin'?'

'Still there I think. I can see mine. Only about twenty cars to go.'

Man and boy waited patiently, man perhaps more patiently than boy, until the last car rolled by, and they watched the back end of the train slide away.

Billy looked down at Sam, who still squatted in the snow, lost in thought. 'Can I get 'em?'

'Yeah. Go for it. Remember they're hot.'

Billy darted forward to the rail as Sam stood and stretched his six-foot body beneath its down-filled jacket: by the way his son was breathily mouthing *wow*, he guessed they'd had a result. He joined him by the track.

'At least eight centimetres, Dad. Look.' Billy passed the flattened disc of yellow metal to his father, eyes wide in anticipation of approval as Sam turned the hot trophy over in his gloved hand.

'Matter that it ain't exactly round?'

Billy shook his head.

'Then I guess it's a record. Official.'

Billy cheered and snatched back the metamorphosed dollar. He ran to where Sam had placed his. 'Sorry, Dad. Yours slipped.'

True enough. Sam's dollar had fallen off the track before the train could do its business. He was glad the glory had all been Billy's but he feigned a little hurt as he pocketed the unchanged coin. 'Gee. This isn't my day.'

Billy came up to his father, put his short little arms around Sam's padded waist and hugged him. 'I love you Dad. You can have mine.'

If love could have weight, Sam thought that freight train would have trouble shifting his. He wanted to squeeze his son so hard his muscles ached at the restraint they were under. 'I love you too Billy. You keep the dollar. There'll be plenty more. I'll beat ya yet.'

Billy broke the hug and ran through the thick snow, stumbling like a cripple to the parked car, making a noise like a train as he went.

Sam looked at the retreating train, the distant sound of its bell clanging as it slowed up through town.

If that driver really had been thinking what Sam suspected, he thought at that moment, he might be inclined to pull the fat bastard from the cab and kill him. But how could Sam know that Wesley Martell was innocent? Martell wasn't thinking *That kid must be crazy if he thinks I'm going to wave at two stinking Indians.* In fact Martell hadn't even noticed them. Nothing had been further from his thoughts.

'The light you can leave on all day. Light 96 CHFM. Stevie Wonder comin' up next . . .'

Sam's hand couldn't get to the car stereo off-button fast enough.

What the hell did Katie do with his cassettes? The radio would kick in if there was no tape in the player, and even after ten years of marriage, Sam still hadn't learnt to turn the goddamn thing off before he started the ignition. Katie always left the radio on, he should know by now. There were only two stations a car radio could pick up this far into the mountains, both of them beaming in from Calgary, and both of them made Sam long for legislation to shoot disc jockeys. He could just about stomach 107 Kick FM, pumping out dinosaur rock music until the signal broke up, but when Katie had been driving the radio mysteriously tuned itself back to this easy listening nightmare.

He remembered how once, exasperated, he had turned it off while Katie was singing along to a Lionel Richie song, causing her to tut and smack him on the head, ignoring the fact he was driving. Sam had done a mock swerve. Billy and Jess in the back had laughed hard at that and he'd growled, and asked her why the hell she listened to it.

'You get a traffic report from Captain Kirk, the chopper pilot.'

'Yeah, but it's Calgary traffic. The guy's flying about above Calgary, Katie. You find it useful, knowing that there's a tailback on Barlow Trail, when you're sitting in the car in Silver, two hundred miles away?'

She'd grinned, and hit him on the top of the head again, making his straight black hair flop over his eyes.

'I like it okay?'

'Right. Maybe we can get your parents to tape the traffic reports from Vancouver and mail them over. That would sure make life a fuller all-round experience.'

She'd laughed and put the radio back on. Sam had winced, but out of the corner of his eye he had watched her singing and laughing, and suddenly Light 96 didn't seem so bad.

Right now, though, it was more than he could stand.

The only solution was his cassettes, but it looked like she'd cleared them away again.

'Dig in the glove box Billy will you? Any music in there?'

Billy opened it and rummaged around. 'Nah.'

'What does she do with them?'

Billy smiled.

'Help me choose some at the gas station?'

'Sure.'

17

Sam turned the car into Silver's main street and headed for the Petro-Canada. Cruising down the wide street, its verge piled high with wedges of old black snow, always made Sam feel like he was being covered in warm syrup. It was comforting. It was safe. It was also breathtakingly beautiful. At the eastern end of the street Wolf Mountain stabbed into the sky, a pyramid of seemingly impenetrable rock. Since Silver was nearly five thousand feet above sea level, and Wolf Mountain officially eight-and-a-half thousand, the stone cliffs that towered over the town were pushing four thousand feet. But its fortress was a lie. The climber braving those crags would be crestfallen to discover that the mountain was all bravado and had been tamed several times over.

Not only did the railroad run right through its guts, but its gentler western flanks were blanketed with ski trails and restaurants, hiding from the town as though Silver might notice the mountain had gone soft and lose its temper.

But to the non-skiing tourists wandering around the sunny sidewalks, looking in gift shops and killing time until their partners came down off the slopes, Wolf Mountain was picture postcard wilderness.

Sometimes Sam thought the mountain looked like it sealed off the street like a gate, even though it sat at least three miles away from town. In fact the very first night he and Katie spent in Silver together, he'd had a nightmare that he was running, lungs bursting, trying to escape from the town, or something in the town, and the mountain kept blocking his exit with a wall of living rock. Weird dream. Weird, since he loved Silver. And he loved Wolf Mountain.

They turned into the gas station and pulled in to a pump, Vince looked up from the till and waved a solemn greeting to them through the window. Billy leapt out and ran into the shop while Sam watched the pump eating up his dollars. Next time he looked he saw Billy inside, earnestly spinning the cassette rack.

A hand-written sign on top of the carousel read, *Truck drivers delight. All country tapes half price. This week only. We must be crazy!!!*

Vince sure was making a mark on his patch. The customer might always be right, but as far as Vince was concerned the customer must also be blind. Day-glo stickers alerting the driver to the great offers now available in everything from mufflers to coffee speckled the interior and exterior of his booth like a fungus.

A woman waiting in the Chrysler New Yorker in front of Sam's old Toyota was obviously unimpressed by Vince's style. She glared at the man paying Vince inside, her face pinched and her eyes narrowed behind wire-rimmed spectacles. Sam smiled over as her gaze wandered in his direction, but the smile faded on his lips as she returned his greeting with a look of distaste. Second time today, he thought. You put out and you get nothing back. He was grateful that this time it was him getting the cold shoulder and not Billy. Sam looked in the booth to check out which poor sucker had to share not only the car but his life with the old snake.

There was a guy in a felt hat at the counter, who kept glancing back at Billy while Vince worked at his credit card. He mouthed a sentence to Vince and laughed. Vince smiled, then caught sight of Sam watching him. Vince saw something in Sam's eyes and averted his gaze. The customer picked up the paperwork and left the shop.

Billy was still spinning the cassette rack when Sam came in to pay. 'Anything?'

Billy looked thoughtful. 'Whitney Houston?'

Sam made a fanning motion in front of his face like he was wafting away a bad smell.

Billy rolled his eyes and resumed his search, as Sam walked over to the desk.

'How's it going Sam?'

'Good. Good.'

'Twenty-eight dollars.'

Sam fished the bills out of his wallet. 'What did that guy say about Billy, Vince?'

'What guy?'

Sam jerked a thumb in the direction of the man strapping himself into the Chrysler beside the wicked witch of the east.

Vince looked out. 'Aw nothing. Just passing the time of day. Tourist.' He held his hand out for the money. Sam put the bills on the counter.

'What did he say?'

Vince sighed. 'He said, am I getting old or are truck drivers getting younger? Funny guy, huh?'

'That was it?'

'That was it.'

Sam looked into Vince's eyes and was confused by the message there. Vince picked up the money and opened the till.

'Need a receipt?'

'No. Thanks.'

Billy joined them, his head barely making it over the counter, his hand clutching a cellophane wrapped cassette.

'Okay, what about this one? Kenny Rogers.'

Sam put a hand on his son's head, still looking at the man behind the till, and tried to repair the damage. 'Jesus Vince, your taste in music stinks.'

'We aim to please.'

'Catch you later. Give my regards to Nancy.'

'Will do.'

'Billy. Put back that box from Hell.'

Billy complied and they left the shop.

They had driven fifty yards before Sam spoke again. 'What did that guy in the shop say to Vince? You know, the guy that was in before me?'

Billy was singing to himself looking out of the window. He stopped singing, and smiled up at Sam. 'He said was he getting old or were truck drivers getting younger? He was meaning me.' Billy giggled again. 'Imagine thinking a nine-year-old kid was a truck driver. Just 'cause I was looking through the cassettes.' He laughed again, and then got back to the busy task of singing to himself.

Sam felt sick. What the hell was wrong with him? That shit-kicking train driver had thrown him off balance by not returning Billy's wave. Why did Sam have to look for prejudice where there was none? He was going to have to learn to trust.

Silver was a nice town. It was full of nice people. Sam thought he should maybe write that out a hundred times when he got like this. Stop him getting so cranky.

Yeah. It was full of really nice people.

He turned the radio on.

'. . . not too hard, not too soft, just light. This is Daniel, Elton John . . .'

Truth. Silver *was* a nice town. Regular population eight thousand, twice that when the seasonal tourists poured in.

In summer they came in camper vans, bringing the main street to a standstill while the passengers peered at maps and pointed, and the drivers constantly wheeled round in their seats, either shouting at kids in the back or looking for somewhere to park like predators stalking game. They were a pain in the butt.

They turned the town into a zoo.

Winter, right now, was better. Skiers travelled by car or on tour buses, and somehow they weren't so cheesy, didn't wear so many shiny leisure suits, didn't picnic in dumb places.

But then the winter trade was altogether different. Even the Japanese who skied all season, wearing identical white ski-suits like Elvis's last days in Vegas, were different from the packs that roamed Silver in the summer. The summer Japanese were on tours, herded around by fierce guides, photographing pretty much anything their diminutive leader pointed at. The winter ones came in couples. They had more money to spend, stayed in the big Canadian Pacific hotels on the edge of town, and no one minded them a bit.

Winter also brought the ski bums, the Australian and American kids who worked just enough to buy a lift pass and ski the season away. They packed out the staff accommodation shacks hidden well out of sight of the tourists in the backstreets, revealing their residence by the stinking T-shirts and ski suits they hung out their windows to air.

Sometimes Sam had to take the staff minibus and pick them up; all part of the menial work as an employee of the Silver Ski Company. Other company guys minded plenty when it was their turn, but Sam kind of liked it. The Aussies were funny. In fact last season he'd gotten real friendly with a guy called Bunny Campbell from Melbourne, who'd invited Sam, Katie and the two kids out to Australia for a vacation. They'd never go. Sam knew that. But he got the occasional card from Bunny and it made him feel cosmopolitan, knowing someone half way round the world.

Jess loved Bunny, her two-year-old hormones already tingling to the six-foot, golden-tanned antipodean hunk. Occasionally he would come and drag Sam out for a beer after work, sweep Jess into his arms and do a mock tango while Sam fetched his jacket. Sam had watched Katie watching Bunny and preferred not to examine the emotions he felt. Bunny was a good guy. A friend of the family.

The last card had come from Hawaii where Bunny was surfing. There was a picture of a model with big breasts holding a surf board under her arm, which Bunny had defaced by drawing a beard on the girl's chin. The card had been addressed to Sam Two-Dogs-Fucking-Big-Chief-Skis-Like-A-Cow, and after initial irritation, Sam had laughed and stuck it on the door of the ice-box where all the other postcards lived. He hoped Bunny would be back this season. Sam never thought he'd have friends like that. Big, funny, happening.

White.

That was the truth. White friends. That's what made him happy. And unhappy at the same time. Real unhappy, remembering what big tanned guys like Bunny used to mean to him when he was young – a time that didn't get head space – not if Sam Hunt could help it.

Still, winter was good.

Like most Silver residents, the Hunts preferred winter to summer, but whatever the season, it was a bitch of an expensive town.

When the grimy railroad workers had built Silver over a hundred years ago, original name Siding Twenty-three, it was nothing more than a collection of tin and wooden huts in a clearing cut in the pines.

Now, any real estate agent's window in town would make the ghosts of those guys swoon. Photos of houses were displayed like pornography, their doors open wide, their interiors on show to the casual viewer. And printed below, in discreet blue type, were prices that read like telephone numbers.

Little surprise then that the big houses by the river were mostly holiday homes, owned by rich city people; people who dressed expensively, and seemed built on a different scale, the way the women's bones were so fine and the men's shoulders so broad and square.

You could sometimes see them in summer behind their hedges, the way you might glimpse a shy wild animal in the trees, catching them talking and laughing in low voices round rustic garden tables. But in winter the only evidence that they were in residence was the thin blue lines of smoke from their chimneys and the shiny hire cars sitting in the drives.

Since only the seriously rich owned nice property in Silver, the workers who kept the town ticking lived in Stoke, ten miles away, in cheaper accommodation. But the Hunts were lucky. Really lucky. Katie's family had vacationed in Silver all their life, and when her father bought a holiday house in 1955 it had cost about the same as a good canoe. It was their daughter Katie's house now, its holiday function forfeited so that their grandchildren could have a house and a home. And it was a great house.

Sam thought for possibly the ten thousandth time what a great house it was as he and Billy pulled into the drive.

It sat high on Oriole Drive, south of main street, looking across the roofs of smaller houses to the mountains that hemmed in Stoke. You could just make out the railroad as it appeared between the pines on the edge of town, but the Trans- Canada highway was hidden, reminding the Hunts of its presence only when an easterly wind brought the distant sound of trucks to their door. Sam had painted the two storey, detached house powder blue last fall, a choice that Katie had first disputed loudly in the lumber store, then applauded when she was enchanted by the result. Yes, it was a great house, and for the most part its wooden walls echoed to adult laughter, children's squeals and the good-natured barking of Billy's husky, Bart.

Bart was out there before the car stopped, bounding round the Toyota, as Light 96 died with the engine and Sam stretched into the back seat to pull out the groceries.

Inside, Katie Hunt chopped tomatoes and silently rehearsed a grouchy reception for her tardy partner, while Jess earnestly dragged crayon across paper at the end of the table.

Sam and Billy had been rehearsing too.

Sam began.

'Okay. You want an explanation. It was a dinosaur in the super-market. Billy spotted it first, in the canned vegetable aisle. Took us nearly an hour to fight it off with a roll of kitchen wipe.'

Billy nodded, smiling.

Katie stopped chopping. 'Aw come on, guys. I needed that stuff light years ago. They'll be here in an hour and a half.'

Sam put down the brown bags and from behind circled his arms round his small blonde wife, and kissed her ear.

'Sorry babe.'

She was softening, but not quite soft.

'Yeah, well sorry's not going to fix dinner for six.'

'For sure.'

'Where were you?'

'The railroad.'

'Dice those onions.'

'Okay.'

Bart, outside, watched through the kitchen window as the Hunt family reunited and got busy. He whined once and lay down in the snowless patch at his kennel door to watch the sun slide away behind the peaks.

4

'. . . okay, so let's just get this straight . . .'

There was a communal moan from the other five diners.

'Come on! this is serious.'

Gerry was leaning forward on the table, using his fork which still speared a tube of pasta, to emphasize the importance of his words.

'We agree that *Bewitched* was a subtle statement about the rising threat to men from feminism in 60s America. We agree that Samantha was subduing her massive and powerful superiority over Darren in order to keep him, the man as child, happy, and the home stable. But we can't agree whether the programme was pro-woman or anti. Am I right?'

Gerry's wife Ann mumbled through a mouthful of food.

'Of course it was anti-woman.'

Katie jumped in again.

'No way. It was the most important piece of feminist TV ever made. It said men are weak, women are strong. Men only just manage by the skin of their teeth to keep women in their place by emotional blackmail.'

Across the table Gerry's sister Claire threw her husband Marty a look, as if pitying Katie, and moaned again. Gerry waved his fork again, clearly deciding he was chairman of this debate.

'Right. Right. But by portraying Samantha as an individual only interested in shopping and hoovering, was that itself not undermining the women's movement? Saying quite categorically, it doesn't matter how strong women may be, at the end of the day they just want a credit card and cushions that unzip for cleaning?'

Katie shook her head. 'Totally wrong. Women understood the sub-text of that show.'

'I took it as an anti-woman subtext. Quite clearly as a matter of fact,' said Claire, raising an eyebrow.

Sam stood, dropped his napkin on the table and cleared two empty wine bottles from the centre of the debris. 'Anyone for more wine?'

Marty chucked himself in. 'You see, there was a lot of angst going down then. Guys didn't know the score.'

Sam, realizing that grabbing their attention would be as easy as getting Bill Clinton to come and mow his lawn, took the bottle and walked into the kitchen. He opened the ice-box and pulled out another cold Chablis while the voices from the dining room shouted each other down. To the sober man, the drunk is a curious beast. Sam always wondered why alcohol affected people's volume control. An hour ago they were all talking normally, but now five of them were shouting like they were trying to be heard over a baseball crowd. Sam couldn't imagine why, but then Sam had never had a drink in his life. Worried about the noise, he sneaked out of the kitchen and upstairs, the bottle still in his hand, to check on the kids.

The shaft of light from the open door to Jess's bedroom illuminated one tiny hand on top of the comforter holding the arm of a fun-fur monkey.

Sam waited until his eyes adjusted to the contrast of light and dark, and was rewarded by a glimpse of the small dark head of his daughter lying peacefully on its pillow.

As he watched her chest rise and fall beneath the cover, he heard a whimpering from next door. He backed out of the room and stepped quickly to Billy's door. Pushing it open, he saw Billy writhing on the bed, his comforter lying on the floor in a heap where it had been thrown off. Sam put the wine on the floor, picked up the bedcover and laid it gently over his dreaming son.

Billy was obviously in some distress. With the door fully open his face was clearly lit. It was light enough to see he was suffering some imagined agony. Sam toyed with waking him up, hugging him and telling him his dad was here, but his decision was made for him as Billy sat up suddenly with a yell.

'Hey, hey, hey. It's okay. Everything's okay, Billy boy.'

Sam had him in his arms before the yell died on the boy's lips. He held the small panting body close to his chest, rubbing his back with a large hand.

Billy's tears came. 'Dad. Make them stop. They have to stop.'

'It's just a dream Billy. Nothing's happening.'

'It is happening Dad. You have to warn them.'

Sam hugged him closer. 'Okay. Okay. You tell me, and I'll make them stop.'

Billy was sobbing, his whole body heaving under its Calgary Flames T-shirt. 'They're gonna let it go, Dad. You can't let them.'

'Who is Billy? What are they going to let go?'

The boy started to cry again. 'I don't know. I don't know. The wolf told me. I just know it's going to be bad. I saw them. Two of them.'

Sam rocked him back and forward, his hand now stroking Billy's hair. He sat that way for a minute or more. 'Sshhh now. I'll stop them. It's just a dream. Go back to sleep.'

But he was already asleep. In fact, Sam wondered if he'd been awake at all. Billy's body was a dead weight in his arms, breathing steadily, arms hanging at his side.

Gently Sam let Billy back down on to the pillow and pulled the comforter up to his chin. He stood by the bed for a while, waiting to see if Billy would go back to the dark place he'd been in, but the crisis was over for now. From downstairs, a roar of indignation reminded him of his other duties, and he walked slowly out of the room, retrieving the wine as he went.

Looked like he hadn't missed much. Ann was hard at it.

'Well you can say that, but the kids I teach, and the kids Gerry teaches, haven't a fucking clue what the whole movement was about.'

Katie was in a corner, holding the lions back with a chair. 'Then it's your duty to remind them. Unless you want all those little guys to grow up thinking they rule the world.'

Claire laughed sarcastically. 'They do Katie. And they will.'

Sam picked up the corkscrew, opened the bottle and started filling glasses. 'Yep, we do. Take it in turns as it happens. When it's my turn I'm going to make it illegal to have waiters tell you their names before they bring the menu.'

Marty and Katie laughed. Claire was annoyed not to be taken seriously. 'Yeah. Cute.' She paused, taking stock. 'Now I don't know you Sam. In fact, this is the first time I've met you. But I'd say you're an old-style kind of guy. Am I right Katie?'

Claire picked up the wine glass that Sam had filled, and half-emptied it again.

Katie looked up at Sam with love. 'No. You're wrong. He's cool.'

Claire was undeterred. 'Gerry, Ann, help me out here. You've been friends with Sam and Katie how long?'

Gerry smiled and made a space between his palms that stretched, the way a fisherman lies about his catch.

'So is this guy for or against women?'

Sam took his seat again, and looked cheerfully round the company with a smile of comic innocence. He beamed across at Katie. 'Oh go on, honey. Tell them how I leave you the key to the chastity belt when I travel.'

Katie smiled again. 'Yeah, but leaving it in the men's washroom at the Bus Depot doesn't count.'

Claire didn't laugh. She folded her face into a mask of censure. 'You know, in my job women have eighty-five percent less chance of promotion than men. Eighty-five percent. That's no joke.'

Sam took a swig of soda. 'Don't that put you right off being a lumberjack then?'

Everyone laughed this time, and the fact that Marty sniggered into his wine let Claire out of the cage. She ran a finger round the top of her glass. 'I would have thought that given your background Sam, you'd be slightly more sympathetic to a statistic like that.'

Katie shot Sam a glance. Sam held Claire's gaze.

'Sorry. Not with you.'

'No. I'm sorry. Sorry if I'm the one to remind you that Native Canadians don't do too hot in the promotion stakes. That is if they can get a job at all.'

Sam looked steadily at her. 'I got a job.'

Marty put a hand on Claire's. 'Claire.'

She pulled her hand away. 'No, come on folks. Let's face up to it here. What kind of a job have you got exactly Sam? A good job?'

'Yeah.'

'Oh well pardon me once again. Gerry led me to believe you were a manual groomer. Not exactly executive status, unless Silver Ski Company's started recruiting from Harvard.'

Sam said nothing.

Claire softened her voice, and if the intention by doing so was to paper over the cracks, it was wasted.

'Look, all I'm saying is that I know how you people must feel. I'm a woman. I get shit on too.'

Sam looked into his soda like there was something dead in there. 'I can believe that. The last part anyway.'

Marty wiped his mouth with his napkin. 'Okay, time we were hitting the road. Listen, it was real nice meeting you. We're staying with Gerry and Ann another week. Maybe we can all ski together.'

Katie was still looking at Sam. She slipped a hand beneath the table and wound her fingers between his. 'Yeah. That'd be neat. I don't know if we can take time off, but if we can, sure.'

Sam looked across at Claire. 'If we can't, I sure look forward to sweeping the snow off your car.'

Marty stood up, and the others followed his example, scraping their chairs on the wooden floor, and fussing over their possessions. Marty moved round the table, kissed Katie and put a hand on Sam's shoulder. 'No hard feelings Sam. Lighten up. Everyone's a little gassed.'

Sam nodded solemnly.

There were polite noises made and Katie herded everyone out without the assistance of her husband who remained seated, staring into the middle of the abandoned table. He heard the door close and their footsteps crunching in the drive, and was aware of Katie standing behind him, leaning against the door frame.

'She was a jerk. Wasn't it enough to just let her be one and leave it at that?'

'Should have been.'

Katie pulled up a chair beside him and put her head on his shoulder. He slipped his arm round her.

'I didn't even get to serve the after-dinner mints.'

'I should do it for a living, huh? Dinner parties cleared in minutes. Call Freephone 0800 Sam Hunt.'

'Tell me what's wrong.'

Sam sighed. 'I don't know. I've been kind of cranky all day.'

Katie undid the top three buttons of Sam's silk shirt, ran her hand over the bone amulet he wore round his neck on a leather thong, and let her hand rest on his warm belly.

'In fact cancel cranky. Replace with asshole.'

'Can I help?'

He smiled down at the blue eyes in her pale oval face; the face of a Victorian china doll.

'Sure. You can load the dishwasher.'

She guffawed and bit his shoulder. He lifted her head and kissed her small rosy mouth.

When Sam and Katie Hunt got to bed an hour later the dishwasher was still empty. The cushions on the sofa however, were going to need some recovery time.

Billy heard his parents climb the stairs and lay awake in the dark listening to their hushed voices as they turned off the hall lights.

His forehead was beaded with sweat and his hands were fists, clenching and unclenching across his chest. He knew he'd had a bad dream, nothing more, but the taste of it was still with him. Lying awake now, he wondered why he didn't call out to his parents, bring them into his room to sit on his bed and talk to him in calm voices. But he didn't want to see his parents right now. He wanted to see Bart. The wolf had told him to trust Bart, but Bart was in the yard, banished nightly from the house. Billy waited until he heard Sam and Katie's door close gently. He gave it a minute and then reached out and turned on his bedside light.

He paused to see if the light from his room would bring an enquiry from next door, and when it didn't he slipped out of bed and pulled on his plaid jacket.

Finding a torch in the toy box and opening his door carefully, Billy picked his way downstairs and through the house to the kitchen door by the light of the slim beam.

The sky was clear outside, a million stars glittering behind the black jagged silhouette of the mountains. Bart was standing outside his kennel, ears high, nostrils blowing clouds of vapour, face staring toward Wolf Mountain. There was only a tiny twitch of recognition and a small noise from the back of the animal's throat when Billy knelt beside him and put his arms round Bart's thick spiky coat.

Boy and dog looked out towards the mountain. Upstairs man, woman and child slept.

5

Lenny Sadowitz shifted a rogue piece of gum from between his cheek and back teeth before squinting up at the mountain, preparing to holler at his colleague.

'C'mon Jim. I got a life to lead!'

The word *lead* bounced off the rock, returning to his ears in a thin piping voice barely recognizable as his own. He watched his breath swirl in front of him, blew a few rings of frozen air, sucked the cold between his teeth and continued to chew. He leant forward on the handlebars of the snow cat and watched his companion's silhouette move silently between the other cat and the unexploded charge he was investigating.

Lenny hated being on avalanche rota. What was the point of being a ski patroller if you ended up miles away from the action on the trails, stuck in godforsaken gullies like this one with as much chance of getting some skiing in as Jim had of pulling that dreamboat waitress in T.J.'s Diner?

Having a white cross on your back impressed the public. It did nothing for the coyotes and the whiskeyjacks, and that was all there was for company in this part of the mountain.

This whole exercise was getting on Lenny's tits. Why they should have to avalanche the cliffs on Wolf was anyone's guess. If the loading slopes were a risk to the railroad, then the frigging railroad workers should come up here and blast them themselves. Lenny sure didn't recall railroad maintenance as part of his job description when he signed up as a patroller.

He glared down the cliff at the thin track just visible between the tunnel mouths, and expelled a white globe of spit in its direction.

Lenny pushed his Ray-Bans up onto his forehead, narrowed his eyes and looked back up at his partner with disgust. The rule was that unexploded avalanche bombs get their location noted and then stay put until spring, when the patrollers simply wander over and pick them up out of the grass. Digging around in eight feet of powder for something the size of a shoe box is not a sensible course of action, especially when that shoe box could just blow your legs off. Not good enough for Jim. He knew where the bomb was and he was damned if he was going to let it lie there until the snows melted.

This was the second bitching day they'd been at this. Jim had thrown the charge yesterday, delighting in the formality of shouting *fire in the hole!* and then was puzzled and disappointed by its failure to detonate. He knew any danger of it exploding now was nil.

No, stubborn curiosity and a determination to put his house in order were the factors that made Jim decide to go and fetch that wayward bomb, before they carried on with their legitimate day's work, to blast the bollocks out of the double black diamond run down Spangle Couloir. That's where Lenny wanted to be, and that's where Jim was stopping him being.

Jim's fascination with explosives made Lenny despise him more. Jim was the incendiary expert in the resort but he was a pig on skis. Lenny and the two other guys who took turns to help out 'lanching in the high season, got all the revenge they needed for being pulled off the trails to do this shit by scoring with any girl Jim looked at sideways. Girls don't care much about dynamite when they get a chance of a guy with a tan and thighs like iron.

'Aw Christ. What is he doing up there?'

Lenny got off the snow cat, sinking up to his knees in the soft snow, and cupped his gloved hands to a mouth ringed with white lip salve. 'Jimbo! I'm losing toes down here. Get a fuckin' move on!'

He saw the stooping figure of Jim look up, and then Lenny felt the explosion an age before he heard it.

Jim's body dissolved rather than blew apart. His flesh pushed tennis-ball-sized holes in his Goretex smock, and the face that he had washed for twenty-six years and shaved for ten, remained nearly intact as the skull to which it had been attached splintered into a macabre approximation of a fibre-filled breakfast cereal. Lenny had just enough time to watch one of Jim's arms windmilling through the air on its own like a stick you threw the dog.

32

Before the pieces that made up Jim McKenzie could attempt a landing, they were lost in the fountain of snow and rock that was heading towards Lenny. He didn't run or shout, but then that would have been hard with only half a face left, the eye on the remainder of his face hanging uselessly down his cheek. The rock hit him on the left side of the head, knocking him sideways, and as his exposed brains quivered, ready to obey gravity, the snow melted into every orifice, as though it were disinfecting the wounds.

Six heli-skiers on their way to some dream powder in the back country saw the explosion from the air and thought nothing of it. The pilot, Abe Foster, thought a great deal about it. Avalanche explosions are small, and the avalanches they cause rumble, roll and then stop. This was a mother of a bang, with plumes of thick black smoke spiralling up from Wolf Mountain as though terrorists had hit an oil terminal. The whole hill seemed to be disintegrating.

Abe took the chopper up another five hundred feet and banked west to take a better look. It was bad. Christ help any poor sucker in the vicinity of a blow like that. Abe got on the radio and called patrol, then turned the chopper round, and, ignoring the whining from his dumb-assed stock-broker passengers, headed back to Silver.

Getting the kids out of the house was like playing with one of those mercury-filled hand-games where you tilt the piece of plastic until you manoeuvre the shiny sliver of liquid metal into a hole. Every time Sam shovelled a son into a coat and herded him into the back of the Toyota, a daughter had taken her coat off and was back amongst the wreckage of the breakfast table.

He was never very good at those hand-games, and he was no better at rounding his family up.

Sam Hunt was losing his temper. He stood in the driveway, his hands on his hips, as Jess waved happily to him from the kitchen window clutching a piece of toast in a starfish hand.

'Honey. Jess isn't ready. This happens every damn morning. Could we get Jess ready? Would that be too much to ask, that Jess's ready? How hard can that be?'

Katie appeared at the door, wearing a wool, chequered coat and that smile she kept stored for occasions like this. The sight of her extinguished his ire.

'It's not hard Sam. I'm the one who's not ready. Just put her in the car and I'll be right with you.' She stepped out onto the drive and kissed him before flitting back inside on her mission to make him late.

Bart lay inside his kennel, his head on his paws, looking dolefully towards Billy inside the car.

Billy glowered back at him from between his Walkman earphones, rubbing a circle clear in the frosted window in the back of the car, whose engine was running unsteadily in an attempt to clear the windshields.

Sam, hands still on hips, shook his head and smiled, looking at his feet in mock defeat, when the explosion thundered in his eardrums. Katie stepped back outside, surprised. 'That sure was a big 'lanche blow.'

Billy poured himself out of the car, his mouth making an *O* shape. 'Look Sam. There's smoke.'

A black plume rose from the cliffs on Wolf Mountain. 'Lanchers didn't make smoke. Just a bang and a rumble. There was a lot of smoke.

Jess was crying in the kitchen. Whether it was due to the explosion or because she had dropped her toast was unclear, but Katie went to attend to the matter.

Sam remained silent. He had felt that explosion somewhere very deep inside. Not just in the regular way that a loud noise seems to come from inside your head, but in a sick, unholy way, as if someone had whispered something filthy and inhuman to him.

His head was swimming and he felt nauseous. The smoke was still rising in a black column, its source hidden by the Hunt's snowy roof. Sam could almost make out a form in the smoke. It was not a form he wished to look at for hours, the way he might look for shapes in the smoke of a log-fire, but it was the last thing he saw before he passed out.

Sam realized he was looking at the bedroom ceiling. Two familiar lozenge-shaped pieces of plaster that had been threatening to fall since the pipe burst last winter comfortably filled his vision. He sometimes looked at those two shapes when Katie was on top of him, not irritated by the reminder of repairs to be done but soothed by the part they played in being bits of his house. The house they owned, well at least

Katie owned. The house where he ate his dinner, watched TV, made love to his wife and brought up his kids. The house he had tried to make his own for ten years, lovingly patching its tiles, painting its flaky wood and scooping leaves from its gutters. Yes his house. Their house.

'Are you awake honey? I think he's awake, doctor. Sam, are you all right?'

Katie was bending over him now, obscuring the plaster shapes with her pale face. Sam smiled dreamily, remembering the photos they had taken in a booth in Calgary airport, waiting for Katie's parents to arrive from Vancouver. The booth's exposure had been set for Katie's fair white skin, and Sam's dark Indian face had come out as a featureless brown blob. Katie had laughed hard at the four useless snaps of herself kissing what looked like an old brown football propped on the shoulders of a suede jacket. Sam had laughed too, but had stopped laughing when he saw the look on Katie's parents' faces as they realized that the Indian guy standing next to their daughter was not the cab driver waiting to relieve them of their luggage, but the man she had told them so much about. The man she had thrown it all away for. The man she had married.

'Can you hear me, Mr Hunt?'

Alan Harris was leaning into Sam's vision, bringing with him a faint smell of linoleum.

'Sure. I hear you. I hit the deck, right?'

'Right. How does the head feel?' The doctor put his stethoscope to his ears and pulled back the goosedown comforter to put the cold metal to Sam's chest.

'Okay, I guess. How long have I been out?'

Katie's face bobbed back into view. 'A big scary fifty minutes, you wicked man. The doctor's been in and out of here all day like he's planning to move in.' Her voice softened, and she put a hand to his brow. 'We thought you were a hospital case. I can't tell you what I've been going through or how glad I am to have you back.'

Sam closed his eyes again. Fifty minutes. What made him black out for five hours? His head was starting to hurt now, and the realization that he must have junked a whole day's work was starting to make itself known in that area in the pit of his stomach reserved for anxiety. He opened his eyes abruptly. 'Jesus, Katie. What about my shift? I was standing in for Ben. Did you call the office?'

'Sure I called the office. They said they hoped you were okay and not to worry. And I called the museum, so I can take a few days off if you don't feel like getting up right away. Stop chewing over it.'

Sam closed his eyes again, listening to the doctor making soft cooing noises to Katie about how everything seemed fine and when he was to take the painkillers and how she was to let him know if Sam's head got sore and how were the kids and shit.

As he heard Katie closing the front door and the front wheels of Doctor Harris's car having big trouble helping him leave the Hunt's icy driveway, Sam drifted into gentle velvet sleep quite unlike the cold dark place he had been for the last fifty minutes.

Katie looked in from the bedroom door at her sleeping husband, his face no longer contorted as it had been since Andy next door helped her carry him inside, calm the children and call for help. For hours he had sweated and moaned as though someone were roasting him over a spit, but now he was just plain asleep.

His straight dark hair, damp with sweat, lay over the face she loved, and she exhaled lightly with relief that he was going to be all right.

But two things still bugged her. First, why he had passed out at all, and second, that for nearly fifty minutes of his blackout he'd been shouting and muttering in Siouan. Sam hadn't spoken a word of Siouan since before they were married, except once when they'd had a minor car accident while Billy was a baby. He'd sworn briefly and violently in the ancient Indian tongue as Katie screamed, clutching Billy, and the car skidded off the highway, to rest harmlessly and mercifully on the verge.

He never used it again. The language of losers he called it. Whatever was bugging him in his dreams was powerful enough to turn back the clock for Sam and pull that long-abandoned language out of his past and into his mouth. It made Katie uneasy, although right now she couldn't say why.

In half an hour she would go and collect Jess from Mrs Chaney, but now she could use a coffee and some time to herself. In the tiny kitchen, she switched the TV and the coffee machine on at the same plug. The local cable station was talking about the blast. Two ski patrollers killed, half the mountain gone above the Corkscrew tunnels, the railway blocked by rubble and ice. It was also a mystery. Some nervous reporter in a big anorak was standing in the car park beside Ledmore Creek stuttering that so far they could find no explanation for the size or violence of the blast but that theories included a pocket of methane gas detonated by chance.

Behind him blue lights flashed and people walked about pointing aimlessly. Katie poured herself a coffee, smiling at the ineptitude of local news, but deep down she was still worried why Sam had measured his length on the path not at the precise moment that pocket of methane had gone up, but moments later when they looked up at the smoke. The doc said it could have been the shock waves if Sam was already feeling light-headed from an encroaching infection. Katie didn't think so. Shock waves don't take that long, and Sam sure didn't look like he was coming down with anything other than usual early morning grouchiness.

Katie had stomached enough of goddamn blasts and blackouts for one day. She switched off her worries, switched channels and sat down at the table to catch half an hour of a Green Acres re-run.

When Gerry turned up at the door, the snow was falling so thickly Katie could barely make him out. The snowman on the doorstep handed a conical shape to Katie and said, 'Peace offering.'

She smiled, took the flowers already frosted with snow, and pulled Gerry in by the elbow.

Gerry shook himself like a dog in the kitchen. 'Christ. This is going to make the ski company wet themselves.'

Katie already had the coffee machine back on. 'Yeah. And not a whisper of it on the forecast. I want my money back from the weather channel. Grab a seat.'

Gerry installed himself at the kitchen table. 'I heard from Billy at school. Is Sam okay?'

'Yeah. He's fine. We don't know what all that fainting was about. Probably saw the hockey scores.'

She turned her back on Gerry and fished out a couple of mugs from the dishwasher.

'Listen Katie . . . about the other night . . .'

'Forget it, Gerry. It's no big deal.'

'It *is* a big deal. Claire's my sister. Uptight corporate woman maybe, but my sister nevertheless, and I'm ashamed she upset Sam.'

Katie sighed and joined him at the table, toying with the defrosting flowers in their soggy paper wrapping. 'You know the problem, Gerry. You've known us for nearly ten years. Sam just doesn't think he's an Indian.'

'Kind of hard to forget. Especially when you look at Billy and Jess.'

Katie laughed.

'I know. Sometimes I'm glad I can remember giving birth to them, or I'd think I had nothing to do with their creation at all. The Crosby DNA's sure got mugged somewhere along the line by Sam's.'

'Is he mad at Ann and me for bringing Claire?'

Katie shook her head. 'No. He's mad at being born a Kinchuinick Indian and growing up on a reserve.'

'Claire's real embarrassed. She wondered if we could maybe have you all round to our place for supper before they head back to Montreal. But I guess if Sam's not well . . .'

'Let's leave it, Gerry. But thanks for the thought.'

He nodded. The coffee machine gurgled its message that the brew was up.

'So how's school anyway?'

Gerry lightened up, his duty done. 'It's shit. As usual.'

'The kids all talking about the explosion?' She put two coffees in front of them.

'And some. Of course now they're also talking about this blizzard. They figure they'll get time off if it keeps up.'

'Billy seems distracted right now Gerry. Have you noticed?'

Gerry cupped the mug in his hand. 'Can't say I have. Was he upset by Sam collapsing?'

'I don't know. I just detect something disturbing him. Probably nothing. I thought you might notice, but I forgot teachers just practise riot control these days.'

'Up yours. '

Katie laughed and drank her coffee. Gerry took one sip and stood up.

'Look I really have to go. Just came to leave these.'

'The coffee that good, huh?'

He kissed her on the ear and made for the kitchen door, then paused when he looked through the glass panel. 'Hey, I think you should loosen up with the disciplinarian dog-owner bit and let Bart in. He's carrying more snow than a blue trail.'

Katie came to the door. 'I tried this morning, thanks Doctor Doo-little. He won't come in.'

Gerry stepped into the blizzard again.

'That's huskies for you, huh? Bye!'

Katie waved goodbye, and looked over at Bart. Gerry was right. The dog was outside his kennel, almost completely covered in snow.

'Here Bart. Come in boy.' She patted her thigh.

Bart looked at Katie and then resumed his vigil, staring towards Wolf Mountain as if it were made of prime sirloin.

'Jeez, a dysfunctional dog. That's all we need. Next stop the *Oprah Winfrey Show*.'

Katie brushed the snow from her hair and shut the kitchen door.

6

Frank Sinatra was giving it all he had in the chorus of 'It Happened in Monterey', when Ernie Legat's horny hand stretched out to the cab's stereo and cut the cassette. Ol' blue eyes was God to Ernie, but he liked to hear what the engine was up to when he hit Wolf Pass. In weather like this, with a full forty-ton load of frozen seafood behind him, he would be lucky to see second gear. That would be on the way up. On the descent into Silver, he could probably do with a parachute.

The snow was coming at him in the headlights like a corny asteroid storm on *Star Trek*, hypnotizing him with flakes that became rods of relentless white motion as they streaked past the windshield, and despite the work of the snowploughs, the road wasn't giving away many clues as to where it stopped being road and started being ditch.

Ernie coaxed the eighteen-wheeler into a first cautious gear change as the gradient started to introduce itself.

'Come on you bastard. '

Ernie reached his paw out again to turn up the heater, figuring getting more heat in the cab would take some of it out of the engine. The truck was doing its best.

In the back, two hundred lobsters bound for plates on the east coast, slid backwards an inch on their plastic pallets as the Peterbilt started its journey up the one-in-fourteen pass.

The snow was getting thicker with every foot Ernie climbed, making him curse that last coffee he'd had at Mabel's. No wonder he hadn't seen another truck for twenty miles. The sneaky sons of bitches waving hello to him back in Lanark must have known how bad stuff was up here and either left hours earlier or cut loose for the night in the parking holes down on the Trans-Canada. Not a sniff of trouble on the C.B.

Well shit on them. Ernie liked to get where he was going, and even though this was shaping up to be one of the worst winters he could remember, it would take more than a blizzard to knock the stuffing out of his schedule.

He was getting near the summit now, and the old tub hadn't put a wheel wrong. Nice and slowly, that was how to take it. Ernie could feel the road flattening out, and even though all he could see in the dark and through the snow was about fifteen feet of white featureless ribbon, he'd worked this godforsaken road often enough in daylight to guess he was right underneath the peak of Wolf Mountain. That meant at least two miles of even cruising before it was hang on to your hat for the slide down into Silver.

The chorus of 'It happened in Monterey' started to form itself into a hum on Ernie's lips. It died just as quick as he saw the figure up ahead. Standing at the side of the road was a man in a long black coat with his ungloved hand out, casual as you like, thumbing a lift. Ernie figured it must be at least minus thirty-five out there, but this guy was just standing in the snow like he was hitching a ride from some pals in a beach buggy on Sunset Boulevard.

Ernie started to brake. It was real fortunate for the guy in the coat that the truck was on the flat. Braking in snow like this was jack-knife city, but this was an emergency.

What the hell was a guy in a coat doing up here near midnight in a snowstorm, at least ten miles from anything remotely resembling civilization?

The truck managed a standstill about twenty yards past the man and Ernie watched in the wing mirror as the figure walked, not ran, but walked, slowly up to the passenger door, his face lit only by the red side-lights.

The company didn't allow hitchers, but this was life or death and the way Ernie saw it, he had no choice. He hadn't seen another vehicle either way for at least two hours. How long had the man been standing here, casually waiting for his lift?

Ernie braced himself for a hospital job, wondering how many fingers the guy would still be able to call his own after a minimum of two hours without gloves. He was already planning the detour to Silver's RCMP station when the cab door opened.

A rush of cold air entered every part of Ernie Legat as the man held open the door and looked up at his driver.

'Jesus Christ buddy, get in and shut the fuckin' door will ya!'

A pale, thin face held two ice-blue eyes that looked straight into Ernie's soul. The man's age was hard to place. A line-free face crowned with white hair, and skin that was almost translucent, belied a look in his eyes that seemed a great deal older.

The only illumination, from the single weak cab-light, was not doing much to help this guy's bid to get a bit part in a beach movie, but despite his pallor the hitcher's smile was disarmingly warm and charming. Not the smile of a man who has just cheated death.

Ernie motioned to the man with a hand that was already losing feeling in the tips of its fingers, and as the stranger looked calmly around the cab like a man buying a secondhand car, the cold was becoming more than he could bear.

'Silver?'

'Sure,' he replied impatiently. 'Get in.'

Huge flakes of snow whirled into the cab, settling on the dumb kidney-shaped plaid cushion on the dashboard that Amy Legat had sewn for her husband, for use when his behind got numb after ten hours of non-stop.

The man climbed carefully into the passenger seat, closed the door, folded his hands on his lap and looked straight ahead.

The cab was colder than Hell and Ernie's breath was coming out in fast, thick clouds. Fast, because for some reason he was a little breathless after the excitement of finding the guy way up here. Thick, because the temperature had dropped to something that would freeze the balls off a polar bear.

He groped for the heater. It was already on full. The cab would heat up again once they got going. Once they got going. God, why was he driving at two miles an hour? Get this thing moving.

The truck shifted a gear and picked up speed, but Ernie was driving without seeing. All he could think of was the guy in his peripheral vision, lit only by the instrument panel now, sitting silently three feet away.

No explanation seemed like it was going to be offered, but Ernie was damned if he wasn't going to be repaid for the rule-breaking ride with at least an interesting tale. 'So what the hell you doin' out there fella?' Ernie settled back into his brown bead seat cover to enjoy whatever the hitcher had to offer.

'Just working my way towards Silver. Thanks for the ride. Looked for a while like I was going to have to walk.' The man beamed across at his saviour, and before Ernie could demand an expansion, the man continued in his soothing pleasant voice. 'Do you know Silver well, Ernie?'

Ernie shot a surprised glance at him. 'How do you know my name?'

The man leant over and tapped Ernie's company I.D., a plastic card hanging from a chain that also supported a tiny cowbell with *Austria* painted on it, that his daughter brought back for him from a school trip fifteen years ago. Ernie's photo glared out from the I.D. like a man in pain, and the real Ernie glared over at his passenger, his face matching his picture. 'It's right here. Unless that's not you.' The man seemed pleased with himself. 'Silver?' He reminded Ernie, who remained locked in his frown.

'Oh I know it well enough. Right now it's choked with folks slidin' around on the hills with wooden sticks stuck to their feet like damned fools, but in the summer it goes right back to bein' the no-shit-happens, assholes in RVs, railroad town it always was. You got business there?'

The man smiled and looked out of his window, his face turned away from Ernie. 'Yeah. I've got some business to take care of there.' He turned back, beaming that smile again. 'Thought I might pick up some work.'

Ernie saw a chance. 'Well you sure would be plenty suited to skiing work, fella, being able to stand out there in minus God knows what without so much as a chilblain. How come you ain't frostbitten, with no gloves or nothin'? And if you don't mind me pryin', how'd you get up there? Didn't see no car.'

The man picked up Amy's cushion, turning it over in his soft white hands, examining it as though it were made of porcelain. 'Got dropped off from another ride a few hours ago. Didn't expect it to be so cold, so I dug a snow-hole. Just off the road back there.' He looked across at Ernie, studying the driver's face closely. 'An old Indian skill I picked up years ago. Outside, forty below. Inside warm as toast. Don't even need a coat once you've sealed the entrance. Heard the truck coming and I just strolled on out to borrow the ride.'

43

Ernie mulled it over. 'So the Indians dug snow-holes? Good to know the useless drunken bums could do somethin'.'

'That's a truth and no mistake,' replied the man with a new tenor to his voice.

Ernie looked across at the man in his truck and his gaze was returned with an unfaltering stare that even in the dim light of the cab Ernie could read as a warning.

He changed the subject.

'What kind of trucker would let you out there? It's only ten more miles to Silver, and the road ain't exactly goin' no place else.'

The man's face creased into a smile. 'Did I say it was a trucker? It certainly was not, Ernie. Like you say, no knight of the road would make such an uncharitable drop. It was a goon in a four-by-four pick-up, and I guess he just got tired of my company. Driver's pre-rogative. Still, mustn't grumble. I'm going to get there anyhow.' He grinned. Hugely. 'Thanks to you Ernie.'

Ernie grunted like an old dog in response.

The truck was already well into its descent, nosing down the other side of the pass, and Ernie turned his attention to making sure his baby wasn't going to end up a forty-ton chrome and steel toboggan, heading for Silver the short way, straight down the cliff.

The heater was being a bitch. They'd been in the cab with the doors shut now for at least ten minutes, and Ernie could still see his breath. If this carried on he'd have to stop in Silver when he let his passenger out, get the thing fixed himself, or stop over until he could find someone who could.

He shifted down a gear, as he felt a slight give under the front wheels.

'Are there many Indians in Silver?'

Ernie didn't enjoy the last exchange about Indians. He wished he'd never brought the subject up. 'Yeah. One or two.'

'Assiniboine, Kinchuinick or Blackfoot?'

'Kinchuinick mostly, I think. Hey, I don't know buddy. Do I look like Professor of Native North American Studies at Princeton?'

The road, which hadn't seen a snowplough for hours, was having one last go at slowing up Ernie Legat and his seafood, boasting a drift of at least three feet across the last serious bend before the run out to town. Ernie could see the lights of Silver just starting to poke through the blizzard, and decided to ram the sucker. Without touching the brakes, he slammed the eighteen-wheeler into the snow bank and hoped it was only this high for a few feet.

Somewhere in one of the back axles, a set of wheels complained enough to shove the rig alarmingly to the left, but the truck held on and ten feet later they were clear. Silver twinkled ahead. Ernie knew his was the last thing on wheels that would get through that for a while. The ploughs wouldn't even look at this until the storm calmed down and nothing he could see was hinting at that. He would drop his passenger and head for the truck stop at Maidston Creek, five miles down the valley. It looked like he'd have to sit out this tempest for a day or two.

'Well, that weren't too tidy, but we made it okay. Where d'you want off?'

'Town boundary'll do fine.'

They crawled up to the edge of town and the hydraulic brakes started hissing and puffing as soon as Ernie caught sight of the aluminium sign that read through a thin sheath of snow *Welcome to Silver. Ski a bit of history!*

'Sure this is it?' asked Ernie as the truck stopped by the sign.

'Yeah. This is where I need to be. Thanks Ernie.'

He put the cushion he had held for the last few miles on the seat beside him, opened the door and hopped out, still holding the clutch-handle.

'And don't drive too long that you need Amy's cushion now, hear?' He shut the door and moved off into the darkness.

Ernie smiled at that. He picked up the cushion to put it back on the dash. He dropped it quickly back onto the seat. It was frozen into a solid, kidney-shaped block of ice.

A blast of hot air from the heater hit Ernie in the face. Seemed it was working again in a big way, and the sudden rush of heat gave him goosebumps, then something approaching a flush.

Suddenly Ernie Legat's heart started to beat a little too fast. How did that guy know Amy made that cushion? How did he even know her name? He hadn't said anything about it at all. Couldn't explain that one from an I.D. in the cab.

And there was something else, something at the very back of Ernie's mind that had bothered him all the way down the pass, but he couldn't get a handle on it. What the Hell was it?

He threw the truck into gear and started to move off, grateful, though he couldn't say why, that the stranger had been swallowed up by the dark and the blizzard.

It was three miles out of Silver that Ernie had it. Even though the cab had been colder than a whore's heart, it was only Ernie's breath that clouded. He didn't like to think about that. So he didn't.

It was twenty minutes after two in the morning that Staff Sergeant Craig McGee stood at the edge of the Trans-Canada highway, looking at the single set of truck tracks already filled with snow, and realized that his sergeant, Joe Reader, was in big trouble.

Joe had been due back around ten, after a routine call to Stoke, on the other side of Wolf Pass. The guys at the store in Stoke who'd called him said he'd left around nine, and since there was a radio in the pick-up, he'd have called for help if he'd gotten stuck in the snow.

Craig didn't like this. Joe was a radio junkie. He'd call up his boss just to say he'd seen an elk in the road, and if he was out there in a drift, Craig would have had an irritating call every two minutes plotting the exact minute-by-minute progress of his entrapment. Of course the radio could be down, which meant that Joe had a cold night ahead, but the truck tracks were evidence that something had got through the pass in the last two hours. If that were so, why hadn't Joe clambered from some trucker's cab hours ago and shambled into the office with a sheepish grin? A trucker wasn't going to ignore a stranded pick-up, especially not one with the RCMP logo painted on the doors and blue and red lights on its roof.

The blizzard was approaching nightmare force, and Craig McGee could hardly stand against the might of the wind and the stinging bullets of snow. He ran back to the Cherokee, sitting off-road with its engine still running, and climbed back into the driving seat. There was no way a chopper could fly in this and it would be crap in the dark anyway, even with the spots on. Nothing for it but to wait for dawn and hope that Joe's wife Estelle didn't go hysterical on him in the meantime.

Craig turned the patrol vehicle round and headed back into town.

The Indians called the gash in the rock that ran from the top of Wolf Pass down to the Silver Creek, Makwi-ochpeekin, the Wolf's Tooth. Fifty feet from the bottom of the gully what was left of Joe Reader's pick-up lay wedged in the fissure of rock like a broken filling in that tooth. Joe's head was almost severed from its torso but a stubborn sinew kept it hanging there, banging against the bare metal of the cab where it dangled upside down. The snow eddied round the remains of Sergeant Reader in tiny cyclones as the ragged, gaping holes in the vehicle allowed it access to the carnage.

Two crows perched on a tiny ledge on the cliff watched the meat hanging from its metal larder, swinging gently with the wind. Perhaps when they were sure it was safe, they would fly over there and explore.

But for now only the snow and the wind explored Joe and his vehicle, and from the look in his eyes, which were two frozen balls in his battered head, Joe Reader didn't mind a bit.

7

When Katie Hunt's phone rang, she jumped. She hoped it was Sam, and it was. Only two days back at work after his blackout and the ski company had sent him to Stoke for fencing in one of the worst blizzards she could remember. That seemed to Katie to be a slice of a raw deal, but the Hunt family had long since learned to lock away resentment at raw deals in a mental box marked *Leave It*.

Right now, she was just glad he was safe.

'So where you going to spend the night honey?'

Sam sounded tired. 'Well it's either the Stoke Hilton or I can bed down in the ticket office. I'm gonna go for the ticket office. Room service is quicker. Seems like I'm the only homeless one round here, so I get the place to myself. It sure beats the hell out of sleeping in the ski truck in a twelve-foot drift. You okay?'

'Sure. You okay? No headaches?'

Katie heard Sam smile through his voice. 'No. No headaches. No drooling down my chin like a lunatic. No writhing on the floor in a fit.'

Katie ignored his mockery of her concern. 'When do you think you'll make it home?'

'If the blizzard lets up I guess the pass'll be open by about noon tomorrow. You can wear my wool shirt if you get cold in bed without me.'

'Sam?'

'Yeah?'

'I love you.'

'I love you too babe.'

Billy yelled from the other room, and Katie said her goodbyes and hung up. Some chat show host was smarming through his front of show stand-up, while Billy Hunt ignored him in favour of a hand-held computer game. He yelled again as Katie came into the L-shaped room that was the biggest living space in the house.

'Nine thousand Mom! I got nine thousand! Yeees!'

Katie stood behind her son, and ran one thoughtful hand through his straight black hair. 'Bed, Billy boy. Now.'

'You said I could wait up and see Dad,' he replied without taking his eyes off the grey plastic block in his hand.

'Dad's stranded in the storm over at Stoke. He's coming home tomorrow, so that means bed for you, right now.'

She leaned over and switched off Billy's game.

'Aw Mom!'

'I said now, Billy. Your hockey kit's at the foot of your bed. You forget to put it in your bag again tomorrow then you're on your own, kid. I'm not driving round to school with it.' She turned to leave the room.

'Mom?'

'Yeah?'

'Dad won't be at home tonight at all?'

Suddenly he looked worried. Katie went back and joined him on the sofa.

'It's okay. Like I said: he'll be back tomorrow.'

'Can Bart sleep with me tonight?'

Katie tried to look hurt. 'Oh, so Jess and I won't do for company then? I keep forgetting, we're just sappy girls.'

Billy put his hand in hers, and looked into her eyes with such concern she already regretted the joke. 'You do fine. I just want Bart with me. It's important.'

Katie squeezed his little hand. 'Sure. If you can get him in. Good luck. You know what he's been like.'

'Great!'

'Now go get ready for bed. I'll be up in a minute.'

Her son bounced up and hopped on one foot to the door, singing as he went. His nine-year-old mind had already moved on to other matters. Likewise, Katie's thirty-four-year-old mind had drifted back to her husband, worry and anxiety drilling into her. It was wrenched back to reality by the sound of Bart bounding up stairs with Billy, as the dog knocked over the frosted glass vase on the landing.

She smiled, and went to play at being stern.

When dawn came on January tenth it revealed the best snow conditions Silver Ski Company had seen for fifteen seasons. It also brought Estelle Reader the worst day of her life.

When they brought back what was left of Joe around one thirty, Craig had been first at Estelle's door, his face a grey mask of grief. Craig thought about the kind of suffering you see in the movies, where widows thank the policeman, squeeze his hand, and sit quietly in a chair absorbing the news. He thought about it as Estelle fell to her knees gurgling like a pig being bled, clutching at Craig's jacket with fists like claws. She writhed on the floor and tore at the rug, saliva running from her mouth as she grunted and panted in the pain of her despair, until Craig hooked his hands under her armpits and lifted her onto a chair.

Life wasn't like the movies. In fact life in Silver over the last week had been real bad.

Two ski patrollers killed in a freak explosion, and now Joe. He would, of course, have to tell Estelle that Joe's death hadn't been an accident, but not now. Time for that later, and time was going to bring her more pain. She would have to suffer the wait before they could lay Joe in the ground, while an autopsy was performed on the grisly remains.

From what they recovered in the gorge, there wasn't much left to fit in a coffin, and after the forensics had been at him, Craig suspected a Safeway's bag would probably be big enough to bury his ex-sergeant decently.

He waited with the moaning shell of Estelle Reader until her sister got there, then left and headed back to work.

Half a mile from the office, Craig McGee pulled off the highway into a back road, stopped the engine and cried like a baby. He would be all right in half an hour. Right now, he was broken up.

'No kidding? Well if it's a problem we can send a car to the airport to bring her luggage separately.'

Pasqual Weaver watched her own reflection in the office window as she spoke. An elegant, if angular, woman in her thirties looked back, the grey fleece zippered top with the Silver Ski Company logo embroidered on the left breast doing its best to undermine her executive status.

The hand unoccupied by the telephone played with the zipper at her neck.

'Sure, we want her to be real comfortable. And can I say we're already over the moon she's even considering it.'

Eric entered the room and Pasqual mimed at him to sit down.

'Okay James, you put those things to her and get back to us when you have an answer, but please tell her from us that we're all huge fans and are really hoping she can make it. Okay, you too. Take care.' She hung up, and gave the phone her middle finger. 'Jesus. The fucking old bitch is acting like she's still a star. Make my day, Eric. Tell me you've come to persuade me this celebrity ski week idea is a crock of shit.'

Eric Sindon had not come to say any such thing. 'You've heard about the accident?'

Pasqual's body changed shape. No longer lounging in her leather chair, it was now sitting forward like a cat watching its prey before striking.

'Tell me.'

'Craig's side-kick. His truck went over the gorge on Wolf's Pass last night.'

Pasqual sat back in her chair with relief. 'Fuck. Don't give me scares like that. I thought we'd had a fatality on the slopes. I think we can live with a cop in an auto accident.'

Eric looked at his boss with distaste. 'It's the third death in Silver in a week. I'm getting rumours that there's more to it than just an automobile accident.'

Pasqual opened her top drawer and fished around until she found a packet of M & Ms.

'Want one?' She tossed the packet over the desk to Eric after filling her mouth with chocolate.

'No. Look I'm telling you this because I think it will have a negative effect on the resort. Skiers don't get off on reading about death when they should be reading about snow reports.'

'Eric, I think our visitors are big enough boys and girls to cope with the fact that sometimes people die in cars.'

'What about Lenny and Jim?'

'Accidents happen. They were patrollers for Christ's sake.'

51

Eric looked at her and she knew that look. Pasqual stood up and turned her back to him, looking out of the window at the last of the die-hard skiers stepping out of their bindings beside the lodge after stealing the last run of the day.

'What do you see out there, Eric?'

'A lodge that needs a re-clad and a nursery area that needs two extra tows.'

She laughed, and threw another chocolate peanut into her mouth. 'Well, maybe so, but I see the best fucking snow we've had in years, and a season that's going to do business like a cold beer stall in Hell.' She turned back to him. 'Now what exactly are you worried about?'

'Someone has to.'

'Meaning?'

'Meaning you shouldn't underestimate negative vibes in a fun resort Pasqual.'

She sat down and smiled a wicked cat grin at him. 'Are you telling me my job, Mr Sindon?'

Eric sighed. 'Okay, forget it. Just thought it was worth mentioning.'

'Thank you.'

Eric shoved some paper at her.

'Here's the shop stock-taking list, and there's a guy outside looking for work. Do you want me to see him?'

'Nope. I'll see him. You fax more celebrities. Try and get something more famous than someone who voiced over an AT&T commercial. Remember the blackmail bit about the kids in wheelchairs. Lay it on as thick as you like. Where's the guy?'

'In the ski school.'

She emptied the last of the chocolates into her mouth, threw the packet in the waste bin and moved to the door. 'Oh and Eric . . .'

Eric looked up expectantly.

'No more drama-queen stuff unless a gondola full of customers spontaneously combusts. Right?'

Eric held her gaze without reply for a few more moments than was polite.

'You're the boss.'

'Yes. I am. Aren't I?'

She smiled and shut the door behind her. Eric looked at the door for a long time until the phone rang.

*   *   *

As Pasqual left the seclusion of her inner office, walking through the shop and past the ticket booths, she ran the gauntlet of questions and greetings from every member of staff in her path.

'Oh Miss Weaver! Got a moment?'

'Pasqual! Can you call the top station?'

'Miss Weaver – any thoughts on this display?'

She loved it. She adored being pursued by a team of courtiers, anxious for her approval or instruction, and she treasured it all the more when the public saw her in the middle of it.

As she left the building and crossed the darkening nursery area to the ski school shed, she tossed her short brown bobbed hair, waved and shouted 'Hi!' to anyone who would respond.

The man was waiting inside. He greeted her with a smile.

'Hi there. You're the job hunter.'

'Yeah. You must be Pasqual Weaver. Moses Sitconski. Pleased to meet you.'

He extended a lily-white hand, which she shook.

'What kind of a name is that exactly?'

The man looked at her, neither offended or defensive. 'My name.'

'Well, Moses,' she said, pronouncing the word as though it were a shared and intimate joke, 'You've done your resort personnel home-work. Now what kind of work are you after? We're nearly half-way through the season, you know.'

'Sure, I know. Looks like it's going to be a great second half. Long time since I've seen snow conditions this good. I guess the powder in the back bowls is like spun sugar right now.'

He smiled, crinkling two ice blue eyes in a face so pale Pasqual figured the guy had never been near a ski trail in his life. She was used to dealing with people with mahogany tans that stopped where their turtlenecks started, but the easy charm of this man was making up for the fact that he was obviously no ski bum. Nor was he dressed like anyone who wanted to be near snow. A long black wool coat hung over what Pasqual noted was a powerful frame. She wasn't looking at a potential ski instructor, but maybe he'd be some use in the PR office.

'You a skier Moses?'

'Sure. I can get down most things.'

'So where have you worked before? And what as exactly?'

The man looked into her eyes very deeply indeed.

Pasqual was aware of an acute sexual stirring begin around her nipples that shifted down over her belly to an area she didn't have much time to explore these days. He was turning her on with those eyes, and she was ashamed. Why this encounter should have such an effect was a mystery, and made her squirm beneath her fleece with discomfort and irritation. After all, she was surrounded all day by pieces of meat on skis that she could have just by looking sideways at them. If she chose to, she could fuck any instructor on the resort, but sex was never high on Pasqual Weaver's agenda. Right now, however, it was standing at the front door ringing the bell.

'Tamarack. Two seasons. Manual grooming mainly.'

She looked at him suspiciously. How could he have worked out doors all day as a manual groomer and still have stayed as white as a baby's ass? She wasn't going to be bullshitted. Tamarack just happened to be Silver's biggest rival right now. So much so, even the name got on her tits.

'And who was the big white chief at Tamarack? Just in case I want to call him up?'

The man who called himself Moses smiled widely, revealing milky white teeth behind his pink lips. 'I'd be glad if you called him up, Miss Weaver. His name is William Cole. We called him Hill Billy.'

She knew damned well it was Bill fucking Cole that ran the show over there. Same as she knew that Tamarack had stolen nearly a fifth of Silver's day trip custom with three new high speed quads. She would drink piss before she would phone up Cole for a reference. The fact that the guy knew his name and his slang name, was enough proof for her he was telling the truth. Plus he would be useful in the office if he knew exactly what was going on with the competition.

'So are you hoping for manual work again or does something with a desk and a fan heater blowing hot air up your fanny all day interest you?'

'Anything you got really. I understand you lost a couple of your ski patrol.'

She frowned. 'Yeah, well we're on that one thanks. The rest of the guys are still cut up about it and I don't think they'd take too kindly to me sticking a sits. vac. ad in the local newspaper before they've got their two buddies in the ground.'

'A real tragedy.'

'It's a dangerous job.'

His eyes were boring through her skull. She looked away, pretending to study the blackboard for tomorrow's ski class rota. 'Okay Moses, why don't you come see me tomorrow at eight thirty and we'll fix something up. Can't promise ski patrol, but I'll be honest and tell you we can use some extra help right now. Things are going to get real busy when the snow reports hit the cities.'

Moses stuck his hand out again and she took it without thinking. This time he held on to it a little longer than she would have liked.

'Well that's just great, Miss Weaver. I look forward to that.'

She withdrew her hand as the door threw open to admit five laughing instructors clopping in like carthorses.

'Robbed the public blind today I hope guys?' she said in a tone higher than she had planned.

'Yo, you bet,' laughed the biggest and brownest of the pack, unzipping his suit with a baroque flourish.

Pasqual smiled once at them, once at Moses, and left.

The tall pale man watched the flimsy wooden door close behind Pasqual and then glanced across at the five faces eyeballing him.

'Hi,' he smiled.

Only one nodded back.

Moses Sitconski put his hands back into his pockets without dissolving his smile, then followed Pasqual out into the night.

8

The ploughs went past with the invincibility of a fleet of Newfoundland trawlers putting to sea; lights flashing, funnels blowing out plumes of snow, their metal bows pushing back the ocean of white in huge, semi-solid waves.

Snaking behind these yellow leviathans was a line of nineteen cars, two trucks and a bus, and right in the middle Sam Hunt sat behind the wheel of the company pick-up.

As he drove slowly behind a big shiny Ford, Sam's eyes were narrow slits of dismay. Not because his progress home was painfully slow, but because last night, alone on the bench in the ticket office at Stoke, he'd had another dream.

So far, it was the worst. Since his blackout three days ago, every night had furnished him with dreams so distressing and unendurable he was beginning to dread sleep. But last night was the pits. It was almost real.

It had been different in detail of course, but the creature was still there. Still fixing him with its unholy, vindictive, glacial gaze as it set about its grisly business. Always the business with the heart. That was the bit he couldn't take.

There was more last night though. A lot more. Sam made a dry swallow as he remembered.

The office that smelt of wet floorboards and hot dogs during the day was a different place at night. Fierce heating dried the wood after the last customer had left, slowly evaporating the puddles caused by skiers dragging the snow in on their moonboots. For a while it made the room steamy and sour. But once it had dried, and the cleaners had done their stuff sweeping up discarded sticky backs from the lift

56

passes, the office was a pleasant and inhabitable room, and when Sam had called Katie he was comfortable. There was, after all, something soothing about seeking refuge from the storm in a commercial rather than a domestic setting, appealing to that childish excitement of bedding down somewhere alien and forbidden.

The first time Sam had been in a church in Calgary he felt that way. He was fifteen years old and the luxury of the interior, the cool but ornate splendour, had astounded him. There had been no sense of God to the young Sam Hunt, just a million opportunities for making tiny living spaces in the dozens of marble and oak corners the building boasted. He sat on the hard pew, imagining creeping in to that fabulous building when everyone was gone and unfurling his sleeping mat beneath the high, carved wooden pulpit. It was like a palace. What would it be like to run barefoot on that marble floor in front of the minister? Think of the feasts that could be laid out on those huge stone steps, and the dancing that could go wildly out of control in the vast empty space between pews and altar. The pragmatist in him figured that cooking could be accomplished quite safely on the stone-flagged floors, since the smoke would have ample space to rise and dissipate high above, amongst the barrel-vaulting. Sam knew he could live there like a king.

The Reverend and Mrs Jenkins were delighted by Sam's expression of wonder and awe as he sat between them that day, his black-button eyes roving over the architecture like a blind man seeing for the first time.

They were not to know his thoughts were on a flight of fancy as to how he would live secretively in such a place, instead of an awakening to the glory and love of their God: but they often misinterpreted their young charge. They never really knew him at all.

The Silver Ski Company ticket office in Stoke was no comparison to the Calgary Church of All Saints on Third Street, but as Sam selected a place to sleep, his instincts were the same as those of twenty years ago. All these interesting nooks and corners to sleep in. Areas to make your own.

He had three blankets in the truck and found a long, foam seat cover from the back of the office where the staff took their boots off. More than enough for a bed. He made his nest beside the radiator pipes at the back wall, where he faced the big digital clock above the ticket windows.

Outside, the blizzard battered at the windows, the snow hitting the glass like shotgun pellets. Sam turned off the overhead striplight and wriggled, snug beneath his blankets. The big green digital numbers of the clock cast an eerie illumination on the room, reflecting dimly on the floorboards. They were reading 10.07 when he settled down, his hand beneath his head like a child. Sam had decided he was feeling better. Dreams aside, there had been no further blacking out, and it was that void of consciousness that held most terror for him. Brain tumour? Cancer? All the demons of modern medical knowledge had plagued him like a hypochondriac since that numbing collapse. But it was over now. He was well. Sure of it.

When he woke up after the dream and threw his load, the green digits were reading 10.45. Sam found himself on all fours, hunched like a dog over a pile of his own hot vomit. He was sweating and panting, and the stench of the wet bile beneath him made him retch again.

The memory of it made Sam clutch the steering wheel like a life-line. But it was what came after that was making Sam's heart thump in his chest like a trapped bird. Nothing. That's what happened after he woke over his own sick. At least nothing until he woke a second time. At 7.30 a.m. Fully clothed, standing outside his truck.

When Craig saw the guy that stepped out of the car he'd been more than disappointed. Not in his whole term as staff sergeant in Silver had he ever had to call in forensics from Edmonton, and this small bald man in a suit jacket covered by a cheap nylon parka didn't look much like the cavalry.

That was six hours ago. Craig was going to give him the benefit of the doubt. Dr Brenner had been working at Joe all day, talking into a tape recorder as he did so, and now he was standing in Craig's office with a styrofoam cup in one hand ready to pronounce sentence.

Craig was calm as he offered the doctor a seat.

Brenner ran a delicate hand over the pate of his bald head and sat down heavily in the chair by the window.

'How's it looking out there?'

Brenner gesticulated with his coffee to the outside world behind him. Craig glanced out of the window.

'It's okay. Cold. What have you got for me?'

'Time of death around 11.30 p.m. Cause of death, a violent blow to the head followed by lacerations to the chest. Further damage, probably after the initial blows, and due to the incisions, indicates massive loss of blood.'

'Incisions.'

'Incisions, Staff Sergeant. The cuts he made to get into the heart and remove the genitals.'

Craig looked at him, unblinking, forcing himself to believe in what he was hearing. Yes, this was Joe they were discussing. Joe who should have been in here glowering at Brenner, looking at his watch and making doe eyes at Craig to let him away for his bowling night. But Joe was never going to dog off early to go bowling with a cold beer in his hand again. Right now, Joe was the collection of meat cuts lying four doors down the corridor on a table covered in polythene sheeting, and how he died wasn't making sense.

No witnesses except maybe whoever drove through the pass after Joe. They were on that one already. It wouldn't be hard to find the driver that made the tracks Craig saw. It could only have been a truck, and there were three constables phone-bashing every trucking company in the book right now.

'And the crash?'

'Happened after death. The lesions and breakages incurred by impact with the falling truck all occurred after he died. The way the blood clots always reveals that. The truck must have been pushed over the edge by whoever carved him up.'

The doctor drained his cup, and met Craig's horror-filled gaze full-on.

'What about the mutilation?'

'Looks like the murderer had plenty of time on his hands. The heart was so tightly compacted up the anus, even with the tiny incision he made to get it in, it implies someone took great care to make sure it would stay there. It's a big organ. I'm amazed how the assailant achieved it. Must have been a turkey-stuffer.'

Brenner grinned at his joke, receiving nothing but silence, and continued more coldly as he lost his smile, 'The penis was torn off rather than cut, and it appears to have been in the mouth, although it had fallen out by the time you guys finished hauling the body up.'

'How do you know it was in the mouth?'

'His teeth closed on it. Left tissue inside. I reckon if you guys send a climber down there you'll find his pecker where it fell.' Brenner stuck his nail into the styrofoam cup, making a popping sound that delighted him sufficiently to make him do it again. 'Yeah, it's an X-rated one this, all right.'

Craig responded coldly. 'When will the full report be ready for our inspection?'

Brenner caught the coldness in his voice, and smiled. 'The report will be ready soon as I get back to Edmonton to write it, but I'll wager with a murder like this you boys will be playing host to a bit of city help. Guess they'll read it first. Tell you everything you need to know.' He stood up to go.

'Sit down, doctor.'

He continued to stand.

'Until we hear who will formally head this investigation, I'm the officer in charge and the sole officer to whom you make your report. There are plenty of facilities here for you to have your taped report transcribed and printed out before you leave. Now, I understand you must be tired, so if you like we can arrange for some hotel accommodation for you while we organise the paperwork.'

Brenner glared at Craig. 'I was planning on getting back tonight, Staff Sergeant, if that's okay with you.'

'No, I'm afraid it's not okay. Not until I know all the facts and can question you in detail about the autopsy. If that takes for the rest of the week then so be it.'

'With all due respect, I work out of Edmonton. I'm not at your beck and call.'

'In the time it takes you to get back to the city, doctor, our murderer could be hundreds of miles from here. Even worse, he could still be here ready to strike again. I'm sure as a senior member of the Edmonton forensics team you hardly need me to remind you that police work is a race against the clock. Now, can I organise that hotel for you while you give your tape to Holly?'

Brenner looked at Craig for a few seconds and smiled. 'Very well, Staff Sergeant. I'll just call my wife, then I'll call my superior officer in Edmonton. Just to let him know what's happening of course. May I use your phone?'

Craig waved a hand. Brenner came forward a pace and picked up the receiver and punched out the number.

'By the way, I think you'll find the murder weapon's going to prove problematic.'

'In what way?'

'No traces to indicate any metal instrument whatsoever. There are usually tell-tale signs that can lead us to identify at least the nature of the weapon. You know, serrated or unserrated, steel or base metal and so on. Everything leaves minute particles behind. In this case, nothing. Yet the incisions were as fine as scalpel cuts . . . Barbara? It's Larry.'

Craig waited expectantly, until Brenner put his hand over the receiver and turned to face him. 'May I?'

'Sure. Go ahead. I'll be right outside.'

Craig McGee closed the door on his own hessian-lined office and poured himself a drink from the water cooler. From the other side of the door came the sound of Brenner laughing on the phone.

Craig McGee couldn't phone home and laugh because there was no Mrs McGee any more to pick up the phone and smile at the sound of his voice. The phone would ring alone and unanswered on the blue painted table by the front door, secure in its secret plastic knowledge that Sylvia wasn't ever going to come running out from the kitchen again, wiping her hands on a dishcloth and pick it up. Why phone home when your wife is dead? In fact if he didn't have to feed her cats, Craig sometimes wondered why he went home at all. Everything there had her mark on it, her smell on it, her touch to it. Her absence mocked him, from the coffee jars full of shells she collected on holiday in Scotland, to the rid- iculous carved magazine rack she bought at a heart foundation sale. Sometimes he woke in the night and stretched out to touch her neck, only to find the empty strip of bed as cold as marble.

He wondered if Brenner knew how lucky he was to be able to perform that simple but delicious act of phoning home.

Staff Sergeant McGee let his forehead rest against the wall above the cooler. He crushed the waxed paper cone in his hand and let it fall to the floor.

'Don't know why they don't just send us out in a carton pulled by a sow. Be as much use as this heap of shit in the snow.'

Constable Sonny Morris was not enjoying trying to control the Ford Crown Victoria in the thickening blizzard, and his partner Dan Small made a nasal sound in agreement. Highway patrol was a joke in conditions like these. They'd be lucky to find anyone moving, never mind speeding.

'You got to drive fast to keep control. I keep telling you. Drive fast.'

Sonny glanced sideways at Dan.

'Uh-huh?'

'Sure. It works. You see, the slower you go the more traction you lose. Tried it last winter in my wife's Honda. Got the thing all the way up to Ledmore in one go. Three feet of fresh fall, and I made it in one go. You have to drive fast.'

The driver remained unimpressed, and maintained the stately twenty miles per hour that was taking them back to the detachment in Silver.

'Like to have seen that.'

'God's truth. In one go.'

'Nah. Not the driving bit. Just the fact you were in Moira's Honda.'

Dan squirmed.

'Hey come on. The pick-up was bust. I had to get to Calgary. What was I goin' to do? Walk?'

'Better than being in Moira's Honda.'

Dan gave him the finger and was formulating a riposte when they saw the truck. Ahead, a tear in the white curtain of snow revealed an eighteen-wheeler sitting in the viewpoint parking bay. By the depth of the snow on it, and the fact that no tracks led from the highway to its current position, it had been there a long time.

Sonny brightened considerably, moving forward in his seat as though the action would turn the Crown Vic into a Land Cruiser.

'Lookee here. Some rough-neck's sure going to be glad to see us.'

They glided to a standstill behind the truck, and Sonny reached for his hat on the dash. Dan got on the radio. 'Two Alpha Four Calgary. We're ten-seven on the Trans-Canada, 'bout two miles west of Silver. Over.'

There was a crackle, a long pause and eventually a female voice. 'Calgary Two Alpha Four. Read you. Over.'

Dan looked at Sonny.

'Nice to know they care, huh?'

Sonny made a wide-eyed expression of horror. 'Oh no! Could it be that here in Alberta we're not as professional as the detachment you worked with in B.C.? Now I don't think I've heard you mention that before.'

Dan grabbed his hat. 'Yeah, well you'll eat shit when you pull over

62

a maniac one day and no one knows you're out here or what the plate is. That's all I'm saying. They should make you tell them. Run it through the computer. This could be a stolen truck. That's all I'm saying.'

Sonny looked sardonically towards the Peterbilt. 'You know you're right, Dan. Guess we just don't know the half of it way out here in the sticks. Never heard of a joy-rider stealing an eighteen-wheeler for kicks. Still, police work is a learning experience. Now shall I go fetch the poor stranded hauler, or do you think we'd better call for assistance? Could be a gang of Hispanic drug dealers using a twenty-ton trailer as cover.'

'Fuck off, Morris.'

Sonny laughed and opened the car door to a flurry of huge snow-flakes. Dan followed him from the passenger door, battling to open it against the wind.

There was little sign of life from the truck, which sported a two-foot crown of undisturbed snow. The blizzard whipped mini-storms under its belly, blowing the snow out between the axles in random but concentrated blasts.

Sonny approached the driver's door and stepped up on the foot plate. The window was more ice than glass, impossible to see through. He shouted and tugged at the handle. Frozen. Dan walked round the front, kicking his way through a drift that had built up round the front wheels, while Sonny continued to tug uselessly at the handle.

Fishing in his breast pocket, Dan found his lighter and put it to the handle of the passenger door. The ice gave way in ungracious rivulets and when he pulled on the metal the door creaked open reluctantly.

It had been a man. Now it was ice. The eyes were swollen horribly, the result of their moisture freezing and expanding, and they stared, boggling, out of the windscreen into nothing. The tongue protruded like a gargoyle, long and pointed and white, and the hands still gripped the wheel as though this man of ice was shouting maniacally at a driver who'd just cut him up bad.

Dan stared at it for a long time, his own mouth open, almost aping the frozen figure he beheld. Sonny, unable to open the driver door joined Dan at his elbow.

'God almighty.'

Dan stepped down, still staring at the nightmare, and let Sonny in. He climbed up and touched the figure gingerly with a gloved finger. It was hard as rock.

Sonny looked round the cab. Full of snow. Snow on the floor, snow banked up on the seat against the door, snow in a cornice along the windshield. What the hell had this guy been doing?

Why would you let the cab fill with snow, shut the doors, and then sit at the wheel until you froze to death? He cleared the dash with the back of his hand and found the driver's I.D.

Ernie Legat. Fifty-five years old.

He sighed and backed out of the cab. Poor Ernie. The guy must have planned it like this. Probably had gambling debts or something. Sonny had seen plenty creative suicides, but they never got any easier to deal with. Poor Ernie.

9

Keeping the yard from clogging with snow was impossible. That was probably why Wilber Stonerider had been given the task. Flakes the size of golf balls were driving through the chicken wire in the compound as though his shovel were their sole target. No big deal. He would have a drink soon. He felt the half bottle of whiskey in his jacket pocket bumping against his thigh with every thrust of the shovel and let himself imagine the moment when he could slip behind one of the dismantled buses in the compound and take a long, delicious mouthful. Inside the shed, the engineers were clattering around their machines, shouting to each other and playing the radio loud, their noise echoing round the huge tin building as though they were in a drum.

The buses that ended up here were like sick animals. They stood passively inside the shed and out in the yard, waiting to be attended by the gang of mechanical surgeons who would strip back their bodywork and probe their insides. Wilber, meanwhile, got to sweep the yard. But then Wilber was not exactly a regular employee of Fox-Line Travel. Wilber was putting in some community service hours, penance for being drunk and disorderly in the Empire Hotel when he managed to smash three chairs and assault a waitress called Candy.

He'd figured this would be preferable to a couple of days in the slammer but now, with the snow making his task Herculean, he wasn't so sure. The RCs didn't dare touch you these days. No way. The band had hired that fancy lady lawyer from Edmonton who'd throw the book at them if any Kinchuinick Indian came out of their custody with so much as a scratch. Sure, they would call you every name in the book and some that didn't make it into the book, but they couldn't break your face. She was the best thing the band ever bought. Even looked after off-reserve Indians like Wilber. All you had to do was use your one phone call to her and, bingo, she'd get you off the hook. Of course from Silver, calling the band office was long distance, but that didn't matter none. So far Wilber had called the lady lawyer four times. He was really getting value for money. Okay, value for the band's money. Except this time, he wished he'd taken the days in pokey. You got food and sleep, and it was warm. Of course there was no liquor or tobacco, and that was hard to go without for three days. He felt the bottle again on his leg and decided that he'd made the right choice. He ran his tongue over dry lips, catching a flake as it tried to fly into his mouth. Now was as good a time as any to step quietly behind the bus and have a small refreshment. He shovelled noisily towards the bus and slipped behind its great frozen flanks, out of sight of the open shed door. With his back to the chicken wire, he propped the shovel against the bus and fished in his light blue parka for the bottle. Even the warmth of his body hadn't made any impression on the whiskey, and it was as cold as a beer straight from the ice-box when he put it to his lips and threw his head back.

'Tasty?'

Wilber choked on the liquid burning down his throat and coughed like a consumptive. His eyes were streaming as he pirouetted round to see who had addressed him from the other side of the wire.

A man, a man just like him, stood smiling from the sidewalk outside the compound, his eyes piercing Wilber like skewers.

'What the fuck . . .'

The man put one hand up to the wire, coiled his fingers through the diamond-shaped hole and with the other hand put a finger to his lips to make a hushing mime, as if to a baby crying in its cot.

Wilber was confused and not a little pissed off. He wrestled his coughing under control, and blinked at the guy like he was crazy. Still hanging on the fence the man put his hand back into his pocket and spoke deliberately, in the manner of someone making an announcement.

' I am . . .' he paused as if for dramatic effect, and smiled, '. . . Sitconski.'

Wilber blinked at him at again. He screwed the top back on his whiskey and stepped back slightly from the wire. 'Yeah?'

The man stood perfectly still, waiting.

Wilber flicked through a mental filing cabinet of what this guy wanted. He took a guess. 'You from Welfare?'

There was an almost imperceptible change in the man's demeanour, but Wilber Stonerider picked it up. Was it anger? Why would a total stranger be angry at him? He'd done nothing. Well, nothing he wasn't already paying for. But there it was in this guy's eyes. Anger. Definitely.

This time the man spoke softly, and if Wilber were honest with himself, menacingly.

'My name is Sitconski.' He scanned the forty-two-year-old Indian's face as if searching for a concealed message, a smile forming on his lips again. This time, an unmistakably cruel smile. 'Moses Sitconski.' The smile gave way to a dry laugh, like ice cracking under a boot.

Wilber was out of his depth here. The guy was obviously a nut. And he was a nut interfering with the only serious drinking time he might grab this morning. Any moment now the foreman would walk out of the shed looking for him and it would be too late to take another swig. If he wasn't here to pin something on him, this guy could get lost.

'Nice meeting you, Mr Sitconski.' He turned his back on the guy and picked up his shovel. There was, after all, eight feet of wire netting between them. The voice that came back at him this time made Wilber freeze like an animal in headlights.

'Do you know my name?'

What was wrong with that voice? It was a human voice. Was it though? There was something horrible running beneath the syllables, like a sewer running under a sidewalk. Frightened, Wilber turned round slowly to face the man again. The snow was falling thick and silent between them and Wilber's breath sent white clouds billowing between the flakes. If the man was breathing at all it was like an athlete. There was no vapour from his mouth or nose at all. Wilber realized the hand holding the shovel was shaking and that he still held his bottle in the other. He leant the shovel on the fence, unscrewed the bottle and took a long draught. Of course he could always run away, but something told him no one would ever run fast enough from this man.

The whiskey hit the spot and gave him back his voice. He laughed nervously. 'Sure. Sure I know your name Mister. You just told me it. Moses Sitconski.'

Wilber thought he saw ripples in the man. That was the only way he could describe it. Like the guy had something under his clothing. No, under his skin. And it was stirring, getting restless.

'Do you know my name?'

He wanted to cry now. What was this? Something was happening to the air between them, and all the alarm bells had just gone off in Wilber Stonerider's brain. What did he mean? The crazy son of a bitch had told him his name about three times. He found himself looking to the side to see if anyone in the shed could see them from here, but he'd made sure they were well out of sight when he'd sneaked behind the bus. Through the wire, he could see the white blanketed scrubland on the other side of the road. In short, no one could see Wilber Stonerider and his insane visitor Moses Whatever.

'Look Mister. I don't want no trouble. I know your . . .'

'DO YOU KNOW MY NAME?'

The force of the words, spoken quietly, almost gently, was so unexpected that Wilber fell back against the side of the bus. The voice had come from somewhere distant and dark and although its volume was that of an explosion, he knew somewhere deep inside him, that only he, Wilber Stonerider, had heard it. It contained so much malice, so much rage, it stunned him. He started to weep. There was something happening to the man, something Wilber couldn't even begin to address. It wasn't so much that he was changing, more that he was becoming what he was. The tears rolled down his cheeks as he pressed himself against the bus.

'Are you pullin' your pecker back there, chief?'

It was the foreman. Wilber opened his mouth to yell, but found he couldn't. The thing through the wire looked back at him with a wrath that promised to erupt into frenzy. It whirled its head round to where the shout came from and as it broke contact with his eyes, Wilber ran. He ran, skidding in the snow, round the bus and into the chest of foreman Taylor. They fell together in the snow, Wilber's bottle smashing with a thud instead of a tinkle in the snow a few feet away. The alcohol melted a tiny patch of snow round the shards before it disappeared into the ground.

'Ah! You fuckin' moron.'

Taylor, clad only in his work jeans and an ex-army sweater, tried to peel the jabbering Indian off him as he rolled on his back like a turtle. Wilber clutched at him like a two-year-old, making gasping noises and dribbling from the mouth and nose. Taylor pushed him off and struggled to his feet, leaving Wilber on the ground, his arms covering his head.

'Get up! I said get up, you drunken shit.'

Taylor was really angry. An Indian with DTs was not what he called help. He was cold and wet now, sweater soaked through, jeans covered in snow, and it was this snivelling idiot's fault. How did the numbskull manage to get so sauced in such a short time? He'd handed him the snow shovel only twenty minutes ago and the Indian had been sober. Look at him now.

Wilber peeled one arm from round his head and pointed to the bus. 'He's there. He's goin' to get me. Crazy guy. Keeps asking me his name.'

He was still weeping. Taylor swept the snow angrily off his thighs and marched over to where Wilber was pointing. Nothing. Of course. He came back round the front of the bus, stood over the wreck of a human being and hauled him up roughly by the arm. Wilber resisted, but Taylor was a powerful man and the Indian was on unsteady feet before he could protest further. Taylor shook him by the collar of his frayed and dirty parka. 'Now I don't need to tell you there's nothin' over there. And I also don't need to tell you you'll be back with the RCs faster than you can say I fuck dogs unless you pick up that shovel and shift this snow.'

Wilber looked towards the bus, then up at Taylor. 'He gone?'

'Don't give me that. Get shovelling.'

He let go of Wilber's jacket with a push and stood with his hand on his hips until the sniffing man walked gingerly to the edge of the bus and peeked round. It was true. No one there at all. Just the shovel lying on the ground where it had slid off the fence.

He walked round the back of the bus, looking left and right as though expecting an ambush, picked up the shovel and scurried back into the foreman's sight. Where did the guy go? There was no-one in the road at all. Not even a car. Unless he'd run off into the scrub, he couldn't have just disappeared. There were no tracks leading to the scrub, but then as Wilber looked back at the sidewalk on the other side of the fence, he noted that there were no tracks at all. Anywhere.

Taylor spat, and tramped back into the shed in search of dry clothes, leaving Wilber Stonerider with the horror that maybe it was true, the sauce was hitting him bad. He looked forlornly at the smashed bottle in the snow and scooped it up in the plastic snow shovel.

A large black bird was perched motionless on the wing mirror of the broken bus and it stared at Wilber.

'What the fuck you lookin' at?'

He resumed his shovelling.

The bird looked back at him for a long, long time, then flapped its waxy wings and flew off.

10

Alberta 1907
Siding Twenty-three

'Well? Are they going to move?'

Angus McEwan looked up from his makeshift table in the centre of the cabin, glaring past the man who stood in front of him as though speaking to a ghost at his side.

'I fear it is more complex than that, Mr McEwan.'

McEwan allowed his eyes, raising them slowly and insolently, to find the face of the speaker. What an absurd figure the Reverend Henderson made. His considerable height, twinned with a slight build, made a mockery of the sombre black clothes he wore. He had the appearance of a gangly adolescent forced into ill-fitting Sunday best for a relative's funeral, the white dog-collar rendering him almost comic, aided in its farce by a nose and cheeks turned purple by the cold. But he spoke these savages' language, and the man was indispensable.

'Complex in what respect Reverend?'

Henderson stamped his great feet in a vain attempt to keep warm, and cleared his throat.

'I have already explained their campaign to you. That is unchanged. I think it unlikely they will move at all. Not without force that is, and that would clearly be inadvisable, not to mention illegal.'

Angus McEwan paused to consider why he disliked this man so much. They were both from Scotland, albeit different parts of the country. Henderson was an east coast Church of Scotland minister, and McEwan was a west coast engineer. But there was little patriotic bonding between them, even though some such comfort would have been welcome in this distant, alien continent in which they both found themselves. It was Henderson's stubborn and naïve allegiance to these base heathens that irritated McEwan so deeply. Any Christian man could see the Indians were not civilized beings, not fit to be treated as equals, and yet this ridiculous man treated them as though they were Lords.

To see a white man, a Scot, so humbled before savages, was disgusting to McEwan.

'If we are to discuss legality, perhaps you would care to mention to your new flock that their forebears signed a treaty concerning this railroad and its building many decades ago. Mention that approximately ten minutes from now, when we kick their bloody behinds off the mountain.'

Henderson flushed slightly, giving new life to the broken purple veins the frost had drawn on his cheeks. McEwan often cursed to rile him. Not this time though. This time there was too much at stake.

'I'm afraid I cannot allow you to do that Mr McEwan.'

McEwan looked interested, and mildly excited.

'And how do you propose to stop me?'

'I will have words with the men. If they are for me, who will do your kicking of behinds?'

McEwan rose from the table and walked to the small pot-bellied stove at the back of the cabin. Turning his back to the minister he knelt down, opened the door and threw in a log. Facing the wall, he spoke in a low voice.

'You underestimate these men. They want this job finished as much as you and me. The weather is against you, Henderson.'

It was true. The blizzard that had been raging for over three weeks now, had cut off siding twenty-three from the world. No trains had been through since the snow built an impenetrable barrier at the top of Wolf Pass, and McEwan had been there when a futile attempt was made to break through with a snow-plough on the engine, bearing witness that passage was now quite impossible.

But with or without communication, they would have to begin the initial blasting of this tunnelling operation immediately, or the whole project would be in jeopardy. But it was not the snow holding them back; it was a band of thirty two Kinchuinick Indians, taking it in shifts to squat night and day on top of the very rock that had been drilled, ready to receive the dynamite.

When McEwan turned round to receive the minister's response, Henderson had gone. He smiled. Well let him try, he thought. There were nearly fifty cold, homesick railroadmen out there. Christians or not, they would not take kindly to being kept away from their families an extra month or more by a bunch of unwashed barbarians. Henderson would soon see how much authority his God had, over men who dreamt nightly of their homes, tossing in their bunks and calling out the names of their wives.

Through the tiny ice-coated window he could see Henderson stumbling through the snow to the gang of men hacking at rocks with picks, the wind tugging at his black coat as he went.

McEwan resumed his seat at the table and flattened out the crumpled plans in front of him, the creases throwing flickering shadows in the light of a guttering lamp. Henderson could do as he wished.

They would blast tomorrow.

The man was coming again. Chief Hunting Wolf pulled the blanket tighter around his shoulders and composed himself. His warriors said nothing as they watched the tall man in the flapping black clothes scramble up the rocks towards them, but Hunting Wolf sensed them shift uneasily beside him in anticipation.

When the Reverend James Henderson reached the small group of natives, he was battling for breath, sweating with the exertion of the climb.

'Big walk I do,' he gasped.

Hunting Wolf laughed internally. This man's command of their tongue was quite preposterous.

'Sit down then, Henderson. You will not regain your breath by remaining on your feet.'

The Reverend made a small and silly bow with his head and joined them in the shelter of a rock, where six of them were squatting in the snow. Despite being out of the wind, the temperature on the mountainside was unbearable. Henderson could never get used to this dry, biting cold, not after so many years in the wet and windy land where he grew to manhood.

He looked at the six dark men, sitting calmly in the snow with nothing more than buckskin and wool to keep them warm, and wondered at their constitution.

'And is there news from the man McEwan?'

Hunting Wolf fixed him with his deep black eyes.

'He big trouble with me. I no can tell him you think. He take rock tomorrow. Men come.'

Hunting Wolf took time to decipher this jumble of words from the frowning Scot, then spoke slowly and as simply as he could to help this white man's poor comprehension. It was like dealing with a child.

'This is very bad, Henderson. You realize that we cannot allow the mountain to be opened. I have explained. We will remain here. You must tell him that. We will remain.'

Henderson sighed, the cold hacking at him through his coat.

'No more I do. Men with man McEwan. Danger for you. Please to come with me now.'

Fishtail and Powderhand exchanged looks of mirth, crushed quickly by a glance from their chief.

'I am sorry, Henderson. We will remain. There is more danger for you if we do not. If we let you open the mountain, you will all die. This way, we save many lives. Not merely our own.'

Henderson looked deep into Hunting Wolf's eyes.

'You not change story? Trickster still?'

It was Hunting Wolf's turn to sigh.

'Yes. The Trickster, Henderson. We have told you plainly, many times.'

'Think you about Great Spirit I tell you. Good Lord Jesus Christ?'

'Of course. We have thought a great deal about your spirit and his teachings, as you asked us to. We do not believe this.'

Henderson looked as if he might cry.

'Is truth. Is only truth. Jesus Christ your great Spirit. He bring love to you. You have must to him love. He save you. Save you from Trickster also. Trickster not true.'

Powderhand gave a snort and crossed his arms beneath his blanket, fishing under one armpit for a mite he could feel shifting in the warmth.

This time, he was not reprimanded by Hunting Wolf. Hunting Wolf was growing tired of the well-meaning foolish white man.

'We thank you, Henderson, for your kindness and concern, but you must understand that we are well aware of what is and is not true. You should explain these things we know to be true to the man McEwan again. We will remain.'

The seven men squatted silently for a few minutes while Henderson wondered what he should do. He was a failure. A spectacular failure. Was God testing him? All he longed for in this life was to save more souls, gather more precious gifts for his Lord Jesus Christ. He knew he could save these people if they would just listen, just believe the words of joy he had to share with them. He'd learned the complex rudiments of Siouan, slowly and painfully from a logger in Montreal, in preparation for his task ahead. The task of bringing these people to Jesus.

But he was failing. It was James Henderson at fault, not the natives. An English Catholic had saved an entire band of Blackfoot Indians a few hundred miles away, building a mission school and converting every last one to Christianity. The Catholics were good at it. They used the weapon of fear, something these natives seemed to understand.

Henderson's weapon of love was going nowhere.

No, it was Henderson's own failure that was condemning these people to Hell, and he was finding it hard to live with.

Meg was right. Her words had been in anger and through tears, but she correctly predicted that he would achieve nothing here. Perhaps he should have listened to her and not to God, when she insisted he stay in Edinburgh, ministering to the souls as much in need there as here. But if she loved him she must have known how it was suffocating him, killing the spirit in him a little more every day, with the smothering middle-class indifference his parishioners had to the word of God and His purpose.

She had refused to come with him. A chance to do missionary work in the new world and she had refused. James thought of Meg, forever taking tea in Jenner's on Princes Street with the ladies of the parish, gossiping over fine china and fresh cream confections, and admitted to himself for the first time that she did not love God in the way he did. He was quite certain now she did not love him either. If he were honest, he'd always known she had married him because he ministered in a fine part of the city, to people who had money and what Meg constantly referred to as 'respectability'. She kept three servants busy maintaining their respectability, putting a strain on

James's church stipend, but she regarded it as a major part of being a minister's wife. No wonder her world had been shattered when he had rushed home that breezy April day, cheeks burning with fervour, to hold both her hands in his and tell her of his plans to work for God and Canadian Pacific Railways. She pulled her hands out from his large fists and put them to her cheeks in horror. He had looked at her for the first time then. Really looked at her. Dressed in her heavy expensive skirts, her hair tied in a fashionable twist, her face lightly powdered and rouged, she was in every way a model of those hideous Edinburgh women who loved nothing but themselves and their position in some imagined pecking order of that 'respectability' James was not privy to.

So he had left without her. And now here he was, squatting on a mountain with six Indians, who not only refused to accept Christ as their saviour, but also harboured some insane superstition that was bound to result in violence. He had lost the love of Meg, and now it seemed he had lost the love of God.

Hunting Wolf spoke first, breaking the silence above the soul-chilling howl of the blizzard.

'You should go now, Henderson. Night is falling. There is nothing you can do.'

Henderson looked tragic. 'You pray with I?'

The chief smiled and looked to his warriors. They returned his gaze impassively. He looked back at the minister, huddling in the snow. He was like a crow that had been broken and smashed against the rock, the dark fabric of his big coat spread crazily around him.

Hunting Wolf spoke gently. 'Can your prayers protect you? Do they have power against great and terrible evil?'

'Yes.'

'Then let us hear them, Henderson. We will join you.'

James Henderson stood up, raised his right hand, held his coat shut with his left, and closed his eyes. He spoke in English this time. What did it matter if these men understood him or not? He was praying for them, not with them. It was all he could do.

'Almighty Father . . .'

11

The blond boy stared up at the wolf with a mixture of awe and expectation. He jumped about three miles high when Katie spoke softly behind him.

'It's a female. She's protecting her cubs. See? Behind her there.'

The boy breathed out hard, whirling round to look at Katie.

'Did I give you a fright? I'm sorry. Guess I shouldn't sneak around like that. Do you like the wolves?'

The boy's heart rate had slowed enough to speak. 'Sure. They're neat.'

'That's the male over there. Do you notice he's a bit bigger and a slightly different colour?'

She had an arm round the boy now as they both stood looking up at the stuffed animals whose dry, painted jaws gaped back at them in silent roars.

The boy's mother appeared from behind a snarling grizzly bear to join them, her face registering curiosity when she saw Katie with her arm conspiratorially round her son's shoulders.

'Will the male wolf eat the cubs?' The boy's eyes were wide.

'Well sometimes they can, but the mother wolf is a pretty strong force to be reckoned with. If I were him, I wouldn't mess with Mom.' Katie looked round to greet her young charge's mother. 'Hi. Hope you're enjoying the museum. Can I tell you that we'll be closing in about twenty minutes? Don't rush on out or anything, but if there's something else you need to see, now's the time.'

The woman smiled gratefully and politely. 'Sure. That's fine. We've just about covered it all. It's been very enjoyable, thanks. Hasn't it, Randall?'

The boy was awe-struck by the wolf again. 'Sure. It's neat,' he said absently.

Katie smiled and left them to it. One quick circuit of the railroad display on the balcony to check everybody was out and she could cram in a coffee and a sit-down before locking-up time. The wooden stairs to the balcony creaked in protest as she mounted them, but offered her a view of the whole ground floor as she climbed.

The vantage point told her that the mother and son were the last ones in, and if the boy could tear himself away from the stuffed wolves she should have the place cleared in five minutes. Already she could hear the comforting sound of Margaret cashing up the till on the front desk, counting out the few dollars and cents that the handful of visitors to the Silver Heritage Museum had spent on postcards, pamphlets and bookmarks.

Katie cherished this time – the feeling of the museum having done its job, as though all the exhibits were silently shaking hands, or paws, congratulating themselves for another successful day intriguing, entertaining and educating the visitors. During the winter, this was where the vacationing wives and children who weren't skiing came to look round, while Dad perfected his parallel turns on the slopes, or the stray family and seasonal worker who passed by and entered on impulse. All left delighted by the display of unpretentious, idiosyncratic mixture of local information that Katie had put together over the past five years. Stuffed animals raged beside solemn Indian artefacts. Posters trying to win the custom of potential Canadian Pacific Railway travellers in the 1900s were framed beside ancient and tortuous-looking wooden skis. Fossils, millions of years old, sat happily in cases with blown bird eggs.

The Silver Heritage Museum wasn't going to win any prizes for academic excellence, but for the entrance fee of a dollar it certainly gave its best shot at being value for money.

This year, Katie had managed to get a grant from the Alberta Tourist Board that would keep things ticking along financially for another two years, an achievement that had spawned a hilarious celebration party for the staff amongst the stuffed animals that made Katie smile every time she thought of it.

If the stern Alberta Tourist Board woman who'd written the letter to her congratulating them had seen her with a glass of cheap wine toasting the museum from the back of a mangy bull moose she might well have changed her mind. She didn't. Things were doing just fine.

The balcony that ringed the main ground floor space of the museum was a mixture of displays that hadn't quite been rationalized. Katie had acquired some Victorian glass cases from an auction in Edmonton and these were now filled with an assortment of items that couldn't be crammed in downstairs. She had wanted the theme to be the building of the railroad in the late 1800s, and Silver's important part in it. However, lack of space had made them include the history of the Kinchuinick Indians from the area; how they broke away in the eighteenth century from the larger Assiniboine and Stoney tribes to live here in the mountains. And although the native Canadians had no part in the building of the railroad, Katie dug up a tenuous historical tie-in about how tribe members had apparently hindered the largely Scottish railroad work-gang during the final stages of building the Great Corkscrew Tunnel. The tunnel was the engineering feat of the century, that saw CPR blast that mad doubling-back tunnel two miles long right through the centre of Wolf Mountain.

In fact the centrepiece of the balcony display was a working model of the Tunnel; a papier-mâché masterpiece they had commissioned from Calgary, where a tiny model train wound its way through the half cut-away mountain when you pressed a red button on the side of the case. The kids loved it. They would stand for an age pressing and re-pressing the button, making the train spiral its way round the tunnel until a bored parent dragged them downstairs to the bird display.

With the mountain cut in half you could see exactly where the line went, a luxury not available in real life. The papier-mâché world was much easier to understand.

Katie knew the whole floor should have been railroad history, but she had all these great Indian domestic tools, and artefacts to do with tribal worship and mythology to show and nowhere to show them. So she banged them in the cases and hoped for the best. Sam, of course, called the Indian stuff junk. She had watched his face as he walked round the display for the first time with her and the clouds of emotion that blackened his normally smooth brow were hard to fathom.

This contempt for his Indian past was something Katie had struggled to understand all their married life. Since it was virtually a taboo subject in the Hunt household she didn't reckon she would ever be permitted to cross that bridge into the secret place that fed Sam with his self-loathing. Nevertheless, she grieved for him when she saw it manifest itself.

Often she would look at the two unmistakably Indian faces of her children Billy and Jess and mourn that they would never enjoy the rich part of their heritage provided by their father's blood. But Sam could barely say *Indian* or *Kinchuinick* without spitting the words and she loved him too deeply to provoke the wrath he so readily turned on himself. If he thought the valuable Indian artefacts were junk, they would just have to agree to disagree. She made sure that all her Kinchuinick studies were done at the museum, keeping the facts to herself and her burning interest in the past of her husband's race a jealously-guarded secret.

The beautiful carved bone amulet Sam wore round his neck, a very ancient Assiniboine charm, gave Katie her only tiny glimmer of hope that one day he would face up to his roots. She knew it had been his father's, the male half of the dead parents Sam never spoke of, and the nature of her job told her it was valuable beyond its role of sentimental keepsake. But he offered her no explanation, no anecdotal family history, and he took it off only once, when he was forced to replace its leather thong after snapping it while swimming in the creek.

What kept her from prying too deeply were two things. First, she thought the ivory-coloured circle of bone hanging on the tight brown skin of his hairless chest was the sexiest thing she had ever seen; and secondly, she loved him so much that anything that made hurt flit across his broad innocent face made her die inside. So the history of Sam's amulet was safe. Sam would never know she had located its origin in more than one book. She knew lots about that charm. One day she would talk to him about it, but not now.

Katie walked clockwise round the cases, completing her little ritual. She wandered past the display of beaded cradleboards, noting that the model baby, strapped into the most ornate example was starting to go yellow on one side of its face. Dummies were a pain. They never looked real, and when they did there was something frightening about them. This mangled thing wasn't going to fool anyone, but Katie had insisted on the baby, just to educate the public about the human side of her objects. It wasn't enough to show visitors the old crumbling piece of wood and beading and make them admire the handiwork.

You had to make them stop and think. Think about what life was like. Think about how their life was much the same as our life. Even make twentieth century Mr and Mrs Leisure Suit consider that although things were harder for the average eighteenth and nineteenth century Kinchuinick Indian, in some ways it was better then than now. She looked at the flaky yellowing face of the plaster baby. The real thing would have been strapped into one of these cradleboards from the moment it was born and taken out occasionally to stretch and kick and be cuddled, then strapped back in and attached to its mother. Secure. Loved. Cherished. Forest moss for a diaper, with the plant's chemicals providing a natural barrier to diaper rash and a whole tribe providing love, attention and security. Pretty different from the Kinchuinick babies now. Nothing about their modern lives would sit happily in a mahogany case. The plaster baby looked back at her as if it mourned for them too. Needs a clean, she thought. Get rid of that yellowing with some turpentine. It went on her mental list.

Then on to the medicine bundles. Strange, small leather pouches full of herbs, used by shamans for good and bad medicine. All present and correct, except maybe one of the bad medicine bundles was responsible for a label peeling off at the back of the case. Bad medicine plays havoc with glue. Note two on the list. A stroll past the eagle feather wands and pipes completed her circuit, and ended, as always, with the model.

Just before closing, before she turned the model off at the wall switch, she always pressed the Corkscrew Tunnel's red button and smiled as the tiny train started its last journey of the day through the mountain of paper: her own ritual.

Ritual was important to Katie Hunt. Perhaps not quite as important as it had been to Katie Crosby, but it was still up there along with breathing and eating. But if that love of ritual had endured the years, lots of things had disappeared forever; and they started to disappear when the twenty-three-year-old Katie Jane Crosby had first gazed into the delicious, mischievous black eyes of Sam Hunting Wolf. Mostly bad things. Things she was glad to have shaken off like dandruff. Things like Tom.

That had been close. Whenever Katie thought back about how close, she shuddered.

Was it really her who thought a Friday night barbecue at Tom's sailing club was the height of sophistication? Yes it was. And it was Katie Crosby who used to practice signing Mrs Tom Clark on the telephone pad when she was doodling during a long call. A real close thing. She recalled her parents' faces that night. Expressions of almost catatonic shock, the night she let them all down. But also the night she set herself free.

It was her own fault. She should never have let Tom own her the way he did. But the things you know as a woman are different from the things you believe as a girl. He bullied her. She knew that now. Then, of course, she thought he loved her, was telling her things for her own good. Christ, she'd lied to herself all those years. Lied when she saw a line for a blockbuster movie she ached to see, when she and Tom were heading for the art-house theatre to sit through a long dark European film with subtitles. Lied to herself when Tom told her that her college friends were young and silly and he couldn't tolerate them, that his boat-owning friends were more interesting. Lied about liking to push weights, ride expensive mountain bikes and go roller-blading with the big muscle-bound dumb geeks Tom admired. She ate low cholesterol food to please him, and agreed with Tom that bed by ten thirty was a good thing to help with a personal training programme.

A whole series of lies and self-deceit. It had left her awash and confused, wondering who the hell Katie Crosby was. Did she like Sylvester Stallone or Ingmar Bergman? Would she rather go to the private view of an exhibition of Corbusier drawings, or go and fly a power kite in a storm? Why did she long to skip 'training', sit up until 4 a.m. drinking beer and arguing with friends whether Kojak would look like Barbra Streisand if he grew hair? Her confusion had made her pretend she was full of certainty, boasting to her friends that she was settled and sure of life, that she had the answers. She was grown now and the answer was, she could like anything she wanted. No reasons necessary. But then, the answer had to be Tom's way. It wasn't his fault. It had been hers. She didn't think she was at all pretty, and no one changed her mind. In fact everyone remarked on how handsome Tom Clark was. She was 'lucky' to have snagged him. He said he loved her because she was funny and bright and full of life, but in private moments, in subtle ways, he made it clear that one of them could have anyone they wanted, and the other one should be damned grateful.

He treated her degree in archaeology and anthropology as a curious and charming little hobby. It was his yacht chandlery yard that would keep them solvent, and she needn't worry about a thing.

But she had loved him. Slim, tall, handsome Tom. Tom who bought endless magazines about boats, who wanted to be thought an expert on books, architecture , design and civilized living, but really only knew about his resting pulse rate. Tom who was like a child, as a direct result of trying so hard to be a man. And she very nearly married him. Warning bells had been sounding long before she met Sam, but she hadn't listened to them. Sex with Tom had started to be so infrequent and awkward she dreaded him even trying. His clumsiness made him treat it like a chore, and every bungled attempt left them beached further apart on some strange shore. It was, after all, her fault. He told her so, often.

'You never initiate making love.'

She hated that term, 'making love'. Sounded like a school's sex education lecture. It took the lust, the dirt, the fun out of it.

'That's the problem,' he would say. 'You have to start it sometimes.'

But for some reason she didn't want to start it. She wanted him to want her more, to grab her like a plumber in a dirty movie and make her ache for him. But that was never going to happen. Remember, Tom could have anyone he wanted. She was 'lucky'.

And all the time her parents welcomed him like he was the son they never had, never once noticing their happy-go-lucky only child growing increasingly more insecure, miserable and bitter.

Then there was Sam. The first time Sam had really made her laugh, she thought a flood-gate had opened somewhere inside her. A joy so profound and delicious burst from her that she felt intoxicated. It was almost as if she'd forgotten how to laugh like that. Crying with mirth, sides aching from elation. With the laughter, always a stirring of sexual passion that made her lightheaded.

And to think she nearly didn't join her parents in Silver that year. Tom had asked her to forgo the yearly family vacation in Alberta and stay in Vancouver as his partner at some charity ball, and she had nearly said yes. Her parents didn't expect her to come with them any more. She was a grown woman after all. The ball was tempting. Tom's friends and business acquaintances were rich. There would be a marquee, and she could wear a taffeta ball gown and long silk

evening gloves with a bracelet over the wrist. She would drink sparkling white wine and maybe break away from his iron-pumping idiot
pals for a moment to find someone who would talk about something
more than their own flesh and how they were keeping it healthy. But
somehow Katie wanted to be a little girl again for a few weeks. She
longed to wear an old sweater and stack her dad's woodpile neatly
for him, the sensual touch and smell of the rough pine delighting her.
Her routine. A routine that had survived for two decades. And she
wanted to sit with her mom as Mrs Crosby in her silly cotton hat
made another futile attempt to capture Wolf Mountain in watercolour
from the porch. She wanted all that warmth and security that Tom
seemed to provide but really didn't. So she went to Silver with her
delighted, but surprised parents. And she met Sam Hunt.

He drove a bus. That's what Sam was doing when she first saw
him. Katie remembered everything about that day. It was hot as hell,
and she was wearing khaki shorts, a plain white T-shirt, a tiny tartan
rucksack on her back, making her way to Lazy Hot Springs for a
hike. And she was waiting to board Sam's bus in the depot.

A big sign on a stand read *Passengers wait here until driver checks your
ticket*, and so she waited by it. Funny thing was, everybody else just
walked by her, out through the glass swing doors to the sidewalk and
got on the bus. It sure was filling up. There were lots of Japanese, a
few hiking couples and some elderly tourists. But they were all getting
on the bus before her. She saw the seat she fancied was already gone,
the front one opposite the driver where you can look out front from
the big windshield, and she started to get annoyed. Where was the
driver? Why didn't someone in charge come and tell all these people
to wait in line like the sign said?

Then a young man appeared in the blue company overalls, holding
a styrofoam cup of coffee. A young, impossibly handsome man. Sam
was twenty-five, six feet tall, his black shiny hair swept back from a
noble forehead. His blue tunic top was open by three buttons,
revealing a T-shirt beneath and the suggestion of tight brown pec-
torals. He was obviously Indian and to Katie's surprise, he was also
undeniably gorgeous.

This driver from the planet sex stopped and looked at Katie, and
then at the nearly full bus through the glass doors. Walking over to
her he handed her the coffee. 'Can you hold this, Miss? I'll be right
back.'

She took the cup, astonished.

He boarded his busy vehicle and she could see through the doors people standing and milling about on board. In seconds the passengers were pouring off the bus, back through the doors into the depot concourse.

Sam was at their back, waving his hands and shouting, 'Come on, that's it . . . hurry along . . . quick as you can . . .'

The passengers milled around grouchily, complaining under their breath, in front of Katie. She was going to be last again.

Sam pushed his way through to where Katie stood, took her by the hand not occupied holding his coffee, and led her to the front of the line.

He cleared his throat, and clapped his hands together twice. 'Could I have your attention please, ladies and gentlemen?'

They grew silent, some fishing around in bags for the tickets they were now going to have to present.

'I'd like to introduce you all to a very special person.'

Katie looked at him, horrified. What was this? The crowd started to look curious.

'This young lady is unique in Canada and it's a great honour to have her with us today. We, at Fox-Line Travel, always knew that one day she would grace us with her presence, but now it's happened, and all I can say is that I'm humbled to find that I'm one of the people to witness it.'

The crowd started to buzz with low conversation, heads bobbing up to get a look at the woman this bus driver held by the hand.

Katie was blushing to her feet. What on earth was this man doing? Who did he think she was?

Sam held up a finger. 'Now I know there's not much time for speeches or nothing, what with the bus already a few minutes behind schedule, but let me, on behalf of the bus line, just say this.' The crowd were expectant. Sam turned to Katie, smiling, and under his breath said, 'What's your name?'

Stunned by the warmth of his smile, she replied. 'Katie Crosby.'

Sam looked to his audience. 'Ladies and gentlemen, please join me in welcoming Katie Crosby, the only, and I mean only, woman in Canada . . .' he paused. 'Who can FUCKING READ!'

There was a stunned and shocked silence and then Katie burst out laughing. The crowd exploded into an irritated hubbub of noise, peppered with *well really* and *cheeky son of a bitch*.

Sam smiled and stood defiantly by the sign, tapping it with a finger. He let go of Katie's hand and waved her through. 'Keep the coffee. It's milk, no sugar.'

She smiled and got on the empty bus, into her favourite seat. Opposite the driver.

Through the window she could see Sam smiling at his frowning passengers, and lip-read him saying *tickets please* as though he hadn't a care in the world.

That was a great journey. They talked, of course. All the way to Lazy Hot Springs, until Katie had to get off. She'd gone off the idea of a hike by then. All she wanted to do was stay on that bus and talk more to the handsome funny guy at the wheel. But she got up and made to leave and when he asked her for her phone number she told him. He smiled, opened the hydraulic doors and said, 'Fox Line wishes you a nice day. Driver Sam wishes you a shitty one for not taking him with you.'

She laughed and waved goodbye, still waving as the bus pulled away, with windows full of glowering people staring at her like she was the Anti-Christ.

All she thought about on the hike was Sam. Her head was spinning and she walked further than she intended, striding out in a trance. Why would she give a bus driver her number in Silver when she practically lived with Tom? But she didn't regret it, and when the bus back that evening was driven by a middle-aged pot-bellied man with a moustache, she was crestfallen.

The phone call came the next day, her father getting there first. He asked who was speaking in a very careful and deliberate way and then called Katie to the phone in the parlour. He held the receiver out to her as if showing a child something it had damaged and waiting for an apology.

'A Sam Hunt. For you.'

Katie's heart had started pounding. She was as excited as a sixteen-year-old on her first date and her father could see it through her mask of indifference.

She took the receiver without putting it to her ear and said *thank you*. Frank Crosby understood the gesture and left the room.

With that first *Hello?* she knew it was over with Tom. She and Sam met that afternoon in town and walked up through the trail in the forest to the old fire look-out hut. And they had sex that nearly made Katie die with ecstasy. She'd known Sam for less than twenty-four hours but her appetite for him was insatiable and she thought as she lay in his powerful dark brown arms between all that rapture, that she would never be able to live without him again. With Sam it was fucking, not making love, although each act contained more love than Tom had given her in her whole life. And they talked. They talked so much Katie felt she'd known Sam since she was born.

She didn't tell her parents a thing. Her father never asked about the phone call, and neither seemed to show any signs of suspecting that each time she went out she was meeting an Indian bus driver who would alternately make her laugh until she cried, and then cry out again in pleasure when he peeled off her clothes, high above town in the pines, or in the tiny wooden bed in the staff accommodation hut behind the depot. ·

She knew the ugly name for it of course. Indian-struck. That was what white people said when any white girl fell for a native Canadian man. But Katie wasn't Indian-struck at all. She was in love with Sam: the man, not the Indian, and she wanted to make sure he knew it.

The night before the Crosbys were due to leave she met him at the fire hut. She held his hands and looked into his black eyes very earnestly indeed.

She was going back to Vancouver, she said. She was going back to tell her boyfriend that it was over and then she would come straight back to Silver and be with him.

Katie braced herself for Sam to be sceptical, to dismiss her as a middle-class girl who'd used him for some rough-stuff vacation fun, and to be angry and hurt. But Sam looked straight back into her eyes, and said, 'I know you will.'

They did what their bodies told them they had to do about four or five times, and then, exhausted, crawled back down the trail to town. Sam said goodbye at the end of her street, and walked away as if there was absolutely no doubt they would see each other again. Katie knew that was the truth.

She thought about Tom on the car journey all the way back to Vancouver, about how she could tell him without hurting him.

She loved him still, in a nostalgic kind of way. She'd been his girl almost half her adult life. A life together was taken for granted. But now the thought of him even kissing her made her wriggle with discomfort. She would tell him the moment they got back.

He called twenty minutes after they returned and said he'd made a dinner reservation in Denton's. Where better to tell him, she thought, than in the best restaurant in town? Her parents seemed excited, asking her ridiculous questions, like, what time Tom was picking her up and what was she going to wear? Perhaps if Katie's mind hadn't been on Sam Hunt's brown body and warm lips, she might have detected something was up in the Crosby household, but she slung on her green dress and grabbed a jacket when the door chimes announced Tom was there.

Tom held her and kissed her on the lips the moment she answered the door, as her eyes screwed in a grimace that he couldn't see.

'God I missed you, you hick.'

She gave him a weak smile.

'Let's eat.'

He was looking unusually smart. He wore a grey Italian suit and a silk tie that she hadn't seen before, and as he opened the passenger door of his Volvo for Katie she saw him raise his head and wink up at her father waving from the bedroom window.

They went to a wine bar first and Katie let him talk for three quarters of an hour. He talked about the ball and how everyone had missed her. He told her about the trouble he'd had with his new PA and how James had a new car. He told her that she should enrol in this new health club on the coast that everyone was joining. It would do her good. Get her in shape. She watched his mouth move but struggled to concentrate on what the words meant. Katie was back in Silver, smelling the pines, hearing the woodpeckers knocking out a rhythm in the distance, feeling the rough dry earth beneath her back and buttocks as Sam blocked out the sun above her with his body. But here she was. Sitting in a bar full of vacant young men in crumpled designer suits and women pretending to be young and cool until they could revert to their true suburban colours the moment they hit thirty.

As she gathered the courage to say what she had to say, he motioned to the barman for the check and told her it was time to go. It could wait, she thought. She would tell him at dinner. Give him time to take it in.

They drove to the restaurant in near-silence, Katie staring ahead,

Tom smiling and humming. She'd been to Denton's only once but the head waiter greeted them as if they were long-lost friends. Tom took Katie's arm and halted her in the marble-floored, plant-filled lobby.

'You go in darling. I'll be there in a minute. I love you.'

He held her face and kissed her deeply. She was stunned. Weird behaviour, but the head waiter was already guiding her through the lobby into the restaurant before she had time to ask Tom what the hell he was playing at. Big shock. Her parents and Tom's widowed mother were sitting at a big round table for six. They stood up and greeted her. Katie was completely and utterly lost. The restaurant was full, faces looking at her as she sat down heavily on the blue velvet seat pushed into the back of her knees by the waiter.

She looked open-mouthed and helpless at her mother for an explanation, but Mrs Crosby put a finger to her lips and smiled at something behind Katie's shoulder.

The lights in the restaurant were dimmed, and behind her she heard Tom's voice. My God, he was talking to the whole restaurant. 'Ladies and gentlemen, there's someone very special here tonight.'

She was going mad. What was happening? Her mind tossed in a frenzy to make sense of it. Had Tom somehow read her thoughts? Was this mockery of her first meeting with Sam to punish her, to make her pay for her betrayal? How did he know? How could anyone know her secret?

She spun round. He was standing with a guitar in his hand, his best friend James at Tom's side holding a lit candelabra.

Tom continued while Katie looked on with the expression of a witness at a road accident.

'I'm sure you'll forgive me for interrupting your meals, but I'm hoping that this special person here, Miss Katie Crosby, is going to say yes to what I'm going to ask her in a moment.'

There were noises of people going *aw*, and *ah*, and before Katie could move or shout *no*, her horror was completed as Tom started to play the guitar. It was a clumsy attempt at Harry Nilsson's 'Can't Live if Living is Without You'. She only barely recognized it. Katie's easy-listening habit stretched way back and Tom naturally scorned her for it, but occasionally relented and bought her albums she liked, always among albums he thought she should listen to. She didn't, however, like Nilsson. If Tom was being generous, he was misdirecting his energy. He started to sing, becoming embarrassingly and comically way off his limited vocal range when he came to the chorus.

Katie had descended into Hell. The nightmare of a song went on for about ten years, and then it stopped. There was a burst of applause from the diners, and Tom dropped onto one knee while James grabbed the guitar. He took Katie's limp hand in his and said it.

'Katie. Will you marry me?'

There was a cheer from some of the more inebriated diners who were clearly enjoying this spectacle.

Katie's parents beamed and Tom's mother dabbed at an eye with her napkin.

She thought then that she would like to die. Time stood still for Katie Crosby at that moment. It seemed that all the faces staring at her had frozen in the middle of some action, like an edition of the *Twilight Zone*. Surely Rod Serling would walk in any moment with a cigarette, and introduce the first story?

She saw through the dimmed light a fat man in the corner with a fork raised half-way to his mouth. There was a woman leaning her head on an elegant hand by the window, grinning with the slit of a red-painted mouth. A couple who were holding hands at the next table smiled at her as though she were their daughter graduating from high school. But she could hear nothing except the beating of her heart and the buzzing of her own blood in her ears, and there was Tom's face, still gazing up at hers in theatrical expectation.

Katie stood up. Her mother made a happy *O* shape with her mouth over at Tom's mother.

She spoke quietly, but nobody in the restaurant missed a word. 'No. I won't marry you, Tom. I love someone else and I'm going back to Silver tomorrow to ask him to marry me.'

There was a tiny scuffling noise from the table, but mostly silence. 'I'm sorry. I really am.'

She pushed back the chair and walked calmly from the room. She walked more quickly through the lobby and by the time she got to the street she was running as hard as she could in her high green silk shoes. She ran gasping down the sidewalk, tears of humiliation and horror streaming down her face and she didn't stop until she got the ocean in sight.

She cried like a child for at least five hours, walking the streets until she could have dropped, before she dared hail a cab and go home. By the time she crawled out of the cab and stumbled up the front porch steps she looked like a hooker on a busy night: her jacket mangled and creased from being clutched to her chest and her face streaked with make-up that had dissolved hours ago in salty tears.

There were no recriminations from her parents – she loved them for that – they were just glad she was safe. But there was talking to be done as her father put it, and never mind them, he thought Tom deserved an explanation.

So she wrote it all down in a letter and posted it to him. Nothing about Sam, just about her and Tom and why it could never work, then packed a bag and made a rail reservation. She didn't tell her parents who she'd fallen for. She wanted to see if it was enough for them that she needed to be free, that she yearned for something else other than a middle-class life in a Vancouver suburb. And it seemed to be. They asked no questions. They gave her the keys to the house in Silver and kissed her goodbye. When Katie Crosby stepped on that eastbound Via Rail train she had never felt so free in her life.

The miracle was there. Sam was at the station.

Katie saw him from the window before the train stopped, a tall, solitary figure leaning against a wooden parcel trolley. She was completely unable to decipher the emotion that the sight of that patient, hopeful man standing alone on a train platform stirred in her. It was more than love and gratitude. It was more than the very real need to weep. It seemed as though he had always been there, waiting for her to realize who she was and come and find him. But even that could not fully explain the complexity of her passion.

She stepped down from the carriage and waited motionless for him to see her, her bags at her feet.

Katie watched as Sam scanned the crowd of passengers weaving their way from the train to the street. He saw her. The invisible beam of light between them set fire to his face, but he walked rather than ran to her. They said nothing for nearly a full minute as he held her, then he held her face in his hands. 'I thought I'd check the trains every day for a month.'

That was his explanation. Simple.

'And then what? What about the fifth week?'

He looked down into her eyes, milky blue jewels, swimming with tears. 'And then I'd check them for another month.'

They married nine days later, and Mr and Mrs Hunt started married life in the tiny staff accommodation room that Sam rented from the bus company. He wouldn't use the Crosby's house and Katie respected his wishes. It wasn't hard for Katie to get a job in Silver. Everyone knew Frank and June Crosbys' girl, and within a month of having run out on Tom, Katie was a happily married woman, selling fossils and loose gemstones to Japanese tourists in a lobby arcade shop in The Rocky Mountain Chateau, the massive Canadian Pacific hotel on the edge of town.

Of course there was tension on the day they picked Frank and June up from Calgary Airport, but it was a lot for the Crosbys to take in at once. She forgave them, like she hoped they would forgive her.

And two beautiful grandchildren had subsequently softened everything. Now, her parents liked to think of themselves as shining white liberals, proud their daughter had rejected the shiny prize of North American conspicuous consumption for love.

Oh it was love all right. A deep, enduring, growing and generous love. He had never once let her down in any aspect of their life, and she hoped he could say the same of her. She loved Sam and her children more than anything in the world, and the snarling female wolf downstairs would have tough competition from Katie when it came to who was more terrifying in defending their family.

Which was why her antennae were twitching now. Sam wasn't himself. It wasn't just the blackouts, it was as though he was fighting some secret battle.

Katie ran a hand over the top of the model mountain's glass case and then walked to the wall to unplug the cable.

The snow was piling up outside and she looked forward to kicking her way home through it, letting the big flakes settle on her hair and the cold making her cheeks blush with cold. Katie Hunt loved the snow. But Katie Hunt did not love secrets, which was why she was going to keep a watchful eye on her family. The stuffed wolf continued to bare its teeth silently downstairs, in a lifeless tableau of female solidarity.

Eric Sindon's formidable rota hadn't taken Sam's involuntary stopover at Stoke into account. There were no points for getting stranded in the snow, and certainly no favours for manual groomers, a species regarded by Silver Ski Company as only slightly further up the food chain than lichen.

Sam found his welcome back to a full day at the depot consisted of being assigned to the bottom station of the Beaver chairlift, on the day of the fun-run. The Beaver run, an easy green trail, was in shade all morning until the sun crept up and hit it around two-thirty. The geeks in fancy dress would come down then, racing for some dumb prize, dressed like morons. Another idea of Pasqual Weaver's. But that wouldn't happen until the sun came round. That meant Sam had to freeze his balls off in the shadow of the mountain for six hours while he loaded untidy, grouchy herds of beginners onto the creaky old chairlift. Meanwhile, the lucky guys who drew a longer straw with Sindon basked in the sun on the south-facing slopes, saluting happy passengers on the high speed quads, and topping up their tans.

As Sam shovelled more snow onto the chair run-up platform, Eric Sindon's rota of injustice was far from his mind.

Dreams were one thing. Blackouts that left you unable to account for your actions were another. Sam had wrestled with his damaged memory since waking at Stoke, trying in vain to recall how he came to be in the truck. The part of it all that stung him hard was the blood. There was no escape from the fact. His face, his chin to be exact, had been covered in thick, dried, blackened blood. Sam had woken in the warm truck to find himself half-way up the pass from Stoke, on the edge of the highway with the engine running. He had sat in the cab for at least five minutes trying to figure out what the Hell had gotten him there, until a glance in the rear view mirror let him catch sight of his face. Everything below his nose was black with it. It caked his face like a kid's first chocolate brownie at a party.

His first thought was that he was dying. The panic that rose in his breast sent images of Katie and the kids whirling in front of his eyes, and although he wasn't aware of it at the time, he had croaked Katie's name as his hands flew to his face.

But the blood was old, and Sam was not wounded. Half-falling from the cab into the road, he scrubbed at his face with handfuls of snow until the blood, and what felt like most of his head, had finally disappeared.

Now, faced with the grinding normality of the first of the morning's skiers clattering onto the chair, the incident felt like a distant and vile nightmare. Except that Sam knew it had been real.

The cold was real, too. And the conditions were hellish. All this snow might be good for business, but only if it would damn well stop.

It was clear right now, but the blizzards had been rolling in and out of Silver like they'd been ordered. Huge dumps aren't much use if the pass keeps closing. This morning, it was minus twenty at the lodge and Sam shovelled like a fevered gold prospector to keep his circulation going.

The Beaver took three-at-a-time on a chair that should have been junked ten years ago. Skiers were arriving at his hut in ones and twos, warming up with the first run of the day down what the instructors called a pussy run. This was where Sam was supposed to say *have a nice day* and *enjoy your run* as he steadied the chair for them and swept the snow off the seat with a broom. Today, it was unlikely Sam would win bonus money for being employee of the month. In fact, the skiers would be lucky if he looked at them. Sam Hunt was in a very far away place.

Two early morning ski patrollers, Baz and Grant, who'd been laying the slalom poles for the fun-run, skidded up to the chair, coming to a halt with whoops in a high spray of snow directly and deliberately aimed at Sam, with the misguided intention of making him laugh. Mistake.

'Go fuck yourselves,' Sam barked at them from beneath his new mantle of snow, like a snowman possessed by a demon.

'Hey. So the customer relations course went well then, Sam, huh?' Baz laughed with an abandon that came with the knowledge he'd soon be skiing in the sun with girls looking at his butt.

'Sure. Soon as I see any customers I'll give 'em a hug and ask them back home for dinner. Meanwhile all I see are assholes with backpacks.'

Grant smiled. 'Whoooeee, Baz! Let's hope Mr Hunt don't break a leg when *we're* on duty. So long, Sam. Keep smiling, you hear?'

They slipped forward onto a chair that Sam kicked as it moved off, leaving the boys rocking their way up the hill, their laughter dying in the deeper shadow of the pines.

Sam ran a hand over his face in exasperation. No point taking it out on his buddies. He already regretted the exchange, but it was too late to do anything about it now, short of growing wings and flying after Baz to apologise. What would he say anyway? Sorry guys. On edge today. You see I've been blacking out lately, and yesterday I may have just gotten into the habit of packing away a live coyote for a snack while I'm out cold.

94

He leaned on his shovel and looked out towards the mountains of the back bowl. The peaks of the Rockies looked back at him with a beautiful indifference. Sam turned the key in that little space at the back of his mind for a moment, allowing himself to wonder what his ancestors dreamed, planned and worried over as they moved about these peaks and valleys.

He knew what his immediate ancestors thought about. A bottle of fortified wine in a brown bag. But the ancient ones, the ones who told stories round fires instead of shuffling out of their prefabs to play bingo for liquor money, did they ever guess that life would be so different, so impossible, for the grandchildren of their grandchildren?

As if in answer, a chill wind with a cargo of drifting snowflakes eddied round the hut and tugged at Sam's jacket. He resumed his shovelling without looking up to greet the couple of skiers who climbed onto the Beaver in a miserable silence that echoed his own.

12

He had seen that movie, *The Wizard of Oz*, many times before. It was always on at Christmas, when they would sit round the big old teak-boxed TV in his sister-in-law's place, drinking beer solemnly and silently.

Calvin Bitterhand thought it was a pretty special movie, but the bit he liked the most was when the woman with the braids saw the big green city for the first time. Viewed it across some poppy fields as far as he recalled. The first time he saw Calgary he thought it was just like the green city. Not on account of being green, which it wasn't, but the way the big tall buildings stuck straight out of the prairie, huddling together as though height was a crime on such a pool-table flat land. But then maybe all cities looked like that. This was the only one he'd ever been to. It sure didn't look much like the green city when you were inside it though.

Right now, as he leaned against a mail-box on Centre Street, watching passers-by alter their route to walk round him like there was an invisible fence in a semi-circle ringing his sixty-one-year-old body, he thought it was a cruel and terrible place.

Five hours to go before the hostel opened up. That meant five hours trying to panhandle a few coins that could get him inside somewhere out of the biting cold that was threatening to lose him a few more fingers. The fact that it was around minus ten even here on the sunny street meant nothing to these folks. They'd just stepped out of a heated car or a heated building and were experiencing the cold as a minor inconvenience until they were back in their offices, their shops or their vehicles, and warm again.

To him the cold was a very real enemy. It had nearly killed him a couple of times. Worst one was two winters ago, in that alley in Chinatown. He'd hung around the trash cans behind a restaurant, hoping the men who came out of the kitchens for a smoke would give him food, tobacco, or in his wildest dreams, a drink. A Chinese guy in the hostel told him they sometimes did that. Didn't tell him that they only did it for other Chinese, that they shooed Indians away like rats. The manager had come out, shouting at the smoking men in a burst of short, fast, staccato noise and then, seeing Calvin, pushed him roughly against some crates by the wall. Calvin's tank was already reading full on a vicious moonshine he'd bought from another hostel Indian, Silas Labelle, and the push had made him topple and fall heavily behind the crates. That's all he remembered.

The Eagle woke him up. Told him he was going to die if he didn't try and move. Of course he didn't want to move. He was comfortable and warm there, lying on the ground in the alley, but his spirit guide was real insistent. They flew together for a while, low over the reserve, where the children were playing by the river, and then high up into the mountains, circling in the sun with the snowy peaks glittering beneath them, until the Eagle said it was time to go back.

And he had come back, drowsy with hypothermia, two of his exposed fingers lost forever to frostbite, but alive. He'd stumbled from behind the crates, out of the alley into the street, where someone had found him and called the cops. Calvin's left hand was now like a pig's trotter, a remaining thumb, first and little finger serving him as best they could.

But then it was never required to do much more these days than hold the brown bag while he unscrewed the top of a bottle. Not like the old days, when his hands had had many tasks to do. Then, they gathered herbs for his magic in the woods. They cast bones and mixed powders. They took the gifts that people brought and handed over the potions they needed. Often they ran over his wife's body and gave him pleasure. But they never held his children. The Eagle had told him many times that there would be no children. Maybe children would have stopped what had happened to him on the reserve. But maybe not.

Two businessmen were getting out of a cab on his side of the road, and Calvin hoped they would come this way and give him money. He held out his hand as they passed and the older man hesitated, put his hand into his big, warm, brown coat pocket in a hurried gesture, and threw him a dollar. The men looked away, embarrassed, as the tossed coin tinkled onto the sidewalk and Calvin bent his stiff, sore body to retrieve it. A drink would help him now, easing both the cold and his humiliation, but he hadn't had a drink in a week. The Eagle had been quite clear about that. He had to be strong now. There had been enough self-pity, enough hiding in the sweet, deadening anaesthetic of alcohol. He needed thinking-time to decide what he was going to do about the Hunting Wolf boy.

Forty years ago of course, there would have been little to consider. He wouldn't have taken a week to think and act: he would have known exactly how to handle this emergency. Calvin Bitterhand had been the only medicine man on Redhorn, the twenty-five square miles of Kinchuinick reserve. His house was right in the middle of Redhorn, the central village, and he had another cabin high in the hills, where he spent months practising his art and gathering herbs. They were all believers then. Sure, the white man had corrupted the tribe with his bribes and lies, turning the chief and his flunkies into puppets for their own political use. But the rest of them, the five bands who lived out their lives there, they were still Kinchuinicks, still knew who they were.

Life had been good for Calvin. He'd learned his art from the greatest of medicine men – a shaman – Eden Hunting Wolf. When Calvin's prayers at puberty for a spirit guide had brought him the Eagle, Eden James Hunting Wolf had sought him out and taken him away from the Bitterhand band to train as his assistant. There was never any question that Calvin would be the next medicine man. Not with the Eagle choosing him. Hit Eden's son, Moses, pretty bad though, and Eden had to sit Moses down and explain that the spirits chose whom they wished. Moses said he'd dreamed the Eagle had been his guide too, but Eden said he was lying, and Calvin could see from Moses face that he had. Eden had been harsh with his son.

'The wolf is your guide, son of mine. The wolf and nothing else. You deny him at your peril. Go now, fast for four days and run with him across our land, listening to what he tells you, seeing what he shows you. Then return and we will speak again.'

Eden had then dismissed his son and his protestations with a wave. But Moses did not build a sweat lodge or fast. Moses had sulked like a child half his age and grew distant from his father and resentful of Calvin. How he would laugh if he could see the great medicine man now, scrambling on the concrete for a thrown coin, nearly dead with cold, hunger and a liver that was ready to explode. But it was unlikely that Moses Hunting Wolf would laugh, unless laughter could come from the grave.

The wind, as if reminding him of the present, caught the hem of Calvin's matted, stained coat and made it flutter like a diving kite.

No point in thinking about the old days and how he was respected and revered. It was now he had to think about, the last act perhaps he could perform for his people, and possibly the most important. Why, he had asked the Eagle, why would you ask an old drunk to do this? What use am I to my people? My powers have long since drowned in my impurity. But there had been no answer. It was essential. He was the only one left, and he must do it. He must do it soon.

Calvin held the dollar in his good hand and thought about how to spend it. There was a coffee shop over on First Street that wasn't fussy who they let in. He would go in there and get warm. He needed to be warm to think.

Such great cliffs of mirrored buildings downtown, and not enough room in any of them to let Calvin Bitterhand in out of the biting wind and deadly creeping cold. The Calgary Tower peered impassively at him over the skyscrapers, standing sentinel like a white man's totem, as he walked unsteadily along the street.

Calvin walked like a cripple, his feet dragging from ankles that were swollen and bitten by vermin, but he clutched the dollar, still warm from the businessman's pocket, as though it held the secret to life.

The girl in the coffee shop thought about not serving him for a moment, then thought again and took his money. He found a stool in the corner and waited. She took her time, watching him out of the corner of her eye, and after what seemed like an eternity, sauntered down to his end of the counter with the jug and poured him his coffee.

Calvin cupped the mug in both hands, feeling its heat before he put it to his lips. He swallowed the hot liquid, savouring the delicious sensation as it slid down his throat into the freezing empty core of his body. He would be able to think now. He had to decide today. He knew he was already late.

It had been a week now. Seven days since he'd blacked out and had the vision; but its pungency had left a mark on his heart and on his dreams. The problem was how to get to Moses' son before the evil went too far. That was his task. He'd flown with the Eagle to where Sam and his family lived in Silver, soaring high above the town until he'd spotted the Hunting Wolf boy going about his business, and he'd seen the great and terrible blackness there. It had been like looking down on a great black hole in the land, shooting up from the ground in a column that was growing and extending, threatening to darken the entire town. But it was two hundred miles away. And what use would he be if he got there?

Calvin looked round the room from behind his mug of coffee. None of these people would ever be safe again if he didn't act. That darkness would reach them all eventually, one way or another, once it had been released for good. Did he care? They certainly didn't care about him. He saw himself through their eyes. A useless, drunken old grey-haired Indian, stinking of his own dried urine, a face lined by abuse and tragedy, wearing clothes that were like diseased and peeling skins instead of fabric. He was no saviour. But the Great Spirit, he knew, cared about them all; the girl behind the counter, the two surly young men in the corner in leather jackets and jeans, the working man on the next stool wearing the overalls of an elevator company, and Calvin Bitterhand. Loved them without question or prejudice. Prejudice was man's invention.

Yes, even though the people in this room would never know that he thought of himself as their brother, it was his duty to act on their behalf. What else could he do? To ignore the Eagle and stay would mean life would go on as normal. He could peacefully spend the last few years of his life as scum on the streets, drinking himself nearer death and crying himself to sleep in doorways.

He must go to Silver and he must go now. But he was not pure enough to face what he knew was waiting for him. Nineteen years had passed since he'd left the reserve, and in all those years he'd never performed a sun dance, or fasted, not even prayed. He was tainted with self-abuse. Broken by booze. There was only one solution. Penance. He would walk. If he didn't make the two hundred miles, then the Great Spirit had other plans for him. But he was going to try.

Calvin swallowed the last of his coffee and managed a weak smile at the girl moving some cakes around the display.

'Want another, chief?'

He shook his head, climbed slowly and painfully off his stool and walked over to where she stood on the other side of the plastic-covered counter. She stopped toying with her cakes and straightened up to confront him. Calvin put his hands on the counter to steady himself, noticing her eyes flicking to the gaps where his fingers used to be. He held up his head and spoke to her softly.

'I have a long journey now. No more money. You give me food?'

The waitress, Marie-Anne MacDonald, looked back at him and found herself hesitating. Normally she gave old bums the treatment they deserved. If they couldn't pay they hit the street. You slipped one of them an old danish or a doughnut past its sell-by, and before you knew where you were you had a string of them hanging around the door expecting to be fed like dogs. It was her butt on the line and if Jack came in and saw her giving charity to any old scrounger it would certainly be her who'd get it in the neck. Okay, it wasn't a great job, but it was a job. The shop shut at four so she had all afternoon to watch the soaps and then get ready to go out with Alan. Suited her fine, and she wasn't going to lose it for a bum. Anyway, these people could work if they wanted to. They just didn't want to. Look at her. She had to work didn't she? Sure, she'd like to stand around all day drinking, but she came in here at seven thirty every day to earn her crust, and she hated these Indian bums who thought life owed them a living. She let them in so she could take their money off them, the money they'd begged from some sucker, and then throw them out when they got comfortable. Marie-Anne sometimes wished she could teach the useless pigs that white people weren't all one big welfare cheque.

At least that was the rule she lived by normally. This guy was different. When he looked at her just then, his black shiny eyes fixing her with a stare, there was no self-pity in them, no pleading or cajoling. More like defiance, as if he were ordering her to do something she knew she had to but had forgotten.

And she caught a strange scent from him, not of piss and liquor, but of a fresh wind and trees, the way washed sheets smell when they've been out on the line blowing in the spring breeze.

Made her think of when she was little and she and her father picnicked on the Bow River, way out of town. The mountains were like a jagged cut-out in the distance, and she would run through the pines, laughing as she fell in the long grass in the clearing between the trees. The smell was the same. Green, wet, fresh, delicious.

Marie-Anne, still looking into Calvin's watery black eyes, put a hand absently into the refrigerated display case in the front of the counter, scooped eight cling-wrapped sandwiches into a bag and handed it to him.

Calvin took it, nodded to her and slowly, wearily, left the shop. She watched him go, transfixed as his hunched figure pushed the door open and shuffled past the window out of sight.

Eight sandwiches. She was in for it if she couldn't account for how eight sandwiches walked right out of the cool shelf. Each one was worth a dollar sixty, in fact one had been a jumbo shrimp mayo, worth two dollars seventy five. Without thinking she went into her pocket book under the coffee machine, took out thirteen dollars and put them in the till. Jack would never know. The elevator maintenance man called for another cup of coffee and Marie-Anne went to pour it, with a smile on her face that would last her until closing, although then, as now, she couldn't tell you why.

13

It would be out of his hands in a few hours. The worst thing, as always, was that the media would go apeshit. Craig stared at Brenner's slim report as if it told him he had a week to live. Instead, it told him loud and clear that Joe hadn't died in a car accident, told him that Joe had been ripped apart and then tipped over the gorge as an afterthought.

There had been some grim excitement when the truck driver had been found, the one who kicked his own bucket on the highway. But when they hauled in the body there had been absolutely no sign of blood, a weapon or even a struggle. Zilch. The guy was clean as a whistle. In short, that poor bastard was certainly the last guy over the pass and probably the only witness they were going to get; but Craig was sure that no way did he murder Joe Reader.

He put his hands to his face and mashed the skin round his eyes. They would send someone from Edmonton now. The rules said you couldn't lead an investigation if you were personally involved, and boy, was he involved. The guy who did that to Joe would know how involved if he ever found himself in a room with Craig.

He let his gaze wander from the document of doom on the desk to the window, where the falling snow was thicker than the fake stuff they used to chuck around on a John Denver Christmas special.

How to deal with the media. That was the next big one. Craig could just imagine how the ratings-hungry louses were going to cover this. What made better copy than a murder in a tourist town, where the biggest stink is usually some skis getting stolen, or some guy winning a busted face in a bar brawl? Suddenly, there's a jackpot;

two patrollers dying in a freak avalanche explosives accident, then a murder that would make Stephen King say *yuk*. All against a backdrop of folks having winter-wonderland fun in the snow. Christ, it would have the American networks circling Silver like crows round a carcass.

Bad thought. It made him see Joe again. Or what had been left of Joe. Craig sighed and replayed the tape in his head one more time. Joe's pick-up was the second last vehicle to cross the pass that night. The truck came after. He was sure of that. Seen the tracks himself. The murderer couldn't possibly have survived up there without a vehicle, so either he was in Joe's car, or Legat's.

Or both. Craig's mouth opened slightly. Or both. In Joe's truck as far as the gorge then hitched a ride in the Peterbilt. He got excited. Then he stopped getting excited. Joe's truck had been pushed over the edge. Something really powerful had pushed it. A single killer and some old truck driver with a dodgy heart couldn't possibly have done it by themselves. It would have taken either ten men or another vehicle, at least another pick-up. The snow that had fallen relentlessly for at least ten hours after the event made sure they would never know the answer to that one. A murderer couldn't have chosen better conditions to cover his tracks. And anyway, why would someone like the Legat guy have taken part in such a foul deed? His records showed he was just a regular trucker: no record, nothing untoward, and strangely, for someone who just took the coward's way out, nothing to suggest he would want to. The suicides Craig had dealt with in twenty years of policing were usually caused by drink, gambling debts, sexual problems or mental illness. Ernie Legat didn't seem to suffer from any of them. Was he forced to do something despicable? Was that why he had committed suicide? Didn't make sense. He would have just driven straight to the RCs if there had been any funny business and he'd survived. Craig pulled himself up. Legat wasn't murdered, remember, just died of the cold. For the hundredth time he asked himself what the Hell were they dealing with here.

The local TV and radio stations had covered the ski patrol deaths and Wolf River Valley Cable had run some crap about the dangers of avalanching. But this was the real thing. A bloody, messy, unexplained, motiveless cop-killing, bound to go network, and he shrank at the prospect. If their man was a psycho, headline news wouldn't help. Where was the piece of shit now? That's what he needed to know. The son of a bitch could be walking round town collecting for the blind as far as Craig knew, since right now Silver had more strangers than residents. That was, if he was still here. What if he was going the other way? To Stoke. He dismissed it. Instinct told Craig McGee the murderer was headed towards Silver.

He pushed the button on his phone. 'Holly, I'm going out for an hour or two. Tell Sergeant Morris to hold the fort.'

It crackled back. 'He's out here already. There's some messages. Do you need them now?'

Craig smiled. His wife used to say Holly was like something out of *Twin Peaks*. Even if he wanted to dispute it, his secretary gave him cause every day to give in and agree.

'Well that's for you to say. You know what they are.'

'I guess they can wait.'

He released the button and grabbed his storm jacket from the peg.

Outside the privacy of his room, in the open-plan office, the place was buzzing. All eighteen constables were on duty, leave cancelled, and what looked like most of them were milling round the operations board like they were waiting for something to happen on its own. It seemed like colour marker pens were more fun than getting out there and doing some police work.

Craig searched for Morris. He saw him sitting on the edge of a desk talking into a phone like he was a Hollywood theatrical agent, holding the phone beneath his chin and gesticulating to whoever was unfortunate to be on the other end with both hands. Not today, thought Craig. Today he couldn't find the energy to play boss with this herd. Constable Daniel Hawk was at his desk studying the photos of Joe's truck. Craig flicked him on the shoulder as he passed.

'Going up to the pass to look round the site again. You want to get me up there in your Ford, constable?'

Daniel got up without speaking, put on his hat and followed his superior officer out into the car park.

The snow was getting silly now. Ploughs were doing their best, with the skiing traffic crawling behind them like ducklings after their mother, but it looked as if the snow would win by dark. Silver was going to be blocked off again. At least by road. A long discordant hoot from the distance sounded like the freight train on its way down the mountain was laughing at the cars. The tracks were clear now after the explosion, and those mile-long iron snakes of coal kept rolling through like nothing had happened. Daniel drove slowly and silently, accepting his place humbly in the line of cars.

Craig glanced across at him. 'So how many colours have we managed to get on the wipe-clean?'

Daniel smiled. 'We're working on ten. But there's still a debate about whether the truck driver should be pink or green.'

'I wasn't being funny Hawk. I was expressing displeasure.'

'I know sir.'

Craig looked out the window, paused a while. 'How are the guys coping with it? The fact it was Joe, I mean.'

Daniel made a little shrug, his eyes fixed on the white mess ahead. 'They cope. You know. Angry I guess, but they figure we'll get him.'

'And you.'

'The same.'

Daniel was putting up a defence shield. Craig could feel it, but he carried on.

'Joe wasn't seeing anyone else or anything, was he?'

'Not to my knowledge. You knew him as well as me.'

'Sure. But you bowled with him. He would have said if anything was wrong.'

Daniel took his eyes off the road for the first time, and shot his staff sergeant a look. The traffic slowed behind the plough in sympathy.

'Why don't you just say what's on your mind, sir?'

'And what's that?'

'That Joe was half-blood Cree and I'm full Kinchuinick, so we must have been best of buddies. That's what you're getting at isn't it? The only Indians, even half-Indians, in the detachment, and we're bound to stick together.'

Craig lowered his eyes. 'Come on, Hawk. That's not what I meant.'

'I think it's exactly what you meant. Sir.'

Daniel Hawk was right of course, but Craig wasn't going to let his clumsy mishandling of the constable stand in the way of what he wanted to know. 'Okay.' He gave in softly, paused again, thinking. 'I just wondered if there was anything cultural, anything particular to Native Canadians I wouldn't know. Something that might have escaped me.'

Daniel Hawk continued to look straight ahead. Craig, over his embarrassment now, was starting to get annoyed. 'Aw Christ, Hawk. I'm fucking sorry if it's not politically correct to notice the fact that you and Joe happened to share some Indian blood.'

'We didn't. I repeat. He was half-Cree. I'm full Kinchuinick.'

'Whatever. Quit acting like I just swindled Manhattan off you for a dollar and answer the question. Was there anything going on with Joe I should know about?'

Constable Hawk threw him that look again, then decided he'd turned the knife enough. He looked at last like he was thinking instead of brooding. 'Nah. Nothing. He was pretty stable with Estelle and all. I didn't notice anything weird.'

Hawk's boss nodded solemnly. It was just as Craig thought. He'd have known if there had been anything wrong with his sergeant. It was just that niggling little maggot of insecurity that white cops have when dealing with Indians that made Craig even bring the topic up. He was sorry he had to. He never thought of Joe as anything but Joe. And whether Daniel Hawk believed it or not, he thought only of him as a damned good constable. So what that they'd been the only two Native Canadians in the detachment? The detachment also boasted one Sikh, a German and a half-Japanese. It was worth checking. Anything was worth checking. They had precious little else to go on.

Daniel drove on in silence but he was still thinking. Craig could practically hear the wheels turning in there.

'What? There's something. Isn't there?'

Hawk shook his head. 'Nah. It's nothing about Joe. It's the cultural bit that made me think of something.'

'Tell me.' Craig was hungry for it. Whatever it was.

Daniel looked grim, fighting to analyse whatever it was he'd conjured up.

'Okay, like I say, it's probably nothing. In fact, given the time involved it's absolutely, definitely, nothing. But the way Joe died. It made me think of something else. That's all.'

Craig turned his body towards Daniel. 'Go on.'

'I saw something like it. While I was policing on Redhorn. But it happened around twenty years ago.'

Craig tried to work it out. Daniel Hawk was only thirty-five years old, tops. How could he have presided over a murder at the tender age of fifteen? They were recruiting young into the Mounties, but not that young.

'I don't understand, Hawk. What do you mean you saw it?'

'I said the murder happened over twenty years ago. That's what the forensics guys came up with. We only found the mutilated remains of the body six years ago. It got dug up by some white construction guys who were pile driving for the new rodeo centre. Course if it'd been found by Indians it would never have been reported. That's the Kinchuinick way. Keeps the reserve a tight community. Makes police work almost impossible. The person, whoever it was, hadn't even been reported missing.'

Craig tried to work this out. 'So you uncovered an old body killed over two decades ago that was similar in its disfigurement to Joe's injuries?'

'Not similar. Identical.'

'Indian?'

'They couldn't say for sure. No dental records or nothing.' He looked across at Craig. 'Contrary to popular white Canadian myth, we're kinda the same as you under the skin.'

Craig ran a hand over his mouth, ignoring the dig. 'Why didn't you mention this?'

'I only thought of it recently. I've been wondering if it's relevant.'

Craig exhaled. 'Fuck.'

'Sorry. It just didn't seem that important.'

'Where are the Native Police files kept, Hawk? At Redhorn?'

'Yeah. The Tribal Administrator keeps them, but since the Mounties from Stoke were called in they got them too.'

'Remember the year?'

'Sure. Larry was born that year. 1987.'

Craig drummed the dash impatiently, his desire to have that file on his knee right now, eating at him like a hunger. The traffic was as terrible as the snow. The tailback behind the plough stretched for at least a quarter of a mile, every vehicle apart from theirs revealing by their ski racks that they contained humans in the search for fun and thrills in this white stuff. Daniel looked across at him and read his discomfort.

'You still want me to head for the site?'

'No. Carry on to Stoke.'

Daniel nodded as if reprimanded and fixed his eyes on the road again. He wasn't looking forward to seeing those photos again, but it served him right for bringing back the whole sorry affair. Maybe the Kinchuinick way was best. Maybe he should have kept his trap shut. But then he wasn't really a Kinchuinick any more. He was a policeman.

Constable Benson, stamping his feet in the snow, raised a heavily-gloved hand to the Ford as they cruised past the taped-off site. Daniel waved back. It was wilderness up there. The Trans-Canada and the rail track sneaked over this high pass like intruders, as if they knew man had little right to be here and should think twice about leaving his mark. This was the highest point, and from here they could cruise all the way back down to Stoke, still trailing the city skiers as they slid about after the plough.

Craig had driven up and down here about two dozen times since the murder. If he was waiting for that movie-cop's moment of divine inspiration he was going to have to wait a long time. Nothing about being there, about experiencing the physical presence of Wolf Pass and its inaccessibility to the pedestrian, lit a fire under his cold, empty ignorance.

This was new territory. There had only ever been one murder in his time in Silver. A pathetic, sad murder: a summer tourist battered to death in a rage by a drunk redneck from the mines up north, allegedly for insulting his girlfriend. Ugly and savage. Sylvia's death had been neither. It had been what they described as peaceful. Craig disagreed. There was somehow more peace in brutality, a natural order where the ripping or tearing of flesh logically and visibly resulted in the escape of the human life-force from its prison of solid matter. The insidious creeping death in which the body was attacked from within was to him a thousand times more violent. He did not associate the hollow white cheeks of his once rosy-skinned wife with any form of peace.

When the doctor had told him, in that stupid pink-carpeted room in the hospital, full of plants and shit as if that made what got said in there any better, that Sylvia's cancer was in the womb and that it would be a matter of days, he'd experienced a kind of elation. It was anger, and unimaginable grief, but it fired him up. He would go in there and get that cancer the way he went out and pulled in a thief. Yes, it would all be okay. Staff Sergeant Craig McGee to the rescue. We Always Get Our Man. Except you couldn't arrest cancer. She'd died so doped up with morphine Craig doubted if she'd even known he was there. But he was. He held her cool thin hand as she let out one small breath and never took another. That was her death. Banal and pointless. He didn't even call the nurse, just sat and looked at her, knowing it was over, that she'd gone. What was that garbage some writer said about not really dying, just going into another room? She was dead. There was, as far as Craig was concerned, no other room. This life was the only room there ever was, and Sylvia had left it and shut the door quietly behind her.

He envied Estelle Reader her grief. The grotesque and spectacular end to Joe's life seemed to have a drama, a showmanship that gave it meaning. He could never say it to anyone, but he felt it. Sylvia's death meant nothing to anyone but him, and even then it was more about his grief than her life. Lots of people died of cancer. The hospital in Calgary checked them in and out like library books, and nothing made those guys in white surgical trouser suits raise an eyebrow. But they would have raised an eyebrow if they'd seen Joe Reader. That made Joe's death special and Sylvia's ordinary, and sometimes Craig could hardly bear to think that anything about Sylvia could have been ordinary.

If anyone was ordinary it was him. At least he had been. Now though, he could hardly remember the thick-skinned unthinking cop he'd been for nearly two decades, letting the extraordinary events of life and death that were unavoidable in his job float past him as though he were immune. Not the kind of immunity that made him feel immortal. More as if he didn't really notice he was alive. Taking things for granted. That time in Scotland, they'd walked on the beach in the Outer Hebrides and Sylvia had lain down on the cold wet sand, sifting through some shells. She'd picked ten tiny, delicate half-moon pink shells and laid them out in front of her.

'Look. Babies' fingernails.'

He'd crouched down behind her, his arms round her neck which was swathed in woollen scarves against the ridiculous weather, and looked at those beautiful fragile things.

She reorganized them earnestly, as though the order mattered. 'Our baby will have tiny nails like that and you can bite them for him. Stop him scratching his face.'

Yes, he'd thought. That's right. We will. No doubt about anything. The McGees were married, they would have children and they would grow old and proud of those children. That's how life went.

Craig was not superstitious then and nor was he now, but the memory of the gust of wind that ripped across the sands on that huge, freezing, empty beach, came back to him often, the wet wind that had whipped away those paper-thin shells and made Sylvia laugh as she tried in vain to gather them up again. He thought about that a lot now. His life, no longer on those invisible oiled rails that carry a person through without having to ponder direction, was now as fragile as those shells. The wind would come, he knew, and swipe him away too. And what kind of wind would it be? Joe's had been a hurricane. A huge, angry hurricane. That's the way Joe went, and he was jealous. Joe, Joe, Joe. Must keep thinking about Joe.

The murder on the Redhorn reserve could be nothing or something. But he was anxious to know, and by the time they viewed the squat grey town of Stoke beneath them, he was bursting with impatience.

Daniel had been quiet throughout the journey, the pair of them sitting like eavesdroppers as the police radio occasionally spat out other people's conversations. When he spoke, they had been silent for at least three-quarters of an hour.

'You ever police a reserve, sir?'

Craig was hauled back from the pit of his thoughts.

'Nope. Ten years in Vancouver, two in Banff, eight in Silver.'

It was Craig's turn to be defensive now. 'Why do you ask? Does it make me a bad cop 'cause I didn't spend twenty years chasing illicit whiskey stills and locking up wife-beaters?'

Daniel didn't smile. 'Guess not. It's just a different kind of police work, that's all.'

'And you're saying this because . . . ?'

Daniel made a dismissive movement with his shoulders. 'Sometimes what white cops think is abnormal on a reserve is pretty normal for the Indians who live there.'

'Like wife-beating and child-abuse.'

'Sometimes.'

'Bull shit. Violence and abuse isn't normal anywhere, Hawk. I don't give a damn if it's an Indian, a Caucasian or a fucking Martian. Anyone who jumps the bones of their five-year-old needs locking up till they rot.'

'Sure. But they don't see it that way.'

'Big deal. Who cares how they see it? They have to learn to stop doing it.'

Constable Hawk sighed and shifted in his seat. 'Yeah, but that attitude's not going to help you if you have to get them to co-operate.'

Craig snorted and put his hands up in mock surrender. 'No. No you're right. Hey, it's okay to beat your woman into a pile of bloody mush if you just tell me everything you know about this corpse. Is that what you're saying? Is it?'

Daniel shook his head as if Craig was a lost cause. 'Listen, I'm no social worker. I just know a lot about these people since I am one of these people.'

'No you're not, Constable Hawk. You're a Kinchuinick Indian, but you're not a filthy piece of scum who fucks kids and hits women. Try to separate the two. Native Canadians don't have exclusive rights to those crimes. Whites do it too.'

Daniel looked impassive. 'And a lot more besides.'

'Yeah. A lot more besides. But our behaviour doesn't excuse theirs. We're all human. We're all trying to be better at it.'

They were arriving in town and Daniel gratefully peeled off from the traffic and headed for the Stoke Detachment. It was a low, modern building in the centre of town, the compound piled high with snow that wasn't going anywhere until spring. Daniel pulled up to the line of Crown Vics abandoned outside and stepped on the foot brake.

'You want me to wait here sir?'

'No, Constable. I want you to come with me.'

Hawk reached for his hat and put it on while Craig studied his face.

'You don't want to see this stuff again, do you?'

'Part of the job I guess.'

They left the car and walked up the concrete ramp to the door. Part of the job, yes. But Constable Hawk could have lived without it.

'That's it, Craig.'

The file, a thin one, slapped onto the table.

Sergeant Cochrane rested his hand on the metal back of Craig's chair, looking over his shoulder at the pastel green cardboard cover.

'Thanks Bob. Any chance of a coffee?'

'Sure. Dan, you know where it is. How's about it?'

Daniel Hawk took the hint gratefully and left the interview room. Bob Cochrane sat down on the other chair as Craig flicked open the file.

Hawk was right. Not similar. Identical.

The photos and the autopsy report told the same story. The corpse, found in a buckskin sack, had been slit up the spine, the organs removed, the heart stuffed up the anus, the penis in the mouth. Twenty years had concealed a lot of detail, but miraculously the body was mummified and still sufficiently intact to tell a tale. A man. They thought about fortyish and possibly, though not definitely, Indian. Interviews with almost every family on the reserve and surprise, surprise, nobody knew anything.

The ground the body had been buried in was unusual in two ways. Firstly, in its extreme dryness – almost pure sand, in fact. A geologist would recognize it as the million-year-old, raised dry remains of the Horn River bed, whose modern course now ran peacefully only a quarter of a mile away. That had been the factor that left the poor bastard looking like Tutankhamun. Even Craig knew that extremely wet or arid land leaves bodies even hundreds of years old whole enough to shake hands with. This corpse's skin was stretched tight like parchment with barely an inch tainted by decay or infestation, leaving the grisly evidence of what had happened to it well preserved. The other unusual factor was that the ground was sacred. That was interesting to Craig. There had been big trouble from some of the elders when the Chief had chosen that ground as the sight of the rodeo centre. It had been in the local rag. Everyone knew Chief Powderhand was a corrupt old piece of ass-wipe and the money he would cream off the rodeo centre made the sacred nature of the ground a joke. What chance did the spirit world have against the mighty buck? Powderhand drove a big shiny Buick and wore suits, and no amount of protest from the elders and their supporters could stop him if he wanted to do something. He held the purse-strings and even though the visitor could be forgiven for thinking Redhorn was one of the poorest places in Canada, it was a pretty full purse. Strange how none of it got to anyone on the reserve. Not until the Chief's elections rolled round that is, when suddenly there was a lot of coinage kicking around to those who voted the right way.

He was one irritated chief though, when the white workers dug up that body. Apparently he'd offered them money to keep quiet and bury it again. The Mounties at Stoke thought about prosecuting the old stoat for that little indiscretion. Then they thought again. It didn't do to go upsetting the chief of the local tribe. Not with the government breathing down your neck. Keep them happy, keep them poor, keep them drunk, keep them quiet. The unwritten constitution of Canada.

So the file was opened and closed. With no reported missing persons on the national computer who even remotely fitted the vital statistics of the corpse, and no one in Redhorn with anything to say at all, the file was stacked away as an unsolved.

This was bothering Craig a lot. The use of the organs was the worst part. Methodical. Repulsive and methodical. Two murders, within twenty years, but more importantly within one hundred miles of each other, and the same bizarre, nauseating outrage. It had to be the same person. And it looked as if Joe might have died for being half-Indian. Only problem with that was why the Indian-hating killer would wait twenty years to strike again. It wasn't as if there was a shortage of Native Canadians to tempt him to take one out. Why now? Why Joe?

Bob Cochrane interrupted Craig's nightmarish thoughts. 'You think there's a connection?'

'Of course.'

Cochrane leaned back on his chair, swinging on the two back legs. 'Heck of a long time ago. You'd think if it was a serial killer, he'd have killed again before now.'

'Maybe he has. But not here. Can we run this on the computer?'

Cochrane leaned forward, his chair coming back to earth with a thump. 'Craig. I know how you feel but you know you're not supposed to be doing this.'

'I haven't been told who's going to be the investigating officer from Edmonton yet.'

'But you will. Leave it for him. You were too close to Joe.'

Craig looked across at Bob Cochrane. He had known Joe too. Yet it would be deemed suitable for Cochrane to investigate and not Craig just because they were in different detachments. It was stupid.

'So what would you do, Bob? Just leave it if you thought you had a lead?'

'Yeah. I think you should. You don't want your wrists slapped. This isn't much of a lead anyhow.'

Craig laughed in a hollow sarcastic way. 'You think an identical murder only a hundred miles away, albeit twenty years ago, is no lead?'

'We came up with nothing last time.'

'So we have a chance to nail the bastard this time. Joe's body wasn't lying there for twenty years. It's fresh in the morgue, Bob.'

Daniel came back in with three coffees and a sad little plate of cookies.

'Don't like to hurry you sir, but the pass'll be pretty much blocked when the ploughs stop.'

Craig snatched a cookie from the offered plate while still looking angrily at Cochrane. 'Can I take this file, Bob?'

'You know you can't, Craig. It's here for when the investigating officer needs it.'

Craig crunched his cookie and nodded. It wasn't the investigating officer who was going to have to go back to Silver right now and fob off the press with *maybes* and *don't knows*, while all the time knowing they had something that looked like an Indian-killer on their hands. An Indian-killer who'd got away with it maybe more than once and then made a big mistake. He'd killed a cop.

Craig kicked back his chair and shut the file. 'Thanks, Bob. We'll get back to you.' He looked across at Daniel Hawk, holding the cookie plate like a mother at a child's birthday party. 'Through the proper channels, of course.'

He made to leave, and then hesitated. 'Incidentally, how long from the discovery of the body until they stopped investigating?'

Bob Cochrane swung back on the chair again. 'Two, maybe three months. Like I said, there was nothing to find out.'

Craig looked across at Daniel Hawk, then back at Cochrane.

'They closed it because it was just an Indian, didn't they?'

'No. Like the file says, they can't be sure it was an Indian.'

'The file says the body was wrapped in a stitched buckskin sack. Is that an Indian burial, Hawk?'

'It's an old way. It's pretty unique to the Kinchuinicks. Usually used for someone important. They use pine boxes now like everyone else.'

'And the investigating officers at the time knew that?'

'Sure they knew it. I worked on this case, remember?'

Craig grunted and looked back at Cochrane.

'Doesn't mean it was an Indian. We got no proof of that.'

'Get real, Bob.'

Bob looked at Daniel with some embarrassment. Both Craig and Daniel saw that it was true.

The two men left the room, bracing themselves for a fight through the snow back to their homes on the other side of Wolf Mountain, and for the storm that they felt brewing between those green cardboard sheets.

14

She was always waiting at the window and Katie always pretended to hide behind the big englemann spruce in Mrs Chaney's front yard. Katie peeped from behind the trunk and saw Jess laughing behind the glass, while Mrs Chaney approached from behind with her tiny coat as though it were a net in which to snare her.

Jess was all dressed and ready with her mittens on when Katie stomped the snow off her boots in the lobby of the big old house, its floorboards thumping to running feet, and the high rooms booming with the shouts and shrieks of the other children still waiting to be picked up.

'Here she is, Mrs Hunt.'

Katie swept her daughter into her arms. 'Thanks again, Mrs Chaney. Have you been good, sweetheart? Have you had a nice day, huh?'

'We don't speak through the children at this crèche, remember, Mrs Hunt?'

Katie was so desperate to laugh she buried her face in Jess's coat. Sam did an impersonation of their fierce childminder that blew her away. So she was an old ratbag to the parents, but she was all they could afford. Jess liked her and the climate of chaos caused by dozens of children running wild in a big house, but Katie and Sam reserved the right to think the woman was a jerk. The phrase Elsie Chaney just delivered was the one Sam used when he wanted to crack up his wife. Sometimes he would duck beneath the comforter in bed and re-emerge as Mrs Chaney.

Katie recovered and withdrew her face.

'No you're right, Mrs Chaney. I'm sorry. Has Jess been good?'

The wide fifty-year-old woman crossed her hands in front of her and smiled. 'This little pixie has been a perfect gem. A perfect gem.'

Jess shrieked in delight at the bare wall over Katie's shoulder, deafening her mother in the ear nearest the outburst.

'Okay. I'll just pay you now if I can Mrs Chaney. I think we owe you for last week too.'

'No, your husband settled up last Friday thank you. Just this week is due. Shall I?'

She held her arms out for Katie's wriggling child, so that her customer could get to the cash in her pocket book.

Katie handed over the beaming Jess and dug around for her dollars.

'I believe this blizzard is one of the worst I can recall.'

Katie was still fumbling.

'You're right, Mrs Chaney. It's a stinker. But you have to admit the snow's real pretty.'

Mrs Chaney wished to admit no such thing. 'Claimed a life a few nights ago I hear.'

Katie looked up. 'Oh?'

'Joe Reader. You know. Estelle Reader's husband.'

'My God. What happened?'

Katie was horrified. She knew Estelle Reader to nod to in the supermarket, no more, but she was genuinely shocked to think of her being widowed so young.

'Few nights ago, Tuesday it was, his pick-up went over the cliffs at the top of Wolf Mountain.'

'My God,' repeated Katie.

'That's the blizzard for you. For all his conceit, man hasn't a chance against the forces of nature you know, Mrs Hunt. We have to learn to respect it.'

Katie handed over eighty dollars in twenties and scooped Jess back into her arms. Jess, however, had other plans. She'd spotted a small frightened-looking child in the doorway and struggled to be let down to go and greet it. Katie released her.

'You know, that was the night that Sam was in Stoke. He got stuck on account of that storm. Thank God he stayed put or . . . well . . .' She trailed off, shrugging, and watched her daughter trying to hug the small boy behind Mrs Chaney's bulk.

'Or it might have been him? Yes indeed it might have been, Mrs

Hunt. And well might we thank God. He moves in mysterious ways. Mrs Reader's loss, your gain.'

The childminder tucked Katie's money into the big pocket on the front of the apron she never took off.

Katie got annoyed. 'Hardly, Mrs Chaney. I don't think that was the deal. I'm sorry to hear about it. Please tell Estelle we're thinking of her if you see her.'

Her attention was focused on Jess now, and she used it to change the subject. She didn't want to discuss poor Joe Reader with this woman any more. 'Hey. Is this a new man in Jess's life?'

Elsie Chaney looked down at the two children. 'That's the Belling boy. You know.'

Katie didn't know, but she knew she would be told. 'No. I don't believe I do. He looks a bit lost.'

'The son of that man. You know.'

Katie still didn't know.

Mrs Chaney sighed. 'Put away. For abuse.' She mouthed the words as if they were too foul to be spoken aloud.

Katie's heart dropped down a rib or two in sympathy.

'Oh. The poor darling.'

She leaned towards Katie.

'Welfare pays his bills here. The mother can barely cope. Heart-breaking, though, to know it'll all happen again.'

'You're kidding. You mean they're letting the guy see the boy again?'

Elsie Chaney looked at Katie as if she were one of her children. 'No no. He won't be back. I mean when the boy grows up he'll repeat the sins of the father.'

Katie looked open-mouthed at the innocent blue-eyed mite, now having one of his cardigan buttons sucked by her daughter. 'You can't say a wicked thing like that, Mrs Chaney. He's a tiny child for heaven's sake.'

Mrs Chaney was clearly irked by the accusation of being wicked. She straightened up, no longer keeping her tone soft. 'Seems you don't know your social psychology, Mrs Hunt. The abused always becomes the abuser. Text book.'

Katie held her gaze for a moment, itching to challenge her. But this was the only crèche that suited them. She couldn't blow it. She bit her tongue and went to pick up her daughter.

The little boy backed away as she bent down to Jess. Katie looked into those frightened eyes and wanted to cry.

What had they seen?

'It's okay pumpkin. I'm Jess's Mom. Would you like a hug?'

He turned and ran. Jess shrieked in delight again.

Mrs Chaney looked triumphant. 'Same time tomorrow, Mrs Hunt.'

Katie hesitated, still looking into the empty door frame where the boy had stood. 'Yes. Same time.'

Elsie Chaney went back into the cacophony of tiny voices, smoothing her apron as she went.

Katie's mood was very different now as she walked along the snowy sidewalk with her daughter kicking the snow up and hanging on her hand. Scary thoughts were bouncing around in there. Thoughts about how it could have been Sam's truck losing control and crashing in the dark.

But it wasn't, and it wouldn't be. She got rid of that one before they turned into their street. The one she couldn't shake off was still there when they reached the house. The abused always becomes the abuser. The stupid woman. The stupid, stupid woman.

15

Only three trees felled. That had been Don Weaver's boast and marketing slogan when he started the Silver Ski Company back in sixty-eight, for the absurd investment of a hundred and twenty thousand bucks.

The turn-over now in ninety-three was in the millions, and they'd sure felled more than three trees in the last twenty-five years. But the picture of Don that hung in Eric Sindon's office was the photograph of a principled man with dreams, who despite the changes that had happened to his fantasy resort, would not be happy to be remembered as anything other than 'three-trees-felled Weaver'.

Eric was sitting back thoughtfully in his canvas-covered office chair, gazing up at the picture of Don. He saw a black-and-white, ten-by-eight photo of a tanned young man on long wooden, hinged binding skis, smiling in front of an almost unrecognizable Beaver Lodge. Eric grimaced as he scanned the picture of the old lodge with its Alpine porch and cute carved window-boxes. The present-day lodge was more like a bus terminal but it did hot business and what shareholder would want window-boxes over profits?

The tree Eric wanted felled real bad was laughing its head off on the other side of the thin partition separating their offices. If he'd known that Don's daughter Pasqual was to come in and run the company after Don died, Eric would have tied his spotted hanky to a stick years ago and headed for another resort. It wasn't as if he hadn't been made offers. There had been plenty, but he hadn't jumped. Like a fool he stayed put, trusting in Don's judgement and friendship, only to find himself number two yet again, but this time to a privileged, brainless bitch who couldn't run a shoe-shine stand.

The big question was what to do now. He was forty-seven years old and time was almost up. Pasqual had been running the resort for a season and a half and things weren't going to get any better for Eric.

She knew what he thought of her and he was just as sure she was going to make a move soon to pluck him out like a bad tooth. Sure, the resort would suffer, and sure, she would be sorry when she discovered the guy who really ran the place had gone. But it would be too late. He would be pushing fifty with no shareholding partnership in the business he'd helped build up from nothing, and Miss Dumb-ass would be moving some twenty-six-year-old business school graduate into his office.

He remembered Pasqual two decades ago when she was a cute kid, hitching a ride on the back of her Dad's skis down to the lodge, squealing with delight as she hung on round his broad waist. If he'd known that apple-cheeked kid would one day turn into the hard-faced vixen, who overturned every good decision he made in this resort, he might have done something about it.

Eric sat upright in the elderly chair. What did he mean by that, he wondered? He felt suddenly uncomfortable.

He swivelled the chair round to face the desk again and shuffled some papers around. Next door, Pasqual was shrieking down the phone, not a business contact by the sound of it.

'C'mon. He did NOT!' She guffawed like a horse snorting.

Eric got up and left the room. If there was no business that needed to be done in the front office he would make some up. He had to get away from that farmyard braying or he would do something he might regret.

The administrative block of Silver Ski Company was labyrinthine and depressing, a series of what amounted to no more than concrete sheds, growing at random from a central two-storey lodge like barnacles on a shipwreck. Eric stalked through its corridors on his way to the front office, his fists clenching and unclenching in frustration.

When he arrived, only one person was where they were supposed to be. Betsy was on the phone, the new guy Sitconski, gone from his desk.

'Where's the rest of the shit-hot team?' Eric addressed the question to the empty desks.

Betsy gesticulated sternly that she was listening to someone on the line. She cupped a hand over the mouthpiece. 'The fun-run. They're all up at Beaver.'

Eric made a small noise of discontent, more because he'd forgotten than that he disapproved of their absence, and sat down heavily in an empty chair. Two lines rang simultaneously. Betsy hung up her call and answered both of them before he could make it to any of the phones on the desks.

Eric left her to her ridiculous martyrdom of efficiency and let his eyes wander round the empty office. A pile of posters lying on a desk for the fun-run that was already under way suggested that the publicity department hadn't been bothering their ass much. Eric was annoyed. He'd put that poster together with the designer. Two colours, advertising the fancy-dress race down Beaver, prizes highlighted in red. Why bother? The lazy bastards obviously hadn't distributed them to the local hotels and shops as ordered. They'd be lucky if anybody showed at all, even with this tiny break in the weather. Betsy finished one call, punched up the other, dealt with it and hung up.

Eric pointed at the posters. 'So are the public just expected to come in here and take one? I thought a poster meant you posted it some place.'

Betsy looked at him with disdain, sliding a pencil behind her ear. 'They're left-overs.'

'So they posted them all over Silver?'

'All over Silver and Stoke. Even took some to Calgary.'

Eric gave in. If he needed someone to take out his temper on today, Betsy wasn't going to let it be her.

'That new guy up at Beaver too?'

'Guess so.'

The phone warbled again and she picked it up , still looking directly at Eric. 'Silver Ski Company, Betsy speaking. How may I help you?'

Eric got up and wandered over to Sitconski's desk. Looked like he'd been working on the rota, very thoroughly indeed. Beside two names there were pencil marks. Of course there was nothing odd about making pencil notes beside names that needed attention. There was plenty wrong with making marks so hard that they ripped through the paper and left shards of broken lead embedded in the paper like shrapnel.

'Hey, hey, hey! Here comes Sean! Would you get that!'

The high-speed quad delivered an eighteen-year-old boy on skis dressed inexpertly as an Indian chief. His gaudy feather head-dress fluttered madly in the breeze, and a makeshift loincloth that was wrapped around tight ski pants was lifted to his friends in a burlesque gesture of vulgarity that passed as a greeting. Eight people hollered and fell about shrieking with laughter as the blond boy skied up to them performing a mock war-dance with knees wreathed in neck-ties, then toasting them with a bottle of cheap whisky he fished surreptitiously from his pocket.

'Shit on you white men. Me pray to um spirit for heap big powder. Me drink fire water. Make me win dumb fucking race.'

The gang of laughing youths were in no position to mock. Two were dressed as cowboys, one as a clown, three girls attempted to look like Playboy bunnies, diminishing the effect by the thermal tops they had on under the bustiers, and the remaining two, a couple, had made little more effort than buying masks of a Jurassic Park velociraptor and ET.

Sean was the best, which wasn't saying much. But with the odd assortment of clothes he wore combined with that huge waving head-dress, he was more like a real Indian chief than anything Hollywood could come up with. Apart from his pink Rossignols and ski-boots, he could have stepped out of a sepia photograph from the town museum. Those long-dead men had sported the same rag-bag inattention to detail that Sean boasted, though they were saved from ridicule by a glint of power and nobility in their eyes that was plainly absent from the boy's. Yes, he looked like an Indian. The wrinklies lining up a few yards away thought so too. Their frowns and muttering indicated they were offended.

One of them, a woman in her fifties dressed in Victorian skirts and a bonnet, skied over to where Sean was busy being slapped on the back by the cowboys and touching the heads of the genuflecting girls in front of him.

'That's in rather poor taste don't you think?'

Eight young, golden-tanned faces looked at the woman, then at each other, and burst out laughing.

The woman's voice became shrill with anger and embarrassment. 'Our native Canadian heritage is not a joke.'

The kids laughed even louder and kicked up the snow, until the woman's husband in Victorian plus-fours and a motoring cap skied across to rescue her. 'You guys are way out of order. Try and show a little respect. Come on, honey.'

She slid away, hot and bothered. 'God help Canada,' she said in a loud voice as they retreated.

'God help America, lady! We're from California!'

That sent them into a new wave of hilarity, interrupted only by Mike Watts, the ski patroller at the start line, clacking his ski poles together for attention.

Sean hid the whisky.

'Okay guys, welcome to the Silver Fun-Run. Well, well, we've got some neat costumes here today.'

The kids started imitating the patroller. Neat was not how they liked to be described.

'Hey, Barney. Neat costume, man.'

Hoots and shouts of mirth. The patroller smiled wearily and carried on. Kids. They could give him as hard a time as they liked. Soon as they started moving on those skis, Mike would have their respect. He could ski the fanny off any of them and they could shove their Californian tans. It was always the ones who made most noise standing at the top of a trail who went very quiet on their way down the hill in the meat wagon, strapped into that stretcher after breaking their bodies in dumb accidents. Despite the temptation, Mike Watts never leaned over the stretcher and said *I told you so*.

'Yeah, right, guys. We're goin' to start out from the line here . . .'

The Californians were finding Mike's Canadian flattened vowel sound on *out* the funniest thing they'd heard. From the group came lots of *oowt* sounds accompanied by cries of *neat*. Mike sighed before continuing. It was going to be a long day.

'. . . and then the race will commence down the Beaver run, through the slalom poles you see there, ending at Beaver lodge, where you'll be judged not only on your time, but on the originality of your costume.'

The wrinklies looked smug, their nods and smiles telling of their conviction that their Victorian skiing-party theme would win the day with dignity. The kids whooped and hollered *neat*.

'So if you want to register here now, pick up a numbered bib, then there's ten minutes for a practice run, just to get those legs warmed up. Okay, everybody. Have a great fun-run, remember to ski safe and good luck.'

The older participants applauded Mike politely while a scuffle of wrestling and jostling kids ignored the end of his speech and hurried to the starting post to pick up their bibs.

One of the girls in the pathetic bunny outfit brushed Mike as she passed, letting the hand not holding her poles run across his buttocks. 'Sorry Mr Canuck. Hand slipped.'

Mike swung his ski round in front of hers, making her jolt to a halt and caught her round the waist before she fell.

He spoke in low voice, right in her ear. 'Missy, if I fucked you, you wouldn't sit down for a week. So if you're really gagging for it, you best stick with these faggots if you want to go home with your buns still touching.' He flashed a huge grin at the horrified girl as if he'd just read the snow report, and let her go with a gentlemanly flourish. 'Have a nice one, you hear.'

The flushed bunny hurried to get her number and hide in the sanctuary of her young companions. Mike smiled and pushed off down the trail to man his post at the slalom.

The clown and the two cowboys were trying to step on each other's bindings and unclip them while the girls tied each others' bibs on. The Victorian party had already registered, been numbered and were pushing off for the practice.

As Sean fooled around, registering with a tolerant patroller, two guys in Mambo suits slid past on Volkl P9s. They looked like pretty hot skiers. Sean turned to smile at them, maybe give them an *O* with his thumb and forefinger to let them know he was part of the brotherhood of hot skiers too.

The older guy looked back impassively. 'Fun-Run, huh? Guess that's goin' to feature big in the next Greg Stump video.'

His streamlined companion laughed and they slid past, making sure the costumed contestants, but not the patrollers, saw them when they slid under the ski-trail tape and jumped off the cornice.

Sean squirmed with embarrassment. It had been his idea in the bar last night to enter this dumb thing. Thought it would be a hoot. But the old crumblies took it seriously, and the cool guy was right. This was for kids. 'I'm not going to wear a dumb piece of cloth with a number,' whined Sean to Barney the clown, who had lost the bindings war and was trying to step back into his ski with a boot clogged with snow.

'So don't wear it, man. You won't win anyhow. You ski like a girl.'

Sean spat, squinting towards the cornice. 'Yeah?'

Barney looked where Sean was looking and understood. They checked out the patroller, busy putting a bib on a seven-year-old dressed as a witch, and pushed forward towards the tape. Beneath them, a double black diamond mogul field stretched all the way to the foot of Beaver, running parallel to the easy green trail. It was a bitch of a run. Bumps as hard as rocks, narrow and hemmed in on both sides by trees that kept its challenge out of the sight of the beginners on the green trail. The fun-run wasn't taking them anywhere near it and it had been closed to stop the kids slipping in by mistake on their way to the start of the big safe highway down the hill. But it was nothing they couldn't handle. Sean looked at the tracks of the two guys who'd just leaped in there, snaking through the bumps in perfect semi-circles, then glanced across at his clown companion.

'Let's do it.'

They slid beneath the tape and dropped in.

Barney whooped and absorbed the first big bump with a grunt, losing it slightly but recovering in time to make a series of three small turns that checked his speed. The Indian chief on his heels was going for it in a big way. He wanted those guys to see him. He wasn't a soft kid. He could ski the bumps like the best of them, even in this crazy cheap head-dress Shelly had got for him. He jumped off the top of the first bump and overtook Barney on the next, finding time in the air over the next to give him the finger.

Barney was hot on his heels, laughing and shouting, 'I'm there, man! I'm there!'

Sean misread the next bump and it threw his weight back. His thighs screamed with the effort of recovery but it gave Barney the time he needed and put him ahead. They were half-way down the trail now, the Beaver lodge and chairlift in sight in the narrow gap between the pines. Barney sliced on ahead and then Sean caught an edge. It was all over. He flew over the top of his skis, arms out like a genuine priest giving benediction, landing on his chin with a dull wet thud, and carried on tumbling sideways into the trees. Sean's world went white, sharp and ice-cold, gasping for breath as the fall winded him, punching the air from his lungs with a frozen fist.

The fall was short but violent, and Barney was gone as Sean finally came to a gasping, groaning stop between two tall pines well off the trail.

'Jesus Christ!' He groaned and slowly and methodically checked that his limbs were all pointing the right way. Nothing broken. No harm done. He wiped his snow-covered face and started to laugh, lying where he came to rest, in a huge drift beneath the tree. Sean was thankful he was right in amongst the trees, but not wrapped round one with his skull smashed in. Lucky, lucky, lucky. No one would see him here. Not even if they were skiing past. The humiliation of one of those guys popping their heads over him and asking if he was all right would be more than he could bear. He was safe here. He pushed himself up on one elbow and started to brush the snow from his chest.

Around him were all the sights and sounds of normality, the melancholy creaking and banging of the Beaver-chair twenty yards away on the other side of these trees and the low voices of people talking on that chair. The pines above him swayed in a light wind and far away shrieks of laughter accompanied someone wiping out and enjoying it. Everything as it should be.

He laughed at his plight, and shook his head, thinking of the tale he would have for the guys.

And then behind him, in the trees, a dry rustling sound.

He swung round to locate it and the feathers of his broken headdress turned with him, like the plumage of a wounded and frightened bird. His eyes widened, and the metallic taste of adrenalin coated the inside of his mouth as he distended it to make a sound that it had never made before.

The Beaver-chair was noisy, all right. So noisy that the people swinging up the hill on the gunmetal-grey seats didn't hear Sean Bradford.

Even though when Sean's screaming started, he screamed for at least half a minute until the biological machinery enabling his scream was silenced forever.

The big man from New York in a lemon yellow one-piece ski suit was not pleased that the chairlift station was unattended. He turned to his wife snowploughing to a halt behind him with their daughter and made a face. 'Guess they don't go big on safety or service in Canada.'

He unhooked his poles from two fat wrists and ushered his equally fat, sullen daughter towards the clanking chairs, turning solemnly on their own round the pylon and jerking empty back up the hill. The tiny wooden hut was deserted. There was no one around at all. No one to shovel the snow onto the mounting platform. No one to wipe the snow from the seats. No one to say *have a nice day and ski safe.*

'I tell you Marsha, if any of us fall getting on this contraption I'll sue the balls off this resort.'

Marsha nodded in agreement, too tired from following her portly partner around the mountain all day to argue or disagree. She and her daughter stepped herring-bone fashion, clumsily like ducks, up to the snow-covered wooden plank that was the primitive mounting platform. Heads turned to look behind them, they waited for the next chair to scoop them up.

It did so without incident, and the father slid forward to catch the next one.

Out of the trees a man in a Silver Ski Company jacket stumbled towards the station. The father stepped back from the chair and let it go. He had a few words to say to this guy all right.

Sam Hunt gasped as he made it to the snow fence surrounding the hut, his head still spinning, his vision trying to sort itself out as his eyes swivelled in their sockets. He was going crazy. He didn't even remember blacking out this time. Just waking up staring at the odd shapes of sky made by the gaps in the tree-tops above him. The branches had swayed and bowed, changing those shapes of sky for a least a minute, accompanied by Sam's breathing and the sound in his ears of blood coursing round his body, before he had realized that he was on his back in the snow, in the trees above the Beaver chairlift station.

Sam had felt like screaming. He had sat up and looked wildly around him as though something might be waiting for him to stir. But he had been alone. Alone and cold.

He had stood up with difficulty in the thick drift and stumbled towards his station, tripping and being whipped by low branches as he'd waded through the snow-covered deadfall to where he was last conscious. When he saw the chairlift station and its one customer in a yellow suit, his vision was still swimming, and his heart was battering in his chest.

The New Yorker looked at this man with distaste. An Indian. He might have known. He leaned on his pole and waited for the figure to reach the place he was paid to be. When Sam got there, his line of travel heading for the hut, a lemon-yellow arm with a pole barred his way.

'Hey, buddy. Don't you think you should shut the chair down if you want to take a leak?'

Sam stopped and looked into the man's face. Cold grey eyes looked back, full of contempt and aggression.

Sam found his voice, and his manners, in that turmoil that was still churning in his chest and stomach. He took a breath. 'Sorry, mister. Got sick back there,' he gasped.

The man was unimpressed. 'Sick huh?'

'Yeah. Sick.'

'Sick as in ill, or sick as in loaded?'

Sam swallowed. He fought back that dark feeling coming from the base of his spine and clenched his fists inside his work gauntlets. Not now. No hassle now. Please.

'Just plain sick. Want a chair?'

The man remained leaning on his pole, in the manner of a ski tutor instructing a class. 'No, buddy. I want an apology.'

Sam said nothing. He looked back up at the trees, his mind wandering back to what had happened to him. With his eyes still on the close-packed pines he said absently, 'Sorry for any inconvenience. Have a nice day.'

No use. Not enough. Lemon Yellow wasn't budging. 'You call that an apology?'

Sam looked back into his scowling face 'Sure I call that an apology.'

The man stood up straight, taking his weight off the pole, and pulled back his shoulders like a bodyguard defending the hut. 'Maybe you people don't understand English so good. When white folks say *apology* they mean saying sorry for something.'

Sam's brow darkened. He spoke softly. 'Gee. So that's what white folks mean. Tell me, what do they mean when they say fuck off you fat ass-hole?'

The New Yorker's voice was bubbling with controlled rage when he replied. 'Okay buddy. I'm not leaving this resort today until you're out of a job. You sure picked the wrong wagon to burn.'

He turned and skied off down the hill, clearly indicating he was off to the base lodge. Half-way up the Beaver chair his abandoned wife and child swung their way back up the mountain, unaware that they were on their own for the rest of the day. Sam watched the yellow suit disappear down the hill and lurched into his hut. Right now, he didn't care about his job. He cared about his head. Sam Hunt didn't want to die.

Slumping heavily down on the folding plastic seat inside the hut, Sam bent forward and held his aching head in his hands. A brain tumour could be treated. He just needed a scan, that was all. Something to look in there and see what was wrong. Because Sam now admitted to himself something was very wrong indeed. Would he have to go to the hospital in Calgary, he wondered. What if he never came out? It was time to tell Katie just how bad things were. He sat up. If that guy in the yellow suit did what Sam suspected he was going to do, he might have to tell Katie they were short of one salary, too. What did that matter, compared to the possibility that her husband, Jess and Billy's father, might be dying of a brain tumour?

It wouldn't be the first time he'd been in trouble for losing his rag at a moron. His own mouth had been his biggest enemy back in the days of driving for Fox Line. The depot manager, Jim Henderson, had often pulled Sam in and had a word in his ear. He was a nice guy, Jim. Gave Sam the job in the first place. Meant well. But he didn't know what he was talking about.

There had been that incident when a passenger who'd called Sam *chief* complained to the company about the colourful response he received in front of his children.

Chief. The Canadian answer to the American south's *boy*. At least the black American had done something about that. Let's see a Beverly Hills housewife pull over in the Mercedes and call a black twenty-year-old man *boy*. No chance. Black Americans scared the shit out of the whites. The Canadian Indian scares no one. You could call him *chief* and he'll just run back to his reserve and sulk. Well, unless you were Sam.

Jim had sighed when Sam answered his call and entered the office. 'You have to realize that sometimes people don't mean what they say, Sam. They don't mean to be hurtful.'

'Uh huh.'

Jim hardened. Or tried to. 'Okay, even if they do, the customer is always right.'

'Specially if the driver isn't white, huh?' Sam's face was dark and inscrutable.

'Look. If a customer lashes out and you're a bald guy, he's gonna say, *Hey! Bald guy!*. If you're fat he's gonna say, *Hey! Fatso!*. So you're an Indian. What do you think they're gonna say when they want to insult you?'

'Beats me. I got all my own hair and I weigh a hundred and eighty-two pounds.'

'Quit acting up, Sam. I know what it's like for you. Just cool it.'

But he didn't know what it was like. How could Jim Henderson know what it was like to be born on the Redhorn reserve, to be a man treated like a child by the world on account of his skin? Or the hoops of fire children went through in that place on the way to being grown.

Did he know what it was like to be in that cabin high in the aspen wood one night, aged fourteen, standing over that thing on the rough wooden floor? The thing that had been his father. The thing that was cut open in a lake of blood, and had its organs in brand new places. Places you wouldn't dream of.

No, no, no, no, NO! Jesus! Where did that come from? Push the thought away. Fast. It mustn't come back. Sam was shaking in the hut. He knew now he was really sick. He'd kept that memory buried pretty successfully for over twenty years in a sealed black pit. It was a very deep pit, and for the most part it kept it quiet. How come it was crawling out?

The walkie-talkie hanging on a wall peg crackled into life. 'All stations, this is patrol. Can you guys look out for a skier from the fun-run dressed like an Indian. His buddies are worried they haven't seen him. Seems the dummy did the closed double black down Beaver. Anyone got a sighting? He could have just legged it off resort. Also, two manual groomers to the top station please. We got a bit of a bare patch on the drag-tow needs shovelling. Over.'

Sam looked at the radio numbly. He was too sick for this. He needed to go home. He reached up, unhitched the radio and pressed talk. 'This is Beaver chair. Can someone relieve me? I need to go home sick. Over.'

The long black box spoke back. 'This is patrol. Mike here. That you Sam? Are you okay, man? We wondered where you were. Karen's on her way already. Thought you'd deserted your post. Over.'

All Sam could manage was a light press on talk and a weak, 'Thanks Mike.'

He sat quietly in the hut as some customers skidded to a halt at the pylon. They looked expectantly at the manual groomer in his wooden shell. A haunted, black pair of eyes gazed back at them. They slid forward and got on the chair themselves.

16

Alberta 1907
Siding Twenty-three

No Indian blood. At least there had been no Indian blood. The Reverend James Henderson had prayed as the men dragged Hunting Wolf and his men off the mountain. God must have answered, for the Indians had not resorted to violence, and ugly and undignified as the scene was, there was no bloodshed. At least not then.

Henderson's heart was heavy now as he stood amongst the large group of natives, all of them staring up at the newly blasted hole in the rock.

Three men dead. Killed by the unexpectedly fierce power of the blast, which despite the men's experienced calculations, did not allow them sufficient time to retire from danger. They were blown apart and the gaunt, harrowed minister would be burying them tomorrow. After the successful removal of the Indians, Angus McEwan had crowed about his triumph. Then he had raged at the accident. How could his men have made such an error in the quantity and positioning of the explosives? Obviously they had, and his work gang was now three short. Two Scots and a Chinaman who would never see their homes and families again.

The natives had watched impassively as the body parts had been gathered like berries and brought back to the camp, and now they congregated at the base of the rude scaffolding, keeping vigil over what amounted to no more than a jagged black tear in the rock.

Henderson spoke to Chief Hunting Wolf at his side. 'You go home now?'

The chief's gaze remained on the black hole. 'No. I cannot go. We must wait. And prepare.'

The minister was weary. He nodded as if he understood, which he did not, and left the band of natives to their vigil. The snow could not possibly become any heavier without falling as a single unbroken sheet. It covered the head like an ermine hat in seconds of a person remaining stationary. Henderson swept his frozen hat away with a hand and started back to his cabin.

McEwan's foreman, Duncan Muir, was waiting for him. Henderson was relieved it was not McEwan himself. His energy for confrontation was low, and unlike his superior, Muir was a civilized and pious man.

'May I come in, Reverend?'

Muir stood at the door of Henderson's tiny cabin, which like all the other cabins, had no lock. McEwan would have been in there by now, his feet on the stove. Muir had more manners.

'Of course, Mr Muir. Please.'

They entered the small hut, its bare wooden walls boasting a single decorative fancy: a cross made from birchwood and twine. A bed, table and two rough stools were the only furniture Henderson possessed. A battered storm lamp and a stove provided the luxury of heat and light.

Muir stood by the stove, his fur hat in his hands.

Henderson wiped the snow from his black coat and closed the door against the colourless desert outside.

'I'm afraid I can offer you little refreshment, Mr Muir. The supplies are low as you are aware, and my few edible conceits have already been donated to Cook for the benefit of all.'

'Och, I am not in search of sustenance, Reverend. It is matters of the spirit I wish to discuss.'

'Be seated.' The foreman's reply was a surprise. Henderson had assumed Muir was here on McEwan's business. Another order perhaps to make the Indians move away from the blasting site.

'How may I help you Mr Muir?' Henderson sat opposite his stocky, grey-haired fellow Scot.

Muir cleared his throat and looked grave. 'I fear for the men's morale, Reverend.'

'The deaths.'

'No. Well, yes. The deaths. But more than that.'

'What then?'

'They are becoming superstitious.'

Muir said this as though he had admitted the men were for the madhouse.

'Is that so unusual? Especially in a wilderness encampment, cut off from the world by this infernal weather?'

'The manner of their superstitions is becoming unusual. Yes.'

James Henderson looked at the weatherbeaten man on the other side of the stove. This was not a man who was frightened of anything. Respectful of the elements, yes, but unsettled by the unknown like a Aberdonian fish-wife, no. He was baffled. 'I am afraid I do not understand, Mr Muir. What precisely is dismaying the men?'

Muir leant forward slightly, his hands still turning his hat. 'The Trickster.'

Henderson was now astonished. 'The Trickster?'

'The thing the Indians say was locked in the mountain.'

Henderson was annoyed now. 'How can the men know of the Indians' fears, Mr Muir? To my knowledge I am the only Siouan speaker on this camp, and the Indians have no English whatsoever.'

'Mr McEwan told Bailey about it, in preparation to remove the natives from the rock. He told the rest of the men.'

This was unfortunate. Henderson had indeed related the whole ridiculous and primitive myth to McEwan, in order to let him understand these people's deepest fears and the reasons, in fact, why they were adamant that the blasting be cancelled. He had not expected McEwan to be foolhardy enough to repeat the nonsense to a gang of simple, uneducated men. Muir's face was testimony that it had been an error.

'And do they believe this nonsense?'

'They would deny it, Reverend, but I know it is colouring their behaviour.'

'What do you wish me to do about it, Mr Muir?'

'You need to settle their minds at the funeral, Reverend. Could you find a way in your sermon of reminding them that the Christian man has no room in his heart for such heathen beliefs?'

'It is affecting their work, I trust.'

He hadn't meant the comment to be barbed, but Muir took it that way.

'I would ask you even if it were not, Reverend. I care about their souls as well as their labours.'

Henderson was sorry to have his remark draw blood from this man but somehow the request to bury the Indians' beliefs along with the bodies of the three men made him defensive and irritable. It was his own fault. He should never have told a man as deceitful and untrustworthy as McEwan anything about the Indians at all. If McEwan had hoped the men would find the Kinchuinicks' legend amusing and idiotic then it had rebounded on him.

There was irony in the fact that Henderson may even have relayed some of the details incorrectly. Trickster, for instance, was the best translation he could come up with. It was most likely incorrect. His grasp of the language, after all, was primitive in the extreme. Hunting Wolf had squatted with him for two hours one dark, cold night, explaining the nature of this thing, the four-named demon, and he thought he had mostly made sense of it. But he could not be sure.

Creator and destroyer. It could be both. There were many Tricksters apparently. Some figures of fun, who could be deceived in a hilarious fashion as well as deceive, providing endless stories of great ribaldry, almost always involving sex or defecation. Others were figures of the deepest terror, demons who destroyed and murdered as naturally as a mortal breathes in and out, clever, shape-shifting, vengeful, evil beyond imagination. Hunting Wolf told of the latter. Henderson had listened politely and not without interest. The demon described was not unlike those of early Christian belief. Certainly it was as grotesque and terrifying in its true form as those nightmares dreamed up by the medieval Jesuits to petrify their flock. The physical description Hunting Wolf gave made Henderson uncomfortable – if he were honest, made his shoulders crawl like a child being told a ghost story. But it was an animal-like cunning, twinned with human intelligence and adherence to a strict pattern of the elements, that separated the heathen demons from the Christian. Hunting Wolf explained that their Trickster was of winter. Colder than ice. A heart harder than rock. Their demon was clever to conceal its true form, enjoyed shifting shape. And it loved to taunt and tease. Oh, it could be tricked, and sometimes defeated, but only by the Keeper. At that point Henderson lost his way in the maze of alien words.

The whole thing was of course preposterous, the product of fear and lack of education. Men of science were putting a lid of reason on all such fancy. His own beloved Edinburgh University was even now full of men of letters who could laugh at the notion of demons and provide evidence backing the misinterpretation of perfectly natural occurrences. The love of God in these modern times did not require a belief in scaly demons from Hades. He and his fellow theologians in Edinburgh enjoyed many a discussion on the topic, usually over a fine port and good cigar. However Edinburgh University, with its gaggle of whiskered, rational men and its comforting neo-classical granite domes, seemed distant and dreamlike as he had sat there that night with Chief Hunting Wolf.

He should, of course have kept the whole thing to himself, but he needed to explain to McEwan why he sympathized with the Indians. He had tried to impress upon the engineer that their beliefs were as deeply held as his, that they believed the Trickster was as real as the engineer believed Christ is our saviour.

Muir was sitting still, waiting for an answer.

'I know you care, Mr Muir. I am sorry if I seemed to suggest otherwise. My only fear is that by mentioning this fanciful notion it will further inflame the men's imaginations.'

Muir nodded. 'My thoughts initially, Reverend, but let me enlighten you as to how far this has progressed.'

Henderson was not sure he wished to hear.

'They are saying they will not enter the hole in the rock to set new charges without you being present.'

'This is not completely eccentric. I believe the gang which built the two-hundred-mile stretch of rail east of here would not set any charge unless first blessed by a priest.'

'I am not done. They also want the Kinchuinick shaman.'

Henderson took a deep breath and sighed. Muir was right to be concerned. He had watched horrified on many occasions as the men had laughed and made ribald jokes at the expense of the solemn and ever-present Kinchuinicks. A Kinchuinick shaman would have been treated with as much respect and belief as a hopeless jester by those men. Obviously these were changed days. Henderson stood.

'I see. I will think carefully about the sermon, Mr Muir. Thank you for bringing it to my attention.'

Muir stood to go, putting his hat on as he pushed back the stool. 'Thank you.'

He made to leave. Henderson spoke. 'Mr Muir. May I ask you something?'

'Certainly.'

'Do you share the men's fears?'

Muir reddened slightly. 'As I said, Reverend. There is no place in the Christian man's heart for such beliefs. Good day.'

He opened the door, stepped into the snow and was gone. So Muir was as frightened as his men. James Henderson sat down again and began to prepare a sermon.

The dark figures standing only a few hundred yards away from the graves were disconcerting. Today, however, the men seemed unmoved by the watching Indian presence that was never far from any of their activities. Three rectangular pits in the ground were in danger of filling with snow as the railway workers stood over them, hatless heads bowed and gloved hands clasped.

The makeshift crosses were rustic and three wooden coffins sat tidily at the mouths of the graves, waiting to be lowered and covered, as Henderson brought the service to a close. Muir was watching him hopefully, his eyes, unlike the rest of the men's, raised to Henderson's face instead of gazing at his feet. The only face turned from the ground was McEwan's. He was watching the watchers.

The group of Indians were framed by a copse of delicate aspens, bending into graceful arcs under the weight of the snow, their balletic posture often resulting in a sudden snapping in the night as the trunk gave up its fight against gravity. It was a dramatic graveyard but the graves had been almost impossible to dig in the iron-hard ground. The men had stabbed at the earth for hours with pick-axes and now stood unhappily, ringing their handiwork as the minister spoke.

'. . . and as we commit their bodies to the ground, we trust in the everlasting life granted to us by the love of our Lord Jesus.'

Twelve fur-clad pallbearers heaved the boxes up on their ropes and lowered them into their rough-hewn holes.

'Ashes to ashes, dust to dust . . .'

Henderson tossed a ball of frozen earth into the middle grave, which bounced comically off the wooden lid and clattered down the side of the pit. He carried on regardless, looking up at the grim snow-flecked faces surrounding him.

'Our colleagues will know the mercy and grace of our Lord Jesus Christ, for they were, as you all are, true believers in the risen Christ.'

Muir looked relieved.

'It was Jesus who taught us that there is but one God. It was Jesus who warned us against the sin of idolatry and false Gods, false beliefs. It was Jesus who reassured us that though we walk through the valley of death, we need fear no evil, for He is with us. He told us, brothers, that so long as we shall believe in Him, and believe in no other, we will have everlasting life in the presence of our Father.'

The men looked dolefully at Henderson. From the corner of his eye he saw a small, quick movement through the snow that made him flick his eyes left. A whiskeyjack, a still, watching bird, was standing in the snow a few feet from Henderson and the graves. He looked back at the men and continued.

'To believe in other gods, other spirits, is a sin, as taught to us by Jesus. Our brothers here, the Kinchuinicks, have their gods. But we as Christians know they are false and that in time Jesus will bring these men and women to his bosom to renounce their false spirits and worship with us the one true God, who through love sent us His only son. That knowledge is our greatest gift as educated, civilized, Christian men.'

The bird, curiously in the presence of such a crowd, hopped twice towards Henderson, its head cocked to one side.

'So I say to you, do not concern yourself with the false gods of less fortunate, less civilized men. Concern yourself instead with the message of Christ, who . . .'

There was a thin whistling sound in the air and a dull thud, as an arrow speared the whiskeyjack cleanly through the breast. Henderson stopped mid-sentence, looking on in horror with the rest of the mourners. Henderson looked open-mouthed towards the Indians. How could they do such a thing? He felt insulted and betrayed. Then, it became worse.

Henderson and the men watched, appalled, as something happened to the snow around the doomed bird. From the dying creature's yawning beak came a deep guttural groan so loud and deep one would not even expect it to emanate from a bear in pain, and the snow for at least three feet around its body thrashed as though churned by paddles.

The men watched with horror until the phenomenon stopped and the bird's body lay still, skewered on the arrow like a chicken ready for roasting. Henderson denied himself the truth of what he had just seen. He stood wide-eyed, breathing hard, as the men milled around, shouting in panic.

Then he held up his hand and bellowed above them. 'Be still. You see how you are? The Indians who know nothing about the sanctity of a funeral service interrupt it to hunt for food and you panic for no reason, your heads filled with nonsense. Be still, I say.'

They looked back at him doubtfully, but his authority and the power of his voice stayed their panic, and they were silenced. Henderson continued, watching the men keenly, praying silently that his voice would not break with emotion. 'The message of Christ is what you must think of. To love one another and worship no other but God.' He was trembling. Chief Hunting Wolf was walking towards the dead bird, his bow in his hand. What now, God? What now? 'And so we bid farewell to our companions in the knowledge that we will meet again. Let us pray.'

Some men bowed their heads, but most looked in fright at the disturbed snow round the dead whiskeyjack. Henderson raised his voice again, almost shouting in very real anger, 'Let us pray!'

They complied, reluctantly.

'Our Father, which art in Heaven, hallowed be thy name.'

Hunting Wolf was nearly there.

'Thy kingdom come, thy will be done on Earth, as it is in Heaven.'

He was at the bird. McEwan was glaring at Henderson as though this were all some elaborate and disgusting charade he and the Indians had plotted together.

'Give us this day our daily bread, and forgive our debts as we forgive our debtors.'

Hunting Wolf stood over the corpse and sprinkled a ring of what looked like herbs round the body. There were two funerals going on now.

'And deliver us from temptation. For thine is the kingdom, the power and the glory, forever and ever. Amen.'

The men muttered *Amen* and instantly turned their attention back towards the Indian and the bird. The body lay prettily in its new dark circle, the snow already coating its lifeless feathers.

Chief Hunting Wolf looked at Henderson.

The white-faced minister thanked God that the Indian could not speak English, when the chief pointed down at the poor broken creature and said softly in Siouan,

'It has begun.'

17

'Quit that Jess, would ya!'

Billy pulled Jess's tiny fists out of Bart's substantial fur, where she had buried them up to her chubby wrists. It was her second attempt to pull out handfuls of the coarse grey coat and she went at it as though it was her job. She chuckled as Billy held her arms, but her brother was annoyed.

'Leave him alone.'

Bart was unmoved. His pale blue eyes watched brother and sister wrestle while he sat sphinx-like on the rug, mouth shut and head erect.

Billy loved Bart, and although he loved Jess too, well kind of, he wasn't going to let her bug him. Sam had bought Billy the dog for his seventh birthday and it was the best birthday present in the whole world. A guy at Sam's work bred huskies and Billy was allowed to go and choose from a litter of four pups squalling and mewing under their mother, their eyes barely open. He saw Bart right away. Bart, because he was just like Bart Simpson in the cartoon, the way his hair stuck straight up like that from his head.

Sam and Katie had laughed.

'Yeah, cool, Billy,' said Sam, balancing Jess on his hip. 'Don't call one of nature's majestic miracles anything noble like Prince or Nanook. Just go right ahead and name him after a drawing that says *eat my shorts*.'

But it was his dog and he could call him what he wanted. So Bart it was and Bart it stayed. Billy was amazed, almost to the point of ecstasy, that Sam had said he could have a husky. How could Sam have known that his son had been dreaming about a friendly wolf who looked just like Bart? The wolf was stringier and meaner-looking than the cuddly dog, but it seemed to have the same sort of kindness behind its eyes, animal eyes that seemed to know more than they should. And it could take Billy places. At night when he was asleep he would run alongside the wolf and they would go fast, and real far. It felt like Billy almost became the wolf, had the same power in his legs and jaws, the same senses, open to scents that could tell you almost anything, tell you if someone was lying, or if they were sick. Or if they were bad. He was never sure if he became the wolf or if they were two wolves running alongside each other. He just knew they were joined in some way and it seemed as natural as sleep itself.

He never told his Mom or Dad about the wolf. It was private. Not bad private, like when he'd broken Katie's shiny china pot-pourri apple and hid it from her for a fortnight. Good private. Like being good-mannered enough not to mention something that didn't concern others. Anyway, they wouldn't have believed him.

Only once he'd nearly said something, but he knew they'd think he was lying. His Grandpappy in Vancouver was ill. Billy had put his head through the banisters at the top of the stairs as Katie took the call from Grandma. He'd watched her hunch over the phone and knew she was worried. He had heard her say that there was nothing they could do that night, that they would all drive out there tomorrow, and he could tell by her two hands holding the phone, and the low voices of her and Dad talking later, that it had been something serious.

That night Billy went running with the wolf. They ran and ran through the mountains, out into the rocky foothills leading to the coastal range and the sea, splashing through rivers, picking their way through the trees and into the big city of Vancouver. He could smell the ocean, feel the salt in his lungs. And although the child in Billy could never have found his grandparents' house in that concrete maze and endless patchwork of suburbs, the wolf in him found it with ease. He padded up the big, creaky, wooden stairs, past the framed butterflies and the big droopy palm in its copper bucket, and went into his Grandpappy's bedroom. His Grandma was sitting by his bed holding his hand. She looked terribly old, and her arms were scrawny beneath the thin satin nightgown she wore.

She didn't see Billy or the wolf, but they were right beside her.

And Billy sniffed. Sniffed the air round the sweet bald pink head of his Grandpappy and knew that he was okay. He knew his Mom and Dad would get a call tomorrow to say *don't come, he's better, it's all okay*. Billy put a hand that felt like a hand but looked like a paw, on his Grandma's lap and left it there for a few minutes, hoping to comfort her, the way she so often comforted him after a fall or a disappointment. And then it had been time to go. They had run back to Silver and when Billy woke up with the phone ringing he had known it was true.

His mom had come into the bedroom and sat on the edge of his bed. 'Grandpappy's better, sweetpie. He's sitting up and moaning about Grandma's coffee right now.'

He loved to see his Mom all smiles and joy like that, and he had snuggled back into his pillow with satisfaction as she'd kissed him on the cheek. He had wanted to tell her what he'd seen, tell her what Grandma had been wearing, that he knew all along. But he hadn't. The wolf was a good friend. But he was a private night-time friend.

His daytime friend was Bart. But even Bart wasn't helping right now. Billy Hunt was on edge. Lately the wolf hadn't been coming. Not since it had said something bad was going to happen and Bart would be Billy's only friend. It frightened him. Especially since his Dad had been acting strange too.

Billy thought his Dad was excellent. He was a gas. Sometimes he would make Billy laugh so much that tears rolled down his cheeks and his sides would ache like he had a charlie-horse. And he was tough too, even when Billy didn't really understand what was going on.

There was that summer when they went canoeing on Lake Winni-kanka, and a lady had come up to Billy and Jess in the canoe while Katie and Sam were picnicking on the shore. He was younger but he remembered that the lady had had a funny accent, German or some-thing, and had wanted a photograph of Billy and Jess in the canoe, each with a feather in their hair. She had the feathers ready, a couple of mangy things she'd found on the shore. Duck tails he thought. Billy said sure and was about to put one of the feathers in Jess's hair when his Dad had marched over and gone crazy. And when the woman's husband came to join in, he'd taken one look at Billy's excellent big Dad, standing there without a shirt on, his wide brown chest glistening above his cut-off jeans shorts, and had turned and fled. Billy hadn't known what the fuss was about over a photo, but he had sure been proud of his Dad. Seemed like his Mom was too, 'cause he remembered they lay down in the grass and hugged while Billy paddled Jess round the lake some more.

But his Dad was cranky right now. Every night he'd come home looking like he'd seen a ghost, and Mom would try and cheer him up with her stories about funny museum visitors. But he was looking ill and it was making Billy sad.

At least Bart would come in the house now when he was allowed. For days he'd stayed outside looking towards the mountains, and Billy had joined him at night sometimes when he couldn't bear the thought of his friend out there alone. But whatever was bugging him up there seemed to have passed and he came in and let Billy stick his face in his fur, just like he always did.

Jess tottered off to the TV table to stick her hands into the video recorder as Katie came into the room wiping her hands on a dishcloth.

'Aw come on Billy. Keep an eye on her would you?' She swept her daughter up just before the saliva covered hand could enter the inviting letter-box slit in the video.

'I was. She was bugging Bart.'

'Yeah? Well you're bugging me lying around doing nothing. If you won't keep an eye on Jess for me why don't you go out and bring in some logs? Your Dad'll be home in a minute and there's no fire.'

Billy hated bringing in the logs. The woodpile was the other side of the yard and it seemed miles away in the thick snow. But he knew his Dad liked a fire in the hearth and he got up and went to put his Sorrels on.

The snow was chucking down and although it was dark the white blanket was so reflective that the small kitchen light illuminated the whole yard like a floodlight. Billy ducked his head and ran for the logs. They were piled under the two big lodgepole pines, kept dry by the canopy of branches that hung over them. Great system, his father bragged, for seasoning wood, letting the wind dry them quicker than if they were in a shed, and keeping the rain and snow at bay. But those long, springy swaying branches made it real spooky. The heavy wooden limbs cast deep shadows over the pile and Billy sometimes thought he saw things moving in there as the branches swayed, but it was just shadows on the gnarly logs. He scooped up an armful of dry wood, balancing as many as he could in the crook of his arm before turning to make the dash back to the warm kitchen.

He spun round and then yelped. There was a figure standing right behind him in the yard. Billy dropped the logs in fright. False alarm. It was his Dad. Sam looked at his son as if seeing him for the first time.

'Dad? Are you okay?'

Sam looked down at the fallen logs then back up at Billy. 'Yeah. Yeah. I'm okay.'

He seemed far away, his eyes glittering like spangles in the freezing blanket of snow. But he was coming back from wherever he'd been and he was starting to see his startled son in front of him. 'Here. Let's get these guys picked up.'

He stopped to pick up the logs embedded in the white where they fell, their location only visible by the log-shaped holes left in the snow like a cartoon character's body outlined in the dirt after a cliff-fall. Billy bent and joined him.

'You gave me a fright Dad.'

'Sorry Billy.'

They shared the cold logs between them and went into the house, Sam walking slowly in front like an old man. This was the same man who would normally throw a snowball at the back of his son's head to announce his arrival, would probably have wrestled Billy into the snow and made him shout *surrender!* Now he seemed to be making the habit of standing alone outside his own house in the dark, his eyes reflecting the lights from the window as he looked at Billy, but radiating none of the warmth that used to flood out of those two dark pools into his son's heart.

Billy decided that tonight, whether it wanted to or not, he would make the wolf come. He and the wolf would have to pad into Sam's room and check out if his Dad was okay. Sniff around for the scent of what was wrong. Tonight. No more delay. Tonight.

Walking was warmer than standing still. That was for sure. But Calvin Bitterhand's legs were swollen and aching, throbbing behind the knees like they were going to explode. The cowboy boots that he'd worn for eighteen months, through every season then the same again, slipped in the snow as though they were skates. Nothing was left of the sole on the left boot except a thin piece of split leather and that had come away from the seam round the heel. It slapped loose and then snapped shut again with every step, shovelling snow into the boot like it was meant to. His feet were in worse shape than his legs.

Only fifteen miles west out of Calgary and his old ruined body was yelling at him to stop. Getting this far in the storm had taken him a ridiculous fourteen hours, twelve of those through the night, and three times now since dawn, when he'd seen a pick-up or car driven by Indians and had been tempted to thumb a ride. But his heart and his knowledge told him that he needed to be pure, to atone for his sins. And walking was the only way.

His food was gone now. The stomach that hadn't eaten properly for two days had at first rejected the sandwiches the girl on First Street had given him, making him puke up shrimp outside a motel on Sixteenth Avenue. But gradually he packed away the rest, devouring the dainty deli sandwiches like an animal, ripping at them, cramming handfuls into his gap-toothed mouth as he walked, caring little if people saw him and turned away in disgust. But now the sandwiches were gone and he was hungry again. Hungry, cold and tired enough to lie in a grave.

He bent against the wind and kept walking, cars throwing up slush as they cruised past him on the country road. He'd long since left behind sidewalks and was now in the commuter belt, the land of ranches that weren't really ranches at all. Just city people who like to play at being ranchers by having a big brown and white stallion sitting out in a stable and a white corral fence round a bit of grass. Even when it was just a horse and a house.

And there sure were some big houses out here. The mail-boxes at the end of long snaking driveways only hinted at the luxury those names painted on the sides enjoyed. Through the driving snow he could make out the elegant proportions of those big houses, their arched lobby windows, the wide stone chimneys and porches you could park a pick-up in. The big white one he was passing now had those chime things hanging above the porch seat. The noise was eerie but beautiful as they tinkled in the snowstorm and Calvin stopped to look over the white fence at them as they swung in the wind. Milligan, said the mail-box. *Pretty lucky Milligans,* thought Calvin. He would have liked a porch with chimes on it. One where he could sit in the summer and smoke, with grandchildren scrambling at his feet, where he could greet people who'd come to buy his magic. They would have stood respectfully at the bottom of the stairs like they used to do for

Eden Hunting Wolf, and ask him if he would use his good medicine to save their baby, make a baby, bring back a lover, heal a foot, find a lost calf, make a win at bingo, stop a toothache. He'd have liked some chimes like that to tinkle as he weighed up the customer and decided whether he would help or not. But there was no porch now, and there would never be any chimes tinkling for Calvin Bitterhand.

No use wanting what wasn't to be. The status of elder was one that Calvin took for granted would be his, but now would never have. Moses had fixed that. Moses had wasted both their lives.

His fingers curled over the top of the fence, as he looked at what he couldn't have, and remembered why he was here.

Roddy Milligan was squeezing some oranges for breakfast when he realized his briefcase was in the lounge. A piece of toast between his teeth, he wandered through to get it.

The snow was worse. Its wind-driven descent filled the huge window, creating an illusion that the whole house was a vehicle travelling sideways at speed through some weird white sea. This weather was making commuting a nightmare, and his temper short. He picked up his leather case and wandered past the huge lounge window, looking down the virgin white paddock to the grey snow on the road. There was somebody looking up at the house from the fence. Roddy narrowed his eyes and chewed his toast. A tramp. Shit. So much for the neighbourhood's strong police presence that the real estate agent had bragged about. *What about security?* he'd asked the weasel of a man in an Italian jacket as they went over the plans at that sales lunch. *No problem*, he'd said. *Rosevale has a very strong police presence. Rosevale leaves all the problems of the city behind you but gives the resident the convenience of its proximity.* Very strong police presence. Bullshit. Looked like bums could just hang about and peer into your house when they fancied.

But you didn't get bums out here. In fact you didn't get bums where they couldn't beg. Roddy felt apprehension stir. Maybe he wasn't a bum. Maybe something worse. Were there more of them? Were they casing the joint to break in as soon as he'd gone to work?

Maybe they knew he was alone in this big house, not even a dog to bark at footsteps on the drive. What if he went to work and brought Nicole home from the office for his weekly lay, only to find his hi-fi swiped?

Roddy swallowed the last of his toast and went to the phone. The police had better get here fast enough to let him get to work. If those bastards made him late, he'd fax their superiors in town first thing he did. Someone would get it. There was a cordless sitting on the coffee table in the lobby. He picked it up, pulled out the aerial and walked back into the lounge to keep an eye on his latent intruder. The figure hadn't moved.

Should he dial 911? It wasn't exactly an emergency, a tramp looking over your fence. But it was a potential emergency if he was going to rob your house, and Roddy was in a hurry. He thought for a moment and decided to go for it anyway, punching in the numbers and watching the dark, hunched figure in the snow as he put the phone to his ear. Even though the man was too far away for Roddy to see the details of his face, he felt the man's eyes sweeping his face like a searchlight. He felt a little lightheaded. The phone was making a buzzing noise now that made him feel strange. It calmed him, made him think of sweet summer smells, the scent of choke-cherry blossom dancing in white clusters on the end of thin green branches even though he stood in a towelling dressing gown only a glass pane away from a blizzard.

'Roddy?'

A woman's voice on the phone. Roddy was only mildly surprised. Must have misdialled. This certainly wasn't the police but he felt pretty good about it.

'Roddy? Is that you?'

'Mom?'

Why hadn't he phoned his Mom lately? he wondered dreamily. He remembered she'd been dead twelve years, that was why. But it sure was nice to talk to her again.

'Roddy. Ask the man in. He needs clothes and some sleep.'

'I thought he was a thief, Mom.'

'Don't be silly, Roddy. He needs to come in right now.'

He was sure he could hear larks in the background. There was certainly a feeling of summer, like his Mom was calling to him from the house to come in and get his lunch. He could feel the sun on his face, and smell honeysuckle in the air.

'Okay, Mom.'

He took the phone from his ear and went to the window. The man seemed to be waiting for a sign. Roddy banged on the glass and beckoned him forward with a smile. Calvin Bitterhand opened the white wooden gate and slowly shuffled up to the house.

18

Sometimes you just have an instinct as a patroller. Mike wished his instinct had been wrong. But it wasn't. The guy in the clown suit said that his buddy was right behind him on the mogul field and that he waited for him at the bottom. Couldn't have missed him if he'd come down, he'd said. He got a rocket up his Californian ass from patrol, of course, for skiing a closed run, but the poor kid seemed upset enough. They let it go and didn't take away his lift pass.

'There's no way I could have missed him, man,' he'd whined. 'I stood right here at the base and he just didn't show. Ain't no other way down.'

Patrollers knew different. The boy could have skied past without being seen if the clown was looking the other way for even a second, or could have cut through the trees onto the green run. But they had to check anyway. His gang were getting concerned. Mike had skied the trail a couple of times, but there were no signs of a wipe-out and no stray poles, gloves or goggles which usually told a tale of woe.

The thing to do was to leave it until the end of the day, just in case he was chilling out in a mountain restaurant, and if the kid still didn't show they'd start getting serious about a search.

He hadn't appeared by three and they got serious all right. The trail was at least a mile long. A lot of trees to search, but that's where Mike's instinct told him to look. The kid could have crashed into the pines and, God forbid, be lying there with a broken back. The snow had started again just as the fun-run ended, and that would have covered any signs of a major wipe-out, but if he was in there, Mike was going to find him.

Betty and Lachlan took the east side of the run and Mike took the west. He side-slipped down the first hundred yards, where you could at least see right through the pines to the other side. Then it got thick. Nothing for it but to get in there and poke about. Mike unhitched his pack and swung it round in front of him. He unbuckled a pair of snowshoes he took from the patrollers' hut, and stepped out of his ski bindings while there was still hard pack to support his weight. One step off the trail and you were up to your waist in snow that held you like a man-trap. He strapped his long skis on his backpack where the snow shoes had been, and legged it into the forest.

There was a strange kind of silence in amongst the trees. When his radio crackled it was like swearing in church. Almost like life became muffled for the time you were in there, softer round the edges, like it didn't matter what went on out there in the other world you could glimpse through the branches. This primeval place sat secretly like a sanctuary beside the highway of snow that carried tourists up and down the mountain every day. A green-and-brown secret full of twittering birds, scuffling animals and that thick syrupy silence.

It was Mike's favourite place to ski, in between these massive old grey-green gods, and when the spring powder fell in April he and his buddies would slice through the pines, leaving their ski tracks like autographs, watching nervously for submerged branches and roots that would rip their feet from under them.

He hated resorts without trees. Couldn't stand Europe. Apart from the fact that the Europeans were gloomy, bad-tempered bastards who wouldn't spit on you if you were on fire, they skied big, white, naked hills that made Mike agoraphobic. He loved the trees, but he loved to ski in them. He didn't much like walking through them. It was tough going in there, with branches whipping him on the legs and face as he plodded through their constantly changing corridors. He kept a line about twenty feet in, parallel to the trail, from where he would at least see a point of entry if the kid had crashed. He knew Betty and Lachlan would just poke a head into the trees on the other side of the trail looking for signs of disturbed snow and leave it at that. It was Mike's instinct that told him he might find the boy here. The fall-line made it more likely he would have slid or tumbled this way. It was that instinct that made him walk rather than ski, as unnatural a choice of locomotion to a patroller as swimming might be to a buzzard.

It was that instinct that also made him hesitate when he saw the ski sticking up in the snow between a gap in the trees. Mike stopped and looked for a second. It had to be the kid. He saw the pink flash of the Rossignol ski he remembered from this morning. This year's model. A hundred and ninety centimetres, if he knew his stuff. Too long for the kid. They always thought long skis made them look like experts. Sad. Only skiing like an expert makes you look like an expert. Skis that are ten centimetres too long only make you look like a jerk with long skis. Yes, he remembered that ski. It was going to be bad. If the kid had been lying here for that length of time he would most probably be dead or dying from the cold, whatever his injuries. But somehow, Mike Watts didn't want to rush forward pull out his first aid kit and get to it. His instinct told him something was even more wrong than a skier lying injured deep in the trees. He pressed *talk* and spoke to anyone who would listen.

'Mike here. I'm in the trees about half a mile down Beaver black diamond. Looks like I found him. Not quite there yet, but it looks bad. Over.'

A crackle of static, and Mike was still standing, not moving.

'Read you Mike. Do what you can. Blood wagon's on its way.'

Mike thought about marking the trail outside the trees with his skis first. Just so the wagon could find them. But even as he thought about it he wondered why. Every patroller worth the white cross on the suit would run instantly to the injured skier and assess the situation. Not pussy about with skis when someone was lying there needing help. He was nervous. No explanation. Just nervous.

Grabbing the picture back into his head of how the boy might be alive and in pain, Mike moved forward. He heard Betty and Lachlan shouting, somewhere, in another time.

He shouted back. 'Here! Through here! Below you.'

That pink Rossignol. It had *Sean* painted on it in big fat clumsy letters with a windsurfing sticker of a cartoon piranha partially obscuring the *n*. He remembered everything about that ski. The scratches, the stickers, the angle it jutted out of the snow. He remembered it very well indeed. When he got to what was left of Sean Bradford, and saw the mess of flesh, guts and bone that was loosely attached to that ski, Mike could barely remember his own name.

*　　*　　*

'Jesus fucking Christ! Jesus Jesus Jesus!'

Good in a crisis, thought Eric sarcastically as he watched Pasqual Weaver shrieking and clutching at her breast. The police incident tape made a whirring sound as it fluttered in the wind where it was attached to the trees, and more than twenty people tried to stand upright on the treacherous edge of the darkening trail.

Pasqual leant against her snowmobile, a female constable's arm round her shoulder, and continued to practise her mature managerial skills by making a series of sounds from the back of her throat that sounded like *ga*. She'd made the mistake of marching across the trail, ducking under the tape and making straight for McGee. She needed through there. This was her patch and they would damn well let her past.

She got through and saw what the policemen were seeing as they crouched round it, trained lights on it, took photographs of it and wrote about it in notebooks. Now she was a tearful, hysterical wreck who was going to heave at any minute. Eric didn't want through. He knew what was in there. The head patroller had told him. Well, more or less. Enough to know he wanted to stay on the trail, well away from the action. Eric was just here watching, taking stock, grateful that the porridge that was an eighteen-year-old kid hadn't been found until the end of the day when the resort was closed and all those curious happy skiers had gone home to soak in a hot tub. Eric knew his skiers. They were attracted to incident tape like flies round shit. Keeping them from tragedy was pointless. They loved it. But luckily they were gone. At least those whose got off their mark sharp were gone. The rest were being held by the roadblock McGee had set up at the exit road from the resort. Even now, the Trans-Canada was sealed off in both directions by the highway patrol. That, if nothing else, would guarantee the media would be here in a matter of hours. Eric took a few careful steps on the precipitous trail towards the huddle in the trees. He didn't want to go ass over tit in front of all these Mounties. It was bad enough for the company that their managing director was coming on like Fay Wray. They didn't need any more childish displays of weakness.

It was practically dark now, and the ski patrol were setting up halogens on the trail and in the pines for the RCs to continue their grim work. McGee looked up, saw Sindon pick his way over the bumps to the edge of the wood and went out to greet him.

153

'Don't come in, Mr Sindon,' he said from the tree side of the tape. 'It'll live with you a long time.'

Eric looked past Craig into the forest, lit now like a Spielberg movie, the beams from the halogen lamps making fans and girders of solid blue light between the trunks.

'I wasn't thinking of it. Believe me.'

Craig nodded towards Pasqual. 'Is she okay?'

Eric smiled. 'Sure. How's it going in there? Anything?'

Craig ignored the question, since it was asked the way a house-holder asked his gardener how the hedge trimming was coming along. 'Was it snowing up here this afternoon?'

Eric shifted his weight, felt himself slip and shifted it back again. 'I couldn't say. It was certainly snowing at the base lodge but as you know, it can be chucking it down up here and sunny down there, so that doesn't mean much. Why do you ask?'

Craig looked away, nodding. 'Routine. We're going to need a lot of co-operation from you, Mr Sindon. I'm sure you're aware of what's going to happen when the press get a sniff of it.'

'I'm aware of it.'

Craig didn't like Sindon's tone. He pushed the tape up and ducked beneath it, joining Eric on a little platform of snow behind a rock-hard mogul.

'We need a full list of everybody that was working on the resort. We need names, locations, times, and we're going to need to speak to every last one until they're hoarse with telling us the details of their day.'

'We still have a resort to run, Staff Sergeant.'

'Then we can close it if it gets in the way of our investigation.'

'I don't think you can do that.'

'Watch me.'

Sindon suddenly wondered why he was being so protective about what was, after all, Pasqual's company. Force of habit. He changed tack. 'We'll co-operate fully. I'll make sure they're all available first thing tomorrow.'

Craig shook his head. 'Too late. We're knocking on doors tonight, Mr Sindon. Can you let my constables have the names and addresses right now?'

Sindon sighed. 'I'll take them down to the lodge if they want to come now.'

'Thank you, sir,' Craig said without much feeling. He looked back over his shoulder to the lights in the wood. 'Hawk! Bell! Here, please.' He turned back to Eric. 'That includes you and Miss Weaver, and all these guys here.'

'Of course.'

Craig looked beyond Sindon to where their bodies threw gigantic and grotesque shadows over the blanket of trees on the other side of the trail. He spoke softly as though Eric had already gone.

'We need to get this animal.'

19

The lodge cafeteria was bad enough as a place to eat. It was even more horrible as an interview room. The long concrete room had windows along one wall looking over the nursery area and a serving counter along the other. In the poorly-conceived space between were twenty ten-seater wipe-clean tables with permanently-attached plastic seats, those evil little moulded shapes that are problematic to get in and out of with any dignity in regular shoes, and impossible in ski boots. But the rosy glow of cheeks and cordial shouting of buddy to buddy, lover to lover and child to parent usually made the restaurant bearable, providing an aural interior decoration of happy echoes that overwhelmed the spartan facilities.

Without that joyous babble it was a grim room, and right now there was nothing going on that was remotely happy.

Constables Daniel Hawk and Jeff Bell had set up their posts at the table nearest the till, their notebooks and a photocopied list of names open in front of them as they worked their way through the employees of Silver Ski Company. Those waiting their turn to be questioned had arranged themselves into groups declaring the rigid class system that exists in ski resorts. The patrollers sat near the darkened window, apart from the horde, their unclipped boots on the floor as they sat with their steaming, socked feet on the table. They tried to look like they knew exactly what was going on. Patrollers always did that. Tell a patroller something he didn't know and he'd move his gum around a cheek a little and say, 'Yeah. We heard.'

Anything at all.

'Hey Baz! Giant soldier ants from Africa have taken over the world.'

'Yeah. We heard.'

Patrollers figured it was part of the image to be the centre of things. They sat and tried to look like they were in control again, but for once the uniforms on the two Mounties' backs were trumping their white crosses.

Standing round the closed serving-hatch were a cluster of manual groomers, the ones who drove the trail bashers, shovelled the snow, fixed the fences and drove the lifts. They didn't care about image. They wanted home. So did the catering staff, the office staff, the bus drivers and the shop people. But it was going to be a while.

'So, Karen Howe.'

Daniel ran a finger down a list of names in the staff rota.

'Your job is . . . ?'

Karen looked nervously at Hawk, who was flicking open a new page in his book with his free hand, not looking at her.

'Manual groomer.'

Her voice was higher than it should have been.

He looked up. 'Hey. Don't worry. This is just routine.'

He smiled a big white smile. She smiled back.

'Sorry. I get nervous speaking to policemen. Always think I've done something. You know? When you haven't? Like when you're stopped for a ticket you think they'll shoot you?'

'Sure. Get that way myself when I go through customs at airports.'

'You do? Wow. A cop feeling guilty.' She giggled. Not unpleasantly. Hawk turned his eyes back to his notebook.

'Where were you between the hours of 11.30 a.m. and 3.30 p.m. today, Karen?'

She swallowed, moving forward in the plastic seat that didn't move with her. 'Uh, I was here mostly, on the quad. Then I went over to Beaver to relieve the groomer on the chair.'

Hawk looked up. 'Uh huh? How so?'

'Oh he got ill or somethin'. I did the chair till it closed at three forty-five.'

'And who was it that you relieved?'

'Sam Hunt.'

Hawk raised an eyebrow. So Sam was a groomer then? He knew Sam briefly when he drove buses at Fox. Met him every time there was a violent passenger or a theft. Would have been hard not to, since Sam and a handful of others were the only Kinchuinicks living in Silver. There was the poor old guy they locked up weekly, a guy who cleaned rooms with the Filipinos up at the Chateau, two more working at the ski company and that was about it. Bit of a rough deal for the people who once called this land their own, that if they wanted to run a social club in Silver for Kinchuinicks, they could all meet comfortably in a phone booth. But he hadn't seen Sam in years. Not socially at least. Nice guy, Sam. Married white, same as Joe. Hung up about his roots though, that was for sure.

Anyway, it made him pleased to see Sam making something of his life, even if it was only shovelling snow. At least it wasn't stealing for drugs and booze like most of the guys he'd dealt with when he policed Redhorn. And it looked like he was going to make Sam's acquaintance again tonight. If this girl's calculations were correct, Sam had been the man on the spot when the boy was being sliced.

'What time did Sam sign off?'

'That would be about, let's see, uh, around one-thirty I think. Yeah. One-thirty.'

'Okay, Karen. You see this guy in the Indian outfit at all?'

'Yeah. I put him on the quad on the way to the top of Beaver. Listen, I just can't believe that poor kid's dead, I mean . . .'

'That was before the fun-run?'

'Yeah. That was just at twelve I guess.',

Daniel became aware of a man watching him from the door into the kitchens. A tall fair man, with very blue eyes, leaning against the door frame, staring straight at him. There was something in that gaze he didn't like. It was more than just the patrollers' sulky sneers and childish smirks as they sauntered up to the table when called by Hawk or Bell. It looked like hatred. Deep, unfathomable hatred.

Daniel noted the chillingly dangerous look in his professional mental file and vowed to make sure he, and not Bell, got that guy to interview. You don't look at someone that way without reason and Daniel wanted to know what that reason might be.

'You notice anyone suspicious? Anyone looking at the boy maybe? Following him? Anything like that?'

'Nah. He was acting like a bit of a geek. But nothing we don't see every day, know what I mean.'

He knew what she meant. *Try police-work, lady*, he thought. He looked up at the door of the kitchens again. There was no one there. Why had he looked across there? He struggled to remember. Was someone there before, he wondered? He had a vague memory of seeing a figure there, but he was mistaken. The door was empty.

'And his friends. Were they with him at the time? On the quad I mean.'

'No. He was alone.'

'Okay, thanks, Karen.'

'Is that it?'

'That's it.'

When the constable looked up again to call up the next interviewee, he would have thought you were crazy to have said there had been a tall fair man in the doorway shooting hate at Daniel with aquamarine eyes. Daniel Hawk always remembered a face and he didn't remember seeing anyone like that. Would swear on it.

'Les Ivan, please.'

Daniel wasn't surprised at all that his staff sergeant wanted to come with him to interview Sam Hunt. He'd been interested that the groomer driving the chair had gone home sick almost half an hour after the time of the boy's death, but he became like a pointer dog spotting a wood pigeon when Daniel threw in the fact that Sam was an Indian. An Indian who grew up on Redhorn with him.

The detachment had never seen anything like this in its history. Edmonton had a team on its way. They would be there by midnight. The same bastarding team that should have been in Silver days ago to investigate Joe's death. Craig winced when he heard how fast they were getting here. So now they were hungry to help were they? On the trail of not just one cop-killer, but a seriously psycho serial killer. Craig figured they liked serial killings in Edmonton. Made them feel like Harrison Ford instead of ordinary policemen doing routine donkey-work to find what usually amounted to a drunk who'd made one violent mistake. Good press in finding serial killers. And as if to prove the point the press were already baying at the door of the detachment and jamming the lines to find out why a bunch of country patrolmen would block the Trans-Canada both ways.

Craig didn't want to waste any more time. He would have to go public with this soon. So when he'd wandered over to the big table and asked Hawk and Bell the standard *anything stink yet?* and got the snippet about Sam, he wanted to move fast.

'Okay, Constable Bell. Yardly will sit in with you for the rest of the interviews. Hawk, you come with me. You got Hunt's address?'

'Sir.'

'Get the Ford out front. I'll be right there.'

Craig walked back to where Eric and Pasqual were drinking coffee with the office staff to give them instructions and keep them calm while Daniel did his best to swing his legs out from the plastic seat without banging a shin, and failed. Bell grinned, and carried on writing down everything a ski patroller who'd been nowhere near the incident, hadn't seen the boy and didn't know what time he'd finished, had to say to him.

Outside in the almost empty parking lot eight Crown Vics sat like unpopular arcade games, their lights flashing aimlessly. Here and there the darkened silhouette of a police officer stood beside or leaned on their vehicles, as the red and blue licked across the blackened snow like disco lights. Even more uselessly, an ambulance sat poised for action. Daniel mused, as he crunched across the frozen lot, on what they thought an ambulance could do for that assortment of meat cuts.

He'd parked the Ford at the edge of the trees, well away from the lodge. He always did that at an incident – parked a distance away to leave room for whatever needed to get close in there. Ambulances, fire trucks, whatever. Courtesy really.

The Ford was a dark square by the trees, its presence betrayed only by a snow-dusted roof, courtesy of another flurry, and the reflections of the winking red and blue lights on those surfaces not dulled by mud or frost.

As he approached the shape and put a hand out to open the door, Daniel heard a sound. A low, ugly, animal sound about fifteen or twenty feet away from the car. He paused, his hand an inch away from the chrome handle, his heart starting to beat a little faster. The noise stopped. He listened, not breathing, his hand losing interest in the door handle and instinctively creeping towards the gun at his hip.

There it was again. A snarling, low, throaty growl accompanied by a tearing sound. It was straight ahead of him. The back of Daniel's neck crawled. He was sure he was being watched. He could feel it. Something malicious was looking at him, assessing him, weighing him up. He tried to deny the sensation, asking himself where that ridiculous abstract concept of *being watched* comes from? How do the prey of the world's greatest predators know when the lion is in the grass or the snake is hanging from the branch? They do. Some sixth sense, some ancient inherited skill tells the dinner that the diner is reading the menu, and Daniel Hawk could feel it right now.

The noise ceased again, but he could sense it was merely an intermission. Slowly, carefully and quietly, Daniel opened the car door and slid inside. With the door still open he turned the ignition key and the lights burst into life.

Two saucer-shaped red eyes reflected the light back at the car. A coyote, ripping its way through a trash bag left carelessly at the side of the lot, was glaring at the car, its head as still as stone, ears up like antennae, body poised to fight or flee. Still hanging from its jaws was the remains of a burger, the soggy bun dangling like a stomach lining. Daniel laughed, breathed easy, and pumped the horn. The animal leapt sideways and fled from the headlights like a bad comedian being booed off stage. Hawk was still smiling as he slammed the door shut, started the engine and drove off towards the lodge.

Jeez, but he was getting jumpy if a scavenging coyote could scare him. He smiled to himself, feeling foolish as he bumped the big Ford over frozen ruts of snow. He was still smiling, as high in the pines overhead, the tiny bird that had been watching his every move with glittering eyes watched some more, then settled back into its roost.

20

The logs were hissing in the grate. Sam stared vacantly at the weak tongues of flame that danced impotently around the wet birch bark. Jess curled up on Sam's lap, her head leaning on his chest while her father's arms made a secure hoop of flesh round her small chubby body.

Billy was watching TV. Katie was watching her husband.

'I could have it printed on a T-shirt if that would help.'

Sam looked down at his wife, all legs and woollen sweater as she sat on the floor at his feet beside the hopeless hissing fire.

'Huh?'

She swallowed a mouthful of coffee from a spotted mug. 'It'll say *you're not going mad and you won't lose your job. You just need a quack check.* Save me telling you every time you get that look on your face.'

She won a weak smile in response.

'Will the T-shirt be wet?'

'Soaking.'

'Let's get this sack of tired bones to bed first. Then you can tell me some more.'

He stood up, Jess still a floppy dead-weight in his arms. Katie leaped to her feet and scooped the girl from him in a practised, fluid movement that didn't let Jess stir as she was transferred between parents mid-air.

'Give it here. You relax by this roaring log fire, if you can bear the heat.'

Sam sat down again, heavily. Gratefully.

Katie glided towards the door, stabbing a finger in Billy's shoulder as she passed.

'And you get ready too, Billy boy. We don't forget you're there just 'cause you're quiet.'

Billy looked across at Sam. 'Okay.'

Katie halted in the doorway. 'Now there's a result. Take a note of whatever it is I said there, Sam. Sure beats the cattle-prod.'

But she'd lost him again. His eyes focused through the flames on something that was beyond sight. Katie looked at him thoughtfully for a second and padded upstairs with her sleeping burden.

Billy wasn't really watching the flickering screen in front of him. It was only a TV movie – some pile of junk in big houses with one of the actresses that used to be in *Charlie's Angels*. He was looking at his Dad. He'd listened from the sidelines to everything Sam had told Katie about his day. The rude man that his Dad had been rude back to, and who could lose him his job. The buzzing head and the fainting. The hours in between when Sam had walked along the railroad in the snow before coming home.

And he didn't know why his Mom was being so cheerful. He was real worried about his Dad, even if she wasn't.

He turned off the TV with the remote and trotted over to Sam's chair. Billy slid his little hand beneath the large, rough, weathered one that was resting limply on the arm of the chair and smiled as the big fingers closed round his.

'Guess the logs got wet when I dropped them.'

'Guess so.'

Billy let go of his smile and studied Sam's face.

'Dad?'

'Uh huh.'

'Is everything going to be okay?'

The adult concern in the child's voice snatched Sam out of his reverie. He sat forward in his chair and took Billy's other hand. 'Course it is, Billy. Nothing's wrong. I'm just tired, that's all. Come here, you.'

He pulled his son up on to a lap that was still warm from his daughter's body-heat, and kissed Billy's smooth forehead through his hair.

'Why don't we go to Calgary soon? Catch the Flames.'

Billy lit up. 'Yeah? You can get tickets?'

'Probably not. Doesn't stop us trying.'

'Crucial!'

Billy bounced off Sam's knee, his anxiety momentarily forgotten as he danced a series of mimed hockey passes on the hearth rug. That made Sam laugh. Felt like he hadn't laughed in a long time.

'Okay Wayne Gretsky. Get to bed.'

'Who's Wayne Gretsky?'

'You taking a correspondence course in how to make me feel old?'

Billy surged forward, kissed his father on the mouth and ran out of the room. The wet ghost of that kiss stayed there for minutes after the boy had left, and Sam savoured it as its sweetness slowly evaporated from his lips.

His children. His wife. The things he lived for. He wasn't going to lose them. He couldn't lose them. Sam leaned back into the old recliner and looked at the ceiling. The fire-light, weak as it was, made a shadow of the mantelpiece flicker on the plaster.

It wasn't as though he didn't deserve what he had. Sam thought he more than deserved it. Nothing had come easy to Sam Hunt.

Even this house that wasn't really his. Sometimes, when he caught sight of some corner he hadn't yet made his own, some little physical reminder of holidays another young family used to share in this house, the memory of meeting its owners nearly a decade ago was still ripe.

He'd known by Katie's face, that night ten years ago when he came home from work into the tiny plasterboard-lined room in the staff quarters, what she was going to tell him. She was shining. Joy was dripping from her like syrup. He'd put down his battered tin lunch-box on the bed and held her before she even spoke.

'Sam.'

Her voice was muffled, her face pressed against his chest.

'Katie.'

'I'm going to have a baby.'

Then they'd kissed and laughed and kissed again. They'd lain on that sagging old bed and carefully done again what made it happen in the first place. Afterwards, Katie said it was time to tell her parents everything. Sam knew she'd been in touch with them plenty and was glad. The boy in him would have fought anyone, friends, foe or family, to the death to keep her. But the man wanted her to have all the old securities she enjoyed in her Vancouver life. His love was passionate and deeper, he thought, than even Katie realized, but unlike Tom's, it wasn't suffocating. He was pleased that she wrote her parents weekly. She wrote and told them everything she could, on postcards of bears and porcupines she swiped from the free guest carousel in the hotel. Told them she loved someone called Sam Hunt, told them how good he was for her, but no more. Told them she was working, assured them the hotel shop job was temporary, and most importantly told them she was fine, loved them madly and missed them. She replied to the mail that she picked up weekly from the empty house on the hill where they thought she was living and never revealed otherwise.

Time, she thought, to put things straight. She hadn't been deceiving them deliberately. Katie had just been caught in that happy time-warp lovers find themselves in, where nothing matters except that other precious person. Now, though, they were going to be a serious family.

She sat down that night and wrote them a note. Sam read it over her shoulder, nuzzling her ear, his hands on her belly that was still flat and hard.

Darling You-Two,

I am now Mrs Sam Hunt. I am also Mrs Sam Hunt who is going to have your grandchild. We don't live in your house. I just get the mail from there. We live at 281 Lynx Trail, room 5. I miss you both terribly. Will you come and see us? You'll love my husband. I do. All my love, Peach.

P.S. I'm so happy.

She mailed it off and in their joy forgot all about it.

Two days letter they got a telegram.

Katie. On Air Canada flight 127 2.45 p.m. tomorrow. Congratulations my darling. Us-Two.

The telegram, like an omen of good will, had been addressed to Mr and Mrs Sam Hunt. Katie was thrilled. Sam was nervous.

'Have you told them anything about me?' he asked her that night in bed, lying like spoons.

'Of course I have. Lots.' She snuggled in, muttered, 'You'll love them,' and fell asleep.

Sam had lain awake, thinking. A darkened door creaked open in his head that let a sliver of memory about his own parents escape. He slammed it shut again. Any whiff of his past was like noxious gas. He thanked God the woman in his arms would never peek through into that terrifying world. Never encounter those two walking nightmares that had called themselves his mother and father. More importantly, he would never have to protect whoever was inside Katie's womb from the kind of mind-numbing horror they had inflicted on him as a daily ritual.

That was in the past. Another life. A different Sam.

With Katie he could live again. He wished shamefully at that moment he could change his skin. Do a Michael Jackson in time for their flight to touch down. If Katie could have read his thoughts she would have chastised him for that. But she couldn't read them. She was softly and safely asleep in his arms, her hot sweet body primed with life. He stayed awake until dawn, waiting for the light to spill through the thin ragged curtains, feeling her stir, listening to her breathe.

Sam took an honest half-day off work and Katie phoned in with a dishonest sick headache and they took a bus into Calgary Airport to meet his new family.

Those sliding doors. Those unthinking, impassive sliding doors behind the metal barrier. They opened every few seconds, spewing out busy people, tired people, but mostly happy people who were met and embraced. A human lottery. Who would come through next, and who would claim them? The doors didn't give a donkey's hole. They just kept right on pumping them out; but they seemed to glide open in slow motion for Sam as the two elegant, elderly people spotted their daughter and waved like children on a ride.

What must it be like, he wondered, to be greeted with such smiles? The smiles of parents who love their child so much their hearts ignite on sight of that face. No one had ever ignited like that for Sam the child. Not ever.

And this time was no different. He was invisible. They didn't see him at all. He stood right beside Katie, his shoulder touching hers, and yet they didn't see him. Not until he let Katie wrap herself around her mother's neck like a shawl and he stood behind her waiting to pick up her father's case. There was a beat. A second's pause while Frank and June Crosby looked at him and assessed the situation. Their faces were still happy, open, as they looked at him with that grateful expression polite liberal people reserve for workmen. He knew then they thought he was a cab driver. He heard Katie say in a distant and far away voice, full of a pride that seemed so misplaced, *This is Sam. My husband*, and he watched those faces change.

Mrs Crosby's hand went into a small fist between her breasts, and

Mr Crosby stood with his legs apart, looking at Katie like she'd dropped her panties in public.

Katie was still smiling up at Sam with love.

No one moved. Sam put a hand out to Katie's father. 'Pleased to meet you Mr and Mrs Crosby. Katie's told me so much about you both, feel I know you.'

If Sam thought that talking in white middle-class cliché was going to help, he was on the wrong lawn. Frank Crosby looked at the calloused brown hand on offer and then at Katie again. Katie said 'Dad?' in a small quiet voice. Not small and gentle with pleading, but loaded with a warning Sam had never heard.

Her father looked back up at Sam's face and took his hand. He didn't speak. He nodded once and then let the hand go. Sam looked at June Crosby and decided not to put her through a handshake with an Indian. He lifted their two cases and stood waiting for Katie to drive the situation.

She slid between her parents and took their arms in hers, marching them towards the exit. Unwittingly, despite the smile she flashed him, she left Sam in the role he'd been cast, a servant, following behind the family with the cases.

Sam knew the driver on the bus of course. It was Henry. He greeted Sam like a long-lost friend even though they'd shared a pizza and watched a hockey game on the wide screen, in the bar at Siding Twenty-three only yesterday lunchtime. Katie was pleased. Her parents less so. Sam didn't introduce anybody to Henry. Sam had fallen pretty silent. The new family unit sat at the back of the bus, Sam at the window and Katie in the aisle so that she could touch and speak to her parents sitting stiffly on the two seats opposite.

He held Katie's hand all the way back to Silver as though she were his protector. And in a way she was. He knew how to deal with ugly prejudice when it came from strangers. His tongue and fists had been his defence for long enough. But he was lost when it came from two people he wanted desperately to like him. He sat and watched out the bus window, as the prairie turned into mountains and the hopes and dreams of success for their only child turned to dust for two retired middle-class Canadians.

At the Crosby's house, he waited alone in the parlour for its owners to settle back in. He heard Katie speak to them in the kitchen, after a long silence where the only sound had been of tins being moved around in shelves and plastic bags being rustled into drawers.

'Isn't he fabulous?'

Mrs Crosby's low voice. 'You're going to have to give us time, Peach. Married, a baby, everything. Let us catch our breath.'

'Are you mad I fell in love with a Native Canadian?'

A sarcastic laugh from Frank. 'Native Canadian. Is that how we have to address them now?'

'How would you like to Daddy? Wagon-burners? Squaw-fuckers?'

'Katie! That's enough.'

'No it's not enough. I know I've put you through it, what with running out on Tom and all.'

Her mother sounded close to tears. 'That's a bit of an understatement.'

'I know. I'm not sorry about any of it except the bits that hurt you. But you're hurting me now. Is that what you want?'

'Oh, darling. We don't want to hurt you. Try and see this from our point of view.'

Sam felt like a spy. He couldn't help overhearing and he was rooted to the spot.

'Which is?'

'Which is we want the best for you. We always have.'

'And you don't think that sweet, darling, funny, generous, clever man out there is the best thing for me. Is that it?'

Her father sounded tired. 'What does it matter what we think Katie? You'll just do as you please anyway.'

There was a silence again. Sam could only imagine what was happening. He felt utterly and completely impotent. Katie sounded composed when she broke that silence.

'Oh I'm sorry. I thought I was talking to the two people I loved most in the world all my life. Obviously there's been an invasion from Mars and my parents have been replaced by aliens. 'Cause you guys are sure making a good job of behaving like strangers right now. Can I just rewind a tape here, folks? *We want you to be happy. That's all.* Ring a bell? You said it often enough. Didn't you mean it? Well let me tell you that for years I've been trying to make you two happy as well. Ever think of that? That it works both ways. Did I do anything wrong? Did I embarrass you or shame you? Did I disrespect or disobey you? Or did I love and cherish you both, as I do now?'

Her mother was crying now. He could hear her sobbing. 'Peach darling, we're not saying . . .'

'No. Come on. Let's face it. You let me down. You must have seen how unhappy I was with Tom, but you never said anything. You never said *we want the best for you darling* when he was ordering me around in front of you like I was a retarded child. Did you? Did you?'

Silence. Sam held the window-sill. His hand brushed a pine cone animal, a little body and head made from different sized cones, tiny feet made from wood shavings, mounted inexpertly on a sliced log. Katie Crosby, the child artist, on vacation in a different life. He touched it gently with the tip of his forefinger as he heard his wife continue on the other side of the door.

'So I made my escape on my own, without your help. And now when I know what is good for me and I've never been happier in my whole goddamn life, you trot out the *what's best for you* crap. I thought you were better than that, Dad.'

'Are you surprised?'

'Gutted.'

Her mother was sniffing. He heard Katie say softly, 'Come here,' and knew she'd taken her mother into her arms. Her voice was gentle now, her temper spent. 'Do you remember the time you took me to the rodeo on the Kalinka reserve one summer, Dad?'

No response.

'Well I do. I remember it real well. You were so moved by those people's horsemanship. That woman, remember, who rode round those barrels like she was nailed to the horse? I recall you picking me up and putting me on that high wooden fence to get a better view, and you said, *We owe these people a debt we can't repay, Peach. We can just marvel now at how their dignity and nobility has survived. There it is out there for anyone with eyes to see.*

'That's what you said. I was so proud of you. I thought you were so compassionate and understanding and big-hearted. Now you're standing here like you got a white pointy sheet on your head. What's gone wrong, Dad?'

'I guess I was being romantic, Katie. You were too young to see what was going on out of the arena. The drunks. The fights.'

'Yeah. None of us have ever seen white Canadians get loaded and act like assholes at a rodeo. Right?'

'We love you Katie.'

'Then love him too. He's the father of your grandchild.'

Another pause.

'If you hurt Sam, you hurt me.'

There was the sound of a chair scraping across the floor, and Sam imagined someone was taking a seat. The kitchen door opened and Katie's father walked out, stopping abruptly as he viewed Sam, surprised to see him standing at the window. His eyes told the tale that he realized and regretted that Sam had heard everything.

That irked Sam. Where did they think he'd been? On arrival, they'd just abandoned him and retreated to the kitchen, leaving him like a tradesman to stand in the parlour. Did they imagine he'd gone to squat outside in the dirt, wrapped in a blanket to dry buffalo meat over a fire?

Frank Crosby crossed the room to his new son-in-law and stopped in front of him. Oh God, thought Sam. Here it comes.

Katie's father held out a liver-spotted hand to him. 'Sam. Will you accept my apologies for a rather unpleasantly cool reception into the family?'

The kitchen door was open. Katie was standing in the frame looking at the back of her father's head with blazing eyes.

Sam looked down at the hand on offer, and back up at Frank Crosby's face. I should lay him out, he thought. I should spit on his hand and walk out of this house a man.

The whole action was a charade. A scene out of a bad soap opera that Frank Crosby obviously thought he had the leading role in. What a fool he was, if he thought he could wipe out all that prejudice and ignorance with a handshake like a plantation owner to the freed slave.

But he could see bits of Katie there. The fold of skin at the corner of the eyes that stopped them short of being almond, the pointed chin, albeit surrounded by a few more folds of flesh in this face, the small-lobed ears.

He knew then that his love of his wife and unborn child was greater than any hurt that this confused, guilty and bigoted white man, or any man, could inflict. He loved Katie, and for her he would build a bridge over these white people's ignorance so that his child could run between them all.

His hand touched Frank's and they closed their fingers together.

Do I feel less of a man now, thought Sam. Am I tamed and constricted by this handshake?

Katie's face suggested he was still very much a man. He marvelled at how these two ordinary people could have created such a perfect exotic flower.

When she had spoken to him that first day on the bus, he had waited for the let-down. The bit when all the white girls who got the hots for him broached the subject of his race and his past. Katie had leaned over to him and said, 'Can I ask you something real personal?'

He'd nodded, waiting for it. Would it be the tipi question? *Say, did you ever really live in one of those pointy tents?* Or maybe the other crappy one about some initiation rites they'd seen in westerns. That seemed to turn on some of the bimbos at the ski company, the ones he'd laid occasionally out of boredom and loneliness. He didn't want Katie to be like that.

Please God, no. She had cleared her throat, and his heart had sunk in case this woman he felt he knew, was going to let it all slip away.

She'd looked serious, really studying his face. 'You know the robot in *Lost In Space*? Were you frightened at the end of every show when he waved those arms around and hollered, *Warning! Warning! Danger!*'

Sam had looked across into her solemn eyes and held them with his own as long as he could without crashing the bus. 'I used to shit my pants,' he replied.

She had bloomed into a grateful smile and sat back in her seat. 'There. I knew we were separated at birth.'

That was who he took that handshake for. That was why two years later he accepted the gift of the house from that man who shook his hand. Was he to deny his wife and children a comfortable life to keep his fragile pride intact? No siree. Sometimes Sam Hunt felt like he didn't have much to be proud about at all except his family. Fuck all that stuff about whose house it was.

He leaned forward and stabbed at a log with the brass poker that leant against the stone chimney. The wood hissed back at him like a snake.

Katie went to draw the curtains in Jess's room as quietly as she could, now that her daughter was safely in her towelling sleep-suit, tucked up and asleep. With a hand on the blue fabric dotted with flying pink ponies, she hesitated as she looked out of the window. There were flashing red and blue lights way over to the east on what must be the Trans-Canada. She could just see the dancing beams above the roof-tops reflecting on the low, heavily laden snow clouds. There must be a hell of a lot of lights. Jesus, thought Katie. Looks like a pile-up. People drove like morons in the snow.

She drew the curtains over the scene and hoped it wasn't as bad as it looked. There had been a lot of sad stuff in Silver lately. More than its fair share. She had enough to worry about on her own door-step without having to ponder on what automobile carnage was happening on the edge of town.

She crossed her arms and leaned against the window-sill, looking into the room at her daughter's bed.

It could be a tumour. It could be something simple. But if she had to knock him unconscious and drag him by his ear, Katie Hunt was going to get her husband into the hands of someone who'd take a look and help him out. She hadn't seen him like this before. Sam was the strongest man she had ever known. Not physically, but in his resolve. He could take things on the chin that would knock most folks down like bowling pins. And he'd shared every rap, every blow with her since they met. Nothing was secret. This time though, it seemed there was gear he wasn't telling her about. And that worried her more than anything else in the world. Okay, some things in his life were private. His past life on the reserve, sure. She got bits from him now and again, usually funny stuff. Like how the kids ripped off the cars that white officials were stupid enough to drive onto the reserve, stripping them down to the axles and then running off with the parts, into the safety of hundreds of square miles of cover. It didn't matter now if that was all she got. She hadn't been there. She had no right to demand a slice of his history. There was plenty she hadn't told him. Mostly out of shame. Stuff about high school, and what her life was like with Tom. All that existed someplace else. But nothing in their life together since they met was private. Nothing.

She crossed to the bed, kissed Jess and went next door to Billy. He was already in bed. 'Ooops. Sorry. Wrong room. I was looking for Billy Hunt, but he'd still be dressed, playing with his computer.'

'I'm tired.'

She sat on the edge of his bed and put a hand on his brow. 'Feel okay, B.Boy?'

He smiled up at her, enjoying her cool palm on his head. 'Sure. '

'Good.'

'Is Dad sick?'

'I'm sure he's fine, Billy. We'll get him sorted. Don't worry.'

Billy smiled up at his Mom. She took her hand off his brow and fussed with his comforter. 'Do you want Bart in here tonight?'

'No. Not tonight.'

That threw his mother. Billy turning down the offer of having that big ball of fur at the foot of his bed was as likely as him offering to sweep the yard. She was puzzled, but finished her fussing and left him with a kiss, too weary to pursue any more irregularities in the Hunt house. Billy turned over as she switched off the light and half-shut the door. He wanted Bart there of course, but when Billy was the Wolf he preferred to be alone. Just in case.

21

'Should we stop?'

The tail-back from the roadblock was solid. Horizon-to-horizon solid. A cop was waving Daniel and Craig on through the gap between patrol cars, but the pack of reporters had spotted them and surged forward. They were local. Craig recognized most of them. The networks hadn't made it yet. But they would.

He sighed. 'Give me two minutes, then hustle me away. Any excuse.'

Daniel Hawk pulled up on the verge. Craig stepped out and motioned to the two constables holding back the gaggle of storm-jacketed reporters to let them at him. Jesus, but they could go some once they got let off the leash.

'What's going on up at the ski area, Officer?'

'What are you looking for in this roadblock, Staff Sergeant?'

'Have you heard that an elderly couple were helped from their car back there with the first signs of exposure? Care to comment?'

Craig let them holler and hoot until they stopped, then he took his hand from his pocket and gesticulated up the mountain behind him. 'I can tell you we have a serious incident up on the hill and we are continuing the block until we've cleared all vehicles that may have been in this area at that time.'

Another burst.

'What's the nature of the incident?'

'Is it a murder?'

Then, 'Was it another cop?'

Craig looked over at the questioner to his right. A tall blonde woman.

'Ma'am?'

'Was the death another policeman? I believe you lost one of your detachment on Tuesday.'

Craig's heart sank. He looked her straight in her pale blue eyes. 'I can't at this time divulge the nature of the incident and I have no further comment. You'll be kept informed. Thank you.'

They went berserk. That woman had really stirred their blood. He glanced across at her as he turned to walk back to the car and the constables herded the shouting reporters away. A delicate creature, despite her height, dressed not in the day-glo shell-jacket uniform of the regular press hound, but in a long black coat. Nor was she shouting questions at his back. She was looking at him with an expression that was doing something to a very private part of his head and his balls.

He was still looking at her as Daniel drove across the central verge and onto the empty slip-road to town.

'Give them what they wanted?'

'Nothing like.'

They drove in silence for a few minutes while Craig wrestled with his reaction to that face. For a man who had been celibate more than two years it maybe wouldn't make headline news, but it bothered him like Hell. He filed it and dismissed it.

'So. Sam Hunt. What do we know Hawk?'

'An apple.'

'An apple?'

'Red on the outside, white on the inside.'

'What's he done to deserve that slander?'

'You think that's slander?'

'Yeah. I do.'

Daniel shrugged. 'He married white. His wife runs the Silver Heritage Museum.'

'Okay. I've seen her. So that's his big crime is it? Marrying someone who can't hold their own in a chicken dance.'

Daniel nearly smiled this time, then decided against it. 'I didn't say it was a crime. It's a state of mind. If you want to live off-reserve sometimes you have to work pretty hard at staying Indian. Sam just chose to forget it.'

Craig studied Hawk in the illuminated gaps between the half shadows of the street lights. His profile was unmistakably Indian, although his eyes had enough of an oriental slant to give him the frequent inconvenience of being taken for an Asian, and his short black hair, cut like a sixties astronaut, was not helping give the constable the image of a Hollywood Comanche. If Hawk was working hard at being an off-reserve Indian he needed to work harder still. He just looked like a cop.

'How do you manage?'

'It's easier for me. My family are all full Kinchuinick. We talk Siouan at home. We keep up with a lot of the old ways.'

Craig put his folder on the floor at his feet. If he were honest, he didn't care if Daniel kept up with the old ways or not. The old ways were gone.

'You knew Hunt when you grew up?'

'Nope. Met him for the first time in Silver.'

'But you knew of him?'

'Yeah. We knew all about his family. '

'Anything interesting?'

'Bad mother-fuckers, every last one of them. His father was a shit on legs.'

'Want to expand on that? I mean how bad are we talking here? Jay-walking or international terrorism?'

'We're talking a Mrs Hunting Wolf with a face so regularly rearranged by her husband that she lost an eye, and a son who spent most of his childhood roughing it in the foothills rather than go back to that cabin . . .' He paused, as if ashamed to have said so much. 'So they say.'

'Hunting Wolf. That his name?'

'Was his name. He changed it when his father left. That's all I know. Gossip mainly.'

They pulled into Oriole and cruised up the snow-clogged street looking for the Hunt house.

'And has Mr Sam Hunting Wolf inherited his father's very special manual skills?'

Daniel hesitated slightly.

'No.'

Craig picked up the hesitation.

'Except?'

'He hit someone once when he drove for Fox. No big deal. No charges brought.'

'Drinker?'

'Not that I know.'

They were there. Daniel pulled the car a little forward of the drive-way, parking it between the two properties. Made it more ambiguous which house they were visiting. A kind habit.

The minute Katie Hunt opened the door and saw who it was, Craig realized she was thinking accident and bereavement. He hurried to reassure her. He knew that feeling. 'Just some routine questions for your husband, Mrs Hunt, if we may.' McGee flipped open the ID no one ever bothered to look at.

'We're having to talk to everyone who was on the hill today. I'll explain further.'

She loosened a mouth that had become a tight slit of fear, and let them in.

Craig recognized Katie all right. He'd wandered round her museum a couple of times. Seen her messing about there and round town. He didn't recognize Sam when the tall man got out of his seat and greeted them stiffly.

She'll offer us coffee now, thought Craig. She didn't. Katie took a seat with the men and waited expectantly.

Craig looked around the cosy, simple room. A lot of books, a TV with one of those computer game things plugged in, some car maga-zines and kids' toys scattered on the rug like flotsam. It didn't look like nasty stuff went on. But then psychos didn't usually have framed photos of their hobby over the fireplace, or gory heads with an axe between the ears mounted on the wall. You had to work a bit harder than that to find them. Craig gazed longingly at a pick-up enthusiasts' magazine with a picture of a '56 Chevy on the front, and faced up to the fact that this was an interesting, but frigging obvious lead. Craig suspected he was going to be disappointed.

'Now that's class,' he said, picking up the glossy and holding it out like a grandfather examining a high school photo of his grandchild.

No one was going to agree or disagree with him.

He gave it a second's pause. Let the silence breathe. 'I'm Staff Sergeant McGee of the Silver Detachment and this is my constable, Daniel Hawk.'

Sam nodded, suspicious. 'What's up?' he said wearily.

Craig McGee replaced the magazine and cleared his throat. His constable opened a notebook.

'There's been a serious incident on the mountain, Mr Hunt. Happened today. We need to talk to everyone who was there. See if you remembered anything that might help us.'

Sam withered. 'What kind of an incident?'

Craig looked to Daniel and then pulled at his face with a hand. 'A murder. Kid killed in the trees.'

Daniel Hawk raised an eyebrow. Since when did the interviewing officer reveal the nature of the crime to a suspect? His superior had obviously spent too long behind a desk and lunching with the mayor. He looked down at his notebook, annoyed.

Katie was watching Sam. His face looked as if the flesh had been sucked from behind the skin, his eyes focusing somewhere outside the room.

Sam spoke softly, as though trying the words for the first time. 'In the trees.'

Craig narrowed his eyes and continued. 'You were on the chairlift station below the area of the incident at the time of the death, Mr Hunt. Did you hear or see anything unusual?'

'Nothing.'

'Are you sure ? Take your time.'

'I was sick.'

Hawk was scribbling as Craig continued.

'So did you leave your station at all while you were taken ill?'

Sam swallowed. 'Yeah. I left it for a bit.'

'To go where, Mr Hunt?'

Sam's world was shrinking. If his worst fears had been stalking him, circling him in the dark, they were on him now, pulling him low. He left to go into the trees, for Christ's sake. Into the fucking trees. And what were they going to make of that?

A murder. A dead kid. In the trees. This wasn't happening. But three people looking at him like they'd paid money to stare, assured him it was.

He raced to find an exit from this nightmare. The guy in yellow. He would tell them he'd been in the trees. What was he going to say? I blacked out at the time you're talking about, and I woke up on my back in the pines ? Nothing suspicious so far, eh Mr McGee? Want to see my other truck trader mags now?

He looked at Katie who seemed smaller than usual. Sam wanted to shout *Help!* at her, to have her cradle him in those soft arms and make these big guys in their big dark anoraks go away. Their rustling massive presence in the room was like an assault.

But she was waiting to see what he would say. She knew everything that happened to him today. He'd told her. He'd wanted to tell her, because this time the burden of fright and dark fancy was more than he could carry alone. If he was going to lie now he would have to do it in front of her. Not an option. He swallowed.

'Into the trees.'

If he expected Craig McGee to spring forward and cuff him he was wrong. The policeman looked unmoved.

'What were you doing in the trees, Mr Hunt?'

'Beats me. I blacked out. I woke up there.'

Craig nodded as though that were a perfectly reasonable explanation, as though Sam had said he went for a soda.

'Good alibi, huh?' Sam said weakly.

'You're not under suspicion here, Mr Hunt,' Craig lied.

Katie looked relieved. For a moment the ugly thought had crossed her mind that Sam was going to lie. What then? What would that have meant? All this had to be just a hideous and woeful coincidence.

Craig looked at Katie and back at Sam. 'Are these blackouts common? Do you have a medical condition?'

Katie jumped in. She could see Sam was on a spit being roasted. 'Sam fainted about a week ago for the first time when that avalanche explosion thing happened. The doctor thinks he had a virus. We're kind of worried, if you want the truth. This isn't fun.'

'No. I can imagine, Mrs Hunt. You must both be very concerned.'

Sylvia lying on the bathroom floor. Sylvia whose blackouts were not blackouts but faints from the pain she was concealing from her husband. Sylvia who told him she'd just fallen and hit her head. Yes, they must be very concerned. Craig breathed deeply through his nose and dragged his wailing soul back from that bathroom.

'What do you remember about when you woke up? What time was it for instance?'

Sam leaned forward, his legs wide apart, his hands clasped between his legs. 'I think it was around one.'

'Anything else?'

'Like what?'

'Like were you hurt? Were you bleeding or showing signs of having maybe been hit?'

'No. Nothing like that. I was just on my back in the snow.'

Katie looked away from Sam to the two policemen. 'How old was the kid?'

Daniel spoke quickly, beating Craig. 'We can't divulge anything about the victim, ma'am.'

Craig over-ruled him. 'Yeah, well you'll see it on the breakfast news. He was eighteen years old Mrs Hunt. And he didn't die very quietly or gracefully.'

Katie crossed her arms and rubbed her elbows. 'Shit.'

'Where did your footprints lead, Mr Hunt?'

'What?'

'In the snow. When you woke. Did they lead from the station to where you woke up, or did they suggest you'd been somewhere else?'

Sam hadn't thought of that. 'Christ, I don't know. I didn't think to look. I panicked and ran back to the hut.' He struggled to remember. Good question. Fucking good question.

'Can I ask where you were on Tuesday night, Mr Hunt?'

Bad question.

Sam had to think. So he thought, and when he remembered he wished he hadn't. Sweet Jesus. Another blackout. But the one he hadn't mentioned to Katie. 'I was stranded in Stoke Tuesday. Couldn't get home for the storm.'

'Were you with anyone who can verify that?'

'No. I spent the night alone in the company ticket office.'

Sam thought how an innocent man would make a fist and bark at the cops *Now quit this shit, what are you guys getting at?* But he had the feeling of a thick silt shifting in his stomach. This was a strange and hostile land and he'd lost his compass.

Craig stood, his constable still smarting from the betrayal looking up at him with a scowl.

'Okay, folks. Thanks for your time. Sorry to have troubled you.'

Daniel closed his notebook and got up, his face telling the tale that he thought his staff sergeant had gone crazy. He looked across at their interviewee and Sam knew Daniel Hawk thought he was looking at a murderer.

Katie was as surprised as Hawk, but she struggled to conceal it in case they changed their minds. She got to her feet to show them out.

Craig smiled at her, then at Sam. 'I might have to get back to you, Mr Hunt. We've got a whole heap of people to talk to.'

Katie pursued them as they headed out. Craig paused in the doorway.

'By the way, my constable here tells me you two grew up on Redhorn together.'

Sam nodded from his chair. Katie looked at Daniel with interest. 'Really?' she said pleasantly.

'You still use the name Hunting Wolf when you go back, or do they know you by Hunt? Just in case we have to make any routine enquiries.'

Sam turned away, looking into the fire. He spoke quietly. 'I don't go back.'

Craig had not been prepared for what he read in Katie Hunt's face. She didn't know. Sam hadn't told her who she'd married. Her eyes were blazing, her back still to her husband, as she fought to keep herself under control. Craig was sorry for her, but the revelation was useful. He buttoned the wind collar on his jacket and left the room, his companion following like a thunder cloud.

The front door closed quietly and Katie stood for nearly a full minute before she turned and faced Sam, and the truth that their lives were changing in a way she didn't understand.

It was a seven-minute drive to the detachment from Sam Hunt's house. They did it in silence. Hawk pulled up to the door and waited for his staff sergeant to get out.

Craig stayed put. 'You think he's guilty.'

Hawk shifted forward, resting his chin on his arms as he leaned on the wheel. 'Nah. I think it was the butler.'

'Karen thingumybob relieved him at one thirty. Right?'

'Yeah.'

'The boy died around twelve thirty to twelve forty-five.'

'Yeah.'

'You saw how that kid died, Hawk.'

Hawk wasn't as far behind as Craig thought.

'He could have been wearing some kind of protective clothing. Hidden the weapon and the blood-soaked garment somewhere before coming back down to the station.'

'Having swung through the trees?'

A quizzical look from Daniel. Craig opened the door to get out. 'No footprints, Hawk. One set belonging to the patroller, some deer tracks and the signs of the skis entering the woods and crashing. That's it. Nothing else. Not one damned bootprint for hundreds of yards.'

Daniel looked ahead. 'He's involved.'

'Maybe. Tell me how or why and win the candy.'

Craig slammed the door shut and went inside. Daniel sat for a second then drove the car round the back of the building to park.

The woman reporter was by the trash cans. She approached the car as he stopped, and opened the door.

'Not now, lady.'

She got in and Daniel sighed. Her action let a gust of cold air in with her that nearly took his face off.

'You're wasting your time. You'll get a story when the staff sergeant makes a statement.'

The woman looked at him through pale eyes and smiled. 'I've been waiting for you. I know your name, Constable Hawk. Constable Daniel Hawk.'

'Neat detective work. Considered a career in the Mounties?'

The woman's demeanour shifted into an unfamiliar gear.

'Do you know my name?'

'I don't give a fuck. Get out of the car.'

Her voice dropped an octave and hummed with a menace alien to the strong but pretty face that mouthed the question.

'Do you know my name?'

Daniel was perplexed. If the woman wanted a story, acting like a nut wasn't the best way to extract it. He stared her out in the freezing car with little success then jumped when Craig opened the car door.

'Left my folder, constable.'

Craig smiled over at Daniel without looking at his new passenger.

'How about getting lost, missy.'

'She was just leaving.'

The woman extended a pale hand to Craig. He ignored it.

'Marlene Sitconski. News International.'

'Craig McGee. Pissed cop about to throw book at reporter.'

She flicked another look at Daniel and slowly stepped down from the car, her coat pushed aside to reveal two long, willowy limbs in black stretch leggings that disappeared into her snow boots. Craig felt that stirring again. He fought it and this time he won. He won easily, because there was something else about her now that she was so near.

A tiny creaking slit opened in a door Craig McGee kept locked in his mind and he struggled to shut it again. It was a door that could sometimes show him stuff he didn't want to see, and he didn't want to see anything now, out here in the dark lot. He didn't want to see what he thought he'd glimpsed behind those eyes.

Marlene Sitconski had a laugh like ice cubes tinkling, and she used it as she walked away from the car towards the street.

Craig watched her go while a finger of inexplicable fear traced a cold path down his spine and turned back to Daniel. 'The A-Team have arrived from Edmonton.'

He scooped his folder up from the floor of the car and went back inside, leaving Daniel in the dark wondering why he wished Craig had waited for him.

22

Alberta 1907
Siding Twenty-three

'What does it want of us?'

Powderhand threw the questioner a look, and inclined his head towards the woman pressing herbs to the bloody cheek of Hunting Wolf. She caught the look and made a snort. Powderhand might treat his wives as children who must be protected from truth and starved of knowledge, but Singing Tree was not accustomed to such nonsense. Her husband, a chief, a shaman, was also her friend and life companion, and she, above his two younger wives, was always privy to his business. Two Young Bears looked anxiously to his chief to see if Powderhand's recrimination would be supported by the elder to whom he had addressed the remark.

Hunting Wolf smiled with his eyes. 'Not of us. Of me.'

His wife withdrew the crushed herbs from his cheek and surveyed her progress. Three dark, deep gashes cut a pattern diagonally across the man's face like a macabre imitation of war paint, the lesions now clogged with tiny fragments of leaf and root. Although Hunting Wolf's face had clearly been clawed, it was as though each cut had been performed with the sharpest of knives.

He looked up at Singing Tree with affection. 'It pains me no longer.'

'Then I will prepare more of the same. Before the pain returns.' She looked over at Powderhand. 'As you talk.'

The young warrior grimaced and threw his braids behind him with a toss of the head. Singing Tree lifted the wooden bowl of herbs and carried it to the edge of the tipi to mix another poultice. Her husband watched her tiny figure bend to its task and his eyes softened with love.

Two Young Bears decided it was safe to continue. 'Then what does it want of you?'

Hunting Wolf looked into the fire smouldering in the centre of the floor. 'It is a paradox. I am both its enemy and the gate to its release.' He shifted his weight towards the fire and spoke softly, almost to himself. 'I pray that the Great Spirit grants me strength to give it nothing.'

Powderhand looked angry. 'It is already released. Those white-faced fools.'

'You know little of the Trickster, Powderhand. Were you thinking of your stomach or your penis when the legends were told to you round the fire? It seems you were not listening to the elder telling the tale.'

'I listened.'

It was Singing Tree who spoke impatiently from her crouch. 'The tales were of fun and laughter. I recall nothing of this darkness.'

It was Powderhand's turn to snort. 'Women's tales. What do you know of the spirit world?'

'And what does a mere man, a being who cannot make life, only destroy it, know of this world, never mind that of the spirits?'.

In spite of her anger she looked as if she would cry. Hunting Wolf's heart stabbed him with the memory they both fought to bury each day. There could be no place for it now. His heart and soul were bruised enough.

'Wife.'

She was silenced. Reluctantly. Looking at his face with regret in her eyes that she had spoken of what must not be spoken, even obliquely. Her husband addressed her gravely. 'This is not that spirit of mockery and laughter. This is of another time. Older.'

Singing Tree was chilled by the undercurrent in Hunting Wolf's voice. She thought of those childhood tales of the Trickster, the wicked fool who was always suffering at the hands of man or nature for his evil and uncontrollable behaviour. She had laughed until she cried at the tale of the Trickster being paid back for a deceit by being rendered unable to stop defecating until he was above the trees, sitting stranded on a column of his own waste.

Perhaps Powderhand was right. That the darker tales were kept until the women were occupied with their chores and their children, the tales that would explain away the terror that was gripping them now, in the trap that winter had sprung. As if proud of her fears, the wind blasted the skin of the tipi with an arsenal of snow, shaking the poles that supported the hides like a threat.

Two Young Bears was still staring at his chief with eyes that implored an answer. He ran a tongue over his dry lips. 'But it can be defeated?'

'It must be defeated. I cannot run from it. There is nowhere on earth I can hide now that it has recognized its gaoler.'

Powderhand and Two Young Bears exchanged glances. Hunting Wolf smiled to himself, although his handsome, wounded face remained set hard as rock. 'And if it defeats me, my brothers, it is free to release its chaos into the world.'

Powderhand drew himself up. 'You are the shaman. It is in your hands.'

Hunting Wolf nodded. 'You think also that I bring it, do you not? You think that to leave me here and take our camp back to the reserve would save you.'

The young man looked anxious, the heat rising to his cheeks. Hunting Wolf made a small gesture with his hand. 'I saw as I flew with the Eagle, my friend. I meant not to hear your words to the company, but the spirit guided me down to your shoulder as you spoke to them. Understand me. I lay no blame at your feet.'

Powderhand stood up abruptly, his face blazing now.

'So you use your magic to spy on us? It seems that is a more simple spell than the one you cannot conjure to rid us of this demon.'

He pulled his blanket over a heavily-belted woollen jacket and left the tipi, a flurry of snow entering the warm circle as he let the flap of hide flutter in the wind after him.

Hunting Wolf put a hand to his wounded cheek and spoke softly to Two Young Bears. 'I am tired now, brother. Follow him and calm his anger which grows from fear. I cannot.'

The thickset young man stood, put on his wide-brimmed hat and touched his heart in salute to his chief, leaving the warm tipi with more grace than his companion.

Hunting Wolf let himself slump back on the piles of skins that made up his bed. He closed his eyes, listening to the sound of the wind and snow against the tipi and the small noises of Singing Tree working in her wooden bowl.

Powderhand had touched a raw nerve. Why indeed could his magic not send this fiend back to the Hell whence it came? The Eagle had shown him the nature of the thing many years before this, a sight which made him shrink in terror even now as he recalled it as a distant dream-like memory. And his father, and his father before him, and every descendant since the Kinchuinicks began, had all prepared each other for the possibility of the fiend's return. Oh, the ugly misfortune that it should have befallen him to meet this abomination that had been spoken of through the centuries. Why not his father? Why not any one of the Kinchuinick shamans that had gone before? How he envied them their lives of peace, the lives they led using their magic and calling their spirits only to perform the simplest of domestic tasks. To save the sick. To heal broken love. To find the buffalo herd. These men were the ones who knew of the Trickster, but only in fireside stories and in the darker, more secretive information passed down amongst those whose task it would be to face it. But they never faced it. He was facing it now and he was resentful and child-like in the depth of his terror.

Why had his father made Hunting Wolf know its names? He had been a conscientious student, listening to and memorizing the scanty details that were known of this dark and ancient spirit. He knew the nature of its blasphemous violence. But now, in the darkness of the night, lit only by the circle of fire, he was in despair that he knew little else. Nothing that would save them. For he was certain that it would destroy as nothing else had destroyed before were it to shake loose the fragile chains that he alone seemed to bind it with and bind it without knowledge as to how he was able to contain such a force.

What was the nature of those chains? Why did it not just kill him and be done? Today, in the tunnel, he had thought that it would kill him. His cheek began a faint throb as if wakened by the foul and almost unbearable memory.

The white men who would not work unless Hunting Wolf was present, were nevertheless resentful and suspicious of him as he had squatted by them at the rock, watching them silently with glittering eyes as they swung their picks against the stone. They were frightened men. He could not understand their clumsy guttural tongue, but Henderson had told him that the men were spreading stories that animals had spoken to them. That had made Hunting Wolf's heart sink with dread. If he so wished he could make the very rocks speak to him. But there were methods to it, and payments due for such communing with the spirits of nature, and the white men neither knew them nor would believe in them.

To speak with a creature or a plant required a heart of purity and a lifetime of learning. Only then would a ceremony of four days in a sweat lodge bring the shaman close enough to the spirits to speak thus with those that were insensible to human communication.

Of course Hunting Wolf also knew how to shapeshift into the guise of an animal or bird. But he did not *become* that being, only a mere approximation of the beast. Anyone with the eyes to see could tell that it was not a real animal, that it moved in a strange way or was incorrect in its detail. And to produce such a trick took such fasting and praying and purification that the act was scarcely worth the toil. He had done it but once, and then only when they were in dispute with the Blackfoot. Their shaman spotted him at once and it was over. It had drained him. But to possess the living, as he suspected the Trickster was doing, was a sin beyond measure. He thought of the dead and wasted body of the bird and sent up a prayer for its defiled soul.

Yes, if animals were indeed talking to the white men, he knew it was not their genuine spirits speaking, but something dark, powerful and malicious. He knew it for certain now.

It was natural that the Trickster should blaspheme so, for to speak through a beautiful creature created by the Great Spirit, with a filthy and obscene tongue, was a trick so loathsome it struck at the heart of Hunting Wolf like an axe. The white men were right to be afraid.

He had watched their faces as they worked, their glances to him a mixture of contempt and apprehension. How easy it was to look into these men's hearts. How easy to read in their foolish minds that they regarded him as little better than a dog. It bothered him little. He knew much about their world. More than they would ever suspect.

He had flown with the Eagle one night, to James Henderson's land to understand the nature of the man and his desire to meddle with their affairs. They had soared over a green and wet land perpetually under a blanket of grey cloud, with mountains small in scale yet more ancient than his own, and full of spirits so old and complex his senses quivered to be near them in his animal guide form. They wailed and reached up for him as he flew past the jagged mountain tops, making the Eagle soar higher and faster to escape the invisible forces that sensed their presence and yearned for their contact.

When they reached a grey stone city, Hunting Wolf was alive with wonder. Huge stone buildings, laid in squares, in circles and half-circles over many miles of land. And so many people and horses. People as numerous as the buffalo once were.

They had landed at Henderson's house and Hunting Wolf had entered the strange dwelling, marvelling at the contents, excited by the strange and wonderful objects that filled the house. Henderson's wife was there by a fire, drinking from a glittering glass. He had looked at her for a time, reading the coldness and bitterness in her heart: bitterness that there were no children by the hearth for callers to admire, that there were no brightly-lit gatherings in the house with her as the hostess. Hunting Wolf read her hatred of her husband and a deeper hatred of the God that had called him away from her side. She wanted him there, but she did not want him. He was saddened when he returned, but he told Henderson of everything he had seen except the contents of his distant wife's heart.

The tall Scot had turned pale and his eyes had opened as though to fall from their sockets.

'This not true,' was all he could say to Hunting Wolf, but the chief knew that Henderson had indeed recognized every detail to be the truth. He thought that Henderson would be pleased, but he was not. He would not speak of it again, and Hunting Wolf let it be. But he knew now of the land that these men came from, and he wondered why their thoughts were so full of hatred of Hunting Wolf and his people. How could his tribe of Kinchuinicks pose any threat to these men and women, who were more abundant than the blades of grass that pierced the snow in spring? He squatted silently musing on it each day as the white men chipped their way into the mountain, the mountain they had opened against his will and against the laws of nature.

It had been ten days since they had buried the workers. Ten days since he had recognized the thing that was in the bird. But since then it had shown itself only to frighten and confuse the unbelieving white men. He knew it would show itself to him soon, and today it had. Oh Great Spirit save him, it had.

He had squatted inside the tunnel, at the far end in the dark, watching the men as silhouettes as their picks rose and fell, the great din of metal against rock ringing in the man-made cave they had created. It was as if the men were a shadow-theatre, the kind his mother had made with her hands on the tipi wall from the light of the fire to amuse them as children – exquisite shadows of birds and animals, made alive by her delicate fingers. These were dark figures of men at toil against the arch of blinding white that the snow fashioned with its glare. The man McEwan had been in and out of the tunnel all day, glaring at Hunting Wolf, often fanning away a smell from his nose when he was near, and once spitting close to where he crouched. No matter. He would remain. Not because of these faceless white men and their childish fears, but because he had to remain, to face whatever there was for him.

The light was fading. The white arch was growing grey which meant that the men would soon abandon their task and return to their cabins. Nothing the man McEwan could say to them would make them continue their work by torchlight. The fools. As if the weak winter sun behind its storm clouds, could protect them from a spirit as powerful as this. As Hunting Wolf had watched the men at their toil a small motion on the ground at the entrance attracted his attention. A ground squirrel entered the tunnel, its tiny stripe-backed body erect on two hind legs as it surveyed the warm interior of this hole in the mountain.

The man at the entrance saw it and kicked at it thoughtlessly, making it scuttle for a crevice in the wall. Hunting Wolf felt the blood drain from him. He had seen a ground squirrel at this time of year only once or twice in his life. They were sleepers. They slumbered through these ferocious months, until spring woke them gently with the sound of dripping meltwater and the scent of sap. This one could be like the few he had seen: lost, disorientated, doomed unless it found its way back to the nest, but he knew it was not. Oh it was doomed for certain. But only because something evil had ripped it from its slumber and entered its innocent body.

He stood up and shouted at the men, waving his hands in the air and stamping his feet for them to get out. Though they could not understand his words they understood clearly his message.

Several of them shrieked and dropped their picks, and their panic sent waves through the rest like a flame under twigs. They ran from the tunnel, skidding in the rubble and pushing each other roughly to escape. But from what? Every sense in Hunting Wolf's body had told him he was in the presence of a greater evil than he had imagined existed. But he could not identify its source or its nature. His nerves were singing with it. He was giddy in the ripples of its power. Within moments he had found himself alone in the darkened cave, hearing only his own hurried, sharp breathing and the dripping of water from the rocky walls. He knew the men would not be far away outside, that they would wait to see what would happen from their imagined sanctuary of the light. But their proximity was as nothing. They could not help him even were they at his side.

There was no sign of the creature. His eyes had strained on the crevice he'd watched it disappear behind, but there came no sound or movement. He'd prayed then for strength and guidance and had been answered by the soft brush of his guide's wing on his neck, and its touch gave him vigour.

Then there was a noise. It was faint at first as Hunting Wolf strained to interpret it. A tiny, tinkling, brittle sound. He narrowed his eyes to its source. From the entrance a soft wind seemed to be blowing the small particles of icicle that littered the floor. Each morning the men smashed the icicles that formed on the roof overnight before they began work, leaving the floor scattered with the shards, where they lay frozen and unmelted until ground down by boots and metal. It was these glittering rods of ice that were now tumbling towards him, picking up speed as they came, yet he could feel no breath of wind to blow them. But they were moving. The pieces of ice bounced along in a fury to a point behind him in the tunnel. There was something hideously wrong with the way the ice was behaving. All through the tunnel there were smaller and lighter pieces of rock on the floor, yet they remained still, undisturbed by the breeze that seemed to be animating the ice. It was only the thin, sparkling wands of frozen spring-water that were moving. But he realized then that they were not being blown at all. They were being sucked. Sucked towards something. Something just behind him. He was aware of a crawling warning between his shoulderblades, a sensation that made him swallow back bile that was rising from his stomach in unnamed terror. The ice battered against his legs in its effort to reach its destination, making tiny cuts on his flesh as it flew. Its noise was hideous. A tinkling from hell.

Slowly he had turned round to face the darkness at his back, his eyes swivelling in their sockets, fighting to see in the blackness of the cave. Nothing could have prepared him for what he saw, and he was only half-seeing it in the darkness. He had muttered then, through his blind terror, 'Great Spirit save me.'

Forming itself out of the ice in the black shadows was a thing so huge, mis-shapen and abominable, that Hunting Wolf fought to remain conscious against the forces that would have him swoon. It reeked like rotting flesh, and its grotesque form crackled under its icy sheath as it shifted in an unholy mockery of life.

Then it had spoken to him. Though the thick rasping sound seemed to come from both it and Hunting Wolf himself.

'Do you know my name?'

Hunting Wolf knew its name. He had always known its name. He prayed for the power to speak. His bladder had emptied down his leg, and the sordid sensation of the hot, acidic urine running over his knee had granted him that power.

'You are Inktumi.'

It laughed: a foul sound that he felt at the back of his own throat while it continued. He fought back a retch as it replied.

'Am I?'

'And you are Inktomi.'

It was breathing and rasping in the dark. Waiting.

'And you are Inktomni.'

It waited still.

'And you are Sitkonski.'

Silence sat thick and vile in that rock prison. The power of the spirit was overwhelming. It pulsated. It throbbed. Hunting Wolf's mind had raced then, sifting through the knowledge his father had given him, searching for escape. Nothing had prepared him for this. This was an invincible spirit, not a lowly spirit of the kind that any medicine man can call for his own mundane uses. They were easily tamed and dispatched: this was something he had never encountered, a spirit of such malice and power that it baffled him as to why it addressed him at all rather than crushing him like a fly.

It spoke again. 'And you are the shit your mother squirts in the dirt of her grave.'

It laughed again, a sound like a man dying on his own vomit. Then, a pause, a long pause followed by a new voice. A voice of kindness and gentle love. His father's.

'Boy? Are you there? Are you there, my smiling boy? '

Hunting Wolf's heart soared. His father. Back from the spirit world to save his son. Hope had entered his soul.

'Father. Help me, father.'

His father's voice had then spoken about the things it would like to have done to his son. The things no man should say and live. This was not his father. The abomination was playing with him.

Hunting Wolf's hands flew over his ears and he screamed to shut out the obscenities, but they were being spoken from inside his skull now, impossible to escape. Tears of rage, shame and terror were pouring down his cheeks. Suddenly, as he had feared he would go mad with the horror, it stopped. The crackling half-seen form shifted before him, the sound it made grating on the rocky floor only hinting at its terrifying bulk. Its voice was low and mocking this time, coming from the rock as well as the icy black form it had fashioned into a body.

'Do I displease you, son of a diseased dog?'

Its breath was of the grave. 'Destroy me then, vermin.'

Hunting Wolf, breathing heavily, had composed himself then to think. Destroy it? What had his father warned? No. He must not be tempted to that course of action. Above all not that. He spoke with a throat that threatened to close against the stench of decay surrounding him. 'I will die first.'

The ice crackled and the rock began to crumble from the walls around them. It roared from the darkness, though the roar was silent. 'Destroy me!'

He stood facing this thundering nightmare, his brow soaked with sweat, his hands clenched into useless fists. 'No, foul spirit. I will not.'

From the darkness a huge, taloned limb shot out, its savagely curled claws made of ice, but ice that betrayed dark putrid fluid flowing beneath its sheen like black blood through rotting veins. Three huge talons slashed Hunting Wolf's face open with an ease that was in itself an affront.

'DESTROY ME!'

Hunting Wolf staggered backwards, his hand over the gushing

wound, blood spurting between his fingers. There was a sudden shiver in the air and a tremble as though before a clap of thunder. The profanity of ice before him exploded into a thousand particles, shooting out its borrowed matter like a cannon and blowing him fifteen feet or more along the floor towards the entrance.

That was all he had recalled. Henderson had been there somehow, had picked up Hunting Wolf's battered body and stumbled away from the tunnel with his slumped flesh held inexpertly in long, thin arms. The men had become near-hysterical when they saw the minister struggling towards them with the limp body of the bloodied shaman, and they ran from the two figures rather than rush to their aid.

Now, here by the fire, Hunting Wolf gathered his courage, assembled all the pieces of the incident and tried to make sense of it. He could make none. His body felt broken, but his spirit was wounded more severely. The ignorance. How could he fight with no knowledge of what he faced? He was impotent as a shaman, and powerless as a man. His face spoke of his terrors as Singing Tree knelt over him, a new poultice in her fist, and applied it to his face.

'You may speak of it to me husband. I do not judge you as they do.'

He wrapped his hand round hers as she held the soft soothing herbs to his wounds. 'Singing Tree.'

'I am here.'

'Before this is done, you will doubt me.'

She looked at him with a half-scolding, half-bewildered expression. 'I will never doubt you my love. You must rest.'

And he closed his eyes. But there was no rest.

His thin hand shook as he held the bible. Turning the pages in the yellow light of the lamp, he mouthed the words he read, as though being spoken out loud would give them meaning. James Henderson was far from being comforted by their message. His mouth was reading for him, but for all he knew it could be a cheap novel he held in his cold pale fingers, so opaque was his mind with fear and turmoil.

A sudden gust of wind rattled the flimsy shutters of his cabin and he looked up with a start, making an involuntary noise of fright which shamed him. Nothing but the wind. He realized he was breathing too fast and he let the bible rest on the table, laid both palms flat on the wooden table and tried to calm himself.

What had he seen? In God's name, what had he seen? It had been a man of reason, of learning, who had boarded that ship in Glasgow for Canada, strong in his faith and sure of his salvation in Christ. Now he sat in this miserable wooden refuge, believing that no walls, perhaps no Christ, could save him from the horror he had witnessed in that tunnel. He was huddled and broken. An outlaw running from his own logic.

Henderson took a deep breath through his nose and straightened his back. Not what he saw. What he *thought* he saw. He kept hold of that thought, clung to it like a log in a swollen river. *Thought* he saw. He stood up, walked to his small, hard bed and knelt before it to pray. A mouse he had been unaware of scampered for the safety of the wall lining-boards as the toes of his great boots scraped the dusty floor. He watched it go with dull eyes.

Of course the whole thing was illusion. The pungency of the Indians' beliefs were affecting everyone. His imagination had been ignited even more passionately than the simple-minded men of his flock, through constant and intimate contact with Hunting Wolf. This is what he told himself, hearing the words in his head, pretending they were being spoken by his colleagues in his club in Edinburgh. They would smile over a brandy and explore with gusto the intricacies of the human mind until it was time to hail a cab and return home to their townhouses where they would be safe in their beds, secure that God's universe was a place of order and sanity.

But he was not in his club. The wind was screaming outside as he bowed his head to pray to the God that he felt in his heart was growing distant from him.

No prayers would come. Each time he closed his eyes the imprint of that half-glimpsed thing drew itself on his inner lids. He could see it, writhing and moving like a bed of snakes at the back of the rock hole. Dear God, had it really been there? Something had been there. Hunting Wolf's face was the physical proof.

He had been on his way to the tunnel when he had seen the men running like pigeons scattering before a horse and he had run past them, ignoring their pleas and their clutches at his coat, lurching through the snow to reach the mouth of the tunnel. And then he had seen it. A dark mass of malice with the figure of Hunting Wolf standing before it like a scolded child. He must have glimpsed it for only a few seconds before the explosion.

The impact had thrown him into the snow, but he had regained his feet and rushed to the injured man before he had time to consider the danger or the madness in what he had witnessed.

Now, he could not shut it out. The nightmare of that thing was beyond reason. He, who had sighed when the men had related their tales of devilish talking animals and reprimanded them for their wild fantasies of being watched in their beds, had seen something that defied description. Something that made him question not merely his faith but his sanity and he was left with the minister's problem of explaining away the inexplicable, and the man's problem of finding peace of mind again, sufficient to sleep again in tranquillity.

None was forthcoming. He could not even pray by his bedside. Henderson let his head fall onto the rough brown coverlet that hung over the edge of the bed. If he let himself spiral down into this pit of derangement, there might be no escape. With all his self-discipline he pulled back the man of reason, the man who could deny and disprove that such horrors stalked the Lord's earth.

He lifted his head in defiance and imagined himself in that leather armchair in Edinburgh, with the smoke of his university friends' cigars blowing around his ears and their logical theories echoing in the high-ceilinged room. They would never allow themselves such self-pitying despair. Nor would he. His head snapped up. It was as though they heard him over the ocean and responded.

He thought again about what he had heard. That had been the worst of all. The obscenities. For the thing had spoken in perfect English.

Hunting Wolf, a man who could neither speak nor understand one word of Henderson's tongue, had been conversing with it. But it had spoken in *English*. Henderson had understood every filthy, disgusting word. He snapped his eyes open and held his mouth and chin in a hand. Surely no more proof were needed that the whole thing then was a product of his own fevered and sick brain? He was, after all, a man trapped alone in the wilderness with an engineer who loathed him and men who regarded him as eccentric. It was hardly inconceivable that James Henderson was claustrophobic and ill.

He was delighted with his observation, if horrified that his mind could conjure such sick and loathsome vocabulary.

Yes. He would see Hunting Wolf tomorrow and end this lunacy. He must tell him once and for all that his hysterical beliefs in things supernatural were adversely affecting not just the men, and he himself, but his friend and supporter, James Henderson. That simple, uneducated man must be made to realize that this was the twentieth century, when such fancies could and should not survive, and did so only in the deluded brains of those who fanned the embers of dangerous fabrication. Psychology. He must introduce Hunting Wolf to the understanding, however primitive, of psychology and hypnosis. The man's injuries were most likely self-inflicted. It was not unknown among hysterics that they injured themselves to make real their fantasies. He and Hunting Wolf had clearly experienced a form of communal delusion, probably brought about by shock from the explosion. He felt better already. Hysterical hypnosis. That was the explanation, and its effects would end as of now. He clasped his hands again to pray, this time in thanks for the relief his Scottish university education had afforded him in this dark and ungodly place.

'It hurts, James.'

He couldn't move. Henderson stayed still as stone staring at the wall, hoping he hadn't heard the voice behind him.

'James. Fetch mother. James. I'm scared. It hurts.'

He was aware that his blood was pounding in his ears and his clasped hands were now clenched so tightly the fingers dug into his own flesh like claws. He turned to see what he prayed he would not. But it was there.

In the corner of his cabin the small figure of a twelve-year-old boy lay slumped like a broken doll, his head spilt down one side like a melon opened crudely with a machete, blood soaking the cream shirt all the way to the waist in a thick, black, congealing ocean.

'No,' was all Henderson could breathe.

This was not Alexander. This was not his beloved Alexander. But it was. He was there in the room. Dying as he had done before, his frail hand lifting to his brother in a desperate appeal for help. Henderson's mind spun in its frenzy. This could not be, and yet it was. The body was as solid as the crude pine wall it rested against. It was no phantom. And the face. That face.

The one he had loved so desperately. It was looking at him now. Imploring him. Begging him.

'It hurts, James.'

He was still unable to move. Tears pricked his eyes, but his terror

197

and shock kept him nailed to the floor by the bed. His own voice sounded alien to him when he found it.

'Sandy?'

'It hurts, James. My head. I want mother.'

Henderson was back there, back in his uncle's croft where they whiled away the summer months, in the barn with the kittens mewling in the hay and the sunlight bursting through the wooden slats like fingers of joy. And he was there to remember that it was his fault.

'You can't.'

'I can so, you scaredey cat.'

He was looking again into the face of his beloved younger brother, that face with its blue eyes and curling lip, always ready with a smile or a burst of laughter, and he was daring it to do something it didn't want to do.

'Prove it, shrimp.'

His sweet Alexander, Sandy, tiny imp of fun, looked nervously up at the great plough hanging from the beams by its chains and licked his lips.

'All the way up?'

'The whole way.'

He looked into his older brother's eyes and took comfort from something he saw there. Was it love? Trust?

Alexander stepped up onto the hay bale and spat on his hands. The rusting metal hulk hung impassively on its chains, the single chain that had broken free of its beam hanging enticingly down about four feet from the highest bale. It was a rusty old thing, sure enough. It hung there the way dead moles hung on fences, as a warning to newer ploughs that their fate was sealed unless they performed. Stored high up in the rafters along with other junk to make room for things that had yet to fail in their duties. All Sandy had to do was to jump up and catch the chain, climb it and crawl along the plough to descend on the upper level of the barn from which it was attached. James had done it. He did it while Sandy watched. That beautiful joyful creature had clapped his hands in delight and appreciation when his older brother had leapt to safety on the upper floor of the barn, leaving the plough swinging madly in his wake. And now, as reward for that loyalty and affection, he was going to make Sandy do it against his will.

He didn't tell the small boy that the contraption had groaned and creaked under his weight, or that the height was terrifying once you pulled yourself up onto the back of the redundant red metal monster. He didn't say any of that. He wanted Sandy to find it out for himself. He wanted him to suffer. And he did. He watched as Alexander weighed up the height of the chain and jumped five or six times until he finally caught hold of the metal link. He listened as his young brother whimpered with effort and fear as he pulled himself up on to the back of the plough, conquering his fear purely for the admiration and attention of his older brother. And then that adored older brother watched as those chains broke, tipping Alexander onto the floor below before following him with half a ton of plough which sliced away half of his head as it fell. If he had only fallen a few feet away. Just a few feet and that rusty blade would have missed him. But he fell as if landing on a target, and James had watched as the metal clipped off the side of his brother's head as neatly as the grocer pulled wire through cheese.

He watched it all. And it was all his doing. And now Sandy was here to implore him to fetch their mother again. A mother who had died seven years ago, silently blaming James for the death of her son as James himself did to this day. Henderson would surely go mad if this apparition stayed to torment him.

'It hurts.'

The figure lifted its hand again and turned its head, so that James could see the quivering grey of the brain that was somehow continuing to function as its body died beneath it. It was Alexander. And he must go to him, try to keep him warm and safe.

Henderson stood up and walked towards his tiny imp of fun. He knelt before the boy and breathed his name. 'Sandy?'

He looked back at him for a moment and then a smile played across those pink lips. Sandy's eyes seemed less imploring. They glittered in the light of the lamp. But it was Alexander's voice that spoke.

'You murdered me.'

Henderson stopped breathing, his terror pressing on his chest like a vice. This had to stop. Please sweet Jesus let it end.

'Would you like to see what it's like to be murdered, you cunt?'

The voice was becoming less like Alexander's, and the figure before him was starting to change. Henderson wanted to cover his eyes and ears but his body could not move. He was paralyzed and rooted to the floor, his bony knees only just supporting him on the wooden boards. He knelt feet away from the thing and watched as it rotted and peeled before him, stinking and writhing with worms. Pieces of flesh fell on the floor with wet sickly thuds and the worms that had burst through those beloved eyes dropped down to work on them.

Henderson found his voice and began to scream. He screamed from a place in his chest that made the delicate vessels of his throat rupture. When they burst into his cabin the screaming had stopped. James Henderson lay unconscious in an empty corner of the room, his chin wet with saliva delicately laced with his coughed-up blood, his thin limbs tangled together like tossed bones.

23

It had taken twelve years to mature the Dalwhinnie malt whisky. Somewhere in Scotland, the man who had watched it being bottled would have clucked his tongue in disgust if he'd seen Katie put the glass to her lips and swallow its contents without thinking.

She let the alcohol burn its way down the back of her throat and put the glass down beside the bottle on the kitchen table. She didn't really want a drink. It was all she could think of to do when the RCs left her with the black cloud of doubt and fear they'd brought into the house. And she needed a space, a beat, before she spoke to the man she loved, sitting still and quiet through there by the fire. The snow had started to fall gently again. She watched dumbly as the big flakes caught the light from the kitchen window on their way to the ground. Bart would be out there catching the flakes in his coat as usual. Everything as normal. Except that everything was not normal.

Sam Hunting Wolf. Katie Hunting Wolf. Billy and Jess Hunting Wolf. So it was no big deal, a name change. But he hadn't told her. She wondered now if she had spent these last ten years in a dream, an adolescent cloud of happiness, where nothing mattered except this family and their love. It was a kind of selfishness, that shutting out of the past. It excluded everything except the life she and Sam had made together. The children they had made together. It said that nothing else that has gone before mattered. Now, perhaps she was wrong.

Why had she never really questioned Sam about his childhood? She drank in anything he had volunteered, but never pushed him when it looked like it was hurting. She knew why. If she were honest, Katie didn't really care. It was a stark and awful truth. She had won

Sam and she didn't give a damn who had him, loved him or hated him before. He was hers. The days of questioning for Katie were over after Tom. She had found her life again and she wanted no more soul-searching. It was childish, but it was true.

Now it looked as if the past was going to pay her back for her indifference. The name wasn't important. No. It was a good name. Hunt or Hunting Wolf it was Sam's name and she'd made vows to take it. It was the horror and the mystery of what was happening to Sam. She felt a creeping fear that he had other secrets. Secrets that would matter more than his abandoned Indian heritage.

The swing door to the kitchen pushed open and Sam stood holding it there with his foot. He looked at the back of his wife's head and longed to touch the golden hair. She didn't turn round when she spoke.

'I just needed to think, Sam.'

He swallowed a dry lump in his throat. 'Have you had time enough?'

She turned and looked up into his face. That darling face, now contorted with fear and hurt and bewilderment, and she stood up and stepped into his arms.

He stroked her hair and held her face to his chest. 'I can tell you if you want.'

'It's not important.'

'It was long before we met. I was sixteen.'

'I don't need to know.'

He put a hand beneath her chin and pulled her face up to him. 'Katie. I'm scared.'

In ten years her husband had never said those words. Sam. The man who was strong enough for them all. The father who loved his wife and children as if they were the last on earth. He was scared. That made Katie more scared than she could stomach. She broke away from him and braced herself. 'Sam?'

He sensed what was coming. His eyes implored her not to say it.

'Did you kill that boy?'

The words sounded ridiculous. She could scarcely believe she'd spoken them. His reply was even more unreal.

'I don't know, Katie.'

'. . . and although there is no official word as yet from the Royal Canadian Mounted Police we can exclusively reveal that this sleepy

ski resort has yet again been shaken to the core by a grisly murder
. . . Aw shit, Brian, don't get in my eye-line. I hate it when you get
in my eye-line.'

The snow-covered CNN reporter gestured to the sky with a gloved
hand and turned his back on the cameraman to compose himself for
another take, while a boy with a clipboard raised his arms in a protest
of innocence.

Craig watched, though he couldn't hear, through a gap in the blinds
he'd made with a finger, until the guy started the same spiel again.
He turned back into the room where Staff Sergeant Becker was still
talking.

'So the 23.00 hours shift will now take over that duty and the
constables on duty now will have to work right through.'

There was a groan from the roomful of tired police constables.

'We don't have a traffic violation here, folks. You don't need me
to remind you your buddy was one of the victims. It's going to take
as long as it takes.' He looked over at McGee. 'Staff Sergeant McGee.
Can you address the detachment on the suspect please?'

Craig looked at this guy. So Edmonton thought this fifty-year-old
desk man would make a better job of catching a killer than he would.
Simply because he knew Joe Reader too well. Assholes.

'We don't have a suspect, Staff Sergeant.'

Becker caught his tone and remained polite. A teacher to a pupil.
'Okay. You interviewed the Kinchuinick. What do we have?'

Craig saw Daniel Hawk flinch at Sam being called simply *the Kinchuinick*, and for once thought that it was not an over-sensitive
reaction.

'We have a mystery. Damned if I know what's going on.'

Becker looked at the men who were waiting for instructions and
guidance and was irritated by the unprofessional resignation in
McGee's tone. He hated these clean-up operations, working with
people you'd only just met, usually bristling with resentment at your
presence.

But it was his job and he didn't like being hindered.

'Well perhaps if you can brief the team on what you learned, maybe
someone can start to clear it up for you.'

Someone laughed at that. It could have been one of Becker's men,
or one of his own. It didn't matter. McGee sighed. He was behaving
badly. Maybe he *was* too closely involved. He moved forward and sat

on the desk in front of Becker, one foot on the floor and his hands clasped at his knee.

'Constable Hawk and I interviewed Samuel Hunt of nine Oriole Drive at nineteen-forty. We ascertained that he had been not only in the vicinity of the murder at the time but was in fact in a state of unconscious collapse in the trees during the kill. No one saw him at this time, but we have witnesses who saw him emerge from the trees approximately half an hour after the boy's estimated time of death.'

There was a murmur from the assembled room.

'Furthermore, Hunt claims to have been alone in the ticket office at Stoke during the murder of Joe, without witnesses or proof he remained there.'

Becker spoke behind him. 'And we don't have a suspect?'

McGee continued to look straight ahead. 'Nope. We surely don't. There was no sign of blood or injury to Hunt when he left the trees. There were no footprints round the boy's body, or indeed any traces on the corpse to intimate Hunt's involvement. Plus whoever killed Joe had to not only get up there on to the pass in a blizzard that had all but closed the road to do the deed which involved just as much gore as the boy's death, but would have had to push the truck with Joe in it over the cliff and get down off the pass. Now the truck could have been pushed over with another vehicle, but that would have left marks and the truck that Hunt was driving that night has already been checked by Benson and shows no signs of even a scratch.'

Becker was silent at his back.

'We think there is a remote possibility the killer may have hitched a ride with a truck driver who we subsequently found dead of natural causes in a parking pass on the Trans-Canada. It can't have been Hunt, since he was spotted driving back from Stoke behind the ploughs at ten the next morning.' Craig left a pause then turned his head to address Becker sitting back in the leather armchair Craig used in the briefing room. 'Messy. Huh?'

Becker nodded. 'Uh-huh.'

McGee continued, knowing this was going to cause a stir. 'There's the other problem of motive, of which there appears to be none. The murders are of course gruesome but unconnected. In the case of Joe there was a deliberate manipulation of the remains.'

He paused here. He remembered when Joe used to sit here on these plastic chairs taking notes and grinning at the guys who liked to make smart ass comments during briefing. His throat tightened at what Joe would have made of being the subject instead of the investigator.

Craig swallowed and went on. 'But in the boy's case it appears to have been a less calculated frenzied attack. The head of course was sliced open down one side first, we know, but it seems as though the killer then went on to destroy the entire body even though the victim was clearly dead.'

Constable Laing coughed at the back. It sounded like it was covering a retch.

'Now the only similarity in Joe's case was a murder that happened on the Redhorn reserve twenty years ago. The corpse was found in a state of near-mummification and the manipulation of the remains was identical to that of Joe's. Sam Hunt grew up on the Redhorn reserve, and would have been there at the estimated time of that death.'

That caused a big buzz, and it sounded like an angry buzz. Becker took over.

'Is that it so far, Staff Sergeant?'

'So far. Yes.'

'Okay. Well before I formally take over now I just want to thank you and your team for taking it to this point and handling what must be a very alarming and alien situation to such a small detachment with such professionalism and calm.'

McGee glared at him. 'You're welcome.'

Becker stood. 'Can I have Bob and Dennis in my office and would the rest of you get your duties from Sergeant Leonard? Let's get moving.'

Craig remained on the desk as the room cleared before him, Becker putting an unwelcome hand on his shoulder as he passed.

Good luck, smartass, thought Craig as he watched Becker close the door of the conference room. He put his hands to his face and kneaded the tired flesh like dough.

Hawk was still in his seat when he finished his rough facial.

'You're part of the B-team, Hawk. I guess you can go home. They'll wonder where you are.'

Daniel Hawk stood up and stretched. 'No they won't. Tess has taken Larry to her sister's place in Calgary for a few days. She don't like being alone in that house up there when I work late on a case.'

Craig nodded. Hawk's house was a spectacular log construction high in the woods above Silver. He built it himself and Hawk always boasted that in the summer the scent of pine and cedar knocked you out as you drank a beer on his porch. Craig had been there only once and he was impressed by its solid and solitary countenance. But he could understand Tess wanting out if her husband wasn't coming home every night on the dot. There was one lonely trail up to the house and that was it. In a winter like this, that made socializing pretty unlikely, and the snow must surround the place like a wall.

'Looks like I'm surplus to requirements now, constable. If you fancy braving the gentlemen of the press as we leave, you're welcome to share a three-week-old frozen pizza I noticed at the bottom of my ice-box.'

Hawk smiled. 'Thanks, sir. I got the Hunt interview to type up and then I'm gonna get back up home before the snow stops me. I ploughed the trail this morning, but it won't last long.'

Craig shrugged as though he hadn't meant the invitation, and Hawk left the room and shut the door. So the frozen pizza was going to have be eaten alone. A beer in Siding Twenty-three was out of the question too, with all these news hounds filling up the town. Craig McGee sighed and went to fetch his things. The psycho wasn't his problem any more. Facing another night in his big empty house with its big empty ice-box was.

24

There was only one TV and video store in Bootle, but it was on the main street with a big window onto the sidewalk. Seven TVs were going in that window and three of them had the same thing on the screen. The old Indian staring at those screens as if they were holding him there by force cut a strange figure to the passers by who altered their routes instinctively to get round him. He was wearing an odd assortment of clothes – a good pair of leather Timberland boots with yellow-and-red laces, a woollen checked jacket that looked new, and a pair of beige corduroy trousers with a crease down the fronts that would be at home at the bar of a smart golf club. And yet the man had the air of a drifter about him, a shiftless, haunted look that flits over the faces of countless street people, or refugees being driven in trucks like animals. It was the air of the displaced. The pedestrians avoiding him may have thought simply, on account of his old un-washed Indian face, that this was a bum, but if it was, it was an expensively-dressed one.

Calvin Bitterhand was distraught. Silver had ignited. The man on the three screens was telling how the town was in the shadow of some terrible murder. Calvin could read the words easily on his lips though there was no sound here in the street. In fact, he could read them even when his face was turned away from the camera. The TV man standing in the snow looked pretty pleased about the whole thing for someone who kept saying the word *terrible*. It was too late. He wasn't going to make it in time. He slumped forward and let his forehead touch the glass as he watched. The pictures were back inside now, of a woman with a stupid face like a painted doll, sitting at a desk with a box floating up above her left shoulder that said *SKI TOWN HORROR.*

Calvin stood erect and walked away from the store window. He had a hundred and twenty miles still to go. There wasn't time. He shuffled down the sidewalk and past a bar, the sour, warm aroma of beer floating out to him as someone opened the door and entered. Maybe he should just give up. Just panhandle some dollars, go in that bar and get wasted, and let whatever was going to happen take its course. What did he care? He was an old man. He would be dead before the thing that was upon them could ever make its real mark on the world. And he was tired. His powers were returning, but they were slow and rusty and he was not pleased to be using them again. He stopped and leaned against a snowy hydrant. He could get there faster of course, but he would have to prepare. And what if that preparation robbed him of the strength to do what he must on arrival? He made a decision.

He closed his eyes and prayed silently to the Great Spirit to forgive him for what he was about to do. He could carry on no longer, and his eyes filled with tears that found their way out of his tightly shut lids as he faced his failure. He opened his eyes and choked back a sob.

Up ahead, the door of a food store burst open and two little white girls ran out into the snow ahead of their harassed and laden mother. They slid along the sidewalk as best they could, foiling snowboots designed to stop them doing that very thing and their laughter as they stalled and stumbled carried in the evening air like lark song. Calvin sniffed away his tears, wiped his nose with the back of his hand and braced himself to beg from their mother.

She would be worth a couple of dollars. Just to be rid of him and get her groceries into the car. He'd learned that one in Calgary. Get them when they couldn't walk away from you. A bus queue, people paying a cab driver, girls waiting for their dates. Any time they were forced to confront a man who had less than they had and couldn't escape from his pleading eyes. And those big brown bags of food were the perfect things to make her feel bad about a man who might not have eaten for days. As he assumed the posture of a beggar the smaller of the girls took a run and managed to complete a huge slide along the icy sidewalk, stopping right in front of him, her cheeks ruddy from the cold, her eyes shining under her red woollen tammy. She could be no more than five or six years old.

Before he could react, she slipped a hand into his and looked up into his face, speaking in a tiny child's voice that was both earnest and comical. 'There's still time, you know. They can wait for you.'

He stared at her as if she was crazy, until her sister threw a snowball meant for her that exploded instead on Calvin's shoulder.

'Lorna!' The mother was furious. She put down her bags on the roof of her car and ran to where Calvin stood staring at her daughter.

'I'm so sorry about that.' She grabbed the culprit by the arm and the smaller girl by the hand.

'That was very stupid and very rude. Now say sorry to the gentleman, Lorna.'

Lorna looked up at Calvin and back at her mother. Quickly she stood on tiptoe and kissed the Indian's lined brown face. Her sister hesitated, looking deep into his eyes, then did the same. They broke loose from their mother's grip and ran laughing to the car.

The woman was bewildered but charmed. She looked at Calvin who had remained fixed to the spot in a trance and put her hands in her coat pockets with a shrug.

'Kids.'

He looked at her dumbly.

'Are you okay?'

Her face was full of concern and compassion. He nodded his head.

She smiled at him like the sun breaking from behind a cloud. 'Take care now.' She turned to join her daughters. They got in the car and drove away, skidding in the snow as the night swallowed them up.

He stood like that for minutes, the circle of white from the snowball gradually crumbling from his jacket. He would have liked to pretend that it had been his imagination, but he knew it had been real. There was to be no escape then. It must be done. He was part of it. His tears came unchecked then, and he stood and cried like a child. He cried for the love that was in those three strangers' hearts, and for the hatred and evil that would one day seek to destroy them. And he cried that a weak and sick old man was the only thin and useless straw the Great Spirit would use against a force that could end him with a thought. But through his tears he knew he had been spoken to by something other than the child, and he wiped his eyes and took a deep shuddering breath. He looked once at the wooden door of the bar with the blue neon Labatt's sign glowing above it, then walked slowly along the street towards the woods and the hills.

She swallowed her M&M and slapped the desk with her palm. 'Jesus, Eric, this is the end.'

The phone was off the hook to stop the reporters getting another chance to con a statement from them, and the television set on the office wall was full of the CNN guy, live outside the office complex, pronouncing doom on their ski company. Who was going to bring the family skiing to a resort where the kids got sliced up?

Sindon sat in the strip-lit office, listening to the phones next door being answered by the cops in the outer office, tired and hungry from the long wretched day, wishing she would shut the fuck up and let them both go home. There was no more to be done. The police had asked them everything except their goddamn inside leg measurements and he'd had enough.

Pasqual pushed the mute button on the remote and slammed the rectangle of black plastic on the desk.

'If it was that fucking Indian the cops are so interested in, I tell you I'll break his dirty neck with my own hands before they get him behind bars.'

Eric thought that unlikely. He also couldn't believe that Sam Hunt had anything to do with this horror. But the RCs had plainly thought otherwise. They had wanted to know everything. Sam had been with the company for years and though he was only a groomer, Eric knew him and Katie pretty well. Sam a killer? No way.

'You know Sam well as I do. Don't be crazy.'

Of course she did. In fact she'd had the hots for him a few years ago until she realized she was drawing a blank. It had irked her bad. 'It's Indians, Eric. I told you they're more trouble than they're worth. How many we got now?'

He sighed. 'Three. We don't have them Pasqual. They're not Mandingos, for Christ's sake. Three Kinchuinicks work here. Sam Hunt, Endel LaBelle and Perry Nine Saddles.'

'Shit. They deserve everything they get with dumb names like that. Perry fucking Nine Saddles.'

'Perry sure doesn't deserve what he's got.'

That was for sure. Big strong guy like Perry. Look at him now. The doctor thought he might have meningitis and they'd rushed him to Calgary. But it wasn't that at all. The poor guy had been having horrible hallucinations about all sorts of weird shit. The shop staff found him screaming out back in the stock room, drooling and pointing at something he thought he saw in the corner by the snowboards. They were doing tests but he still had a fever that was wringing him dry. Of course Pasqual hadn't even noticed he'd been off sick, even though she must have seen Sally standing in for him in the shop. Eric's department, personnel. That's what she always said when things got difficult. At least when there were people to sack or dirty jobs to do. Oh, she liked to hire, but when they were on board they were his lookout.

She snorted, ignoring him. 'No more, you hear? No more wagon-burners on this resort.'

He played with a pen, watching the TV news switch to something about Europe. 'Come on. They were only questioning Sam since he was on duty at the time.'

'Yeah well I think they're all crazy enough to do anything. Moses said they're trouble on any resort and I should have listened.'

Moses? The way Pasqual spoke, he suspected she was on pretty chummy terms with their pale employee. Come to think of Mr Moses, where was he? Eric didn't recall seeing him in the canteen during the staff interrogations. In fact he hadn't seen him all day.

'Did the cops speak to Sit-whatshisname?'

She caught an edge in his voice. 'Sure. Well I'm sure they did. They spoke to everyone.'

Eric knew that was true. He'd gone through the whole staff list personally with that Indian cop, Hawk. Just as well he wasn't around now, to hear this pillar of Silver society deliver her thoughts on the native Canadian and his role in the workplace. He'd have like to see how she'd wriggle out of having her bile overheard by that six-foot-tall crew-cut Mountie. And he seemed a pretty thorough cop.

Hawk had made sure no one was missed out. Not even those that were on vacation. He wondered what Sitconski had to say to them.

Eric didn't care. He wanted home. He would have to fight a path through the waiting reporters, but that seemed preferable to sitting here listening to Missy Asshole. 'Look Pasqual, I'm bushed. I'm going home now.'

'Great. Leave me. I'll just run this crisis single-handed.'

'There's nothing you can do tonight. It'll be worse tomorrow. You should get some sleep.'

'I'll tell you what I'm going to do, Eric. I'm going to make sure our celebrity ski goes ahead. I'm going to phone round the agents that are still in business hours time right now, and make sure their babies don't pull out.'

Eric was amused. She was mad. 'Go ahead. I'll catch you tomorrow. And by the way, if I were you I'd go the back entrance into your house. They'll be waiting for you at the front no matter what time you get back. Remember: don't say anything.'

'I'm not a child, Eric. I've dealt with the press on this scale before.'

Oh yeah? he thought. *In your dreams maybe, lady.* He left her in the office very much a child, and one that saw her toy being broken in front of her eyes.

The darkness was soothing. With his eyes wide open like this it lapped round the edges of his vision like a thick black oil. Only the tiny red light on the radiator thermostat intruded into this velvety balm. Sleep was not happening for Sam. Beside him, Katie's regular breathing told him that she had escaped into oblivion but he was far from such a release. Neither of them had known what do after Katie's question. They had sat unhappily in the kitchen trying to find a road out of this nightmare, and Katie had held his hand silently for an age, as though her touch could make it all go away.

'You're not well, Sam,' she'd said to him when she thought the silent contemplation was enough.

He'd looked at her and nodded. 'I know. But what does that not being well mean?'

'It means we'll find a way to make you better.'

'That's not my point.'

'I know.'

She'd let his hand go for a second and ran her fingers through her hair. 'Can I tell you something?'

He'd blinked at her.

'Do you think I would be sitting here at this table, with our two precious children slumbering upstairs in their beds, if I thought you were even capable of what's going through your head right now?'

He was unmoved.

'Then why did you ask me?'

'You looked like you wanted it said.'

That was true. He thought he hadn't, had prayed at the time that she didn't ask him, but really he wanted someone to scream it, to break the big thick silence of suspicion those cops had woven. She'd leaned forward again and taken both his hands into hers, his big hands that had rested like dead weights on the cheerful yellow formica of that table – a scratched and ruined thing that had seen the Hunts laughing and feeding and joking round it for years. The table where Billy had taken his first solid food, dribbling the mashed carrot down his tiny pointed chin from a gummy smile that would break your heart. Where Jess sat in her clip-on chair and offered her parents pulverized pieces of bread and butter from a chubby hand with squeals of delight. Now, just Sam and Katie, and a lump of horror that sat between them like stone.

'Sam. Listen to me.'

He'd listened, afraid of what she was going to say.

'You've never killed anyone.'

Then, although his face had remained rigid and blank, he'd screamed inside like he'd been waiting to scream all his life, *Jesus, Jesus, Jesus, but I have! My God I know I have. It's happening again. These ten years of happiness have just been a cruel trick. Dear God, let me die before it happens again.*

If Katie could have read the contents of his heart she would have recoiled. He knew it. But she could not. And instead, she got up and held him from behind, and they'd climbed the stairs and put out the lights and got into bed like everything was okay. Sex was out of the question. They'd both known it somehow, neither one wanting to make those first tender suggestive touches that would lead to the inevitable. But they'd held each other and Sam had held her even more tightly when the sudden jerking of her body meant she'd fallen asleep in his arms. And now he was here, alone in the dark, believing he'd been alone in the dark his whole life, his time with Katie and the kids a brief step into the light to which he had no right.

If only he could know. He thought of the faces of McGee and Daniel. Daniel knew something more, Sam was sure of it. He'd seen the expression of disgust on his face when he looked at Sam and he had to know why. He was a straight guy, Daniel Hawk. Sam had liked him though he hardly knew him. It was important not to know him.

There were no Kinchuinicks on Sam and Katie's long Christmas card list and that's the way he wanted to keep it.

Had to keep it. Maybe Daniel knew why. He gulped at that thought. Sam shifted his arm from Katie's shoulder and waited to see if she would stir. She made a small noise as she exhaled then settled back into her dreams.

He could barely see her in this blackness but his heart filled with a passion for her as he touched the warm curve of her neck and smelt her hair.

He swung his legs gently over the side of the bed and felt for his clothes on the chair. The buckle on his belt rattled, and he paused to see if had woken her. No. He was safe. He massed the bundle of cloth in his arms and quietly slipped from the room to dress downstairs.

In the hallway, Sam pulled on his jeans and the big turtleneck sweater that his hands had found in the dark. Some instinct told him not to turn on the light. He pulled back the curtain of the tiny window by the front door and looked into the street. The snow had stopped, leaving the houses and their yards under a picture-postcard mantle of glittering white magic, but the sky looked laden and ready for another dump. There was a car across the road, sitting in the shadows under the pines outside the Neasons' house. Two figures sat in it.

Cops. He let the curtain fall and leant against the wall. So they weren't sure it was him, but suspicious enough not to let him out of their sight. A wave of panic swept over him. He padded softly into the dark kitchen and felt around at the door for his boots. The glowing clock on the microwave was reading 00.52 a.m.

Getting the car away was going to be impossible. Of course, he could just let those guys follow him. He was only going to see Daniel Hawk, a man who might not be that pleased to have his family woken up at this time in the morning. But he had to see him. And he wanted to see him alone.

He grabbed his jacket from the wooden peg and felt in the pockets. The spare keys to the company truck were there, and he knew where the truck was. It was two blocks away outside Marty's place. As quietly as he could, he opened the kitchen door and slipped through. There was a low growl as Bart's head raised from his paws, until he saw and smelt his master and remained lying as commanded by Sam's insistent and frantic hand gestures.

With ears erect and tongue panting in the freezing night air, Bart watched Sam creep through the yard and scale the wooden fence and kept watching until his master was completely out of sight. He put his head on his paws and gave a tiny whimper.

As he hung up the phone, Hawk glimpsed McGee through the open door, moving about in his office with the gait of a man who is looking for something to do. He felt bad about knocking back the invite of a meal. His staff sergeant's loneliness was so acute sometimes it was almost solid, pulling down Craig's shoulders like a rucksack. But he really needed to get home. If he didn't get the plough on the front of his truck and shift the snow on the trail every morning, it'd close for sure.

Although the snow was looking like it would let up for an hour or two, he wasn't even sure what kind of a battle he'd face getting up there.

Tess had taken Larry down around lunchtime, and since she'd seen the news she was coming onto him on the phone like Daniel was a child who couldn't cross the road. Yes, he was okay, yes, he'd be careful, no, they didn't know who it was, yes he remembered the chicken in the foil wrapper needed eating before it started to rot.

She had been bad over Joe's death. She still couldn't talk about it without blubbing. Craig was right. They'd been buddies all right, and Tess had liked Joe. Never got on with Estelle so much, but he thought that was on account of Estelle not being Indian. She was pretty hot on their roots, was Tess. She used to scold Joe for not speaking more Siouan or Cree. Maybe that's what rubbed Estelle up the wrong way.

He loved Tess, but part of him was looking forward to a night on his own. They had satellite, and since it was going to be late, real late by the time he got home, he figured he could watch a hockey game and have a beer without worrying what the hell time it was. They showed those games all night long. Worth the thirty-nine dollars a month.

He shovelled his papers around the desk and undid the top button of his shirt. It was ten before midnight and the room was still buzzing. But Craig was right. The regular detachment guys were definitely B-Team now. Seemed like the squad from Edmonton weren't too impressed by the wipe-clean board and the coloured markers, judging by the fact it was back to being white and blank. Daniel pushed back his chair, picked up his jacket and walked over to Craig's door. He tapped his fingers lightly on the wood. 'I'm outta here. Need me for anything?'

Craig looked up from a file. Joe's file. 'Nope. On you go.'

'Right. Bye.'

'See ya.'

From outside, the long melancholy horn of a freight train filled the valley. Daniel left and Craig watched him go, wondering why he trusted Hawk, a mere constable, more than the sergeant who'd stepped into Joe's shoes since his death. Indian-struck. First Joe, now Daniel. People would start to talk soon. He smiled to himself, then stopped smiling when he resumed looking at the photos of Joe.

This was a great drive in the summer. The road went all the way round the back of Silver and then started to climb up through the trees, before the dirt road for the Hawk place turned off to the right and climbed another half mile through the pines. Of course the geeks in campers spoiled it in the high season. You never knew when you were going to swing round a corner and find them parked in the middle of the road, looking at a bird or a view or sometimes at nothing at all. They sure got a fright when they realized the truck they'd nearly caused to crash had some blue and red lights on the cab and that the angry guy getting out had his hat on and a book of tickets in his hand. But they were a small price to pay for the beauty of the sunlight filtering through the trees and the elks and the white-tails dancing across the road in the morning.

In the winter it was still breathtaking, but it was a bastard to drive. Especially at night. Daniel was still about three miles from his drive end, and the snow had started again with a vengeance. He was just going to have to take it easy. He let his mind drift back to work as the snow came at him like bullets.

Sam Hunt. Everything Craig said at the briefing was true, but his gut was yelling at him that Hunt had something to do with this. A lot to do with this. It was the Redhorn murder that was bugging him.

He told Craig in truth that he hadn't known Sam or his family, but how could he tell him that the Hunting Wolf family were so notorious you didn't need to know them? Moses and Marlene Hunting Wolf. The scum you scraped off your boot after stepping on a carcass.

There were so many rumours on a reserve, rumours about everything and everyone, but some of them had substance. And there had always been a rumour that Moses had bumped off his old man. Eden Hunting Wolf's body had been found battered to death in his cabin with the clear marks all over his head and body from the handle of an axe. But as usual no one knew anything, no one saw anything, no one would say anything. The ashes in the stove told the story of where the murder weapon had gone. Moses Hunting Wolf's drinking buddies all swore blind he was with them at a moonshine session over at the east end of the reserve and that was that. Never mind that those buddies all seemed to suddenly come into some spare drinking money for the next month or so that no one remembered them winning at bingo.

But Sam. The first time he'd met him at the Fox Line depot he couldn't believe that Marlene and Moses could have spawned this good-looking, pleasant guy. The women used to talk about him. In fact as soon as Sam's voice broke he recalled a hell of a lot of the women used to talk about him. Seems after Moses ran off to the city to pursue his drinking career, that priest guy and his wife took a shine to Sam. Used to take him skiing, that was all Daniel knew. Sam was crap in rodeo they said, but he was a mean hockey player and took to skiing like he was meant for it. Weird thing for a Kinchuinick to do though, and Daniel guessed that's why everyone thought Sam Hunt was an apple. That, and changing his name of course. Mind you, if Marlene and Moses had lived up to half of their reputation Daniel figured he would have wanted that name buried too. He thought of his own father, a weatherbeaten, quiet gnome of a man whose craggy face was always ready to break into a smile the moment he caught sight of Dan, and now Tess and Larry, and Daniel's heart went out to Sam. Then he hardened it. Didn't matter what your childhood was like. Nothing excused what happened to Joe and that kid. He'd had enough liberal bullshit for a lifetime from the social workers that hovered round the reserve when he policed it. He would say different to a white man, and that included Craig, but the truth was he thought a lot of asses needed whipping on that reserve.

An animal ran from the trees ahead. A coyote. Its eyes flashed in his headlights as it stood still, side on to the oncoming vehicle, before it bounded into the cover on the other side of the track.

Daniel loved that too. Being up here with all the animals and birds. He'd worried about Larry growing up off-reserve. For all the bad things about it, the space and the freedom was wonderful, and he would have grieved if his son couldn't have grown up with the same love of nature that he'd oafishly taken for granted. This was the compromise. White life in town. Kinchuinick life in the hills. Pretty damn good.

He was nearing the turn-off and the snow was drifting badly. If needs be he could leave the truck and walk the rest of the trail way to the house. He'd done it often enough.

But it was worth having a go. He could always dig himself free in the morning. He checked he was in four wheel drive and gave it a bit more gas. He wanted to get home.

25

It was taking longer than Billy had expected. Maybe it was because he'd had a regular dream first. He'd dreamed that he was the little freckled kid in that old sci-fi TV series *Lost in Space* they were always rerunning, and the big robot was waving his arms about shouting *Warning! Warning!* Dumb really. But he'd woken for a few minutes, just long enough to reprimand himself for not concentrating properly to bring the wolf. He closed his eyes and let his eyeballs roll backwards under the lids, like he'd taught himself to do, and tried to find it. He never used to be able to do it like this, but then he hadn't known that the wolf was his spirit guide. He knew that now. His teacher had taught them all about Indian stuff one afternoon during cultural studies and Billy was proud that he and Cindy LaBelle were the only Indians in class. He could tell the other kids were envious. She'd said they used to have a really different religion and that although they no longer believed these things, what they used to think was pretty interesting. He'd gotten kind of bored with the part about treaties and reserves but he was so excited about the spirit stories that he'd asked Uncle Gerry about it when he saw him in the corridor at lunch-break.

He'd looked at Billy with a raised eyebrow and then sat with him on the big steps in the atrium, watching Billy eat his sandwiches and telling him about animal spirit guides and the Indians' love of nature and all kinds of stuff.

Then he'd looked at him and said, 'It's some heritage, Billy. No matter what your dad thinks, and I'm sure he has his reasons, you be proud of who you are, son.'

Billy had nodded solemnly and knew it was true. It made him sad sometimes that his dad didn't even like the word *Indian* being said in the house and they never talked about it. Yes, it made Billy sad all right. He thought being an Indian would be neat. The stuff Uncle Gerry said about the animal guides sure made sense and for a moment he'd almost told him about his wolf. But he didn't. It was private. And he knew Uncle Gerry would think he was making it up. But he'd called the wolf that night with a new feeling of confidence, like it was all right to call him instead of waiting for him to come. He wondered if his dad had an animal guide.

His dad.

There was work to be done and he concentrated hard to begin it. No dreams this time. He felt his closed eyelids flicker as his eyeballs swivelled back in his head, and the soft waves of sleep starting to break over him again as he snuggled into the warmth of his comforter.

The Ford took a run at it but Daniel knew it was going to lose. At least six inches of snow must have fallen in the time he'd taken to get from the detachment to his turn-off and it wasn't letting up. He'd managed to coax the truck about eight hundred yards up the drive before it had slowed down and slithered around like a puck. But a quick shovel round the wheels meant he'd got going again, and this time he had to keep her moving, and moving fast.

It wasn't going to happen. Another hundred yards and the gradient made a pact with the snow to defeat this man-made hulk of steel and its man.

Daniel sighed and wondered about letting it slip backwards, just so the useless box on wheels would be clear to join the main road again in the morning. But he was bushed. He wasn't going to waste time and lose himself all that ground. The walk up to the house through this stuff would take about half an hour. He gathered his things, zipped up his storm jacket, pulled on his gloves and left the truck to its fate. With the flashlight, he checked there was nothing in the back he needed, then started the trudge up the trail to that beer and some centrally-heated loafing. The snow was just stupid now. It was more like a solid thing with holes in it than independent flakes and he could barely see ten feet ahead, even in the jerky yellow beam of his light. He pulled his hood up and tightened the drawstrings. The snow was up to his mid-calves and he cursed the ploughing he was going to have to do to clear this crap if the snow didn't give him a break.

On either side of the drive the trees formed a sombre, impenetrable wall. He flashed the light in there from time to time to look into that dark labyrinth of trunks and its smooth, undulating white floor. It looked so luxurious, that interior, in spring and summer when the forest floor was a carpet of emerald-green sphagnum scattered here and there with cones. And in winter, in the thin morning sun, it looked so secretive and cosy between the pines that he envied the white-tails the beauty and simplicity of their domain. He sure liked to hunt in there. Stepping like a ghost over the deadfall, knowing the snap of one tiny twig would make the difference between coming home empty-handed or dragging back a deer with a rack on it like a tree. Yes, it was a different world all right, but he knew how to move around in it.

As he swung the flashlight back onto the trail ahead, the beam clipped something dark, moving quickly behind a fallen trunk. He swung it back and stopped in his tracks. Whatever it was it wasn't moving until he did. He switched off the flashlight and listened, waiting for it to break cover in the silence. Despite the snow, the darkness was profound and for some reason Daniel Hawk began to feel uneasy. This wasn't like him. He'd walked up and down this trail in the dark more times than Imelda Marcos had visited a shoe store and he'd never even flinched at the sounds of the night.

Now, however, he wasn't enjoying the dark at all. For a few seconds there was so sound at all, then a rustling noise came from his right, in the trees on the opposite side of the road to where the shape had been. He switched the light on quickly and swept the beam across the dark regiment of wood. Movement again. Behind a tree. Daniel was puzzled. Were there two animals in there, either side of him? Nothing could have moved so fast as to reach the other side of the track and be well into the cover of the trunks in the time the flashlight was off. There had to be two. As if to answer him a branch ten feet up a pine rustled and bounced wildly ahead of him, shaking the snow from it in tiny waterfalls. It made him start, taking a breath of bitingly-cold air sharply into his lungs. This was crazy. Animals both sides and something up there in the branches. Daniel wasn't liking this. Animals didn't roam around in little gangs, keeping abreast with humans, their most fearsome and universally-loathed predator. Crazy.

He put the flashlight under his arm, cupped his big gloved hands over his mouth and hollered. 'Go on. Whooooo! Gerrroutta here!'

He waited for the creatures to crash away, fleeing in panic from this bold declaration of his presence, but his shout was muffled by the oppressive weight of the snow all around him and if they heard the cry it hadn't unduly alarmed them. If, of course, there was a *them*. Somewhere in the back of his mind something dark was suggesting to Daniel Hawk that there might only be an *it* and if that was the case, it could move faster than anything on God's earth should.

He was being ridiculous. The stupidity of his fears suddenly overwhelmed him and he laughed at what a ridiculous figure he must cut, standing shouting at animals in the middle of his own driveway. The grim day's events had really got to him, and he thought again how much he needed to be at home, chilling out and calming down. He grabbed the light and waded ahead with a new sense of purpose. The man in him felt he should walk on without the flashlight, just to prove to himself he was being an asshole, but somehow the feeling that eyes were boring into his back stopped his fingers from pressing that black rubber off button. Murders made you jittery. That was all. He kept the yellow beam on the trail ahead, and continued the muscle-wrenching trek to the house.

It was alarming how quickly it all came back to him. The sneaking through the dark where no one could see you, the holding of your breath when you think you've been spotted, and above all, that overwhelming feeling of loneliness. Oh yes, that had come back to him very strongly indeed as he'd scaled Dave's fence like a criminal and run low behind the cars until he reached the end of the street. And now, as he stood looking at the Silver Company pick-up, parked innocently and thankfully behind Marty's Dodge Ram, Sam wondered what the hell he was doing. There had been a reason back then for all that hiding. Being caught just wasn't an option. Did he really have to hide now? Why didn't he just go up to those two cops outside his house and ask them to give him a ride up to Hawk's house? And why in God's name hadn't he woken Katie to tell her he was going to speak to him? Because she would have told him not be crazy, that's why. Well maybe he was crazy, but he needed to speak to Daniel and he felt he needed to do it quickly.

Sam groped in his pocket for the keys and ran quickly and quietly over to the truck. The door wasn't even locked. No one in Silver locked their car doors much. Maybe they'd start doing it now. And locking their porch doors real tight too. He kept his eyes on Marty's windows as he started the engine, the noise exploding like a cough into the still, snow-laden air. No lights came on. Thank God. He chucked it into drive and moved away slowly down the block. If he took a left on Argyll the cops wouldn't even see the truck. They might wonder where a Silver Ski Company truck was going at one in the morning.

As Sam drove it down on to Main Street, he wondered that too. This was a crazy scheme. The snow was so thick that the wipers were just moving it around instead of clearing it and he knew what kind of a road there was up to the Hawk place. But if Daniel could just tell him anything, anything at all that would help him understand what was happening, then he'd walk to the fucking North Pole in his flip-flops if he had to.

So Joe Reader hadn't died in an accident? That was what they were getting at wasn't it? Asking him about where he was that night. Jesus. His hands gripped the wheel like a lifebuoy. His thoughts were hot coals now, searing him as they insisted he heed them. Who was he? Was he Sam Hunt, loving and loved husband and father? Or was he really, and in fact always had been, Sam Hunting Wolf? An altogether darker proposition.

What was it the Reverend Jenkins had said to him that time on the double black diamond? The time he wanted to go home after a bad fall. The thin white man had skied to his side, picked him up and dusted the snow off his cheap and frayed parka, despite Sam's humiliated tearful protests.

'Sure you can go back and give up now, Sam. But it'll go back on the bus with you. You'll wake up tomorrow and the fact you gave up will be right there with you. No escape. But if you get up and do that run again till you get those turns right, then that's what you'll wake up with. You can carry success around with you as much as failure. Which is it to be?'

Stupid to think that he might not wake up some day from the dream of perfect happiness with Katie and still face what he'd tried

223

to forget. The Reverend was right. Success or failure. Good or evil. You carried it right along there with you on the bus.

He was on the forest road now, heading uphill gradually through a curtain of snow that made him dizzy watching it fly towards him like boulders. The road was treacherous and indistinct, without a single set of tracks to follow. He took a deep breath, wound down the window an inch to let some air in, and a few flakes swirled in and brushed his face. Only a mile or so before Hawk's place and he willed himself to concentrate. The end of Hawk's drive could be missed so easily, especially in this weather, and he had to make sure he didn't drive past. But God, the snow was making him feel bad. His head was buzzing and his eyes were narrowed to slits to see where the hell he was going. And then, without warning, his soul was being sucked into a twister, and the blackness came and took him.

The sinister black shape of the log house changed instantly to the warm brown thing it was as Daniel broke the beam of their yard-light sensor and stepped onto the porch. Silently he awarded himself points for fitting that thing last fall. It was a marvel for switching itself on, letting you see what you were doing as you got out of the car in the dark before you opened up the house, but right now it had been better than a marvel. For the last quarter of an hour he'd felt like running. He knew he was behaving like a schoolboy, but that feeling of being watched, no, more than that, being *stalked*, had been living in between his shoulderblades the whole way up.

Well now he was home, and he was going to shake off his boots, get this jacket off that he was sweating like a hog under, and crack open a beer. He stamped on the wooden slats of the porch and turned off the flashlight. The yard-light would stay on for forty seconds until he either switched it on permanently from the lobby or broke the beam again with his body. He took off his gloves and found his key from the bunch on his belt. It felt good to open the door and get stuff going. The house was warm as toast, the big oil-burning stove going like a dream back there in the kitchen. Daniel turned the lobby and living room lights on, fingered a few letters Tess had left on the telephone table for his attention, and hung up his jacket. He let the yard light go out of its own accord. It had served its purpose.

It was weird not having Tess and Larry home. She usually heard his truck droning up the hill and waved to him from the sitting room window. And Larry would crash into him like a train, shouting at him in English and Siouan about the kind of day he'd had.

'Pick a language,' Daniel would laugh, and to his delight, Larry would usually choose Siouan. Not tonight. Tonight it was real late and the house was still and empty.

Lord, but he was tired now. He sat on the bench and pulled off his boots. Maybe it was too late for a beer and TV. Maybe he should just sleep and try not to dream of that mess of flesh he'd stood over in the woods. He put a hand out to the front door beside him and turned the lock. Never usually did that but tonight he felt like it. One quick look at what was on the sports channel, he decided. He stood up and walked through to the sitting room, slumped down on the sofa and punched the remote. Volleyball. Christ. Did he really want to sit and watch a bunch of faggots pushing a ball about on a beach? He sighed and sank into the cushions. It was something to watch. Something to help him unwind.

The windows filled with illumination. The yard-light had gone on. Daniel sat up. That happened sometimes when a big animal broke the beam. But not often. He'd fixed it so you had to be at least as big as Tess. Even Larry couldn't do it. Only a big deer or a bear would make it read their movement and neither made a habit of coming that close to the house. He went to the window, expecting, hoping, to see an elk blinking in the glare. Nothing. His heart started to beat a little faster when he looked at the thick snow, and one set of human prints, his own, meandering up to the porch, filling up quickly with the huge drifting flakes. No hoof prints. No paw prints. There was obviously something wrong with the sensor. He stood there for its forty seconds of light until it clicked off again and the virgin snow in the yard was lit only by the square of light from his window, his figure making a bulky shadow in the centre of the square.

Behind him in the room the TV was shouting about someone getting the ball over the net. Daniel shook a shiver from his shoulders and sat back down.

It clicked on again. He thought about ignoring it, but he couldn't. He leapt up quickly this time, in case there was something fleet-of-foot evading his gaze, but the yard was as still as before. Daniel waited stiffly until it switched off into darkness again then pulled the curtains roughly across the window. He wasn't going to get up and down every time the damn thing went on. He'd look at it in the morning. Get a new sensor from Hardy's tomorrow.

He sat down heavily with a groan and gazed dumbly at the big tanned blond guys dancing around in the sand. The commentator kept referring to them as *players*. Looked like pricks to Daniel. He smiled thinking how long one of those blond fairies with their big golden pecs would last out on the ice with a hockey stick in their hand and Grady O'Farrel at their heels.

From deep inside the house there was a low noise, a scuffling growling sound. Daniel didn't move. He waited, every sense on its toes, and it came again. He still had his gun on. Thank God, it still hung there on his hip. Slowly, silently, he slipped off the sofa onto his knees and faced the door, with the big green cushions between him and the opening. He unclipped his holster and slipped out the gun, holding it to his chest as he listened again. The guy on the TV was yelling again about the great strategy from someone called Neddy, and Daniel left it that way, but when the noise came again he could hear that it came plainly from the kitchen at the back of the house. It sounded like tearing. Something being ripped.

He stood up and quickly got his back against the wall behind the door, his gun up at his shoulder and ready. He slipped the safety catch off and cocked it. He waited until he heard the sound again, then while it was happening, leaped through the doorway into the lobby and slid along the wall to the kitchen door. The lights were on in the kitchen. They hadn't been when he got in, but they were now. Jesus. He had an intruder. His mind worked fast. Maybe more than one. What if the sensor wasn't broken? He whirled his head round to see if he was being trapped from behind. No one there. The lobby was clear, the front door still closed and locked. Daniel Hawk took a gulp of air, closed his eyes briefly in a silent prayer, and leaped through the kitchen doorway.

'FREEZE!'

He landed crouched with his legs apart, both hands on his gun, pointing at the source of the noise.

A coyote. A thin, leggy, hungry-looking animal, tearing away at a broken and spilled plastic trash bag all over the floor. It looked up at him, something white and wet hanging from its mouth. Just like the coyote in the ski car park. Just exactly like it. A stupid, hungry scavenger, taking advantage of Tess's sloppy waste disposal. He wanted to laugh with relief, and at the farcical sight he was creating, standing like a Secret Service marksman, pointing his hardware at a dumb coyote. And then he remembered the kitchen light. The one that had been turned on somehow since he'd got home. The animal grinned up at him with a leer.

'Helps to see what you're doing, doesn't it, Daniel?'

It had spoken to him. In a voice that was deep and dirty and disgustingly raspy. It had spoken in Siouan. And it had read his mind.

Daniel was panting hard through his nose now, his hands starting to tremble. He let it have it. Three shots, two in the head and one to the body. It slumped to the ground, its legs buckling beneath it, the head a bloody mess where his bullets had torn away half the skull.

Then as he watched with his mouth hanging open in horror, the body started to shift and quiver, being pulled up like a puppet on wires until the mess of grey fur and red blood was on its feet again. It was a foul thing. No longer an animal. A sack of fur and bones that had something else inside it, making it writhe and twitch like a body in agony.

He was an Indian. He knew about bad medicine. This was really bad medicine and he had no tools in his hand or his heart to fight it. The thing in the coyote's skin faced him again with a terrible grimace from its half-face. He could see the inside of its upper palate, the few remaining teeth glinting on a red sea of mucus and blood, the one eye hanging from its socket on a tendril of tissue.

'Care to join me in my meal?'

It made a jerky movement of its head, like it was struggling for control and picked up the white-and-pink morsel it had been gnawing when Daniel burst in. A small shoe clung to the end of the dangling matter. Larry's shoe.

No. No. Larry and Tess were in Calgary. He'd spoken to her less than an hour ago. He was in bed she said. Fast asleep. No. No. No. No.

The coyote that was no longer a coyote pawed at the black plastic trash bag . Something big and round rolled out of it across the white vinyl floor, leaving a trail of black-red sticky mush as it went. The eyes were dead and staring in the head and the black hair stuck to his son's severed head in matted points. It stopped between Daniel's spread legs.

227

Then the coyote that defied its place in the food chain, smiled up at Daniel. Not a leer that dogs can make by panting, but a very real, very human smile.

And it watched him as it laughed, a sound that filled the back of Daniel Hawk's throat as if he were making the diabolical sound himself from a stomach that was rotting and on fire with disease. His vision swam with the horror and he fought a battle to stay conscious. Illusion. That's all it was. None of it real. Someone was sending him bad medicine and he had to fight it or it would destroy his mind.

He screamed and rushed at the thing with his full weight. But before Daniel Hawk could reach the other side of the kitchen, the thing that was as solid as him was bigger than him, bigger than the kitchen, and enjoying proving that the denial of its existence was of little consequence.

26

He wasn't there. His mom was sleeping in an empty bed. Billy sniffed round the place his dad's head should have been and then round his mom. She was hurting inside. He could feel it. Something was churning around in her mind and she was wrestling with it even as she slept. Billy felt sad and worried, but he was keen to find his father. The wolf was tugging him downstairs and reluctantly he left his mother with the thought of a kiss on her cheek. She stirred as he left the room, as though feeling its phantom touch on her skin.

They were hurrying now, through the town and up onto the road that went through the trees on the forest trail. There was something making Billy afraid. A huge, dark, sick feeling in him that made him want to stop and run back home. But the wolf was pounding ahead. The wolf that was there ahead of him, and yet he was the wolf. He was outside it and part of it. He could see the loping stride of the animal as it bounded through the thick snow, and at the same time feel the icy cold through his own paws, see the road ahead through the wolf's eyes and smell the air with his keen and twitching nostrils.

The lights of the town that would normally twinkle and blink through the trees, were shut out by the thick sweeping blanket of snow that was falling from a laden sky. They ran on, the wolf's legs not long enough to keep its body out of the deep drifts, and with every bound making itself a pit from which it had to leap and start anew. It left a curious trail in the snow, although Billy knew in his heart that no such trail would be there at all once they'd gone. But they were covering ground at a tremendous speed, and they were getting near the thing was making him afraid. Too near. Billy stopped in his stride and the wolf that was him stopped too, the breath they shared steaming in the frozen air.

There was a truck up ahead that had slewed off the road. The Ski Company pick-up his dad drove around town sometimes. Billy had been in it plenty of times, sitting proudly on the long, slippery bench-seat, mucking around with the CB till his dad told him to quit it. And he knew that his dad was in there now. It was silent, the lights still on, its nose stuck harmlessly in a big soft drift at the side of the road where it had so obviously swerved.

Billy wanted to rush forward to the truck and check out his dad but there was something in the way. All round the truck and in the truck. Something big and inky-black and bad. So bad he could hardly bear to be near it. The wolf was whining, its ears pinned back flat on its skull. And as they looked on, the bad thing, the big, black, dirty thing, felt they were there. He was sure of it. It was like a mad dog tearing away at a rabbit, suddenly swinging around and smelling you creep up behind it. Billy felt a nameless fear rise in his guts as the blackness round the truck started to gather itself. That was the only way he could interpret the thing it was doing. It was gathering.

And there was something worse. He recognized the core of the badness: a pulsating, dark energy that was swallowing and gulping and consuming, ripping and tearing at the night.

He could feel it flashing through his body like electricity, in every blood vessel and nerve ending, in every vein and muscle.

It was his father.

Blackened by this throbbing hate, his father was there right at the heart of the horror. An empty shell of a thing, yet full of bitter and acrid malice.

Billy thought his heart would burst. He struggled to make sense of the thing. So many sensations and dense, ugly, swirling veils of blackness to see through. But through the confusion there was still the truth of what he could feel. That it was the blackness, and his father, and they were intertwined like the hair in a braid.

Then a hissing half-thought, half-spoken voice sizzled in mockery through the blackness.

'And who is this?'

Billy and the wolf were as still as the stones. They felt tendrils like the touch of limp dead flesh brush their fur, and the probing of that fur to see if there was a way inside.

The wolf was baring its teeth in a snarl of ferocity that Billy had never witnessed.

The black, the badness, the thing that was around and in his father, was trying to get in to them, trying to take them over, to have them and *be* them.

It was all over them now. Everywhere. The wolf writhed and snarled and growled, thrashing on the snow as though pinned by a skewer. And it was so close, so nearly in them . . . and . . .

Katie sat bolt upright, her eyes wide open with the scream of her son. It was a scream that could make a mother's heart stop: not the cry of a child dreaming of the boogieman, but one of excruciating torment. Her hand shot instinctively out to Sam and met an empty pillow.

Billy.

Sam.

She leaped from the bed and ran to his room. Jess was already crying, but she ran past her door, burst in on her son and slammed on the light.

His tiny figure was huddled in a foetal position against the wall under the window, eyes staring open, mouth ready to scream again. She ran to him, scooping him up her arms and held him close. The boy was soaking in sweat.

'My darling. My sweet, sweet lamb. Shhh now. It's okay. Everything's okay.'

He was gulping for air, his eyes rolling madly in his head as he gasped out the words.

'Don't let him in me, Mom. Don't let Dad in me. He mustn't touch me.'

She froze.

'Shhh. It's okay. Mom's here lamb. Shhh.' And she held him pressed to her like that until she realized with a heart as heavy as an anchor that Sam wasn't going to come to Jess's cry. That Sam wasn't in the house at all.

It must be given and not taken. And of course, it was given. The boy in Wild'n'Free, Alberta Ltd, had handed over the display tent, the axe, the shovel and big serrated hunting knife to Calvin with a dreamy and kindly smile. He would pay for them out of his wages. He knew he could. The tent was less than half-price and they wouldn't have shifted it until spring anyhows. The old guy really needed those things. And that delicate gentle lemon smell of the sweetgrass he brought into the store with him made him think of camping with Angela. Oh that smell. He was there again, deep in the valleys between the mountains, with the larks singing in the sky a million miles above them, trilling as they lay in that sweetgrass and kissed.

He'd watched the old Indian go, longing for him to stay so he could carry on filling his nostrils and his heart with that sweet lemon-scented memory. But even when the glass door swung shut, and the bell stopped tinkling above it, he could still smell it. He smiled and sat down on the boot-changing bench to dream.

Calvin lit the fungus, purified his hands and prayed. Then he purified the axe and laid down the tobacco he'd carried for nearly eighty miles, offering it to the spirit of the willow. He crouched for a moment to gather his strength and then set to cutting the willow saplings. He cut twenty, leaving the shiny red branches on near the tips, and laid them in a stack. His breathing was laboured at the effort, panting out of him in great whirling clouds of steam, and he pulled his muti-lated hand over his face to wipe away the sweat.

This was as nothing compared to what he would endure when he started. How was this abused old body going to take the strain? He thought little of this preparation when he was young. To prepare, and prepare correctly, was vital, but back then, with the Hunting Wolf boy busying round, assisting him in that earnest and eager way, it had seemed a joy building the sweat-lodges in the clearing between the delicate dancing aspens.

He was in just such a clearing of birch, aspen and willow now, all slumbering beneath their false winter masks of death. Those brittle black branches, bowing and snapping beneath the weight of the snow, held soft tiny green miracles of buds that would cease to be secret when spring unlocked them. Calvin touched a frozen birch branch with a cold finger and closed his eyes as he felt a subtle and deep tingle of its life force enter him. The tenuous pulse of life, shivering inside a wooden husk.

He prayed again, left the branch and bent to start collecting rocks. He would need twenty-five. One for each of the willow saplings, and five for the five most important Grandfathers; Earth, Water, Light-ning, Thunder and Wind. Scraping at the snow with naked fingers, he felt around and selected his stones. There were logs ready to receive them when he had found the rocks that pleased his hands, and he knelt forwards to allow a wider sweep of his arms under the white, freezing blanket that concealed them. Since dawn he had been collecting and gathering the tools of his art, clearing snow to clear the site and dig for roots, and walking far and deep into this forest, searching out the few lichens and grey-green stalks of plant life that he knew thrived beneath the winter layer of white.

Of course there was no buffalo skull and that would make his altar weak. But there had been a gift in the night as he slept in his snow-hole. An eagle feather. He had awoken to find it on his breast, a brown-and-white miracle trembling with the slightest movement of air as though it wished to fly again. A gift indeed. But one that mutely spelled the impossibility of escaping his duty.

So the roots were chopped and ground, the mound of earth that would be his altar was built, and the feather would be his centrepiece on that altar. Not as powerful on its own, but he had little choice.

His stones chosen, he laid aside and blessed five of them, four for each of the cardinal directions, and one for the sky.

All the rocks were then placed on the piles of logs, east of the altar, then surrounded by more timber and kindling. Calvin took a knot of lichen to the small fire a distance away from the lodge site, lit it and returned to the pyre around the stones. He placed the burning lichen beneath the twigs with a prayer, and watched until the wood had fully ignited.

The desire to hurry was still beating in his guts, but this was too important to defile by an imprecise gesture or a hasty shortcut. He knew in his heart, that this would be his last building of a sweat-lodge. He would ensure, therefore, that it would be his most pious.

Calvin returned to the site of the lodge and lifted the shovel. The hole would have to be two and a half feet across, and a foot and a half deep to hold the rocks when they came red and glowing from the fire, but it was tough, real tough, stabbing at the iron hard ground, even with the shiny new blade of this tool. He narrowed his eyes and shut out the pain of the effort as he dug, letting his mind drift from the task.

Red-hot from the fire.

An ugly memory was there before he could push it away, bobbing to the surface of his consciousness like a bubbling carcass surfacing in a pool. Too late to force it back down. He hacked at the earth with a hatred that was not directed at the innocent, if ungiving soil.

They had been drinking heavily that afternoon, Moses and Marlene. Wayne Longpaw was there too, squatting cross-legged on the floor, smoking a roll-up and raising his drink in a cheerful toast to more or less anything his host said.

Moses sat in his greasy coffee-brown chair by the oil-drum stove, his jar of cloudy moonshine resting on one thigh. He was an ugly sight, sitting proudly with the pantomime demeanour of a king, the way drunks do in their own house. Stick-thin legs beneath his jeans gave him the appearance of a fairground stilt-walker, as though he concealed two wooden poles beneath the grimy denim. His whole haggard and pinched body was ravaged by a lack of any nutrition other than the booze he swallowed down like a suckling pig, and the odd piece of dismal food that Marlene made him eat when she was sober enough to remember they had to. Looked like he'd already been sick once, down the front of his pointy pocketed rodeo shirt, and there was something matting strands of his long black un-braided hair that fell forwards on his shoulders. This was round two of the day, Calvin figured.

Marlene was nearly out cold. Her jar lay on its side on the cracked linoleum floor, the caustic contents around her feet in a puddle as she lay slumped back on the pile of old clothes she'd been sitting on.

Calvin could hardly bear it. He had only come up there to that vile cabin to look for the boy and ask for his assistance but Moses had welcomed him in like a member of the family.

And so he sat with them, holding a broken cup of moonshine that was given by the grinning Wayne, looking on in horror and pity as Moses gesticulated and slurred insults at his semi-conscious wife, laughing at his own witless remarks with a mouth full of black and broken teeth.

Calvin had gulped down the filthy brew, knowing to close his nostrils to the stench as he drank, and waiting for that burning hot stream of pain to slip down his throat into his chest, before the blessed release of the raw alcohol started to pad out his head with a dull cushion. It had been practically pure ethanol. Another brew from the still of Milton Destaville, a big silent half-French Kinchuinick who moved his cabin monthly to foil any RCs that might find his popular laboratory.

The room was oppressively hot from the stove, but no warmth

could make this dingy space feel homely. There were some curling black-and-white photos of Marlene in a barrel race tacked to the plasterboard wall opposite the curtainless window. Calvin thought she sure did look something in those days. Braids out at right angles to her head, her face clear and unlined as she gripped that nag with her knees. Hard to believe it was the same girl when you looked at the face of Marlene Hunting Wolf now. Her lifeless left eye-socket was closed and sunken, the skin scarred and fused together over it in a hideous reminder of what Moses could do when his tank was full.

And she was as thin as her husband. A tiny wizened bird. The womanly flesh that had modelled her pretty oval face and sweetly rounded body in those black-and-white photos was long gone.

Those sad, curling stained documents of the past were the only decoration in the room. On a drop-leafed table in the corner was a bundle of rags and newspapers spilling over onto the floor. The lumber from a broken gate leant against the table leg, and it looked like that was what was burning in the stove. Surrounded by trees, and the lazy bastard chose to find a gate to break up and burn.

Moses lorded it in his chair. The remains of some kind of meal were on the floor at the back of the stove. Bits of stale soda bread that seemed to have been dipped in a gravy. It made Calvin sick looking at it.

And even now, it made Calvin sick thinking of it. He stopped digging for a moment, realizing he was attacking the earth like an assassin. He let his breath return to his normal half-caught wheeze and steeled himself to continue. He sliced at the soil rhythmically, and the memory was still there. He was back in the cabin again,

The boy had come in. Sam had opened the door the way Calvin guessed he opened it every day of his life. With caution. A hunted thing, watching warily to see if the predator would strike. Moses's eyes had glittered. Calvin saw that thin, barely-perceptible line of evil intent flit across those deep-set black eyes and had been afraid for the boy. But they had guests. Sam was to come and join them. The boy had looked at Wayne, then at Calvin with a mixture of relief and shame. He clearly didn't want his shaman teacher there in the house, but he knew he was glad to see him nevertheless.

Sam was like a creature from another planet in this household. At fifteen he was already six feet tall, gangly, waiting to fill out as a man.

But he smelled of the open air, and his clear, nut-brown, almost femininely beautiful face was all the more attractive for the smears of mud on its cheeks.

He was clutching something in his fist and Moses spotted it, anger starting to rise in his face.

Then Wayne raised his newly replenished jar and toasted Sam's entrance incoherently. Moses's face relaxed from anger into something more approximating cunning.

'This here boy been throwin' away dollars on the railroad, Calvin.' He motioned to Sam with his drink. 'Go on. Show 'em your prize.'

Wayne toasted them again, wheezing out a laugh and babbling to himself as an encore. Sam looked to Calvin for help, but there was nothing the medicine man could think to say. Besides, the second gulp of moonshine was making him soften round the edges. Sam opened his fist and showed the company the shiny flat disc of metal that had been a dollar. He waited for whatever was going to happen next, and Moses through his haze of drunkenness was somehow able to time that wait to its excruciating limit.

'Fix the guests somethin' to eat.'

Relief swam into Sam's almond-shaped, black eyes and he closed his fist on his coin. Marlene was stirred by the cold air that came into the cabin with her son and she propped herself up on one elbow, squinting at him, trying to focus. 'Is 'at ma darlin'? Ma darlin' come home to his mama? Come here ma baby.'

Sam walked quickly into the back room to escape. Calvin heard him moving about, shifting objects on a table, presumably looking for something edible to offer them. His mother sank back down onto her arm again, making a cooing sound as though chucking a baby under its chin.

Moses took a long swig of his drink, gritting his teeth and saying *gaaaar* through them as it slipped down his throat, then leaned across to Calvin with a cunning conspiratorial glint, his voice thick from the burning liquor. 'You want to see somethin' good? You watch this.'

He leaned forward in his chair, nearly toppling out of it, put down his jar as though it were the finest wafer thin porcelain and felt in his jeans pocket for something. The operation took a long time, but eventually he fished out a coin. A dollar. He winked at Calvin, kicked at Wayne to pay attention to what he was doing then winked at him too. With the concentration of a chef putting a cherry on top of his cake, he placed the coin on top of the raging hot stove and sat back in his chair with a contented and triumphant expression. He put a finger to his nose and tapped it at Calvin, then sank another drink. Calvin watched the yellow of the dollar start to discolour and tarnish with the extreme heat.

'He don't do nothin' for his ol' man.'

Moses shook his head solemnly. For a moment the sly face softened into a mockery of self pity, like he was going to cry. The maudlin tears of a drunk.

'Nothin'. Flattens those dollars he earns in town so's I can't use 'em. I know it. I know it.'

Calvin had poured the remains of his cup down his throat. He'd wanted another. Just to blot out the misery of the room.

Moses sat shaking his head to himself for a few moments, then drank deeply from his jar and put it back down again, the action seeming to signal time for his mood to return from self-pity to sly prankster. He made a small sniggering sound and booted Wayne to watch him again as he picked up a small black shovel by the stove, slid the hot dollar onto it and into an empty tobacco tin on the floor by his chair. He grinned, his eyes on Calvin as he called out.

'Sam. Get in here.'

The boy appeared in the doorway behind his father, sullen and expectant.

'Got somethin' for you, boy. Get in here.'

Sam came round to his chair.

In the half-light of that room, the evening approaching fast, Sam looked so handsome and vulnerable that Calvin, man as he was, had wanted to kiss those tight pink lips. It was the light on his face, the way it glanced off smooth high cheekbones and shone in his straight black hair. And the set of those broad shoulders with a boy's lean body hanging below them was sculptural.

It was a strange feeling, all the more aberrant for the absence of shame he had experiencing it. Calvin had never felt it for a man or boy before. But it was there. Sexual perhaps, but at the time it was not his crotch on fire, but his heart.

'You want dollars to spoil? Have mine. Jesus knows I owe ya.'

Moses chuckled like an indulgent father and picked up the tin, offering it out to Sam to show him the contents.

Sam looked at his father and then at the dollar, suspicious but

237

seeing no trick. He went to pluck it from the tin, when Moses pulled it back.

'Ah ah! Hold yer hand out and say *thank you, Pappy!*'

Humiliated and yet scared to detonate this drunken time-bomb, Sam did as he was ordered. 'Thank you.' A pause and a small tight mouth. 'Pappy.'

Moses kept his grinning eyes on Sam and tipped the searing hot metal disc into his son's palm. There was a fraction of a second before Sam's skin got the message to his brain and he dropped it and grabbed the wrist of his burnt hand, his teeth bared like a fighting dog. No sound, no cry, no yell. Just teeth clenching in agony, eyes screwed up, fighting for control.

Calvin was digging hard at the ground now, gulping to fight off the face of that boy in the room and the sound of those two drunken men laughing at his pain.

The shovel split a last clod of hard earth apart with a thud like a blade splitting a skull. His hand was a fist round the shaft of the shovel.

The hole was big enough. It would take the stones.

Calvin straightened up, and massaged the small of his back with his knuckles to relieve the aching.

The saplings would have to be woven together into a dome, then the canvas he'd cut from the tent, draped over it to make a loose roof. There was still a great deal to do, and between the delicate branches of the trees, the grey sky announced the day was waning.

He stood up, faced east and offered up a prayer for the Hunting Wolf boy. It was not the first time he'd done it, and with his eyes turned to the darkening sky, he knew in his heart it would not be the last.

27

The soft grey leather bound round the steering wheel in a spiral had absorbed enough saliva to make a dark, wet stain. But then Sam had been slumped forward drooling, with the wheel between his teeth like a horse's bit, for an hour.

He was clear-headed this time when he'd woken. Although woken was not quite the right word for that mercurial return to consciousness that left him gasping as though winded by a punch. Sam groaned, almost whimpered, as he lifted his head from the wheel and rubbed at his aching jaw.

An hour. The lights were still on, illuminating the spartan instrument panel, though the engine had stalled, and the clock told him the unpalatable story of the time he'd lost. His mouth was dry and sore, his neck muscles throbbed, but those minor physical irritations were of little consequence compared to the nugget of alarm in his heart, that it had happened again.

For a moment he sat blinking in the darkness, allowing an overwhelming sense of hopelessness and resignation to wall him in. His hands fell to his lap and he stared at the snow wall through the windshield like a child at a dull adult TV show; mouth hanging open, eyes glazed and distant, yet too drained to look away.

Awake again. Alone, in the dark. Paralyzed with terror by the potential an hour could hold.

So sad. Waking had been his pleasure for ten years. How many ways had he woken with Katie? There were big sunny awakenings with bird song, the sounds of neighbours' cars leaving outside, kissing and sex and jokes. There were cold, cosy mornings when waking up meant he could enjoy falling asleep again, tucked up in the skin and hair and silk of her. Waking to children crying and comforting them back to sleep. Waking to children laughing, bouncing on the bed. Waking in the yard on a lounger with his soda gone warm in the sun beside him and Katie rubbing factor thirty-five on his unburnable chest for a gas. Opening his eyes in the sitting room to find the TV still blaring, the fire low, and Katie sleeping beside him with a book over her eyes.

But now there was this. This is what he woke to. The madness of uncertainty, the horror of not knowing and the deeper fear of knowing. This time there had been a silver shard of light in that great blackness. A dream perhaps, in the void. Someone he loved close by. He looked forlornly at the snow avalanching down the glass in front of him and watched as it slid gracefully down to join the wedge that already reached half way up the wipers.

Loved ones.

Soon, he thought, they will doubt me.

An alien thought, a phrase from nowhere. It snapped his torpor. Sam opened the cab door and stepped out, thigh-deep into the snow and the air thick with flakes like fortune cookies. He didn't want to see Daniel any more. He wanted to get away.

The truck was not badly stuck. It appeared to have left the road slowly, as though Sam had taken his foot off the gas, kept his hands on the wheel but ceased to steer. The drift had halted it safely, if inconveniently, in its breast, and it needed digging out.

He fumbled about in the back until he found the shape of the shovel under the whiteness. Sam was thinking like a criminal now. There was still time to get the truck back before Marty missed it, if he could just get the snow shifted, and if, please God, the battery wasn't flat. He opened the door, the shovel in his other hand, and from outside the cab turned the key. A churning cough. Again. Two churning coughs.

'Come on. Come on, you bastard.'

Two, three, four coughs and a result. He leaned his head against the door with relief. Yes, a criminal now, without a crime. What was he so desperate to get away from? He hadn't even left the truck for God's sake. But he knew the whole scheme had been crazy, and would look crazy to anyone who knew he was here. Nothing he was doing made sense any more. He wanted to get home, erase the night's lunacy and make a space to think.

He dug frantically as the truck ticked over to itself, chopping a rectangular escape route at the front and clearing miniature runways behind each wheel to reverse out of trouble.

It wasn't hard. He'd gotten out of worse. In under ten minutes he was snaking his way back down the trail towards town, the snow already filling in and healing the vandalism he'd performed on its perfect undulating coat.

It was five after three when he got to Marty's place and parked the truck right where it had been. Not that it mattered. The relentless snow had done a lot of work for him, and it would be a first if someone like Marty, who had trouble remembering his name, noticed the pick-up was three inches away from where he left it last night. He waited breathlessly to see if the truck's return would make those dark windows above the porch roof, light up into yellow squares of enquiry. When it didn't, he pocketed the keys, closed the door as silently as a thief, and headed back home.

Maybe he should have gone on up to Hawk's. What the hell was he playing at? All that way for nothing. If he had another blackout up there, so what? Hawk could call for help. Sam was in turmoil, no longer sure what he wanted or why, what he was thinking or if it made sense.

But he was doing a careful and constant job of keeping that big black thought out of his mind. The big insistent one that said, people die when you're out cold, my boy. Yes they do. People have died every single fucking time.

No. That wasn't true. Not this time. This time he hadn't gotten out of the goddamn truck. No one was dead and there was no room for a thought as despicable as that. All he knew was that he was creeping around his own neighbourhood after three in the morning like a tom cat.

It was beautiful in the still streets. All these timber houses, blue and yellow and pink, coated with white snow like confections. And the people sleeping in those big safe wooden cradles were good people he liked. That was the Ritchies' house there. Billy played with their son Dillon and Katie could rarely get away from that house without an armful of jars of preserved things they could never quite identify.

And ahead, in the three-storey house that was way too big for them, that was where Pat and Benny lived. Block Parents who had no kids. Their little round Block Parent sticker in the window was like a declaration of defiance in the face of their infertility. He saw Pat's face when she opened the door to the kids that abused the sticker by asking for the bathroom and cookies instead of help in a crisis. It wasn't a face annoyed by the intrusion and exploitation, but a face that said she ached to wrap them in her arms and own them. It wasn't fair. They were such good people.

It struck Sam that he was reminiscing. That was exactly what he was doing. Thinking about his friends and neighbours as if they were dead and gone. Or he was.

He squinted against the snow, denying himself the masochistic luxury of punishing himself further, slipped into Dave's yard and over his fence like a robber.

The Hunt house was still and dark as Sam retraced his steps to the kitchen door. He bent down in the dark by Bart's kennel, fumbling for the invisible dog to stroke, hoping to comfort himself with the warmth he stored concealed under his snow-dusted fur.

Bart was gone. Sam crouched, uncertain, by the kennel opening, his eyes adjusting from the lit street to the dark pools of shadow in the yard. There was no way the husky could get out of the yard unless the gate had been left open. But Sam had climbed over the fence and the gate was shut tight. Jesus, Billy would have a fit if he found his dog gone. There was no time to deal with it now. Sam would face it when the sun came up.

He pushed open the door and stepped into the dark. Sam started to step out of his boots and stopped.

There was someone else in the room with him. In the dark.

Sam remained absolutely still, trying to contain his breathing but knowing his entrance must have betrayed him. For a second, he felt like screaming, running from the room and far away from the house. God, he was jumpy. After all, *he* was the criminal. His senses were on overload.

'Where've you been?'

He let out a breath that had been festering in his chest for an age, fumbled for the light switch behind him and threw it on.

'Katie! Jesus. I nearly died there.'

She was at the table, her hair mussed from sleep, but her eyes glowed like those of a cornered animal, ready to strike.

'Katie. For Christ's sake, what you doing sitting here in the dark?' He sat down on the chair opposite her with a heavy thud and moved to take her delicate hands, rested on the table top like a judge's. She moved them away. He withdrew his as though stung.

'Katie.'

'Where have you been Sam?'

He looked into that pale, lovely face and felt the spit dry in his mouth. In the back of his mind it was as though a hellish fanfare were sounding. This is it, he thought. The end of all that joy. As the lie formed on his lips, the first lie he had ever uttered to this woman whom he loved beyond measure, he felt the quiet and sickening noise of a door closing on his life.

Tight small mouth. 'Couldn't sleep. I walked round the block.'

And it was over. Everything was over. He had lied to her. Over.

His head buzzed like radio static.

'Sam? Sam? Baby? Is that you? Where you been Sam?'

Safe. His father wasn't home. Just Marlene. Watching from the field above the cabin he'd seen her come out and empty slops in the yard and Moses didn't seem to be around. Safe. Thank you, Great Spirit. Thank you, Jesus, too.

He walked cautiously into the room and he knew by his mother's tone that he wasn't home. She would never be so flamboyant, never shout in case it got up the old man's nose. She was sober. She'd tidied a little round Moses's chair and her braids were done again with a bit of silky stuff in the ends like she'd made an effort. He looked around, checked again and went straight to the stove, trying to get some warmth back in his hands.

She was on him. Fussing, kissing, brushing imaginary objects from his dirty shoulders. 'Sam. My baby. You can't go doin' this to your mama, baby. I thinks you was dead for sure this time.'

He shrugged her off and saw her hurt. Marlene looked at him like a little girl for a while, swinging her foot behind the other then turned back to what she was doing at the table.

'You got nothin' to say after it bein' close on five weeks? You think I don't got no heart.'

'I don't know, mama. He get that too?'

She turned on him, her face full of a pleading that Sam could no longer ignore. 'I know it's been bad, my baby, but we ain't gonna do the booze no more. I swear. I ain't had nothin for weeks.'

He knew she was lying, could see it in her yellowed eyes, but he

243

stopped rubbing his freezing hands over the oil-drum stove and stepped forward to hold her. It was like holding sticks in a sack. 'You have to get away, mama.' But as he said it he knew he was lying too. She was part of it . As bad as him. That was where the pain was. She was part of Moses's madness too, and he knew what she would say. She had said it so many times before.

This time she said it in a muffled voice into her son's thin chest. 'He be not such a bad guy, your pappy, Sam. He be okay when the booze don't hit him bad.'

He said nothing. Then that thin reedy voice again.

'Where you been, Sam?'

The fifteen-year-old Sam Hunting Wolf had laughed sardonically to himself over her greasy black head. Where indeed? Did she think he'd wanted to build a shelter of branches and turf, high in the hills away from this torment? Living alone, off fungus, roots and rabbits, and once killing a lowly weasel in his hunger and eating its two mouthfuls of tasteless flesh like an animal himself.

It was too late to blame this wreck of a human being. He would just lie to her. Make her pain easier. The truth, that she and her husband drove their son in horror and pain from their house was not something he would skewer her with now. Not while she was sober. A lie.

'I was fine, mama. I was over at the Reverend's place.'

But not entirely a lie. He had certainly been outside the Reverend Jenkins' cabin one night. A small cabin the chief had let him have after the reverend's church gave a stack of money for the privilege. He was a Baptist something or other, here with his wife and daughter to save Indians.

Sam had seen a light in their window and squatted on the dirt rise behind their rough yard to watch them take their meal. Scrutinizing a real family held endless fascination for Sam. There was Mrs Jenkins talking to the Reverend as she drained off the potatoes and their daughter Darcy was just sitting at the table writing something in a book. He'd gazed enraptured as Mrs Jenkins cleared the book away from under Darcy's nose and Darcy didn't even flinch.

She'd placed a big steaming plate of food in front of the girl while still speaking to her husband and then took off her apron and sat down with her own plate. Then they'd bowed their heads and the Reverent had said something and they'd all tucked in. Darcy was talking, waving her fork, and get this, the Reverend and Mrs Jenkins were listening and laughing. Sam couldn't imagine what that would be like. He'd sat in the dark, watching them right up until Mrs Jenkins had cleared the plates and put out the light. Then he'd sat there for an hour in the dark, hugging his knees, before he went back up the hill to his shelter and a hungry sleep.

Where you been, Sam? That's where he'd been.

Katie was still looking at him across the table with those hot, hard eyes. Had the door closed for her too? Had she read the lie in his eyes?

'Long walk, huh?'

'Uh-huh.'

He looked at her, aching to smash whatever it was sitting between them, but knowing that he was its architect. 'How long have you been sitting here in the dark?'

''Bout an hour.'

'Bart's gone from the yard.'

'He's in with Billy.'

'Oh.'

'Sam. Did you see Billy before your walk?' There was sarcasm in that last word, and sarcasm was not a tool that Katie often used. Certainly never on him.

'No. Why? Is he okay?'

Sam's face was suddenly in that dimension where anxiety can shift a gear to distress with just one word. Katie looked at him for what seemed like a very long time. Sam's eyes glittered, his own woes temporarily forgotten as he searched her face for a hint of news about his only son.

Katie put her hand out and took his. 'No. He's fine. Just had a really bad dream.'

Sam looked down at her hand holding his. She was confusing him. The wall seemed to have crumbled.

'We're going to the doctor's tomorrow, Sam. Together.'

He nodded and lifted her hand to his lips.

28

Alberta 1907
Siding Twenty-three

'Take a good look at them, for the love of God!'

The men, instead, looked back at McEwan impassively. He was angry. But they were frightened, and that was by far the more dangerous and volatile of the two emotions.

In front of him, thirty-one strong men who had downed their picks to watch what these reeking savages were doing, were now waiting for their engineer to tell them that all was well. He was trying his best, attempting like an alchemist of the emotions to turn attack into comfort.

'Go on. Look. So it is these barbarians and their wild tales that have turned you from men into children, is it? Look at them. Look at them, damn you!'

They looked out of duty, although the scene was no different from the one that had ceased their toil. In the thick, relentless snow, seven Indians were constructing a small wooden dome from willow saplings and laying out all manner of foolish trinketry that made McEwan despise them more.

Observed with a cool eye the Indians were a bizarre sight; huge wide-brimmed leather hats and ill-fitting wool coats and vests they had traded from loggers, the material bunched tight around their waists with shiny belts from which hung a variety of knives and pouches. On top of this cacophony of cloth they wrapped highly-

coloured blankets which fell to their soft hide-bound feet. It enraged
McEwan to think that such a band of comical fools could be bringing
the most important engineering project of his life to a standstill. He
was snorting steam from his nostrils as he gathered himself to address
the men again.

From the back of the group, which was huddled, scattered beneath
the shelter of the red cedars as they watched the proceedings, Strachan
spoke in a low voice. 'And what o' the minister, Mr McEwan? Is he
tae be told he is a child an' aw?'

Angus McEwan winced. To tell the men what he thought of James
Henderson and his hysterical tantrums would be to lose their respect.
Religion to the Scots, trumped authority as paper wraps stone in the
child's game. He would bite his tongue and play this carefully. 'The
Reverend Henderson has nothing more serious than cabin fever, Stra-
chan. A month of snow like this does not often occur in the parish of
Morningside.'

There were one or two short laughs from those men who knew
Edinburgh and understood the jibe at Henderson's naiveté. McEwan
continued, encouraged by the response. 'Aye, and it is the same afflic-
tion and nothing more that is making you all see and hear what is
not there. You must shake yourselves from this indulgence.'

Strachan was not convinced. 'Ah've been in snowstorms that wid
bury a man in minutes Mr McEwan. An' four of us here have been
stuck under a brushwood shelter for nigh on seven weeks wi' the
rations doon tae biscuits an' bacon. If ye're tellin' us that we dinnae
know cabin fever when we see it then you dinnae know the crew ye're
workin'.'

McEwan looked around the faces, searching for an ally amongst
the nodding heads. His search was fruitless.

Strachan hammered home the last nail. 'Naebody's got cabin fever.
And naebody's workin' till we see what they're gonnae dae next.'

McEwan stared him down. 'Then you'll not be wanting work at
all when the snow stops long enough to let an engine through and I
send for a new crew.'

A few anxious faces, but not many.

'Maybe that's so.'

Chanting from behind him broke McEwan's studied glare and
made the men resume their wide-eyed vigil.

The Indians had thrown a sewn buckskin cover over the wooden structure and the chief was shaking some damnable stick over it as he made incantations. In front of the tent on a small mound of earth was a buffalo skull and what looked like the severed wings of a large bird.

McEwan ran a hand over his beard, where snowflakes were trying to hide and looked back at the group of his men. 'You forget how long I have endured this wilderness. My tales will match yours and more, Strachan. And I tell you this: if it is not cabin fever then it is the worst case of men behaving like old women I have ever come across. When you search for work in the cities I would advise you to adopt the former as reason for your dismissal. It is better than the truth.'

He read their faces then turned and walked back towards the camp, making a deliberate detour that would take him through the circular site of the peculiar tent.

Damn the treaties. And damn the delicate touch they were advised by the company to take with these filthy creatures. He should have frog-marched them from his camp the moment they showed their unwashed faces. Then perhaps this nonsense could have been prevented. He would make do instead with kicking the ridiculous buffalo skull like a rugby ball as he passed. If it made the men laugh, it would get them on his side, and that would be worth any risk.

McEwan waded through the snow towards the dark figures in their circle of herbs and stones. The Indians took no notice of him, bending slowly and passively to their various tasks like men dreaming.

When the tall, bearded engineer reached a point about four feet from the edge of the circle, Hunting Wolf broke off his chanting and without looking at McEwan held up a hand in warning to come no further. Angus McEwan paused. The Indian turned to face him. McEwan looked into the brown, horribly scarred face of this simpleton and weighed up the peril. The eyes of his men were burning holes in his back, but the eyes of this Indian were worse. Two black, burnished jewels stared out at him, glittering with a fierce and unexpected intelligence that made McEwan recoil. Something at the base of his spine wanted him to turn and run but he battled with the sensation and faced the savage like a man. His words, though he knew they could not be understood, nevertheless came from a dry mouth.

'You are on Canadian Pacific Railway's property.'

The Indian continued to stare.

Angus McEwan shot a furtive glance back to where the men were gathered, then walked quickly forward into the circle and kicked the skull from its mound. It was heavier than he had anticipated and the yellowing head seemed to gaze at him through its empty sockets as it toppled and rolled heavily into the snow. It was not the gesture he had hoped for. He had imagined it soaring into the air like a ball, with Indians chasing after it, as his men roared with laughter.

Instead, there was a silence. Seven Indians looked at him through the falling snow with inscrutable black eyes, and thirty-one railroad men watched with their breath drawn to see what would become of their sacrilegious overseer.

Hunting Wolf raised his hand slowly and McEwan backed off imperceptibly. The Indian moved his fingers together and apart as if his hand was talking and said something low, though it was said in a voice that to McEwan did not sound as if it belonged to the man. It made him more fearful him than any shouting. In fact it made him very fearful indeed.

The thick muffled silence of the snow made McEwan's head beat with the rhythm of his own blood and he stepped back from this madman and his talking hand. The men were beginning to mutter from their shady grandstand beneath the trees and through his inexplicable fright Angus McEwan realized that he had played a bad hand. Friendless, he turned quickly from Hunting Wolf and steered his awkwardness towards the camp.

The eyes that followed his progress betrayed a variety of emotions. There was pity and anger, and glinting in one or two were the first signs of malicious delight at his error. But in one pair of very deep and dark eyes, there was naked hatred.

Angus McEwan, however, saw no one's eyes as he stumbled through the snow while the Indians at his back destroyed their defiled site and went in search of a new one.

The boy turned the wooden crucifix over in his small brown hands, his fingers gently tracing the relief ivory figure of Christ. It was a curious object but he liked it. The white of the little bone man's flesh against the dark wood fascinated Walks Alone, which is why he had been sitting on the floor for at least an hour, holding it and stroking the figure.

At the foot of the flesh-and-blood white man's bed, his mother,

Singing Tree, was squatting, chewing dried meat to soften it and replacing the masticated pieces carefully in her hip pouch. She alternated her gaze as she performed this ovine task between her son and the figure of the thin white man lying asleep on the bed, his chest rising and falling beneath the ragged brown blanket.

Henderson stirred, groaning slightly as he turned in his sleep.

'Put the totem back, Walks Alone. He will wake soon.'

He looked up at her with huge black eyes then past her to the bed as Henderson awoke, brought back to consciousness by Singing Tree's growl at her son.

As though pulled by wires, James Henderson sat up from the waist and shrieked. She was at his side with one swift movement, a thin dirty hand on his shoulder.

'There is nothing to fear. Lie down and know you are safe.'

Henderson looked at her with wild eyes, then swept the room with his stare like a man expecting attack. He gasped when he saw Walks Alone looking up at him with a furrowed and solemn brow.

Singing Tree followed his terrified gaze. 'That is Walks Alone, our son. He is here also. He has fetched wood for your fire.'

For a moment Henderson was lost. Where was he? Why was he in bed in the daylight, still partially clothed, with two Indians in his room?

And then he remembered Alexander. He fell back onto his hard pillow, and covered his face with his hands. Dear Jesus, he was sick. Sick and alone. He sobbed beneath his fingers, and Singing Tree threw her son a glance, nodding her head at the water boiling on the stove.

Walks Alone stood up and went to the task. He pulled his hand into the big sleeve of his wool jacket to protect his fingers from the hot metal and carried the steaming vessel to his mother.

'Put it there.'

He laid the dull copper pan on the wooden floor at her feet.

Singing Tree opened a small leather bag and took crushed green and brown foliage from it, which she scattered on the surface of the water. Instantly, the room was filled with a thick acidic aroma which made Henderson appear from behind his hands, blink and attempt to sit up again in alarm. The small dark woman looked at him with a half smile. 'It is for your brow, Henderson. You do not have to drink it.'

Walks Alone opened his mouth to laugh but he did so without noise. It was a strange sight, this earnest little boy, making the motions of mirth with his face, dark eyes crinkled, but his breath coming in short soundless panting bursts.

Henderson looked at the couple as thought they were his tormentors, not his comforters, as the woman bent to soak a piece of cloth in her pungent brew. 'Where Hunting Wolf? Why . . . ?'

'He is building a sweat-lodge. He will call the spirits and the Grandfathers to help him.'

Henderson closed his eyes and concentrated on fighting the sharp pains of nausea in his stomach, caused only in part by Singing Tree's aromatic concoction. His confusion was exhausting and he struggled with his eyes closed to bring together the pieces of himself that were scattered and torn.

Sick. Sick, and now being nursed by two dirty, alien individuals, who although uninvited, were welcome to Henderson for their simple human presence.

The brain was a cruel organ when it was sick, he mused. Now, with the weak grey light filtering into the cabin through slits in the wood and a clogged, drift-banked window, he could see how it had played warped tricks on him. Alexander was dead. He had never lived or breathed, or died, in this cabin. Only in the fevered imagination of his surviving brother did that little heart still beat, those liquid eyes still implore.

In the imagination of his murdering brother.

No.

He opened his eyes and clenched his fists around the frayed edges of his blanket. James Henderson wanted to be in the wide brass bed of his townhouse in Edinburgh. He thought of the soft embroidered quilt and the lace-edged pillows that Meg always removed from the bed when James or she were ill. How sumptuous it would be to sink into that luxury, with the fire going in the hearth and the maid bringing tea. Even Meg's contempt would be better than this hell of loneliness and despair.

Sweet Jesus, was God testing him? Was he being punished?

The man of reason was calling to him over his abyss of fear and he held a hand out to it.

He was suffering from a fever and Hunting Wolf had sent his wife to tend him in that fever. He was not mad. The world was not ending.

He sat up and tried to compose his face and recall his grasp of Siouan. 'Hunting Wolf?'

Singing Tree wrung out the cloth and pressed it to his head, forcing him to lie back down. 'He is strong. He will win.'

The boy looked on with eyes like a woodland animal.

To avoid the closeness of Singing Tree's pretty face, which made the man in the Scottish minister uncomfortable, he turned to the child. 'You help your father?'

The boy looked back silently. Singing Tree answered. 'Walks Alone does not speak. Not since . . .' She broke off, looked at the boy quickly, and then back at her charge. 'He is a shaman child. He needs no words.'

A *shaman child*. Little wonder that Henderson's brain was fevered, surrounded as he was by so much primitive fear and superstition. The very air he breathed was charged with it. His resolve must be to avoid its seduction.

Hunting Wolf's wife lifted the cloth from his head, pulled back Henderson's blanket and began to undo his shirt. He grabbed her hand round the wrist with a roughness he had not intended, but she looked at him with barely disguised mirth again. 'The balsam must be laid on the skin of the whole body. Is it the cold you fear or your nakedness?'

Henderson was reddening. Her proximity, and the physical link that his hand made on her thin wrist, was already approaching what he would have classed as improper. But to have her strip him and lay her hands on his body would be an outrage. He loosened his grip on her wrist, and wrestled for vocabulary. 'No. You must not,' was all he could manage.

Singing Tree pulled her hand away, kept her eyes on his florid face and bent to dip her cloth in the steaming water again. 'White men are shy like women are they not?'

Walks Alone was smiling. She looked once at her son, then again at Henderson, who had curled his body into a defensive arc.

'The Kinchuinicks believe the heart and the penis to be the sacred parts of a man Henderson. You should be shamed by neither. We have a saying, that a man gives life with his penis and lives life with the heart.' She snorted to herself at some hidden thought. 'Though I have seen men who live life for pleasure only and give life with nothing.'

Henderson's high colour had left him, but he was unchanged in his resolve. 'I not Kinchuinick.'

She shrugged, smiled, and wrung out the cloth. 'Then it will be the head only. The heart and penis will have to soothe themselves.'

He lay back, relieved, letting the woman continue pressing and dabbing at his forehead and then noticed that the boy's attention had returned to something he had stuffed down his beaded belt and was now retrieving surreptitiously. It was his crucifix, the beautiful mahogany and ivory gift that his father had given him on his graduation day.

'You like?' He gestured weakly to the object in the boy's hand.

Walks Alone registered alarm at being caught and looked to his mother for reproach or defence. She offered neither, dropping the cloth back into the cooling water to administer more attention to the pale man.

The boy looked back at Henderson and nodded.

'It is son of . . . it is Great Spirit. He come here and we live because he die.'

Walks Alone stared at Henderson's mouth as he said this, trying to make sense of the words, and failed. He looked back at the figure of Christ as if it would speak more clearly, and when it did not, to his mother. Her interests were elsewhere.

'Does the balsam water soothe your fever?'

Henderson looked into her black, almond-shaped eyes. Although it stung the skin, making it tingle, it was soothing his brow, there was little doubt. Somehow he felt more calm now, his thoughts beginning to recover from their turbulence. 'Yes. Thank you.'

She shrugged in reply as though his thanks were of no consequence. The boy still clutched his precious crucifix. Henderson very much wanted to bring this young soul to Christ, but the base human in him wanted his keepsake back. He could read the child like a book, the face waiting to be told he could have the trinket, but Henderson could not bear to lose it. He held his hand out for the cross and slowly the boy gave it up into his big pale palm.

The minister's fears were creeping on his flesh again. This strange couple would not be with him forever. And then what? What would come with the night, and with his dreams?

James Henderson's fingers closed around the wood and he held it tightly to his breast. He expected the boy to have a tantrum now. He could be no more than eight or nine years old.

Instead, those large dark eyes fixed on James with an expression that was adult and wise, an unmistakable expression of compassion. He put his small brown hand out and laid it on top of the man's fingers that held the cross, then put the other hand to his own heart.

Henderson felt a phantom sun on his face. He could smell the delicate scent of heather blowing on the hill above his uncle's croft. Sweet, like honey, filling his nostrils and his lungs.

There was the faint drone of bees rustling in the tiny dry bell-shaped blooms, as though they could smell what Henderson could, that thrilling sharp tingle of autumn in the air. And in the distance was the sound of Rory barking. Oh, it was so sweet. So sweet. He closed his eyes, and his dreams filled up with hills of purple and green, and the warm damp smell of the beloved collie's muddy coat.

'A shaman child,' he said in English as he drifted away, and Walks Alone smiled at his mother.

29

'Relax those for me, would you?'

Sam's toes twitched under the doctor's hands and he looked over at Katie to see if she was smiling at the ludicrous spectacle of her husband having his feet tickled.

She was not. Katie Hunt was sitting low in a red plastic chair, gazing at the frosted-glass window as though there were a view to see. Her arms were crossed, the hands clutching their opposite shoulders in a hug that was more defensive than relaxed.

But then why should she be relaxed? It was a shitty day.

This morning, breakfast had been an ordeal. That first meal and meeting of the day for the Hunt family had always been a sack of laughs. Sam usually held Billy's pop tarts between a thumb and forefinger and pinched his nose with the other hand in a gesture of disgust as he dropped them into the toaster with a retching noise. That never failed to make Billy laugh. And the ice-box magnets. Billy and Jess loved moving those dumb magnets around, and she and Sam would laugh dutifully when the Mr Fruity magnet was shifted to stand on his head on top of some innocent human posing seriously on a postcard.

Not this morning. This morning Billy hadn't come down for breakfast at all. Bart came down all right, hungry and looking for his pound and half of chuck steak. But no Billy. When Katie had called up stairs again, she'd glimpsed him sitting fully-dressed on the landing. She was about to call up at him to get his butt down here, when she saw the look on that little face, framed between the white wooden spindles of the banister. He was frightened. She'd gone upstairs to him then, and gently put an arm round his shoulders.

'What's up, Billy Boy? Not coming down for something to eat?'

And he'd looked up at her and said, 'Has Dad gone yet?'

A simple, innocent question. So why did it strike a terror into Katie's heart that made her hold her breath? 'No lamb, he's still here. You can see him before he goes to work.'

Billy had leapt to his feet and yelled 'No!', before running back into his room and slamming the door. She'd heard him sobbing behind that wooden door, and had stood looking dumbly at the wooden barrier between them, with its poster of Sonic the Hedgehog grinning malevolently back at her with a two-fingered salute.

Sam had looked concerned when Katie returned to the kitchen, but accepted her explanation that Billy wanted to be left alone.

Would he have accepted that a month ago? Or would he have been up there poking his son in the ribs and asking what was up? Sam had looked like he was someplace other than the kitchen, so she'd let it be, battling back her darkest fears and misery as she watched her coffee go cold. And the three of them, Katie, Sam and Jess, had sat in a silence broken only by Jess's occasional babbling, until Sam had left the house.

Billy had heard the door close and had crept carefully and tentatively into the kitchen. It made her freeze, to see her son so desperate to avoid his father. The same boy who would fight to accompany Sam to the bathroom if he let him. Could a dream be so real? And what had happened in that dream?

Katie Hunt was adrift, and it felt bad. Today, Sam was like a stranger trying to be her husband. He said the same stuff he usually did, smiled at her from time to time with those white even teeth and kissed her when she came to pick him up and drive him to the doctor. But it wasn't Sam. Or more accurately, she wished it wasn't. Her Sam didn't lie, or frighten their son, or look hunted and dark when he thought he was unobserved.

She could feel him now, trying to catch her eye in this small beige surgery, and yet she couldn't turn to meet his gaze.

'Okay, I'm just gonna prick the sole of your foot here. Just relax.'

Sam braced himself. Doctor Alan Harris did the business, made an *uh-huh* sound, and put Sam's foot gently back down on the vinyl bed he was lying on. 'Okay Mr Hunt, you can put your shoes back on. What I'm going to say is that I want you to get checked out by Neurology in Calgary.'

Katie sat up and lost interest in the opaque window. She uncrossed her arms and leant forward.

Her action had the effect of making the doctor turn to address her, as though Sam were a child in her care.

'I can't find anything wrong with Mr Hunt's reflexes, and there's no immediate evidence of epilepsy. But blackouts of the severity you're describing need more investigation, and I think all three of us here would be a lot happier if we just get the possibilities of any blockages on the brain cleared up.'

Sam swung his feet off the vinyl bed, catching the white human-length piece of tissue that covered it with a heel and tearing it.

'How soon will they see me?' he asked, recapturing Harris's attention, and peeling the white paper from his foot.

'I'll get on it this afternoon, and I'm going to ask that they see you within the week.'

The doctor crossed the room to wash his hands, and the running water from the chrome hooped tap accentuated the silence between the people in the room.

Katie looked at Sam then and the sight of his face creased with a defeat she seldom saw woke her from her torpor of self-pity. He might be sick. Her darling Sam. What if it were a tumour? It wasn't just her life falling apart. It was his. Katie was awash with guilt and she smiled across at her husband with a heat they both recognized. Sam kept the smile as he bent to put on his socks and boots.

Harris wiped his hands and motioned to the door with his head. 'Okay. If you want to sort yourself out through there Mr Hunt, I'm just going to check Mrs Hunt on a few points. Just in case we got a virus here.'

Sam nodded, picked up his remaining boot and headed out the door. Katie looked puzzled but as Harris sat down with that searching look in his eyes, she started to get worried. There were no points to check on. He was going to tell her something that Sam wasn't to hear. She knew it.

'Your husband doesn't drink, does he, Mrs Hunt?'

'That's right.'

'I have to ask you this, but it's for medical reasons and its purely confidential.'

She raised an eyebrow.

'Does he use any abusive substances?'

'You mean like Kraft TV dinners?'

Not funny. The doctor ignored it.

'Does your husband take drugs?'

'No. Of course not.'

'Are you sure?'

'Of course I'm sure.'

'You're aware that unlike alcohol abuse which is impossible to conceal, drug abuse can remain a secret even from those closest to the abuser.'

The abused always becomes the abuser. God. Get that dumb thought out your head, Katie.

'You're saying this because he's Kinchuinick, right?'

Alan Harris looked at her like a stone with eyes. 'Yes. That's one reason I'm saying it.'

'He doesn't take drugs. Believe me. I'd know.'

Another pause and the doctor sat back in his chair.

'I'm sorry if you're offended. I'm also sure you'd rather be offended than be a widow through wrong diagnoses.'

That hit home. Sure, she could live with offence. She could never live without Sam. She nodded, and Harris continued.

'It's just that, as I'm sure you know, the Kinchuinicks use a great variety of drugs in their religion and ceremonies, most of which are hallucinogenic and extremely dangerous. You know also that their purpose is to bring about the kind of blackouts your husband is experiencing in order to allow communion with the spirits.'

'You're teaching your grandma to spit tobacco here doctor. I write about this stuff at the museum. Remember?'

'So we can rule drug abuse out.'

'Yes.'

'His behaviour hasn't been erratic, secretive or out of character?'

She touched her nose lightly.

'No.'

Harris studied her for a second then tapped the table top with a finger. 'Okay. I'll call you with the appointment when I hook up with Calgary. Everything else okay with the family?'

'Yeah. We just want Sam better.'

'Sure.'

He stood and showed her out of the door. Sam was in the outer room, both boots on, his hands clasped between his legs as he waited innocently for the conspirators. Katie took his wide brown hand, and unlike the way they came in, they left together like lovers. She was a weakling to doubt him. There would be an explanation for Billy's behaviour. An explanation for Sam's blackouts. An explanation for the police watching him like wolves smelling an elk. As they left the surgery down snowy steps, and saw the plain clothes RCs in the brown car start their engine, she hoped the explanations would start coming soon.

It was still dark when Craig woke. He lay there in the blackness letting the sharp pain of being alone that always hit him first thing subside into a dull ache. It was hard to get up this morning. He knew what was waiting for him. Nothing. Becker and his team would be milling around, making statements to the press and trying to find reasons to arrest Sam Hunt. Meanwhile, he would be expected to get on with the important business of making sure ski-theft was stamped out in Silver.

Craig McGee was not Eddie Murphy. He wasn't going to take a couple of days leave and solve the crime with a zany Indian side-kick and a blonde love-interest. He was a quiet, methodical policeman and he wanted to solve this systematically and officially. He wanted to answer the riddles, but most of all, he wanted the killing to stop.

This was the best time to think. The dark and the warmth, and that soft bridge between consciousness and sleep, was a safe place to look at hard things. Thoughts were like runny syrup in this cocoon of heat, dark and quiet. Must buy cat food; Sylvia; is it still snowing?; that dumb TV show about a news crew; what's it called? *ENG*? blonde woman camera operator my ass; Sylvia; haven't bought any clothes for about six months; Daniel Hawk should be more than a constable; mouth ulcer again, just under my tongue; Sylvia; that kid.

That kid.

His thoughts were focused involuntarily.

What, apart from a blade the size of a sword, could have chopped half his head off so cleanly? How the hell did a man escape without leaving foot or ski prints in that thigh-deep snow? The animals couldn't do it. There were deer prints all round the carcass like it had come sniffing round to see what all the mess was, but not a single mark from a human foot. He'd gotten the trees checked out. No broken branches, and the snow was found to be undisturbed on all the branches. Any aerial escape, any monkey-like acrobatics would have left a trail in the trees that would have been easier to see than prints on the ground. And the brains and the blood. Jesus. So much blood.

In other words, the atrocity was impossible. It couldn't have happened without breaking the laws of physics. It made him feel cold as he admitted it to himself for the first time. Just like Joe's death. Impossible.

Deer prints. Would a deer come near a carcass? A crow maybe. But a deer? And when was the last time anybody saw a deer on the ski-side of the mountain? Craig thought he would like to have another look at where those tracks started and ended. The team had photographed the whole area in the trees for at least a five hundred yard radius, so tracking the animal's progress should be easy.

A murderer walking on sticks with deer print shoes was crazy, but it wasn't as crazy as a murderer who could fly. He realized he was clutching at thin air and squirmed in frustration beneath the covers, remembering that the whole preposterous case was out of his hands.

Fuck Edmonton. He'd look at the photos anyhow. A long look at them later with Hawk. Craig turned over in bed and stared at a ribbon of orange light on the wall that had sneaked through his curtains from the street lamp outside.

There was no such thing as an impossible crime. He tried to sleep some more on that thought, but sleep was tricky with both your eyes wide open and staring.

'. . . And the proper name is prism. P.R.I.S.M.' Miss Root scratched the word on the board behind her and stood back to admire it. 'Okay? Prism. So light of all colours travels at the same speed, but just as there are big waves and little ripples in the sea, so light of different colours comes in waves of varying size . . .'

Billy stared at the back of Andy Weiss's head. There was a big zit there on his neck, just above the collar of his sweatshirt. Billy watched as Weiss shifted about, the stiff stitched collar threatening to burst the zit each time they met.

'. . . and when it passes through one side of the triangular prism and comes out another, it's checked and spread out, like the rolling waves on a beach, so that all the colours appear in a rainbow band.'

The fabric won. It sliced the top off the zit and released some pale yellow liquid into Weiss's collar. Billy watched miserably as the hand of the zit owner crept round to the back of his neck and massaged the new wound.

'Can anyone name the colours of the rainbow and put them in order?'

Agnes Root stood with a pleasant, expectant look on her face as she surveyed her class of eighteen pupils. She glanced at her wristwatch surreptitiously to see how long it would be before lunch, and her heart skipped a little when she remembered her legs round Martin, when he had given her that thin gold-plated watch last week. She would call him at lunch-time. But lunch-time was a long way off. There was painting to get in next. The smile never left her lips as she lifted an elegant hand to Tony Spender. 'Yeah. Tony. Want to have a go?'

Tony pushed his spectacles up on his squat nose and cleared his throat. 'Uh, red, yellow, orange, green, purple, blue . . . uh . . . that's it. I think.'

'All right. Good. But you missed one and this is the order they appear in when we see them in the rainbow. Write it down with me.'

She turned to the board and started to scrawl the words below her drawing of a triangular prism. Heads in front of Billy bent to their task of copying the names of the colours in their notepads. Billy carried on staring at Andy Weiss's neck.

Miss Root turned again to watch her class write down the colours. Only one head was up. Billy Hunt. 'Billy? Want to write these down please?'

He continued to stare.

'Did you hear me, Billy? Write these down please.'

A few heads looked up this time, their faces expectant, hoping for a confrontation. Billy continued looking at that neck, with its red raw zit and pus-stained collar.

Agnes Root walked to Billy's table and bent down to his level. 'Are you feeling all right, Billy?'

Billy nodded, not looking at his teacher.

'Well, do you want to write down what I've put on the board then, please.'

Billy just stared at the neck. The young woman scanned his face for a few seconds, searching for any mischievous defiance and saw none.

'Are you ill?'

No response.

A child by the window sniggered and Miss Root turned and threw the culprit a look that stopped the laugh like a bell jar on a candle. She turned back to the small boy and spoke softly this time. 'Aren't you going to speak to me, Billy? I'm asking you a question.'

Billy turned his head and looked at his teacher. His liquid black eyes held the expression of a much older person and they had a bruised quality that dismayed Agnes Root. He opened his mouth to say something and then closed it. This was not a rude and naughty child. This was a disturbed one. Billy Hunt was normally a lively, funny, spunky little guy. She didn't like to think about what might be wrong. But she'd deal with it later. His teacher put a hand out and laid it on his shoulder. 'It's okay. You chill out for a minute.'

She stood up and returned to her board, facing the class with a forced jollity to cover Billy's distress. 'Alrighty then. Let's see if we can paint some pictures on the theme of prisms. Think of rainbows and all those bright colours, and let's see what we come up with. Paint monitors please.'

Little bodies sprang up and got busy with the hardware of making paintings. Before they turned the neat pile of painting equipment into chaos, Miss Root rescued a piece of cartridge paper, a white plastic palette with big circular indentations, and a wide soft brush and carried them over to Billy.

'Do you think you could do a picture sweetheart? Huh?'

Billy slid the paper towards him silently and nodded.

'Good. Go get some lovely colours for your palette then, Billy.' She ruffled his hair and left him to it. She had a class to watch and if she didn't watch them closely they'd paint the walls, their faces and every flat surface in the room. Her watch said there wasn't much more of this and she sat down at her desk to dream of Martin's mouth.

30

Sometimes – correction – lots of times, the human race made him sick. That RCMP incident trailer, sitting there in the middle of the ski car park, ought to have kept the public a million miles away from this resort. Did it, fuck. The car park was full and Eric Sindon was watching three of his guys trying to squeeze more cars in behind the shop loading-bay. So they liked to ski with the scent of blood in their nostrils, did they? Or was the fact that news crews were nearly outnumbering skiers providing the big attraction?

As if to answer his question he saw a cop being interviewed by a CBC crew out in front of the lodge, while behind him a family in crap ski-suits took an unnaturally long time to slide past. Their tiny dumb attempt at immortality. Get in the shot. *Look kids! A camera! Get in the fucking shot.*

What did they think it would gain them? That maybe in the year two thousand and ninety Martians would examine all the earth's news footage and those grinning morons behind the interviewee would be picked out and discussed? Sad, sad, sad.

Sadder still was Pasqual gloating that everything was okay after all. 'You see you worry too much, Eric. When did you see a week-day car park like this huh? And look at the bitching snow!'

But this wouldn't last. It was day after a death hysteria. And if the cops didn't catch this guy soon, or if he killed again, Silver would be as empty as a kid's party át Michael Jackson's.

Eric thought the cops were wrong to let them open for business immediately but Pasqual had argued that they always carried on after any death on the mountain. Company policy. The time that guy from Norway had wiped himself out at forty-five miles per hour straight into the pylon in front of the whole quad-line the resort hadn't even blinked. The bits were scraped off, loaded into the meat wagon and away before the screaming had stopped. Surely murder was different? When people said skiing was dangerous, they didn't mean you had to watch your back for a psycho who'd slice your head in two.

He sighed and turned to walk back into the lodge just as a rusty Toyota drew up and spat out Sam Hunt. The car park guys were waving their arms and shouting *Move it!* to the driver and Sam barely had time to wave goodbye as the vehicle slithered away.

Sindon stopped to greet him.

'Hi, Sam.'

He looked up at his boss standing on the concrete steps. 'Mr Sindon.'

'Feeling better?'

'Yeah.'

'They catch you last night then?'

Sam stared at him with horror. What did he mean? His mouth went tight, and inside his fleecy his heart did a flip. 'Excuse me?'

'The cops. They were coming to see you.'

Sam breathed a relieved plume of steam through his nose, and kicked at the snow. 'Yeah. They came. Don't think I helped much.'

'Uh-huh.'

Sam changed the subject, although the subject was all around them, an all-singing, all-dancing murder hunt.

'Am I lodge-side or up at the top station this afternoon?'

Eric took his hands out of his pockets and turned up his collar. 'Neither Sam. We have to talk seriously about a complaint from a customer yesterday. Did you think it would just go away?'

'Guess not.'

'Grab a coffee. My office in five.'

'Okay.'

Eric walked into the lodge and left Sam breathing in the cold air, watching him go. A glance to his left, at a brown car pulling up behind the taped area at the incident trailer, told Sam he still had his two companions with him. Let them watch, he thought. They could watch him as he lost his mind, his job, and in his worst nightmares, his family. Enjoy, he thought bitterly, and marched up the steps towards his beating.

* * *

The office was still full of RCMPs. Christ knows what they were doing with that trailer when most of them seemed to be hanging around here making calls and scribbling in note books. Only one of the cops looked up when Eric crossed the office and Betsy rolled her eyes to heaven in a call for sympathy as he passed her desk. Sitconski still wasn't at his. Eric stopped and backed up to Betsy.

'He didn't show?'

She shook her head.

Eric raised an eyebrow, carried on to his office and shut the door behind him. The absence of their weird office assistant was no sorrow to him, but it was interesting. There was something wrong about Sitconski. Maybe the police should know he didn't come in. Mind you, they must have grilled him last night, and his disappearance was not exactly front page material. He seemed to come and go as he pleased. Eric didn't hire the creep or he'd have kicked his butt out of here on day two, but Pasqual either didn't notice his erratic attendance, or she didn't care. He knew she just wanted to get into his pants.

So what was it that was wrong about the guy, because *wrong* was the word that formed itself in Sindon's mind. Eric sat down on his revolving chair, swung around for a moment and let himself think about that. There was something about Moses Sitconski's features that bothered him, even from the first time he saw him. They were plain, maybe handsome, but . . .

He rubbed the stubble on his chin. Yeah. That was one thing all right. No beard growth. His face looked like it was made of something else other than skin. Crazy. But yes, that was it. It looked like a pretend face. A kid's face. Eric caught sight of his own sour, ageing face in the window reflection and realized how jealous that one would sound to a sober listener.

Tough. It was true. And he could never quite remember that face after Sitconski had left. All that was left was a vague impression. Did bland features do that to a person?

A negative personality. That's what the management assertiveness course that Pasqual had forced him to attend, taught all the way through that waste of a week. He pictured that stupid red-lipped woman in the blue suit that had brayed at them in the banqueting suite of the Balfour Hotel, and he winced.

Don't have a negative personality, ladies and gentlemen. Make them remember you when you leave the room. She said it daily, wagging her finger with its painted nails at them like they were mentally deficient, which of course they were to have parted with six hundred dollars for the privilege of listening to her bullshit.

A negative personality test. Moses Sitconski would have failed that one all right. Eric could hardly picture his features accurately at all, even now.

And his temperature. That guy just didn't feel the cold. He never came in with a rosy face or stamped his feet or blew on his hands. Eric didn't like that. He hadn't really added all these things up before, and it was making him uneasy. Because there were other things too, and for some reason he didn't really want to think about them. No, he didn't. A knock at his door saved him from having to.

'Come.'

Sam stepped in. Eric waved a hand for him to sit down, and he pulled the chair out, sat down gracefully, flicked his hair back and stared at Sindon. Now here's a man with a positive personality, thought Eric. Hard not to notice six feet of handsome Indian with eyes that bored you to the wall.

Sindon sat back and swung a little more.

'You first, Sam.'

Sam unzipped his jacket and ran a hand through his hair.

'Look. Mr Sindon. I've been sick, you know? That's why I just got back from the quack. The guy was a jerk and I lost it. Now if you want to step on me, take a number and get in line. I've kind of had enough.'

'Some apology.'

'I'm not going to apologize. I should have stuck his skis up his flabby ass.'

'This is the . . . what is it? . . . fifth time?'

Sam shrugged.

'It's a service industry, Sam. We serve the public. You know that. You can't do your job barking at paying customers like they just kicked your cat.'

'Guess not.'

Eric sighed and leaned forward on his desk. 'Look. I know the cops are bugging you 'cause you were there when the kid was killed, and . . .'

Sam's face hardened slightly.

'. . . and you're an Indian. Not exactly RCMP mascot material.'

Sam's face softened again. But not much.

'So I'm gonna let this one go. But I warn you, and I fucking mean this, if you shit on any of our customers again I'll drag you to the door myself and fire a shotgun at your ass. Understand?'

'So no Happy Smile Staff bonus?'

'Don't push me.'

Sam shifted in his seat, looked down and floor, and spoke quietly. 'Thanks.'

'You're welcome.'

'So top station or lodge-side?'

'Top station. It's as cold as a whore's heart up there and it's all you deserve.'

'Right.'

He got up to leave.

'So did you see anything yesterday that's going to help the Mounties get their man?'

Sam looked dolefully over his shoulder. 'No.'

Eric made an upward nod, and swung away from Sam on his chair. Sam closed the door softly.

That wasn't true. He did see something that the Mounties wanted. He saw it every morning when he looked in the bathroom mirror.

He walked through the office and felt eyes follow him across the corridor of oatmeal carpet. There was a small pause as he closed the outer door, then the bustle of noise continued as before, and a policeman got up and knocked on Eric Sindon's door.

Behind the till, Margaret was eating cake. She tucked it out of sight as Katie came through the doors and pushed through the turnstile.

'Hi!'

Her greeting was thick, from the spongy confection sticking to the roof of her mouth.

'Hi, Margaret. Busy?'

Margaret opted for the easy option and just shook her head. It gave her time to swallow. Katie stopped at the counter and tidied a pile of flyers advertising the new Japanese restaurant on Carlisle Street.

'How bad? Two people, three people, or no people?'

The cake was on its way to Margaret's stomach. She could speak

again. 'All day we've had eight. There's one woman upstairs. That's
it.'

'Any messages?'

'No.'

'Denholm still in?'

'Gone to his aunt's. She asked him to cut wood. His uncle's in bed
with flu.'

'You know, Margaret, it's a challenge being a high-powered executive, but sometimes the stress is unbearable.'

Margaret said, 'Hey,' and put her hands out like a Jewish mamma,
as Katie smiled and walked away, taking a path through the stuffed
bears to get to her office. She opened the glass-panelled door and
threw down her bag on the chair.

She was glad the museum was empty. There was a lot to think
about and she didn't have the energy today to introduce snotty-nosed
kids to the miracles of fossilization, or phone up the computer contrac-
tors for the tenth time to complain about her screen flicker. Katie
needed space to start a bit of damage limitation. She went to the
window and looked out as she peeled off her coat. There wasn't much
of a view. It looked out onto the yard of a car hire company, but if
you looked past their brick wall and chicken wire, you could just
make out the big lodgepole pines on Main Street. She dropped her
coat on the chair with the bag, crossed her arms and stood gazing at
three snow-covered, un-hired Buicks.

Okay lady, she thought, let's get it all in proportion here. Number
one. Do you trust Sam?

Yes.

Number two. Will Sam die?

No. Not if I can help it.

Number three.

Will everything soon be back to normal?

Yes.

There. Nothing to it really. Except she knew that every single one
of those black and white questions and answers had a million grey
areas. Little niggles and twisting implications that would send her
spinning back into that pit of confusion and apprehension again. But
this is what she was built for. She was strong. Sam Hunt had made
her strong when she thought she would break and here she was letting
him down when he needed her most, by doubting him and backing

off. Not good enough Katie Hunt. Not by a long way. Kids were weird. Billy could be upset by all kinds of stuff. Nothing would let her believe that Sam would hurt his children in any way. He fathered those kids like they were the last two hopes for the human race.

She scratched vacantly at her ear and decided to do a tour of the museum to clear her head. There was work of sorts on the desk, but it could wait half an hour.

She opened the door and breathed in that hot woody, floor polish smell that pervaded the museum and made for the stairs to the balcony. They'd catch the guy soon. They had to. She couldn't bear the thought of those two cops following Sam around like he was a criminal. But at least if the guy struck again soon, while they were watching Sam, it would get her husband off the hook.

She paused on the stairs, her hand on the banister, stunned at the evil of her thought. So she would like to see someone else die to clear her husband's name? Jesus, Katie. This business was turning her into a monster. What if had been Billy or Jess skiing up there, huh? How'd you like that psycho to cut them up?

She put a hand to her temples and took a breath. Katie didn't wish anyone dead. What was wrong with her? That ugly, warped thought had just floated in from nowhere and she would never entertain it again. She pulled herself up the stairs, flushed from her shame.

All quiet. So quiet that Katie's boots made a squeaking noise on the highly polished floor as she moved across to the glass cases. Katie leant against the wooden rail running round the balcony, gazed up the fifteen-foot length of the Indian artefact case and sighed. Funny how she had never questioned her happiness before. She thought it had somehow been her right, that she'd earned it after suffering with Tom. But had she suffered? Think of the parents of that kid. Think of Estelle Reader. That was suffering. She'd never really suffered at all.

Something caught her eye, moving on the edge of her vision, through the glass of the case. She turned her head in curiosity.

Katie's mouth opened and her blood beat in her ears.

For one fraction of a second, a beat in time, Katie Hunt thought she saw a body, a substance, a moving entity reflected in the end panel of glass. A ridiculous illusion. It was the fragmented image of something horrible, something dark and fluid and insubstantial, that seemed to have nothing but jaws and teeth . . . and . . .

A woman in a dark coat stepped out from behind the far end of the case. Katie blinked at her, dazed by her foolish misinterpretation of the play of light and shadow, in this cluttered reflective balcony.

The blonde woman seemed unaware of Katie's fright, and flashed her a smile as she carried on slowly down the case, hands in pockets, looking at the Kinchuinick religious artefacts.

Katie walked away from the balcony and stood where she could see the whole length of the case from the front. The blonde woman turned round and smiled again, looking Katie quickly up and down with two pale ice-blue eyes.

'Good display, huh?'

Katie's mouth was still dry from her fright. She moistened it. 'Thanks. It needs some attention though.'

The blonde woman, tall and pretty, took her hand out her pockets and crossed them in front of her. 'Well then! You work here?'

'Yeah. I'm the curator. Glad you're enjoying it.'

The woman turned back to the case and pointed, tapping the glass. 'This is great. These things are really old.'

Katie took the cue and walked over to join her customer, looking into the case where she pointed; medicine bundles, animal bone amulets and some sacred hides painted with the symbols of animal and bird spirits from an eighteenth century sweat-lodge.

'They are. Most are Kinchuinick, but a couple of the bone amulets are Cree and Assiniboine. Much, much older.'

'How'd you get 'em?'

Katie laughed, relaxing now, and enjoying the interest of a visitor as she always did. 'With great difficulty. I negotiated with a Kinchuinick elder for months to get a lot of this. It was just rotting away in a rug chest in the guy's cabin. When he finally agreed we brought him here and he blessed the display with some prayers. It was neat.'

The woman still smiling, shook her head and said, 'A wonderful thing, faith.'

Katie smiled warmly, gazing into the case. 'Yeah. It is, isn't it?'

'Are you the Indian specialist here then?'

Katie laughed again. 'Kind of. Take my job so seriously I married one.'

There was a subtle and sudden change of air pressure around Katie, that movement of oxygen that can be felt when you stand inside a building beside a revolving door. Not enough to ruffle the hair or lift the corner of a stray newspaper, but enough to caress your cheek with its progress. Katie noted it and ignored it. It was gone as swiftly as it came.

The woman was fixing her with a huge grin, her head cocked to one side – the kind of grin that Mormons turn on like a switch when you open the door. The aquamarine eyes were crinkled in that smile but her smooth skin was devoid of wrinkles. Lucky gal, thought Katie. Try raising two kids and see if you've still got time for a moisturising routine.

'Fabulous! I'm Marlene Sitconski by the way. Pleased to meet you.' She held out a pale hand.

Katie felt somehow that she didn't want to touch that hand. But manners always overcame inhibition with her and she took it and shook it lightly. Cold. Really cold. Get some gloves, lady.

'Right. Pleased to meet you too. Katie Hunting Wolf.'

Marlene Sitconski's eyes flashed with some enigmatic emotion for a second and then the light in them was gone. Katie stared at her. What on earth did she say that for, for Christ's sake?

Hunting Wolf? Who did she think she was? Kevin Costner? But it was her name, really, wasn't it? Whether Sam wanted her to know or not, it was her name. She felt lightheaded and a little sick. This whole afternoon was becoming too weird to handle. Maybe she was getting ill too. That's all they needed. Katie wanted to go and sit down quietly somewhere and stop seeing shadows and feeling draughts and telling strangers she was someone she wasn't.

'That's a very romantic name. '

'Yes. I think so,' said Katie weakly. There was a buzzing in her head, and she put out a hand to lean on the case.

'You know, it's amazing how these people's dignity and nobility has survived. We owe these people a debt we can't repay.'

Katie was feeling giddy now, and her hand was leaving a cloudy greasemark where it was pushing against the glass. Was that her father who just said that? It sounded like him. No. No, don't be stupid. It was this Marlene woman who'd said it. This visitor she was talking to. That was her job. Talking to visitors. How they sucked you dry, these visitors. Sucked and sucked, like hungry, black, pulsating leeches, until they had everything inside you, and still they sucked until your core was bone-dry and you crumbled like dust.

What? What the fuck was she thinking about?

Katie put her free hand to her hot head. 'I'm sorry. You're going to have to excuse me. I'm feeling a bit faint.'

Marlene Sitconski looked concerned, said *Oh*, and put a hand out to Katie's elbow. Katie stepped back before the hand could touch her sleeve.

'I'm sorry.'

She turned and lurched away, fumbling for the banister as she stumbled down the wooden steps. Marlene Sitconski watched her go, standing motionless until she heard the door of Katie's office bang shut, then she turned back to the case and put her cool hand on the glass with a smile.

31

This time, the force of the spirit's visit blew him onto his back and held him there. Calvin lay panting on the floor, his teeth gritted in pain as he fought for control of his naked sweat-soaked body. In his good hand he gripped the crude pipe he had fashioned, clutching it fiercely against the potency of the spirit's weight and wind, which threatened to tear it from his fingers.

Calvin's chest was heaving with the effort of staying alive. Inside the sweat lodge, the temperature was that of a furnace, but the atmosphere was not the agent of his imminent destruction. It was the presence of this rogue spirit who was finding him unworthy. He groaned a prayer, begging for the strength to endure the onslaught, and writhed in his torment as the pressing on his torso became unbearable. A rib was on the point of snapping. He felt it bowing under the pressure, and arched his head back in agony, concentrating on staying conscious. To swoon now would be disaster. He cried out, bellowing like a bull, in a voice that would have chilled any who heard it. But there was no one to hear it at all. No one for at least fifteen miles.

Then, like the first sounds of rain on a roof, the beating of wings came, softly at first, then building until the noise filled the lodge, thrumming against the canvas, the air moving under their phantom flapping, and the weight was lifted from Calvin's chest like a stone being rolled off a cliff. His eyes flew open and he fought back the bile that was rising in his throat.

'Thank you,' he whispered, coughing as he lay on his back staring through the steam at the tight blue canvas roof above the willow branches.

He had passed this new test, and now the trick was to stay conscious long enough to welcome the Thunder Spirit formally, whose invisible wings were beating so loudly now that Calvin felt his ear drums move with the pressure.

The shaman tried to sit up but his head was as heavy as an anvil. He must sit up and put more water on the hot stones before the temperature dropped. He tried again, and this time managed to raise himself onto one elbow, grunting at the effort, and feeling the stab of his bruised rib-cage as he bent his body.

He leaned across the floor with his gap-fingered hand, grabbed the bark container of water and with a flick released an arc of water onto the rocks, reeling back as the wall of hissing steam hit him like a fist.

But it was in time. The spirit was still with him in the lodge.

Calvin waited for a few seconds until he could breathe in the new heat, then pushed himself fully up and slowly resumed his cross-legged position in front of the hot rocks.

He closed his eyes and spoke in a croak. 'Thunder Spirit. I thank you for your presence. I am your unworthy servant and I offer this tobacco to you.'

He put the pipe to his soaking lips, blinking to see through the salty sweat and puffed four times, sending a prayer up with each cloud of smoke. The beating increased in frequency until it became one continuous deep humming throb, then Calvin's eyes rolled back in his head, his arms falling limply to his sides.

He was at one with the Thunder Spirit now.

Safe and secure, Calvin Bitterhand was wrapped in the awesome power that was generated from the very air itself, the pain of his body forgotten as he floated in the spirit's caressing, encompassing crystal web. He would not be able to sustain this for long and there was much to know, but, oh, the luxury of being without pain was so beautiful. If he could just sleep for a few moments in that soft place, surrounded as he was by the vibrations of sweet health and goodness, and the proximity of such irrepressible life-force. But no. He jolted as his will reminded him of his mission, scolding his flesh with a spasm, and he retuned his mind to the request he sought from this powerful spirit. It responded with a shiver. He could feel it was in readiness to answer him.

'Thunder Spirit. Is it the spirit I fear that I seek?'

The web that held him, shifted, and he was rocked gently within it. 'The same.'

His own voice answering, but the words were not his own. 'And the keeper is the boy?'

'He is.'

'Will the keeper accept me?'

'No.'

'Why?'

'Because he does not accept that he is the keeper.'

'Then what is my part in this?'

'To tell the truth.'

'How, if he will not hear it?'

'You must tell it so he has no choice but to listen.'

The language Calvin spoke in his out-of-body state was an ancient tongue, the oldest form of Cree, and his questions sounded stiff to his own ears.

'Will the keeper succeed if he knows the truth?'

No answer. That sparkling crystal web was starting to tear, and he could feel gravity beginning to work on the body he had forgotten he owned.

'Will he succeed, Spirit?'

Nothing.

'Answer me, I beg you.'

Calvin was becoming aware of his physical presence again, and the ecstatic state of being free of his flesh was disappearing, like the tingling return of sensation to a numb limb. A rivulet of sweat ran down his nose as he struggled in a panic to liberate himself from his body again. But it was over. The pleasure of that ethereal state left him, and his whole being grieved for it. His eyes opened and Calvin knew the spirit was gone from the lodge.

He slumped forward, exhausted. His hair, stringy and soaked with sweat, hung down over his face like slender thongs, and he watched the moisture drip from the ends in beads of cloudy water and he sat bent and dejected.

The truth.

How could he make the boy know the truth, when Calvin Bitterhand was barely sure of it himself? So many truths. So many.

Eden had spoken of truth the night before he died. Before he was murdered. Did the old man know what was going to befall him? It didn't take a shaman to know.

275

Anyone with eyes to see could have seen the drunken, insane fury with which Moses Hunting Wolf had looked at his father that night and seen that the devil was in him. He, Eden's pupil and closest companion, should have known.

Calvin fed Eden every evening, coming to his cabin around six to fix some dinner for the walnut-skinned man. For an elder whose very being was driven by retaining the tradition of his people, he sure was a man for junk food. Pemmican may have sustained his forefathers, but Eden liked a burger and no mistake.

It was no burden, serving Eden like that. Calvin stood and cooked up the burgers over the bottled gas stove by the window, while the old man sat in that big winged arm chair beside the sink. He loved that chair. Got it as a gift from Dean Morning Star for saving his baby son and Eden had grinned from ear to ear when they unloaded it off the pick-up and carried it up the steps. It was just a cheap plastic thing, made to look like leather, and the arms were worn through where your hands rested. But Eden had seen some film where an English minister nearly lost his wife to an angel, on account of not giving her enough of what a man ought to give a woman, and the English minister with the thin moustache had sat in a big chair just exactly the same. Eden was real proud he had a chair like the one in the film. Specially as the minister turned out the good guy and got the woman back after he decided to give his wife a good time instead of building a church. He would just sit in the chair all day, greeting the visitors that came with a nod as they let themselves in the screen door.

And there were plenty of visitors. Before he passed his mantle to Calvin, Eden had been a powerful and respected medicine man. Sure it was changing in the seventies, with the young folk sneering at the old ways, but even they came to him occasionally when they couldn't get a girl or were worried they had venereal disease. One guy had even come asking for cowboy boots; a young lanky kid, with big flared Levis and a denim vest over his T-shirt. Seemed he couldn't afford the boots he'd seen in town and couldn't figure out a way of stealing them, so he came to ask Eden how to get them. Calvin had thought he'd be shown the door, but the old man had leant back in his chair and smiled.

'You got to walk off the ones you got on, and give thanks.'

'What you talkin' about?' the kid had asked.

'What I say. Don't eat nothin' for four days, just water, then walk till your boots wear through, keep your heart pure and the spirits will give you the boots when you give them thanks.'

The boy had made a tutting sound and looked at him like he was crazy, but Calvin had caught a look in his eye that told him the boy believed Eden. A week later Calvin heard that the kid had won sixty dollars at bingo, and next time he saw him at the community centre pool hall, he was kicking the boards with a pair of silver-capped cowboy boots that would set your heart racing. Calvin had told Eden who just wheezed out a laugh.

'All you got to do is say thanks the way they want. Boots be nothin' to the spirits.'

The women were never out of there. His linoleum, with its patterns of fish and suns, was as shiny as linoleum could get without wearing through to the wood. They scrubbed anything that didn't move and Eden watched them, smoking his pipe and nodding in his big plastic chair. And Calvin liked to cook for him.

It was one of the few times the two men were alone and that was important to Calvin. It was those times that Eden would tell him things, things that helped him understand why he'd chosen Calvin as his apprentice and not Moses. He struggled to piece it together from the old man's memories, which became more disjointed and rambling as he got older.

'You don't be picked, Calvin. You be born a shaman. I be born Walks Alone, and I don't have no choice in it. Change my name don't change nothin' about what I got to do. A man can change his name all he likes. Changes nothin'.'

Eden had made a noise in his throat then, sucking up snot from the back there and swallowing it.

'When that piece of shit comes back, and he gonna come back, believe me, everyone better know what's in their heart, 'cause he don't be called the Trickster for nothin'.'

Calvin had pressed him often about what had happened back then but Eden would only nod and smoke and tell what he wanted to tell. The strangest thing was that Eden James Hunting Wolf still loved his son. He would say nothing judgemental about Moses at all, even when the women who cleaned, or the visitors who called, would tell him what new atrocities he'd performed on his family. That caused talk. Why didn't the old man save his grandson? He knew what Sam was suffering at his son's hands, and yet he sat in his chair and just looked on as the reports came back. He loved Moses and he loved Sam, but it was as though the events were out of his hands.

Calvin had been in Eden's cabin the night Marlene lost her eye. Betty Sandtail had run over and told him, near-hysterical as she gasped out what happened, clutching and clawing at the folds of her cheap floral-print dress.

'People is cruel and dumb,' was all Eden said. Nothing more.

Yes, Eden was a mystery. He told Calvin often and long about how he carried the honour and the weight of being the keeper, and how his father before them had saved them all, or they wouldn't be there now, eating burgers and drinking cheap watery beer. Calvin, as an apprentice to Eden, expected any day to be handed that keeper's key and given his blessing. But he didn't. Calvin had pressed the old man gently on when Moses would be handed the knowledge and the responsibility, secretly hoping that it would prompt him into bestowing it upon him. But it never did.

'Moses don't need it,' he said and changed the subject.

So that night, when Moses arrived, drunk and mean, Calvin had felt no duty to leave. He hated Moses Hunting Wolf, and he stuck around to make sure the bum didn't end up dealing some nasty stuff up to his pappy. Eden could stop a man's fist mid-air with just a look, but sometimes he seemed meek in the face of his sly and useless son.

The pan was on, sizzling with onions, when the screen door flew open to admit Moses. Calvin took the battered implement off the gas, and Eden just took another draw on his pipe, his backside squeaking in the plastic chair as he shifted his weight. Moses took a good look round.

'Got yer squaw cookin' again?'

He grinned with his dirty teeth closed. He smelled bad, Moses. A mixture of piss and alcohol that swirled around him, reaching the nostrils of those nearby in random wafts.

Eden smiled. That hurt Calvin. The power that man had was awesome. Why didn't he defend his chosen apprentice? Calvin was a medicine man and a shaman now. Maybe he should defend himself, but when he looked at Eden's calm face he knew he did not have the licence. Moses took a seat on the pine bench against the wall, took out a cigarette and lit it with the flourish of a movie star. He'd looked at Calvin for a long time with those narrowed eyes, then decided that he didn't exist.

He turned his attention to his father. Eden was a beautiful old man. The lines in his face were so deep they were trenches but they radiated from the corners of his eyes in fans of laughter and the skin that joined them was still smooth and the colour of walnut. His eyes were not yet milky with age, but sparkled like jet when the crinkled skin surrounding them let in sufficient light to bring them alive. The braids of silver-grey hair were still thick and long, and he let whoever wanted to, take them out and comb them, as though he were a girl.

'You thought about what I said?'

Moses squinted through his own smoke. Eden kept his pipe in his mouth and smiled, holding the wooden stem between his teeth.

'Don't need to think. You ain't the keeper, Moses.'

Moses's eyes had flashed with malice and hurt, and he threw down his cigarette and stood. 'You old fuck. You give me that fuckin' thing an' let me at its power. I'll show you what a real man can do with it.'

'You ain't gettin' it, Moses. You go back home.'

Moses took three steps towards the old shaman and made two fists. As Calvin watched, Eden gently raised one gnarled finger to his son like he was a teacher making a point in a lesson. Moses stopped.

'I be dead before you ever get this off me. You know that.'

Moses seemed to be wrestling with an invisible force, holding him back from the old man like a net. 'And Sam? You'd give it to Sam?' He spat the name of his own son like he was cursing.

'Sam ain't never asked.'

'But you'll fuckin' give it him, won't you?'

'Looks that way.'

Calvin had been amazed. Nothing had made him think that Sam was in line for Eden's bizarre inheritance. He'd stood silently, watching father and son stare each other down. Moses broke first, and turned away as he spoke. 'You be such a dumb old fuck, havin' medicine like that hangin' round your scrawny neck and usin' it for nothin'.'

'It ain't such good medicine, Moses. I told you plenty times.'

'That's what you say. You just keep it for yourself, but you don't never use it.'

Eden's face had changed then, growing darker than Calvin had ever seen it, his old eyes fixing his son, but looking through him. 'If you'd seen your grandpappy usin' it you'd pray every day of your life like I do that you don't ever be the one to use it. This don't get you no beer, son. This take away your soul.'

Moses had just looked at him, then across at Calvin as if seeing him for the first time, then lurched unsteadily out the door and into the night.

This take away your soul, Eden had said softly to himself as the screen door banged and Calvin had turned to the cooker to put the pan of onions back on the ring.

They had eaten then, and Eden had spoken for at least three hours. More than he had ever spoken at one time. He told Calvin about the days of being Walks Alone, and the railroad and the tunnel. He spoke warmly of the white man, the tall, thin minister his mother had honoured with the renaming of her only son. And he had spoken of truth, and how truth was the food and drink of the spirits.

He'd leaned forward, one elegant old hand circling a red plastic picnic tumbler full of beer, and touched Calvin's hand with his other.

'You know mortals always think there be lots of truths. You know the thing. Oh, there be this way or that way of lookin' at stuff. Ain't so, Calvin. The spirits know there be only one. Them that twists it and tricks you, they be mostly from beyond where we can get, and we got to keep away from 'em. But they be part of the world, same as a tree or a moose is. Trickster just doin' what he does. We just been chosen to stop him doin' it to us.' He'd laughed, remembering something. 'That white man, he didn't understand nothin'. But he want the truth real bad too. You see, killin' comes from the man. He couldn't kill so much as a bug if it wasn't that killin' comes from the man. He just makes you reckon he could kill you soon as look at you, but he can't. The killin' comes from the man. And that's the biggest part of the truth. That's the part that kills the man too, if he don't know that. You understand? Huh? you understand?'

This point had seemed to be important to Eden, who'd paused to make sure it had struck home, and although Calvin didn't understand at all, he'd humoured him and nodded. Eden seemed satisfied. He lifted the bit of burger he'd pushed aside on his plate and chewed at it. 'He try to make you hate him, but you can't do that. You do that and you die for sure. Just keep rememberin' that he as old as the world and the world be the greatest creation the Great Spirit ever done.'

Calvin had squinted at Eden under the lamp, trying to make sense of what he meant. 'You mean you love the Trickster, after what happened to your pappy?'

Eden chewed some more at the cold grey meat. 'I just saying he be part of the same stuff that you and me made of. White men know him too. They just got a whole heap of different names. 'Cept they don't believe no more and that make them be weak as kittens.' His eyes lit up. 'I ain't goin' to be the one to meet him again, Calvin.'

Calvin thought he recognized an old person's tone in the statement, the forced cheerfulness about dying that they adopt to make relatives dismiss it as folly.

'You don't know that, Eden. You got plenty years in you yet.'

Eden just looked at him. There was a pause. 'Sam teachin' good?'

Calvin had been relieved at the change of subject. When Eden fixed you with his gaze, it was as if he were reading your soul. 'Sure. I don't know that he be a shaman, but he be making a fine medicine man some day.'

It had been on his lips to add *if Moses doesn't kill him first* but he knew he would get nowhere with Eden attacking his family.

Eden looked like he could hear Calvin's thoughts anyway. 'Sam be fine. He be a shaman okay. You teach him everythin' you know.'

Calvin had nodded, and they had drunk the rest of the beer in silence.

At half-past ten, Calvin gathered his stuff up and made ready to leave. He cleared the table, left the pan in the sink for the women and helped Eden back to his chair where he would smoke for an hour more before going to bed.

As Eden sat down, his hand grabbed Calvin's and he looked at him with such a kindly loving expression it made him stop and stand before him in surprise.

'When we meet in the spirit world, Calvin, you be known as my son.'

Calvin had swallowed, moved by the first real display of affection Eden had ever declared. He could find nothing to say in response.

Eden smiled. 'Don't go wastin' money on burgers tomorrow. I won't need nothin'.'

Then he'd closed his eyes and lain back in that plastic chair, a sign that the evening was over.

It had been Rita Powderhand's turn to clean next day and she found the body on the floor by his chair, with its head split open like soft fruit.

No Kinchuinick called the RCMPs, but no one moved Eden either or touched anything in the house. It only took nine hours before the news reached someone off-reserve who fetched the police. And then the place had crawled with cops, asking questions and getting no answers from anyone. They couldn't prove it was Moses, and Calvin knew they didn't really care. Just an old Indian. Sure they would have loved to have banged up some Kinchuinick for the murder, but it wasn't like someone white had died. So after they'd taken Moses away to interrogate him and brought him back again, they mooched around the reserve for another six weeks before the visits started to tail off, and they went back to keeping white folk safe. The rumours were all that Moses had done it, and there was scared talk that Moses Hunting Wolf was now powerful with a bad medicine. Maybe that's why no one challenged him. Calvin had been distraught. The RCMPs didn't even return the body so they could lay him down in the sacred land by the river. They held on to it, and since there was no family to ask for it back, it never came back. Calvin didn't like to think what they'd done with it, but he knew Eden's soul was strong and pure enough to get to the spirit world without their earth-bound ceremony, though he wept that he couldn't help it on its way with dignity.

Only six months after the murder, Calvin saw Moses wearing the keeper's key round his neck. He was in the bar of the Craigellachie Hotel that lunchtime, drinking miserably on his own when Moses and Buster Fishing Bear walked in like a pair of swells and ordered beers. Moses leant on the formica counter with both elbows and looked around like a predator while his eyes adjusted to the gloom of the shabby, sour room. It had taken him a minute or two to spot Calvin, who was sitting at a table by the iron pillar, but when he did he fixed him with those narrow mean gashes of eyes and smiled. Moses said something to Buster who laughed in a high pitched giggle, then he grabbed his beer by the bottle neck and walked over to Calvin. Moses had seemed pretty sober, when he'd pulled out the chair and sat down.

He slouched there for a moment, letting Calvin's horrified eyes take in the sight of the ancient bone amulet sitting on his throat, then he took a swig of beer, wiped his mouth and laughed.

'Suits me, don't it?'

Calvin had been speechless with hate, but his fingers had tightened round the neck of his own beer. Moses leant forward slightly and tapped the amulet with a finger.

'You think I don't know how to use this, huh? But you and Eden teach Sam good, and if I have to beat it out of your spineless little shit of a boyfriend, I gonna get to know the secret.' He laughed again. 'How you be likin' that, medicine man? Huh? How you be likin' that?'

If Moses had not been sober, perhaps the bottle that Calvin swung at his face would have made contact with those high cheekbones, would have split open the flesh and made the blood spray. But Moses had been too fast. Calvin came to on the sidewalk outside the hotel where the barman had thrown Moses and the remains of Moses's handiwork and lay there sobbing for at least half an hour until the barman came back out and moved him on with a kick.

Eden's cabin lay empty for years, until someone burned it down, the women saying it was 'noisy' with spirits which scared the children who played in the long grass inside the fence.

But Calvin was back there now in his mind, his sweat trying to sneak inside his eyelids, as he sat with them screwed tight thinking of everything Eden had said on the eve of his death.

He could not call the Thunder Spirit again. It had spoken and it would not speak again. He would have to call the Eagle Spirit and begin his transportation without the benefit of any further knowledge. Calvin gasped for air and bowed his head again. How could he continue? If he were to make any more errors, let just one more rogue spirit into the sweat-lodge, he knew it would kill him. He began to chant and prayed silently that his impure thoughts of hatred and revenge be forgiven by the love of the Great Spirit.

Outside the tiny dome of canvas and wood, the snow started to fall again, and the aspens and birches and willows prepared themselves for their own battle, with the brilliant white weight that would threaten to snap their delicate limbs.

32

'Life goes on.' Becker, passing by with papers in his hand, said it with a smile as Craig emerged from his office to ask Holly for four more coffees. Life going on for Craig McGee meant an annual meeting with the heads of security from the three biggest hotels in Silver. He made a crooked mouth at the remark and went back in to his office, where Jeff McIntyre, the goon from The Rocky Mountain Chateau was taking out a pack of cigarettes.

He looked up at Craig. 'Mind if I . . . ?'

'Yes I would mind, Mr McIntyre. The detachment went smoke-free in October.' Craig closed the office door and sat back down.

The tanned man in his expensive grey suit looked embarrassed and put the cigarettes back in his pocket. Craig did nothing to ease his discomfort. These guys had been here an hour and he ached for the idiots to take a hike and let him get on with thinking about murder. They were promised a couple of hours of McGee's time, but he'd had enough already. The coffee was to remind them to go and if they didn't get the hint he'd open the goddamn window and climb out himself. Outside Becker and his men were thinking about murder. In here, they were thinking about ski-theft and credit card fraud. Craig unsuccessfully stifled a sigh.

'Okay, Mr Katzenberg. To sum up, you were outlining the problems a police presence at the hotel brings you during an investigation.'

Stephen Katzenberg cupped his hands over his knee and cleared his throat.

'Sure. All I was saying was that the problem we have up at Sun Springs is the same as Jeff's. Basically, the Japanese in particular, and let me tell you we care what those guys think, well the Japanese

284

get upset if they see a whole bunch of cops mooning about in the foyer. But they get just as antsy when they think nothing's being done about their thousand-dollar skis being swiped.'

Craig looked at him with cool eyes, then to the third man, David Blessed from the one hundred and fifty bedroom Family Inn. 'We get on your tits too, Mr Blessed?'

The man laughed. 'He's got a point.'

Craig spun a pen on its axis on the top of the shiny desk. 'I hear what you're saying, gentlemen, and as always we very much appreciate the contact with you. Obviously in a resort town like this it's our job as much as yours to keep the visitors happy and above all safe.' He paused to see if any of them would laugh at the irony of that one. Right now, their own hotel TVs would be beaming the news round the bedrooms just how safe they kept visitors in Silver. No. Irony was not a feature of hotel chain security chiefs. 'But we have this discussion every year, and every year I remind you that a large part of that responsibility rests with you also.'

McIntyre made a gesture that he was going to interrupt. Craig continued. He was getting impatient.

'You need better ski-lockers, you need to tell your guests to beware and stop pretending that ski-theft is not a problem, you need to keep your receptionists on their toes with your credit to cash transactions, and then, Mr Katzenberg, maybe you'd have less cops mooning about in your foyers.'

Holly brought in a tray of coffee, and there was a pause while the men fussed over who took cream and who didn't. Craig bit his lower lip against an urge to scream. He looked through the open door, caught a glimpse of that milling herd that made up the investigating team, and felt a stab of frustration, made more acute by the insignificance of his present audience.

Save your breath gentlemen, thought Craig as he watched them drink their coffee. Save it and just tell the Japs that Silver is free-ski-city for the young kids who drive in from Calgary with an empty covered pickup, and drive back again with enough skis to start a hire shop. Easy. End of problem. Now get back to your nothing jobs, patrolling miles of air-less carpeted corridor talking shit into walkie-talkies, and leave me alone.

Craig suddenly realized that the contempt he had for these men was most likely echoed by the Edmonton crew, with him as the target.

Get back to your nothing job of catching ski-thieves, you small-town cop.

He swallowed back his contempt and tried to regain a semblance of professional demeanour. He noticed Daniel still wasn't at his desk as Holly went back to the open door with her empty tray. What had Becker got him doing, he wondered? Craig really wanted to talk to Daniel, and he made a mental note to do it as soon as he shovelled these gorillas out of the office and back into their hotels.

As Holly closed the door, McIntyre spoke first. 'And does the responsibility also rest with us to ensure the guests come back to the hotel on the ski bus instead of in a body bag?'

Cranky addict, thought Craig. Deny a smoker their nicotine and what do you expect? 'No, Mr McIntyre, it doesn't. You stop them shoplifting the fluffy moose from your arcades. We'll stop them getting murdered.'

Blessed took offence. About time. 'Not doing such a hot job so far, are you?'

'Seems not.'

McIntyre sat up, as if height were superiority. 'Well if someone here doesn't start doing their job, we may not have many guests left to frisk for fluffy toys, Staff Sergeant. Have you any idea what this is going to do to our business if you guys don't get off your butts and catch the loony?'

'Sure.'

'And?'

'We'll catch him. You think about ski-lockers.'

McIntyre stared him out and lost. It was time to stop this crap. Craig wanted Daniel Hawk in here. His mind was constantly straying back to Hunt's involvement in all this.

An apple.

Why would a clever, good-looking young Indian like that change his name and try to live a white life? Daniel sure didn't. He was doing just fine as an Indian. And Craig had seen enough young Kinchuinicks in town with licence plates on their trucks reading *Indian and proud of it*, or *Bad Mudda*, to know that there was little evidence of shame amongst them.

So why did Sam Hunt hate himself? That bothered him. He needed to know everything there was to know about Hunt, and if Daniel couldn't tell him, he'd know someone who could. But there were still three morons to shift.

'Well, gentlemen, we've covered everything I think. If you want to keep an eye on the situation, we'll talk further into the season and assess the size of the problem. But you have to call us and report thefts. All thefts. Remember that. You can't keep it in-house.'

He stood up, signalling that the meeting was at an end. Katzenberg and Blessed gulped down the coffee they'd only just been handed, pushed back their chairs and stood, but McIntyre remained seated. He took another sip from the white mug with the RCMP blue logo the side, and cupped it in his hands.

'As heads of security, don't you think it would be appropriate to give us any information you have on the murder? What if the killer is staying at one of our hotels?'

Craig went to the door and opened it. 'If you think he is, you tell us and leave him alone. Then I'd tell housekeeping to watch he doesn't steal the little soaps.'

The two men on their feet laughed at McIntyre's expense. Jealousy that the carpets he patrolled were thicker than theirs and had the hotel logo printed on them, made them quick to join Craig, and McIntyre had no choice but to stand and put his mug on the table. The men shook hands with Craig and filed out, but McIntyre hung back a little and spoke softly to his crude host.

'You know, you need the town behind you in something like this, McGee. You got an attitude problem.'

Craig didn't smile. He imagined this man back in his small office at the Chateau telling some underling that he'd be out all morning at an important meeting with the police, and he felt a niggle of sympathy. The untalented, the mediocre and the stupid always elevate themselves to the fantasy of importance, and it was shooting fish in a barrel to bring them low. He regretted it. 'Maybe you're right, Mr McIntyre. We get tired. This is a tough job. Of course I'll keep you informed if we need your help.'

McIntyre looked surprised, but a big shit-eating grin spread across his face and he shook Craig's hand warmly. 'No worries. Hey, we live it in the fast lane too.'

Craig watched the sad dickhead leave, wondering why it was he managed to raise everybody's hackles these days. It was easy to be nice. He needed to practise it more. He mussed his hair and walked to the duty board to see where Hawk was. He hadn't been assigned, which looked like he hadn't come in.

'Holly. Where's Hawk?'

'Not in yet.'

'Did he call?'

'Nope.'

It was after two. Craig walked to Hawk's desk and sat on the edge. There were three yellow post-it stickers from Holly on Daniel's phone.

'Dan. Phone Tess please. 9.05.'

'Tess called again. Can you call her back? 11.30.'

'Call your wife, asshole. She and Larry will be at Lizzy's number after one, and she says put your answer phone on when you go out next time.'

A small alarm went off with Craig. Tiny, but insistent. Hawk wasn't here, and he didn't seem to be at home either.

Unless he wasn't answering the phone. Of course the phones could be down with the storm and he might be snowed in. Unlikely. Hawk would get to work if you tied his ankles together and poured concrete in his boots. Snow wouldn't stop him. Craig's heart started to beat a little too fast.

Indian. He's an Indian. Daniel Hawk is an Indian. Please God, no. Craig reigned in his dark thoughts.

'Lenny! Get a car up to Daniel Hawk's place right now and get his ass in here. I need him.'

'Right now?'

'Right now.'

'No free cars, sir. It'll have to be highway patrol.'

'I don't care if it's space patrol. Get him in here.'

'It's happening.'

Craig fingered a dumb plaster figure on Hawk's desk that held two broken pencils and a thin felt-tip. It was a squat little man with crossed eyes, a lolling tongue and a bare belly, and a sign below him, mimicking a carving in stone, read, *World's Greatest Dad*.

Craig looked at it like it would bite him, then got up and went back into his office.

Agnes Root was not dressed for the cold. Her cashmere sweater was letting the wind cut right through to her thin white body, and she cursed herself for being too lazy to go to the staff room and fetch her coat before she came outside. She stamped around on the top step, holding Billy's hand, and peering through the small crowd of parents to try and make out Katie Hunt.

'See her yet, Billy?'

The boy shook his head, but he was looking at his feet. Miss Root looked down at the top of his head, encased in a cute hat with a blue and yellow pom pom, and wondered what she was going to say to his Mom. Maybe this was mad. None of her business. But she couldn't let it pass, in case, well, in case something happened and she'd done nothing.

A woman was striding across the snowy yard towards them, smiling at first, then the smile fading as she grew nearer and saw her son's head bowed.

'Mrs Hunt?'

'That's right. Hi Billy! How's it hanging?' She bent down to his level and put her gloved hand under his chin to bring his face to hers. He dropped Agnes Root's hand and threw his arms around her neck. Katie looked up at the young teacher. 'Has something happened?'

'No. Not really, Mrs Hunt. I just wanted to have a word with you. Do you have time to come inside for a moment?'

'Of course.'

Katie picked Billy up in her arms and followed her in to the school. The sounds and smells of schools were the same as hospitals, Katie thought. As Agnes Root walked ahead of them along the corridor, her low heels made a clicking noise on the tiles that echoed off the hard walls, and added their small contribution to the din made by shrieking children leaving the building.

They turned into the glass-doored classroom, and Agnes Root made a gesture at one of only three adult-sized chairs in the room, for Katie to sit down. She put Billy down and he rubbed his eyes like a tired baby. Miss Root bent down to him.

'Billy. Why don't you go look see if the gerbils are okay for a minute while I talk to your mom?'

He looked uncertain. Katie touched his cheek. 'We'll be here, lamb. Go on.'

He looked at Katie to see if that was true, then turned and left the room. They listened to his boots squeaking along the corridor to where the gerbils were imprisoned in their glass cage.

Katie concentrated on looking calmly at this younger woman,

although her heart was already sinking in anticipation of more bad news. She still felt like shit. That turn she'd had in the museum had upset her more than it should have, and every time she thought of the weird conversation she'd had with her visitor, she felt sick. Poor woman. Imagine coming for an afternoon's innocent museum browse and ending up talking to a raving lunatic who said she was the curator. God knows what the woman must have thought of Katie. The problem Katie was still having, was the sick but strong feeling that she'd somehow betrayed her family today. Crazy. Plain crazy. She had nearly fainted up there on the balcony, and even when she was pregnant she never fainted. Did Sam have something catching? Sam. There was still the hard nugget of worry about Sam.

It had been a bad day all right, but she had thought it couldn't get worse. Wrong. What was Billy's teacher waiting back to tell her?

'I'm Agnes Root, Mrs Hunt.'

'Yeah. I know, Agnes. We met at the PTA.'

'Of course. Sorry. I keep thinking no one remembers you at these things. You know, with all the head teachers hogging the speeches and stuff.'

'What's up with Billy?'

'Right. Probably nothing. But I just wanted to tell you he'd been unusually withdrawn all day, and more importantly I wanted to show you this.'

She leant over her desk, picked up a big sheet of paper and handed it to Katie.

'We did science and painting today. I wanted them to paint rainbows and prisms. This is Billy's.'

Katie took off her gloves and accepted the paper from Agnes Root. She held it in front of her in silence, and her mouth opened slightly.

There was a triangular shape in the centre of the picture, just like the one on the board behind Miss Root's desk. The picture was familiar. Katie still had that ancient Pink Floyd album, *Dark Side Of The Moon*, that Tom gave her years ago, the one with the cover that had a beam of white going into a triangle and coming out as a rainbow. Hippy stuff, but Billy liked that cover. This was the same. Except that a rainbow was going into this triangle, and bursting out the other side was a snaking, scribbled nightmarish gash of black, that filled the rest of the page and had been so savagely applied to the paper it had torn it near the triangle. Katie swallowed. Beneath the horrible painting was Billy's scrawled writing.

'Dad.'

Agnes Root was watching Katie's face. 'I wondered if there was a problem at home.'

Katie could hardly speak. She croaked her words. 'A problem?'

The teacher shifted in her seat. 'Well, any . . . difficulties perhaps with Billy's relationship with his father.'

Katie was still staring at the hateful painting, unable to believe it came from her son's hand. The same hand that had painted his parents as bright, colourful stick figures with smiley faces and a sun constantly at their shoulder. The same hand that had written an essay that had made Katie and Sam blush, when it revealed that his mum and dad were always kissing and his mum went all weird when his dad kissed her slow. That little hand was the one that had drawn this abomination. Dear God. What was going on in his head? Katie looked up at Agnes, fighting for control.

'No. Not that I know of.'

The young woman was scanning her face for a lie. 'It's just that this looks like the work of quite a disturbed child, Mrs Hunt. He won't talk to me about it. I thought you might be able to tell me something that would explain it.'

Katie replied in a cold voice. 'I'm afraid not. But thank you for your concern.' She stood up unsteadily. 'May I keep this?'

Agnes Root stood. 'I'm sorry. No.'

Katie nodded and handed it back. The young woman rolled it up and held it to her chest. 'Where are the gerbils, Agnes?'

'Second on the left. Follow the smell.'

'Thank you.'

She turned to go. Katie stopped at the door and looked back. 'He has dreams you know. They're just dreams.'

It was Agnes Root's turn to nod, and it seemed to satisfy Katie as she left the room and went to fetch her dark artist.

Agnes let out a whistling breath. She'd met Billy's father at the PTA all right. She'd remembered him for two reasons. The first was that the Hunts were friends with Gerry and Anne and she was curious to see who her boss counted as chums. The second was that Sam Hunt was a number one lay if ever she saw it, a man so delicious it made her clench her buttocks at the thought of him. But an Indian lay. And everyone knew what Indians did to their kids, didn't they?

She unrolled the painting and looked at it again. Katie Hunt's face had so clearly signalled a lie she would have been more discreet taking out a billboard.

Agnes Root thumbed the edges and decided that if she was right, no matter what it took, Mr Gorgeous was going to be a very sorry Indian. Very sorry indeed.

Ski restaurant lines cracked Sam up. Were people really that dumb that they didn't know to unclip their ski boots? They clattered along like robots, stiff-legged and walking like Boris Karloff in *Frankenstein*, spilling everything they had on their tray before they got anywhere near the till. There was an elderly woman in front of him now doing just that, walking from the yoghurt display to the coffee vending machine with a laden tray, holding it like the lives of millions depended on her not spilling a Coke. He gave in.

'Here let me. I got soft boots on.'

She beamed up at him, her red face crushing into a smile. 'Weeel thank yooo!'

He put his own Coke on the tray, carried it across and laid it safely on the runner under the machine. She clumped eagerly behind him like a cow in splints.

'Try loosening your clips. Here let me.' Sam bent down and unclipped her tight rear-entry boots, as she held his shoulder for balance. 'There. Try that.'

She shuffled forward and smiled. 'Gee! Much better. Thank yooo!'

'No problem.' He grabbed his Coke and went to the till. Neil was behind it.

'Going down on old ladies now, Sam? Katie know?'

'Hey stop it. My sides might split.'

Neil laughed and rang up the Coke. 'How's it going?'

'Could be better.'

'The cops grill you too?'

'Sure.'

'Gruesome as fuck man, but it's kinda exciting. Wonder if they'll get the mother.'

'Wonder.'

Neil leaned across the counter, twisting in his seat, and inserting a cocktail stick in between his neat white teeth.

'You know how Mike found the mess? Said there were no footprints in the snow. Can you get that?'

Sam stared at him. 'How would Mike notice something like that . . . like why is he looking in the snow?'

Neil leant back with his arms out. 'Jeez. Come on, Sam. First thing Patrol check is the footprints round a casualty. You should know that. In case the injured party had a companion that wandered off, got into trouble, needs help, da dum, da dum, da dum.'

Sam gripped his Coke. 'And there were none?'

'Zilcho. Just the kid's ski tracks, and some deer prints.'

Sam's lips were parted, and he felt his heart knocking. 'Deer prints?'

'Prints from a deer. Deer prints. Four legged fuck with hooves. You probably got one in the family. D-E-E-R prints.'

Neil cupped a hand over his mouth. 'Hello! Houston! Can you hear me!'

Sam snapped out of it. 'Yeah, yeah. Right. So Mike told you this?'

'Nah. He's all to pieces. He told Baz. Baz told me.'

'Right.'

'Hey Sam. It's a riot talking to you man. Not!'

Sam smiled weakly, saluted and walked away. No prints. Shit. Why did that make him feel cold? He had planned to take his Coke and get back out to the snow fence he was fixing, but now he wanted to sit down and think. In fact he needed to sit down. He wandered over to the packed seating area to search out a space.

Behind him the woman approached the till. Neil grinned as he rang up the mound of food and drink.

'Okay. That's a big fifteen dollars twenty-five.'

She fumbled in a black bum-bag, pulled out the notes and paid him. Neil handed her the change and looked past her at the next tray. The woman clutched at his arm. 'Could you give that Indian boy this for his trouble please? I know every penny counts for them and how proud they are.'

She handed Neil fifty cents. Neil concentrated very hard on not throwing back his head and laughing. Sure he could give Sam the money and watch an old lady fly backwards through a plate-glass window. Instead he said 'Sure', waited until she'd gone then dropped it in the till with a delighted chuckle. That was a woman who would never know how close she came to a native Canadian fist. Neil composed himself and reached out for the next tray full of crap.

Sam was having trouble finding a seat. Any gaps he spotted had the old hat and glove reserved sign on them when he approached. Pissed him off, that trick. Sit down, take off anything that comes off and lay it on all the seats around you. Sorry, seat taken. No room. Didn't you see the goggles? He tried a few more spaces, then with a sigh, backed away from a clothing strewn bench and walked round to the window area from where he could see the whole seating plan of the restaurant.

It was real busy. A weekday like a weekend, not even lunchtime and nearly the end of the day. Murder was obviously good for business. He scanned the crowd for a gap, his eyes skimming the bobbing heads.

It was like a jagged fingernail catching in fabric, the way his eyes went back to that face in the crowd. No reason to single it out, and no reason to notice it. But Sam Hunt was now standing staring at the blond man sitting half-way along a bench who was returning and holding his gaze as though it were a solid column of steel between them connecting their eyes.

The clattering of boots and cutlery, the babble of conversation, the whooshing rush of the cappuccino machine, were all one vicious, buzzing white noise in Sam's ears as those eyes held him. His breathing was cancelled and his hand was dripping with the Coke that was being forced from its crushed waxed cup as Sam's fingers involuntarily closed round it into a fist.

'Hey buddy! Your soda!'

A man at the end of the nearest table was leaning out and tugging at Sam's jacket, as the drink cascaded down his arm and dripped into its own pool on the floor. But the voice only reached Sam in a dream. His consciousness was so thick with the presence of that other being, he was impervious to the man's concern.

Sam Hunt knew what he was looking at. Lots of bits of him tried to tell him that he didn't. His eyes told him he was merely looking at a stranger who was staring right back at him.

Staring with a malicious twist to his smile, but just staring nevertheless. And his head, his bone box of reason, told him that the stranger was probably someone Sam had seen before, which was why that nondescript blond face was so familiar, so instantly intimate.

But Sam Hunt knew.

His everyday senses that said *look out for the dog crap on the sidewalk, careful with that boiling pan, put your hat flaps down or you'll lose your ears,* those senses could tell him what they wanted. They were all wrong. He knew.

The guy who cared about wasting good Coke was shaking his head at his wife as Sam let the crushed cup fall and bounce away, splattering the rest of its contents on the tiled floor.

Sam's arms hung limply by his side, as useless as the rest of his body, caught as it was in the radar of that obdurate gaze. He had never felt so alone. There were at least a hundred people in that barn of a room, but they could have been chocolate bunnies in ski-suits for all the comfort they were affording him right now. No one was going to rush at that man and pull him to the ground with a football tackle. No one was going to raise the alarm with a yell and empty the restaurant. No one. Because it was just a guy in a black coat sitting at a table. That's all.

But then who can predict a miracle? The seven teenagers who stood up at the next table, rustling and jostling to get their gear together for a last run, performed that miracle. They could have gone out behind Sam. He was, after all, standing within arms' length of the table, and behind him lay three feet of free passage to the exit. But then kids know little and care less about personal space, never guessing they're getting in your face until it's too late and someone ends up throwing a punch. So with the choice facing them of a polite clear passageway or shoving right past the big Indian guy, they chose the latter.

Four bodies pushed past him and broke the invisible beam. For about five or six seconds those pale blue eyes were blocked from Sam Hunt's view by woollen hats, anoraks and the sullen slack-jawed faces of Canadian youth. Sam suddenly discovered he had the power to take air into his lungs again. He gasped in a shuddering breath, turned and ran.

Neil looked up from a tray of omelettes and mineral water to see his customers scattering as if about to be mowed down by a buffalo, and the buffalo looked like Sam Hunt. The big crazy guy was careering through the crowds like his shorts were on fire and Neil watched him, open-mouthed, until he crashed out of the restaurant through the wooden swing doors, leaving a group of indignant people in his wake who shouted 'Hey!' and brushed their arms as if his rough contact had left them marked. Neil shook his head, shifted the cocktail stick to the other side of his mouth and went back to adding up food.

Nowhere to run. Sam stood with his legs apart and his arms by his sides, staring at the skiers around him as though surrounded by dangerous lunatics. The restaurant here at the top of the mountain was always busy last thing, as people congregated to have a snack before the last full run of the hill, happy that they were good and high, even if lifts closed.

They slid around outside the restaurant, finding their skis from the forest of bright plastic and wood stuck in the snow or leaning against racks, and they shouted greetings and happy words to companions, the sounds making that deadened flat noise that shouts always do in the open air.

Far below, the valley was already filling with evening mist, a thick white mantle settling on the pines, punctured occasionally by a rogue tree, that pushed through the cloud as a reminder of the rugged grey-green texture the cloud concealed. It was snowing on the other side of the valley, and the massive glacier that crowned Mount Fraser, usually glittering with green and blue, had turned a grey that rendered it indistinguishable from the leaden sky. It made it seem all the more colossal, the way its bulk was swallowed up by the sky. Sam had seen it in every conceivable light and weather, seen its summit tipped by a delicate roseate light at dawn, watched the full summer sun glancing on its broken ice like a laser on diamonds, and the purple shadows creep along the jagged crags with the fading of the evening light. Even in this oppressive unstable weather, it was a ragingly beautiful sight, but as if to tip the balance of the view from savage grandeur into melancholy, a train's horn sounded below, long and low in its chord of three mis-matching notes, as it left the valley and headed west.

Sam put his hand over his mouth and closed his eyes. What was he running from? A face in the crowd. He let his legs buckle and he slumped down to the snow on his knees as if in a prayer.

Weeks ago there used to be a Sam Hunt who'd just be tapping in the last post of that snow fence, looking forward to going home and hugging his kids and crushing his wife in his arms. He'd probably have jawed with the guys on the night trail groomers for a time, then picked up some groceries on the way home if it was his turn for the car. And there might be steak and spinach salad for dinner. Katie would have books to read after they'd pigged out on cheesecake, and he might just watch a hockey game on TV or muck around with Billy and Jess before bed. That was what it used to be like. It wouldn't make a feature on *Lives of the Rich And Famous*, but it was heaven. So where was he now, that Sam Hunt?

Who was this frightened man on his knees in the snow? Frightened of death by brain tumour. Frightened by cops who thought he was a killer. Frightened by a look he saw behind his wife's beautiful eyes. And now frightened by a face in the crowd. No. Not frightened. Terrified.

He got to his feet like a new-born calf, and knew he had to get home. Fuck the snow fence, fuck the job, he had to get home.

A look round told him the snowmobile he'd come up on was gone. Dean had gone for more orange netting. If he went down using the chairs it would take him the best part of an hour, and that calculation relied on the chairs still running at Half-way, which at this hour was doubtful.

No problem. He'd ski down. Five miles of trail, but he could do it in less than fifteen minutes. He knew his crappy old black boots were in the Patrol hut behind the restaurant, and there were dozens of skis in there that could have their bindings tweaked to fit. Sam loped towards the hut, going round the back of the building instinctively, out of sight from that huge expanse of plate-glass window, that might or might not still contain a pale face with ice blue eyes.

It was windy back there. The asshole architect of the monstrous concrete building had created a pretty effective micro-climate between its ugly back side and the patrol hut.

Regardless of which direction the prevailing wind blew from, the space between the two structures screamed with its own private whirl-wind, throwing eddies of sugar-fine snow into the air, and piled the small hut's door high with drifts. Sam put his shoulder to it and barged in. The warmth of the room was soothing as he closed the door behind him and scanned the box shelves for his boots. It was a tiny hut. One door, one small square window looking out over the valley as if the hut was flying, and the rest of the room a jumble of skis on racks, ropes, backpacks and climbing equipment. Sam loved the smell in there. It was woody and waxy, and when the thermostat on the electric heater decided it was time to come back on again, it made that acrid, nostalgic singeing smell of burning dust. But you couldn't swing a cat, and it didn't take long to spot his boots. They were shot to pieces, lying sad and neglected beside someone's pair of metallic turquoise Rossignols he'd coveted but couldn't afford last season. Sam rescued them from their shame and sized up the assorted skis at his back. He found a pair of 210s that fitted the boots like a dream, and sat down on the long leather padded seat to get his Sorrels off. It was that physical act of sitting down that interrupted the anaesthetic of his practical mode with a mental tap on the shoulder.

Hey Sam! A face in the crowd. Remember? Sam sat forward, one boot off, and held his head in his hands. It had been a hard-learned skill, that trick of keeping memory at bay. He was good at it. But after so long being denied access it flooded his senses like a dam bursting, and he fought with his eyes screwed tightly closed to keep Eden out of his head.

Too late.

'Was you afraid?' Eden had asked him that day, in a voice that didn't mock, but was genuine in its curiosity. Fifteen-year-old boys want to be big and tough and grand, and Sam had ached to say *no grandpappy, I wasn't afraid*. But you couldn't lie to Eden. Eden could smell a lie before you'd formed it.

'Yes.'

'What of?'

'It didn't sound like it was Calvin talking.'

'It wasn't. You know that.'

Sam had looked at his feet. A pair of plastic track shoes with the big toe of the left one worn all the way through to the canvas, encased his long feet. He kicked at a loose corner of the lino with it. 'Uh-huh.'

'So who was it be talkin'? Look at me, boy.'

Sam had looked up at his grandfather, sitting back in his big chair, gripping the arms like it was going to take him someplace.

'I guess it was the Thunder Spirit.'

Eden looked at Sam for a long time, then turned his attention to gazing through the window as though his tall, dirty, half-starved grandson had ceased to be of interest. Sam waited. He knew he was not forgotten. Eden was either thinking, or remembering.

They sat in silence for a minute, until Eden spoke again. 'You build a lodge with Calvin, you does all the right things to purify yourself, and you be bringing the spirits to speak with you. But you just be guessing it was the Thunder Spirit?'

Sam looked at him through his long dark lashes. 'I know it was.'

Eden nodded.

'You knows a whole heap boy. Beats me why you always be tellin'
yourself it ain't so.'

Sam had shrugged, sulky like a child. Eden let go the arms of the
chair and crossed his gnarled hands on his lap.

'This here thing be real important I goin' to tell you, and you best
listen' hard. Hear?'

It was Sam's turn to nod. Eden stared into Sam's eyes with that
fearsome inky black gaze, until he saw something there that satisfied
him his grandson would listen. 'You and me and Calvin, and some
others who be all around the place but we don't knows them, we be
the ones who can see it's him when he comes playin' around.'

Sam didn't need to ask who *he* was. His grandfather was obsessed.
He had sighed internally, bored with the old man's hobby horse. 'You
see he ain't good at makin' human shapes. Get's it wrong enough for
a shaman to spot him like a bear in a flock of geese. Plenty be fooled
by it and he be enjoyin' himself doin' it, but you and me, we be seein'
him right off.'

Sam humoured the old man by feigning interest. 'So why's he do
it? Why don't he just stay inside animals or be the shape he is?'

Eden had pursed his lips then, and scratched at something in his
pants. 'Don't know. When I sees him he was doin' it to hurt your
great grandpappy. But I guess he does it sometimes to find the likes
of you and me when he ain't sure who we are.'

He never knew what it was he did wrong, but Sam's face must
have betrayed some kind of scepticism or worse, boredom, because
Eden had gone crazy. He sat forward in his chair and slapped both
his palms on the arms of the chair, and hollered. 'You start actin'
like an Indian, Sam! You be born Indian, you gonna die Indian, and
unless you knows that, that excuse for a face gonna come at you in
a crowd some day and you gonna walk right past it. You hear?'

Sure he had heard. Born Indian. But fifteen years of being born
Indian had been enough. Those white guys he saw in town, same age
as him, same everything as him except their skin, they had homes
and families and jobs, and no one filled their heads with all this shit.

He would watch them sometimes, from the steps of the food store
where Sam sat with Randall and Harry doing nothing but kicking
the dirt and watching the cars. The sight of those white guys filled
Sam's throat with a thick envy that stopped him swallowing, when
they hung their elbows out of their new trucks and the girls would

come over and do that cute twirling thing with their hips while they stood and spoke to them. They would drive away to things Sam could only imagine, things like they did on TV. Parties maybe, with big tents and chairs and tables on lawns. Or picnics in blowy meadows with ball games and rugs on the grass.

He saw the TV sometimes over at Randall Fishtail's cabin, and there were always white kids like the ones in town doing great stuff. And what did Sam get to do, because he was born Indian and would die Indian? Sam got to hide from Moses's fist in the trees until Calvin found him, and then build sweat lodges to help him bring spirits that scared the living shit out of him.

If the spirits that spoke to Sam and Calvin could do anything for him, it would be to change his skin and let him ride around with those kids. Change his skin and kill his father. That would do, thanks.

Eden must have read his mind. He went deadly calm. 'Two paths, Sam. Shamans got only two paths. Good medicine or bad medicine. Nothin' in between. Other folk can go all kinds of ways and still be kind of good. But we got only two paths. You let that dark one inside get you, you be ending up much worse than your pappy.'

And he'd stared at Sam real hard then, until the boy had been so ashamed of his thoughts a film of tears had formed in his jet-black eyes. Eden had just closed his eyes and leant back in the chair.

And Sam's eyes were closed now as he wrestled for his sanity.

Indian shit. Just a pile of steaming, festering, stinking, made-up Indian shit. These were the nineties. That was a ski restaurant out there full of people eating fast food, who came here in hatch-back cars along highways and went home to brightly lit houses with central heating. It wasn't a fucking tipi full of old men who still believed in wittiagos and demons and spirits.

And he was Sam Hunt, for Christ's sake. He went to the cinema. He had an electric toothbrush. He played Pac Man on Billy's Nintendo. Fuck all that ancient bullshit.

If Eden James Hunting Wolf had been such a powerful shaman how come he couldn't even save himself? All bullshit. There was no face in the crowd except the demons of his own sick and fevered mind and from now on those memories were going to stay where they belonged. In the place in his heart where he'd buried Sam Hunting Wolf the Indian, and given birth to Sam Hunt the human. As if in reply, his father's amulet pressed its small bone weight against his chest, and Sam made a fist and muttered out loud, although under his breath, 'Fuck every last one of you. I'll be who I want to be.'

The door of the hut burst open with such violence, the window rattled and the wild wind that burst into the room knocked a rack of skis backwards, sending them clattering to the floor.

Sam bellowed in fright and leapt to his feet. A figure was filling the doorway, the light from the snow making it a silhouette in a frame. Sam, his heart pounding, struggled to make out the features against the impossible glare of white.

'Just two seconds to get a fucking Coke, huh?'

It was Dean. Sam nearly wept.

'There's half an hour of light left and an hour of fencing to do thanks to your Coke-break and ten minutes to track you down here, you lazy bastard.'

Sam found his voice. 'I have to get home fast. I was getting skis together since you had the mobile.'

The figure in the doorway put out an arm and leaned on the post. 'Jesus, Sam. I can't finish it on my own, and Baz'll bite our balls off if that fence is still down tomorrow. Can't it wait?'

'Please, Dean.'

The figure stood for a moment, having the advantage of seeing Sam's face and seeing its pleading distress.

Dean made an upward sweep with his hand in exasperation. 'Sure. Don't mind me.' He turned and walked away. 'Have a nice ski, y'hear?' he said sarcastically into the wind.

Sam watched him go, sat back down and pulled on his ski boots. He could get down to base with the snowmobile now that Dean was back, but he wanted to ski. He needed something to clear his head and help him flush out this garbage that was making him ill. Keep moving, Sam. Every time you stop those black clouds from the past get you. The door banged in the wind and Sam kicked it shut with a foot as he snapped the clips of his boots closed.

33

Alberta 1907
Siding Twenty-three

Even as the snow fell, the wind was blowing it from those two straight rail tracks, and in the thick pillow of white that covered every other trace of topography it was as though two infinite charcoal black lines had been drawn on a white sheet.

Tall pines, fronted by scrub birch, formed a lugubrious wall on either side, and Hunting Wolf felt them imprison him as he staggered along between the tracks, his chest heaving for breath as though it would explode.

Over the pounding of his own heart and the rasping of his elusive breath, he could hear this new abomination gaining ground behind him. He could hear its paws beating in the snow, its breath grunting with every bound. Great Spirit, he had no prayers left for these poor creatures. How much more? He lurched forward and his foot caught a sleeper, pitching him forward, spread-eagled into the snow. He could run no further. And running was a pointless conceit. Hunting Wolf lay gasping, waiting for his torment.

A bear cub this time. A bear cub roused from winter slumber by its mother's side for this atrocity. It bounded a few feet ahead of the Indian's body, lying half-submerged in the crystalline snow, and stopped in front of him.

'Look at me, you worthless scum.' The voice was forced from the bear's unwilling and violated vocal chords, grumbling in its throat like a growl of pain.

Hunting Wolf kept his eyes shut and began chanting a prayer for the bear's soul to the Eagle God, his outspread palms grasping the snow into balls.

'LOOK AT ME!'

He chanted louder, grimacing as the cold of the snow started to burn his face with its sting. A theatrical pause, as the evil in the animal enjoyed the wait, and then that noise – the ripping of animal flesh, the snapping of bone and the sickening wet slick of fur being torn by teeth from the viscous membrane that attaches it to skin. The animal roared in agony as it devoured itself, and Hunting Wolf felt its hot blood splash his face and hands.

He threw his hands to his ears, but his frozen fingers could not muffle the sound of the creature in such tortuous pain. It bellowed and screamed and the snow churned around its doomed body as it writhed in the pincer of its own jaws and talons.

It was worse this time. He knew it was going to leave the creature half-alive. Hunting Wolf felt the Trickster leave the cub's body and the animal ceased its frenzy of self destruction. But it was still scream-ing. He opened his eyes and pulled himself up out of the snow. The cub was propped up on the edge of a crater of snow it had created with its own death throes, and it sat looking grotesquely comical, like an old man in a hammock. It had torn its stomach open and bitten off both its feet, the bone protruding in sharp spears of ivory from the seeping dark stumps. Its muzzle was ripped by those razor claws and one eye hung from its socket. Hunting Wolf could see the young animal's exposed rib cage, and the organs that had spilled out were steaming gently in the cold snow.

It bellowed and shrieked as Hunting Wolf fumbled in his belt for his long knife. He took it out with a shaking hand, held it by the blade and aimed. With one strong throw the knife spun through the air and pierced the cub's remaining eye with a wet thud. It screamed again, twitched, and was released.

The man stood staring down at the pitiful remains of the once-beautiful animal, clenching and un-clenching his fists. He turned and glanced down the track behind him. The bodies of the others lay in dark patches, all the way back to the point on the horizon where the two black lines of track met. Shapeless sacks in the snow. So much death. An obscene entertainment for his eyes alone. The cougar had been the worst. It had destroyed itself in seconds and the noise had been unearthly.

Hunting Wolf knew it would not take his demon long to find and command another innocent creature, and he ached with regret for his madness in running so far from the camp along the tracks. It was growing dark and he would soon be unable to see anything but the subtle difference between the snowy ribbon of his path and the dark wall of trees. He would not make it back to camp in daylight, even if he had a horse. But how to stop the slaughter? Running like a child would solve nothing. He walked forward, retrieved his knife from the cub's skull, knelt beside its violated husk and offered up one last prayer for its soul.

It was as though the spirits had forsaken him. What good had the sweat-lodge build done? None. The Thunder Spirit would not come after the white man had defiled their original altar, and it would take four days again to purify and fast before they could try again. How foolish he had been to think that he was prepared. Sitting at his father's side, listening to the stories and being taught the truth was of little use to him now. There was so much he did not know. His father had said this spirit was weak. Weaker by far than a man. How could that be?

Only the spirits could help him and they were as silent as the falling snow that was floating around his face like feathers on the wind. Hunting Wolf wiped the blade of his knife on his leggings, and stood erect. He was a shaman. And a man. Enough of this running. The Trickster was feeding on his fear, and he must contain his horror. He would walk back to the camp, slowly, like a warrior. He was shamed by the cowardice that had made him flee in the face of these nauseating displays, and ultimately, he was weakened by it.

The killings could become no worse. Already his heart was hardening to their frequency. From now on, he would keep his eyes open and show the monster it meant little to him. He had, in his medicine bundle, a powerful herb that would aid his courage, and as he replaced the knife he fumbled for the pouch with his freezing fingers, opened it and took out some shiny blackened pieces of plant. His tongue stung with the acid from the small bitter leaves, and he bit into them to release more of their natural magic. He waited, and when that soft hand of sopor started to caress his temples, he placed two more leaves beneath his tongue and started to walk back along the tracks, treading carefully in his own untidy trail as he retraced his steps.

From his left, there was a crashing in the trees, and a red fox burst out of the forest and scampered, panting and white-eyed, onto the tracks in his path.

Hunting Wolf blinked at it slowly as he approached, pulling the blanket round his shoulders and keeping his steps even and unhurried. The animal bared its fangs and slavered like a mad thing. Hunting Wolf did not stop, even when, inevitably, it spoke to him.

'Going back to pick over the bones, son of shit?'

The shaman looked away and replied, 'Why waste good pelts?'

The animal remained still, quivering faintly with the power of its uninvited guest, watching the Indian until he drew level with it and then passed. Hunting Wolf carried on along the track, and when the sound of fox teeth tearing at fox flesh began behind him, he merely blinked and focused his hugely dilated pupils on the snow between the tracks, as it blew across the frozen metal.

He bit into the second leaf, and stepped aside to continue as his foot kicked the twisted carcass of a mink.

The tipis made their own miniature mountain range, clustered together as they were about half a mile from the railroad camp. The poles protruding from the apex of each triangle splayed out in irregular fans and delicate tendrils of blue smoke played between them. As he approached, Henderson mused on the perfection of the tipis' gradient and design, how the snow could gain no hold at all on such a surface. Hunting Wolf had told him they rarely used them now. He and his family had a cabin on the Redhorn reserve, at least eight days' hard walking from Siding Twenty-three, and they camped in tipis only when moving the cattle or horses to distant summer grazings. But for this exercise, the Kinchuinick disruption of McEwan's great tunnelling project, the tipi had enjoyed a winter resurrection.

Deep in his pocket, James Henderson's fingers toyed with the small crucifix he had whittled from a piece of seasoned jack pine, and rehearsed in his head the Siouan words he would use in the giving of the gift. The huge flat flakes of falling snow were so light they hung on the minister's hair and face like flying summer seeds.

He felt good. Singing Tree and her silent, doe-eyed boy had stayed with him and soothed away his fear. There had been no recurrence of the nightmare from three days ago and he knew now that he had been feverish, ill and deluded. Strange that the people who had induced his madness with their tales could also cure it. But he wanted to show his gratitude to them, and he felt a stab of guilt that he had not granted the prize of the ivory and mahogany crucifix to the little boy who had fetched his wood and filled his cabin with his childish humanity. He hoped his own amateur effort in carving would suffice, and possibly help bring the heathen child to his God. And he wanted to speak with Hunting Wolf, to try to make sense of what had happened to his mind after the incident in the tunnel. If there had been an incident. McEwan suggested that Hunting Wolf's injuries had been self-inflicted and the university-educated Edinburgh minister, who was the pilot of this thin, stranded soul, had to agree.

A dog barked as he approached the camp, its yelping muffled in the thick snow-padded air, and a woman wrapped in a rough, striped blanket stepped from behind the first tipi. She stared impassively as he raised a hand in greeting, and went back inside her shelter. He let the disappointed hand fall as he entered the encampment, and walked along the flattened snow path between the cones of hide that concealed the occupants, grateful to be out of the knee deep snow.

There was no mistaking Hunting Wolf's tipi, painted as it was to mark a great chief and shaman. A primitive eagle spread its wings above the entrance and a band of reddish brown paint encircled the whole structure, dotted with white circles and vertical lines.

Henderson stood outside, looking up at the wisps of smoke from the tipi's fan of sticks, unsure what to do. He cleared his throat, and said in Siouan, 'It is Henderson.'

He heard low voices inside, and a man's hand pulled back the stitched hide door-flap. Powderhand's face followed. He looked up at Henderson with a mixture of contempt and disinterest, then made a small head movement for him to enter.

It was gloomy inside, and when Henderson's eyes adjusted to the amber light that filtered through the walls, he realised there were about half a dozen people in the tipi, sitting silently round the edge, looking up at the tall white man as he entered in a clumsy stoop. By the small fire in the centre, Hunting Wolf lay on some crudely-cut and stitched furs, his eyes closed and his mouth open, panting. Singing Tree was kneeling by his side, and the boy, Walks Alone, crouched at his feet.

Henderson, feeling the awkwardness of his height, knelt, looking anxiously at Singing Tree. No one spoke and he swallowed as he tried to formulate a question that would not result in his ejection. He had never been invited into a tipi, and he was lost as to the etiquette and formality of such a visit. But concern for Hunting Wolf won over his fear of error and he risked speech.

'Hunting Wolf sick?'

Singing Tree looked back at him silently with black, liquid eyes that reflected the firelight and, though he fought to deny it to himself, made sparks ignite in James Henderson's heart. She said nothing. It was Powderhand who replied.

'We found him on the path of the iron horse. He does not wake.'

Hunting Wolf was panting hard now, his eyeballs moving rapidly beneath their lids.

'How long since?'

Powderhand sighed, as though it were a chore speaking to such an imbecile. 'Not long. This morning.'

Henderson's face crushed with anxiety. If the man had been lying out there all night as Powderhand seemed to imply, he was lucky to be alive. He leant forward to feel Hunting Wolf's pulse, but a tiny hand shot out and blocked his way. Walks Alone did not want him to touch his father.

'I must feel for his life. In his hand.'

The boy shook his head slowly. His mother spoke in a quiet voice. 'We must not touch him. There is a dark spirit upon him. Walks Alone can feel it in his father.'

Henderson felt his world start to crumble again. More talk of spirits and darkness was not what Henderson had come here for, and he ached to be free of this superstitious foolishness that had led to his own sick visions. He withdrew his hand and settled back on his knees. This time, though he knew the boy could not speak, he addressed the question to those big serious eyes. 'Will he wake?'

Walks Alone nodded and turned his attention back to his father. Henderson decided he would wait. If they asked him to leave he would, but right now, he would wait. The faces around the edge of the tipi were divided in their interest between the white man and their chief, but all remained silent and the only sound was the laboured breathing of the unconscious man on the floor.

*   *   *

307

Cook cursed at the stove as the cauldron of broth showed little signs of boiling. Those men. They didn't realize the miracles he performed daily, that was the trouble. Nearly a month now without any contact from outside this white prison, and he was still serving up good eats. Did the ungrateful pigs not realize that his repertoire was based on getting fresh supplies from the trains that should have been passing through here three times a week? But without trains, with their crates of vegetables and meat, he was reduced to famine cooking. And he was doing a damned good job. But what thanks did he get? No buggering thanks, that's what. The Scots were a dour race, and he should know, since his new Canadian blood ran thick with old Highland stock. But he'd had enough of those long, bearded craggy faces sitting around the refectory table in the canteen cabin, never once saying *thank you*, or *that sure tasted good, Saul*. And Saul Campbell had cooked for plenty of miserable railroad crews in his time. Yes, these long-faced goats took all the prizes.

The snow was getting to them too. All this frightened muttering of ghosts and Indians and talking animals was more than he could stomach. It was like cooking for old women. If he didn't know for sure that there wasn't a drop of liquor for at least fifty miles in any direction, he'd swear they were all suffering the tremors.

Oh, but Indians are cunning. He'd seen their schemes at work before, when he cooked for the repair crew on a section of rail on the other side of these fearsome mountains. The darn weasels would squat alongside the rails watching the men working, staring straight at them without talking or moving, and unnerving them so that they were given gifts of food and clothing to make them go away. They knew what they were doing all right, and this concoction about spirits and ghouls was the same kind of conspiracy. Yes, he was sure of it.

The disappointment was that a man like Angus McEwan hadn't put a lid on it. Saul had heard about what he did to the Kinchuinicks' religious ceremony. About time, thought Saul, and had secretly applauded him. The unhealthy thing was that the men talked about the incident as though McEwan had transgressed. In fact they talked about it as though they were afraid of unspoken consequences.

A thick lazy bubble surfaced in Saul's broth and burst with a splatter. Boiling at last.

He stirred it with a copper spoon and a smile, tasting it with a small pointed tongue. More salt. He'd made it from some ham that had been frozen in the larder, lentils, and the last of the onions. And it was delicious. Mr McEwan liked his broth, and this was day three of the thick soup's life, but he didn't come to supper last night. That was unusual. It took a lot of food to keep the big bearded engineer going, and he hadn't even requested a meal in his cabin. McEwan had just failed to show. This morning too, no sign of him at breakfast.

If the engineer didn't make it out of his quarters for lunch, Campbell would go over there with a bowl of this broth and make him eat. Sometimes you had to act like these men's mother, and when Saul was most cranky and impatient with them he was teased that he stopped just short of picking them up after a meal and making them break wind. No matter. It was his job.

He watched the bubbles start in earnest now. He would wait until the cauldron was at its hottest, cover it with the copper lid and drag it up to the tunnel mouth on the big sled, where Jamie would have the fire going to re-heat it. A daily ritual, but an exhausting one.

Cook worked it out. If he got to the tunnel and McEwan wasn't there, then the men would most likely finish the broth before he could get back and serve him a bowl. He should check now, and if McEwan was indeed sitting brooding in his spartan quarters at least he would have first shout at the soup. The man must be starving. Plus, he was the man who hired and fired, and the pragmatist in him knew it was worth keeping him sweet.

Saul scooped up a tin plate from the stack waiting for their cold sled ride, and filled it with broth. He broke off a piece of the coarse unleavened bread he'd made yesterday and dropped it in the plate, and with his free hand put a spoon in his pocket and placed a cloth over the dish to keep the snow out of his creation.

He opened the door and stepped out to make a dash through the snow to McEwan's cabin, which lay about fifty yards away between a clump of lodgepole pines. Cursing the thickness of the falling snow, the cook tried to hurry without spilling his steaming burden. The cabins all sported brownish stamped areas of ice surrounding the doors, where the men came and went, foiling the snow's attempts to cover their tracks. Off the main pathway between the wooden structures, McEwan's snow had won. The thick, unbroken wall of snow covering the track that led to his door suggested he had not left his hut since yesterday, although a glance at the smokeless chimney seemed to imply he was absent altogether.

Saul waded through the drift, soaking his thin cotton pants to the thigh, and kicked on the door with his foot.

'Mr McEwan. It's Cook with some broth.'

There was no reply.

'Mr McEwan. May I come in?'

Nothing. Obviously he wasn't there. All the signs said he wasn't there. Saul turned to go back, and then stopped. What if McEwan were ill and no one had checked? Everyone would simply assume he was somewhere else. The man was forever striding out in his snow-shoes to the head of the pass like a scout, to see if the lines were showing any sign of clearing, or visiting the tunnel at dusk when the men had stopped work.

He could be in the cabin, weak and cold in bed, waiting for someone to come and tend him and re-light his stove.

Saul sighed, put the broth on the snow bank and pulled down the latch on the door. It swung open and he held it there with his foot while he bent to pick up the tin plate.

He stood and walked in, letting the door swing shut behind him with a bang. It was almost black inside with the door shut. Black and cold. The only window was completely blocked by snow and the light coming through the gaps in the logs was negligible. But Saul knew the layout of McEwan's cabin. The table was in the centre of the room, where the engineer would sit and hold court, and Saul knew there would be a candle and matches there. The least he could do would be to light Mr McEwan's stove for him, whether he was here or not. No one let their stove go out in Siding Twenty-three unless they wanted to freeze to death in the night. He walked carefully across the dim room towards the dark shape of the table. The floor seemed sticky and icy. Saul placed the dish on the wooden surface and felt around for a candle, withdrawing his arm suddenly when his hand touched something soft and cold. It felt pulpy and unpleasant and Saul recoiled at its contact.

The experience stopped him wanting to feel around on that table any further, and leaving the soup there, he retraced his steps to the door, to prop it open and let in the thin grey daylight.

The floor was definitely sticky, and there was the unmistakable crunching of thin ice on a puddle, as if something wet was down there that had partially frozen. Saul's senses started to alert him to something he could not place, and did not wish to. He fumbled for the wooden latch, finding himself panic slightly when he failed to locate it first time, then breathing hard with relief when his fingers found the big hinged slat that opened the door. He pulled it up, threw the door open and blinked in the light, narrowing his eyes to peer into the newly-illuminated interior.

It was a full thirty seconds before he screamed. Thirty seconds in which Saul Campbell realized many things. The first thing he realized was that the cold object he had touched on the table was a piece of meat. A large piece of white-skinned, fatty, bloody meat, about seven or eight pounds in weight, his cook's eye told him, and meat that had pieces of fabric sticking to it.

The second thing he realized was that the silvery-grey wooden floor of McEwan's cabin was indeed stained with huge splashed patches of something dark. Something wet and sticky and half-frozen.

But it was the third thing he realized that made him scream, since the other observations took on new meaning. McEwan's head, neck and one shoulder lay in a black puddle by the wall, the mouth pulled back into a rictus, a white knob of spine protruding like a handle from the severed neck. The upper half of his torso was half-concealed beneath the bed and part of a leg showing behind the stove suggested that the other half might be found there.

Saul's scream was thin and reedy, and as he fled from the cabin he stopped making the piping shriek only when he gagged and retched, finally vomiting into the snow as his legs gave way and pitched him forward.

His throat was burning with the acid of the bile and from the gasping breaths of a runner, as he flailed up the icy trodden trail to the tunnel.

From a distance, his white face was a cartoon, with its down-turned black crescent of gaping mouth and wide boggling eyes. And the men who watched him come stood still and waited, as though delaying whatever disastrous news this staggering madman ran to deliver, would make it better when it reached them.

Duncan Muir watched the cook's approach with the others, and when the hysteric arrived and fell at their feet he fought back the moisture that was rising to his eyes in fear. Behind them in the rock, the tunnel entrance yawned like a mouth, and below them their cabins between the trees waited silently in the snow for their return.

34

The wipers heaved against the snow, each sweep testing the strength of the motor. Billy watched them scraping back and forward as his mom drove slowly in silence. His straight hair poked a few exploratory tendrils out from his woollen hat and he toyed with one that hung over his eye.

Katie was still wrestling with the urge to ask Billy big questions. But just the asking risked wrecking her family, never mind the answers. She had to believe in what she had. Any other way led to an abyss that was too deep, too dark and terrifying to even contemplate peering over its edge. Billy shifted in his seat, and she used the tiny movement as an event to kick start a normal conversation.

'Okay over there, Billy Boy?'

Her son nodded, not looking at her. Where was the boy who sang terrible pop songs in the passenger seat, and whose childish chatter about his day couldn't be silenced at any price? She swallowed and braced herself to be cheerful, but her voice still sounded unnatural and high when she continued.

'Miss Root showed me your painting.'

Billy stared straight ahead. She glanced at him as she steered the Toyota down the busy main street towards Mrs Chaney's.

'What was it about Billy?'

He tugged harder at the strand of hair and looked away from her, out of his window. Where was she taking this? She was asking him things she didn't want to know about. The abyss beckoned.

'It didn't look like a very happy painting.' They stopped on a red light and Katie turned to face him, her hands off the wheel reaching to touch his slumped shoulders and the little unoccupied hand that rested limply on one thigh. 'Talk to me, lamb.'

He looked at his feet, but didn't shake off his mother's warm hands. 'It was a prism. We got taught prisms.'

'And was the one you painted Dad's prism?'

He nodded.

'Why?'

'Just was.'

She stroked his hand gently. 'Is my prism like that? All dark, like you painted?'

He shook his head.

'So why is Dad's like that then?'

A car hooted behind them. Damn it, the light was green. Katie withdrew her motherly hands, changed into drive and moved off. 'Huh, sweetheart? Why is it like that?'

Billy's chest was rising and falling now, as though he were struggling with something. He said nothing for an age until Katie thought of repeating the question. But he beat her to it and replied in a small broken voice. ''Cause something big and dark's got inside my Dad.'

When Katie glanced at him in horror, she saw two huge tears rolling down his brown cheeks. She pulled the car over and grabbed her son in a bear hug. He cried then, sobbing uncontrollably as Katie held his hot woolly head with one hand and circled his body with the other, patting and rubbing his back.

Her own tears were threatening to spill, but she had started down a road from which there was no turning, and she decided she was not going to lose her way.

The engine, as it always did, guttered as though it wanted to cut out, and its labouring, plus the squeaky wipers and the splash of passing cars, made such a normal, everyday aural backdrop to Billy's sounds of distress that Katie prayed this was not really happening. But it was.

'Tell me, lamb. Tell me what the dark thing is. Does it make your Daddy hurt you?' There. She'd said them. Those impossible words of revulsion and horror she'd never even imagined could be formed on her lips. Does it make your daddy hurt you? How could Sam Hunt hurt anyone?

She remembered Sam in the labour suite at the county hospital in Stoke the day Billy was born. How strange and silly he'd looked, standing awkwardly over her as he watched her face contort in pain with each contraction, unable to soothe or offer any comfort other than his presence, and the squeezing of her clawed fingers with his big rough hand. He made gags that made her mad, since laughing was sore and broke her concentration, and he looked like he wanted to be somewhere else, somewhere very far away from all this pain and blood.

And then when Billy came slipping and sliding out, a purple-and-white wrinkled scream of a thing, Sam had been transformed, his restless nervousness replaced by a man made of granite, and he watched silently as Billy was freed from the cord that linked him to his mother and was placed at her breast. Katie was panting through her teeth with relief and joy at the touch and sight of their child, and when she looked up at her silent Sam she saw that the man of granite was crying fit to flood the room. His cheeks were stained with salty tears and his eyes were already puffy and small. She'd held out a hand to him, and he took it.

'Do you want to hold him?'

He looked at the nurse who took Billy and wrapped him in a white rigid sheet that did nothing to absorb the goo he was covered in, and handed him to the big weeping man. He held his son's tiny body in his arms and looked at him as though Billy were telling him something very important no one else could hear. And then Sam had said in a whisper to the baby, 'I'll keep you so safe. So safe.'

The man who said that to both his children at their birth was a man who had meant it. To ask the grown version of that baby who had communed so closely with his father on his entrance to the world *does it make your daddy hurt you?* seemed an obscenity. But she had asked it and it was done now.

Instead of the world crumbling with a rumble and a flash as she expected, there was a curious lightness on her chest and throat, as though the weight that had pressed down on her had been lifted with her dreadful words. Katie held Billy tight, waiting for the answer.

He trembled with a sob. 'It wants to hurt us all.'

And then he wailed like he was being skewered, and she hugged him hard enough to break and told him not to worry, that nothing was going to hurt any of them. But when she calmed him back to a sob and they continued on to pick up Jess, she wasn't sure that was true.

*   *   *

A small crowd had gathered to watch the interview and they stood around, leaning on their ski poles, looking at Pasqual as though she were going to tap dance. She smoothed her jacket nervously and cleared her throat as the guy in the camel coat and red scarf, who was called Ritchie or Roger or Raymond or some damn thing, spoke to the cameraman as though she didn't exist.

'Give me a wide for three or four questions then zoom in to her for a tight, okay?'

The cameraman with a neat beard and bored expression nodded, then winked at a good-looking company groomer in shades, who was leaning on her shovel and smiling with a big white grin. Pasqual glared at her and made a gesture with her hand and eyebrows to get back to work. The girl raised a hand, palm out in surrender, mouthed *sorry* and wandered back to the closed quad station where she was shovelling snow on the worn run-up.

The newsman turned to Pasqual. 'So, you ready to roll?'

'Sure. Do I look at you or into the camera?'

'You just look right at me. I wouldn't ask anyone without a welder's mask to look directly at that ugly son of a bitch.'

The cameraman smiled a smile that said he heard that gag every time he took the lens cap off. He bent to look in the eyepiece of his locked-off camera, both hands in his pockets.

Her interviewer shook his shoulders and made a choked coughing sound in his throat. 'Okay. Running?'

The cameraman took one hand lazily out of a pocket and turned his camera on. A little red light winked on at the top and Pasqual realized that she was nervous. Her mouth was dry and her heart was beating too fast, betraying her by the rapid clouds of vapour that puffed from her mouth as she waited.

'In ten.' He turned his back to Pasqual as he waited for the sign from his companion. A lazy hand again from the pocket. Ritchie, Roger or Raymond was off. 'A week ago, Silver, Alberta was just a sleepy ski town in the Canadian Rockies where the biggest event was a moose on the road.'

Funny guy, thought Pasqual. *Ha fucking ha.*

'But now, following the horrific death last week of Constable Joe Reader and only the day after the murder and mutilation of tourist Sean Bradford . . .'

Yeah that's right, you bastard, she thought, angry now. *Play up the dead tourist bit. God, why was she doing this? No publicity is bad publicity. Remember?*

'. . . the town is on the world's map as the home of a possible serial killer. Here, they're calling it the ski-riel killings.'

You mean you're calling it that, you shit. She frowned.

'Pasqual Weaver is the managing director of the Silver Ski Company.' He turned to her, surprising her with his newly-assumed, phoney expression of professional concern and interest. 'How are they coping here, Pasqual?' He thrust his boxed microphone at her like a witch-doctor thrusting a wand at someone he wanted to hurt.

Her heart pounded, but he'd made her cranky and that was good for getting over your nerves. 'Folk are coping just fine. In fact we were busier here today than we've been for a long time. I think people are smart enough to know that this was one awful but unrelated incident that will never happen again. There's certainly no danger.'

'Two incidents, surely. How can you be certain the killer won't strike again?'

That wand again.

'Of course I can't be sure, but he'd be a pretty dumb killer to strike again when the town is crawling with police and you guys.'

'There's been some criticism that you opened for business the day after such a death.'

'We always open immediately after a fatality.'

Jesus. Wrong thing to say. She saw his face light up.

'So nothing new about death at this resort? You're used to tourists dropping like flies in Silver?'

'What I meant was that with the inevitable fatal ski accident . . .' she ignored his advice and looked straight into the camera for the next bit, '. . . of which let me say there are fewer here than almost any Canadian or American resort because of our rigorous safety standards . . .' she looked back at him triumphantly to continue, '. . . we have to carry on as normal. And I'm afraid we had to carry that through even with the tragedy of Sean Bradford's death.'

The camel-coat with a mouth looked annoyed she'd wasted his tape with a commercial. 'Surely you may have to face the fact that your business will suffer in the long term from this horror.'

She'd waited for this. 'Absolutely not. In fact only today I've been able to confirm that our celebrity ski week, in aid of the Alberta Living Time Charity Foundation, and packed with stars, will go ahead as promised in two days from now. How about that?' *Ask me about the stars next*, she thought and gave the kind of smile to the camera she'd seen anchorwomen do when they handed over to sports. But the man with the mike decided finally he was dealing with an imbecile. He stepped in front of her and turned to camera.

'Thank you. So Silver struggles on in the face of the fact that a silent killer is stalking its quiet streets, its quaint bars and restaurants. In fact as we stand here at the foot of the trails, the day waning, he could even be amongst the folk coming down off that hill of fear, looking for his next victim in the happy crowd of tired skiers. This is Robin Tyler, W.C.B.N. Back to you, Marty.'

Pasqual exploded. 'Oh come on! That's a piece of bullshit!'

The camera was off, the neat beard already unscrewing it from its tripod. Robin looked innocently at her. 'What's the problem?'

'You're kidding! Are you deliberately trying to lose me customers? You said this was going to be a positive piece about how we're carrying on in the face of adversity.'

'That's right. It was.'

The cameraman was folding the tripod up. Pasqual held up a hand and pointed a finger at him. He smiled up at Robin.

'You just hold it right there buddy.' She turned back to the man with the mike, her finger still pointing at the cameraman as if it were keeping him there. The small crowd of onlookers had evaporated with the pay-off, gone to catch their ski bus or load up their cars. Pasqual was on her own. 'Now we're going to do that again, Mr Tyler, with a little less of the hill-of-fear crap, or I'm going to boot you and your crew right off this mountain and make sure that every other goddamn news unit here gets access to this location except you. You know I can do it.'

He looked at her, then at his cameraman who raised one laconic eyebrow, and knew it was true. 'Okay, calm down. I'm real sorry you feel that way, and I must say I think you're wrong. It was positive and I think you would have been happy with it when you saw it go out. But if you want to do it again, hey, we'll give it another shot.'

He pulled himself up into his broadcasting posture again, and waited for the camera to be screwed back on. Neat-beard gave him the nod.

'Okay, Frankie, just for variety let's have the strawberry filter on this one.'

Frankie half-smiled, and flicked a switch.

'In ten.'

Ten was up.

'A week ago, Silver, Alberta was just a sleepy ski town . . .'

Good. They would do the interview again and this time she would make no mistakes. She'd make sure she told the shitty American rat bag that she'd got a great big yes on the celebrity ski from Del Parkinson no less! *That's right, you slimy nobody. A real TV star coming to Silver. His agent knew all about the murders and said that Del wasn't scared, that he'd love to come and help the town get its balls back.* Pasqual was delirious with victory. And she'd mention it this time. All it took was to lose your nerves and concentrate real hard on what you were going to say. In fact she concentrated so hard on remembering to mention it that she didn't notice the strange effect using a strawberry filter had on a news camera. It stopped the little red light from going on, and the tape inside the camera didn't go round at all.

There was a tap at the door. Becker poked his head round.

'You busy, Craig?'

Craig was not busy. Craig was fretting, avoiding his next meeting which was with the warden of some far away national park about poachers he suspected were coming from Silver. Craig was waiting for Hawk to get picked up and hauled into work so he could ask him something. Meanwhile, what did Edmonton's finest want?

'No. come in.'

The squat man in his fifties let his body follow his head into the room, and shut the door behind him. 'How's it going?'

Craig looked blankly at him. Be nice. Remember. 'Good. You?'

'Nice and slow but sure. The motto of all good policemen. You know it well enough.'

No he didn't. It was the motto of an old guy who had authority, experience and could see a big pension coming up on the inside lane. The motto of a man who did the job and didn't take risks. ' Uh-huh.'

'I think we have a suspect, Craig and I'm thinking of bringing him in.'

That made McGee sit up. 'Take a seat.'

Becker waved a hand, still standing by the door. 'No time. This won't take long. I just had to run this past you.'

In other words, what you think is not important. I'm merely required by

RCMP etiquette to let you know who I'll be locking up behind your bars. Craig gnashed his back teeth and the muscle in his jaw protruded through his cheeks as he did so. 'Go on.'

'I guess we both know, you and I, that this is probably the work of an Indian.'

'No. I don't know that.'

A half-smile from Becker.

'Sure. We don't know for certain. But you get my drift.'

Craig did not reply. That unsettled the man in his office. He dropped the buddy act.

'Wilber Stonerider. A drunk and a nuisance. You've had him in here plenty.'

Craig groaned. 'No way. He's a harmless old guy. Gets loaded, lays one on whoever's nearest and gets slammed up till he dries out. How in God's name did you come up with that one?'

Ernest Becker looked at Craig with something approaching anger. 'We came up with that one, as you put it, by careful police work. You know, we were working our way through all the Kinchuinicks in Silver since your interesting interview with Hunt, and it came up with something. The man has no alibi for either murder date, and he seems to know a hell of a lot about Joe Reader's death.'

'Like?'

'The organs. We haven't released that information to anyone, have we?'

'You're telling me Wilber knew about the mutilation in detail?'

'Not in so many words. But I believe the man is psychotic. The transcript of his interview with Sergeant Lenhoff this afternoon makes pretty interesting reading.'

'I'm losing you here, Staff Sergeant.'

Becker changed his mind and sat down. 'Look. This is a man who tells Lenhoff that a bird came to him, followed him everywhere, and told him that it would carve him up. That a man's heart and penis were, and I'm quoting now, the bits that should fuck each other. Seemed to believe this bird was coming to get Stonerider.'

Craig's eyes widened, mocking, but Becker didn't catch it. 'He said that did he?'

'He said that.'

'And he was specific about Joe's death, you say.'

'He didn't actually mention Sergeant Reader or the murder, but the heart and penis connection are pretty convincing don't you think?'

'Curious, yes. No more.'

Becker was already regretting this conversation. His face hardened and his voice dropped half an octave like a father giving a wayward son a row. 'Well I happen to think it's a little more than curious, Staff Sergeant. The man is obviously a fruit, and he sounds like a fruit we should have safely in here.'

Craig was silent for a time, leaning back in his chair and rubbing the edge of his desk with both hands. 'You're right. We should talk to him some more. But not in custody.'

'Because?' It was Becker's turn to mock with a tone.

'Because those guys out there with cameras and notebooks are just salivating to see who we're going to pull in. And if you pull in an Indian they'll go apeshit. Especially if it's an innocent Indian.'

'And you of course, are so sure he's innocent.'

'Pretty much.'

'Want to enlighten me, McGee?'

Oh-ho! No more Craig or Staff Sergeant. Craig rubbed the side of his nose and looked down. He wanted to be nice. Remember? 'You think an old drunk like Stonerider could have gotten on to that pass in a blizzard, murdered Joe then pushed his truck over the Wolf's Tooth gorge on his own? Then you think he somehow found his way onto the ski hill without anyone seeing him, snuck into a bunch of trees and took out a fit young Californian kid with what looks like a blade the size of a sword, and escaped without leaving any footprints? Jeez, Becker. Some talented fruit all right.'

Becker stared back at the impertinent. He took a conspiratorial line, sounding vaguely excited, as though imparting thrilling infor-mation that he shouldn't give away. 'We think he may, just may, have been in cahoots with Hunt.'

Craig did the unforgivable. He leaned back in his chair and laughed out loud. He laughed like a fairground clown, his sides shaking and his eyes crinkled in mirth. Then he threw his arms out wide and faced Becker with the laugh still on his lips. 'For why? What the fuck do you think they're up to?'

Becker stood up. He was very calm and very quiet. 'I'm sorry for disturbing your busy schedule, Staff Sergeant. It was my duty to tell you we would be arresting a man and bringing him here to your detachment. It is not my duty to discuss the details with you.'

Craig stopped laughing. He hadn't done a very good job of being nice. He regretted it, and wondered if it could be fixed.

The two men sized each other up, contemplating how they could proceed when the difficulty was wrenched from them. The door burst open.

It was Constable Bell. Craig knew in his guts what he was going to hear. He stayed very still, waiting and breathing.

Behind Jeff Bell, through the wide open door that he didn't knock on, the office was churning like a tidal race. He could see one of Becker's men holding Holly, who was crying. He could see three police constables standing in that inert way you stand when you don't know what to do next. He could see arms flailing and heads being hit with the palms of hands. And he could see worse things in Bell's contorting face as it formed the words Craig was praying he wouldn't hear.

'It's Dan. He's got Dan.'

35

Eden had once said that if you doubted we were all part of the same thing you had to ask yourself why every natural scrap of the earth looks like an old familiar face. Sam hadn't understood as a boy. He did as a man. A rock patched with lichen, a cloud blowing across a peak, a stem of buckbrush bouncing in the rain; they all possessed a face of sorts.

Sam scanned the Rockies remembering Eden's observation, and knew exactly what he meant. These massive pieces of rock were the same. He knew as he looked at them that they didn't look back, but there was something about them which reminded him that he was connected, and that they, the mountains and the man, were inseparable.

Sam pushed himself forward to the lip of the small cornice and let his eyes follow the infinity of pink peaks that stretched away to the north. The eerie clanking of empty chairlifts and the odd shout from a distant homebound skier was all that broke the silence. He had chosen the hard route from the top station, knowing that only Patrol would risk it when the sun went down.

A face in the crowd.

He was running from shadows, and the shadow he was most afraid of was his own. Big tough Sam Hunt, afraid to the point of screaming of a face in the crowd, and too scared to let his past through and pick it apart. Was he born a coward? Perhaps. But at least he'd been born a robust coward. His two other siblings had died. One born dead, the other mewling its last breath at only three weeks old. He had survived, and until he met Katie he'd wondered why. Moses had made him wonder daily why he bothered to live.

Calvin had said Moses hadn't always been that bad, that he went bad when Eden rejected him. Said that Moses Hunting Wolf was strong and funny and good-looking in his young days, maybe with a streak of cruelty in his humour, but okay really. But if he had been okay, Sam didn't remember it. He'd wished he'd never been born so many times it became a comforting ritual to think it instead of a cry of despair. But then came Katie. Katie, his blonde saviour, and beautiful Billy and gorgeous, chubby Jess and all the things he'd never dared dreamed of having back in that cabin on Redhorn. And now he was being proved right again. That those things were not for him. He could practically hear Moses's drunken wheeze of a laugh from the grave.

Heh, heh, thought you could be havin' what them white boys have, didn't ya? Well like your grandpappy says, you be born Indian and you gonna die Indian, and now there be a face in the crowd gonna make you lose your mind. Heh, heh, heh.

Born Indian. Was there ever a time when he wasn't ashamed to be Indian? Yes. There had been times when he had been proud. Eden and Calvin had sometimes touched a part of him, an atavistic nerve that made him proud, although pride wasn't an exact enough description for the emotion. It was more like the thing Eden meant about the substance of the earth. A sense of belonging, of understanding who you were and being glad that you were part of it all. Eden had almost gotten him to believe that Sam was part of a very special family. A family who if they only knew it, held a power that was as important to the world as clean air and fresh water, for keeping mankind alive and safe. White men didn't know it, on account of them no longer understanding the old world and the way it worked, and what's worse, they didn't care. But they'd care plenty if it wasn't for folks like Eden and his pappy and his grandpappy and so on before him. You just don't know you've been safe, Eden said, until the man holding back the dog lets go.

But now where were the Indians that Sam had been proud to belong to for that brief moment? Did the Indians who staggered, shouting and fighting from the Craigellachie Hotel bar respect anything, except someone who'd get in another beer? And their repayment for that search for oblivion, was short lives and a legacy of misery and despair to their children. Those were the Indians now. Brown faced Canadians who drank and ranted, who hit their kids, or worse. Brown underprivileged Canadians. Nothing more. Who cared if white Europeans did it to them? Why did they let it happen? What was there to be proud of in that? And if Sam were part of such a frigging special family, what had Moses been? It was all horse shit. All of it. Except . . .

A face in the crowd.

Sam's head buzzed faintly as he stood looking at those darkening mountains. He closed his eyes and leant on his poles, his head resting on one arm. He had recognized it, just like Eden said. What he had to decide now was whether it had happened, or whether he was projecting some weird fantasy from the past into his conscious mind because he was sick.

But the face had not been human. What did Eden say? A bear in a flock of geese? Yes. That was good. Exactly right. There was no mistaking it. Other people had been fooled all right. Only Sam saw what lay behind that milky white membrane that pretended to be skin and he felt a twist of nausea in his stomach as he remembered what he'd seen.

Hate. Swirling dark, naked, hate, bubbling in its own blackness like viscous oil disturbed in a vat. But it was not a hate that stemmed from anger or fear or jealousy: it was that familiar thing again, a malice that was happy being malice itself, the way a rock is happy being a rock. It was something that lived to hate and loved to hate. And it had looked at Sam for a long time as though it knew him.

He pulled his head up off his arm, as though those pale blue eyes were boring into him again, and took a sharp breath of freezing evening air into his lungs to clear the vision. It was snowing down in the valley now. The yellow lights that had started to twinkle into life in the distance were obliterated now by the thick cloud dumping its white load. Home. He had to get home.

Sam stood upright, gripped his poles and pushed off over the cornice. He dropped into the icy trail and got his speed up with a path straight down the fall line. The trail narrowed ahead, and swept left through a gap between the tall pines, and he made three short turns to check his speed as he approached. It was nastier than he had anticipated, and he grunted as his thighs burned, cutting the blunt edges of the old skis into the shiny unforgiving blanket of blue green ice. The wind ripped at his face as he flew down the mountain, alone on the trail, and the sound of his skis slicing into the snow was all that accompanied him.

He burst through the trees onto the wide part of the trail that snaked beneath the stark pylons of the Serendipity Chair. Sam was surprised to see it still running. It was well after four now and those guys closed it at three forty-five on the dot. What was weirder was that there was a solitary figure in the chair, swinging his way up slowly towards Sam, poles clutched over his lap and swaying one ski lazily beneath him like a pendulum. That made Sam turn his skis side-on to the hill and sweep to a halt in a wave of snow the height of his waist.

Not a patroller. Just a skier. A man by the look of it. What were they doing down there, letting a member of the public up the hill so late? The tortured, confused portion of Sam released him for a moment, and he slipped back into Silver Ski Company-employee mode.

He waited for the figure to reach him, to check the guy hadn't hopped on the chair without someone knowing he was there. It had happened before. Some girl from Germany last season had sneaked onto the quad from the unmanned half-way point and got stranded thirty-five feet up in the dark when they switched it off from the base not knowing she was there. She nearly bought it with hypothermia, and would have for sure if the guy driving the night trail-basher hadn't got out for a leak and just heard her cries over the roar of his engine. Big changes after that. You count them on and you count them off, and no station is left unmanned while the chair is still running. So how come this guy got through when it was nearly dark? He'd find out. The chair was getting close, clanking its solitary passenger over the tops of the trees towards the expanse of flat snow between the pylons.

Sam waited, leaning forward on his boots, taking the opportunity to get his breath back after the effort of the run.

The chair stopped. Now there is one lucky guy, thought Sam. A few minutes later and he'd be long gone down the Serendipity trail. Sam pulled himself up and moved off down to where the guy was swinging in the air.

Strange though, that the guy was sitting so still and quiet. He didn't raise a hand to Sam or look behind him to see what was up. He just sat there waiting and something about him looked like Sam had seen him before. The suit. That was it. As he drew nearer, even in the half-light, Sam recognized that old black suit with red and navy flashes on it. What a dinosaur from the seventies that was. They'd never heard of day-glo or fuchsia and peppermint back then. Every ski-suit had been black, navy or red and they were awful. And the one this guy was wearing was just like the one the Reverend Jenkins used to wear. Exactly like it.

Two more turns and he'd be right underneath him. The hat was the same as the Reverend's too. An orange hill-walker's woollen affair with a tiny bobble that clashed horribly with the suit. And the skis were the same. Beat-up Dynastars. And the gloves. And the blue scarf that was wrapped round the lower half of the man's face obscuring all but his bespectacled eyes. And the spectacles. All the same.

Sam stopped sharply about twenty yards from where he was going. His heart was racing. Not from the skiing, but from the black things that had started to form in his mind again. It was crazy. The Reverend Jenkins had died eleven years ago. Mouth cancer. This was not him. It was a man dressed like him. But it was not him. Sam panted to control himself.

Go and help the man. Stop this lunacy, and go and help the man. He pushed forward again, although every nerve in his body told him not to, and skied up to a halt on a spot in front of the man's chair where he could speak to and see him comfortably. The chair hung, swaying gently now, about fifteen feet above Sam. He cleared his throat, and held a gloved hand up to cup his mouth.

'Are you okay, mister?'

No reply. Sam peered up at the figure in the gloom waiting to see what he would do. He knew the man was looking at him; saw his spectacles glint as his head inclined slightly towards Sam. He tried again. 'Do the chair attendants know you got on?'

Nothing.

'Hey mister! Can you hear me up there!'

'I can hear you, Shammy.'

Sam's heart stood still. His hand dropped from his mouth to his side, letting the pole that was attached to his wrist bang uselessly against his boot.

The figure in the chair shifted forward slightly, leaning on the safety bar. He raised an arm and pointed a finger at the man below him. 'You didn't hear me when I shcreamed for you though, did you?'

Sam's mouth was opening and shutting now, his lower jaw trembling with the unauthorized movement.

The figure's voice sounded strange. Oh, it was unmistakably the Reverend's voice, but the words were distorted, lisped, strangled in some way that gave them a horrible, wet, indistinct sound. Sam croaked a noise. 'What?'

'You heard. They called you, didn't they? I ashked them to. They told you what ward I wosh in and shtill you didn't come.'

Sam was making this up himself. He had to be. They would find out why or how when they looked into his brain with that machine in Calgary and then everything would be fine. No more faces in the crowd, no more blackouts, no more nightmares hanging from iced steel cable in the twilight.

He could barely breathe, and he closed his eyes and gritted his teeth. No good. When he opened them the figure was still there, hanging in space, alive when it should be dead.

'I know why you let me die like a dog without shaying goodbye. Don't think I didn't know, Shammy. Did you think that your dirty filthy fornication with Darshcy had been a shecret? Did you? You thought she'd be there at the hoshpital, and you didn't come. In cashe she grabbed you by the shleeve and begged you to fuck her again.' The figure that could not possibly be the Reverend Jenkins, laughed a coughing, slick and wet sounding guffaw. No. This was not him. He had been kind and good and forgiving and cared about Sam. What was this thing that Sam stood beneath, staring up at it like a baby watching a mobile? It was real, and it was talking again in that thick, slurred slurping voice.

'One fuck from a shtinking Indian and she was heartbroken. Nothing to you, Shammy, eh? You didn't want to know after the deed. But she cried for you every night. You knew that. And that'sh why you shtayed away, washn't it?'

And he would never have cursed, the Reverend Jenkins. No no. Not if he caught a finger in a car door, not if a coal fell from the fire onto his slipper, not even if his lascivious daughter *had* won herself an afternoon of clumsy pointless sex with someone he thought of as his son. Never.

The figure put a hand up to its face. 'Well you misshed yourshelf, Shammy.' It pulled away the blue scarf. Beneath the spectacles and the bridge of the nose was a void. There were upper teeth and part of a lower jaw, but the flesh was eaten from the cheeks all the way back to both ears. The obscenity grinned at him with its diseased half-face. Bits of the remaining blackened flesh moved around what was left of an ulcerated and rotting tongue. 'Yesh, you misshed your-shelf, boy.'

Sam opened his mouth to scream and found nothing there. The horror grinned on at him, laughing in its wet throat. The message of panic from his brain that didn't reach Sam's mouth in time to scream, reached his legs instead and he threw himself forward with a lunge. The skis did the rest and in seconds he was accelerating down the fall-line with the sound of that wet cackle dying behind him.

A variety of creatures stirred in alarm from their evening chores as Sam crashed past their haunts in the high pines.

They were nervous creatures tonight. They could smell a fierce danger in the air. They lifted their snouts and beaks, cocked their ears, and waited until he was past, then resumed business in their secret places.

The bell on the microwave made her jump. Katie had been thinking about that woman visitor in the museum; her face, the way she smiled, and the thing she thought she saw through the distorted end of the case. The pizza would stop her thinking about it, so she got up to scoop it out of the revolving stage on which it had starred for the last three minutes.

'Billy! Pizza, honey!'

Jess was in bed. It had taken a while but the wriggling laughing little bundle had eventually given up the good fight against sleep and was safely folded into her Care-Bears comforter. Katie was shamed that she was about to feed herself and her son a revolting frozen cheese and pepperoni smeared disc of dough, but Sam wasn't home. She cooked nice things for all of them when Sam was home but she didn't know when he would be home, because he wasn't here like he should have been when she got back and he hadn't called. Tonight it was going to have been beef stroganoff. She'd bought the ingredients after they'd been to the doctor's, going to three stores until she found all the right things. But that was before she got sick at the museum. Before she picked Billy up and saw his painting. Before everything. So it was frozen pizza for supper.

Billy waddled through to the kitchen and climbed up onto one of the old pine captain's chairs at the table. Katie slid the pizza onto a china dish, dipped her finger in a bit of the melted cheese, put it in her mouth and did an impersonation of the Seller's pizza mom. 'Mmmm hmmm. Does that EVER taste good!'

A weak smile from the boy at the table. 'Yeah. That's funny.'

She ignored the slight, put the dish down and went to the drawer to get a knife. 'You want Coke or milk with that?'

'Milk.'

'Milk, please.'

'Milk please.'

There was a scratching and a whining at the door. Billy looked up at his mother with huge black pleading eyes.

'Go on then. But no feeding him while you eat.'

Billy jumped up and skipped to the door to let Bart in. The husky bounded in, licked Billy like he was a candy, and then shook his cargo of snow all over the floor, his master and his mother. Billy laughed. Katie's heart lost about twenty pounds of weight with that sound and she bent down and hugged him as he hugged his dog. Billy had seemed a little better since that cry in the car, but she'd watched his face as they came in the door, his eyes roaming the room looking for Sam, and she had nearly wept. He had actually looked frightened. Billy had relaxed when he realized that his father wasn't home and she'd thought her heart would break.

Bart panted around excitedly as Billy climbed back into his chair, and finally settled for a place beneath the table at Billy's feet. Katie served a mushy triangle to her son, cut herself a slice and sat down beside him.

The kitchen door was rapped with knuckles, and for the second time that night she jumped. Billy looked at her with surprise. She tried to cover her moment of fright with a big smile even the Seller's pizza mom would have chucked out as phoney. 'Hey. We got a sit-com kitchen door tonight, Billy Boy. I'll bet it's a special guest star who'll get a round of applause when I open it. What do you think? Bill Cosby?'

Billy shrugged and got to work on his soggy slice. He was far too close to his mother not to see straight through her forced cheerfulness. She was as unhappy as he was, and the song and dance act wasn't helping anyone.

She got up and opened it. Not Bill Cosby. Gerry and Ann.

'Guys! Get in here.'

They stamped into the kitchen, spreading as much snow as Bart but a little more politely. Gerry ruffled Billy's hair as he took off his coat, and Billy smiled up at him.

'Pizza, huh! That looks good.'

Katie took his coat and waited for Ann's to come off. 'Don't. I'm not proud of it.'

They fussed around taking more stuff off and finally settled round the table.

'Well this is a treat,' said Katie in that same voice she'd been inflicting on Billy all evening. Ann looked at her like she'd gone mad.

'Jeez. You don't get many treats.'

Billy laughed again. Good. Very good. And Gerry seemed very interested indeed that Billy laughed, looking at him and nodding with a smile. That told Katie all she needed to know about her friends' impromptu visit. Agnes Root.

'Sam home?' Ann asked it innocently, but Gerry never took his eyes off Billy. If he was here to witness the basis of Agnes Root's concern he wasn't disappointed. Billy's face crumpled at the mention of his father's name and his eyes dropped to the table as he put the pizza to his lips again. Katie shook her head. Anne nodded up the way in response.

'So how's it hanging in the school yard?' Katie bit into a piece of pizza and chewed at it.

Gerry took his eyes off her son at last. 'Good. Got through another day without losing a limb.'

Ann sat back. 'There's a lot of buzz about this you-know-what. The news crews have been all over town. Kids can't help but get excited.'

'Yeah. Exciting.' Katie said it through her mouth full of melted cheese, but it couldn't disguise the disgust in her voice. Her friends looked at her now, the way they'd looked at Billy. Katie could see they wanted to talk. 'Okay, Billy. Since you're the oldest son in this house, you win the prize of getting to finish your pizza in front of the TV.'

He looked up, surprised but delighted. 'Can Bart come too?'

'Sure. Long as he doesn't use the VCR and tape over *Citizen Kane*.'

'Neat.'

He needed no more encouragement, and the three adults watched

him and the big dog go in a silence that persisted until they heard
the canned laughter of some game show float in from the other room.
Gerry clasped his hands in front of him on the table.

'What's happening, Katie?'

Katie looked at Gerry's big kind face, then across at Ann's pretty
and worried one, and the flood gates opened. She opened her mouth
in a wail that she only managed to stifle with both hands. Hot tears
streamed down her cheeks like there was a hose behind each ear, and
she gulped and gasped in her sobbing as Ann stepped down behind
her and held her shaking body. 'Dear God, I don't know. I just don't
know. My world's turning upside-down.'

She wept uncontrollably rocked in Ann's arms for what seemed
like an age. And then the grief and self-pity subsided. Katie shuddered, drew in some halting breaths and pulled herself upright and
off her friend's shoulder. 'God. I'm sorry. I'm so sorry. I don't know
what's up with me.'

'Shush, honey. It does you good, a weep. Do you want some water?
Anything?'

Katie wiped her nose with the back of her hand. 'There's a malt
whisky in the left-hand cupboard. I broke it open last night.'

Ann laughed. 'That's what I meant. When I said water I meant
malt whisky.'

Katie laughed through her tears. A strange, shuddering laugh.

Ann had three glasses and the bottle on the table at the speed of
light and they watched as Katie took a big mouthful of the yellow
liquid and swallowed it with a gasp.

'Better?'

Gerry was leaning forward.

'Yeah. Sorry.'

'Stop saying you're sorry.'

'Sorry.'

They all laughed gently. Then they stopped laughing. Gerry put a
hand out and placed it on Katie's. 'Can you talk about it?'

Katie looked down and shook her head. 'I don't think so, Gerry.
Because I don't know what there is to say, and I think I'm going mad.'

'Well let me start. Is it Sam?'

Her mouth did that wide thing again, as she pulled back the
corners, trying to control the crying that was starting again. 'Sure . . .'
She gasped, controlling the sobbing. 'It's Sam.'

Gerry and Ann exchanged looks. Katie took another swig of Dalwhinnie. From the other room a burst of laughter again, this time accompanied by Billy's unbelieving yell of, 'Naw! No way!' and a bark from Bart. It reminded them all why they were sitting there.

Gerry looked back at Katie. It really was a very kind face. 'Agnes showed me the painting, Katie. Told me she had spoken to you.'

Katie nodded glumly, head bowed like a naughty pupil as he continued.

'I don't know what to make of it. I know what she thinks and I know it just isn't true.'

Katie nodded again.

'I know Billy, Katie. He's an imaginative boy. I've lost count of the times he's astonished me with some weird and wonderful tale he's concocted. It's not out of the question that he's just taken a bad dream too far.' He paused, looked at Ann, then back at Katie. 'But what's more, I've known Sam for ten years and if I ever met a man with a purer prism than him then I didn't know it.'

Katie squeezed his hand. 'Thank you, Gerry.'

Ann took her hand away from the whisky glass and put it on top of the pile that was Gerry's and Katie's. 'Is everything okay with you and Sam?'

Katie sniffed. 'The police were here, asking him questions about the murder. He was there at the time.'

Anne raised an eyebrow. 'I had no idea.'

'It was routine, you know. But I found out that his real name is . . .' She was starting to cry again. Two hands patted hers calm. '. . . I found out he's really Sam Hunting Wolf. Can you believe that? He didn't tell me he'd changed it?'

Gerry was casual. 'That's not such a big deal is it? We all know how Sam feels about being Kinchuinick.'

'It's just like I'm scared about what else I don't know Gerry. And in ten years I've never even thought about it. I never cared. Now I'm scared I don't really know him.'

'Come on, Katie. It's a bummer being interviewed by the cops. I know. They grilled me two years ago about that drugs thing the Hendon boy got mixed up in. But like you say, it's routine. It's just the strain.'

She nodded and smiled, and lifted the glass to her lips with the hand that wasn't smothered by other people's flesh. 'I'll drink to that. Positive thinking.'

They lifted their glasses to join her in that happy toast, when the door kept its promise of being the evening's theatrical entertainment by bursting wide open. Sam Hunt stood in the frame, his eyes wild with something that looked like terror, his face scratched and bloody where he'd run through the trees when he took a tumble and lost a ski.

Anne put a hand to her mouth, Katie scraped back her chair and Gerry leapt to his feet. And when his big, exhausted Indian friend staggered forward with a groan into the room, everyone realized there was to be no toast that night to positive thinking. Especially Billy, who stood in the doorway to the parlour, his hand buried in Bart's fur in a tight fist.

36

Calvin Bitterhand's eyes flickered open and he steadied himself to avoid falling forward onto the hot stones.

He struggled not to weep, finding himself once more earthbound after the flight that had seemed to last forever. But now he must have water. His gap-fingered hand reached out to the bark bowl and lifted it to his lips. The water was as warm as soup, but it ran down his throat and soothed his monstrous thirst. It must have been a long flight, since the stones were no longer hot as he imagined, but warm. He needed to heat them on the fire outside the lodge again, but right now he had little enough energy to keep him sitting upright.

To fly, unburdened by the body, with neither the snow blizzards above the mountains, or the blazing sun high in the azure blue sky causing you harm or discomfort, was a heaven that most men would never attain. But the price was this. An old shell of a body, quivering and aching with fatigue, stained with sweat, and near, Calvin knew it, to death. But he had not flown like that since his prime days as a shaman, and it told him he was nearly pure again. The Eagle would not fly to order in such a manner with one who was not pure, and he had soared effortlessly with it for what seemed like an age. But to see what? To see that ancient curse of a thing dig its claws more firmly into the fabric of a world it had no right to. This world. The one that was ruled by the human heart, and would be until such time as it was decreed that the domination must end.

And Calvin knew that it would end, had seen that the dark spirits that were struggling to come through would one day have their time, when man and woman no longer walked the earth, when mankind had darkened it by their actions and would be destroyed by their own folly. But he had also seen that the earth would heal itself in their absence, and spirits such as the one he feared, would have their days freely on earth. But the spirits could see what Calvin could see and they dreaded that future darkness as much as man would if he knew. For what is the purpose of evil when it has no victim?

But that was far away, and the spirit was here now and rejoicing in it, growing in confidence, enjoying its stay. He had seen it as it moved amongst men and women in its inexpert disguise, sometimes shifting into a terrified lowly creature for no more reason than it could, and to pacify its bottomless ire that it could not do the same to a man. At least not yet. Not yet.

But it had found its keeper.

Calvin put down the bark bowl and held his head in his hands. Oh Great Spirit, a keeper who did not know he was the keeper, or at least would not believe the truth in his heart. That was Calvin's doing. His responsibility to teach and to prepare, and what was the outcome? How could he have foreseen what was to happen?

The boy could have been the most powerful of them all, so strong and pure was his heart. But his weapons were blunt without that belief. He was as a white man now, weak and child-like, his belief only in what the eyes could see and the empty religion of science could explain.

It was no use blaming Moses. Calvin was to blame long before that nightmare afternoon. Calvin could have stopped him: he knew what was in Sam's heart, and what was worse, why it was there. But he did not stop the boy doing what he did, and he was as guilty and responsible for it as any. But the boy must know the truth. It was not as Sam thought, and the importance of that information was everything. Everything.

He let his hands fall to his naked legs and breathed deeply. He must find the strength to continue. He was near being able to achieve his goal. His heart sank, remembering how easy it had been for him as a young man to achieve it. How far he had strayed from the Great Spirit's plan. And how he had been punished for it.

With a huge effort, he uncrossed his legs and stood. Every muscle and bone in his body protested, and he left the sweat lodge with difficulty to tend the fire and replace the stones. Outside it was light. Had he been amongst the spirits all night, or was this the same day? The fire would not tell him. He had placed four slabs of cut turf over it to keep the fire smouldering in secret for days and now he knelt and shifted the snow-covered turf, and there indeed were the glowing embers he had left. He bent and blew on them, watching the red glow increase and sparkle with life, then reached into the pile of sticks by the fire and threw on a handful of twigs. An orange flame danced about them, and he fed it with more wood.

Now for the stones. He took off his buckskin loin cloth, standing naked in the snow and walked back into the sweat-lodge. With the cloth, he lifted the first of the warm stones, prayed over it and carried it to the fire, careful to walk clockwise, with the sun. Twenty-five times he would have to do it. Alone.

Sam was the one who used to reheat the stones, allowing Calvin to remain in the lodge, his concentration unbroken and his sweat still running. Calvin thought of the boy's eager and earnest face as he prayed and heated the stones, and his heart ached for him. Sam moved like a young deer, and oh, those shining eyes and that determined pink mouth. Calvin could have watched his young apprentice forever. And then he thought of the face he had seen from his flight with the Eagle. Sam, the adult, standing on that ski hill, staring up at an empty chairlift. Calvin knew the spirit was there. Its filth and its blackness were swirling around the wires and pylons of that contraption. But Calvin could not see what Sam saw. That cáme from inside Sam's head only, and it must have been something that filled him with dread. His face was contorted with pain and shame and fear. What a different face. It looked so old compared to the smooth-skinned beauty that he had been.

Why had Eden not been the one chosen to deal with this? Eden would have laughed in the Trickster's face. Calvin was sure of it. Because Eden knew what it could and could not do. It was not knowing that made the man weak, made it possible for the Trickster to crawl inside its keeper, take his human strength and use it elsewhere for something that was most certainly not an illusion.

He placed another stone on the fire and retraced his steps for the next, gulping at the memory of Sam on the hill.

If he could be so easily frightened by an illusion, he would also easily be goaded into doing what the Trickster needed him to do. And Calvin knew that the goading had already begun. Calvin had called to Sam from the air, trying to remind him of what he had been taught, but he was silent without his body, and his shouted words were as slight as ice crystals hanging in the morning air. But the Trickster had heard them all right.

The shaman had felt its black, sightless sense turn towards the Eagle spirit and Calvin, putting out tendrils to feel them, and he had soared away quickly to the safety of the high peaks. So foolish. He should have remained a silent watcher. It knew now, even if Sam did not, that he was coming.

Another stone, and Calvin was starting to feel the cold, his sweat having been evaporated, and the snow now getting a grip on his freezing naked flesh. No rest. There was no time. He dropped the rock on the heating pile, and laid more wood on the flames.

He stopped and looked at the flames, enjoying their heat on his legs, and before he could beat it back, he remembered his folly.

It was the firelight. How could anyone who had seen the boy's perfect skin lit by the glow of the fire not have wanted to touch it? He screwed his eyes shut tightly, as if that would keep back the pain of memory, but it was there. Back again to haunt him, to torture him.

They had been in the woods for hours that day, he and Sam, collecting fungus and roots. Sam's laugh was merry when he was with Calvin in those days. He hung on his words as if they were precious gifts, and Calvin was careful to make sure they were words that merited such attention.

'Here. This one boy!'

Calvin had called him over to a shrub with bright red berries. He plucked at a maple-shaped leaf without tearing it off the branch. 'This here be Devil's-Club, and it be used for so much stuff I lost count.'

Sam nodded, taking it in and fingering the leaf as though its touch would help him understand its powers.

'The Crow Indians rub these here berries in their scalps to chase off lice. Say it makes the hair shiny too.' He looked at Sam. 'Not that you need that, huh?'

Sam looked embarrassed and tugged at his leaf again. Calvin turned back to the chest-high shrub and continued his lecture.

'Me, I takes the root and mixes it with tobacco and it smokes away a powerful headache.'

His young pupil made a half-twisted smile that was bitter rather than mischievous.

'Best pick some for Moses then. Randall told me he been in the bar since yesterday.'

337

Calvin had bent to dig at the roots of the plant, and spoke without looking at Sam. 'Well then, you camp out with me tonight. You know Moses when he be gettin' home. Specially now that Marlene ain't there to beat on no more.'

Sam stared at his feet. Calvin had no idea how the boy felt about the death of his mother, but he could guess. Such an ugly stupid death. Choked on her own vomit after a moonshine session, and no one in the cabin sober enough to notice she was dead. The RCMPs took the body away to do an autopsy, probably hoping to pin something on Moses at last, but seems like they couldn't. Since it was just Indians they didn't ever bother bringing Marlene's body back to let her family have it buried. Calvin wondered where she'd ended up. Sam must have too, but he didn't talk about it.

'Sure. We can camp.'

Calvin had nodded, and they got on with their tasks.

Over the fire that night, Calvin had cooked at least twenty different types of fungi, wrapping the delicate flesh in birch bark first, then an outer layer of damp leaves, so that the concoction steamed and didn't burn.

He'd watched Sam's face as he ate and was delighted he could give the boy some pleasure. Then it had been time to talk more of the past that would be their future.

'You know Moses has the key now, don't you?'

Sam nodded.

'But he don't know first thing 'bout how to use it. Only you and me be knowin' that, Sam, now that Eden be gone.'

A nod again, and a wide brown hand reaching for more fungi.

Calvin ate a little more and looked into the fire. 'So what you gonna do when Moses be tryin' to get that outta you?'

Sam looked up at him with those glittering black orbs, and made that thin mouth he did when anyone mentioned his father. 'He won't.'

Calvin leaned forward, his arms hanging over his knees. 'You remember what I told you 'bout it, don'tcha?'

'Sure.'

'And you believe it with your heart?'

Those eyes had looked into him, so trustingly. 'Sure. I guess it be true.' Sam had looked down at the fire, avoiding Calvin's eyes. 'You be my real pappy, Calvin. I believe everythin' you told me. Even more than the stuff Eden said.'

338

'That's dumb, Sam. He knew more than anyone. He was there.'

Sam's face hardened. 'Well he ain't around to say it no more, is he? The son he be never keepin' in line saw to that.'

Calvin knew Sam's hurt at Eden ignoring his grandson's plight ran deep as a river, but he'd thought at that moment that maybe Eden had a plan, that he'd known all that stuff had to happen and he couldn't lift a hand to stop it in case his love got in the way. Because Eden had loved Sam. Calvin knew it. He'd seen the pain in the old man's eyes when Sam came in like a beggar looking for food or shelter, but he never showed it to the boy. And that was real dangerous. If Sam didn't believe in what Eden told him, out of some adolescent hurt, then Sam was going to be in deep trouble if the thing ever came back. No. *When* the thing came back.

'You got to believe in Eden, Sam. You gonna be the keeper one day.'

'Maybe.'

'No maybe. For sure.' A sulky silence, then Calvin looked straight into the boy's eyes. 'You know what the key does?'

'Sure I do.'

'Then you be a liar. No one knows what it does, they just be knowin' how to make it call what needs to come.'

Sam's eyes had flashed with boyish anger. 'I know what comes. Eden told me.'

'No you don't. You should listen closer. It be different every time. Eden told you what came to his pappy. Might not be the same to you.' Calvin had looked into the fire, and spoken more quietly. 'And I be real sure it wouldn't be nowhere near the same for your pappy. Nowhere near.'

Sam had squinted at Calvin, as if something had occurred to him, and then quickly looked away into the flames.

They finished their meal and then Calvin smoked a little, enjoying the sweet, warm evening air on his face. Sam had lain down in front of the hot fire on his torn and dirty jacket, and taken his T-shirt and pants off. The warm night needed no fire except for cooking, but Sam had banked it up into an inferno and the boy basked in front of the tall flames like a cat. He lay on his side, staring into the fire, scratching his long muscular brown legs and plucking occasionally at the grass with a lazy hand. All he wore were a pair of mangy-looking grey shorts with a hole in the butt, but as Calvin's eyes roamed over the beautiful brown body, he had thought he looked like a sleek and rare animal. Sam's pubic hair just poked from the waist band of his shorts and the large, but gentle swelling beneath that filthy grey fabric told Calvin that at least one part of Sam Hunting Wolf had reached maturity.

He'd stayed smoking until Sam's eyes got heavy and he rested his head on one arm to sleep. The firelight. It was just the firelight. The shadows flickered across that lean body, dancing over shapes and cavities that Calvin wanted desperately to touch. That's all. Just to touch and stroke. Not to hurt or dominate. No, never that. He loved that boy, and he just wanted to feel that warm brown flesh beneath his own fingers, and maybe for a moment, softly cup that swelling between Sam's legs in his hand.

Calvin was sweating with excitement and he got up and quietly lay down behind the boy. At first he had just watched the rise and fall of Sam's shoulder as he breathed, tracing the outline of his back and hips with his hand an inch away from that elegant body. And then it had been too much. Calvin had slipped his arm round the front of Sam's waist, and running his fingers lightly over that hard flat belly, he had arrived at and caressed the part of Sam that was making Calvin's heart beat in his ears. He closed his eyes with the pleasure of what he felt there, and then it was over. Sam woke.

The violence of his reaction was intense. He threw Calvin's hand off with a strength that nearly broke the shaman's wrist and leapt to his feet with his teeth and fists clenched, eyes ablaze and his breath panting from him like a caged beast.

'Sam. I only . . .'

The boy was close to tears through his rage.

'You dirty scum! '

'Sam. Please!'

Calvin held a pleading hand out to him. Sam kicked it away with a foot.

'You gonna teach me 'bout that next? Huh, Calvin? You gonna tell me that this be part of the magic?' Tears spilled down his furious face. 'I should have known it all be bullshit. You be just like my pappy, don't ya! You be makin' up all that stuff 'bout the Trickster and the key an' all that crap, and now I know it's all fuckin' shit so you can get up my ass! Huh? Is that it? Is it?'

Calvin had sobbed then, clutching at the ground in his misery.

Sam held him in his tearful glare, then he grabbed his clothes from the ground and ran off into the dark. Calvin heard a wail from the boy, like an animal in pain, receding into the woods. And then there was no sound nor sight of him.

Calvin was crying now as he dropped the second last stone on the flames. It had been the firelight. That was all. He loved Sam.

He shivered as the wind bit into him and he did nothing to control his tears as he retreated into the lodge for the final stone. Had he had that transgression purified out of him? That unspeakable betrayal of trust? He doubted if it ever could be. And in his heart he knew it had been more than a mistake. It had been the disaster that could lead to their defeat.

Calvin lifted the last stone from the hole in the ground, and this time in his prayer, he muttered in that ancient tongue that called the spirits from the rocks and made the sap stir in the trees, 'Believe, Keeper! Believe!'

What lunacy to try and stop him going up there. But Becker tried. 'I think it's best if you stay calm and stay here, Craig. Remember. This is not your investigation.'

Craig was standing up, leaning forward on straight arms that propped up the top half of his body on the table like he was going to do a handstand, his head hanging down between slumped shoulders. Becker was talking down to the top of the man's head and the back of his neck, and getting no response. Craig fought a battle against tears that were far from manly. He wanted to wail and shout and tear his breast. But he just hung there on his arms, his eyes shut and his mouth a tight slit like a closed razor. Bell was gone to the car, waiting for the Edmonton officer to follow him.

'We'll keep you well informed.'

Craig spoke in a choked voice without changing his position. 'I'm coming with you Becker.'

'I can't stop you. I'm merely advising you.'

'Then don't.'

'Craig. This is why we're here. To avoid personal involvement.'

Craig's head surfaced and he looked at Becker with eyes that were way too old for his face. 'Yeah. It's real personal now.'

Air moved between them and Becker backed off. 'We'll go with Bell. When you're ready.'

He left the room quietly and Craig opened his mouth in a silent scream that would have broken windows if it had a voice.

The dumb bastards had churned up the snow in the driveway, making such a mess that if there had been tell-tale tracks of any kind, they were gone now. The snow in the drive was flashing red and blue and Craig felt sick.

Daniel. Joe, Daniel, Sylvia. No. Not Sylvia. Only God had messed about with her internal organs. His privilege.

The guy that had messed around with Joe's and Daniel's and split the kid apart was not a god, but he murdered like one. Invisible. Untrackable. Silent.

Craig got out of the car, knowing what he was going to see, and knowing that however prepared for it he was, he would not be prepared enough. He never was. A constable from the Edmonton team hurried past him with a roll of incident tape. Craig stuck out an arm to stop him.

'Where are you going to put that, constable?'

'Foot of the drive, sir.'

'Uh-huh? Why don't you just phone up CNN and ask them to bring a bottle?'

'Sir?'

'Leave the tape until we got ourselves an audience. Don't go looking for one.'

'Sir.'

The constable wandered back into Hawk's house, no longer hurrying since his task was cancelled, and he would have to work hard to find a new and useful one in the standing around that always accompanies a murder. The big log house was ablaze with light, and figures moved back and forth across the beaming windows.

He put his hands in his pockets and went straight in. It was in the kitchen. The men at the door instinctively stood aside when McGee entered, and he stepped past them into the mess.

The World's Greatest Dad lay belly-up by the ice-box. A gaping black hole leered at them from Daniel Hawk's crotch, and what had been there was now in his face. At least what was left of his face. It was ripped and pounded like a tough steak. Please God, don't let them make Tess identify him.

The split down the front of the chest was exactly like Joe's, and

Craig didn't need to have the body turned over to know where the contents of that empty cavity were. Bags of trash made islands in the thick dried blood that coated the floor and Craig watched one of the Edmonton boys pick up a tortilla chip carton with rubber-gloved fingers and drop it in a plastic bag. Yeah, sure, that would hold the answer. *Dangerous things, tortilla chips. Watch out for the extra chilli folks. It rips your pecker off and stuffs your heart up your ass.* He lamented internally at the idiocy of the man with the rubber gloves and spoke to the constable at his right without taking his eyes off the body.

'Where did the son of a bitch get in?'

'We can't say, sir. There's no prints from the back door here, 'cept for a coyote. And it's a dead coyote.'

Craig looked up at him sharply. 'Where is it?'

The constable pointed through the kitchen window.'In the woods there.'

Craig was keeping going. That was good. Just keep it together, and don't think about who's lying there on that kitchen floor. Don't think about anything except the facts, and that murderers can't fly, or appear and disappear at will. They make mistakes, because although their actions are inhuman, their weaknesses are human. He walked around the bloody surface and went into the yard. He found the animal's body easily in the trees, following the flash made by a lone photographer taking shots of the coyote. Craig joined him. This was almost worse than Daniel. He had been prepared for Daniel the moment Bell burst into that bright office with darkness on his lips, but he was not prepared for an animal that seemed to have died ripping its own heart from its chest.

'Never seen anything like that,' breathed the photographer as he focused on the twisted heap of blood and fur. Neither had Craig.

Prints. No human ones, just coyote prints. *Deer prints. Just deer prints.*

He made a noise in his throat to the photographer by way of a reply, walked back to the kitchen door and without re-entering that mock-up of Hades, called Jeff Bell to the door with the wave of a hand. Bell nodded and left the room.

'The prints at Bradford's murder.'

'Prints?'

'The deer prints, Bell.'

The grim-faced constable nodded quickly to say he understood. He

343

had been crying. McGee could see the staining on his cheek, the puffiness of his top lids.

'Did you find the deer that made them?'

Bell looked at him dumbly. 'Eh, no. I don't believe we did.'

Craig blew steam out of his nostrils and looked towards the photographer still firing his flash in the trees. 'Well, actually, maybe someone did. The whole wood was swept for clues. I don't know. It might not have seemed important. You could ask Simon, eh, Constable Ross, in there. He was on the sweep.'

'Get him out here.'

'Sir.'

Simon came out with an expectant fire in his eyes.

'Did you find the deer that made the prints round Sean Bradford?'

'Yeah. We did. It was half-buried in the snow near the top of the wood.'

Craig's antennae started to twitch. 'Did you have it photographed?'

Ross got nervous. He guessed he'd done something wrong now. 'No sir. It was just a dead deer. We left it.'

Craig kept his voice very still and calm. 'And did you see what it died of?'

'No. It was half-buried like I say.'

'And that didn't worry you? That a deer had sniffed round the remains of a murdered human, then walked a few hundred yards away and also dropped dead.' He motioned behind him. 'Like that.'

Simon Ross knew what was being photographed in that wood. He also had never seen anything like it. But then he'd never seen anything like the remains of his colleague in the kitchen either. 'I'll report it to Staff Sergeant Becker right now, and get someone to go back and get it.'

'Uh-huh.'

The young man left McGee with an embarrassed lowering of the eyes, and left him alone on the step. The photographer finished up and walked very quickly to the kitchen door.

'Don't mind telling you, sir, I was pretty glad when you joined me just then. I was kinda getting the creeps out there, know what I mean?'

Craig nodded, as kindly as he could. Sure he knew what he meant. In fact he knew exactly what he meant when the man walked past him and into the kitchen and left him alone in the dark snowy night.

Inside, someone laughed. The public would throw up their hands at that if they knew. A man lying in his own blood, excrement and entrails, ripped open and mutilated, and men are laughing round his corpse. But right then Craig felt like laughing too. Was there an animal near Joe's corpse? They'd never know. They hadn't checked. And why should they? It wasn't usual to check for an animal who might have witnessed the crimes of the century, then collapsed at the scene of the murder.

He'd had a tail on Hunt all last night and today. That was something. Maybe he could rule him out of the picture. But somehow, although he couldn't say how or why, he knew Hunt was part of something. What the fuck went on in that wood yesterday? A man blacks out, a deer dies and a kid gets killed by something that leaves no trace. What the fuck was going on, full stop?

He was weary with unexpressed grief, and his mind was clouded with it. He heard a commotion in the kitchen, and the voice of Ernest Becker cutting through it.

'Keep them on the highway. On no account let them up here, do you understand? Now move it.'

So now the bored constable had his job back for sure and would be happily stringing striped incident tape from the trunk of one tree to another. Craig wished he could tape it across their goddamn mouths. He hated the media.

He remembered that woman, the one from, where was it, News International, that had been in Daniel's car. It might be useless, but he was going to pull her in. She might know something. Anything. He tried to remember her name but it wasn't there any more. That was weird. He always remembered names and licence plates. And she had made a big deal about saying her name to him. Come to think of it, he could hardly remember her face either.

No matter. It would take seconds to track her down. She was probably knocking back her third Caesar cocktail in a hotel in town somewhere, crunching the celery and trying to get a cab to bring her up here and get the story.

Fine. He knew he'd see her again.

37

They were talking in low voices down there, but he could still hear them. He pressed 'start' to pause the screen and turned the volume up. Billy didn't want to know what was going on. He had fled from the kitchen when his Dad came bursting in like that, all scratched and wild-eyed, and his Mom had come after him. He told her he was fine and that he wanted to play with his computer for a while, so she left him. But it took a while to make her go, and he could tell she was frightened by the way Dad was. It looked like she'd been crying real hard. Bart had followed her out and Billy let him go. He knew he'd be asleep on the landing by now, with his big fluffy head on his paws as he lay there on guard outside his master's room.

But they were all down there talking now, and in the kind of voices that people use when someone is sick or dying. Scared voices, of people who didn't know what was going on. He wanted to escape, to be far away from all this confusion and fear, and he was playing *Sonic the Hedgehog* as hard as he could to try and flee those voices. It usually worked if he was worried. You couldn't think about a thing when you were playing good, picking up extra lives and loading up the sparkly gold rings. But right now he was playing like a little kid. Jess could probably do better than this for pity's sake. He hadn't even made it through the Springyard Zone on the last three tries, and that was worse than pathetic.

A door closed and he heard Auntie Ann say something to Uncle Gerry. He turned the volume up again. The kooky cartoon music blared out of the speakers on the tiny TV, and he flipped Sonic into a spin to get him over some scary crabs that could lose you your rings. Except they weren't really crabs, were they? They were little bouncy bunny-rabbits and ducklings that evil Doctor Robotnik had imprisoned in the bodies of bad crabs and bugs. Sonic released them. Billy paused the game and closed his eyes. That thing in his Dad had wanted inside him and the wolf, to make them like the bad crab. He could see it now, feel its touch on him and hear the horrible ugly words it had spoken, although they had only been voiced inside Billy's own head, he knew that.

Billy was too scared to see or speak to his Dad. What if that dirty bad thing were still inside him? What if he was like one of those crabs now? His tears were coming again, and he didn't try to stop them. He was alone now, he could cry if he wanted to.

Billy opened his eyes, let the big hot tears spill down his face, and looked at the screen through a blur. Sonic was high above the palm trees in mid spin and when Billy pressed 'start' again, he reckoned he would come down on top of that ugly spotted bug that was really a bunny or duckling.

He sat staring at it. Why had his Dad let that thing in? His dad was bigger and stronger than anyone in the whole world. Remember how he was when that man had tried to take Mom's pocket-book in the restaurant line? That was neat. Just like the movies. And that time when the big guys that were smoking and cursing had tried to force him and Jess off the swings in that park near Granny and Grandpappy's in Vancouver. They sure didn't count on Billy's Dad then. Billy smiled through his tears at the memory of those boys scattering like scared mice, and the big safe hands of his Dad putting him back up on that swing and pushing him.

So how come he couldn't have stopped the thing?

He sniffed and started the game again. Bam! He got the bug, just like he thought he would. It popped, and threw up a score of a hundred. Billy wished he could pop that dark thing like Sonic did. Pop it right away from his Dad. But it wasn't like that. Billy didn't know if there was a dark thing to pop, at least not without popping his Dad too. They were the same thing, when he had seen them, that darkness and his Dad. The exact same thing. Another wave of tears clouded his eyes. He missed a flying insect that fired a golden ball at Sonic, and knocked all his rings out with a metallic tinkle.

'I wiped out. That's all.' Sam's voice was low and sullen.

Katie, sitting against Sam's chair at his feet, looked up at Gerry who'd come back in with a coffee for her wrecked husband. He tried to pass Sam the steaming mug, and when it was ignored, placed it on the stone hearth and sat down on the sofa next to Ann. They felt useless. They could be good in a crisis, Gerry and Ann. When Katie had gone into labour with Jess, they had been round here, soothing the panicking Sam, looking after Billy and sorting things out. That was what they were good at. But how could they help when they didn't know what the crisis was? Sam wouldn't talk to them. Billy wouldn't talk to them. Katie couldn't talk to them without crying. The Hunt household had gone from the big happy place of laughs and perpetual hospitality, to a vale of tears. And nobody seemed to know why.

Katie stroked Sam's free hand that was hanging limply over the arm of his chair and he withdrew it. She looked like he'd slapped her.

Gerry noted the expression on Katie's face and cleared his throat. 'Look. Wouldn't it be best if we could all just talk?'

Sam raised his eyes slowly to Gerry, as if realizing for the first time that he was there. 'About what?'

Gerry held Sam's gaze. 'About what's up with you mostly.'

In Sam's dark eyes, something like fire kindled. 'Nothing's up with me. What's up with you?'

'Meaning?'

'Got no life? Get off on spending a silent evening in a room, staring at two people who want you to go?'

Katie's fingers closed on her sleeve. 'Sam!'

'Sure. We got better things to do.' He paused and then looked away from Sam. 'You want us to go Katie?'

Her eyes were wide. 'Of course not. Have your coffee.'

Sam was still staring at Gerry as though the man on his couch were brandishing a knife, instead of holding a brown mug with some poorly painted ears of wheat on the side. 'This is my house. I want you to go.'

There was silence, and when Gerry spoke again he experienced a sensation that he had only encountered once in his adult life. Plenty in childhood, but never as an adult. It was that horror of ugly words formed secretly in the safety of your head reaching your mouth before you had time to catch them and replace them with something more acceptable. The words were there and he was standing somewhere inside his own body watching them being spoken as though he were not the speaker.

348

'Actually, it's Katie's house.'

The air in the room almost shifted with his words. Katie replied softly. 'Now I want you to go.'

Sam stood up slowly as if neither Gerry or Katie had spoken at all, and he was merely on his way to get a cookie from the kitchen or go to the bathroom. He took two steps towards the sofa, stopped in front of Gerry, and with one sudden and violent arc of his arm, punched the mug out of Gerry's hand with a clenched fist. The speed sent it smashing against the wall below one of June Crosby's framed watercolours of Wolf Mountain, the dripping coffee on the wall not only echoing Mrs Crosby's painting technique, but in this case better-ing it.

Sam's arms hung by his side, the restrained power in his body visible in the way a puma ripples before striking its prey. 'Get the fuck out.'

Gerry opened his mouth to speak, decided to close it again, then stood up in the limited space afforded him by Sam's looming figure. Ann sprang up at his side, while beside the chair, Katie sat white-faced and disbelieving. The Hunt's two closest friends left the sitting room, and then the house, in silence and misery. Behind them, two figures remained motionless as though waiting for the curtain to fall from a proscenium arch. Katie stared at Sam's back until he turned around.

The tiny cut below Sam's left cheek had started to bleed again, and this time Katie let it. She spoke in a barely audible, breathy voice. 'Welcome home, sweetheart.'

Her voice had a dark, malicious barb in it that had never once been given life in their entire marriage. Sam turned his gaze to Katie, as though surprised that anything was wrong with savaging their friend, and saw the malice was in her eyes as well as her voice. The sight of that pale, pretty face twisted into something approaching hate, brought Sam Hunt back from wherever he'd been, and both eyes moistened as his shoulders slumped into a dejected hunch.

She looked at him for a long time, wondering who this tall stranger was, standing weeping before her, until a large tear rolled down Sam's cheek broke that membrane of distaste she had held up between them, and her own tears flowed for the second time that evening. She covered her face with her hands and Sam walked slowly back to the chair, sat down and put a hand on her head.

Katie gulped on a sob and put her aching head on his thigh. 'Talk to me, honey. Please. Talk to me.'

Sam put his head back, closed his eyes and concentrated on stopping his tears falling from under the closed lids.

'What about?'

'Everything. What's happening here?'

'I don't know.'

They sat like that for an age, Katie trying to find a crack in the wall that always rebuilding itself with bricks of mistrust and fear every time she climbed it. She rubbed her cheek on that long hard thigh, and struggled to make sense of her feelings.

'Then tell me who you are.'

Sam opened his eyes, and the action released another tear he had been saving. She wiped it away for him this time with a delicate finger.

'You know who I am.'

'But I want to know more. I want to know who you were.'

Sam bent forward and took her face in his hands. It was such a beautiful face. Pointed chin, blonde hair streaked with a darker hue that made it change with every toss of her head, surprising dark arched eyebrows, and those eyes, those blue intense eyes with tiny laughter lines creeping from the corners that Sam prided himself in creating over a decade.

'Does it matter?'

She looked up at him, her face cupped in his brown hands like she had a beard made of fingers. 'It didn't used to. But somehow it feels like it does now.'

He let go her face with a gentle stroke on her cheek and looked up at the ceiling. Katie continued, still touching his thigh. She couldn't help touching it. Even in this barren emotional desert they had suddenly found themselves in, she longed for it to be naked against her own. She was drowning in her bewilderment, and spoke mainly to suppress it, to stall the silence and the realization of how her husband had just behaved.

'I haven't told you much about who I was either, have I?'

'Sure you have.'

She shook her head at him, her shoulders giving one more involuntary heave as if hoping she would sob again. Her voice was steadier now. 'No I haven't. Not really. I told you about Tom and me, but that's all. This house for instance. I never told you what it was like to have been a child here, did I?'

'Guess not.'

'It didn't seem right. I wanted this place to have only our memories. Our new family memories. Not all mixed up with mine.'

'Fine. I understand.'

'No. But I want to tell you now. I want us both to know more.'

He looked so weary, her Sam. He brought his eyes back to hers, and reached for her hand. But he was still far away.

'So tell me.'

He said it as though he cared little about what she had to say, but just wanted to hear her speak. And he said it so softly, so gently, she could scarcely remember the villain he had been only minutes ago. She wanted to kiss him. Instead, she told him.

'Over there.' She pointed to the old Shaker dresser, whose perfection of simplicity Katie had ruined by painting daisies on the doors. 'I fell against that when I was four and smashed my front teeth.'

'Ouch.'

'Yeah. It was nasty. Knocked one right back into the gum. I had an operation to get it out before it went septic. And the window there. I used to run to it and watch the trains when I heard them coming. You knew that there were no houses on the other side of Oriole when we bought this place? You could see right across Silver to the rail track and the Trans-Canada then. There was just birch scrub across the street. I used to play at being *The Man from Uncle* in it.'

Sam wondered if the same trains that had flattened his dollars nearly a hundred miles away had been tracked by the eager eyes of a young Katie Crosby. It made him feel warm for the first time that day to imagine it.

'I'd count the stairs with my eyes closed every time I went up to bed and if I got it wrong then it meant I would grow up ugly and never marry.'

'So you always got it right then.'

She smiled at him. 'I didn't think so at high school. I also thought I was gay.'

Sam raised an amused eyebrow, but not very high.

'I was in love with Betty Lendle. She was tall and elegant, and I was small and round. She had these fantastic big tits and I wasn't even in a bra by then. And oh, I wanted her to love me back, but she never did. I don't think she even knew that I used to dream wicked things about her and me.'

'But you weren't gay.'

'No. I guess I wasn't.' She looked away, and Sam felt like crushing her to him when her face reddened a little. 'I fell for a guy called, wait for this, Kirk Mahoney.' She looked back up at Sam with sincere eyes and cheeks still coloured from the memory. 'In fact I lost my cherry with Kirk Mahoney.'

Sam wasn't laughing, so she continued.

'I wanted to die. It was so ugly and sore, and there was blood all over the rag rug that I had to get a cloth and wipe up. It left a big brownish stain that glared at me every time I walked past. I cried and cried and tried to scrub myself clean for days.' She looked at him as if there were a big confession coming now. 'He was the son of the mailman. It happened on holiday, while my parents were out skiing. Here, in front of this fire.' She waited for Sam to be horrified. He put his head back and laughed lightly. Her heart lifted as she watched his face crease, and she laughed too. 'Does it ruin the fireside for you?'

'No, but it'll make me horny every time I poke the logs.'

'I told Mom and Dad I'd spilled coffee on the rug. They believed me.'

They laughed again and it felt so delicious to forget her fear and confusion for a moment that she was lightheaded with the release. Then she caught sight of the coffee stains on the wall where Sam had smashed Gerry's mug, and spoiled it.

'Now you.'

Sam's face crumpled. So those were her dark confessions. Jesus. So innocent and simple. What would she make of his life? Sam rubbed at the cuts on his face. Maybe he should find out.

This woman was his life now. She was everything. The past had already burst through, and it was pounding him to a pulp with its dark fetid force. Making him act like a crazy.

What if he were to share some of it with her? He had always thought that to let it through, to think of it for a moment would destroy him. That somehow the past would sneak up and grab away everything happy and whole and good he had, that it would rip off his mask to the world and shout, *Ha! You see the scumbag that Sam Hunting Wolf is really? Don't expect him to show at the next Silver Cancer Foundation Bowling*

tournament folks, 'cause he's not the nice guy you all thought he was. He's a
piece of shit masquerading as a family man. A stinking scummy INDIAN!

Well it was happening now anyway, wasn't it? What difference
would it make if she knew the foul stock her husband came from?
She was still at his feet, watching his face contort, her hand brushing
his thigh to soothe him. She spoke quietly.

'I'm Katie Hunting Wolf. We both know that now.'

He nodded.

'So who were your family Sam? Tell me.'

His family. His family were here in this house. There had never
been any others. Not really. He closed his eyes, took hold of her hand
and let his head rest on the back of the chair. She waited.

'Marlene Mary Crowfeather married Moses James Hunting Wolf.
They had three children, but only one survived and you're holding
his hand.'

She squeezed it in response. Katie's heart was beating faster. She
was frightened at the tenor of Sam's voice that had taken on an
unfamiliar pitch, and frightened of what he was going to tell her that
made it so hard for him to do so. Strange. She had been shocked and
angry at what he had done to Gerry and Anne, but now she was
scared. She listened.

'I lost my front teeth too when I was a kid. Moses tried to pull me
out from under the box-bed in the back of the cabin while Marlene
held on to his legs, screaming. I could see her face from under there,
and she was yelling at him in Cree to leave her baby alone. Her
baby.' Sam made a sour face. 'Can't recall what I did to make him
so mad. Most likely nothing. And when he couldn't pull me out, he
took an iron fence-post and stabbed it around under there till he got
me. I was lucky it was the teeth. He was aiming to get an eye or
break a bone. I was six. You grow more teeth.'

He kept his eyes closed, but he could hear Katie's breathing and
knew she was starting to cry.

'And the strange thing is I would have lost my cherry on the floor
like you too if I hadn't have grabbed a beer bottle out from under
my pappy's chair and smashed it on his head while he tried to hold
me down. He never did get his old rocks off on me, 'cause I was eight
then and I could run and hide in the woods for weeks and no one
could find me. No, I lost my cherry to a white girl who nearly ripped
it off me. Darcy Jenkins.'

You mished yourshelf, Shammy.

Jesus. No. Sam bit his lower lip at the thought of the horror. Carry on. Get it out. Katie was still there. The world hadn't ended. Yet.

'Moses beat Marlene so bad she lost an eye, then he let her die on her own vomit when he and his buddies were all juiced on pure ethanol.'

'Oh Sam. My God.'

Katie was weeping again now. The hand that was not gripping his like a vice, was over her mouth trying to hold back her grief.

'Had a talent for killing. He killed my grandpappy. Eden James Hunting Wolf. Used to be the Kinchuinick chief and shaman. Killed him for this dumb thing.'

He put his hand inside his clothes without opening his eyes and flicked out the small bone amulet. It flopped onto the fabric of his sweater and hung there innocently while its owner continued to horrify his wife.

'Worth killing an old man for, huh?'

His finger rubbed at it lightly, almost as if the answer were yes.

'I took up with a preacher who was on the reserve trying to save us Indians. He liked me. Used to give me money for odd jobs, clearing the snow from the yard, painting the fence, that kind of Huckleberry Finn shit. And I guessed he thought that if he couldn't save me, he would try and educate me. He taught me to ski at Tamarack. Once we even went as far away as Lake Louise to ski the back bowls.

'And he made me stop speaking like an Indian and made me think it would maybe be okay not to live on the reserve.' He opened his eyes and looked at Katie, whose eyes were tiny with her silent crying. ''Cause you know most Kinchuinicks think like they'll die or something the moment they step off reserve. Think that there's no oxygen out here in the white man's land. But after his daughter Darcy jumped me – okay maybe I was willing too, but anyway I figured the Reverend Jenkins might not want to see me around so much after that – I learned you could live and breathe here, and nothing would ever make me go back there. Nothing.'

He squeezed her hand.

'I didn't want that shit's name, so I just dropped the Wolf bit and hey presto, at least when I phoned up for a job they said they'd see me. Course their faces fell when I turned up, and somehow the position had always just been filled a moment before I got there. But I kept at it and eventually Jim Henderson at Fox Line gave me a job in Silver.'

Katie smiled weakly. 'God bless him.'

'For sure.'

'What happened to your father?'

So it was over then. The honesty. Thus far and no further. The lies would have to start again, and he fell into the pit that he knew had sides of glass.

'Don't know. People say they think he went to Calgary. Probably died drunk in an alley someplace.' Oh God, that he should lie to her again.

Katie detected the change of tone in Sam's voice and rubbed his hand to get him back before he slipped from her again. She sniffed and changed her tone too. 'So your amulet was your grandfather's.' She just caught him.

'Yeah.'

'It's a very old, and very rare symbol. Called an Isksaksin, meaning line or boundary. But I guess you know all about it.'

Sam couldn't help his tone, that of a man who had just heard a child recite the alphabet. 'How'd you know that?'

'You know that place I go to work in every day? Well strangely enough it has this weird word *Museum* on the sign outside. I just noticed it one day and then, hey, I also noticed all the cases had these real funny old things in them . . .'

'Yeah. Okay. Hardy har.'

'Of course I know, Sam. I just never had the opportunity to talk to you about it. Or more like, I knew you wouldn't want to hear it.'

She looked at him to see if that would wound him. It wasn't meant to. And it hadn't. He just looked dazed.

'What else you know about it?'

'You want the full schools lecture tour?'

'Yeah.'

She touched the curious shaped amulet, running her finger over the indentations that scored the not quite circular bulk of it. It was a good excuse to touch Sam's chest too.

'Well yours obviously can't be the original, which is supposed to have been made from the skull of Pitah Annes, Eagle Robe, the greatest ever Kinchuinick shaman, who was around in the sixteenth century. But we've got a book in the museum by an English archaeologist with a drawing of the Isksaksin in it, and this is the absolute double. Bored yet?'

He shook his head, his face darkening. She tapped the bone.

'It's a real curious one, since this is about the only Kinchuinick charm that doesn't come with a list as long as your arm about what it can do. Most of these things, like, you know, claim they can heal, ward off bad spirits or make you babies or something like that. But not this. In fact that English guy, P.R. Nicholson, said that the wearer wouldn't discuss it, and he could find no living Indian who knew its purpose, but all were in awe of it.' She looked up at him with love through her puffy eyes. 'I thought it was just like you to have something as special and mysterious as that round your neck when I read it.'

Sam's head was reeling and he sat in silence staring into space in front of him.

'Sam?' Her voice was thick again.

'Mmm.'

'How did you survive?'

He looked away from her into a nothing distance, and spoke as if the answer were so obvious it was barely worth discussing. 'I breathed in and out.'

She felt him doing it now, and she could barely speak. But she did. 'I love you so much.'

He looked back at her, pulled her up to his knee and kissed her. She was crying through the kiss and the salt ran into their mouths as they caressed each other's lips with slow tongues and gentle teeth.

The door banged open as if it had been blown with explosives, the wooden handle thumping into the wall with such force it left an indentation in the plaster. Sam's body went out of his control and he jumped up with a howl, his adrenalin pumping in his veins. Katie stumbled from his knee, making a small gasping noise.

It was Bart. He stood in the doorframe looking at them, mouth closed, ears cocked and alert. Katie put her hand to her own heart this time and exhaled like a runner.

'Jesus Christ, Bart! Give us a break!' She laughed, got her breath back and ran her hand through her hair.

'That's what I call a dog that wants his dinner.'

Sam was breathing very fast through his nostrils, his mouth a tight line. The husky was looking straight at Sam with steady blue eyes, and if dinner was on its mind, it seemed in no hurry.

38

Alberta 1907
Siding Twenty-three

He wanted to lie. Looking around at all these frightened raging faces, he wanted to say things that would help. But he could not. What was his life if it was not a search and a desire for the truth? This was not a court of law, but it was still a group of men who were watching him like peasants waiting for a decree from a kingly balcony, and they demanded an answer.

'The morning. They found him in the morning. He had been missing all night.'

He said it quietly, but it was as though James Henderson had scored a try at rugby. The men burst into a shout that was triumphant at the same time as horrified. He held his hand up to them, pleading.

'Please. Please! Listen to me!'

They were for no such nicety. They were for shouting their fury and clenching their fists.

'For the love of God ! Listen to me!'

God, or the mention of His love, was more successful. They quietened.

'Hunting Wolf is no common murderer. The man is a great chief, chosen for his wisdom and compassion.'

There was a snort from the back of the canteen. Henderson ignored it and carried on.

'Why would he do such a brutal and unspeakable thing?'

And it was indeed unspeakable. Henderson was only just hanging on to his nerves. Muir spoke again. It was he who had become the inquisitor.

'You know why, Reverend. He defiled their religious ceremony.' He spat on the floor, an uncommon gesture for Muir whom Henderson thought of as a gentleman. 'And pish on their religion. The blasphemous devils.'

The men shouted again, and Henderson hung his head in despair. No. Not Hunting Wolf. It was hard to imagine that any man alive could have wrought the frenzy that had gone on in McEwan's cabin. Even the most ferocious of animals could not have inflicted such mutilation and horror. And it was certainly not the work of a man who possessed deep, wise intelligent eyes as did the handsome Kinchuinick chief. But the motive was there and now he had provided them with the fact that the Indian was abroad and unaccounted for at the time of the engineer's death.

Henderson looked around the room. These men who raged about the savages should look at themselves. How ugly hate was. He had watched their faces often when they ate in here at night and they were the faces of men thinking of home, passive and gentle and human, talking quietly over a stew or laughing occasionally at a jest. Now they were twisted and hideous as they vented their rage on their native neighbours. Henderson wanted it to stop before he went mad. He played a wild card. 'But what will you do if it is true?'

The question cut a slice into their ranting. Muir looked at him. 'We will have them.'

The men fell silent again, watching Henderson, wary at his change of tack.

'And if that abomination is the handiwork of just one of their number, how will we, simple railwaymen, a cook and a man of God, hope to combat their fury with no outside help and no weapons?'

Muir looked around him. 'This snow will not last forever, Reverend. The lines will open soon enough, and when the first train comes through, then we shall see. Oh yes. We shall see all right.'

The men murmured.

'And will you stay alive long enough to see whatever is it you are expecting, Mr Muir?'

He had not meant to say that. He wished it back into his mouth the moment it left his lips but it was too late. He had changed the game with his question. The hunters looked at each other, realizing that they were in danger of being the hunted. Muir stared at Henderson with betrayed, defeated eyes.

'You're saying they will kill again?'

The rabble-rouser was now a frightened boy.

'We do not know that they have killed at all.'

Muir was silent but Strachan raised his voice from the long bench.

'Aye. An' we dinnae know if the sun'll come up in the mornin'!'

James Henderson kneaded his brow and tried to calm himself. He must regain his authority here and he raised his head to do so. 'I must remind you that Angus McEwan is still in there waiting for us to give him a decent burial. There will be time to discuss this predicament, but I must insist that we proceed. The man deserves our Christian attentions.' It was good. They were reminded of the man and not the deed, although it would take a strong stomach to do the necessary and scrape McEwan's remains from the floor. He decided to take the lead. 'And if none of you are man enough to deal with it, I will do it on my own.'

He looked around and then moved off towards the door. Duncan Muir put a hand out to his thin arm, and shook his head. 'Naw, Reverend Henderson. Leave him. We must do it.'

Henderson nodded, and as if prompted a group of men at the back put their hats on and opened the door. He watched their slumped shoulders and shuffling gait and pitied them their grisly task. He had not even been able to fully enter the cabin, the sight of the blackened blood on the floor being more than he could bear. These men were of stronger stuff and he felt guilt and a nugget of shame that he had manipulated them. The cold air seeped in with the opening of the door and the ever-present wall of falling snow was there to greet them. As they filed out, the men at the front stopped.

'Look! There, by God!'

Henderson came to the door and peered over their shoulders to see what it was. Through the opaque sheet of snow, a figure was approaching. A white man. A tall white man in a long black coat walking towards them from a thicket of trees as though he were expected. He raised a hand in greeting and the men looked at one another.

'Hallo!'

Muir pushed through and stared at the figure. He found his tongue in time to answer by the time the man reached the crowd of staring faces and stood before them with his hands on his hips.

'Are you a ghost, sir?' Muir was only half in jest.

The stranger laughed, his pale blue eyes taking in the assembled company, and resting on Henderson's face with a smile. 'No indeed. A trapper foiled by the snow, gentlemen. And a damned hungry one.'

A Canadian accent, but hard to place. The men stood uselessly in a bunch, staring at him miserably until Muir took the initiative again.

'You'll forgive us our surprise sir. We've had a . . . we're in the midst of tragedy today and we expected no one until the trains can get through.'

He looked concerned, and nodded. 'Tragedy follows us like our own shadows out in this wilderness. I'm no stranger to it.'

Henderson was as surprised as the rest of them by this man's appearance, but he was not comforted by his easy manner. In fact, he was made distinctly uneasy by those smiling eyes. But he could tell that Muir was pleased they had a guest.

'There's no hot food. Our cook is indisposed at present. But there's a loaf and some cold ham if you care to have that.' Muir looked around and then back at the man. 'I must say it's a relief to see a new white face.'

'It's a pleasure to see a face at all for me. I can go for half the year and not see a Christian soul.'

The words were forced, Henderson thought. An easy manner, yes, but words that were almost being read from a book. As if he was learning them, very fast, from some unidentified source. He put it down to the fact the man was a trapper, and must indeed, true to his word, be alone for much of his life. No doubt he was just picking up the rudiments of social intercourse as he went. But it was odd, and the minister did not care for it.

Henderson stood aside for the man as he was led into the canteen to be fed, and the men outside burst once more into heated conversation. They looked as though they wished to change their minds and delay the grim chore for the more heartening pursuit of watching this new man eat, when Henderson turned to them and put up a hand.

'It must be done. He should not be left like a dog.'

They made no gesture, but one by one they lowered their heads and moved away through the snow to McEwan's defiled cabin. Henderson went back inside the long, warm wooden building. The trapper was already at table, being brought a piece of ham by Sinclair, a short and dour man from Inverness. A flash of irrational rage shot through James Henderson as he watched this man being waited on but he fought it back. The man was hungry and just new from the isolation of the wilderness. He had a right to their hospitality. He stepped closer to the throng that was around him to hear his words. The trapper was answering Muir's question with a smile.

'Strange to say, I have almost forgotten my real name. Best call me by my Indian name given to me many seasons ago when I was trading with the Kinchuinicks, I believe on account of my hair. They have peculiar notions these savages. But it serves me well and I have used it for so long I have become it. They call me Snowchild Sitconski.'

He grinned to the men. They did not grin back.

He turned the wooden cross over in his hands as if looking for its secret. The Henderson man had carved it well. One piece, and where the bars crossed, a rough and tiny figure of a man with his arms out. It was nothing like the beautiful bone and wood one that Walks Alone had held and hoped to keep in the cabin, but it was good and he liked it.

Henderson had seen him hold it when he came back a few hours ago, but there was no time for smiling or thanking him with his hands. He had brought terrible news. Walks Alone had sat on his blanket next to the wall of the tipi listening to the tall man try to tell his story. His mother, and his father, who had woken and was well, had listened carefully to Henderson's tale of the things that were happening in the white man's village. Then his mother had looked at his father in a strange way when she heard of the death of the man McEwan.

They were all gone now. He was alone in the tipi, tending the fire and touching his cross, trying to discover its magic which he could not comprehend. But there was much he could not comprehend. He had been astonished to hear his sister's name spoken again in the tipi today. They never spoke of her in front of him. At least not when they thought he was listening. But he had heard his mother crying sometimes at night when she thought he slept, and heard her call her name. And today, her name had been on all their lips but his. Walks Alone looked into the fire. They thought he could not bear to hear it. They were wrong. He said it every day inside his head, and he relived her death in minute detail just as often. The spirits had taken his voice with that death, but he would not forget. He could not. Not even if he wished to.

'Take her, Walks Alone.'

His father's tone had been brusque that hot summer evening. The camp was only hours old and they had much to do before nightfall. Singing Tree had gone with the women to the river and the men were in the camp with a few scattered children who were too tired after the long journey to accompany their mothers.

She had put her chubby little arms out to her father and was crying that he would not hold her. He had been busy with his medicine, herbs and roots that he was pounding to give to an elder to whom the journey had not been kind.

'Why must I take her, Father?'

'I must have quiet. Fetch wood and take her with you.'

Walks Alone had looked sulkily at his father but his authority was unshakable. He picked up the one and a half year-old girl and waddled away under her weight towards the edge of the camp.

It was a new summer grazing site, and he was excited that he would be able to explore where he had never been. Narrow-leaf cottonwood and aspens fronted a forest of pine, and he headed for its dense bulk to search for deadfall. She weighed so much and was making his burden more difficult as she gurgled and kicked in delight to be lifted in her brother's arms. Behind him, the sounds of camp were comforting. Dogs barking, horses snorting and the shout of one man to another. He had grunted into the woods with his sister, elated at the thought of the summer that lay ahead.

The edge of the forest with its elderberry and honeysuckle was not interesting to him and he hitched his bundle up in his arms as he headed deeper into the tall trees. It was beautiful. The scent of sweet pine resin rising from the hot forest floor and the sunlight filtering through the high canopy of branches was magical. The undergrowth was full of deadfall as he'd hoped, and the pick of firewood was endless. Then he had remembered that he had not brought the willow basket that he wore on his back. How was he to fetch the wood home with his sister to carry? He sighed and put her down. She fell heavily on her bottom, picked up a twig and put it to her mouth, took it out again and talked to it in that secret language that only she and her mother seemed to comprehend. What to do?

Walks Alone had decided he could run back to camp quickly enough and bring the basket without his sister even noticing. She was happy on her seat of twigs, chuckling and grabbing anything that came to hand. He had broken the sharp branches off a long thick piece of pine and given it to her. She'd closed her fingers carefully on the rough bark and looked at it, then back at him as if he'd handed her a valuable prize.

'Gaaah! Baaa!'

He'd nodded at her and it had seemed to satisfy her. She'd returned to her piece of wood, fascinated.

Walks Alone had turned and run quickly through the forest, surprised it was so far. He had not noticed how deeply into the woods they had come. No matter. He was fast. He'd gained camp and run round the back of the tipi to avoid his father's gaze, had found the basket from the jumbled pile of belongings in the sled, and sped off towards the wood again.

He had been lost for a moment, then her childish sounds had drawn him to the spot. He'd seen her through the trees, crawling expertly on all-fours along and over the undergrowth and fallen branches. He'd slowed his run and walked towards her, slinging the basket off his back making ready to collect the wood.

How could he have seen it? It was hidden. Of course it was. That was its point.

The gin trap was for a bear. A black fearful thing that would hold a thirty stone grizzly. Its circumference was only slightly smaller than his sister's length and when her weight triggered the spring, it had folded her in two, the back of her head touching her own heels as it had snapped her spine in half and severed her head from her shoulders, her feet from her legs. Such a fast, fluid movement, with no sound other than the snapping of bone and the rustle of leaves as the whole trap jumped in the air with its new prey.

The body had not been recognizable as human. How could a human body bend backwards from the waist so the calves were against the back? And without a head, or feet. Just a ragged red circle of neck, pumping blood as though the heart wanted the little life to continue and the stumps of legs that oozed their contents onto the forest floor.

He'd opened his mouth and no sound had come from it. No scream, no shout. Nothing. He had stood over the thing that had been his sister for an age, then turned and walked slowly out of the wood towards the camp.

By the time they had understood that the boy could no longer speak, and had gone without him into the woods to search where he pointed, a wolverine had got to her.

His father had found her and for a moment had not understood what he was seeing as the animal tore another piece from the carcass, then seeing it had human company, picked up the head by sinking its teeth deep into a plump cheek and ran off into the forest.

He remembered it every day. Why should he not? And when Henderson had spoken her name in the tipi they had all remembered her. Strange that it was a trapper who would have her name. No matter. It pleased his heart to hear it again, and he rubbed his cross with a thumb as he tried and failed to say it for himself.

Snowchild. Darling little Snowchild.

39

Outside, everything was quiet at number nine Oriole Drive. The snow fell silently on itself, making a slab on the roof that needed new tiles. The light wind that occasionally sent the solemn flakes into a swirling frenzy shook the branches of the tall pines the yard and made the snow sculptures on their boughs fall to the ground with a barely audible whoosh. Far away in the distance, a train sounded its horn as it pulled its coal through the night.

But inside the house three people were still awake. Katie lay looking at the dim outline of her towelling robe hanging on the back of the door.

Physically she was warm, but far from comfortable, hugging herself beneath the covers, legs curled up to her belly, arms circling her knees. Her thighs were still wet from their sex and she lay completely still, a mile away in the bed from her husband, making no attempt to move and barely breathing.

Katie was sore. Between her legs was a dull ache that was matched only by the one in her heart, the one that was compressing her chest like a vice, making her breathing a chore. She had initiated their sex with a feathery touch and a caress as soon as they climbed into bed a few hours ago. Sam had seemed so small and lost, so weary from his confessions and broken by his circumstances, that she wanted to hold him, to have him inside her and soothe him with the anaesthetic of pleasure.

And it had been pleasurable. To begin with. Sam had returned her touch and she'd burned for him, and if she were honest, a little of her passion was that she was holding a man who had become a stranger to her. It was the same hard body, the same embrace, although she noticed as he moved above her that he had removed the amulet from around his neck for the first time in their married life. But the warm skin contained a man she loved but didn't really know. The thrill had been short-lived. Even now, lying silently thinking in the dark, Katie was not sure at what point she had stopped trusting the large man who had been inside and all over her body. Thoughts had come to her as he stroked her back, she knew that much. Dark thoughts. Thoughts of her son and his distress, of Sam's behaviour, of all the things that were wrong with this picture of a happy normal family. And the darkness of it all had pulled her back from that temporary loss of sentience that sex affords, and made her struggle to move away from him. Had he misinterpreted her squirming? Surely he had. Perhaps he thought she wanted to play rougher; it wasn't unknown in their repertoire. All she could think of now in the dark was the ugly burning violence of the act, of his penis that was normally a part of them both becoming nothing more than a hard intrusive piece of meat that she was desperate, violently desperate, to expel from her body. It made her feel that the centre of all rage was between her legs, that a touch there was a deliberate and scheming affront from someone who would hurt her. Hurt them all.

Billy. God. Please, never Billy.

She had fought with him, clawing at his back and rolling her head, screaming at him inside her head to let her go, but he held her tighter, punching himself into that pit of her wrath until she could bear it no more and bit him savagely on the shoulder.

Sam had come inside her at the same time she drew blood from him and arched back in a mixture of pleasure and pain.

Then there had been silence. No talk. No holding and laughing and kissing. He had put his hand to his bleeding shoulder and turned away like a wounded dog, leaving her gasping through clenched teeth, staring up into the darkness.

The abused always becomes the abuser.

No. Not true. Yes true. Maybe.

She had cried softly, too softly for him to hear, and the movement from his shoulders suggesting that he was already asleep made her hate him for an instant.

Jesus, she was falling apart. He had told her his life, and now she was hating him for the truth of who he was.

What did she think his childhood had been like? Sometimes a glimpse of herself as she really was hit her and she realized that maybe part of her was exactly the type of girl who should have married Tom and given endless fondue evenings for B.C. lawyers and their stupid big-haired wives. Because the pathetic truth was she had harboured a Hollywood fantasy that Sam had ridden about on a horse on some grassy prairie, had lived a life outdoors and grown up tall and straight and handsome with the simplicity of humble but decent native life. The middle-class fool in her thought that he had left it behind because it wasn't good enough, not ambitious enough for a man like Sam. But Sam was not ambitious. Sam was always happy with whatever they had. A tiny room, a big house, a crap job, no job, it made no difference. As long as he was surrounded by his family, and they were well and fed. Not ambitious at all. She had just made it up to satisfy herself and get on with her own little selfish life.

How could a man like Sam love someone as shallow as she was? Sam? Sam who? After her horror in their bed, how could she love a man like that? She writhed in her torment. A man like what? Who was he?

The abused always becomes the abuser. No. No, no, no, NO!

She made herself think the unthinkable. This crazy stuff had all just happened. Abused children were abused for years. Slowly. Gradually. Agonizingly. Billy had only reacted to his father like he was the devil since yesterday. It was nothing.

Was one incident nothing? What if this was just the beginning?

But why? Why would a man like Sam Hunt hurt one of the things he loved most. You mean like just there, like how he just hurt you, her dark side thought. She pushed the darkness away.

Maybe he wouldn't. But maybe Sam Hunting Wolf would. The blackouts. And the murders. Her father-in-law was a murderer. Sam had said so. Like father like son.

Dear God no. That was going too far. She heard his breathing, steady and rhythmic. No. It was all wrong and wicked to even think it. Billy would be fine. The police would catch and incarcerate the psycho and Sam would be better soon. She loved him and she trusted him. Her eyes moistened afresh. Trusted him enough to want to kill him when he penetrated her? She screwed her eyes shut and groaned, concentrating on shutting it all out. But before she could stop herself the dark machine that was running the programme marked *the end of everything* started to run through every detail, every betrayal and sniff of duplicity all over again.

The second person still awake was Billy.

His mom had come and made him stop playing Sonic, and he had gone to bed without a fuss. But he hadn't been asleep yet, and he was making himself stay awake. Billy was afraid. Sometimes the wolf took him places when he didn't ask to go, and he didn't want to go anywhere tonight. As long as he stayed awake he'd be fine. And there was plenty keeping him awake.

His dad was hurt that he was avoiding him. Billy knew it, and it was confusing him. Did that mean his dad didn't know the thing was in him? He so badly wanted to rush into his arms, to kiss him and let those arms sweep him up and hold him. Keep him safe. But he was still afraid. He had never been so afraid in his whole life that night. In fact, he had wet the bed after his mom had come in and put him back in. She still didn't know. He knew where the sheets were in the big cupboard at the top of the stairs and he'd stripped the stained one off, stuffed it in his toy chest and put a new one inexpertly on the bed. He didn't want that kind of fright again. And so he wasn't going to go to sleep. He only wished that Bart could be in with him but Mom had put him in the kitchen and she wouldn't let him upstairs. He could always go next door and get in with Jess, but she would only get excited and start yelling or doing that big loud laugh she did that was more like a scream. So he just lay there and stared into the black night, trying to keep his eyes open and praying that the dark thing wouldn't find him and take him away.

The third thing awake was in the kitchen.

Its memory was a little more fragmented, but clear nevertheless.

'Come on then, boy, here it is.'

A lifetime ago, before they had gone to bed, Katie had put the dish down for the husky. It stared at her, ignoring the food. She looked up at Sam who was watching the dog as if he'd never seen one before. 'Can you believe that?'

'No,' croaked Sam.

She had bent down and grabbed Bart's coat with both hands. 'So, fella! You burst in demanding to be fed and then turn your nose up at it, huh? Well tough. You only get one chance in this house.'

She had buried her face in his fur, and over the top of her head the dog looked at Sam. It was not the look of a low mammal weighing up its master. It was something else. Katie surfaced from the warm fur.

'Hey. I wonder if he's okay. Do you think he looks peaky?'

'No. He looks okay.'

'Well maybe we should keep him in tonight. I'm not going to let Billy have him in case there's something wrong with him.'

'Like what?'

'I don't know. Worms or something. Do I look like a vet? He can stay in here.' She grabbed him again, looking into the dog's piercing blue eyes with concern. 'Yes you can, my darling. Stay in here where it's nice and warm.'

'I think he should be outside.'

Katie had looked at Sam with surprise. He was usually the one who treated Bart as if he was the third baby in the house. She would have to hit Sam on the head with a baseball bat to get him to clear the drive of snow for the humans in this house, but he was always out there at Bart's kennel, making sure he had a nice flat clear patch in front of his little arched door from which to survey the world.

'Let him stay in huh? Think how you'd feel if there is something wrong with him.'

Bart had looked at Sam with that look. The one that was making his guts churn. But Sam was tired. He wasn't functioning properly any more. He was imagining ridiculous stuff. 'Sure. If you think it's necessary. Remember, he's a husky. He's happier outside.'

Katie shook the dog by its big thick neck again. 'Well you get to be happy inside tonight, don't you?' She got up, filled a bowl with water and put it down beside the untouched dog food. 'There. Don't die in the night of overheating or I'll be in big trouble.'

They left the kitchen and Sam put the light out.

It didn't much matter to Bart whether he was inside or outside. He was screaming and barking and yelping deep inside his own body. Trying to bite blindly at something strong and dark and terrifying that was moving his limbs, and seeing through his eyes. Bart shrieked in horror with the punishment of it, but no one heard his cries. His body crouched down silently and sat with its paws out front. Bart screamed as his vocal chords that he used for barking and growling and whining were manipulated into a hideously painful contortion that he couldn't begin to understand, and from its own jaws came a sound that made the dog inside writhe in agony.

'Good night, Sam.'

'Well really because Staff Sergeant Becker said he thought you'd want to deal with it. That's why, sir.'

Bell waited as Craig shuffled some papers angrily. So, Edmonton thought he was too close to be involved in the hunt for the maniac who was giving Silver detachment a staff shortage problem, but Becker thought he was good enough to speak to the grieving relatives? Cheap. Really cheap. Some poor woman constable in Calgary had done the deed with Tess Hawk last night. He was thankful for that. But now Sean Bradford's parents were here from California, fighting off the press and fighting back their grief, desperate to speak to the men who dealt with their boy, just for the sake of it.

'Fine. Don't leave them standing out there. Let's have then in.' He stood and waited for them with the door open.

Bell led them through, and asked about coffee in a quiet voice. They refused and the constable shut the door behind him.

They looked so young. Two tanned, fit young people.

The dark-haired woman couldn't have been more than about thirty-eight or thirty-nine, and the man only a year or two older. Their cold-weather clothes were all new. He could see one of those little plastic T-shaped things that had held the label still sticking out of the man's anorak collar. He imagined their friends bringing them the clothes in mall bags, to get them ready for their trip to Canada where the bits of their boy were waiting for them.

'Mr and Mrs Bradford. I'm Staff Sergeant McGee.' He put out a hand and they shook it, the woman as if she were in a dream, the man as though the hand could bring Sean back.

Craig pulled the chair from against the wall to join the one at his desk, and motioned for them to sit down. 'There's not much I can say, except how sorry I am, and how hard we're working to bring your son's killer to justice.'

The woman was all cried out. She looked at him numbly, probably sedated. But there was still fight in the man. 'I hope for his sake you find him before I do, Mr McGee.'

The sad empty threat of a grieving impotent father.

'Uh-huh. Well we will, sir. It takes time.'

'How much time? '

'Too much time, Mr Bradford. Every minute he's loose out there is a minute too long.'

That threw the father. They were in agreement. The man hung his head and looked like he would cry now. Craig carried on in a calm tone. 'In the meantime we're here to help you in any way we can, particularly in keeping the press from you, if that's what you want.'

The father looked at Craig with an expression that told him it was too late. He'd obviously made that mistake and spoken to them. He didn't blame them. It would have been hard not to. The hyenas were waiting for the poor mugs the moment they stepped off the plane.

Craig continued. 'Now I have to tell you before you hear it on the news, that there's been a third murder. It looks like it happened the same night that Sean died.'

The name of their son. It made her tears come at last. Mrs Bradford started to weep, her husband's arm slipping round her shoulders. 'Yes, we heard. We're sorry. '

Aha, thought Craig. I'll bet you heard, all right. From the same scumbag reporter no doubt who offered you sympathy and an exclusive.

Grieving people should be protected from these animals. They lost their judgement. Spoke confidentially and intimately to people they wouldn't normally wipe their ass on. Sean Bradford's mother was hard at it now. Trying to get the words out as she choked on her tears.

'Why Sean? It was obviously a mistake. I mean Sean's not . . . Sean's . . . Sean was only dressed like an Indian for God's sake.'

Craig's stomach did a flip. My God. So that was the story out there was it? An Indian-killer. He looked at them wearily and wished he could think of something to say. 'No,' was the best he could come up with. It was true. In fact Sean didn't even look like Sean Bradford any more.

'Which interview room are they in?'

The Edmonton man looked surprised. 'Eh, the end one. What's that? Number three?'

'Four, sergeant. '

Craig snapped at him without looking back as he marched towards it.

'Sir.'

The stupid shits. Wilber didn't kill anyone. Why the fuck did they bring him in? But they had, and Craig had only just heard that they had. This was going to turn political if they screwed up.

He didn't knock. Screw them all. It was still his detachment. Still his interview room. Becker threw him a look like Craig had come in with his shorts over his head. Craig ignored him, closed the door and leaned against the expanse of plain magnolia plaster wall. The two other men, Sergeant Park and the quivering wreck that was Wilber Stonerider, looked up briefly and then resumed their dialogue.

'Carry on, Wilber,' said Park, pointedly.

'Can't I get no smokes?'

'No. Concentrate. Two nights ago.'

Wilber had been crying. His filthy face was streaked with the wake of his tears and he looked at the familiar face of Craig for sympathy. He found none. 'I told you. I be sleepin' rough. I be in the train yard, sleepin' over them air vents that come up from the basement at the back. Keeps me warm.'

'But no one saw you?'

'Course not. They'd have moved me on.'

Park looked up at Becker, then back to Wilber with a sigh. 'And was this talking bird there? In the train yard?'

Wilber's face contorted at the mention of it and he looked like he was going to start blubbering again. 'No sir. He don't come that night and I be real scared in case he do. He been a rat too once.'

'A rat spoke to you as well?'

'Yeah. He was laughin' at me with those beady little eyes and he be sayin' real sick stuff about my baby son that passed away years since.'

That did it. He cried. Craig rolled his eyes to the ceiling. This was crazy. He spoke from his wall.

'It's okay, Wilber.'

Wilber sniffed and swallowed some snot down the back of his throat in a great wet snorting sound. Becker chipped in.

'The things the bird said, Wilber. About your heart and your . . . your pecker. What was that?'

It was pathetic. The patronising tone he was using to this man. As if he couldn't say penis to him. Craig shifted his weight onto his other foot in irritation.

'Was like I said already. Said they be the parts of a man that should fuck each other. Said that should happen to me. Me. He was comin' for me.' He sobbed and clutched at the old torn blue parka that hung around his shoulders like it had been grafted on.

Becker looked at Craig with satisfaction, as if this was it, the reason they'd pulled in a poor drunken old man in full view of the world's press. Craig had seen enough. He turned to the door and put his hand on the handle when Wilber spoke again through his weeping, like he was speaking to himself.

'That be filthy talk. Filthy talk. He be knowin' the real rhyme.'

Craig stopped and looked back. 'What rhyme?'

The old man sniffed, wiped his nose and said something in his own language. 'In English, Wilber.'

'It don't rhyme in English.'

'It doesn't matter.'

Wilber looked at the table. 'Kinchuinick mothers. They always be sayin' it to their boys before they's becomin' men. It goes somethin' like, *a man gives life with his penis but he be having to live life with his heart.* It rhymes good in Siouan.'

Craig looked at the man for a moment, then opened the door and left. He was not quite at his office when Becker caught him.

'Did your uninvited visit there convince you?'

He was obviously angry at Craig's intrusion. Tough. Daniel was dead. Joe was dead. The son of those two bewildered broken people was dead. Craig turned and faced him. They were in the middle of the office, and if he wanted an audience, fine.

'Yep. Real convincing.'

Becker raised an eyebrow. 'Good.'

'Convinced me that you've pulled in a sad old dipso, and that right now there are twenty reporters out there, busting their asses to find a word that means murder to rhyme with the word Indian for tomorrow's headlines.'

Becker was calm in the face of his younger colleague's anger. He smiled, well aware of the arena they were in. He rocked back on his heels and crossed his arms. 'How many murder investigations have you led, Staff Sergeant McGee?'

'Jesus.'

'How many?'

Craig put his hand on his hips. It was as well his gun was hanging on the chair in his office or the action would have looked like he was going to draw and shoot.

'One.'

'One. Well I reckon that's pretty standard for a policeman in a small country town.' He enjoyed emphasizing those last three words. 'Want to know how many I've led?'

'Let me guess. The first was when you were six and you figured it was Jack who bumped off the giant.'

Someone laughed. Becker ignored it. He had the upper hand and they both knew it. 'Seventeen. That's how many, McGee. Including solving the West Coast Beach Murders.'

Craig laughed, hating himself for the anger that Becker had raised in him. Be nice, remember? No. He'd forgotten. 'Yeah that was a tough one, huh? Whoever would have guessed that the guy on the beach burger-stall with a twitch and a fifteen-year rape record would turn out to be the one. Now that's good police work.' He'd gone too far.

'And getting an autopsy ordered on a fucking dead deer is good police work? Did you think I wouldn't know?'

Craig looked Becker full in the face. This was not a stupid man. It was just a supremely untalented one. They were the worst. They lived their lives trying not to be found out. 'Call me suspicious. I was never sure about Jack. I'd have finger-printed the beanstalk.' He held Becker's gaze for a beat, turned his back on him and left to fetch his jacket from the office. Shit. Thanks a lot, Constable Bell. So much for staff loyalty.

He was going out. He had a lot to think about.

'Tell them to fuck off and die. You can paraphrase me.'

Margaret put the phone down, staring at it as though it had turned into something other than a piece of plastic. She looked back up at the man and woman in big chunky sheepskin coats and cleared her throat.

'I'm sorry. Mrs Hunt is tied up right now. She can't see you.'

'Aw come on. This won't take a minute.' The man's face was pleading, insistent.

'I'm sorry.'

The couple looked at each other, then the small dark-haired woman with the hard face leant on Margaret's counter and smiled. She was much prettier when she smiled, but Margaret thought she looked as if it didn't happen often.

'Well how about you? You know Mr Hunt? We just need to ask all the Ind . . . all the Native Canadian residents in Silver if they're scared that the killer will strike again? What do you think? Is he scared? Taking any special precautions?'

'Like what?'

'I don't know. Spells maybe? Something like that?'

'Can you go please? We get busy soon.'

The man looked around the empty museum foyer. 'Got the crowd barricades ready?'

The woman stayed staring at Margaret, trying to break her. It wasn't working. She stood up and her face was hard again. Those little lines that shot up from her top lip. Smoking too much, Margaret thought. Horrible.

'Thanks for your help.' Her sarcasm was vicious. Margaret made no reply. The woman led the way out. 'Come on. We got three of them. That's enough.'

The man turned to her, laughing unpleasantly as he opened the glass door. 'Hey there's fights starting in the line out here.'

Margaret watched them go, then stuck out a tongue.

In the safety of the back office, Katie took off her round black spectacles and rubbed her eyes. Her heart had sunk when Margaret said there were journalists at the desk asking about Sam. *What now?* she'd thought. *What's next on the big roller coaster ride through the rough country they'd been in this last week.* False alarm. It had been nothing. Just two dumb jerks looking for a story about Indians in Silver. Tenuous, even for a tabloid journalist she thought, to make an Indian thing out of two deaths, when only one was a native, and even then only half-native.

She put an elbow on her book and held her chin in her hand. This morning, Katie had gotten up feeling like she was still in a bad dream. She shifted in her chair, the physical reminder of her horror still aching in between her thighs.

The stuff Sam had told her last night was so unexpected, so hideous and tragic, she still couldn't believe it was real. And then that brutality. She changed the hand at her chin to a fist and covered her mouth.

Nothing physical in the bedroom this morning had changed. She wasn't sure if she had expected it would. The room was the same.

There was the linen basket under the window, with Sam's socks dripping out from under the lid like they were trying to escape. There was the bedside table, with its dusty digital clock, some coffee cup ring stains and a neglected packet of throat pastels dating back six weeks when she last had a cold. And there was that shiny black hair on the pillow where it always was. Shiny and thick as silk embroidery threads, but attached this morning to a man she now knew grew up in Hell and whom she had suspected last night of trying to drag her and her children down there into the flames with him.

Then Jess started her *Wake up, mama* noises and she crept out of bed without waking Sam to attend to the toddler. Billy was awake on the landing, rubbing his eyes and looking cute in his pyjamas. Katie swept him up and they collected Jess together and went downstairs to start the day. Billy had seemed fine. Exhausted-looking with big dark rings round his eyes that matched the deeper ones round hers, quieter than usual, but fine. Maybe the crisis was over. Katie prayed it was.

Bart was the next problem. She was right. He was sick. The big dog was lying next to a pool of its vomit and it looked up at them with sad, wounded eyes when they came in. Billy ran to it and Bart panted with as much excitement as he could manage in his washed-out state.

Billy was distraught, but Katie promised she'd take him to the vet as soon as she dropped him off at school, and after she'd deposited Jess at Mrs Chaney's she was as good as her word. The antiseptic-looking receptionist at the vet's said they'd keep him and look at him, and she could pick him up tonight. She could see the girl thinking big bucks and Katie sighed, thinking of the bill. Huskies were better business when they got sick than goldfish.

Katie let Sam sleep late. It was spiteful: she knew he would be late for work, but as she watched his body rise and fall under the comforter, her heart grew a shell of stone. She'd turned away and left the room without a sound.

So the Hunt household was back under her tight control as usual. On the surface. This feeling of unreality, of everything being different and somehow broken, was still strong in her, and she was damned if she could shrug it off. It made her want to cry. Damned if she would again though. Damned if she would.

She put her spectacles back on and looked down at Nicholson's book. There it was. The Isksaksin. A beautiful pen-and-ink drawing of the exact amulet Sam wore. He said so little about it, but then Nicholson was more concerned with domestic artefacts than the occult. This entry was by the way. She looked up the bibliography. A pamphlet was mentioned that looked promising. The big reference library in Vancouver could probably help her get it. She noted down the details, wrote a big note to Margaret to get the pamphlet faxed through, and closed the book.

The phone warbled again. It was Margaret. Katie listened with a frown. 'Yeah. Sure. Send him along.'

She hoped her voice had sounded calm. Because she was trying to stay very calm now as she gently replaced the receiver. Jesus. Craig McGee. Another policeman come with more bad news . . .

She took off her spectacles and sat at the desk like a headmistress, hands clasped tightly in front of her. She saw his dark shape through the opaque glass and shouted *come in* before he got a chance to knock.

Craig entered with a smile, his hand that was going to tap the glass held up for her in jest, as evidence of her good timing. Dared she hope this was social? Oh sure. Like she hoped the girl on the cash register at Safeways would ring up her groceries and say, *Hey. Looks like we owe YOU money!*. Policemen did not make social calls. At least not to people they'd interviewed about murder two nights before. Not to people whose husbands they put a tail on day and night. Her throat went dry.

'Hi! Sit down.'

He did. On the old black leather swivel-chair in front of her desk. Its stuffing was coming out and in the sunken crater it had left there was a little hard knob of wood just under the leather where Craig's balls would be. He shifted in it uncomfortably, but she didn't apologize or tell him the secret, that if you sat on one buttock at a time, you'd be fine. No, she let him suffer. Just in case he was going to make her suffer too.

'So?'

He shifted onto one buttock. Policemen. They always worked it out.

'Am I catching you at a bad time?'

'Not at all. What can I do for you?'

'Two things really. Well one that you can do for me, and the other just to keep you informed.'

She listened. Craig thought how pretty she was. There was still a mark on the bridge of her nose from her spectacles and he watched as the creamy flesh of that bump filled itself in again. But her eyes were ringed black, bagginess beneath them betraying that perhaps Mrs Hunt wasn't sleeping so good. He noted that.

'This is going to sound crazy, but I'm here to ask you about some historical stuff.'

'Hey. You don't need to tell me. I can put your mind at rest right now and tell you it's not true what Mounties used to do with their horses.'

That had been unnecessary.

But he laughed and she was relieved to see that he didn't register her aggression. 'No. It's more up your street Mrs Hunt. It's about the Kinchuinicks.'

'Oh?'

Her tone was wary. He tried to look reassuring, to look less like a cop. The radio on his shoulder foiled him as it crackled into life for a second, and he turned it down to a faint buzz with an apologetic glance. 'We talked to a man today, I can't say who for reasons of privacy, but he said there was a Kinchuinick phrase, a rhyme, and I wonder if you've heard it?'

'We have a book full of the things. Let's hear it.'

He looked at his shoes. 'It's pretty crude. The guy said that Kinchuinick women used to say it to their boys before they reached puberty. Presumably to prepare them for manhood.'

She leant back in her chair and smiled.

'Oh ho. You think it's delicate. I wish white women said it to their sons, Staff Sergeant: it should be inscribed in stone above every high school entrance. I know it very well. And I wish I could say it in Siouan, 'cause it rhymes you know, but it goes, *The Kinchuinick man makes life with his penis but he should live life with his heart.*'

Craig lit up. He slapped his palms together then pointed at her with a delighted finger. 'That's it. You know it.'

'Sure. It's still in use far as I know. I think they were trying to teach a primitive form of birth control with it. Fat chance.'

He sat looking satisfied for a moment as she waited for his next question. It was completely unrelated.

'Do they use animals in any rituals at all?'

'Use them? Like how?'

'I don't know. Do something with them that results in their death. Anything. Anything ritualistic at all.'

She gave a bitter laugh. 'You sound like those journalists.'

'What journalists?'

'You just missed two morons who wanted to speak to Sam about how he was preparing himself against what they seemed to think was an Indian-killer. Not very accurate given that the boy was a white Californian.'

Craig's face grew a mask. She noted it and leaned forward. 'What?'

'That was the other thing, Mrs Hunt. I wanted to tell you before you heard it, but seems like I'm way behind here. Daniel Hawk is dead.'

Her hand gripped the edge of Nicholson's book. 'Dead.'

It wasn't a question. She just repeated the word as though it might go away. She didn't need to ask if he was murdered. Of course he was. That guy. He'd been in her living room. Right there on the sofa. Blood pumping through his veins, air going in and out of his lungs.

How did you survive?

I breathed in and out.

The one that had known Sam back then. Back when he was being tortured. The one that gave away the fact he was called Hunting Wolf.

Dead.

Craig shifted his weight onto the other buttock, then looked at her with sympathy. 'We don't need to bother you about it, Mrs Hunt. I'm sure you know, and I apologize for it now, but we had men watching your house. We know it can't have been your husband.'

'When did it happen?' She was stunned.

'Tuesday night. Same night we came round to you. Your husband didn't leave the house that night, did he?'

It was meant to be a rhetorical question. He was not asking her, but telling her. But then he saw it. Huge and unmistakable and written in facial letters the size of a house. He tried not to let it show but she saw that he had seen it. It was the lie forming in her eyes and on her lips. Agnes Root had it right. Katie Hunt was a terrible liar. Craig watched her try and fail.

'That's right. He didn't.'

There was silence for a moment. Craig picked up a leather glove from his lap and turned it over in his hands.

'So. The animals. Anything spring to mind?'

He watched as she gathered up the pieces of herself. She lifted up her spectacles and put them on clumsily, as if to make herself more scholarly, or perhaps to try and put a barrier between her eyes and his.

'Animals?'

She cleared her throat of an imaginary obstruction. Buying time. Craig had seen it often in liars.

'Em, no. They would never do anything to hurt animals. They worshipped many of them as deities. In fact, when they killed for food they would spend days praying for the soul of the creature they'd eaten. No. I can't think of anything that would make them hurt animals in a ritual way.'

Craig nodded, trying to make her continue. Only really now so he could watch her face and see how soon she could wipe off that big tell-tale fib.

She continued, wriggling under the pincer of his gaze. 'Certainly they thought that animals could be their spirit guides. I'm sure you know that's a very strong part of their religion even today. And some shamans believed they could shape-shift into animals to go unseen. But that's about it really.'

'Shape-shift? You mean, possess the animals?'

'Well. Borrow them for a while. They're very strong on that. They say it's only the most evil of spirits who possess without permission. The Kinchuinick shape-shifter asks the animal first. It's a long ceremony. They have respect, these people.' She laughed nervously. Craig seemed interested.

'And they still believe they can move about as animals?'

'Shamans, yes. Not so much believe. They take it for granted. They can also transport themselves , their physical bodies as humans that is, across incredible distances. You'll find the religion of the Australian Aborigine is similar in this belief. In fact, there was documented evidence that an Aboriginal man was familiar with the craters and valleys on the moon and described them in detail to an anthropologist about ten years before the first moon landing. Well, Kinchuinick shamans are the same. They claim they can move around like that. After praying and fasting of course.'

She was calmer now. Enjoying the escape of a subject she was an authority on. A safe place to hide from whatever was going on in her mind.

'And so who are these shamans?'

'Usually the chief, but sometimes just a medicine man or woman. It's a respected position in the band, and it's usually passed down, father to son, mother to daughter, whatever.'

'Is it horseshit?'

She raised an eyebrow and tried to look amused. She was still far away from being amused. This was show. 'Please!'

'Come on. You know what I mean.'

'You're being a science bigot, Staff Sergeant. Modern medicine has a hell of a lot to learn from Indian herbal cures and hands-on healing. Some sceptics who've come to it have been amazed at the results. We have two papers here written by a guy from Calgary University who catalogues some incredible things if you're interested. First-hand reports and observations. It's academic, not speculative.'

'So you believe it?'

'I don't disbelieve it.'

'Can Mr Hunt shape-shift?' He tried a smile with the question. He got the first visible sign from her that everything was far from good. Her voice was acid.

'What do you think?'

He held up his hands. 'Hey. Joke. I was just asking.'

'My husband is not a shaman. He doesn't shake rattles or spread herbs around the TV to make the Flames win the Stanley cup. He's a manual groomer. He shovels snow.'

Craig waved his hands again to say he knew that.

'Why are you interested, may I ask?'

Craig licked his lips. 'Daniel got me interested. It's just kind of my way of dealing with his death, showing respect I suppose. To find out more.' His turn to lie. He was better at it. Much better. She didn't see him struggle under the guilt of it.

'Do you want the papers I mentioned?'

She was cold now. An ice queen offering knowledge.

'Sure. That would be great if it's no trouble.'

'No trouble. They're here.'

She got up and went to the metal filing-cabinet and after some fussing with folders pulled out a bunch of paper tied together at the top with short string and metal binders. She handed it to him. Lots of close print and annotations. It looked like dull stuff.

'I hope you find it interesting.'

'Thank you. I'll bring it straight back.'

'No hurry.'

Katie held the door open for him while she was on her feet and he stood up, grateful to be released.

'Thanks for your help, Mrs Hunt. Sorry to bring more bad news.' He shook her hand. Katie nodded and shut the door after him.

She went to the window, filled like a TV with its neverending show called *Snow Falling*.

She'd lied. He *was* out that night, and not for a walk round the block. Unless going round the block took a couple of hours. Was she going to be the last person to know what was happening with her husband?

Jesus Christ, she was spending all her waking hours swinging from hope and love to mistrust and insanity. It was eating her up like a cancer and she put her hands to her face in pain.

And for the hundredth time she told herself it was unthinkable. Completely and utterly impossible. Sam was not a killer. She loved him. She knew him. Did she? Until last night had she known that the man she loved had been forged on an anvil of torture and darkness? Had she known that her son would fear his father for some unknown transgression that was neither discussed nor explained?

Impossible? Well, who knows, maybe she'd like to tell Craig McGee that anything was possible.

She stared out of the window as a car-hire man tried to clear the snow off one of the Buicks for a potential customer that looked like a journalist. Tourists didn't wear expensive, long storm coats and carry aluminium flight cases. The car-hire guy was using big hand movements to explain the merits of the freezing vehicle to the man in the storm coat, who seemed less than impressed. Those cars hadn't moved for weeks. He'd be lucky to start it. The customer climbed in as the man from the car hire shop stood outside watching him turn the key, no doubt crossing his fingers. It started first time.

Yes. Anything was possible.

40

The pipes made soft ticking noises as they cooled down. The central heating had gone off. Sam opened his eyes and his head worked out that the noise meant he had overslept. Katie was gone. He focused blearily on the digital clock on her bedside table and groaned. Eleven-fifteen. That wasn't late. That was ridiculous. The house was big and empty and silent, and as he started to feel that they'd all cheated him, sneaking out like that and leaving him to oversleep, he remembered last night.

Had it been a dream? His hand went to his throat where the amulet had always hung, and he touched the naked flesh. No. It hadn't been a dream. He had told her about his sick little life, and before she'd joined him in bed last night he'd ripped the cursed thing off and flung it under the bed with contempt, just as he seemed to be tossing away his life in all this madness.

For one fleeting, unbearable moment his world fell from him like a chair kicked away from under a hanging man. Had she left him? He'd told her it all, well nearly all. And although she had listened with sympathy and love she had acted weird in bed. His hand moved from his throat to his shoulder where the scar from her bite was scabbed over now in a crusty black line, and he closed his eyes in a prayer that she was coming home tonight.

She'd been in his dreams last night, and for a time they were good dreams. They'd been on a lake together in a boat, a big green morainic lake like the ones in the mountains, with the glaciers reflecting in that emerald water. Except that this lake, unlike the real ones that were milky and cloudy with the particles that made it that mad colour, this one was crystal clear. They could see all the way to the bottom and it was hundreds of feet deep. Katie was laughing and throwing her head back as she dipped her fingers into the water and Sam was rowing the boat, smiling with love at his wife. He'd been so happy.

And then as he looked into the water, he saw a dark shape down there in the deep. Small at first, but growing in size as it started to float up towards the surface. Like a whale, but bigger and faster. Sam had watched as it started to rush up towards them, its shape becoming a huge mass of dark solid matter, and still Katie was laughing and trailing her fingers in the lake. The boat was starting to toss and pitch as the water churned and he rowed faster, pulling harder to get away, but he knew the shape that was turning the green water black would reach them soon, and he tried to scream to a deaf smiling Katie. And then suddenly he dreamt he had woken. But he had not. He was still asleep. His dreams had been feverish and muddled after that, making him believe he was conscious, wandering around the house looking for things that were not there, when he knew, even as he walked in the dream, that he was asleep. Mild dreams compared to the night-mares he'd been having.

But then his waking hours held more terror for him now than his sleeping ones. Sam was tired but was fully awake now, aching for the touch and the smell of Katie, the sight of her streaky blonde hair mussed up over her face and those dreamy, half-awake eyes full of love and desire. She was at work. She hadn't woken him. He suddenly felt deeply lonely.

He sighed and put his arm behind his head and tried to take comfort from the warmth of the bed. His face was still scratched from the fall yesterday, and he fingered those scabs too. Seemed like everything hurt him these days, cut him and left its mark. But he knew he'd been lucky. He'd been skiing faster than he'd ever skied in his life, pointing his skis straight down the fall-line like a downhill racer, schussing rather than skiing, blind with panic and fear.

He'd caught an edge at the base of the Wildwood trail and the fall had catapulted him across the hard snow and whipped him into the branches of a low spruce. It could have been worse. After all, he was fleeing for his life. Running like a frightened rabbit before a hound. Even if the hound was only in his head.

The tourists on Toby's ski bus had looked at him like he was a monster as he'd climbed aboard in his mission to get home. Wild-eyed, scratched and bleeding, his face running with sweat and melted snow. Toby, ever the half-wit you prayed you wouldn't have to sit beside on the staff bus, had watched Sam get on with a cackle.

'Nope. They surely don't pay us enough.'

Sam had glowered at him and sat down on the jump seat behind Toby, watching through the window as the brown car by the lodge entrance turned on its lights. Had they been waiting here, looking for him among the crowds? Or had they followed him up the hill, maybe even skied down behind him? He caught a glimpse of the fat cop with a couple of chins in the driver's seat and realized that was unlikely. What a tale they'd have to give back at base, he thought. The suspect all cut up and scared.

Now he lay in his warm bed in the darkened room, looking at the irregular patch of grey daylight on the ceiling that was filtering through the curtains, and knowing that outside would be two cops looking up at the bedroom window, wondering why those curtains were still drawn.

Warning! Warning! Danger!

The voice of the TV robot.

Sam sat up with the terror of complete bewilderment in his racing heart, eyes boggling at the source of the voice. A tall figure, in the gloom, sitting on Katie's cane chair by the wardrobe. It laughed. A deep throaty sound that was like a drunk coughing on bile. And the voice again. This time trilling and mocking, imitating a woman's like a burlesque player.

'Did it make you shit your pants this time? Huh?'

Sam could see it now. The face in the crowd again. It was here. In his own bedroom, sitting on the chair laughing at him with those blue eyes that were so poorly drawn, the pink mouth that was so inexpertly realized. At least to Sam. For he could see the machinations behind the pretend skin, and his body and soul were paralysed with fear in the face of it. It moved its mouth again, although the speech seemed driven from elsewhere.

'Smells like it from here. But then who could mistake the stench of Kinchuinick vermin?'

The house. Was it empty? Sam's mind raced, praying that the children and Katie were gone as he'd assumed. The face in the crowd caught his thought as though he'd tossed a ball.

From the next room there was a wail.

'Daaaad! Help me! Please! Dad!'

386

Billy. Then the crying of Jess, that high sweet burbling cry.

Sam jerked in instinctive response, but the thing was grinning and he knew it was false, knew that his family was not here. It was a poor trick. An obvious one. He remained sitting upright like a gaping fool, naked to the waist, vulnerable and nearly out of his mind. His guest crossed its legs.

'Harder to find in these modern times, aren't you? Even though the reek of losers carries across centuries.'

Sam's back teeth were grinding.

'Did you think that you could hide, all you little shits? Hide amongst white men?' It laughed again. 'Oh but I've enjoyed the search. So much misery. Such lost and useless lives. What has become of you, my fine noble people?'

The laugh again. This time the unmistakable sarcastic, bitter laugh of Moses. Heh heh, heh. Sam wanted to close his eyes, put his hands over his face and open them to an empty chair, but his senses would not let it happen. There was real danger in the room and his animal fight-or-flight instinct was in charge. His mind could tell him all he wanted that what he saw and heard was not real, but his body was not prepared to listen. His eyes remained staring and wide, his ears listening to every sound, and his body ready to spring. But at what?

The thing stopped its mockery and there was a flash of anger in its eyes, that Sam could also see as a whorl of oily black beneath the disguise. 'Did you think to trick me perhaps?'

There was a madness in the tone this time, a childish petulance that was unstable and out of control. It looked at the naked area around Sam's neck where the amulet had been, and smiled weakly, the anger and something else, something like confusion, hidden again, the composure of a torturer resumed.

'Well now, my degenerate son of a drunkard . . .' It paused as if waiting for a rebuke, then spoke quietly and with satisfaction. 'Do you know my name?'

Sam clutched the sheet, grasping it to remind his paralyzed spirit that he was still alive, that though the world had gone spinning out of control, the rough linen touch of the sheet was a constant. Real. Here. Under his fingers.

'Do you know my name?'

No. Not this. Not this madness from the past when sticks and rocks and herbs ruled his intellect. When spirits spoke and the air trembled under Calvin's outstretched arms. Not that insanity. He would not submit to it again.

'Do you know my name?'

Such menace in the quiet voice this time. That undertone of madness. Did it think that his silence was a trick? That to deny this horror, a horror that had been predicted as though it were merely a summer storm by his grandfather and his shaman, was a calculated trick? It was no trick. He wanted no part of it. It was the only way.

I survive. I breathe in and out. I will not listen. I will not believe.

'MY NAME!'

The force of its rage blew him back onto the pillow, and he lay gritting his teeth, his hands over his ears, eyes screwed tightly shut. He knew the thing in the room was changing, that it was abandoning its form for another that Sam could not bear to see. He would not see it. Would not speak to it.

The air in the room changed its pressure as it was filled with something solidifying. Something massive.

No. No. He would not. And yet, he could not deny it. He knew its name. Of course he knew its name.

Eden. Looking at him from his cheap chair.

'Say them again boy.'

'They sound the same.'

'They ain't the same. They be different.'

'Why I need to know them?'

''Cause he be clever in one way and real dumb in another. He only ever be rememberin' his oldest name. You gotta tell him his other names then he be knowin' who he is for sure and who you be.'

'What if I don't tell him who he is? '

Eden had laughed.

'Then he just kill you.'

The sweat was pouring down Sam's brow, the sheet beneath his body already damp with the same from his back. The room was full of a roar whose frequency rattled the bed and shook the walls.

As he fought to keep the sound of the nightmare in his house out of his head, there was no escape from the memory of Eden's eyes, boring into him, making him listen, making him believe.

'And he be mighty sorry if he lose you, 'cause then he have to find someone else help him do his killin'. And that get harder to find the more men goes away from knowin' what they used to know.'

Sam, the boy, had been so confident, so sure. 'Then I be lettin' him kill me and everyone be safe.'

Eden looked sad then. 'No one be safe if he be left out there with no keeper to put him back where he can't do no harm. He be the Trickster. Time was we could all trick him back some. You knows the stories. Then we gets to bein' scared and believin' in his tricks like my pappy done. And that be makin' him real strong. No boy. You gonna die Indian, you be doin' it when the time is right. You go ahead and says his names. It be better he knows who you is and who he is, so he thinks he knows who be puttin' him back in his cage.' Eden had sat back with satisfaction. 'He never get that right. Not once. That be our trick, boy. That be our big trick.'

Sam arched his back in his shaking bed, and abandoning all reason, all hope of survival and sense, he spoke through his teeth.

'You are Sitconski.'

There was a hissing sigh through the room, a pressure released, a new one building, and a voice that was like dust talking said, 'And?'

Sam was in Hell. Eden had said it, known it. *'Then he just kill you.'* He didn't want to die. Katie. Where are now you my Katie?

'You are Inktomi.'

'And?'

Sam could hardly speak. His throat was on fire.

'You are Inktomni.'

'And?'

'You are Inktumni.'

He writhed on the bed. His twentieth century bed that had a pine headboard with an acorn carved in it, and a little notch above his side, that Katie had done with a penknife for a joke after they'd done something particularly inventive one night.

His head tossed on the pillows, snug in their pillow-cases that he had thrown in the washing machine and Katie had slung over the radiator to dry. All the familiar ordinary things, that were now rendered twisted, grotesque and misplaced, bathed as they were in the ancient pollution of this nightmare. He would not open his eyes. He would not.

Even though the satisfied voice of a thing who now knew who it was, was addressing him again.

'Then destroy me.'

'No.'

He thought he heard the carpet tearing and the walls splitting. His bed rocked on its legs.

'DESTROY ME!'

Sam screamed at it. Calvin's words this time. In that ancient guttural tongue. The Latin of Cree.

'You will destroy yourself.'

The room stopped its agitation. There was a pause and then the mass was growing smaller again. He could feel it. The sheet was a ball of cloth in his fist. Sam could sense the thing controlling its fury, weighing up the childlike opponent that was hiding his face in the covers. There was an age as it waited. The voice came again, calm and in control.

'Will I? Then before that, we must do some more of what we do best together.'

Sam opened his eyes slowly and turned his head to the chair. It was in human form again. Sam could only croak, hoarse with fear. 'And what's that?'

The pale face creased with a laugh that was not a laugh, and it got up slowly and left the room. Conventionally. Through the door.

Two things for him when he came back from the museum. They'd let Wilber go. *Hip hip hooray,* thought Craig sourly. And the deer. They'd discovered that the deer's heart had burst open.

Bell had been conspiratorial with the news, as though he had been told that it was no concern of McGee's any longer and not to pass on the information. Craig wondered which of the two pathologists that had arrived from Edmonton had done the work. They had the coyote too, although the way it had died seemed all too obvious.

He sat for a moment at his desk and watched the snow fall through the pencil blinds. No mention on the log from Edison and Patel that Sam Hunt had gone out Tuesday night. They'd observed him go to bed and the lights go out and then nothing till the next morning. But he had gone out. His wife knew. What did he do? Sneak out a window? His car didn't move so if he got up to Hawk's how did he do it?

But so what? Even if Sam Hunt had flown out of the window with a fucking gold lamé cloak on and a neon light flashing round his head, what was all this killing about? These dead animals. Wilber's talking animals. Craig held the bridge of his nose between a thumb and middle finger.

Come on then Becker. Solve it you asshole. Make it eighteen solved murders, you smug bastard. Craig was at sea.

He needed to speak to Hunt again. Speak to the apple. He caught sight of the dreary paper Katie had given him, sticking out of his storm-coat pocket, rolled into a disrespectful cone. Craig leaned forward and fished it out, slapping it onto the desk in front of him with a sigh.

A study and history of the occult beliefs of the Stony, Blackfoot, Kinchuinick and Flathead tribes of the Western states of Canada, including field studies, observations and transcripted testimonials. By Doctor Aird Lennox and Chief Cecil Bows With the Wind. 1964.

Catchy title, thought Craig. *Bet the film rights have already gone.* He sighed and flipped the first page over on its binder.

To discuss in context the historical beliefs and surviving indigenous religious culture of the native Canadian, it is important to assess the abstract as well as literal understanding of the word 'reality' to the Indian mentality.

Jeez, this was going to be riveting. He leaned a heavy head on one hand and forced himself to read it. If it carried on as it started he would be comatosed by page three, and it would probably be of little use. But let's face it. It wasn't going to do any harm.

They should have just let him out the front door. He knew those journalists would have given him money for booze if he'd talked to them. But they took Wilber out the back door and drove him away so that those guys didn't see. No matter. He'd find them again and then he'd get plenty drunk. They had money, those guys. Yeah. Big money. You could smell it off them.

Wilber wanted a drink real bad. It was only ten before noon but he'd had a thirsty morning, what with those cops making him cry like that and telling them over and over again about the bird and the thing in it. He swallowed, and looked behind him. They'd dropped him out in the suburbs, by all that staff accommodation for the hotel and ski workers, where there was a hostel for guys like Wilber. But he didn't want a hostel. He wanted a drink. And he knew the guys in town would get him one. So he waited till the cops drove off, and made it look like he was going to go inside the grim wooden shack that he'd slept in before, then when they turned off the block he started to walk back into town. It was less than a mile. About two miles off, high on the hill above the roofs of these hidden cabins and ill-kempt cabins, the towering Rocky Mountain Chateau poked its turrets out of the pines. That was just its big backside you saw from here and it was still something. Yes, it was something, all right. Wilber looked up at it as he shuffled through the snow, and wondered who all the people were that were in it right now. He'd got into the grounds one time and been able to get right into the foyer before a bell-hop saw him and took him by the arm all the way back to the gates.

It was like a heaven in there. All old wood and a big round carpet on a marble floor. There were girls in green jackets all lined up behind a big long bar that was the reception desk, and they were smiling at everybody who spoke to them.

And there was a kind of quiet loud sound. Like, lots of noise, on account of there being lots of people there, but all kind of muffled and peaceful.

And most of the people were those Japanese. How come's they got to be in places like that, thought Wilber, and folks like him didn't? They had dark skin too, didn't they? It wasn't fair. They'd be there now. Drinking and talking in that muffled way, maybe looking out one of those tiny little windows all the way back to where he was. Wilber thought they probably weren't looking at all, and if they were it would be over his head, at the Wolf River snaking its way to the sea. He pulled his parka tighter against the flurries of wind that blew the snow right into his face and picked up his pace.

The sidewalk was lined with big trees here. The houses and shacks hid behind them like the trees were the reason for the street and the houses were expendable. Such big trees.

A branch shivered suddenly above him and shook some snow down on his head as he passed beneath it. He looked up nervously, but there was no more movement. He pressed on, licking his dry lips and thinking of how warm the bar would be in the Keystone Hotel, and how cold the beer.

The branches above his head danced again, with the weight of something moving through them. This time the snow fell like a waterfall. Something heavy. Wilber made a whimper. Up ahead there was a lane between the houses. It went down to the river, away from these big pines. He started to run. The breath swirled from him in clouds as his thin legs staggered to keep up with his body as it leaned forward into the snow and wind. He gained the lane and headed down it as the branches of the tree at the entrance bent and dipped. There were two men in the lane. One, a kid of about twenty in a big four-wheel-drive car with the engine running and skis on the rack, the man, in work overalls, a plaid jacket and a baseball cap leaning on the open driver's window talking to him. They looked up at this haggard Indian running towards them, gasping and clutching his parka round the neck like a Victorian mining widow.

They looked at each other and laughed: he was being pursued by a small black and white domestic cat.

Wilber wasn't looking behind him, he was just running. Stumbling and slipping, but running as fast as he could. The cat bounded daintily behind him, effortlessly keeping pace. Wilber fell over the hood of the kid's car, gasping for breath.

'Gotta help me. It be comin' after me again.' He pointed behind him, at the cat that was nearly there.

The guys laughed, and the man straightened up and crossed his arms. 'You owe it money, chief?'

They both laughed and Wilber scrabbled his way round the vehicle until he was behind the car. The cat jumped up onto the hood, sat down and looked at Wilber through the windshield and the length of the car.

Both men were amused and bewildered. The man walked forward and put a hand out to the cat. 'Come on, puss. Stop givin' the old guy a hard time. He ain't got any fish. Just smells like he does.'

That cracked up the driver, and he hit the wheel in mirth. The cat slowly turned its head from looking at Wilber and regarded the man who was leaning to pet it.

'Don't touch me you ugly cunt.'

The jaws of both men opened, and the hand of the man to whom the words had been spoken stayed frozen in mid-air.

Wilber was nodding like a madman, screaming, 'Ya see! Ya see. I told ya!' He looked wildly behind him, holding onto the back screen-wiper as though the car would go someplace without him. He had got it badly wrong. This was not the lane that went down to the river. That was on the next block. This was a cul de sac behind the staff quarters. It ended in three lock-ups. No way out. A dead end.

The man standing staring at the cat was trying to find his voice. Maybe he hadn't heard that. He looked to his companion through the glass whose face told him he had. He gulped, looked back at the still watching animal and found his voice, albeit a tiny, hoarse voice.

'What you say?' He was nervous, flabbergasted, but excited, willing the cat to speak again and confirm the miracle.

It looked at him with cool amber eyes. 'So you want to die with that human excrement do you?'

Its voice was deeper than should come from anything smaller than a bull and it wasn't saying very nice things. The man with his hand out decided that if this was an illusion he wasn't enjoying it much. Slowly he withdrew his hand and moved back. Wilber was whimpering, scratching at the back window and his face alternately. 'It got us now! Lord. It got us for sure!'

'Pump the horn, Kenny.' The man touched his friend's shoulder and said it quietly. Kenny did as he was told, and only three out of the four beings jumped. The cat looked back at them passively. Kenny broke the spell. This was ridiculous. He opened the door and got out of the car.

Through his tears Wilber whimpered a soft *no* from the back.

Kenny closed the door and threw his older companion a look. 'What we got scarin' us here? A talkin' cat, huh?'

There was no reply. Kenny lifted his hand up and banged it down hard on the shiny metal of the car hood, an inch away from the animal, accompanying it with a shout. It didn't move. He backed off, afraid now.

The cat opened its mouth once more, and instead of a voice there was a dull growl, a vibrating, retching noise that was too loud and too low in frequency to come from the animal itself. The men stumbled back as the tiny body of the feline bulged for a moment, then gaped its jaws as a black sticky ooze exploded from its mouth, splattering onto the windshield with breathtaking velocity and force. The ooze hardened, rising into a glistening, crackling, insane form that was black ice.

Black ice with jaws that yawned and split. Black ice with talons that sliced and slashed. A heaving, writhing serpentine materialization of hate, that quivered for only a second before it speared the two men through with razor-sharp barbs that ripped and pulverized as they penetrated the flesh.

The older man's face attempted a scream as the rapier of ice that had slit him withdrew, pulling the hot contents of his upper body with it, to spill viscously out into the snow. But the scream never happened, since his head was split in two by a second blow that cut it neatly below the nose. The attempted noise died in the *O* of the mouth that was left on its own, the decoration on a bowl of flesh whose contents were seeping grey and red brains.

The younger man was dead before he could react. The black glittering talons caught him under the chin and while the spear of ice held his quivering body, the claws wrenched his head off with one smooth movement. It turned once in the air, then bounced on the roof of the car, rolled down and landed at Wilber's feet. The Indian was collapsed against the back wheel now, dribbling through clenched teeth, and letting the hot urine that was pissing down his leg run into the snow beneath him.

The abomination let its prey drop and engulfed the car, sweeping over either side, scraping the metal with its hellish fluid yet solid body, and reforming before Wilber, whose snot was running over a trembling lip. It had a voice, and the voice was the low thrumming of turning abattoir blades, the suppressed screams of the tortured, the triumphant bellow of the demented killer.

41

The cold snout of the dog poked into his face, nudging him twice before leaving him with a sandpaper lick. His eyes opened and he tried to focus as flakes of snow, grey against a grey sky, tumbled down towards his iris. He blinked as one found its target. Where was he? He tried to lift his head from its pillow of snow, but his numb body ached in protest.

'What ya doin', mister?'

A child's face peered into his swimming vision. A round boy's face, red-cheeked and with its hat flaps tied securely under its chin. A child? A dog? The sound of water. He was lying outside in the snow, but where?

He pulled one elbow painfully back into his body, and with an effort that made him wince, lifted himself up on it. By the river. Of course that's where he was. In the park by the river, just like he'd planned.

A bright red metal climbing-frame and three tall swings stood to his left, redundant in their winter mantle of white. The boy was standing with his hands in his pockets, his dog gone elsewhere to forage, and he watched as Calvin Bitterhand drew his legs up and attempted to stand. There was no helping hand from this little white boy. He watched with the same detachment one might observe a fish flapping on the rocks before being clubbed and bagged, a product of parents who told him that Indians shouldn't be touched or spoken to. He'd already broken one rule but he was keenly observing the other. Calvin's boots slipped in the ice beneath the softer white, and he fell painfully on his knee. He winced and tried again. With greater

396

care he committed his weight to both feet and pulled himself erect. The kid spat thoughtfully.

'You drunk or somethin'?'

Calvin ignored the child and swept the snow from his jacket. How long? How much time had passed since he'd stepped out of the sweat-lodge, dressed, and re-entered its searing heat to fulfil the final part of his prayer for this journey? It should only have been seconds. It used to be seconds. But he was struggling with a body that could barely withstand the weight of its own flesh, and he had passed out as the journey commenced. He was not chilled through, not in that way he had been when he lost his fingers, not the cold that was so intense it was like heat on the skin, so perhaps it had only been seconds. The boy should know.

'How long I be lyin' there?'

The boy shrugged, already bored. He didn't care. 'Dunno. Salty just found ya.'

Calvin looked across at Salty, who was lifting a leg to the plastic slide. Good. The boy had not seen him arrive. That would have been awkward. He looked across the river to the backs of the roofs in Silver's main street. He could eat now. Eat and drink now that his fasting was over. Now that he was here.

He wiped his hands across his face and turned to the boy who couldn't care less if Calvin was hungry, cold, dead or alive. Salty would always get better treatment than any human from a child like this. Calvin could see the cold man in the child's eyes and grieved for what he would become. He looked into those little brown eyes and smiled. The boy hesitated, then smiled back. He could smell chocolate cooking, like when his grandma was alive and she used to make those things with rice crispies and put them in little folded paper cups. There was laughter. He could hear it faintly in the distance and it sounded like the way his Mom used to laugh before Dad left and they came to live here. It was so lovely and warm and safe.

He had three two-dollar bills inside his glove that his Mom's new boyfriend had given him to go and get some candy. But this man needed them. He didn't want any candy anyhow. It didn't taste the way those chocolate rice crispie things used to. He pulled the money out of his glove and handed it to the man. It felt good. He wasn't used to giving folks things.

He stood in the park with Salty licking his bare hand, watching the old man walk away towards town, and the boy heard another tinkling peal of laughter that was so like his Mom's. Or was it just the ice breaking on the river, smashing into shards and bumping and spinning away downstream? It didn't matter. It felt real good.

She couldn't look any more at the little boy that Jess wanted to cuddle. His haunted eyes avoided hers every time she tried to reel him in with a smile. She looked instead out through the window as Jess struggled into her coat and saw her son looking through the passenger window of the Toyota with eyes that were not dissimilar.

She snapped her head back round into the lobby. 'Thanks, Mrs Chaney. See you tomorrow.'

'Prompt if you can please Mrs Hunt.'

'Prompt.'

Katie swept Jess up into her arms and bundled her out to the car. Billy was withdrawn again. Gerry, waiting at the school gates, had brought him to her car ten minutes ago with a grim smile.

'How's Sam?'

'Fine. Look, Gerry, I don't know what to say. How to apologize to you both.'

'Then don't.' Gerry's face was full of friendship and love. She wanted to kiss him. Instead she carried on defending the indefensible acts of her husband. 'He's sick. We all know that now. We're waiting for an appointment from Calgary.'

'And you?'

'Good,' she lied.

'Do you need us at all? We're around.'

Katie had shaken her head, then as Billy crawled into the car she'd enquired with her eyes how her son was.

Gerry shrugged a little and made a look that said *the same*. Agnes Root was watching them from the steps, making Katie uneasy as she drove off.

All she'd gotten out of Billy was that he wanted Bart home. Well now they were going to fetch him maybe it would cheer Billy up. She strapped a resistant Jess into the toddler's seat and headed for the vet's. *Just keep on going Katie*, she thought. *Just keep on going with these familiar family routines and you won't have to think about it. Any of it.* At least that was the theory. The practice was different. How could she stop thinking about where Sam was that night?

Her hand had hovered over the phone so many times this afternoon, to call home and hear his voice. But what if the phone rang out? What if he wasn't there? Did she ever know where he was now, what he was doing?

'Will Bart be okay, Mom?'

'Sure. He'll be fine. I guess he's just got a cold or something.'

'Huskies don't get colds.'

'Whatever.'

They were there. Billy started to undo his seat belt.

'Ah ah. You stay with Jess. I'll just be a minute. Get the back ready for him with that blanket would you?'

Billy sighed but obeyed. She didn't want him there in case it was bad news. You never could tell these days. Seemed like they were cultivating bad news in the Hunt house like most people grew geraniums. She grabbed her pocket-book and dashed through the falling snow to the surgery.

There were two miserable-looking clients waiting on the metal-backed chairs, one with a mewling kitten in a basket and the other without an animal, presumably like herself waiting to pick one up.

The receptionist was doing that really annoying thing of not looking up from the form she was filling in even when Katie was standing right in front of her. *Don't push me, honey*, thought Katie, *not today*.

'Bart Hunt. Husky. Here to pick him up.'

The woman looked up surprised that she'd been addressed without permission. Most people stood patiently and waited until she chose to raise her eyes. She was about to give this blonde uppity bitch a hard time when she realized it was the owner of *that* dog. Mr Adler had told her he wanted to talk to her himself.

'Take a seat.'

Katie looked at her coldly and replied as though the receptionist were four. 'You mean take a seat, please.'

The woman flushed, glancing sideways to see if the other two clients had heard her admonishment. Sure they had. They'd loved it.

'Please.'

Katie nodded and sat beside the fat woman without the animal as the red-faced receptionist punched the phone through to her boss. Katie closed her eyes. Where was he now, her Sam? Waiting for them at home, or gone for another walk around the block?

'Mrs Hunt?'

She opened her eyes. It was the vet, poking the top half of his body round his surgery door, in his white coat and holding a clipboard.

'Yo!'

'Would you like to come in for a second, please?'

Oh no. Not Bart. Please no doggie deaths, she prayed. It would kill Billy right now. But what else could it mean? They usually just led the dog out, gave you your bill, and you never even saw the guy who'd done whatever it was just cost you a small fortune. This time she was going in to see him. Not good.

In his room there was a parrot in a big cage sitting on his table like an ornament instead of a patient. The fat woman's pet, she guessed. No Bart.

'Where is he ? Is he dead?' Her voice was steady. Her hands were not. She put them in her pockets to stop them trembling. The vet shook his head. There was nowhere to sit so he didn't offer.

'No. No, he's okay, Mrs Hunt. He's sedated.'

'What's wrong with him?'

'Nothing, physically. We sedated him because we thought he might harm himself.'

She looked at him quizzically, bewildered. The vet pursed his lips. 'I can't find what's up with him other than a psychological disorder. Now that means you can either risk taking him home and living with the consequences of that, or ... and I only suggest this because of the nature of his disorder, you have him put to sleep.'

Katie was dumbfounded. 'What do you mean, *psychological disorder*? What's he been doing, for Christ sakes?'

The vet ran a hand over his mouth, banging the clipboard against his thigh with the other hand. 'Eh, he seems to want to tear his own heart out.'

Katie's mouth fell open. 'Bart?'

'Can't describe it any other way. To put it in layman's terms, I think your dog's flipped.'

'Where is he?'

'Through here.'

He pushed open the door to a corridor like room lined with big cages. There were a few animals yapping and mewing and sleeping, and there was Bart in the middle, lying in his favourite pose, like a sphinx. He saw her and got up drunkenly but excitedly. His curly erect tail wagged like it was going to fall off and he tried to jump up to her, laying his big paws on the cage.

'Bart, my sweet thing! What's up, boy?' She knelt to the wire. He tried to lick her through it. She put a loving finger through the wire to his tongue, and turned to the vet. 'He seems okay now.'

The man shrugged. 'Can't guarantee what he'll be like when the injection wears off though.'

'And you say there's nothing physically wrong with him.'

'Apart from the damage he did himself, no.'

'What did he do exactly?'

'I can't explain it really. He sort of turned on himself. Started snapping at his own neck and shoulders, as if he were attacking a foe. He only sustained minor cuts before we grabbed him and gave him a shot.'

'What would you suggest?'

'Do you have young children, Mrs Hunt?'

'Yeah.'

'Then I wouldn't risk it. I'd put him to sleep.'

Tears came to her eyes as she turned back to the big beautiful husky, panting now in its joy to see her face. Was it a risk? Bart would never harm anyone. But if he was trying to harm himself, then who knows? But what about Billy? How could she tell Billy? The vet said there was nothing physically wrong. Surely he'd be all right? What if there was a chance he might get better? Maybe he was just freaked to be in here. Who wouldn't be? They could keep him outside until they saw what was up with him. Yes, that would do surely. No risk then. She stood up. 'I can't do that. I'm going to take him home.'

The vet shook his head clearly disapproving. 'Up to you. But I'd watch him carefully, Mrs Hunt. He was wild with it. I mean really wild.'

Katie waited silently while the vet opened the cage and grabbed Bart out by the collar. She clipped on his lead and he showed her out into the waiting room.

The woman behind the desk clicked her computer while Katie waited.

'Thirty-seven dollars.' She looked up.

'Please.'

Katie paid her, patted the panting, woozy Bart and led him unsteadily out of the surgery to the car. Great. Thirty-seven dollars to be told your dog's a loony. This was all she needed. But she couldn't have him put down. No way. Not without even discussing it with Sam. God. So much to discuss with Sam. Where to begin?

Billy went wild and so did Bart. Didn't look to her like a dog that wanted to kill itself. She moved off, stopping abruptly to let past three speeding police cars with lights flashing and sirens going, heading out of town towards the river. Her heart was in her mouth as she started to move off again in their noisy wake.

What now? In God's name what now?

Craig looked across at the white-faced man who had headed seventeen murder investigations and knew he was defeated. He was going to have to declare an emergency, get some more serious police help. So he and Craig were equal now. Neither had ever had to do that.

The mess was unreal. Broad daylight, and it looked like a regiment of Samurai soldiers had waded into these guys. And then there was Wilber. The parts had fucked each other like he'd feared. And some. There, of course, was the animal. A cat this time, twisted and mis-shapen, its spewed guts lying around it on the hood of the car like an offering.

He watched Becker and his men circle the sight like mating birds, stepping carefully and almost ritually around the pieces of human that littered the snow. The woman who'd stumbled across the carnage on her way into the lane with some trash was under sedation. But she'd recover and soon she'd be bleating her horror story out on national TV, her hand clutching her breast.

And what could they do now, these policemen with their guns and radios and cars, that couldn't keep Wilber alive?

They could roll tanks down Silver's Main Street if they wanted but Craig knew it wouldn't stop whatever did this. Above them the chopper thundered back and forward in the thick snow clouds in its fruitless search for a culprit, and the the road-blocks were up again like a sick practical joke on the public.

He didn't need to ask the tail on Hunt where he was. He knew he'd have been somewhere else when these choice cuts were happening.

He bent down and clasped his hands across his knees. The snow fell like Christmas card snow, oblivious to the fact that it fell on entrails, severed limbs and naked bone.

How do you tail a man's soul, thought Craig, and he was glad no one could read the crazy question in his mind.

42

Alberta 1907
Siding Twenty-three

Hunting Wolf would come no further. Henderson stopped, surprised. He beckoned to the man who had paused in the snow behind him, his eyes fixing on the railway encampment like a hawk fixing on a rat.

'Come. Fear nothing.'

But it was not as Henderson thought. It was not the retribution of the white men that Hunting Wolf feared. It was the man the minister had described as being in their midst. Singing Tree had all but swooned when Henderson pronounced their dead child's name. *Snowchild*. Born to his wife in the snows of winter, crying by the fire, or nursing at her breast as the wind howled outside and the animals pawed the ground and starved for want of food. The sweet Snowchild who survived the cruellest of biting cold and then saw but one more winter because of his carelessness.

Henderson walked back to him, turning his face from the snow-filled wind that stung him. He touched the chief's arm under his blanket, trying to see into his black eyes beneath the huge-brimmed wool hat he wore with an eagle feather stuck in its head-band like a jest.

'They must see you not the man kill McEwan. We tell them.'

Hunting Wolf would not move. The scheme was foolish. How could he stand amongst them and let them examine his heart, when he himself did not know the contents of it? He was drawn only by the name of his child, and now he wished to go back. His wife was unsure of his heart also. He saw it in her eyes. Her suspicion was that he had killed a man. He could not tell her the blood that spattered his clothes and face and body when they found him in a trance was from the creatures that had died before him like actors. He scarce believed what he had seen himself. But he made himself believe. He had been warned. All his life warned, and now was the time.

'You go on, Henderson. I have changed my mind. They will not believe me, for I have nothing to tell. But I would see this trapper. I will wait here, and watch.'

The Reverend Henderson looked into the chief's eyes and tried to read them. They were closed to him. Henderson swallowed and blinked against the snow. He had to ask. He had assumed, but now he could not assume.

'Hunting Wolf. You kill man McEwan?'

Hunting Wolf looked beyond Henderson to the cabins, their smoke rising from the metal chimneys. He spoke in a dream.

'I do not know. In truth, I do not know.'

Singing Tree huddled beneath the lodgepole pine gazing through the falling snow to the mountains. *Snowchild.* Sometimes she thought in her sleep that she was with her yet. Wriggling beneath her arm, warm and plump, shifting in a child's sleep. And then she would wake and know that it was not true. She had blamed no one but herself for her child's death. But it had made her doubt her husband in a small way. If he were such a great shaman, how could he not have foreseen such an event?

And this mission they were on now, how much was true? She knew the tales. But she was a practical woman. There had been no spirits in her life other than the one she prayed to, and who came only in dreams. Spirits were of men. Bad and good. Like men.

She would not let herself believe that Hunting Wolf had killed the white man. Such folly, such evil, would be unthinkable. And yet what was she to think? Powderhand had whispered of it as if he were glad. But she was not glad. She wished to be home, on the reserve in their cabin, away from all this madness and magic and fear.

She knew the spirits came to her husband. That much she believed, although her bitterness over their silence on her child's death was profound. But evil spirits could come too, and they may use a man if that man is not strong, not pure in his heart.

The wind swung her braids and she shivered. *Snowchild.* Dearest Snowchild. The trapper who had returned for his evil contraption that summer had been surprised to see their camp, and devastated to know the truth of what prey he had caught. A tall, white-haired man from the north lands across the sea with eyes as blue as ice. He had wept. She remembered that. But none could bear to look at him or speak with him and he had left, leaving behind the pelts of mink and otter and wolf as his offering. She had burned them. That her child's life could be bought for a few pelts sickened her.

They found his body half-eaten by animals in a small lonely camp that fall when they dismantled the tipis and headed back to their cabins. He had been drunk and taken his own life, had blown his head apart with his gun. An earthenware jug lay by his side, the evidence of some foul brew he had fermented himself and drunk in his loneliness and guilt.

The men wanted to take his gun and belongings, but Hunting Wolf would not allow it. He said the evil spirits had already visited this man, attracted by the act of his suicide and despair, and he was defiled now. He said he could smell them on his body, as though the dark ones had been examining, searching, studying.

She was glad. How could she have stood the pain, to have that man's things about her as a reminder of what his trapping had done? She often had nightmares about the man, and Hunting Wolf had too. He told her. It was as though he were setting his traps for them. Singing Tree was not afraid of this man's spirit. He was a sad man whom the wilderness had broken. She had seen many such white men. But she was sometimes afraid of what had been with him after he died, the things that had visited, that made Hunting Wolf shout those crisp, angry warnings not to touch him. She prayed often that they would never encounter such dark things when they were abroad on the night air, and that there would be no such despair for those fiends to feed upon in their simple lives.

And of course she prayed for her tiny girl of shining hair and sparkling eyes.

She sighed. *Oh Snowchild. Where are you now my love?* she thought.

Singing Tree put her head on her knees and wept.

*　　*　　*

'Mr Sitconski thinks we should act now.'

The tall man nodded sagely at Henderson, his blue eyes looking sincere and concerned. His voice was odd, strangely stilted, yet correct in its language. 'I was telling Mr Muir and the men that I have seen these savages turn this murderous way before. It must be stopped.'

James Henderson did not reply. He looked around to find one of the men who had taken care of McEwan's remains and saw George McKay sitting against the wall.

'George. We will make the grave by the other men. I will conduct the funeral tomorrow at noon. Perhaps you could ask some men to dig the hole in the morning.'

George nodded and bowed his head slightly.

'Did you not hear us Reverend? Mr Sitconski says . . .'

'I do not care to hear what Mr Sitconski thinks, Mr Muir. You may take it from me you are in no danger. The Kinchuinicks are as horrified as you that our engineer has met with such a disgusting and mysterious death.'

'Aye. Mysterious is the word, Reverend. If it was not the work of the heathens, then who?' Muir was adamant.

Henderson looked directly at the trapper who was watching the men with detached interest. The man's face was as odd as his speech, but Henderson could not find a reason for his discomfort. He tore his eyes away and looked back at Muir. 'We have been so befuddled by our own fevered imaginings, sickened by occult nonsense, perhaps we may never know. We are men of reason, Mr Muir, and yet we have been talking of animals who speak and demons that live in rock. Aye, and I have suffered perhaps the worst of you all. But I am cured of my brain fever now, and we must start to reason like the civilized beings we are. After all, it may even be someone unknown to us. Mr Sitconski has proved we are not alone out here as we thought. Perhaps a madman is loose in the wilderness, and the Indians are at as much risk as we.'

Muir was not convinced and Sitconski sat with what Henderson could swear was an amused twinkle in his peculiar blue eyes.

Henderson challenged the trapper. 'You disagree, I see.'

'I do, sir. I believe you should beat the truth out of the hound.'

'So you would have us go to their camp and torture their chief until he confesses? Speaking now as a member of the church, we stopped such practices many centuries ago. We no longer burn witches either, sir.'

'But you still hang murderers.'

'After it has been proved that they are guilty.'

Sitconski shrugged in his big coat. 'Do as you please. I would not sleep sound here.'

'Then you do not have to.' Henderson turned and left the long, dark cabin. He could hear the murmur begin even as he pushed open the door to leave. This strange man was playing to the gallery of frightened and confused men and for some reason Henderson could not bear to look at him further.

James Henderson had lied to them. He was not entirely cured of his brain fever. For a moment, just then, when he had been reprimanding the blond man, he had sworn that it was not a human face he was regarding, but some badly-made mask that concealed a hideous blackness, a swirling thing that he felt he had been touched by once before. But the illusion was gone as quickly as it came. It was the fever reclaiming him in his agitation, and it was why he had ended the discussion.

Now he strode away from the canteen to his own abode, where he would have to think carefully and decide how best to proceed. He glanced up to the low hill above the cabins and knew that Hunting Wolf would still be there, crouching, waiting for a glimpse of this uninvited trapper. Madness. It was all madness. He pulled his coat around him and headed into the wind, the cloth that was not clutched flapping around him like birds caught by their wings.

Hunting Wolf was nearer than Henderson thought. He lay only a few yards away from the door behind a great spruce. He was practically invisible, having dug himself into the snow, and staying so still that the birds hopped over him as they foraged in the undergrowth. This was not magic. It was a basic and mundane skill of any warrior, any hunter. He had thought briefly of using his magic to seek out and watch what he feared was here, but how could he shift into an animal after the display of yesterday? His nerve could not stand it. And it would take too long to find the right animal and ask its permission.

So he waited like a hunter for what may not be his prey, but his tormentor. He did not have to wait long. After Henderson had emerged from the long building a group of men had followed. Hunting

Wolf searched their faces, but they were merely the sad bitter faces of these northern men he had grown to know.

Then the man Muir had appeared, and with him, oh Great Spirit, was the nightmare. His heart beat like a caged animal in his breast as he saw that face and knew it. And it knew him.

The man, the thing that was not a man, that had inexpertly copied the form of one that would bedevil his Keeper, stopped and looked directly at him. It smiled and behind that row of white teeth Hunting Wolf could see the jaws. The black, icy, yawning jaws that were hungry and rabid and yearning for more flesh to destroy. Muir saw Mr Sitconski smile with a merry twinkle at something behind a great englemann spruce, but he could see no reason for mirth. He looked at him quizzically.

Sitconski turned to Muir with a pleasant smile. 'I'm sorry, Mr Muir. I have been so long trapping in this great wilderness I often smell a beast's scent on the air like an animal itself. I must be wary of it when I return to civilized company. Christian men would not have me lifting my nose at every musky whiff that comes my way.'

Duncan Muir looked into the woods where his tall companion had been looking and smiling. He saw nothing. All was still. The snow fell silently and sparingly between the trees and the trunks guarded the cathedral-like forest interior as if nothing alive had ever walked there before.

'And can you smell a beast now?'

The Scotsman was full of admiration for this man's senses. In fact he was impressed with him altogether and wished Henderson could see the sense in listening to his wisdom.

'Oh yes, Mr Muir. Something so stinking and foul it can only be a skunk.'

Muir laughed. 'Then I think we'll let it be.'

Sitconski returned his smile and walked on. 'For the time being, yes. I think we shall.'

43

'You can't ski, Del.'

'I ski better than you handle my fucking career.'

'Sure. Look around us. You're struggling.'

Del Parkinson ignored the command to examine his suite in the New York hotel that peeked over the trees of Central Park, and instead hit his forehead with a palm in mock exasperation at his squat balding agent, then turned his back on him.

Lester Golding responded in kind and slapped the arm of his robustly upholstered chair with a square hand, albeit more quietly and with less anger. He'd never liked Del. He liked him even less now that he was on the slide. Lester knew that CBS were going to pass on another season of *The Alley Cat* after they'd finished shooting this run, but if the fifty-something actor with the famously sad face knew it too, he wasn't letting on. Cop shows were ten-a-penny, and Lester wasn't complaining, since his latest client was Shardu Nant, the female lead in the show that looked like replacing it.

Fuck Del and his moods. The goose had stopped laying its golden eggs and Lester was tired of trying to help Del avoid making an ass of himself. This celebrity ski thing in Canada was so frigging typical. Hadn't even come through him. The girl organizer had met Del before at some other stupid skiing thing in Aspen a long time ago and contacted him direct, which was smart, since Lester wouldn't even have bothered showing him such a request. Who wanted to slide about on some Godforsaken hick slope with a bunch of drooling tourists who'd all want Del to say *Lighten up, Cundie* just like he did to his young side-kick every week in living rooms all over America? All that would have been gruesome enough, but now, with the idiotic little town being on every news show in the universe on account of its murders, the whole scheme was crazy.

Lester looked at Del's back as the actor stared out of the huge window over the New York skyline. Maybe Del was a sad old fuck who thought he really was Bernard Cat, law enforcer, instead of Del Parkinson, twice-divorced crap actor whose future in TV was looking rough. In fact maybe Del even thought he would be associated with the hunt for the murderer in the public's eye and it would make them think again. Make them tune in and boost those ratings for that tired old piece of trash that saw Del mooching about New York in a squad car looking sad and tough as he dealt with clichéd black pimps and Hispanic drug dealers.

The letter from the Canadian skirt was lying on the glass-top coffee table. It had a photo with it. Lester reached forward and picked it up. Del was in a chairlift with a young, pretty girl and they were waving to the camera. The girl was obviously the organizer and Lester realized he was wrong. Del just wanted to get laid for the weekend. He sighed and put the photo back down on the table with the letter and the six page fax that was folded beneath it.

'So go! Get murdered! Just tell me, who else is doing it?'

Del turned round again. 'That's just it. No one. I'll be the biggest star, and I'm going to bleat my heart out about how cowardly everyone else was to pull out. They had that old bitch from *Sally's Army* lined up, but she knocked them back when the news broke. Don't you see Lester? Every goddamn network news show is out there right now, and next to the fucking Rockies, I'll be the biggest thing there. When was the last time I was interviewed on network news?'

Lester shrugged.

'Exactly. Watch me this time. You may learn something about publicity.'

Lester doubted that. 'What about the piece of ass in the picture?'

Del smiled with his crowned teeth and flicked unpleasantly at his crotch with his thumb and forefinger. 'Charity, Lester. It's amazing how warm folks get in the aid of charity.'

'Sam?'

It was the second call, and there was still no reply. Katie dropped her car keys on the kitchen table and put Jess's writhing rigid body into her high chair. She noted with pain that Billy was already cowering, as if his father's absence was a trick, and she slipped an arm round his shoulder, pressing his nose with a finger as though it were a button on a machine.

'Want to get Bart organized?'

Billy's face lit up. He nodded his head, this stranger, this boy who was scared of things he used to love. She wanted to cry again but she checked the emotion, driving a spike of adult responsibility into her shifting sands of self-pity. Billy shrugged her off and ran to the big cupboard where Bart's disgusting dog food lived. Billy would be busy for an age now, as he tended his furry love. Katie hoped the vet was wrong. If Bart did anything to Billy . . .

She cancelled the thought. It wasn't going to happen. In the meantime, where was Sam? She turned on the portable TV in the kitchen for Jess, who spluttered appreciatively as it blinked into life beside the coffee machine, although the silent coffee machine, its glass jug stained with a brown tide-mark, had more to offer in the way of entertainment. A woman with a dark top lip was sitting in a chair on a talk show with a caption beneath her that read *Beth. Proud of her facial hair.*

Katie opened a packet of rusks, handed one to Jess and without taking her coat off went to see if there were any messages or notes from Sam.

The house was silent, some lights left on in places that suggested they'd been that way since she left this morning. She climbed the stairs quietly, aware suddenly that she was holding her breath. From the kitchen a shout from the TV as a man yelled, 'Lady! You look like a man!' followed by a roar of indignation from the audience. Jess joined in with a shriek of glee, and Katie let her breath go and almost smiled as she reached the landing. The bedroom door was open but the light wasn't on, and she walked up to it and stood in the doorway. The curtains were still closed and Katie clicked on the light.

There was a mussed-up bed, her side no longer neat where she'd smoothed the covers before leaving her husband with a stony frown this morning. Sam's side was thrashed and crumpled, like he'd been jumping around in there. But no Sam.

She walked to his bedside table, switched on the small lamp and sat down on the bed, her hand smoothing the chaos of creases on the sheet as she gazed vacantly at the light.

Hawk was dead. Killed on the night that Sam went for his walk around the block. Where was Sam now? Another walk?

Katie's body slumped a little at the corruption of her thoughts and she dragged the hand that was stroking the sheet towards her. It touched damp cloth and her hand recoiled. Katie pulled back the comforter and looked at what she had touched.

Urine. Her husband had wet the bed.

As she stared at the oval yellow stain on the white sheet she heard Bart bark cheerfully outside, and a gust of wind sent snowflakes to rap gently on the window behind the closed curtains. Her hand returned to the sheet and clenched the wet linen into a ball in her fist as she closed her eyes as tightly as her fingers.

Esme Fielding was getting worried. She knew that was Katie Hunt's husband out there, but she didn't know what to do about it. She'd waved at him with a cool expression when he first slumped against the window of the gallery about ten long minutes ago, and had been annoyed on two accounts at his lack of response. Firstly it made her look a fool in front of the two customers she was serving that he didn't acknowledge her wave, and secondly, he was smearing the plate-glass window with his big hands, and now his forehead.

The customers were American and unless she'd lost it, her sales sense told her they were going to buy the George Lanson brass buffalo sculpture for three thousand dollars. The American woman smelt sweetly expensive and had a face like a slapped ass, which looked like it only smiled at charity lunches. And her husband was the species Esme tried to lasso into the gallery every time she met one at a Silver summer cocktail party at the Chateau; trim, tanned, neat, and eager to give off the impression he knew about art. Easy meat. He'd already said the word *cubist* three times in connection with Lanson's angular brass, and she'd nodded with eyebrows high in phoney surprise as if discovering a kindred spirit, while secretly sneering at how completely stupid he was. Lanson was no more a cubist than she was a virgin, but if it made the tanned man in his cashmere coat buy it, then she would talk all day about how astute he was to notice the obvious nod to cubism in the great squared-off flanks of the buffalo.

But that Indian guy was going to ruin her sale. He was leaning his whole weight on her window now, pressing his head and open palms against it with his hands out and above his shoulders. He was just out there in the snow, staring in at a primitive native painting on hide that was stretched out for display on willow sticks with leather thongs like a trampoline. It wasn't a good painting, but Esme figured it would pull in the idle rich winter tourist who wanted to take home some native art. It looked good there in the window on its own, classy against the beech-wood panels, lit by concealed spots.

Esme had called it 'The hunt', not in the least shamed by her lack of imagination, and was pleased the way it looked. It was scraped onto the skin in red ochre dye, and showed three highly-patterned stick figures spearing some large animal. Typical stuff. Always sold well.

But she didn't need some big, mad-eyed Indian staring at it like she'd mugged him for it in the street. She couldn't call the police. It was Katie's husband, and he wasn't doing anything wrong except acting weird. Nor could she go outside and chase him. To leave these two for a second would mean losing the sale. She could feel it.

'I think we saw a Lanson exhibition in New York. Did we?'

The American was talking to his wife who was watching the big man slumped on the other side of the glass absently.

'Mmm. I guess.'

Esme was in there. 'Wow! No kidding! Well that's a coup. We thought we were keeping him to ourselves, but he has exhibited internationally so I guess we can't keep him secret from real art lovers forever.'

Lanson had, of course, never exhibited outside Canada, but so phooey. A sale was a sale.

Katie Hunt's husband had sunk to his knees in the snow now, his face still against the glass. This was getting embarrassing.

'Do you think that man needs help?'

The woman was fingering her gold charm bracelet, addressing the question casually to her husband rather than to Esme, but it was Esme who answered. 'I'll go check. Why don't you walk around the buffalo a few more times? Touch it and see what you get from that. I tell you it's almost spiritual, running your hands over it with your eyes closed.'

She turned and headed for the door down a corridor of white wood that blocked her view of the window, wondering what she was going to do. But by the time she'd opened the door and peered out into the darkening snowy street he was gone, leaving behind only an oily mess of smears on the glass to prove he had ever been there.

Esme sighed with irritation and turned to go back in, almost bumping into her two potential customers who were on their way out. The
man touched her arm.

'Thanks. We'll be back.'

Esme's heart sank. No they fucking wouldn't. She tried to look like
it didn't matter, wished them a nice evening and watched them retreat
up the main street. Esme looked in the window at the painting
that had lost her the big one of the week, and cursed the Indian
under her breath in language that would never appear in a fine art
catalogue.

Sam could hardly breathe. He leant back against the shallow alcove
of brick that separated the Japanese-owned Okay Gift Emporium
from the Silver Book Den, and let the skin of his sweating back grate
on the jagged mortar as he slumped to his heels.

Tricks. It was all tricks. He tried to focus his eyes through the
falling snow to the cars parked in the street. Normal cars. Normal
street. He had to keep remembering that none of this madness was
real. Those figures in the gallery window had not really been alive.
He'd seen them before they started to move and they were just ordinary stick figures, playing their sad part on a piece of shit, phoney
ethnic art. Loathsome junk for the tasteless wealthy but no different
really from the bead key-rings and trashy kids' embroidered mocca-
sins they sold in the gift shops as 'Kinchuinick crafts'. But as he
passed, he'd heard something call out to him through the window in
what sounded like a chorus of tiny piercing voices. He'd turned his
head slowly and gawked through the glass.

The ochre stick-figures had become expertly painted images of his
family. Blinking didn't help, didn't clear the picture, but then he
knew it wouldn't. So he'd looked. There was Katie, arms out trying
to protect her children behind her, and they were crying out to him
as they cowered from the great beast that towered above them, its
jaws widened in an outlandish gape, drooling with the anticipation
of its prey. They moved and squealed like tiny cartoons, but they
were calling to him nevertheless.

And he called back, put his hands on the window to show them
he was there, until the tiny, painted nightmare beast turned to look
at him and laughed a laugh like a death rattle.

Sam had fallen to his knees, saliva drooling slightly from his open bottom lip, until the picture faded back into the dumb hunting scene it had been. No not had been. Always was.

Tricks. Just a bunch of tricks.

He squatted against the rough wall now, fighting to compose himself. At the end of the street the barely visible Wolf Mountain stood like a portcullis. He narrowed his eyes at its grey, misty bulk, the top lost in the clouds of the snow storm and remembered a dream he'd had in which this mountain he loved became his captor. It was like he was in that dream now, but it couldn't be. He was not a prisoner. He was free. Free and completely barking crazy. Sam ground his back teeth together and concentrated on truth.

His heart was speaking to him now, and it was telling him that the thing in the bedroom was no trick. Yes, his Indian heart knew that much. He'd known long ago that the things he saw and touched and spoke to in Calvin's sweat lodges were no trick either. Sure he'd wanted to believe they were fake, particularly when they scared him, but his heart told him things back then too.

But his head told him like it had done for decades, that the Trickster was not real. Sam had battled his whole adult life to be more than a superstitious spirit-fearing Indian. More than his parents. More than the heritage of misery and deprivation that formed him. To believe in the Trickster would be to believe in Sam Hunting Wolf the Indian, and in some ways that would be the worst part. Look what happened to Indians who believed in themselves, believed in their proud past and their spirit world: the gaols were full of them and only liquor-store keepers rubbed their hands in glee when they saw them coming. He wasn't one of them. Not Sam.

He had a head that reasoned and saw the world the way it was, and it told him that things like that monster, that face in the crowd, couldn't and didn't exist.

And the tricks, all the tricks today, they were fake. It was a trick when he woke an hour after his faint, ran panting from the house and saw Moses peering out from Billy's bedroom window at him, waving at him with a leer when Sam turned his head to look up at the horror. It was a trick when the mouse-catching cat at number nine turned its head lazily to watch Sam stumble past, as it licked its new born kittens in the snug nest its owner had made from a wool blanket in a dry crevice in the log pile. He'd stopped in his tracks when he saw the dark thing swirling inside the cat, saw a glimpse of the real animal struggling to break free, then watched in horror as the cat slowly tore the heads off each of its helpless screaming litter as if for Sam's amusement. He'd stared at it, paralyzed, until the sight of the second last kitten twitching as thick black blood pumped from its severed neck was too much, and he broke free and ran again. Tricks perhaps, but he knew the mess of five tiny kitten bodies would still be there when the cat's owner came home from work tonight, and even Sam could not wish that one away.

And would these tricks pursue him to the grave? Right now it seemed likely. The thing whose existence he was trying and failing to deny was bent on his torment. He lowered his head and fought the urge to weep. He raised it again quickly when from the end of the street the howling of sirens rose and three police cars raced by, throwing snow up on the sidewalk as they passed. As the sirens died on the evening air, Sam could hear the blades of a chopper flying somewhere near the river and his heart that was already encased in lead, sank further.

That thing in Katie's chair.

We must do some more of what we do best together.

As he thought of its filthy attempt at a human mouth forming the words, he realized with a rising nausea that he knew only too well what that thing they did together was. There was no point pretending any more. A scan at Calgary's finest hospital wasn't going to show jack shit in his head. Sam Hunting Wolf knew now why he was blacking out and he knew what happened when he did. So had they done it again, this team of two, this partnership from Hell? The RCs didn't make that kind of show in this town for jaywalking, so it looked like the answer was yes. One hour. He'd been out this time for one hour. You could get a lot done in an hour Sam thought. Especially if you'd waited nearly ninety years to do it.

He looked into the street properly for the first time, with the keen eyes of a fugitive instead of a roaming madman. A glance up to the left rewarded him. Yes, it was there. It wasn't a brown car any more, it was a blue Ford. But the guys in it were the same two from yesterday. They were sitting on a double yellow in the tow away zone trying to look like they had business being the only car there. Not so smart these cops. Did they see what he saw? Of course not.

But their presence sobered him, and he stood up on shaky legs with new resolve. He would lose them. It hadn't occurred to him before, but it would be easy.

He straightened up, emerged from his shelter and walked a few steps into the street towards the bookshop. The window was good and reflective, and he positioned himself until he could see the Ford in the glass. The display was all tourist books: wildlife calendars with bears catching salmon, maps of the mountains, and books for fatties and morons on how to ski better. But the goods on offer were of little interest to Sam. He waited until he saw in the reflection the men start the car up and move forward, anticipating Sam's slow progress up the street. He waited until they were almost level with him, then turned and walked briskly back the way he'd come. They couldn't do a U-turn on that side, so he marched past the gallery and slipped into the alley that ran between it and the sports shop. He stopped and waited there watching his breath swirl around him like a spell. He knew they would drive to the top of Main Street, hang a left and speed round to where the alley emerged in Cedar Street. He counted to twenty and stepped back out onto Main Street. They were gone. Sam ran across the street and dived into the alley on the other side that came out by the bus station. Easy. He'd be behind the terminal building and on the rough ground by the railway lines where no car could go, long before they admitted to themselves their man had done a skunkeroo. As he went he cast one short guilty look over his shoulder into the street, and his heart started its pounding again.

Another trick.

Standing at the end of the alley was another inconceivable figure of his fevered fantasy. Sam held his breath and looked for the darkness swirling beneath its form, searching for its imperfection that would give it away as a mask. It stared back at him, solid and immobile, hands by its side letting the snow fall and rest on its preposterous impossible head.

Calvin Bitterhand. But of course it couldn't be Calvin Bitterhand. Sam stared at the apparition, desperate at this new skill of the Trickster, that it was able to conceal its true form from his shaman's eyes. The thing that could not be Calvin put his hand out to Sam and said his name in the croak of a tired old man. Sam hesitated for a beat, nearly fooled by those weary soft black eyes, full of what looked like relief and love, until he remembered how all the other tricks had resolved. He tore his gaze away from that face, turned and ran for his life down the alley, not stopping until he was past the bus station outbuildings, had broken free from the sight of roads and sidewalks into the birch-scrub by the railroad tracks and fell to his knees in the deep, drifted snow.

Far behind him, in Silver's Main Street, Calvin Bitterhand stood still like a cigar-store Indian, staring into the alley as though he had lost everything a second time.

A small gust of wind toyed with the edges of a black plastic trash bag leaning against the wall, and the rustling was like autumn leaves. He looked at the bag as though it had spoken, then turned and walked slowly away.

44

'One chopper buzzing the town doesn't mean it's another murder.' Pasqual was glaring at the Australian ski-shop assistant as she spat the words in his face, the face of someone who wished he'd never mentioned it. He shuffled his feet, not knowing what to do with his big body in his discomfort.

'Yeah well maybe not, but like I say, the news crews camping out here went apeshit. Talking into their portables and shouting at each other to get to town fast. That's all I know.'

She leaned heavily against the shop counter with her back to him, knocking a stand of Oakley shades to the floor but ignoring it. 'Fuck. Fuck fuck fuck FUCK!'

The boy was nervous now. Two customers who'd been browsing through the high price all-in-one suits for a long time looked across with obvious disapproval at the small, attractive woman spouting the obscenities. He was going to lose a lucrative end-of-day sale. Correction. She was going to lose it for them both. His boss was pretty pissed.

'Like I say. Maybe it's nothing.' She looked out of the glass door at the darkened lodge-side area where the lights had just come on, and clutched the edge of the counter behind her with hands like claws. 'If that murdering cunt fucks up my celebrity ski, I swear I'll find him before the pigs do and tear his balls off myself.'

The man and woman looking through the suits exchanged looks, stopped feeling the ski-suits and made to leave the shop. Pasqual watched them vacantly for a moment until she realized they were leaving without a purchase. As the door closed behind them, she turned slowly to the big square-built, tanned boy on the other side of the counter and compressed her already tight face.

'You know what would help me here, Donald?'

'What's that, Miss Weaver?'

'Stop gossiping and sell some stuff, you prick.'

He watched her go, expelled all the air from his lungs as she slammed the back office door, and thanked God that his fitness programme would never let him get that screwed up. He came out from behind his counter to pick up the spilled shades and in a few seconds was swinging his hips and humming a Red Hot Chili Peppers track, dreaming of the powder he would shred with his snowboard tomorrow if the weather let up. In the back office a small dark-haired woman was being sick into her wastepaper bin.

Becker looked defeated, and for the first time Craig felt something approaching sympathy as he watched the man replace the phone on its hook.

'They've taken off. It'll be less than an hour.'

Craig moved his eyebrows. 'Even in this weather?'

'Yeah. They'll be here.'

Craig balanced a hip on the edge of the desk that used to be Martin's and was now Becker's, swung a leg and crossed his arms. 'And what now? While we wait for the big boys?'

'We find the son of a bitch and bring him in.'

'On what charge?'

Becker looked up at Craig with eyes that said go to Hell, but his mouth was still driven by a policeman. The sympathy dropped from Craig like a silk scarf from marble as Becker answered him in a cool tone, 'He was out of sight of our men for the entire duration of the three murders. He could have been in his house, but he could just as easily have not. He was then tailed, staggering around like a madman, acting like a grade-one crazy until he deliberately and skilfully slipped that tail. That's enough for me, and more than enough to stall any fucking reserve-bought lawyer who tries to get him bail on grounds of being another untouchable target of white victimization.'

Craig thought of fighting, then thought again. 'The press. They'll burst vessels in their necks.'

'So let them. I want that bastard off the streets. In an hour it won't be our problem.'

Craig knew that if that was true for Becker it wasn't the case for him. He lived here. He liked it here. He'd lost two men. Two friends. The whole fucking thing was very much his personal problem. He looked at the older man for a moment as if waiting for more, and when nothing came but a gaze of indifferent resignation, he stood up and left the room without a word. He could get to Katie Hunt before they started the search for her husband, and right now that seemed important. Important enough not to tell Becker.

The journey from the spare office Becker was occupying to his own, was through a war-zone. The phones rang like alarms and the humans they alerted jumped and scurried from desk to desk as though the cheap teak tables were trenches affording cover.

In the shifting chaos, an Edmonton constable was sullenly clearing out Daniel Hawk's desk, putting the contents into marked plastic bags. Craig stopped and watched. The young policeman eyed his superior with caution as he scooped up a magazine and a packet of indigestion lozenges and bagged them with some papers.

'Sir?'

Craig was hardly aware he had been staring at the man performing his mundane task. 'Huh?'

'You need something?'

Craig looked at him, then down at the drawers and put his hands in his pockets. 'Yeah. Give me a minute with this stuff, will you? Go grab a coffee.'

The constable nodded, put his bag down on the desk, smoothed it like it was something precious and then left. The desk was an island in the babbling noise of the office and Craig sat down in Hawk's chair with his hands on the desk in front of him. Was this what a man's life amounted to? A few small things that could be put into bags and poked through by indifferent strangers?

He pulled open the second drawer, feeling like a spy. Files were stacked in neat rows, the odd yellow square of sticky notepad paper stuck to the spine, marking something for Daniel's attention. Notes to himself. Craig fingered them, his heart sore at the scribbled things that had meant something to the man who was never going to hug his son or wife again.

Chateau. Inc. Thefts, and another, *Int. Faccini bar fight. Bell's witness, comp. lit.*

Who knew what they meant? Who cared now? He flicked another file back, then stopped. A small yellow square was sticking up like all the others. Nothing unusual. Except Daniel's scribbled message to himself on this one, unlike all the others, was not in English. It was not abbreviated notation, but quite obviously a word written in Daniel's native tongue.

Craig looked around him like he was a robber about to take money from a till. No one was watching him. He put his hand into the slit between the files marked by the yellow paper and pulled out what was attached to it.

A photograph. A yellowing ten-by-eight black-and-white photograph of a corpse. Craig held it for a moment, looked across at Becker's closed door, then, leaving Hawk's drawer open, he stood up with the photo held down at his hip and walked swiftly to his own office.

He closed the door and sat down heavily at the desk.

How did Daniel get one of the photos from the Stoke file into his own possession? Did he surreptitiously ask for it when they'd been there, or did he perform the unpolicemanly act of swiping it when Cochrane had left the room for a moment? More importantly, why?

Craig pushed the photo of the Kinchuinick corpse under the angle-poise lamp and turned on the light. He'd looked at this already.

It was the mid-shot of the body, a grisly snapshot of a mummified head and shoulders down to the chest, the skull grinning up at the photographer with that paper-thin, obscene sliver of dried skin between its teeth. The shot just showed the beginnings of the burst chest.

Craig looked at it again. Carefully and slowly. He ran his eyes over every detail of the picture, looking for something he may have missed when he glanced at it in Cochrane's office in what seemed like a different lifetime, but was only days ago.

Then he saw it. Round the neck and on the collarbone. Craig opened his drawer and rummaged for his magnifier. He found it, slid it over what he'd seen and tilted the light.

It was faint, but distinct. There was a mark around the body's neck that looked like a macabre suntan line, as though the wearer sported a pendant around his neck that had left its mark on the skin. Except this wasn't a paler mark where the sun had been blocked from the skin by something solid. The opposite. It looked like whatever had been round the man's neck had singed the skin like a brand.

Craig could make out the line on one side of the neck that suggested a thin string or chain, and then just below the collarbone was the faint but distinct mark of an irregular circle. It was like a hoop. Something almost round with a strangely-shaped hole in the middle like a crude letter *O*.

He stared at it for a minute then sat back. Was that it? It was all Craig could see of interest that he'd missed first time, but it wasn't exactly earth-shattering. So the victim had been wearing some sort of jewellery when he died. Had it been robbed by whoever killed him? Probably. So what?

What about it, Daniel? he thought. *What was so fucking interesting to you?*

He looked again. The mark was quite distinct when you looked for it. He pulled at his mouth.

Why would it have left a mark like that? The pathologist hadn't even mentioned it in the report. No way now of knowing whether it was a burn or some skin pigmentation disorder caused by an irritant. And what was there about it that had made a RCMP constable steal the photo and write himself a note?

Craig sighed and touched the yellow note again. It was written hastily in scribbled letters. He could read it, but he was damned if he could pronounce what it said. It made him remember Katie Hunt, how important it was to get there soon.

Craig got up and put the photo in his drawer, but he pocketed the yellow paper. Maybe Mrs Hunt would not only know how to say it, but could tell him what the Hell Daniel Hawk meant by Isksaksin.

He was careful this time. They could be just sitting in their fat car on their fat asses in the street, or maybe they could be hiding from him somewhere smarter. That would be more likely, now that they knew he could shake them off. So Sam crouched under the car for what seemed like an age, until the kitchen light went off and gave him a dark cloak of blackness to move under and reach the back door. He hoped it would be open like it always was. Why would you lock your door in Silver? No reason at all. Well at least it used to be that way, although maybe folks would start to turn their keys, now that human guts were starting to outnumber dog turds as a sidewalk hazard.

It had wrecked him, the wait to get into his house. He'd watched Katie move around the kitchen like a delicate little animal in its den, and he longed to hold her and tell her he was here in the dark loving her. Once, she'd come to the window and gazed out into the snow as if looking for him, and he prayed she would feel his presence there in the yard, and willed her not to worry.

The bite in his shoulder throbbed as if to remind him that things were tougher than that. After last night, she might not be that glad to see him burst through the door, mad-eyed again, with tales of the dead living, demon paintings and animals that ate their young.

He hadn't thought about their last disastrous coupling for hours, but it haunted him again now, alone in the dark, lying beneath the family car like a bug. He'd felt her hate last night as he came in her, and was lost in it, confused by it, devastated by it. He knew nothing any more. Everything had changed and no one had told him the new rules.

Sam still wasn't sure why he didn't want the cops to know where he was. After all, they were just watching him. He hadn't been arrested. What could they arrest him for? But the nightmare events made him desperate to stay free and mobile. The thought of being in a confined space with nowhere to run from the dark thing that brought that madness was too much to bear. He wanted to move around silently for a while without the eyes of two men noting his apparent eccentricity. And he had to see Katie.

It was important to move now while it was dark, in case an upstairs light came on that would stream into the snowy yard like a follow spot, picking him out for any watchers like a frightened actor on an empty stage. He got up and, keeping low, reached the kitchen door, opened it and slipped inside. The warmth of the room pillowed against his freezing face and hands, and he stood with his back against the door for a moment savouring it. It was the second time that week he'd entered his house like a thief, and as he stood in the dark, feeling the heat and smelling the remains of a coffee brew, a huge and unexpected surge of anger rose in his throat.

Sam Hunt had not expected to feel hounded again as an adult. It seemed to him before he met Katie that he'd been running and hiding for most of his life, disappearing into the forest to sleep on mossy beds, lying in snow-holes with branches of evergreen to soften the icy floor, and returning to his home, as he was tonight, with a troubled, churning heart and a dread of being observed.

He turned around, pulled the blinds in the kitchen, flicked the light on and called out.

'Katie?'

He walked through to the lobby and heard the sounds of the TV from the sitting room. They were all in there, Katie on her feet by the time he pushed open the door, Billy in a curled ball on the sofa sucking his fingers, and Jess on the carpet with a mess of objects for her short-term amusement scattered around her in a semi-circle.

Sam locked eyes with his wife and gulped back a grief that was more profound than any he had known when he saw only two cold blue pools of mistrust watching him. She moved forward a couple of small steps, standing slightly in front of the children in an unconscious protective gesture.

'Where have you been Sam?'

He looked around the room at these three strange people. The days when he would have had to beat them off with a stick to get air from the smothering of their welcome, were gone forever. New rules.

'I'll be in the kitchen. Fix myself something to eat.'

He left the room. Katie watched him go, looked around at Billy whose eyes were wide and glazed, staring at the TV without seeing it, and made the decision to stay in the sitting room. Her numbness surprised her. Part of her had just become deeply tired of following her bruised and beaten husband around asking if he was all right, and she didn't care for his tone.

It said *follow me and I'll tell you where I've been.* For the first time, Katie was not keen to know, and more than that, she doubted if she could take another lie from him. He was in one piece. He could wait to speak to her. She stood for a moment looking at the closed door, then sat back down on the floor next to Jess, who was enjoying the victory of not yet being in bed, and busy deciding which object to put in her mouth next.

Sam was not hungry, but he hadn't eaten for nearly twenty-four hours and the weakness in his body demanded attention. He opened the ice-box.

Normally its white rubber coated racks were stacked with cold cuts and cling-wrapped goodies that could be microwaved and consumed by any bounty-hunter that came upon them. A big, white, happy confirmation that the Canadian way of life was a good way of life. Now, the lit interior displayed stained, empty shelves, a direct echo of the distress and unhappiness in the Hunt house. Sam's heart ached at the sight and he pulled out a carton of milk, shut the heavy door and drank with his back leaning against the humming appliance.

The door from the lobby pushed open and Sam stopped drinking, wiping his mouth with the back of his hand. The door swung shut again. Sam's eyes flicked from head-height at the door to dog-height. Bart's claws clicked across the kitchen floor towards his master. Sam smiled warily down at the fluffy grey and white head. 'Suckered them to let you in-doors again then, huh?'

The dog stopped in front of him, sat down on its haunches and looked up into his face. Its jaws were closed and the pale blue eyes looked up at him without blinking.

Sam Hunt's smile left his face like a footprint in wave-washed sand. The carton fell from his hand, exploding into a fountain of white on impact with the floor, but the passive husky neither flinched in fright nor bowed its head to lick at the milk swilling at its side. It remained perfectly still and watched the man who was forming words with a small tight mouth.

'No, you fucking monster. Not Bart.'

The swirling blackness inside the animal stirred in its dark pleasure, rippling under the dog's skin like an animated disease. When it spoke, Sam could hear in its voice the agony of the animal that was fighting to be let free.

'Bart's been a very bad dog, Sam.'

The foul rasping voice spoke in Siouan, and its timbre was deeper than those small lungs could afford. Cells were bursting in there, sinews snapping and twisting.

'He's been so bad he's going to punish himself.'

The dog looked up at Sam, and for one tiny second it was Bart looking out of the blue eyes in unimaginable pain and terror, before the black thing wrestled back its control. The dog's jaws opened and with a movement of almost balletic elegance, Bart rolled on his back and ripped at his belly with glistening teeth. His jaws were surprisingly wide and the wedge of flesh that he tore off with the first bite was thick and substantial, leaving a hole the size of saucer in which the grey-white of Bart's intestines could be glimpsed. The dog's blood spattered Sam's trousers and ran in thick rivulets from the dark hole onto the floor to mix with the milk like an obscene raspberry whippy. Sam could not move. His mouth worked like a penny-catching fairground clown, his hands clenching and unclenching, but the rest of his body was immobile. It wasn't until the third bite, when the dog's jaws got through to the serious stuff and buried its bloody snout deep in its own guts, that Sam broke free from his shock and jerked into action.

The wet tearing and growling noises from the abomination on the floor at his feet were threatening to make him vomit, but he whipped his eyes round the room, desperate to find something to end this torment. The snow-shovel for clearing the path glinted at him from its place beside the back door. In one bound Sam grabbed it and skidded back to the horror in the pink milk. He held the tool by its shaft like a two-handed sword and lifted it high above his chest. As he brought the shovel down on Bart's head, the animal was ripping its liver. The blade of the shovel came down harder than Sam could have hoped, slicing clean through Bart's skull between his ears. An eye burst from its socket and the brains that had told Bart when to bark, when there was a chance of leftover chicken, where the warm bit in the kennel was, and what his beloved Billy smelt like, spilled out into the soft grey fur like porridge. The body was still, and the air around it moved as the darkness leaked away like the steam off hot urine.

Sam stood with his legs wide apart, panting uncontrollably, hands gripping the shaft of the shovel like a spear. His tear-filled eyes spilled their load and the salty moisture joined the mucus from his nostrils running into his wet open mouth.

There was perhaps a gap of three or four seconds between Katie opening the kitchen door and the beginning of her scream. But when it started, it shook her body like electricity, her arms waving and flailing at her sides as her mouth made that black oval of noise. She jerked as if shaken from behind, and the piercing intensity of her shrieking deafened him as he stood dumbly over the bloody mess, gripping his weapon.

Had she not been screaming she would have grabbed Billy as he pushed past her and fell to his knees in the gore. But Katie did not have the power in her body to raise a protective blocking arm. Billy knelt in the remains of his dog, the blackened blood seeping up the knees of his pants, and with an unflinching face he looked up at his father. The boy opened his mouth and from the back of his throat a tiny thin wail started that seemed to be unconnected with the calm

428

expression in his eyes. It was the noise of a small creature being tortured. Hopeless, forlorn, unfathomable in its agony. Sam looked from face to face and the coil of rationality in him that was twisted seemingly beyond repair or recognition, snapped.

His big hands let the shovel fall as he turned slowly and walked towards the back door, opening it and feeling the cold air rush at him. Sam walked out into the night, and the kitchen door banged behind him like a pistol.

45

Calvin sat in the window of Rib Experience on Main Street, nursing his seventy-five cents coffee and watching the madness outside. The RCMP had blocked every road out of town, and the line of cars stranded in the snow poured out their exhaust into the freezing snow-filled air like angry animals bellowing to be freed.

The cops had been into the restaurant, asking everyone where they'd been and who they were. Of course they'd been real interested in Calvin, but the guy who interviewed him wouldn't even remember he'd seen the old Indian by now. He would look in his notebook later and find a page of scribbles that didn't remotely resemble the words he thought he'd been writing at the time.

But the workings of the RCMP were of little interest or worry to Calvin. He was waiting for something else. He knew it would come. He had felt it reaching out for him on his arrival, probing with a malicious finger at the new uncomfortable bump that had appeared under its dark, deepening skin. And he knew it would deal with that bump when it was done with its other duties. He might as well be warm and comfortable when it got round to him.

Under the tiny round table a ring of dried blackened herbs encircled Calvin's chair, big enough to contain him, but small enough to avoid being kicked by the waitress who came to fill his mug with fresh coffee from time to time. Anyway, her attentions had been wavering when she realized that Calvin was going to be a one-cup-lasts-all-afternoon wonder, and for the last fifteen minutes he'd been alone with his cooling mug. She'd have thrown him out earlier, but there had been all the excitement with the cops, and she kind of liked the smell round him. Weird, but there it was.

So Calvin waited. And when it came he was not surprised, and was prepared enough to hide his fear. The waitress noticed the old Indian guy in the window had a companion she hadn't seen come in, and was quietly pleased. She went to fill Calvin's mug and ask the tall, blond man if he wanted to see the menu. He turned his pale handsome face up to her and smiled, creasing his ice-blue eyes. 'Just coffee, thanks.'

'Sure. Regular, espresso, cappuccino?'

'Regular. Black.'

'Sure.'

She walked away with the plastic menu still under her arm, disappointed there would be no rib experience happening at table nine in the window.

Calvin looked at it with something like wonder. That the waitress hadn't seen what he was seeing now was the most astonishing thing. How had mankind become so blind, he wondered? What else stalked the earth in such naked form that went unseen by the modern car-driving, computer-punching, TV-watching populace? He shuddered with a weary sigh as he studied the crude approximation of a human form sitting in the chair opposite him. Dark clouds swirled and bubbled beneath the illusion of skin and behind the face there were yawning jaws, row upon row of filthy ragged teeth, hungry for something it could not have.

Yet.

Calvin detected an irritated stirring in its obscene, cloudy form. The old shaman's composure was clearly not what it had expected. He remembered Sam's face running down the alley, eyes rolling in his head like a startled horse, and thought how this creature must be getting a taste for the fear it could conjure. He let it speak first.

'Do you like what you see, Indian scum?'

Calvin turned away, looked casually out of the window and sipped from his hot refreshed coffee. When he spoke, it was in the ancient tongue, that long-forgotten form of Cree that only a very few elders and shamans can recognize, and fewer still can use. 'No more than I like what I see when I watch the dung that falls from my shit-hole.'

Although Calvin was not looking at the creature, he could feel the air moving with its ire. The waitress was back with its coffee, and he saw in the reflection of the glass that it smiled at her with that false face as she placed the mug in front of it. Great Spirit, if she could only see what she had served. Its blackness seemed infinite, porno-graphic in its lust for itself and everything it wished to consume. He turned to look at it again, knowing what would come next, and he prayed to the Thunder Spirit that he was right, that a Trickster could be tricked.

It gathered itself, and Calvin knew that somewhere Sam Hunting Wolf's body would be getting ready, against its owner's will, to lose consciousness. His heart had started to beat a little faster now at that prospect.

'Do you know my name?'

Calvin looked into its blackness. 'You have no name. You are nameless.'

He felt it falter. It swirled like mud stirred, and gathered again in a concentration of hatred.

'Do you know my name?'

Calvin laughed bitterly and with every nerve in his body telling him not to, turned and looked away again as though the question was of little consequence. 'You are nothing.'

Dark tendrils reached out for him in the moving air and stopped as he'd prayed they would at the invisible barrier that circled the shaman. There was a roar from the thing behind the mask that could, and should, have stopped Calvin's heart with its sudden volume and ferocity. But he had been prepared for its rage, and had focused his old eyes on a young couple enjoying ice-cream and each other's love at a table far down the restaurant. They heard nothing, for as Calvin was repeating over and over to himself in his terrified brain, it was nothing. The couple laughed at something the young man had said, and the girl put a dab of ice-cream on his nose playfully with her spoon. Calvin shut his eyes with that vision sewn onto his lids. The love of the young. The love of life. Life must be allowed to continue. He was surviving. That was what counted.

When he opened his eyes again, his wife was sitting opposite him.

She was weeping. 'Calvin? Will these never be full of milk?' She was holding her naked breasts out of the buckskin dress that she had always worn covered with a greasy woollen cardigan. Dead, he knew, but back now and imploring him.

'Look! Look at what I must suffer because you shoot no seed.' She squeezed both tits and oozing from them came clots of thick, sticky blood. It spurted onto the table, a great wet globule of it landing in his coffee mug with a slopping sound. Then she put her head back and laughed and her hands became like claws, ripping at her breasts until they burst with a thick tearing sound, splattering stinking black ooze over Calvin's face.

He swallowed hot bile back in his throat, wrenched his eyes away to the couple with the ice-cream and concentrated on their love. The girl was holding her lover's hand now, stroking the back of it with her delicate fingers. He focused on that act. What would it feel like for the boy? Her hands would be cold from holding the ice-cream dish and the boy would enjoy the coolness of it. Yes, he could feel that if he thought hard enough. Soft, cold fingers toying with the hand she loved. Small, well manicured nails, scratching lightly at the skin, fingertips massaging the knuckles.

'He won't listen to nothin' you be sayin', you old butt-fucker. He fuckin' hates you.'

Moses. Slumped over the table with half a face and a mutilated, decomposing body slick with slime, moving quietly with the work of worms.

Calvin faced it again, his eyes seeing the apparition but his heart concentrating on the pulse of life that meant people would always love other people. That girl's fingers, they would probably stroke the boy's face later, savouring every plane of his face, the feel of his rougher skin. Loving him. Longing to be with him, to share their lives and honour their own brief mortal spirits together.

The half-face leered up at Calvin, losing two green teeth to gravity as it did. They fell on the foul, stained formica table with a clatter before spinning off onto the floor. The thing cackled with a throat full of phlegm and pus, 'Want a heart to love Sam with? Here!'

He pulled at the ragged shirt and burst open the thin putrefying flesh beneath it. The bony hand tugged at the strands of cartilage and sinew still attached to the heart and ripped it free. It put the still beating, blackened organ triumphantly on the table where it moved on its own like a skinned animal.

'And how about a pecker to shove up his hole? You wanted to do that bad, huh?' It fumbled beneath the table. Calvin gathered his strength.

'We laugh at you. All through the centuries. Laughing loud at the thing with no name. No power of its own.'

It stopped its fumbling and fixed him with a searching black shaft of malice. The air was singing again, and once again Calvin felt fetid tendrils explore the circle around him.

Slowly, as the shaman watched, Moses gave way to the blond mask. The pale eyes with their whorls of blackness beneath the blue smiled at him. 'You should have stayed in the gutter to die on your own vomit. Your useless drunk's head can't even guess at how long and slow your death will be here. The agony will seem an age.'

'I will die with a name. I will have existed. Your death is eternal.'

Its fury made it careless. For a moment as it roared in Calvin's face, the diners in the restaurant looked up in alarm. Some of them thought they saw something and some of them didn't. But for a fraction of a second, the diners in Rib Experience, Main Street, Silver, found themselves like a herd of antelope smelling a lion, and their primeval senses twitched beneath their modern skins.

It was over before the message reached their conscious brains and the result was no more than a few butts shifting uneasily in seats, a few anxious glances at something they thought they saw at the table by the window. No riots, no peasants charging the beast with pitchforks. But Calvin cheered internally as his trickery worked. He had frightened it and it had retreated.

The blond pretender realized its error and composed its human form more carefully as it stared at Calvin for an age, then stood up and left the restaurant calmly, waving to him through the window as he disappeared from view. Its coffee, of course, lay untouched. Calvin felt in his pocket for the dollars he had left and put two down on the table. He had to move, but he could not. His legs felt as though they were filled with nothing more than liquid rubber. Maybe it was right, he should have stayed in the gutter. His head and his heart were bursting, and all Calvin Bitterhand wanted to do was lie down and give up. The ice-cream couple had paid their check and were leaving now, and they walked to the door, arms around each other's waists. Calvin watched them with dull, clouded eyes. Just before they reached the swing-doors, the boy broke away from his smiling girlfriend as though he realized he'd forgotten something, and approached Calvin's table with an energetic bound. The old Indian stared at him warily, unable to arm himself against any more trickery. The boy leant over Calvin's table and put a hand on his shoulder.

'Thank you. From everyone.'

Calvin gaped at the boy, unable to answer or comprehend, until the girl called her partner back with a coquettish wave and they left the diner as they had entered. Laughing and kissing.

The old shaman put his head into his hands and sobbed with self-pity and shame. He didn't ask the Eagle for help and guidance and he didn't want it now. He wanted out of the task. Why couldn't it let him be? Right now, in the face of a greater darkness than he had ever conceived could be abroad in the world, he couldn't find that pure place in his heart to accept without question the love of the Spirit. Yet that boy's hand on his shoulder had made his legs work again, had calmed his dangerously racing heart, and he knew that the boy and the girl would not be hugging on the sidewalk when he left the restaurant. He glanced across to their table and saw through his tears what he knew he would see. The tiny, soft eagle feather below the girl's chair moved in the draught from the closing door. He had not been alone in here. But he was very, very alone now.

Gerry opened the door and stared at Craig, then past him at the unmistakable police Crown Vic in the street as though he were seeing a ghost. 'But how . . . I didn't call you guys yet.'

Craig tried to piece it together. Why was Gerry Farrel, the head teacher from Silver Junior, answering Katie Hunt's door? And what the hell was he babbling about?

'Were you going to call us for something, Mr Farrel?'

Gerry was still staring.

'Well . . . yes.'

'Is Mrs Hunt home?'

Gerry clued in, and realized it was a coincidence. He ushered Craig inside, embarrassed and flustered. 'Sure. I'm sorry, Staff Sergeant. Come in. How are you?'

'Good. How's Silver's youth doing? My last visit turn them into decent citizens?'

'Nope.'

'Yeah? Guess it's up to you then, huh?'

Gerry laughed quickly and nervously, then let his smile evaporate. He put a hand out to Craig's chest as he moved forward in the hall.

'We got a big problem here. I know it's none of my business, but if you've come with bad news about Sam, she's in pretty bad shape. In fact I don't know if I should call the doc or not.'

Craig looked at the closed sitting-room door and could hear the noises of sobbing and comforting going on.

'Can I know what this is about?'

Gerry nodded and led Craig up the lobby to the kitchen. He looked over his shoulder at him then pushed the door open. Gerry stood to one side and let Craig enter the room, standing behind him as the policeman surveyed the carnage.

'Who did this?'

Gerry looked at his feet. 'Sam.'

'And he's where?' He asked this knowing the answer.

'Gone. He legged it when they caught him.'

Craig turned back to Gerry, his eyes steady and emotionless. 'Who's they?'

'Katie and Billy. He was standing over it with the shovel in his hand.'

Craig nodded as if that happened all the time. 'I really need to see Mrs Hunt now.'

'Like I said . . .'

'Mr Farrel.'

'I'll tell her you're here first.'

Gerry left to convey the news and Craig turned again to the remains of the dog. He walked forward to the edge of the gore and looked carefully at the mess. Looked like nobody had touched anything. The shovel was lying where it had been dropped beside the ice-box, and the carcass lay ripped open on its back, its head clearly split open by the blade of the shovel. But the belly was torn. Craig noted that. Torn away in huge ragged chunks, and what was left of the dog's jaws appeared to contain some of the guts. Did Sam manage to do that with a shovel?

There was a noise behind him, and Katie, held up by Gerry's wife, greeted him in the doorway with a shape made by her lips. She was rough all right. Her eyes were barely visible, lost in the puffy mess that crying had left, and her face had somehow grown older, grey in pallor, less full in the cheek. He could see why Farrel was talking about medical help. She looked like she was going to keel over.

Craig gestured to the hall behind them. 'Let's get out of here. Please.' He steered them back towards the sitting room and Katie sat down heavily on the sofa with Ann. Craig sat in the chair opposite. He looked up at Gerry. 'Can we be alone for a while?'

Ann looked at Katie. The wrecked woman nodded her consent. 'Yeah. Could you check Billy's still asleep? He might wake suddenly if that sleeping pill wears off. I don't want him alone.'

Ann squeezed Katie's hunched shoulder and got up. 'Sure. Call us when you're through.' She threw Gerry a look and he followed her lead. They left the room quietly, and Craig waited until he heard them climb the stairs and open a door.

Katie Hunt looked at Craig through her red-rimmed slits of eyes. The cop-hating ice-maiden had gone. She looked relieved he was here.

'He's good with a shovel don't you think?'

'Want to tell me what happened?'

'What you saw.'

'You burst in and found him doing that?'

'He'd already done it. Bart was dead.' She wrestled a sob back. Her shoulders shook.

'Why did he kill Bart?'

Katie crossed her arms, which had been limp by her sides, and hugged herself tight. She just shook her head, gulping, unable to speak. Craig leant forward and clasped his hands over both knees. 'Mrs Hunt . . .'

She looked up at him like a little girl.

'Katie.' He softened his voice. 'Katie. The officer from Edmonton in charge of this investigation has issued a warrant for your husband's arrest.'

'For this?' Katie was confused.

'For murder. Three more people died this afternoon. Staff Sergeant Becker believes your husband can help with enquiries.'

She stared at him with pleading eyes, begging him silently to say it was a mistake. He returned her gaze steadily.

Katie closed her eyes and let the tears seep from under the lids. She lay her head back on the sofa and bit her bottom lip. Craig waited. There was silence for a long time, broken only by her laboured breathing and the gasps she made when a sob racked her frame. Then she opened her eyes and looked at the ceiling. 'You know he wasn't home the night your man was killed? The man that was here.'

'Yes.'

She looked across at him, almost lazily. 'How did you know?'

'I saw you were lying when I asked you.'

She nodded as if that were fair and obvious, and looked back at

437

the ceiling again. Her tears were still falling, although she had wrestled control of her voice. 'And you all think it's him.'

'Mrs . . . Katie, I came here to warn you about Sam's arrest, but also to talk to you about some other stuff. Stuff that might seem a little crazy.'

'You don't think my husband being a killer is crazy enough for me?'

'For sure.' Craig gestured vaguely at the kitchen.

She sat forward and wiped her nose on her hand. Katie's eyes were growing fierce with something. 'Give me the crazy stuff, Staff Sergeant.'

He tried to smooth the frown off his brow. 'Craig.'

'Okay, Craig. I need to know what you're thinking. There's nothing you can throw at me that'll be wilder than real life right now.'

For a moment Craig McGee wondered what he was doing here. He struggled with what he was going to say next, and yet this woman's gaze was so earnest, so trusting, he felt that he could share this dark thing he'd been harbouring with her.

'That paper you gave me. Do you believe the stuff in it?'

She struggled to understand what he meant. This was not what she was expecting. He watched her think and then turn to him, thrown.

'Some of it. Sure. It was observed quite scientifically by a respected academic.' Her interest had halted her tears, and she sniffed as she wiped away mucus from a streaming nose.

'So you believe in shape-shifting and animal possession?'

'Why? What is this?'

He bent his head and looked at the carpet. 'They're going to try and pin these murders on Sam, Katie, and I'm sure they'll do a good job of making it stick. The strongest thing they have is that he has no alibi, for any of the killings. That's a lot of coincidences.'

She swallowed, realizing that hers was the last line to her drowning husband and she'd just pulled it from him. Then she thought of Bart, and damned Sam to Hell. 'The problem is, it would appear to be impossible for him to have done them. At least not in any sense we can understand.'

'I don't understand at all. What are you talking about?'

'There are elements to these killings that suggest . . . that would point to a belief in the supernatural.'

Katie watched his face for a second to see if there was a joke involved. Not that she imagined he would joke about this. His face was serious and drawn. Katie let out a breath like a diver surfacing. 'What do you want me to say here?'

'Whatever you think.'

'You've lost the place, Craig. Take a holiday.'

He shook his head. 'You're misunderstanding me, Katie. I'm feeling my way through stuff that may suggest the killer believes in it, not me. I'm forty-one years old. I still know the creak on the stairs is just the cat going to take a crap.'

Katie Hunt looked at him for a long time and didn't see a crazy person sitting in her room. She hugged herself again. 'Tell me about it.'

And so he did. He told her about the absence of footprints, and the dead animals. He told her about Wilber Stonerider and his tale of the talking bird and rat, and gently he told her the detailed nature of the Indian mutilations.

'Like the rhyme. Jesus.'

She was listening like a child, not upset, but flabbergasted. He told her everything he could and then he stopped.

Katie bit her lip again and studied his face. 'Why are you telling all this stuff to me? I'm his wife. Something in there might let me help him in court.'

'If he's the killer, Katie, you're not going to want to help him. You're going to want to see him locked away till he rots.'

The language was wrong, and he regretted it before he'd finished the sentence. The notion of someone she loved being a serial killer snaked a trail of confusion and pain all over her face. She hardened towards Craig McGee like drying clay.

'What's this about? What are you telling me? That he's a fucking wizard?'

The surreal nature of their conversation suddenly struck Craig like a slap and he blinked. He stood up. 'Men will be round real soon to take a statement. Don't touch the dog, please. If your husband contacts you at all you're obliged to pass that information on to us.'

Katie held him in her gaze. 'You do. Don't you? You think he's some sort of shaman?'

'I'm more interested in what *he* thinks he is.'

She shook her head and gave a dry hard laugh. Craig winced. 'How's your son?'

Katie sobered. 'Not good. I gave him half an adult dose of mogadon.'

She was aware that Craig McGee was looking at her questioningly. 'Yeah I know I shouldn't have. My mom kept the damn things here in the back of the kitchen cabinet to help her sleep. It was all I could think to do. He was hysterical.'

He nodded. 'You know where I am if you need me.'

She looked small again, and she made a tiny gesture with her hand as if to dismiss the whole visit. Craig made for the door and stopped. 'Can I just ask you one small favour?'

She looked dumbly at him, her eyes freshening with new tears.

He pulled the yellow paper square from his pocket. 'This word. I know it's Indian.' He held it out to her.

Katie Hunt looked at it then back up at the policeman who'd brought so much hurt into her house since his first visit. Her voice was hoarse and weak. 'You heard this from Sam?'

Craig still saw no reason to withhold anything from her. 'No. Constable Daniel Hawk wrote it. A note to himself.'

She looked at him like he was lying and held the paper back out to him like she wanted it out of her hand.

'It means line or boundary. The edge of something.'

'Uh-huh?' Craig was disappointed. What had he hoped for? A word that meant *Sam Hunt's your man?* He took the paper back and nodded his thanks. As he put his hand to the door she spoke again quietly.

'You're wrong, Craig.'

'What about?'

'You said I know where to get you. I don't. Leave me your number.'

46

Alberta 1907
Siding Twenty-three

'Where is he?'

Panting, wide-eyed, his nostrils flaring, Henderson had forgotten in his madness to speak Singing Tree's language. She looked at him with inscrutable black eyes and her only response was to pull her son closer to her, as though she imagined Henderson had come to take him.

The snow swirled around the tall man, sticking to one side of his body as it would cling to the rough trunk of a tree. He clenched his fists in frustration, standing impotently outside the entrance to the tipi he had just searched, watched by the silent woman and child.

Singing Tree might not have understood his words, but Henderson's actions were naked in their intention. She tightened her arms around Walks Alone, keeping her eyes fixed steadily on the hysterical Scot, and spoke to him quietly. 'He will not be back here. He is no longer chief. No longer fit as a husband.'

Walks Alone's huge round black eyes were full of tears at his mother's words but he made no move from the circle of her arms.

Henderson groaned. He did not have the vocabulary to enter into all this confusion and mayhem with the woman. Instead he slumped to his knees in the thick snow and berated himself in English. His temperature was high, and the flakes that flew in his face and landed on his bony forehead returned to water in an instant.

'Dear Jesus. This filthy thing is winning. Give me strength, my sweet, sweet Jesus.'

He wept, his teeth clenched and his arms buried to the elbows in the snow in front of him like a dog squatting on the ground. Singing Tree watched the ragged man's despair for a moment, then steered her son forward and disappeared back into their tipi.

It was not brain fever. He knew now that the men in the leather armchairs in his Edinburgh club were wrong. Men of reason be damned. There was no reason out here in this wilderness that God had abandoned. There was only the very devil and his legion here, as solid and visible as his own body, as cunning and wicked as the worst evil that lives in men.

But not a man. Oh no. The thing he had seen, that he kept seeing even with his face hidden in his hands, was the thing that had killed again and again, and it was not a man. It was here to destroy Hunting Wolf, their only hope.

He had to find the shaman before Muir and the men got to him with their pick-axes and hammers, and their lust for the Kinchuinick's blood. Five more dead since McEwan. That made six horrific, stomach-churning deaths that defied explanation or comprehension. Did they not stop and wonder, these men baying for Hunting Wolf's life, what madness would make a peace-loving chief kill two white men in a frenzy, then torture and mutilate four of his own kind? He stared into the grey spaces filled and vacated by the dancing snow-flakes in front of him and tried to smother the memory of those unspeakable deaths. It was useless. They were fresh in his mind, the recollection of their detail prodding him constantly with their gory thorn.

McEwan torn apart. Then Peter Lorn, a quiet, inoffensive man, his slashed and pulverized body separated from its head in the shadows of the deepening tunnel.

And the Kinchuinicks. Those deaths had been horrible beyond words. Killed in ways James Henderson could not think of without battling down bile. The ritualistic violation performed with the men's genitals and hearts had made the railroadmen who found the remains lying in patches of red snow beside the tunnel entrance almost swoon with the horror of it. Strong men who had seen hands and legs ripped off in working accidents and never flinched. Who had watched com-panions die and buried them in the hard ground, their faces as hoary as the solid soil, could barely stand upright at the sight of the carnage that had confronted them. For the first time in his life Henderson cursed his own God that He let such things stalk the earth. Especially now, as it seemed to be stalking him.

Henderson had seen Sitconski. Seen the real thing behind the skin. No, not brain fever at all. It was real enough.

When Henderson had told Hunting Wolf what he had seen, the dreams he had been having and the fear he could find no release from, the weary battered Kinchuinick had touched Henderson's chest above his heart and called him a white shaman. It was little comfort. James Henderson, Scottish minister who had hoped to live the rest of his small life in the glory of God and the comfort of his green homeland, was not cheered to think he was a magician. But what could he believe or deny any more? Reason had gone with the lives of those men. He could not deny that he saw what Hunting Wolf saw, what no others did, and knew that the filthy abomination that was amongst them recognized Henderson's sight.

It visited him now in so many foul guises, so many obscene tableaux, that he was nearly broken by it.

Only his time with Hunting Wolf, his confession and the voicing of his terror to the dark alien man who had become like a brother in this trouble, had kept him sane.

But that was days ago, a lifetime away, the last time he had seen the chief before he was forced to run from the ire of both the white men and his own people. Now Henderson was desperately searching for his companion in this lunacy to save him from what was real, not imagined. The weapons of frightened men, bent on his destruction.

His hands were numbing from their sheaths of snow and Henderson sniffed as he pulled himself up. He was seeking Hunting Wolf for another reason too. A more insane one. Henderson whirled around at the sound of snow falling from a laden branch behind the tipi, then with a lurch, stumbled off into the colourless afternoon.

His mother was too preoccupied with a combination of grief and mundane domestic duties to notice Walks Alone's eyes roll back in his head. The Eagle came to him in waking now as well as in sleep, and he had no control over its presence or the insistence of its messages. The small boy slumped in the gloom against the pile of skins at the edge of the tipi and gave himself up to it.

He was gliding above the edge of the mountain where the white men were making their great hole, and his father was lying far below in the snow.

Hunting Wolf was naked, except for the bone amulet around his neck, his long body lying like a fallen brown nut on the white pillow of a drift. Even from such a distance above, Walks Alone could not help but think how beautiful his father was, how strong and sound his body seemed, making its dark shape on the featureless ground.

The eagle that was Walks Alone dipped its wings and dropped down to land on a rock at the man's side. Hunting Wolf was conscious, his knife in both hands, the blade pointing at his belly. The great bird and its passenger of a human soul, ruffled its feathers and watched with unblinking amber eyes.

The naked man in the snow was in great pain, although it seemed not to be from his flesh wounds, which were superficial diagonal cuts caused unquestionably by his own hand. It was an internal agony, the cause or result of some fierce concentration. Walks Alone watched with an aching heart and knew exactly what his father was doing. He was cutting himself to prevent himself from becoming unconscious.

This was the black truth his mother did not see. If Walks Alone could speak he would have told her how wrong she was about her husband. How wrong about his beloved father. She feared the man she had loved, and Walks Alone's heart broke at the injustice of it. He feared that darkness which was in his father too, but he knew his father was apart from it, an enemy of it, an unwilling slave to it. Singing Tree's thoughts were a mystery to the boy, and he was tortured by the signs that she had pushed her husband away in her heart.

Walks Alone looked on the contorted face of his father and loved him, praying to the Great Spirit that his mother would know the truth and believe what her dreams must surely tell her, even though her head denied it come the thin dawn light.

Unaware of his spirit observer, Hunting Wolf was writhing in his bed of snow, biting the inside of his cheek until it bled again and rubbing his numb back against the wet ice beneath him. The black sleep was nearly upon him, and he knew who would be the recipient of the fury it would channel from him. His spirit had felt Henderson approaching and he knew that this time the Trickster's darkness was for the white shaman.

He could not let it happen again. He would rather die. Except that to die would be to release the evil on its chaotic tempest that would destroy as nothing had destroyed before, would liberate it from the prison that was also its succour, and let it draw that blackness at random from other unwitting sources. His leaden eyelids flickered shut and Hunting Wolf stabbed the knife at his belly once again, jerking awake with the pain as the blade punctured the skin.

A thin line of blood ran from his body into the snow and fanned out through the crystals in red, ragged fingers. The eagle shifted its weight from one taloned foot to another and inclined its head towards the trees below. The tall minister was struggling up through the pines towards the tunnel, muttering like a madman, his crucifix grasped in his hand like a witch-finder. Close behind him, unseen by the stumbling black-coated minister, a snowshoe hare scurried, keeping a watchful distance until such time as its shaman enemy gave way to darkness.

Walks Alone saw and understood all. Hunting Wolf would not sleep if the white man was at his side to keep him wakeful, but should he fall into sleep before Henderson arrived . . .

Walks Alone gathered his will. He had little control over the eagle other than as a passive, sometimes uncomprehending viewer, from its keen eyes. But he knew what he was seeing this time and hungered to act as his spirit guide's master.

It was in a deep, soft place that his dream-will rested, and he probed it and focused upon it until it ceased to be a soft thing and became a white-hot shard that pulsed in his mind and moved the air around the rock they were perched upon.

The eagle resisted the force of will to begin with, then twitched under Walks Alone's iron intent and spread its great wings like a protest. Hunting Wolf was fading into oblivion, but the eagle driven by his son was in the air and on the shaman's breast before his second torpor-induced breath was drawn. The phantom bird pecked and clawed at Hunting Wolf's face, forces at work that were greater than the mere touch of claw on flesh. He stirred like a baby dreaming and his eyes flickered. The bird put its head back and squawked, digging its claws deeper into the shaman's skin. Walks Alone was bursting with the effort of driving the creature that drove his spirit life, of reversing the natural pattern of existence to something near blasphemy.

But he continued. His father must wake.

Hunting Wolf's body began to twitch and jerk, and as suddenly as he had slipped into the darkness he was in the light again, blinking as snowflakes fell into his open eyes. For an instant he saw the huge wings beating above him, felt a sweeping velvet touch on his forehead, and then there was nothing but grey sky filled with the darker flakes that tumbled into his face.

On his bloodied breast a tiny soft brown feather moved in the wind, catching the breeze and blowing out of his reach before he could move his heavy arms to capture it.

Hunting Wolf suddenly felt warm, and when he narrowed his eyes to focus again, the man Henderson was standing over him panting like a thirsty hound. A dark coat was thrown over his naked body and he felt thin arms beneath him lifting him up out of the man-shaped pit he had made in the snow with the diminishing heat of his body.

It was safe. Henderson had not died. He had not killed again. Hunting Wolf closed his eyes with a sigh and gave way to sleep, knowing the difference between that sweet slumber and the black unconsciousness that brings the unthinkable.

Muir looked down at his own pale, hairy hands clutching the axe-handle and wondered for a moment what they might do. Would the hands that built and mended, pulled and pushed, hammered and dug, be capable of burying this tool in a man's skull? He closed his eyes and thought of Peter Lorn's body. That head that had looked at them from the edge of the tunnel wall, its mouth gaping in agony and its neck a tangle of ragged veins and sinews. There was no question of it. The murdering animal must be stopped. Johnston had seen the Reverend Henderson through the telescope and had reported him heading for the tunnel mouth. So that was where the insane savage would be, then. Henderson was drawn to him like a fly to dung, and they would follow, by God. They would follow.

Behind him, the men clattered and gabbled like farm labourers heading for the fields, but this was no happy gleaning. Their tools were on leave from digging rock and subduing steel, and there was a new ugly purpose to the way they handled these familiar implements.

Muir mused darkly on how they had arrived at such a brutal mission. But the rabble-rouser, the man who had told them to gather their wits and their picks, was forgotten. In fact, there would be none

446

amongst them who could even remember Snowchild Sitconski's face, let alone his sinister warnings of Kinchuinick treachery. Muir was firm that the decision had been his, and he stood by it as he cleared his throat to address the band of men who milled in the snow, a line of slow black cattle.

'We find the savage and we deal with him humanely. You understand? He is to be killed quickly. Remember in all this depravity, we are Christian men.'

There was no response. Muir looked away, above the tall pines to the rock where he hoped in his true heart they would not find the Indian, and an unaccountable fear rose in his gullet. The muffled sound of metal clanking against a buckle moved him to action, and he gestured weakly that they should move. The weak gesture was echoed in the passive tread of the frightened and lonely men who followed him. These were not murderers or even executioners. These were men who laid shining rails and blasted deep and complex tunnels. But then everything was different now. And the falling snow, unchanged and relentless for nearly two long months, reminded them that they were prisoners in that pandemonium, until it, or an early spring, decided otherwise.

47

He should have been frightened. The figures standing around him in a half-circle were the stuff of nightmares and yet he was calm and strangely comforted by their presence. Billy looked around him with his wolf eyes and tried to make sense of the place he was in. He was sitting on his haunches in large a glade of soft sweet lemongrass, a curtain of aspens blowing gently to his right, their shiny leaves flashing in the sunlight, and a green glacial river sparkling over smooth rocks to his left.

But in front of him, the sun behind their towering heads, stood the seven creatures who demanded his attention. The tallest figure was the most grotesque, and should have made any little boy cower or run for his life. It was at least fifteen feet high, with an eagle's head on the oversized body of a man, and when it spoke to him again its voice was kind but fierce.

'Why do you hesitate, Running Wolf? Do you not know us?'

The wolf that was Billy blinked up at the creature and it was Billy who answered, his voice having no sound, but coming directly from his deeply sleeping mind.

'My name is Billy Hunt. I don't know who you are.'

'No. You are Running Wolf, son of Hunting Wolf.'

Billy thought about that in a sleepy way and decided that the bird-man was right. He was Running Wolf. He had always been Running Wolf. He could still be Billy Hunt and yet be Running Wolf somewhere deep down inside where it mattered, and it seemed perfectly logical and natural. He nodded and looked again at the huge eagle head silhouetted against the sun, its feathers fanning over the collar of the scarlet robe that was pinned around its great shoulders with a blue quill hoop.

This sleep. It was so deep and velvety, the deepest he'd ever had, and yet not sleep at all. Running with the wolf was not real sleep. It was like being more real than real. That was the only way Billy could describe it to himself.

'Yes. I am Running Wolf. You are the Thunder Spirit.'

There was a sigh from the figures, although it might have been from the rustling aspens so soft was its touch on the fragrant air. The deep rumble of the Thunder Spirit's voice was addressing him again as he and the wolf stared up at its impossible form.

'Your elders are here, Running Wolf. They would speak with you.'

Running Wolf lay down with his paws in front of him, his jaws open slightly as he panted. The sweet scent of the grass was intoxicating and his head was almost as light as his heart to be in this wonderful place. He waited peacefully to hear whatever had to be said.

Running Wolf could not make out the other figures distinctly. The sun behind their massive heads was too intense, the brilliance of their robes too dazzling. It was as though he could only see the Thunder Spirit when it chose to speak to him, that the creation of a voice was a window to see through into the physical form from which it had chosen to address him. For now that it was no longer speaking, Running Wolf could not focus on the huge creature, he was merely aware that it was there, looming above him in an aura of awesome power.

A new voice spoke and he turned his long snout to the speaker. He could see a wolf's head this time on a man's body, smaller but no less terrifying. Except that Billy Hunt was not terrified at all. He felt a profound and sensational love, for although the voice was a deep growl it was full of compassion.

'You are the descendant of my loins, Running Wolf. Your father is the keeper of the key.'

Running Wolf said nothing.

Inside the wolf, Billy Hunt's heart became sore again at the mention of his father. He listened with sorrow as the growling voice continued.

'I feel your pain, child. But there is much you do not comprehend. You have the spore of white woman in your blood as your father has the spore of white man in his heart. We watch our people's spirit dying with this spore but we grieve not, for we can see far. We are brothers, white man and red man and one cannot be subdued by the other forever.

'A day will come soon when the white man is so rare on the earth as to be like the white moose. And although in his rarity he will still have the power of earthly things, of great wealth behind defended walls, he will run and hide like the moose and be treated with no kindness by the multitudes, the black and the yellow and red and brown hunters who will fill the earth.

'White man's day will be done then, and it will be our day once again. But when that time comes, the old ways, the ways of the spirits and the invisible world, must be the ways of man or we will all perish. There must be shamans who have the wisdom of their own souls, who were mocked before but will be honoured in the new world, as they bring the earth's people together with their spirits to heal the earth's wounds.'

Running Wolf heard the words and was mesmerized by the voice speaking them, but he did not understand. He said nothing. Above all, he wanted that voice to continue.

'The white man has laid our kind low, Running Wolf, but he cannot touch our spirit. Your father's spirit is strong and pure, but he weakens himself with a desire to be something he cannot be. You are confused by what you have seen in his soul are you not?'

The wolf nodded in its mind, and inside, the boy in the wolf felt a band of iron tighten around his heart. He was confused by everything, but with the warm sun on his fur, in this fragrant glade, a million miles away from the horror that was back at nine Oriole Drive, he could easily bear such confusion.

Another figure started to speak and he turned his head to focus on its form. This was just a man. A tall man, in chief's ceremonial attire and headdress who was holding his hand out to Running Wolf.

'Come, my son. I am Eagle Robe. We must walk together and talk of many things.'

Running Wolf looked at this man and he seemed familiar. He got up and trotted over to the outstretched hand. The man could read his heart and his thoughts.

'Yes, I have walked with you before. And your father and your father's father, and his before him.'

Billy Hunt struggled inside his wolf spirit to remember when that might have been, but could recall nothing.

'Your father turned his back on me and would not know me when I came to him often in his animal spirit guide in the night. And your grandfather tried to know me but was not pure enough to make the meeting of spirits. My heart is glad that his son's son knows me.'

Billy was speaking now. 'My father has an animal guide like mine?'

'He has the Eagle, the most sacred of all. Your father is a great and pure shaman, Running Wolf. He is the keeper.'

Billy Hunt's heart suddenly became lighter, and he opened his jaws to pant happily. Eagle Robe turned and walked from the semi-circle of tall figures towards the waving trees and the wolf trotted happily at his heel. In his human mind Billy knew that this sleep was too deep to be disturbed, and he smiled at the prospect of the journey with this man he knew and the things he would hear. The river gurgled in the distance behind them and the trees bowed their delicate limbs in the breeze as they walked slowly beneath their shade.

'People are amazing.'

Pasqual's stage-whisper was unsubtle, and because of the tone of her remark, which was not one of admiration, Eric Sindon looked around furtively to see if any of the 'amazing' people had heard. They hadn't. They were still milling around the Silver Ski Company Celebrity Ski Extravaganza registration desk by the big arched window like Angie was giving away dollars. In fact Angie was taking dollars. A lot of dollars.

These people, here in the deep carpeted arcade of the Rocky Mountain Chateau, woke up this morning in king-size beds to CNN telling them they were in the most famous ski resort in the western world. They pretended to be horrified by the murders but they knew that if they were part of the celebrity ski tomorrow there was more than a fair chance of the folks back home seeing them interviewed on national TV. And of course you got to ski beside Del Parkinson and someone called Brigitte Mackenzie from the Shopping Channel, and that guy who was in *The Love Boat* once.

All for charity of course, and for only five hundred and fifty dollars, with a welcome party tonight thrown here at the Chateau. Yes, people were amazing, and although Pasqual Weaver meant *amazingly dumb*, she was damned grateful they were. The enthusiasm of these rich bozos was keeping her resort reputation above water. Just. She watched as a woman in a mohair sweater with a kitten design picked out in sequins on the front saw the camera whirring at her side and acted out a nonchalant charade. The camera turned away. It belonged to a news channel. It wasn't looking for actors.

Pasqual turned on a huge smile for the line of rich customers and tilted her head to greet the Chateau's duty-manager who was gliding towards them with a similar smile.

'Hi. Doin' great business I see.'

Eric smiled weakly but Pasqual was effusive.

'You bet, Saul. This'll make Tamarack wince. They only got two people from *Thirtysomething* last season. We got Del Parkinson. Did you hear he confirmed?'

'Yeah. Good. *The Alley Cat*, right?'

'Right.'

'Yeah. *Lighten up, Cundie*. Ha Ha. Right.'

Pasqual laughed readily, thinking what an asshole he was.

Saul seemed to want to say something else, and Pasqual arched an eyebrow. He put a hand into an expensive suit pocket. 'I hear they're after your man then.'

'Excuse me?'

'The cops. They're on the trail of your Indian.'

Pasqual looked blank. 'My Indian?'

Saul smiled at a wrinkled old trout in a shiny ski-suit who was gazing at him from the line. She smiled back and adjusted her expensive and ugly shades.

'Yeah. That guy Hunt. Heard a rumour from the news guys that were gassing off in the piano bar upstairs last night until three in the morning. They're saying that he's on the run and the cops think he's the killer.'

Pasqual went cold. A flash of what she'd seen in the trees, the remains of that boy, came back to her so vividly that she felt a thin pipe of vomit trying to slide up her throat. Sam Hunt. She was working beside a guy all these years who at any time could have cut her up into fillets and . . .

'Sam Hunt?'

Saul grinned like she'd just made a booking for fifty doctors on conference.

'Yeah. That's it. Sam Hunt.'

'Saul. This is real important. Does anyone else, any of these hacks here, know that Hunt worked for the Ski Company?'

Saul looked pleased he'd affected her with such confidential and important news. 'No one knows anything. I told you. I get this stuff being on the spot where the news guys get loaded.'

'I'm begging you now, Saul. I tell you I'll work my butt off to fill this goddamn hotel with skiers for the next ten years if you just bear with me. Don't tell a soul. Please. Not a soul.'

Saul put on an expression of mock offence. 'Hey. Why would I?'

She nodded, knowing in her heart that if a nothing guy like Saul Jennings knew about it, the whole fucking world would too. She had to pick up Parkinson from the private airfield at half-past eleven. If they could just keep it quiet till then. Please God.

She turned to see how Eric had handled the news. He was over by the big arched window that looked out onto the Chateau's frozen lake, his portable phone to his ear and his free hand pressed palm up onto the glass.

Eric would sort it. Right now she had to check if the dinner preparations were going okay, and the welcome drinks party people had remembered to put up the Silver Ski Company banners for any cameras that might be there. And of course, make them put out the company napkins with the nibbles.

Yeah. Go count some napkins. That would take away the thought of that boy in the trees.

Maybe.

Katie had waited last night until four-thirty in the morning to phone Craig. She had nearly called him three times before that, but her mind was doing crazy things and it took a long lonely night to decide that maybe they should both be crazy together.

It was hard to make Gerry and Anne go, especially after the visit she'd had from those grim-faced cops that followed McGee's visit, asking questions that hurt, but mercifully cleaning up the remains of sweet Bart. But she'd convinced them she would be okay. Katie saw in one alarming moment on Gerry's face, that he wasn't worried about her spending the night alone, but more concerned that Sam might come back. It was no use any more asking herself how this had come about. It had. Everything had changed, and the only thing to do now was to find a way to deal with it.

She'd dialled Craig's home number first, the one he'd written on the back of his card, and there had been no reply. She wasn't thinking straight yet. A murder investigation didn't let its investigators go home to cocoa and bed. She called his detachment and the noisy babble in the background as the guy put her through confirmed that theory.

'Craig?'

'Yeah.'

'It's Katie Hunt.'

'You all right?'

'Yeah. Nothing's changed here. I just need . . . I just think it would be good to talk about some things.'

'Now?'

'Uh-huh.'

He was over in less than fifteen minutes, stopping briefly outside in the falling snow to talk to the guys who were watching the Hunt house. She let him in like they were both doing something wrong and they braved the kitchen almost as a dare. The floor was shiny where she'd knelt like a peasant and scrubbed the last of the blood off with a bristle brush until her arms ached. Craig said nothing, and sat at her table as though everything was normal.

The old coffee machine went through its noisy faltering cycle and Katie sat down with him while it got on with it.

'They took photos and then put him in a bag.'

'Yeah. I know it seems weird. They know what they're doing.'

She nodded, staring at the table top and playing with a strand of her streaky blonde hair. Then she looked up at him with red eyes.

'Why did your constable write the word *Isksaksin*?'

'I thought you might tell me. I don't know what it means. Well, at least I know you said it means boundary or something, but I don't know what it meant to Daniel.'

She looked away again, thinking. Then as if she'd made her mind up about something she turned back to him. 'It's also the name of a charm. A Kinchuinick charm.'

'What do you mean? Like a spell?'

'No. An amulet. A thing you wear.'

Craig sucked his top lip and bit at the skin. He remained silent, although part of him wanted to shout. Katie got up and went out, leaving him unsure what she was doing. Then she returned with a mess of fax paper and her spectacles and sat down at the table. He kept his eyes on her face. She was going to tell him something she was unsure about, and he wasn't going to roll any barrels in her way by talking like a cop.

He needn't have worried. Katie wanted to talk. Very badly.

She rustled the paper at him. 'It's a rare amulet. So rare I've only ever come across one in my whole career. This stuff is the only research material done on its origins. I had it faxed over from Vancouver yesterday.'

Craig looked down at the shiny roll of paper tumbling over itself, then back up at Katie Hunt. 'The one you've seen. It's round your husband's neck isn't it?'

She nodded dumbly and they looked at each other for a moment before the silence was broken by the final vulgar slurping of the coffee machine. Katie got up and poured two mugs of unpleasantly weak coffee, then rejoined him at the table. Craig fingered the fax paper.

'This tell you anything?'

'Plenty.'

'Keep it simple. It took me an hour and a half to get through the stuff you gave me yesterday. If it doesn't start with *The suspect stated* . . . I lose it after the second paragraph.'

She laughed, and Craig brightened involuntarily at the heat she made with that smile. Katie leaned back in her chair and sipped her foul coffee, and either the murky brew or what she was about to say wiped the sun from her face.

'How about I read you just a bit? I can't paraphrase. Not well enough.'

He shrugged, and she rustled the paper, searching for the desired passage.

'This is an interview recorded in 1959 with a woman elder from a Kinchuinick band in British Columbia. It's an English translation. She would have spoken in Siouan.'

'Right.' He tried to sound interested in the academic shit, but Craig McGee just wanted facts.

Katie opened her spectacles, propped them on her neat nose and started to read in a surprisingly monotone voice. It was unlike her normal sing-song tone and it gave what she was saying a gravitas that he hoped it would deserve.

'It is a bad thing and a good thing.' She looked up at him. 'This is the Isksaksin she's talking about.'

He nodded. She obviously thought he was a complete fool but so what?

Katie continued. 'But mostly it is a bad thing. Only the keeper wears the key and he prays his whole life he is not the one who must use it. I do not know anyone who has the key. This band has no shaman great enough to wear it, but there is one always on earth who does. My husband Turns Calf Around was a great medicine man, and he spoke of the evil spirit that the keeper saves us from, but I know nothing of it. They say it is the Trickster, and we make fun of him in stories to stop our fear of him.'

Craig was staring at her, a child looking at its teacher. 'The Trickster? Like a joker?'

Katie stopped and fumbled again with the paper that was joined in one long scroll. 'Right, this bit . . . listen.'

He was listening.

'The Trickster is bad and good too. He was good once, long long ago, in the days when animals spoke and the forests were alive, and he played with men like their brother. Then men tricked him and he became angry and bad, for he is the good and bad in men. He is only what they are and nothing more. Their evil and their good. A mirror that would kill its own reflection. When he is bad he can come only into low animals unless he can steal the power from a great shaman and become himself. Then he can kill as himself. The sight of his form is too terrible to bear. It is worse than the worst wittago.'

Craig interrupted. 'Sorry. Wittago?'

She looked at him impatiently. 'A fiend made from mud, ice or stones that ate human flesh. Bad medicine men are said to be able to make them.'

'Neat trick.'

Katie ignored him, returning to her monotone. 'When he comes now it is winter, for it is said he is of the rock and ice. The rock can hold him and the ice can make him.'

Craig watched her silently, and she looked up over the top of her spectacles at him, caught the look in his eyes and put the fax down.

'I know what you're thinking. You're right.'

Craig was glad she *didn't* know what he was thinking. It wasn't honourable, but it had been the way she pushed her specs up on her nose and tossed her blonde hair.

'What's that?'

456

'You think I'm hiding in this irrelevant, academic, mythology bull-shit as therapy. Escaping from the fact that my husband may be a psycho and you want to put him away.'

'Are you hiding in it?'

'Yes. Desperately.'

'It's not irrelevant bullshit, Katie. Daniel wrote that word for a reason. It was stuck on a photograph.'

'What photograph?'

'The photograph of a body. Someone who was murdered twenty years ago. The body had the mark of that thing that your husband wears round its neck. Like it had been burnt onto the skin.'

Katie's eyes widened. Craig sighed and gazed into the middle dis-tance at nothing in particular.

'So if you need therapy, you should have chosen something a bit lighter. How about the common grazing rights of the fifteenth century plains Indian?'

'Craig.'

'Uh-huh?'

'You're a policeman. Make sense of this.'

He shrugged, his hands out like a surrender. 'Your husband's a shaman with an iska . . . iksa . . . amulet round his neck that keeps away a bad thing called the Trickster. How'd I do?'

She took her spectacles off and held her forehead in her hand. Her face made him regret the frivolity of his tone. He cursed himself that he was forgetting the circumstances of their conversation. Katie Hunt was looking at him with an expression of utter and total defeat.

'He's not a shaman, Craig. He's a man who likes skiing and bowl-ing, eats celery with a cheese dip while he watches ice hockey on TV and dreams of having a big shiny pick-up with chrome roll bars. He gets on with his quiet simple life and he loves . . .' She started to cry, softly. '. . . he loves his family more than anything in the world.'

Craig put out a hand out and touched her arm. She snatched it away with a grunt. She sniffed back her tears. 'I'm falling for some cop shit here aren't I? You're making me believe that you genuinely want to know about this stuff and really you just want to know some-thing else.'

'Like what? They've asked you everything already.'

She was gulping and swallowing, trying to control herself. 'I don't know. I've watched *Columbo*. I know the nice cop is the one who gets the stuff he wants by pretending to be interested in pottery or architecture or shit.'

It was Craig McGee's turn to look defeated. His voice was small. 'No. I'm not pretending anything. I'm clutching at straws. You want some truth?'

Katie wiped her nose, scrutinized his face and made a tiny nod. 'The stuff there, that fax? If I make the connections that it automatically suggests to me, join up the myths with the facts, it changes everything.'

'Like what?'

'Everything. My whole life. Everything I believe in and everything I know to be true. Nothing will make sense any more, do you understand? '

'No.'

'This cup might not be a cup any more. That window might not look onto your yard any more. The sun might not necessarily rise in two hours.'

Katie was just watching him, her eyes full of tears and a thin line of fear. He leaned forward and looked at her with a steady gaze.

'I can't allow that to happen, Katie, so I can't make those connections. I believe this is a cup because I can see it.'

A tear rolled down her smooth cheek.

'So where does that leave us?'

'Back at square one.'

'But you said that even though you didn't believe in this you wanted to know about someone who did.'

'I've changed my mind tonight.'

'Why?'

'Because even a fanatical belief in all this shit can't make someone perform the miracle of murdering silently without trace or motive, or leave behind the kind of bizarre clues that we're dealing with.'

Katie looked crestfallen. 'You're telling me these murders are impossible.'

'Yes. These murders are impossible.'

'Not even an *if* or an *unless.*'

'Sure. Plenty of those.'

'Give me one.'

'Impossible unless your husband or someone else can turn into an animal, kill, turn back into a human and escape.'

He sat back and looked at her with a challenging glint.

Katie sighed and glanced towards the window. 'I guess the sun will come up okay.'

'I guess so. '

They sat miserably and quietly for a long time, and between them sat two cups that were always cups and would still be cups when that sun came up.

48

A night in a snow-hole so near to town he could sometimes smell the chlorine from the Welcome Inn's outdoor pool, and they hadn't found him. But then nothing the RCMPs had could match his skill. Sure, they would take dogs out and sniff around, maybe pull in some rangers from a nearby national park who thought they knew about tracking. But they would be useless. Though he had spent a lifetime trying to forget it, Sam Hunting Wolf was Kinchuinick, and there were thousands of acres of wild country that he could move through and live in without being found.

But Sam didn't want to go far. Katie and Jess and Billy were why his heart still beat, and he had to know he was near enough to get back. In case . . . in case of what? Why in God's name would they want to see him again?

He squinted up through the snow at the ice-crusted rock-face and put that thought away. Sam's body was tingling, his nerves coming back to life as the blood reached the frozen skin. He had stripped naked and waded through the half-frozen Wolf River for a quarter mile, his clothes in a bundle on his head, the floating wedges of ice banging against his torso, just in case the dogs managed to get this far into the forest. No dog would recover his scent now, nor any ranger pick up his footprints in the thick snow, even if they found the broken remains of his snow-hole. In fact, he was confident no man would find him. But then it was not men that he feared.

He could just make out the top of the tunnel arch from down here and knew that if he scaled this last piece of rock he would reach the dark safety of its black interior, a sheltered haven for another night. He had followed the tracks as far as he could, walking on the rails and leaving no prints, but when the tracks ran alongside the Trans-Canada highway for a time Sam was forced back into the forest. He took a tortuous route between the tall lodgepoles that kept him covered, stopping to listen occasionally as the chopper droned over-head or in the distance, presumably looking for him. It was hellish going and had taken him all day, picking his way through the dense snow-covered deadfall, but it brought him invisibly and safely out beneath a thirty foot slab of rock that led up to one of the higher tunnel entrances. An entrance far from the road. The cliff was icy and sheer, but for one who had spent a boyhood of climbing such rocks to hide in their deeper crevices, not impossible.

Sam sucked his fingers to warm them and scanned the rock for holds. There was a route between the huge aquamarine icicles that looked passable, if he could stretch over the last smooth section and grab some jagged rock at the top that might bear his weight. There was no choice. He took his fingers from his mouth and bent to remove his Sorrels. The cumbersome snow-boots served their purpose well, but not in climbing rock. That he would have to do barefoot, even though the day had produced nothing higher than minus fifteen.

He tied the boots' laces together, stuffed them with his socks and hung them round his neck. He flexed his toes to keep the circulation going, shook his arms, then stepped forward and up onto the first foothold. Cold flesh slipped into the slit of the rough rock, but his hands had already found the next hold and he pulled himself up to a ledge below the bulbous blue ice. Four or five more moves and he would be there on the track.

His feet were numbing now, but his strong toes retained their grip on the ledge and Sam pushed his fingers into a new crack and tight-ened his shoulder muscles for another pull.

He made it to a diagonal break across the slab, pushing his toes deep into the crack and crouching like a monkey on a palm trunk. The next hold would be on ice, and it would have to be no more than a fleeting lever to the six-inch overhang of rock he could see to the right, or he would fall.

For a moment he let himself think about falling, about how his messy death would bring a sweet release and an end to a life that was no more than a shallow lie. It was an ugly thought but he was weary of being strong, and he let it lap around the edge of his pained consciousness. Sam looked down at the jagged rocks at the base of the slab and knew what would happen to flesh and bone hitting them from this height. It wasn't high, but it was high enough. What was he running and hiding from? What good did his staying alive do his family?

If he went back they would lock him away. He knew that. Like father like son. The murdering son of a murdering father.

He gazed down at the sharp rocks beneath protruding from the snow as if in a trance, his eyes resting on his own footprints that the falling snow was already trying to fill. In half an hour, if the snow kept up, it would be as if he had never stood there. If his broken body were to lie down there on the rocks, the snow would cover it as quickly. Then the animals would get to him. They would gnaw at his frozen flesh, carry bits back to their lairs and feast on it as a fresh succulent delicacy. In spring, maybe a railroad worker would find the bones, but Sam doubted it. This was a place to disappear back into the earth. There was a purity to that thought, a delicious relief that his body was no more or less than the rock he clung to, no more than the trees and earth that were moulded and round beneath the snow.

Sam's spirit knew in a giddy moment of joy that he was one with everything he saw and touched and breathed and stood upon, and for the first time he longed to be part of it in death, to give up his brief and tumultuous hold on being a man.

Just the simple action of letting go. That's all it would take. He felt his arm ache, the weight of his body pulling at the muscles as he stared dumbly down the face of the rock. Beneath his fingers he felt a vibration. Slight, but definite, and its throbbing snapped his attention back to the rock that held him. It was starting to quiver, vibrating with a deep internal pulse that was increasing in waves.

Sam knew what that meant. He jammed his hand deeper into the crack and adjusted his weight, bracing himself for this piece of bad timing. If his mind had been contemplating the voluntary release of its life, his body had other plans. Its muscles and sinews tightened and adjusted, altering themselves subtly like a cat's to best hold onto the rock and life.

Sam looked up as the vibrating turned to thundering, and the train he had felt coming burst out of the tunnel entrance. From down here, the engine was massive, its yellow-and-black striped snout pushing through the curtain of falling snow, its thrumming contents filling the air in Sam's ears with a roar. He ground his teeth as his numb bloody toes were being shaken from their sliver of a hold and he wormed them back into the sharp rock with a grunt. The cars being pulled started to roll out of the tunnel, red and black, with their plain CP Rail insignia of a forward-pointing white chevron mocking Sam like salutes as they passed. How long would this take, for Christ's sake?

This train could be a mile in length. It would be an age. Billy would know how long it would take. He always knew. He could squint up at the tunnel entrance nearest Silver and tell his dad exactly how far away it was, and how long the train would take to reach them. But Billy wasn't here.

The thought of his son made Sam ache with longing. Before he could block it he saw that face again, the way he had last seen it, looking up at him from the gory mess of Bart's remains, and Sam wailed out loud with despair into the thunder of the train's bellow.

Then the thought again, cutting through his pain like light. Let go. Just let go of the rock. Your family will never love you again. Never. It's over. He closed his eyes and felt the stabbing of the cramp that was gnawing at his arms and legs and summoned his resolve.

Yes. To die. It was the right time. It was the right place. Fitting that he would make a meal for a wolverine. Was that what Eden had meant about being born an Indian and dying like an Indian? If he could no longer feed his own family, then at least he could feed a beast. They were attached by an invisible bond to the earth, the Kinchuinicks. Time perhaps, to make it more physical.

He opened his eyes and gave one last glance up at the rumbling cars that were squealing and creaking by, indifferent to his agony. Slowly Sam unclenched the fingers of his left hand, pulling them from their jagged crack, and placed his palm on the rock. Simple. Now the right hand, and it would be over. The snow was flying in his eyes, thrown up in a crazy whirling frenzy by the tons of passing steel.

Sam flexed the fingers of his right hand inside the crevice of rock that held them and looked up through the mini twisters of flying flakes. The train was slowing. The car that was emerging from the dark arch was taking its time, but something about its progress made Sam narrow his eyes and lift his head. The car already free of the tunnel was a standard red freight box, CP lettering, white chevron. But already he could see that the next car was different. It looked normal at first, its CP logo gliding out of the tunnel until its entirety emerged from the dark sheath of the arch. On the side of this otherwise ordinary box-car were a series of huge hieroglyphics, painted carefully, beautifully, delicately, in gold.

Sam was sweating on his agonizing perch, his mouth open, eyes narrow as slits. Of course he knew those marks. He had painted them on the canvas of Calvin's sweat-lodges many times. The arrow. The eagle. The buffalo skull. The symbol for a heart. So many more now before him, and all gleaming ridiculously on the side of a freight wagon snaking through the mountains, coupled between its mundane companions.

As the car rolled past they shone and sparkled, almost dazzling Sam with their brilliance despite the fading grey light. He read the marks as though they were on a page before him, watching breathlessly as the car rolled on and was followed by a normal red freight-box sporting only a number and its dirty white lettering.

Slowly Sam's free hand slipped back into its crevice and took his weight again. He panted and pressed his face against the rough freezing rock. Above him the noise of the train continued its clamour and he fought to find breath as it masked his grunts.

Yes, he had painted those marks in many different configurations. The pictorial language of the shaman. Sometimes they had meant war, the preparation for driving out evil and inviting the light of the spirits to battle with the dark. Sometimes they meant knowledge, and often they merely represented a season or a wind. But in this arrangement, the marks wrought in gold on the side of a box-car, they meant something different.

They had spelled the word *love*.

Sam's tears fell, and the hot line of saltwater that ran from his cheek onto the rock to which it was pressed, spread out like ink on blotting paper and joined the water that ran across the ice from the mountains.

What did he feel?

He had not even considered that on his journey. He watched the cars rumble by and knew that on the other side of this solid snake, Sam was walking along the track toward the tunnel entrance. He was safe. Alive. Calvin had stretched out his spirit and felt his pain and sorrow as he climbed that rock towards the track, and knew that Sam's heart was contemplating a dark and unthinkable deed. But his hurried prayer to the Thunder Spirit must have been answered, although he was not sure how, and Calvin had nearly wept when a small gap between the cars had briefly revealed Sam emerging over the top of the rock. He would wait now, until Sam settled in his purpose, choose his time, and then approach.

But what did he feel?

Calvin rubbed at his disfigured hand with his good fingers and bent his head. All his purification, his return to the way of the spirit, his sweat and terror, had left him no time to ask himself that simple question. Now, he had tracked his prize to this place, and the question was burning in his heart.

He stood in the great shadow of a tall pine, and with a mind that was clear allowed himself the luxury of honesty. He was still in love with Sam. His excitement that was almost swallowed by constant terror was the excitement of seeing a lost love.

And how would this object of adoration, this boy that had grown into such a man, react when he viewed this old and broken nightmare from his past? Once, that was, Sam believed it to be truly the man and not an apparition from his private Hell. Calvin could not say, but he braced himself for the rejection that was inevitable, the violence that might occur.

The tree above him rustled, dropping snow onto the drift in front of him with a dull thud. The shaman raised his head slowly and stared into the drooping snow-laden branches of the lodgepole pine, searching for the creature that had betrayed its presence. There was no time to dwell on the pain in his human heart. It was not only Calvin who watched Sam Hunting Wolf with hungry eyes.

He stepped back into the darkening shadow of the trees as the rumble from the tunnel indicated that the train was nearly through. It was just in time. The last car glided out of the dark arch and moved past with a diminishing screech, leaving the track in a sudden and unnerving silence.

Calvin was alarmed to see Sam so near. He was standing only yards away at the entrance to the tunnel, his back to Calvin, staring out over the top of the pines to the lower track, where already the front of the freight train had emerged from the second corkscrew inside the mountain. He stood barefoot in the snow, his boots still strung around his strong neck and Calvin's heart rolled in his breast at the sight of that thick, shining black hair and the set of those square

465

shoulders. The branches above Calvin rustled again. It was time. Because there was no time.

He stepped out slowly from the trees and stood on the edge of the rail that was dripping and snowless from the passage of the train. He could see the breath from Sam's mouth clouding around his head. It was as though he had seen this picture of him before, a picture that might have been painted on velvet and sold to tourists in lobby arcade shops: the figure of a tall man, looking out over the tops of pines to the towering mountains beyond, his breath freezing on the evening air as though he were some frosty prince wearily surveying his magnificent kingdom. Calvin clenched his fists, the good hand performing the act more neatly than the bad.

'Sam.'

He said it quietly, softly. And just as gently, as if Sam's body were responding to the tone of the tranquil voice, he turned around. The face was bloodied where it had grazed against the rock, but it was no less beautiful for its wounds. Calvin's heart lost its light anticipation to become an organ of lead, as those deep black eyes scanned his face with an expression of fear, hatred and suspicion. He spoke again, in Cree, with the same quiet tone.

'Look into my face, Sam. You will see no darkness. This is flesh. Old and tired flesh, but the real flesh of a man.'

Sam looked. He looked hard and long at the old man standing on the other side of the rail track. If this was another trick it was a horrible one. Calvin Bitterhand had been a handsome man. Tall, though not as tall as Sam, his long black hair braided and thick and his eyes always fiery with intelligence and purpose. This thing that stood before him now was nothing like Calvin. It was a wrinkled old bum, stooping and broken.

Sam looked with disgust as a hand that was mutilated and missing fingers clawed at old, papery skin on the good wrist, and watched as a face that spoke of abuse and waste looked back at him with sagging bloodshot eyes. Sam's lip curled involuntarily, but in his heart something was singing like a wire in wind. It was singing that this was no vision. No swirling black pilot drove its form. It was as the old man said, flesh. When Sam spoke, it was almost in the voice of a child.

'Calvin?'

The old man shut his eyes, his mouth moving slightly. Sam slumped to his knees, his legs no longer able to support his weight. He lifted an arm and pointed at the old figure, a painted saint naming the heretic. Sam's head was shaking, denying what his eyes told him. 'No. Not Calvin. You liar.'

Calvin's eyes opened and gazed at him with love. 'Why would I lie, Sam? Who would make the pretence of being Calvin Bitterhand. Only a fool would pretend to be that which no man would gladly be.'

Sam let his arm fall, and as the two men stared at each other for an age, the distant trumpeting horn of the freight train broke the silence, and the last light of the dark grey evening started to drain from the sky as if in response.

Tendrils of smoke swirled in the dark and were sucked into the deeper black of the tunnel, as the orange flames made the rough rock walls dance with life. Cracks and crevices waved crazily, making shadows against the untidy surface, the stone that hands had hewn, the living rock. Sam sat with his arms circling his knees, staring dumbly at the fire. Wasn't it round such a fire that he had last seen Calvin? But that had been twenty long years ago, in the sweet summer woods with the scent of sap and pollen on the air. This was ten feet into the mouth of the upper Corkscrew Tunnel, a miserable fire at the side of the track giving little heat to combat the ferocity of the cold. Both fires however, two decades apart, were hosts to misery.

Calvin poked at the embers with a wet branch and flicked his eyes up to Sam's iron face. He knew what the younger man was thinking. Knew what memories would be stirring in his heart, and he lowered his eyes to the flames again in his shame. Sam had said nothing. A silent figure allowing Calvin to build a fire and settle a camp in an unspoken agreement of co-operation, almost as if Sam had decided this were a dream in which action was useless.

So when Sam finally spoke, it startled Calvin. His voice echoed in the tunnel, joining the dripping rock in making the only sounds in this man-made cave lonely and empty things.

'Why have you come?'

Sam was speaking English, his way of denying Calvin, of forcing him to speak in a language that rendered him inarticulate and simple, and the shaman knew it. Calvin kept his eyes on the growing flame that his branch had stirred, grateful for any words, even ones that might wound. He answered in the tongue that Sam had chosen. An attempt at a bond.

'I be told to.'

He raised his eyes to Sam when there was no reply. It was an acid pause. Sam was staring at him with hate, then he too lowered his eyes as he replied, as though he could not bear to look for long into Calvin's face.

'By who? A lunatic? Why would I want to see you again?'

'You know by who.'

Sam said nothing, and Calvin gulped at the viciousness of his tone. He poked the fire again and tried to keep his voice steady.

'That's the reason. I be here, telling you things you already knows.'

Sam put his forehead on his knees and remained silent for a long time. When he spoke again it was in a voice muffled by the thick material of his sleeve.

'What do I know? I don't even know if you're real. I pray every day I'm making this up, that I've gone crazy.'

'But you know you ain't gone crazy. Don't you, Sam?'

There was a slight nod from the buried head and Calvin lowered his own head in sympathy for the resigned agony that Sam's tiny movement signified.

He looked into the fire and decided to revert to Cree. There was much talking to be done and Calvin needed to talk with authority in his own tongue. He could not be forgiven, he knew that now and cursed his foolish heart for even daring to hope it would happen. Calvin Bitterhand, the man, was beyond Sam's redemption. It was time merely to become the tool that the spirits had wrought.

'He has shown himself to you?'

Sam looked up, surprised by the sudden switch in language and the new authority in Calvin's tone. He blinked at the old shaman through the flames and surprised himself further by answering him softly in Cree.

'Yes.'

'Then there is so little time.'

Calvin crossed his legs, put down the branch and placed his hands on his bony knees. Sam watched like a mesmerized animal waiting for the snake to strike, and Calvin closed his eyes.

'The spirits sent me, Sam. You know that. You felt that. I know you did. But like everything else you can feel and see with your shaman's eyes, you have pushed it away and denied it.' He opened his eyes suddenly and looked straight into the black shiny ones that fixed him with their steady gaze. 'I blame my conduct for part of that denial. I know why you wish to forget who you are, Sam Hunting Wolf, but it is time now to remember. Remember only this of my error that night, that I love you dearly.'

The object of his love continued to stare. Sam's face was devoid of emotion, a silent oval of judgement. Calvin closed his eyes again. Sam's gaze was burning him like a coal.

'Even now he watches. He waits and watches for your weakness and then he will bring the blackness to you and do with your shaman's powers what he must to become potent. You cannot stop him and you must end this before he kills again.'

A branch cracked and spat in the fire and Calvin bowed his head, speaking more quietly now. 'I am here because there is a stone in your spirit that prevents you from being pure. I am here to remove that stone. Without purity you will never defeat the Trickster.'

The name. Sam took a sharp breath and flared his nostrils. The nightmare he had denied and would still be denying if this crazy old man had not returned to haunt him like a spectre. Sam snapped from the trance Calvin's soft words had induced. His eyes flashed and he clenched his fists, speaking in a tone that was more menacing than any shout.

'Love me dearly?' Sam snorted unpleasantly and lowered his voice to a pitch that was barely audible over the crackle of the fire. 'I'm giving you a minute to get out of here.'

Calvin looked back unmoved. So it was time. The tired old man who wanted to rekindle a love must give way to the shaman at last. Sam's dark, raging face stared at him over the flames, the heat of its hate upstaging that of the burning pine.

Calvin raised his arms and in a voice stronger than any young man's he shouted suddenly and alarmingly straight into Sam's face.

'NO! You are the impure one! You will listen! The spirits care little for your childish anger. They care only for your purpose. Be still.'

Sam jumped at the shout and now he sat breathing heavily, gawking at the man opposite him who was exuding a power he had long forgotten, a power he had felt from Calvin so many times and been both awestruck and frightened by it. Suddenly Sam was a teenager again. He could smell the grass and the blowing honeysuckle, and his heart was being released from its heaviness. He gazed more softly at Calvin, sensing the power that bathed him and he gave himself up to it as though he had waited to do so for two decades. Calvin stared at him for a time, then spoke in that new quiet strong voice. The voice of a restrained power.

'Your impurity. Name it.'

Sam blinked. Calvin waited for him to speak and when he did Sam heard his own voice far away as though someone else were talking. 'I am a murderer.'

'Who did you murder?'

'You know who.'

'Who?'

'My father.'

Calvin's face moved only slightly, as though his thoughts were wrestling behind his eyes. He set his lips tightly and then spoke calmly. 'Tell me.'

Sam Hunting Wolf closed his eyes. The honeysuckle smell was not imagination. No. It was in his nostrils now, pungent and real. As real as that morning when he had woken in the woods. He had run from Calvin so fast the night before, crying in horror and shame, weeping at his betrayal, at the loss of his only loved one, and had hidden beneath a juniper wrapped in the sweet tangle of yellow and white honeysuckle. The morning sun had touched the dew on its delicate blossoms and it was the scent more than the light that woke him. He was there. It was real. He spoke of it now as if in a dream.

'I hated you, Calvin. You know I loved you so much before you touched me. Better than any father. Better in every way. Kinder. Wiser. But it was over that night. You left me alone again.'

Calvin was listening as if he was merely a prompt, but his steady face and unwavering eyes did nothing to sway Sam from his dream-like recollection.

'So I went home. I remember looking down on the cabin from the edge of the aspen woods and there was smoke coming from the chimney. I knew Moses was home. Normally I would have run. But you'd left me alone, Calvin. There was no one to run to. Nowhere to go. I wanted to die, and the surest way to die was to walk back into that cabin when the smoke was coming out of the chimney. So I walked real slow down the hill to the paddock and waited outside to see if he would come out. He didn't. The sun was hot already and everything seemed more real than real.

'The grass was bending in the wind, showing its shiny side underneath, glinting in the light. And the pines. The pines were poking out of the mist by the river, sticking their heads up like they wanted to see the sun.

'It was so beautiful, and I felt it was being beautiful for me, kind of saying goodbye to me. 'Cause I didn't care what Moses did to me no more. I'd made my mind up I wasn't going to run. I pushed the door open and it was dark like it always was, but this time much darker. Took me an age to let my eyes see. But when I got used to it I saw that Moses was kneeling in the middle of the floor, and there were blankets nailed over the windows.

'He was butt-naked and he'd cleared all his stuff, all the bits of old table and chairs, the magazines and rugs, all pushed up to the walls. He was just kneeling there, staring up at me like he'd been expecting me, and I stared back at him like he was a mad animal but he didn't get up to run at me or anything, just knelt there like a crazy man. Then I saw he was in a ring. A ring like you used to make of blessed herbs.

'Except this was just grain or tea or cereal or something. Yeah. That's what it was. I can see it now. There was a carton of tea lying spilled in the doorway to the kitchen. The stupid old shit. I could see he was drunk. There was booze spilled all round the pile of his clothes and one of those stinking jars on its side. He made me sick, but I was confused. I never saw him doing anything crazy like this. Usually, like you know, he just got mean. He never got crazy. But here he was, kneeling in a ring of tea-leaves in the dark, the oil-drum stove going like it was February, even though the sun outside was already splitting rocks.

'All he had on was Eden's amulet round his scrawny neck. The Isksaksin. He was clutching it in both hands and he had an erection. He was like a totem of a dog spirit, an ugly shrivelled demon with its charm held in its claws for protection, and he was staring at me like we were both made of wood.

'I didn't know what to do. I wanted to run for a minute. Then I remembered why I'd come home and I did what seems crazy considering, it was Moses in that room. I just put my hands on my hips and I laughed. I laughed at him and pointed at his prick, tears running down my cheeks like I'd never laughed before, and even though I could see him getting ready to go nuclear I just kept on laughing.

'I said "Calling up the spirits, Pappy?" and I laughed so hard I could hardly say it, and slapped my leg.

'I don't remember much about how he moved across the floor, except next thing I was on my back and he was kneeling on me and smashing my face with that fist.'

Sam looked across the flames at the stony Calvin to see if he were still listening. He was.

'How'd he get that strong, Calvin? I always wondered that. He was so strong and fast for a drunk. I never could fight him. Anyway this time, I didn't bother.

'I couldn't move my arms, and I wasn't even trying. I just let him keep crunching that fist into my face, blinking through the blood and still coughing and laughing at his prick that was resting on my chest like a skinned skunk while he hit me. He was kind of gurgling his shouts at me, yelling, "You fuckin' cunt. I'll kill you, you cunt. I'll kill you," and he meant it too. And then suddenly he just stopped and stared at me from up there, panting like a horse, and looked at me real close with those scheming eyes. I could hardly see for the blood. All I could smell was the raw alcohol off his breath, and the blood from my cuts, and I just lay there quietly waiting to see what he was going to do next.

'He was breathing fast, looking at me like he was thinking just as quick, and then he lowered his fist and grabbed me by the hair still sitting on my chest. Then he said, real quietly,"You think you be so fuckin' smart. Don't ya? Huh? Well so fuck if I can't be makin' this fuckin' thing work none for me. You're goin' to make it work. You be making it work right now or I kill you." I looked at him like he was mad. He was meaning the Isksaksin of course, and when I realized suddenly what all that tea, and the stove and his being naked was all about, I couldn't stop myself. I just burst out laughing again, even though my face was so swollen I could hardly move my mouth.

'He went crazy then. He tore at my hair with one hand and then started hitting me again with his other hand. He was shouting at me, just guttural noises this time, like he was too angry to form words. And then . . .'

Sam stopped speaking suddenly as if a thin tape had broken. He focused eyes that had been glazed during these words, and looked back up at Calvin. The old man was still and quiet across the fire, a shaman listening rather than a man. Far down into the tunnel, a drip fell into some dark pool and gave birth to a forlorn echo. Calvin kept his eyes unflinchingly on Sam's until the younger man swallowed and spoke again.

'He stopped hitting me and touched his cock. He looked at me in a real crazy way, then he grabbed my face with one hand turned me over and put my arm up my back. Everything changed. All I could think of was you. Calvin. I knew what he was going to do and I just thought of how I loved you and trusted you, and as I felt him tearing at my pants this deep anger that was bigger than anything I ever had before in my life just welled up in my throat and exploded in my head.

'I moved so fast he didn't know what happened, but I roared like a bull and the anger in my head went into my body. And in a couple of seconds the roles were reversed and I was on top of Moses, my hand at his throat, my knees nearly bursting his chest. I just looked down at him then, spots of blood from my face dripping onto his, and I felt this thing happen in me as I looked into that face that was now frightened and weak instead of strong and cunning.

'It was evil I felt. That's the only way I can describe what it was. It was a warm dark thing that crept up my spine and touched a bit of me I didn't know was there. *What will I do with him*, it made me think. *I can do anything I like. I can torture him, kill him, make him suffer. Anything.* It was such a dark warm feeling, a feeling of power and I guessed that's how Moses must have felt all along with me, and it made the darkness worse. Made the hate worse. He just lay there whimpering, drooling from the corner of his mouth, and I was about to hit him real hard when I stopped. I looked at Eden's amulet round his neck and I just stopped.

'There was a voice in my head, like Eden's but not Eden at all. It was only like his voice the way a peach full of maggots is like a peach. Do you know what I mean? It seemed to come from a long way off, but it was near too, like the voice was using a lot of effort to speak though it was really close. Moses looked up at me like I was mad while I listened. I must have been straining my ears or screwing up my eyes, 'cause he thought I'd let up and forgotten about him, and he made a pretty good go at getting loose.

'So I hit him. The first time I ever hit my Pappy. It was like it happened real slow. I saw my fist swing down and the knuckles smashed into the side of his nose with a snapping wet noise. Soon as

473

I did it, it was like the voice got some new strength. I could hear the words this time, I didn't have to strain to listen. It was real simple. It just said, "Show him how to use it, Sam." Like I say, it was Eden, but I knew it wasn't. Worse thing was, I didn't care. I looked down at Moses's bloody face and I felt how sweet that dark feeling in my spine was again.

'"Pappy?" I said right into his face, my mouth inches from his broken nose, "Promise not to hit me no more?" He nodded at me, gurgling on his blood. Then I said, "Then I be showin' you how to use it. We goin' to use it together."

'Slowly I let my knees off his chest, watching him all the time and let him up. But he was a crazy mixture now, all scared and excited too, like being hit by his son wasn't so bad. He sat up and put his hand to his swelling face. "What we need first?" was all he said. That's all. Like what we'd done had never happened. It made me feel weird. Like he'd planned all this or something, but I knew that couldn't be.'

Calvin held a hand up suddenly, gesturing Sam into silence. There was a scuffling noise behind them in the tunnel. A tiny scratching of claws. Both men stiffened, listening with more than their ears. The silence was profound, broken only by another lonely drip, falling to its pool like a lost soul. Calvin let his hand fall to his knee once more, and looked back at Sam.

'No matter. We are both awake.'

Sam looked back at him with horror, but despite his instant instinct to deny the truth of what the shaman implied, he nodded. He took a breath of cold air and resumed his tale.

'I told him, Calvin. I told him everything and watched him prepare. He was like a kid and I still had this big dark thing sitting on my heart that was screaming I was doing wrong. But I hated him so much I just wanted to hurt and destroy. I didn't know what I was doing. Do you understand that? I didn't know.'

Calvin neither nodded or spoke. He watched Sam carefully, and when the scuffling started again behind them, nearer this time, he merely leaned forward and threw another branch on the fire, letting the hiss of the wet wood drown the sound of those tiny claws on rubble. He looked up from the fire at Sam's twisted face and made a small gesture with his hand that meant continue.

'You know how we prepared. You taught me well. It seemed like blasphemy though, letting Moses do it, and because he was doing it unpurified, making it for bad medicine, it stank of evil, of a badness I could barely comprehend. But I didn't care. I told myself I didn't believe in it, not really. I had decided the night before that this was all bullshit, tossed on the hard ground telling myself over and over again that my curse was not only to be born Indian but to be born at all. That this shit was all made up to keep us pegged down to our grubby beliefs, to keep us out of the white man's hair and away from his rockets and his computers and his money. And I hated the whole fucking thing. Hated every fucking Indian ever born and every bit of our stinking, stupid clay-footed religion.

'So I just watched him, telling him the next step each time he completed a prayer, believing nothing except that I had my Pappy in my power for the first time in my life. He was so hungry for whatever it was he thought the Isksaksin could do for him, he was like a child. Eager, wild-eyed, listening to me like I was special. I tell you, Calvin, I enjoyed it. And then we were ready. He put the Isksaksin between his teeth like I told him, and I waited for a moment before the last prayer. He looked so small and thin, Moses, standing there naked with that piece of bone gripped in his teeth. I thought about Marlene then. Wondered what she'd have been like if he hadn't turned her on his skewer. Would she have loved me and held me, stroked my face and sung to me on the porch like I saw other Kinchuinick mothers do to their children?

'And I looked at his filthy greedy face, and I believed for a second that she could have loved me. That I could at least have had a mother if he hadn't wrecked her and killed her like he killed Eden. Like he killed everything. And my hate was so intense I could feel it inside me like a hard nugget. I clenched my fists and said the words that completed the calling, watching him while he repeated them through his yellow teeth.'

Calvin nodded as though there had been a question. 'She did love you. She was weak.'

Sam's eyes were clouding. He stopped speaking, looking up at Calvin with a face that said there was no more to tell. Calvin prompted him. 'What then?'

Sam looked back at him with glistening eyes. 'You know what then, Calvin. You were there. I killed him.'

'How so? When did you kill him? What with?'

The scratching claws were very close now. Calvin figured the animal was only feet away in the blackness. A bold creature indeed, if creature it still was. But both men suspected different. Sam's tears fell, running over his bloodied cheeks in thin snaking rivulets, falling to rest in smudges on his filthy jacket.

'I don't know. I don't know. I only know I passed out and then he was there . . . like that . . . the way you saw him when I came round.' He buried his head in his knees again and gave voice to his tears, sobbing deeply. 'Dear God. That I could have done that to any human being.'

Calvin leaned forward and picked a smouldering twig from the fire and with an astonishingly nimble movement swung round and threw the burning wood at something behind him. Sam snapped his head up at the action, and as the twig spun into the dark its flames momentarily lit up the marten that was crouching against the rough wall of the tunnel, before striking it squarely on the back.

The animal growled with a noise too deep for its size and bared its teeth and both Sam and Calvin had time to see the dark whorls of the obscenity shine behind its eyes, before the flaming wood extinguished and plunged the tunnel into darkness again.

Calvin turned back to Sam who was looking into the blackness with horror. 'Did you think he would let us be?'

Sam sniffed and wiped his face with his sleeve. 'It let me be last night. I hoped it was over.'

Calvin gave a wry half-smile. 'It had other duties last night.'

The light dancing on the old man's deeply-lined face showed just how sick and broken he was. Sam felt cold fingers of horror on his spine at the thought of what those duties had been, and how Calvin might have dealt with them. He looked for the first time at this figure from the past with something approaching sympathy.

If Calvin caught the look he did not respond. His voice was still flat, emotionless. 'Now it has just one.'

The tunnel remained silent. No claws scuttled away in fear of another blow. No clattering gravel betrayed an animal retreating. The men looked at each other and both knew that when dawn pushed its thin light into the tunnel mouth it would describe the body of a dead marten. Used and now discarded, its heart or liver burst inside it, its veins opened or its spinal cord snapped. Something invisible and malevolent had stopped its small life in spite now that there was no more use for it. Calvin lifted another branch, stirred the fire and placed his hands back on his knees as if nothing had happened.

'Moses' death. You know more. Remember.'

Sam's reply was almost sulky. 'I've told you everything. I killed him. I just don't remember how.'

Calvin sighed, and after watching Sam's face for a few moments he put the branch down, shifted on his crossed legs and reached to his waist for his medicine bundle. With cold fingers he opened its neck and started to finger the contents. It seemed almost as though he had lost interest in Sam's confession, but then he raised his eyes to meet Sam's and answered the question in them. 'We will pray and eat herbs. The Eagle can make you see what you cannot speak. The foul one cannot hear our thoughts when we are joined.'

Sam swallowed, his mouth already dry at the thought. He knew what these herbs and that joining could do. Calvin had made him see many things in the past. The white man he had become told him it was no more than a drug trip, the mind-bending trick of a toxic plant. But the wire that had sung in the wind of his soul earlier was telling him different. The ancient voice buried deep in his soul, that was proud to be Indian, sure of its hold on the earth and its place in the spirit world, was saying yes, it's true: the Trickster could have no entry into their joined minds when Calvin and Sam dreamed together.

But Sam was afraid of what he would see. More afraid than he had ever been in a life that had held so much fear.

Calvin was laying the blackened pieces of foliage on a stone in front of him, carefully, meticulously, almost artistically. He glanced up at Sam as he arranged the leaves and stopped. 'You know the prayer. Begin.'

The man who only weeks ago had sat in his bath flicking through a truck magazine, dreaming of a holiday in Europe with his family, wondering if he should take a course in first aid to help him get on the Patrol; the man who had decided he was white though no one else noticed; this man dug around in his mind and found those ancient and sacred words that had stayed buried for so long under a stone he had constructed from hate. Hunting Wolf, son of Killing Wolf, father of Running Wolf, opened his mouth, closed his eyes and began to chant. 'Sikoch Pik-sik-see . . . Pachitia Inustanatkini . . . Natomachestai . . .'

477

Calvin was closing his eyes, swaying with the rhythmic chanting of his companion, holding his hands above his shoulders and joining in the prayer.

The words came softly from Sam's lips and between them the fire roared with new life as though sugar had been thrown in its midst.

The deer that watched them from outside the tunnel mouth saw two figures bending and swaying over roaring flames, stopping only to lift and eat the leaves that were laid out before them. It saw their massive shadows dance on the walls, and when the chanting stopped as suddenly as it had begun, and the two men snapped upright into rigid positions, the deer scampered off into the woods in alarm. It sensed danger greater than these chanting figures and it ran until it was many miles away, far from the scent of something it feared more than man.

49

Alberta 1907
Siding Twenty-three

He cradled the big man in his arms like a baby. Hunting Wolf lay quietly, his head resting in the thin crook of Henderson's elbow and looked up at the sky. The snowflakes were huge and flat, pirouetting in tight columns where the wind interfered with their descent. He wondered where they began, these flakes. What height were they falling from? He smiled weakly, remembering the stories his mother had told him about the Snow Spirit shaking its bundle and making the white pebbles in its pouch turn to crystal flakes flying down to cover the land. He knew different. He'd flown above the clouds in winter with his guide, seen the clouds below empty their heavy loads and knew there was no Snow Spirit, no pebbles.

But he could almost believe watching them now, that these were special flakes, falling from only a few feet above his aching head, created specially for this ragged white man, and for him, a ragged Kinchuinick. They fell on his brow and melted quickly as he turned his gaze from the sky to the tortured white face of Henderson.

'He was with you. All the way here. Did you feel him?'

Henderson shook his head, and Hunting Wolf lifted a weary arm, pointing into the tunnel. The men lay only feet from its yawning mouth and Henderson did not need to turn to see what his exhausted companion was pointing at.

'He is back in the mountain now. Waiting.'

479

The Scot made a down-turned arc with his thin lips, the action of a man trying not to cry. Hunting Wolf felt the thin body that held him heave and shake as Henderson controlled himself enough to speak.

'They come Hunting Wolf. The men.'

The Indian nodded. 'No matter. It will be done soon.'

Henderson looked down on this handsome brown man, wrapped in the black coat he remembered so vividly buying from Laurie's the Tailor on Edinburgh's Hanover Street. Somehow, it was not ridiculous. Hunting Wolf was the reality. The grey-faced Aberdonian with whiskers, who had made and sold the coat with a tape measure around his neck and a superior glint in his eye, seemed like the dream now. Scotland was the dream. Henderson summoned his resolve and controlled the contortions that betrayed his fear.

'I go in. Stop this.'

Hunting Wolf looked at him as he would at a slow child. A faint, but not unkind smile moved on his lips. 'How, Henderson? How will you stop it?'

The curse of language. That disease from the tower of Babel that so cruelly separated these men was often unbearable to the Scot. How he longed to unburden his terrors, his anxieties, his plans and lunatic schemes to this man. But his grasp of Hunting Wolf's tongue was so meagre that he knew he would sound only like a simple fool. How to tell him what had occupied his every waking thought since yesterday? The Catholics believed in it. He had seen them do it once. Of course he scorned their idolatry and detested the sumptuous and excessive theatre they called worship.

But the part of that theatre they called exorcism, that had started to occupy his thoughts ever since he had crafted the crucifix for Hunting Wolf's son. He had held the wooden cross in his hands and felt something like power from it. The power perhaps, only of his own faith, briefly revisiting him after its desertion that always came with that thing that stalked him. But was it not simply the power of faith that Jesus used to drive out demons?

And this demon, this cunning, spiteful abomination, surely it could be driven before the same power that had cast out its brother imps.

Hunting Wolf had called him a white shaman. If it were true, then his medicine was the cross of Jesus Christ. The minister who had left Edinburgh would have blushed at the thought of descending to this peasant-like belief. Exorcism was, he had always believed, another tool of the misguided Church of Rome to subdue its ignorant followers and keep power by encouraging superstition.

But that was then. A time when he believed the painted demons in the stained-glass windows of his church, writhing and screaming in hell, were only figments of man's fevered and guilty imagination. But now?

Now he would believe anything.

Henderson gently let Hunting Wolf's head down onto the snow and wrapped the coat tighter round his shoulders. The chief looked up at him with heavy eyes, pupils dilated. Henderson picked up the mahogany and ivory crucifix that lay beside him in the snow, and held it up for Hunting Wolf to see.

'This stop him.'

The chief made no movement, merely looked at the cross then back up at the minister with those drowsy black eyes. Then as Henderson started to get up, Hunting Wolf put out a hand and held the thin man's wrist with a surprisingly rough grip.

'He is older than that. Much older.'

James Henderson tried unsuccessfully to make sense of the Indian's words for a moment, then unwrapped the strong, freezing fingers from his wrist and stood up. He looked down at the shaman and Hunting Wolf read the love in the white man's eyes. He stretched out a hand and pointed at Henderson's cross, speaking with more tenderness this time.

'Does it answer your prayers, this charm?'

Henderson bowed his head slightly. No was the answer. The cross never answered your prayers. The western Christian man floundered in the love of a God that seemed never to hear, and certainly never acted upon man's wishes. Indeed to ask for anything material, anything at all in fact, other than forgiveness from the God of the white man was considered impious.

What Indian would continue to love or serve a God that was deaf to their pleas? If a Kinchuinick asked for rain he received it. If he asked for fertility it was granted. How did Henderson's God become so impotent? And more, how did theologians use that very impotence, that silence, to prove that God was still there? Tears began to form in James Henderson's eyes. He clutched the cross as though it were the last piece of his faith and raised his head to the questioner.

'It will answer mine today.'

He turned and waded through the snow towards the tunnel mouth, leaving his only companion in this madness lying in the snow watching him with eyes that were aching to close.

50

When Craig left at dawn, Katie stood by the front window
and watched the news crews gather. A man in a parka was first.
He took up position across the street by the Ritchie's front gate
at around seven-thirty and unfolded a little seat. By eight he had
been joined by at least eleven others, some with video cameras,
some with stills cameras. They milled around on the snowy sidewalk. Katie figured the ones stamping their feet and acting cranky
were the American and European journalists. The guys who just
stood there were Canadians. Canadian journalists stood in the snow
a lot.

They'd already tried ringing the bell but she'd ignored it, and if
they had her number it was a waste of time. Some of them had mobiles
and she'd watched them punching in numbers, wondering if they
were calling her. Who cared? The phone was off the cradle.

She watched them passively from behind the safety of the net curtain with the lights off and decided she couldn't even find a space in
her bursting heart to hate them. In a while she would phone her
parents and warn them about what was going to go down here. June
Crosby had been on the phone constantly since the first murders hit
their TV screen in Vancouver, but Katie had laughed off her mother's
concerns. Time though, to tell the truth. She thought of what she
might say on that call and her heart piled on a few extra weights. But
right now, she just watched the vultures gather outside the window. A
mother wolf guarding the lair.

'They looking for Dad?'

The voice made Katie jump, and she whirled round with her hands
over her breast. Billy was standing in the door to the lounge, his eyes

483

tiny with the remains of his drugged sleep, the Flames T-shirt he'd slept in as crumpled as his face. She studied that tiny oval face, weighing up his condition, wondering if he was able to handle what new horror waited on his own doorstep.

And as she looked, Katie saw in her son's eyes something that had never been there before. He was looking at her with the eyes of an adult. Calm, introspective, mature. It was unnerving her.

'You okay sweetheart?'

He nodded once.

'Come here.' She held out her arms to him and he walked slowly forward, docking in the bay that was his mother's embrace. Katie stroked his head, held his face to her stomach and swallowed. 'Things are going to get a bit tough, Billy Boy. You're going to have to be real strong.'

'Why?'

'Well . . . your Dad's done some bad things.' She hesitated. 'We think. Those men out there think so, anyhow. Things he might not be that proud of.'

Billy's head snapped out of her grasp and he stood back from her, his eyes ablaze. 'He hasn't done nothing bad! Nothing!'

Katie stared at him in amazement. The boy that had seen his father standing over the mangled body of the dog he loved, a bloody shovel in his hand, was now staring at her with accusing eyes. How had she suddenly become the traitor? It was maybe time to serve her mixed-up son some harsh realtiy.

There was plenty of it outside. She spoke as softly as she could. A useless attempt to smooth the edges of the hideous words she formed. 'Billy. He killed Bart.'

Billy opened his mouth and wailed. He staggered back from her and stood against the wall.

'Billy!'

He stared at her for an age, his mouth a tiny *O*, then suddenly, like a grown man controlling grief at a funeral, composed himself again. He spoke as gently as she had. 'He didn't kill Bart, Mom. He was helping him.' Billy turned and walked from the room, and from upstairs a cry announced that Jess was awake.

Katie stood silently in the room for a moment, contemplating the madness and confusion that was her life. Craig was right. She knew nothing any more. Nothing. The doorbell rang and Katie walked out of the room past the front door, and climbed the stairs to fetch her daughter.

The darkness in his house had been profound when Craig opened the front door and stepped into the lobby. Dawn's light was thin and grey through the falling snow, nowhere near strong enough to pierce the black that the drawn curtains in the lobby created, curtains he had drawn nights ago and forgotten about. But that was his life now. A neglected shelter, not a home.

He flicked on the small lamp by the door and dropped his keys on the table. Just a shower and then he'd get back to the detachment. He felt empty and sore, as though something sharp had been scooping out the inside of his head. No sleep, that's what it was. But he'd worked plenty with no sleep. This was different. He moved through to the kitchen and opened the ice-box in the dark. The door opened and lit up his face. A mouldy slice of pie glared out at him. Craig sighed and reached for the freezer compartment. It was solid.

When he comes it is winter, for he is of rock and ice.

The words Katie had read out in that serious monotone were still clinging to the hollow thing that used to be his brain. He stared at the frosty white skin clinging to the freezer box, clustering in defiant pillows round the plastic door making it impossible to open.

The sight of his form is too terrible to bear.

He rubbed his face with a hand, trying to erase all the craziness, trying only to think of food and the glorious effect washing would have on his tired body.

The rock can hold him and the ice can make him.

Craig slammed the ice-box shut and leaned heavily against it, his arms straight as rods, palms against the door in the dark. The Trickster. What the fuck was all that about?

Worse. Why was it nagging at his guts? He let his head hang between his shoulders as he leaned against the big, white, humming machine and let himself bathe in a moment of primitive acceptance. What if he were just to believe what seemed to be screaming for his attention for once? There were no leads in this sick case.

No reason, no motives, no clues. Not even a real suspect as far as he was concerned.

What if . . .

Just what if . . .

Where would a moment of allowing his mind to be simple and uncluttered get him? So much prejudice and bigotry getting in the way. What had she called him? A science bigot?

He stared at the floor, eyes unfocused on the long rectangle lit dimly by the light from the hall, and let his mind loose.

Maybe it was the lack of sleep, in fact maybe he was just asleep on his feet. But Craig McGee started to let go of that intangible, delicate thing that tethered him to common sense, and in seconds found himself in a cocoon of something else, something more than concentration. He let himself accept the fact of a thing called the Trickster, a thing so bad it was *worse than the worst wittiago*. He sucked in the fact of the Isksaksin. And he thought hard about Sam Hunt's face, and how despite his Indian name it was not the face of a hunter but that of the hunted.

Then stuff started to happen to him. He was in a new area of consciousness. He could feel abstract things in an almost physical way with his mind, and a deep liquid feeling, like an egg breaking inside his stomach, engulfed him.

A picture came into Craig McGee's mind. It was the picture of a tall woman getting out of a car. Tall and blonde, with blue eyes like ice. The journalist, what was her name? Marlene something? The one that had been in the car with Daniel. He wasn't seeing the rectangle of light on the linoleum floor any more. He was looking straight at her, into her face. And as he looked he started to see something else, something he didn't want to see, behind the woman's face. It was a dark, swirling thing, like clouds of acrid smoke rising from a filthy garbage fire. Like disease moving and multiplying under a microscope. And it was right under that woman's skin. Plain and visible, and so easy to see when you looked.

Craig realized with a lazy kind of a horror that he'd seen it then, at the time. But his mind was a closed thing. Closed perhaps for sanity, or maybe closed because until now he'd never wanted to open that door. He'd seen something once when he was a boy, too. A tiny thing. A vision of something mundane happening to his mother. Something small and insignificant that was going to happen later. And when it did happen just like he'd seen, he'd been frightened and slammed that door shut again. Just like he had when the wind blew Sylvia's shells away on that beach in Scotland.

It was a door he kept closed because he didn't believe. A door that was kept firmly shut by being a policeman, a man who lives and breathes only facts. And now, with that door wide open he was sweating at what he was seeing behind the paper-thin skin of that woman. No not that woman. That thing. That fucking thing.

He was breathing rhythmically, a pulse beating in his forehead, as he looked again into that swirling blackness behind the pretend face. The one that had been so close to Daniel. And then his eyes focused again. The rectangle of light on the floor was being broken by a dark shape. There was someone standing in the doorway.

He looked up very slowly, eyes narrowing in the dark to focus on the silhouette that was now very still in the frame of the open door. Craig McGee's breath left his lungs. He found air again and spoke without thinking.

'Sylvia?'

The figure didn't move. Craig took his palms from the ice-box and let his arms fall down at his sides as he turned to face what could not possibly be in the lobby. The figure stepped forward a pace.

'Craig? Darling?'

He was sweating heavily now, the salt stinging his eyes. He tried to swallow and failed. The figure moved again, a step closer, coming into the room.

'Craig. Where have you been, darling? I wanted you to see the baby.'

That sing-song voice. Always on the edge of laughter. Yes. so beautiful, Sylvia's voice.

He was unable to speak, but somewhere the lever that turned on the policeman was being pulled by an invisible hand. His eyes tore themselves away from this back-lit shadow and flicked to the side of the wall by the ice box where the light switch was.

'Darling. What's wrong with you? Look at the baby, sweetheart. He has your eyes.'

Slowly Craig shifted a pace to his right and raised his hand to the wall. It met plaster and he ran it back and forward over the smooth surface searching for that square of plastic that would light up this mystery.

'He's been so good, darling. Not a sound while you've been gone. Look at the sweet thing.'

The sweat was pouring from him now, his eyes swivelling in his head as he tried to see the switch his hand could not locate. Suddenly flesh met with plastic and he banged the heel of his palm against the white switch with a grunt. Striplights hummed into life, and when their flickering had done she was still there. Smiling.

He felt his knees give way, but his legs were too rigid to obey the command to buckle. Instead Craig McGee kept his hand on the light switch and a small noise like air escaping from a pressure cooker left his lips.

It was Sylvia. She stood smiling at him the way she always did when he came home tired and grouchy. Her eyes said she knew how tired he was. Her lips said she was ready to kiss that tiredness away. But that was all there was of the Sylvia he remembered.

She was holding something very close to her in a posture that was so unlike her. Closed and hunched, as if she held something she thought was in danger of being stolen.

'That's it sweetheart. Look. Look at our baby we made.'

Craig's eyes slipped slowly down to her huddled arms and as he watched she held them out to him, the smile on her face turning sickly, insane, like a TV evangelist asking for money.

He wanted to scream but he couldn't. There seemed to be no part of his body that would be able to express the scream he needed to give voice to. So Craig McGee made no noise at all, and instead let a string of saliva drool ponderously from his bottom lip.

With her arms outstretched like this he could see that Sylvia was open from breast-bone to hip-bone. A gaping black hole replaced the area where he'd known the firm flesh of Sylvia McGee to be. There was her heart, pumping away. A liver, the glimpse of some grey intestine. And then nothing but a spacious, ripped and ragged black-red hole.

And in her arms, the thing she so desperately wanted him to look at was cradled gently and carefully. Black, shining and viscous. A grotesquely swollen oval sac lay in her arms, black growths extending from the glistening body of the mess like fungus.

Sylvia's womb.

She spoke again and this time it was a voice from the cellar, deep and rasping and so full of malice he felt its heat on his soul.

'Our baby, darling. Isn't he beautiful? Don't you do wonderful things with that policeman's cock of yours? You do know it was your cock that did this, don't you?'

It laughed then, horribly and disgustingly, and because it was doing it through Sylvia's beautiful face Craig lunged at it to silence that laugh. Doorframe met skull and there was no more fight in the Staff Sergeant McGee. The house was quiet again. But then the house was always quiet these days.

There were only five reporters to meet Del Parkinson's plane, and it pissed him off. The pilot had been a jerk. Just the two of them all the way from Calgary Airport and all the guy could do was talk to air traffic control. Del kept jawing to him over the headset, but then the fuckwit would break into one of his anecdotes and speak to someone Del couldn't hear about cloud height or some shit.

It pissed him off. By the time they reached Silver, Del was beginning to suspect this jerk didn't know who he was. But that would be impossible. He was the Alley Cat. Everyone knew him.

But only five reporters. Big fucking deal.

At least the skirt was there. Pasqual Weaver stood on the edge of the snowy runway with an expression that said she'd suck his dick right now if he wanted. Plenty time.

The ape with the epaulettes shut the engine down, leaned clumsily across Del's lap and opened his door for him.

'Thanks, Captain. And listen. Lighten up.'

Del waited for the smile, the knowing bashful punch on the shoulder that meant the guy had just been doing his job and knew all along he had a superstar in his plane.

Nothing. He nodded as though he had just delivered a lunatic and shifted the shades on his stupid nose.

Del glared at him, stepped out the door and went to greet his press. Such as it was.

51

So familiar, this feeling. It was warm and safe, yet he knew it couldn't last forever. He would be back in the freezing tunnel soon and this delicious state of elation would merely seem the fancy it was. Calvin was with him, their minds dreaming as one as they had often done back in the sweat-lodges. Back then they had travelled together to understand so much, and though Sam could never have imagined it, here they were, twenty years later, doing it again.

Sam had fought off the first wave of nausea that always accompanied entering the spirit state, and now he was just hanging, waiting for whatever it was Calvin wanted to show him.

At first it was dark. Then gradually Sam saw that he was in a room. The cabin. He waited until Calvin caught up with him and when he felt his presence join him in the dream room, Sam sighed and settled like a floating seed onto this tableau of the past.

It was him. Sixteen years old with a bloody and badly swollen face from the beating Moses had given him and he was standing staring at the figure in the centre of the darkened room. Points of sunlight intruded into the darkness where the blanket over the window had been inexpertly nailed, and the spirit Sam thought how beautiful they were, these pin-heads of brilliance, like diamonds.

Moses swayed unsteadily in the middle of the floor, Eden's amulet between his rotten teeth, glaring at the young Sam with wide eyes. He barked at his son, and because of the obstacle in his mouth his words sounded comical rather than threatening.

'What now? Come on, you little fuck. What now?'

Sam's spirit watched his younger self wrestle with something and he knew what that had been. It was blasphemy even to have proceeded this far with the mock-ceremony. But there was hate in that young boy's eyes. A hate so deep it chilled Sam to see it from outside.

Calvin was approaching. The younger Calvin. Sam's spirit could feel it. He extended a tendril of his floating mind and saw the shaman running up the hill towards the cabin, the sunlight catching his hair as it swung wildly behind him, free of its braids. Calvin's spirit whispered to him.

'Yes Sam. I was there. As you said.'

The Sam in the room was stiffening now, and Sam's spirit wanted to shout *no!* to stop the boy performing this last act of sacrilege. But he was soundless here. This was nothing more than a reflection of the past, not an event that he could alter or direct. His spirit was here to observe.

And as it observed the boy, slowly reciting the words that his father must speak to complete the ritual, his spirit ached with the wrongness of it. This was as far he remembered. This hideous end to the ritual. What he would see now? What he had always feared? That this boy, previously guilty of nothing more than innocent faith, would become a gory murderer, a psychotic mutilator before the silent witness of his spirit?

Moses shut his eyes, and with the Isksaksin gripped firmly between his teeth, began to chant the words after his son. Sam's spirit could not feel temperature, but his young self displayed the effect that Moses's words had created, clutching his arms to his body as the room became icy cold.

Vapour was coming from man and boy's breath now as the room fell below freezing. Calvin Bitterhand was almost there, jumping over the broken fencing that half surrounded the paddock and running through the thistles that stood sentinel over a long forgotten driveway. Sam's spirit saw it all at the same time, his mind taking in every movement and detail. Even a mouse rustling beneath a crate in the kitchen was observed by this roaming probe that was his mind. He could see it foraging for food on the garbage-strewn floorboards. Calvin's mind touched his again, calling for his attention.

'You must look, Sam. Look and remember.'

The room was changing in more than temperature. Something was growing there invisibly. On Moses's face there was a look of triumph as his eyes grew wide and the amulet dropped from his teeth, swinging back down to rest against his collarbone. Moses was changing too.

491

Subtly at first and then faster as all the watchers, flesh and spirit gazed on.

Sam's spirit saw his own sixteen-year-old body sway and waver as if it seemed to be undergoing some kind of internal physical punishment, and he wanted to reach out to himself and give his young image comfort. Not possible.

But Moses.

What was happening to Moses was too horrible to behold.

The thing that had been Moses was now huge, terrible, crawling with its own degeneration and venom. And its power was beyond measure, filling the room like a yeast growing. The boy was screaming, his body pressed against the plasterboard wall, and his breath panted from his mouth in freezing clouds of vapour.

And then as the young Sam slid to the floor unconscious, the thing started its business, the business that Sam's spirit was here to witness, and yet still could not. His mind recoiled from the vision so violently that he catapulted his thoughts away from the cabin and sent them hurtling up into the mountains that looked down on the small wooden structure containing such profanity.

But he had seen it. That which he had helped to call without purpose or permission. Seen it and remembered.

Sam's eyes rolled in the back of his sockets and his head fell forward on his breast. He sat like that for minutes until he realized he was looking with his eyes instead of his mind, and was seeing glowing embers. The red-and-blue life that was still playing over the burning wood, comforted him with the vividness of its colours in this great darkness that surrounded him.

He lifted his head slowly and looked across the gloom at Calvin. The old man's eyes glittered with the reflection of the embers, indicating that he was awake and staring at him. The sweat that was drying on Sam's forehead suddenly chilled him as much as Calvin's steady gaze, and he lowered his eyes, selected a handful of small dry twigs from the pile and placed them carefully in the heart of the glow. Smoke funnelled from the twigs, then orange flames danced into life, rekindling the fire. He threw two larger branches on and watched as they hissed and smoked and joined the twigs in lighting up the tunnel walls.

He could think of nothing to say. It was Calvin who broke their silence. 'You fled a second time.'

'I saw.'

'What did you see, Hunting Wolf?'

Sam looked into Calvin's eyes, jarred at the formality of his address and the ancient tongue with which it was spoken.

'That which I cruelly released.'

'So tell me now. Did you murder your father?'

Sam bent his head again in shame and horror and struggled with the question.

'Not in the way I thought. But you saw as well as I. Yes. I murdered him.'

'The weapon?'

Sam paused, then spoke the name quietly, but with rancour. 'The Trickster.'

Calvin slapped his knees with a ferocity that made Sam snap his head up. 'NO! Do you learn nothing?'

'But the thing . . . the thing that Moses became . . .'

'What of it?'

Calvin sounded disappointed, almost petulant. Sam was dumbfounded, and yet at the back of his mind he knew why Calvin's voice was weary. He had fled a second time. And he was still fleeing. He was not telling himself the truth.

Sam choked back a tear. 'Calvin. What did I do?'

The old man leaned back. 'Where is the Isksaksin, Sam? You do not wear it.'

Sam didn't even pause to wonder how Calvin could know that, dressed as he was in his thick plaid jacket and another three layers of cotton wool and fleece. He merely bowed his head and replied. 'At home.'

'Then you must fetch it. Quickly. You know that now. Do you not?'

Sam nodded, then spoke in a small voice, still in that ancient formal Cree they used so often in the past, 'Tell me first. Tell me what you saw.'

Calvin sat back and Sam watched the firelight make canyons of the lines criss-crossing the old man's face as he waited for a reply.

'It was impotent. The keeper had not summoned it and so it was trapped in its fury, able only to destroy the impostor who called it, and by doing so, destroy itself. It is so old, so powerful, that none

493

can hold it and it waits its centuries for a chance to break free from one who calls it and who can liberate it.'

Sam breathed his question. 'But it is not the Trickster?'

'No. It is the one the Trickster desires you to call. Do you not remember him whispering to you from his prison of rock when you faltered in your plans that day?'

Sam said nothing but Calvin took his silence as affirmative.

'He is powerless in the rock but he can see and hear and sometimes reach out his black jester's fingers. And he wanted you so badly to call that which you did.'

'Why, Calvin? I am lost.'

The shaman sighed. 'I know, my son. That is why I am here. If you are lost when he faces you then we are all lost.' The fire sparked as if in agreement and Calvin's voice became eager. 'He is a fool. He thinks that if you call that which cannot be contained he will enter you when it takes its leave. Then he would be spirit and shaman-flesh, and his evil would know no boundary. The Isksaksin is his boundary. The line he cannot cross.'

'Why then do we call up such a demon that could release him?'

Calvin put a finger to his lips. 'You have seen why with your spirit, Hunting Wolf. We must not speak it. He is the Trickster that must be tricked.'

Sam stared at him in confusion. 'I do not understand.'

'You do. You will. When it is time.'

Sam buried his head in his hands, exhausted and broken.

'Listen to me, Hunting Wolf,' Calvin said sharply.

Sam looked up, imploring Calvin with eyes that were both desperate and respectful. 'I am listening, Soaring Eagle. Tell me of my father.'

Calvin's heart soared like his spirit-guide's name and he looked across at Sam with love. 'It left him after the blackness took you. I came into the room as it was wreaking its revenge on the body that had let it come this far. You know what it did. The carnage covered you with its mark. You were like a hunter who has spent the night in the carcass of a slaughtered caribou for warmth, no part of you not bathed in your father's blood. But it was not at your hand. It was under the vengeful talons of that which Moses called.

'I saw it and thought I would die at the sight. When it turned its great filthy bulk to regard me in the doorway I thought I would never be sane again. But then it turned away and raged harmlessly over your unconscious body, screaming like a tortured soul as its power dissipated and it faded from the room like mist. Then you woke.'

Sam swallowed, remembering that awakening.

'I could not calm your terror nor stop you when you fled. You looked at me, bloodless and clean, then at yourself. And when your eyes alighted on the torn body that had been your father you made that ill-founded connection and ran from the cabin.' Calvin paused and raised a finger at him. 'Where did you go?'

Sam tried to control his face, but it was twitching in agony. 'The river. All that blood . . .'

Calvin nodded. 'I took your father's body and after I prayed over it I took two of those precious parts, lying severed and torn on the floor, and I violated him with them.'

Sam stared at him. 'What?'

'The penis. I put it in his mouth. The heart I placed in his rectum.'

Sam could hardly breathe. He stared at Calvin with horror. 'Why?'

'Eden told me to.'

Sam was shaking his head, his mouth gaping open, denying what he was hearing.

Calvin remained calm, his tone that of a teacher rather than a madman. 'He told me how Moses would die, and that it was important that when he was found that there should be a sign to the one who can save the keeper.' Calvin's voice dropped. For a moment he lost his lecturing tone and sounded sad. 'He failed to tell me that he would die first, at the hand of his own son. But I obeyed him. I took off the amulet and wrapped the body in a skin. It had left its mark, the Isksaksin. Plain as if it had branded him. I buried the body where Eden had told me to, in the sacred burial ground by the river. The ground was so dry, so sandy I thought I would never make the hole big enough. But I toiled in the hot sun, alone except for the crows that circled above me, and laid him down. Then I returned to your cabin, washed the blood from the walls and the floor and waited for you.'

Sam was still aghast. He could not speak and even if he could, he had nothing to say. Calvin looked across at him, still with love in his eyes. 'I knew you would come back. I had to give you the Isksaksin.'

Sam found his tongue and spat out the words. 'And I took it.'

Calvin nodded. 'You had no choice. You are the keeper.'

495

There was no sound from his young companion. He was just staring at the old shaman as if he had been cheated. Calvin sighed. 'He killed himself, Sam. He died because he was evil. Take the stone of guilt from your soul and cast it away.'

Sam fought himself one last time, then, losing the battle, did what he had waited twenty years to do. He put his head back and wailed. The achingly empty wail of grief, shame, fear and pain filled the tunnel, echoing back at them from the hard rock. Calvin Bitterhand bowed his head and closed his eyes, trying to shut out that howl of agony. But he could not. He sat and listened to it, taking the pain it caused him like a punishment.

52

'Sorry. I only got the message half an hour ago that you called.' She ushered him into the lobby quickly before any of the vultures could get a clear shot of her tear-stained face.

Craig was unsure what to do. Katie had obviously been crying for hours, and his first instinct was to hold her, comfort her. But that was out of the question. Under the circumstances.

She looked up at his face, and gestured at the crudely fixed band-aid on his forehead. 'What you do?'

'Fell against the door this morning. Believe that?'

Katie Hunt shrugged. She believed anything now. Anything at all. She looked at Craig's face and thought how hollow and ill it had gotten since last night. 'Eaten today?'

'Sure. I had a late lunch. Sandwich about three-thirty. You?'

Katie shook her head. 'Anne's been in most of the day. Trying to feed me and the kids. Didn't work.'

'Is she still here?'

'You tell me. Your guys are watching who comes and goes like this is Alcatraz.'

Craig looked at her steadily, refusing to offer the apology she was seeking. Katie relented. 'She went about an hour ago. After she helped put the kids to bed.' She turned and led the way through to the lounge and he followed her silently. The room was uncomfortably tidy. Craig reckoned he knew what Katie's friend had been busy doing all day. The tools of refuge from crisis or grief; the hoover and the damp cloth.

He sat down uninvited on the long sofa and waited for her to speak. Katie stood in front of the fireplace, her back to the empty grate like

497

a detective in a corny country house drama about to unmask the killer. If only, wished Craig.

'I haven't got news if that's what you're hoping,' she said, reading his face. She looked down at her feet and continued in a smaller voice. 'But I've got something.'

'Uh-huh?' He sounded weary, not eager.

Katie looked back at him with blue eyes behind puffy, red skin sparkling. 'Hope.' She walked over and sat down beside Craig before he had time to respond. 'You think I've gone crazy, don't you?'

He studied her face. 'Depends. What's giving you hope?'

Katie sat back heavily into the sofa and stared up at the ceiling. 'Yeah. Maybe I have gone crazy. But it feels better than yesterday. Yesterday I hated my husband.'

'For killing the dog?'

'Partly. Mostly because I thought he'd . . . I thought he'd harmed Billy.'

'So I believe.'

She sat up and stared at him. 'What do you mean?'

'Detachment got a call from Billy's teacher. When the news broke today.'

Agnes Root. Doing her job. Getting her Indian.

Katie looked at the floor again. 'I don't think he did. Harm him I mean. I got it wrong.' She looked up at him with a hint of anger and shame. 'We all did.'

'Billy told you?'

She nodded.

'That's all I needed Craig. I needed to know he hadn't harmed his son. Now I believe in him again.'

'Even if he's harmed other people's sons? Cut them into bits?'

Katie studied his face carefully, trying to see the facial match for the brutality of his words. 'Do you believe that?'

Craig McGee churned inside as he thought about what he did and didn't believe. He was lying last night. Everything had changed. Sure the sun had come up and the cups in her kitchen were still cups. But that was all. Everything else was different. He had seen it.

His mouth was dry. Honesty was dry work.

'No. I don't.'

Katie put her face in her hands, leaned forward and sobbed. Maybe with relief, maybe with the shame that she had doubted her love.

Craig didn't know. She sat up, wiped her face and choked back her sobs.

'The stuff Billy's been saying. It's crazier than anything we talked about last night. But I believe him about Sam. I do.'

'But not about the rest? The crazy stuff.'

'How can I? It's off the scale.'

'Tell me.'

'Why?'

'I need to know.'

Katie looked at this ill, sallow-skinned man with eyes that were now haunted instead of searching. Only last night he looked strong and determined. Something had happened.

Yes. He did need to know. So she told him.

53

Alberta 1907
Siding Twenty-three

The hare watched him enter, and the pure white of its winter coat let him see it almost immediately. It sat, unafraid, unblinking in the middle of the floor.

Far behind it, tiny drops of water running from the end wall of the unfinished tunnel echoed lugubriously as they dripped onto the rubble-strewn floor. Henderson tried to breathe normally, but it was beyond his control. His lungs seemed incapable of retaining oxygen, merely panting the air out again as soon as he drew breath. He stayed framed in the arch of the tunnel for a moment, struggling for that elusive breath, praying for strength, then took two steps inside.

The animal continued to watch him passively. He took another trembling step then stopped, only a few feet away.

Just a hare? An ordinary snowshoe hare evading the biting cold? The tall man narrowed his eyes and looked. The hare's eyes glinted in the dark, but it was impossible in this half-gloom for Henderson to look into them, to probe for that swirl of blackness that he feared would cloud behind the innocent animal's pupils.

For one moment of blessed relief he believed he was looking at a simple hare. Yes. A coincidence that it was sheltering in here. Then, dear sweet Jesus, there would be no confrontation of that deep, unimaginable and malevolent evil. Then there would be a brief respite from this gnawing terror that was threatening to make him vomit. Better. There would be no exorcism.

'Jamesss.'

The hare had spoken. No. It had whispered in a hissing, provocative voice that was almost seductive. God almighty, it had.

Henderson closed his sweating fingers more tightly around the crucifix and slowly brought it up in front of him. His voice was surprisingly steady. 'In the name of Jesus Christ our Lord . . .'

Henderson faltered, aghast at what he was doing. Horrified at the duplicity of it. He was no Catholic priest. But he believed. Surely he had that much. And Christ would be with him. He knew that. Had to know that. Henderson shouted, his voice booming in the hard space, bouncing back at him as if mocking him.

'I CAST YOU OUT!'

The animal cocked its head slightly. A human gesture of curiosity. It was looking at the cross without alarm. Then a laugh. That choking gurgling noise from Hell's sewers. And the whisper.

'And who is this . . . Jesus Christ?'

Henderson took an unsteady step back, the cross still held high in front of him. The hare hopped forward, still looking at the crucifix.

'Is this his totem, this Christ?'

It was almost a friendly enquiry. Except that the deep dangerous voice of the animal was like syrup poured on rotting flesh. The stench of its malicious undercurrent was overwhelming.

There was a comical insanity to his situation that made a hard knot of hysteria grow in Henderson's throat. He stepped back again, nearer the entrance and the light.

The thing was still curious. Far from frightened. When it rasped at him again its voice made him retch and he coughed back bile.

'What does it command, this Christ spirit? The wind? The earth? The water?'

It hopped towards him, once more closing the distance that the trembling minister had instinctively tried to lengthen.

James Henderson's head was light with terror and confusion and as he blinked down at this abomination he began to imagine the sight of himself from outside his body. He saw what anyone would see were they to step through that arch of light and come upon him. A tall, thin Scottish minister, dressed only in a dark woollen vest, thick black trousers and rough cotton shirt, with the cross of Christ held high before him, standing comically brandishing it at a tiny hare. What in God's name was he doing? The arm that held his cross shook.

And then the memory of the dead and mutilated men came to him, the unbearable depravity of those deaths. He thought of the visions that this thing had visited upon him both at night and in the grey daylight, in front of unseeing others, stealing from him even the imagined safety of men's company. The filth, the lies, the obscenities. His anger grew and slowly his arm stopped shaking. He growled down at this nightmare and held his cross tightly. 'He is no spirit, you foul demon. He is the son of God.'

The hare was only feet away from the entrance now, and in the thin light Henderson could see into those eyes.

There it was. The darkness. Turning over on itself like a thunder cloud. Corrupt and venomous and latent with savagery.

From the animal a laugh began that was so internal and intimate that Henderson questioned whether it happened only in his own head. It had no echo in this hard place, so perhaps the hare was making no sound. Instead, it was hot and muffled, touching every nerve of Henderson's in a personal and secretive violation. It was a noise that was in him and for him and he could not rip himself free from its filth.

'The son of God!'

It spoke the words with relish as it laughed on and on, and with that laugh James Henderson felt his last hope trickle from him. His faith. He could see almost straight into the heart of the corruption for a moment, see its amusement at this spirit it knew nothing of, and with terror he understood Hunting Wolf's words.

Older than Christ. Much, much older.

Had no one awakened it from its centuries of deviant slumber to tell it the good news? Did Christ's message not reach back to these ancient creations? He was lost, adrift with doubt and desertion. His Christ. The spirit that demons quaked before in his world was a stranger to the demons of the Indian. How could that be? How could that be if he truly was the son of God? Henderson slumped to his knees and began to weep.

'Oh Jesus. Sweet Jesus.'

The hare stopped laughing and seemed to sniff the air, and from its very core there came a deep bubbling sigh of delight.

The hiss of a whisper again, this time with an air of purpose.

'Ah Jamesss. Our friend sleeps.'

She ran after him, gasping with the effort as the deep snow sent her tumbling with its hidden holes and branches. But panic kept her moving, her mother's heart beating in panic for her only remaining child. The only thing she had left.

'Walks Alone! No!'

She watched his tiny frame leap nimbly over a fallen trunk and dart behind another tree. Great Spirit, why was he pursuing the man Henderson? The boy was running in the tall white man's tracks, and she, like a fool, was running behind like a wolf after a hare.

She would not lose her son. No. Not after Snowchild. She would die first. And she sensed great danger. What instinct had made her follow Walks Alone as he pretended to go out for firewood? A mother's? Perhaps, she thought with a tiny spark of hope in her aching heart, a wife's.

How she longed for Hunting Wolf. But it had been Walks Alone who had made her doubt him. His unaccountable, mute fear of his father tore through her like a summer fire in the trees. And when the braves were slaughtered and the bereaved pointed to him, with his unexplained absences and his bloodstained body, what was she to think? She had a son to protect. She had been strong in making Hunting Wolf go, making him a fugitive. Though she longed for him still. Ached for him. But she would not lose her son: she would follow him to the edge of the world.

Singing Tree pulled her legs from the deep hole and stumbled back into the tracks that the boy was following. They were heading for the white men's hole in the mountain.

So be it. She ran on, and her voice that continued to shout his name was muffled and deadened by snow and the thick solemn pines.

Walks Alone gasped to regain his breath and whirled around in search of his father. The hole in the snow marked where he had lain, but he was no longer there. The man Henderson must have helped him up. Where would they shelter? He looked towards the tunnel entrance yards away and narrowed his eyes.

There, only feet from the arch was a man-shaped curve in the snow, black fabric showing through the mound. Walks Alone gasped soundlessly and sprinted forward. The thick snow had all but covered his father's immobile face and the boy swept it off, almost crying with relief that he swept it from a warm face. Hunting Wolf was alive.

Alive, but dead to the frenzied shaking that Walks Alone employed on his shoulders. He put his face to his father's breast rising and falling and wept.

Too late. Too late to stop the black sleep coming over his father again. And what was the filthy thing he feared beyond reason doing with this slumber? As if to answer him, there came a noise from the tunnel that nearly stopped his heart. A human scream so shrill yet deep, of immeasurable suffering and agony, bellowed from the black arch.

The boy's eyes were wide with terror. He kept deadly still, waiting for more, and when the silence was unbroken, he snapped his head back to his father.

Quickly he fumbled beneath the black coat that covered Hunting Wolf's naked body and found the small medicine bundle and knife that was tied around his wrist with a thong. He fished about in the small leather sack and found the bitter leaves, the ones he had been taught about. Walks Alone placed the leaves on his father's chest, took the knife from its sheath in two hands and raised it above his head. The prayer. How did it go? Would it work, spoken only in his brain and not out loud? He had to try. There was no more time.

He formed the words in his head, repeating them as if with his tongue and swayed his head in rhythm to his phantom chant. There was a new noise from the tunnel. A deep scraping roar. Something on the move.

He raised the knife higher and screwed his eyes tighter.

'NO!'

His mother's tearing scream made him open them with a start. She was yards away, her face a mask of horror. Walks Alone looked at her once, then turned his head back to his father and brought the knife down in a shining arc.

Singing Tree collapsed into the snow, wailing like a wounded animal. The boy lifted the knife and brought it down a second time. The roar in the tunnel increased.

Beneath him, his father's chest bled from the two perfect surface cuts that described the first shape of the Thunder Spirit's mark, the herbs at the point of the crude V it described. And as Walks Alone watched, Hunting Wolf's eyes flickered and his mouth started to twitch and drool.

The boy looked to his gasping mother, a world away on her hands in the snow, and smiled.

When the hare opened its mouth, wider, much wider than the mechanics of the jaw had been designed for, James Henderson realized he was going to die. A paralysis came over him that was mental as well as physical, temporarily stopping his fear as well as very nearly stopping his heart. He watched almost with wonder as the mouth of the ruined animal split and burst, and the black bile burst out of a body that would have required to have been a hundred times the volume in order to contain it.

The fingers of Henderson's hand opened and let his crucifix drop to the ground.

There was no God. How could there be?

How could any God that loved man concoct such a perversion? His mouth was stretched open in a scream, he knew that. But there was no sound coming from it. But then a scream would have been a cry of alarm, a cry for help, an expression of fear with purpose. None of these applied at that moment to James Henderson. He was numb, the scream silenced in his rigid body by the knowledge that he would die and there would be no God to greet him. His body would merely disintegrate and there would be nothing. No consciousness, no love, no purpose. This thing was the truth, not the words written in his bible, because if this thing lived and breathed and killed and tortured, then all else was lies.

No. No God could let this abomination be.

The black, stinking bile was solid now. Within that strange dreamlike state of being beyond terror, Henderson knew that the grotesque Kinchuinick totems he had seen, the wooden nightmares of gaping jaws and rolling hate-filled eyes, were sculptures, not fantasy. Here was their model. The ice was forming it. And the rock, and the ice and the crawling viscous membrane of scum that held the component parts together, combined in one giant creature that now stood on great taloned hind legs and regarded him hungrily, with a pornographic stare.

And no one to pray to. An empty universe, deaf to man's triumphs and failures, where neither good nor bad was rewarded or punished, where life could begin and be extinguished without purpose.

When the talon of ice shot out and pierced Henderson's chest, his scream was as much for that glimpse of Godless chaos and bottomless dismay, as for the agony that seared him and scythed him writhing to the ground.

54

This wasn't what he had in mind. The Victoria function room in the Rocky Mountain Chateau was clattering with the chatter from the Celebrity Ski participants as they filled their fat faces with pastries and wine. But there was no TV crew.

Some dickpiece from the ski company was wandering around the crowd taking a video, but what did that count for? Jack shit, that's what.

Del Parkinson tried to look threatening from the safety of his window-seat as yet another big-haired woman waddled over to him, her hand extended to shake his. It didn't work. The idiot classes never knew when they weren't wanted. That's what made them idiots.

'Del Parkinson in Silver. You know Vera and I can hardly believe it!'

He looked at her with resignation, knowing that Vera would not be far behind. 'Me neither.'

She laughed, although not at his joke. She didn't understand it, he could tell. Del noted the dark lettuce stuck between two of her bottom teeth and felt queasy. She adopted a look of pride.

'We come every year. No killer's going to stop that.'

Del allowed himself the luxury for a moment of imagining exactly how a killer could very quickly and easily stop her coming every year.

Over the woman's shoulder he caught sight of Pasqual Weaver looking at him, her creamy tits pushed up high in that black cocktail dress, and decided the evening might not be a complete waste of time. He turned his gaze back to the woman and smiled, hoping Pasqual would note his charming boyish grin. 'Yeah? Good for you. That's the good old Canadian spirit.'

'Oh, we're from Idaho.'

I'll bet you are lady, he thought, and drained his glass.

Eric Sindon leaned against the wall by the wine table and scanned the room. There weren't very many nice people in it. Same at every celebrity ski. It attracted the ones who didn't give a dog's ball for charity. They merely had cash and a desire to swan around the hotel with their *I'm skiing for those who can't* badges on, getting on the tits of the famous people who for once could neither complain or escape.

He mused for a moment what the count would be in here right now, if St Peter appeared with the trumpet that sounded judgement day. Would this be a room full of good like the badges suggested, or a watered-silk wallpapered holding area of evil?

He thought of the decent families who dropped their dollars as a matter of course into the charity bins in the lodge restaurant, never questioning their obligation to do so. How come they never came to these bun-fights? They didn't. But they would line the ski course and hold their children up to get a view of the skiers, and they were always the ones who stopped and spoke kindly to the poor bastards the money was for in the first place; the cripples and the cancer victims who were always wheeled out to see the *heroes* skiing for their benefit. He had watched those good-hearted people and wished they could see through this crowd of perfumed piranhas pretending to do good.

That guy over there with the Rolex on. What did he do to get his money? Something decent? Some fucking chance. Eric had watched one of the company girls ask him to contribute to the raffle that was an extra to build a conservatory for the hospice in Stoke. He'd watched that mouth spit the words into the girl's face, 'I paid enough for this frigging ticket already, sweetheart.'

That mouth was now being stuffed with pastry and shrimps. Eric had to turn away.

And Del fucking Parkinson. Big-hearted charity man. He knew what the old creep had in mind with Pasqual. Eric looked at her beaming across at him and wondered if she did too. The guy was ancient and ugly. Surely not even Pasqual could stomach that sagging old body on top of her in the name of fucking the famous?

He took a last sip from his glass, put it down on the table and went in search of something to do. His muse was over. St Peter wouldn't find many candidates for heaven here. If Sam Hunt was really the

killer, Eric felt like calling him up and asking him to the party. He'd
be in good company. They could all go to Hell together.

The cry of despair had lasted longer than Calvin could bear. Sam
was like an animal in a gin-trap. He wailed through gritted teeth, his
tears unchecked and seemingly endless.

Calvin buried his head in his arms and waited, praying for his
young apprentice's grief to subside.

So Sam had never grieved. Calvin understood. This outwardly
strong, handsome man had buried his sorrow for betrayal, for a lost
childhood, lost parents, a murdered grandparent and a heart that he
believed to be black with guilt, kept it all so deeply buried for over
two decades that the sudden exhumation of all that horror was tearing
him to bits.

Calvin hadn't grieved either. He had merely drunk. But as he raised
his head and looked across the fire at the contorted face of his beloved
boy, he wished he too had time to release the remorse.

But there was no time.

'Sam.'

The young shaman put a hand to his face and drew a shuddering
breath, quenching the next howl that was waiting to find a voice.
Calvin spoke again.

'Sam. You must return home. Fetch the Isksaksin.'

Sam panted, his eyes closed and his teeth still grinding.

'SAM!' Calvin put aside sympathy and barked his name with
urgency and authority.

Gradually Sam's breathing calmed and he opened his swollen eyes
to regard Calvin. He wiped his face with a sleeve and straightened
his back. 'How can I go home?'

'You must. Go unseen, and return.'

Sam stared at him through puffed eyes, then nodded.

Calvin reached for more wood and found none. It was as though
the small matter of Sam finding his way home and back here again,
when the whole world were after him, was as nothing. He stood
wearily and walked slowly towards the tunnel entrance.

'More wood.'

It was both an explanation and a prompt that Sam should go. The
fire was low and time was short.

Sam looked back at the red, flickering embers and the old man disappeared into the night, betraying his proximity with the sounds of branches breaking and the crunch of feet on ice. He looked into the low fire, took a shuddering breath and his shoulders slumped in weariness. His eyes were sore and heavy with crying and he closed them and put his head on his knees, letting the heat from the glowing wood warm him.

The cold. It was so very cold.

So cold.

Colder than hell.

Cold because the fire was out.

Sam's head arced up off his knees and his eyes blinked in the dark. Not even a tiny red glow lit this deep velvet blackness. Because the fire was out and had been out for a long time. Because the man who had slept alone beside it, for God knows how long, hadn't noticed its embers cool and die.

'CALVIN!'

He leapt to his feet and screamed into the darkness. An echo threw it back at him like a punch.

Sam stumbled towards the entrance, the arch only dimly described by the reflective white snow outside. He staggered out into the snow between the tracks and yelled again.

'CALVIN!'

The falling snow caught his frantic shout and wrapped it in a thick deadening silence. There was no echo out here.

Worse.

There was no reply.

'Where's McGee?'

Constable Bell looked up from the computer with distaste at Becker and the two new guys in suits.

'I think Staff Sergeant McGee has gone back to the Hunt house.'

The reinforcements from Edmonton that flanked Becker caught that heavily barbed reminder of Craig's rank and exchanged looks.

Becker was tired, but his energy was quickly rekindled with irritation. 'Why?'

'Mrs Hunt called. Left a message that he was to call her back. Guess he just went straight there.'

Becker walked back towards his office without response and the two men followed him.

Jeff Bell muttered *asshole* under his breath and resumed his two-fingered typing. The sooner they pulled in this bastard Hunt the sooner these goons from Edmonton would be gone. He looked up from the screen. Then, maybe, they could get back to normal. Maybe bury Joe and Dan decently, instead of letting them lie there in the morgue. Maybe get that travelling circus called the press out of Silver and back under the stones they crawled out of.

He sighed, took a gulp of cold coffee from a styrofoam cup and got back to the dull routine of typing in statements.

Inside his office, Becker was sitting on the desk with his hands out wide, gesturing to the two other men. 'I can't stop him. Not if she asks to see him.'

The younger man looked at him coldly. 'The reason you're here is because officers aren't supposed to investigate cases in which they have personal involvement. You wouldn't call this personal?'

Becker moved his hands again. 'What can I do?'

'Want me to spell it out, Staff Sergeant? Call him back. Tell McGee he can't see Katie Hunt until we've found and arrested the wagon-burner.'

Becker shrugged in his discomfort and called through the open door. 'Alice. Get the guys outside the Hunt house to go in and pull out McG . . . Staff Sergeant McGee.' He looked at his audience of two. 'He turns his radio off. Phone's off the hook. The press.'

They looked back at him, unimpressed.

'Well. You asked.'

Craig remained silent, looking into the empty fireplace as though Katie's voice were coming from there. He'd said nothing all the way through Katie's bizarre recounting of Billy and his crazy dreams. Now she'd finished, she expected some response. Katie looked at him, studying his ashen face. He looked ten years older than he had last night.

'What are you thinking?'

He looked up at last. 'That you shouldn't give a nine-year-old boy sleeping pills.'

She sighed. 'No. You shouldn't.'

Craig watched her writhe on the unintentional spit of guilt he'd skewered her with, and softened his voice. 'You accept his reason for being frightened by Sam?'

'I accept that he was scared by a dream and not by anything Sam did to him in real life. Yes. Very much so.'

'But not the rest?'

'Come on, Craig. He's been in shock.'

'Bart was killed, Katie. You were there. Not a dream. We've got the dog in a plastic bag down in the morgue, with an evidence number tied to what's left of it. You're telling me you believe that Sam was killing the dog out of mercy to save it from . . . what was it . . . killing itself while possessed?'

Katie got up from the sofa and walked over to the window. The curtains were drawn and she fingered them with her back to the policeman.

'No. Of course not.'

'Then why believe Billy about Sam not hurting him? And why did your loving husband kill the dog if it wasn't like Billy said? If it wasn't a demon in there?'

She whirled round at him, eyes blazing. 'I don't fucking know. I'm just telling you what Billy told me. Okay?'

'And believing the bits you want to. Because they make life more comfortable.'

Katie pursed her mouth and lowered her voice. 'And that's so terrible is it?'

'It's not helpful.'

Craig was looking up at her with those tired haunted eyes. Katie almost felt sorry for him. But she was the victim in this room, not him. Her anger rose again.

'So you can sit there, smug in your policeman's scepticism, disbelieving it all and that's somehow helpful is it? Forgive me for reminding you of four little words, Staff Sergeant. Back to square fucking one.'

'That's five words.'

'Whatever.'

'And you're wrong.'

'Yeah?'

He looked at her steadily and there was no humour, no irony, no sarcasm in his eyes whatsoever when he said,

'I don't disbelieve it.'

55

Alberta 1907
Siding Twenty-three

Husband and wife looked at each other from a distance. In Hunting Wolf's face there was no trace of bitterness or reproach. He looked through the curtain of falling snow at the woman kneeling and sobbing, and his weary black eyes filled with love.

But there was no time now. Not for reconciliation or explanation. Time only to face what he had evaded, and in doing so, had cost the lives of so many.

His son stood at his side, his face registering triumph and fear. The man stretched out an arm and touched the boy's thick black hair, and the small face tilted up to look into his father's.

Suddenly, both father and son turned their heads like startled deer towards the thick trees behind Singing Tree. The sound of voices. Distant, but approaching.

Hunting Wolf let go of his son's head and without speaking or looking again at either of his family, turned and walked towards the tunnel. The woman and boy watched the tall, naked man go, then Walks Alone ran to his mother.

There was no sound, except for a lonely echoing drip. It took Hunting Wolf a long time to adjust his eyes to the gloom. He was still dazed, exhausted from his ordeals, but his spirit had purpose. He knew he had lost toes and patches of flesh the size of acorns on his body. He could see the whitened skin, the skin that the cold had destroyed, and knew that those innocent patches of numbness would kill, would turn black and diseased, bringing fever first then death.

But his family must live. That was what kept the fire in his soul. He stood silently, waiting until his eyes could see, and then when they did, prayed that they were wrong.

There was a dark shape by the rough wall, splayed crazily over the fallen rocks like a doll.

Henderson's body lay in a dark pool of its own blood, and the shaman was glad that its face was turned to the wall, hiding the agony that he knew would be frozen there.

'You die like worms on a thorn. You men.'

The pale face was only a few feet from his dark one. It regarded him with a half smile and behind the pale blue eyes it had copied inexpertly from that tragic trapper the clouds of swirling black desecration moved as if stirred by a stick.

Hunting Wolf ignored the vision and bent to pick up Henderson's totem. The cross lay by the body where it had fallen from his hand and the tiny white figure was red with the Scot's blood. The Trickster was not to be ignored. It flared beneath its disguise like a torch.

'Your idiot cock-sucking son interrupted our work. He will die slowly for that irritation. I could have done so much more with this white dullard.'

The shaman opened his medicine bundle, pressed the bloody cross to his forehead where it left its mark, and dropped it into the leather pouch, his eyes still on Henderson's body. The pale thing that was dark underneath, now boiled in its rage.

'Look at me, you cunt!'

Hunting Wolf closed his eyes and knelt down on the hard, freezing tunnel floor. He raised his hands above his head, swayed forward and back and chanted a prayer to the Thunder Spirit for purity. The monotone of his deep intonations bounced between the rock walls, returning to his ears almost as a chorus rather than a single voice.

The darkness behind the pretence of pale flesh was losing its grip on the illusion. It watched the man with a hatred too intense to quantify, and its form shifted like sand.

'Father! Father I can speak. Help me!'

Hunting Wolf twitched but continued chanting, his eyes closed in concentration.

Then a boy's scream, and the sound of flesh being torn and bones snapping. The shaman closed his eyes tighter and finished his prayer, the final blessing making him touch his scarred cuts unconsciously with a finger.

When he opened his eyes the body of his son was lying before him, his torso ripped open and its guts lying fanned out like a display at a feast. He looked coldly on the apparition, then stood again and waited. He was pure now.

Slowly the vision of Walks Alone faded as he knew it would and the pale man stepped back into view from the gloom.

'Destroy me, or see all you love destroyed.'

Hunting Wolf's head was high. 'How may I destroy that which is nothing?'

The pale face was still, but the dark clouds raged. Its voice was no longer coming from the mouth as it lost its hold of the human illusion in its anger. Instead Hunting Wolf heard it as a screaming in his own head.

'I am not nothing, you scum from the cunt of a whore! I am Sitconski!'

'We give you that name. If it pleases us. We can make names mean what we please, for we are men. Now, here, it is the name for nothing. You are nothing, because I choose it.'

'I am Inktomni!'

'No. You are nothing. Only we are something. We have life.'

There was mayhem in the tunnel for a moment as the air around Hunting Wolf's head whipped and churned. Then it became still.

The voice was calm and deep and inside the shaman's head again. 'You fear me because I am eternal. It is you who are nothing.'

'I fear only that which has life and purpose. I fear the nettle more than you.' Hunting Wolf paused, then spoke in a softer, more thoughtful voice. 'Why, when you were once in the light, did you choose eternal death?'

There was sadness in the shaman's voice, and in reply the darkness was hushed and still. It was a moment that the man had not planned or expected. The dark thing was thinking its putrid thoughts, but Hunting Wolf could feel something like pain from the dark tendrils of sensation his mind was constantly reading.

He waited for a reply, and as he stood silently from outside the tunnel mouth there came a clamour.

Men shouting.

515

It was time.

He closed his eyes and spoke a prayer inside his head.

Oh Great Spirit. You who make the dark and the light. I thank you for my flesh and bones. For my penis that gives life, and my heart that guides life. I thank you that my spirit that lives in the flower and the rock and the stream and the clouds that chase across the sky like horses, lives too in the body of this man. I pray for the spirit that is in everything and I carry the joy of my thanks with me in my heart that I may embrace you in the next world.

Hunting Wolf opened his eyes wide, lifted his amulet with a frozen bloody hand and put it between his teeth.

There was a sigh from the darkness, a deep unholy sigh like gas escaping from a corpse.

'Ah! So we are to do battle! The dung-hole chief of shits will at last fight that which he calls nothing!'

It laughed a throaty, delighted rattle and continued laughing as the keeper started the final portion of his ceremony. Outside, in the light, men of flesh and bone and blood howled for Hunting Wolf, and a woman and boy prayed for him.

56

In the dark, the lampshade hanging from the ceiling looked like a face. Billy guessed it was the bulb that made the nose, and the eyes and mouth were just shadows caused by the fringe that hung round the edge. He'd stared at it for a long time now, fighting sleep, and he was still wide awake, listening to the low voices of his mother and the policeman talking downstairs.

The day had been more like a dream than the one he had last night. Except that wasn't a dream. Not really.

They'd stayed in all day, hiding from the men outside with their cameras, Auntie Anne fussing around in a pretend-cheery way, and Billy had tried to make his mother stop crying.

Maybe she would soon. His father was on his way home. He could feel it. He knew it. He needed to be awake to help him if he asked. Because they had to fight the dark thing together. Eagle Robe had said so.

The thought of the dark thing made him close his eyes tight to try and push it out of his head. He couldn't bear the memory of its fingers reaching for him. The dirty, scary fingers that had been wrapped so tightly round his father. He concentrated hard on ordinary things, things that would stop him thinking about the darkness and about . . . Bart.

Too late. From under his tightly shut eyes, tears found their way between the long thick lashes and rolled onto his cheek. Why Bart? His beloved, barking, loyal, handsome Bart. He would never bury his face in that warm fur again. Never run laughing after the big animal as it bounded over the lawn and jumped the fence. He opened his eyes and his little mouth was set in a hard straight line. That dark thing would pay for what it did to Bart. It would pay dearly, and he and his dad would do it together.

Somewhere in his heart Billy Hunt wished he could still be a child. He wanted his dad to come in and tuck the comforter under the edge of the bed like he used to, and tell him those dumb stories about when he played hockey that would make Billy laugh.

But Eagle Robe had told him he needed to be a man now and he knew it was true. His mom had listened and cried again when he told her some of the stuff he'd heard when he walked with Eagle Robe. Not everything of course. She was white. He knew that was different somehow, that it would stop her understanding. It didn't make her better or worse, just different. But this was Kinchuinick business, and Eagle Robe had said she knew some of this stuff in her head but not in her heart. Billy didn't care. Her heart was good to the core, and he loved her so much he just wanted her to stop hurting. So he'd tried to stop that hurt by telling her the truth.

Maybe she hadn't believed it. It must have sounded pretty crazy. But she'd gone all pale and quiet when he talked about the Isksaksin and he thought that maybe she knew he was telling the truth. So what? He loved his mom and dad, and he knew now his dad loved him too. That's all that mattered.

He wiped the tears from his cheek and took a deep breath. Yes, he would be a man for now. The dark thing would be the one to cry next. It would cry plenty.

It was in there, very deep. He probed around in his mind and touched that soft thick area of consciousness that he had forgotten. It was like a layer of peat, that place. Skills and secrets laid down in Sam's head by Calvin over all those years when they prayed and conjured and explored the spirit world together.

And then compressed by Sam, by his guilt, to try and forget. But like peat, it was still there, its energy intact. Now it was time for Sam to dig into it and remember.

He had no choice. It seemed like there were cops everywhere. The brushwood by the rail track was cover for now, but the moment he stepped out onto that wide road that led up towards town, they would see him. He'd watched two patrol cars glide by already and he knew they would be all over town. Sure. They'd see him all right.

How could they not? Sam Hunting Wolf looked like a madman.

His jacket was torn and filthy, and his face was a mass of cuts and grazes from his scramble through a dense piece of birch-scrub in the dark.

Yes, that had been dumb. Running like that from the figure of Marlene that stepped out in front of him between those dark trees. Her eye had hung from its socket, dangling on a sallow sunken cheek, and when she had put a hand out to touch his face and rasped *my baby* at him, he had run. A mistake. But he was ready for its tricks now. He wouldn't run again.

At least under cover of night he'd been able to walk almost the whole way along the tracks, falling to his stomach between the rails when a car on the Trans-Canada briefly lit up the track with its headlights. His detour through the dense pines and back down that wall of rock was not necessary.

But now he was back in Silver and it offered little cover for a six-foot-tall Indian with a bloody face and the clothes of a bum.

Go unseen, Calvin had said, and he knew Sam had the power to do just that, stored somewhere in his dark locker of a brain.

Calvin. Where was he? Sam could barely contemplate the options. He had no time to think about it. He had a task, and the difficulty of that task was the thing that was keeping him sane.

Sam closed his eyes and reached into his mind. The prayer he offered was a chant in his head, a mesmerizing, droning thing that dulled the edges round his conscious mind and pushed him nearer that well of knowledge and piety that he used to draw from unthinkingly as a teenager. Droning on and on and on until his eyes rolled back in his head and his breath came in short, panting bursts. He was numb now, oblivious to the outside world, where the snow fell on his concealed body behind the bushes and the wind howled through the telegraph lines above him. His mind felt sharp, alive, refreshed, and he saw as clearly as though it were yesterday, the way to go unseen.

His eyes rolled back into focus and Sam gave a grunt. Despite the cold, he was sweating. But he knew it would be okay. He was becoming pure again. He felt it. And although part of him kicked and screamed at the thought of what that implied, that he was becoming an Indian again, a Kinchuinick shaman again, he swallowed back his distaste and embraced the cleansing in his heart.

Sam Hunting Wolf stood up, brushed the snow from his torn and ragged jacket, and started to walk towards his home. He walked across the wide street towards the bus depot and the main street that sprawled behind it. There was a driver clearing his wing mirrors of snow outside the depot. Sam walked by. The driver continued his task.

He turned into the main street, full of people as the bars and restaurants closed for the night. Couples ran to snowy cars and groups of young skiers threw snowballs at each other as they waited for one of the fifteen cabs in Silver to pick them up and bundle them back to their hotels; and there were the cops, strolling up the street like they owned it. And every one of the pedestrians, tourists going home, bar owners at doorways taking the air, cops killing time on the sidewalk, walked right past Sam Hunting Wolf as he strode up the street with his eyes fixed on the lights of Oriole Drive that twinkled above the shop-roofs.

And as he walked, Sam saw the street, his own main street, where he shopped with Katie, greeted friends, and looked in the windows of the stores at things they couldn't afford but didn't care, and he knew who he was.

Hunting Wolf.

The Kinchuinick shaman.

The years of self-loathing, of wishing his skin would fall away like a snake's and be as white as Katie's, were such wasted years. Look at these people he had believed were so much better; people so far away from the invisible roots that connected them to this earth they stood on, so sure in their understanding of the world yet understanding nothing. The spirits moved amongst them, touching them with phantom fingers in their grief at being invisible to man, and yet they saw nothing.

Savage. How many times had he heard that word fall from a white man's lips? Hunting Wolf, the shaman, could have wept with joy when he realized that there need no longer be any shame, any horror at the Kinchuinick blood that coursed through his veins. He was no savage amongst civilized white people. It was he, and each one like him, who was civilized.

His concentration was absolute, walking tall in this modern street that was only a dream in the sleep of an earth gone mad. He felt his power come from the earth and the air and the trees that lined the street. And when the snow fell on him, each flake was a whispered prayer, a tiny, perfect piece of the earth's secret that caressed him like a mother, stroking his face, the wind singing to him as it howled through the wires.

It was standing in front of him. But its attempt at Katie was poor. She had a bullet-hole in the centre of her forehead that oozed black blood and was clutching the dead Jess, her delicate brown throat cut open in a red grin, like a sack of rags.

He could see that there was no back to Katie's head, that it had exploded in shattered pieces of bone and brain where the bullet had exited. But there was no bullet. No bloody head.

'Sam!'

It was barely able to keep the illusion of flesh, and as he walked past unmoved the blackness swirled in anger at the shaman's calm demeanour. To be in this state of purity, this continuing prayer that let him go unseen, was to be impervious to its tricks.

The thing that was not Katie slumped against a day-glo poster for Silver Celebrity Ski and the black blood that caked the back of the head smeared the paper like melted chocolate.

Sam Hunting Wolf turned the corner and started up the hill towards home. A house on the corner burst into life as a couple said their farewells to friends and, with a sleepy toddler in their arms, walked down the drive towards their car.

Neither the man or woman noticed the big dark man who passed inches between them on the sidewalk as they put down the little boy and fussed with the baby-seat.

A small fist rubbed tired eyes as the four-year-old child stood on the snowy sidewalk waiting for its transport to take it back to a warm bed. The boy looked up and Sam turned around. He looked straight into Sam's eyes.

'Mommy. Look at the man!'

His mother looked in the direction the small finger was pointing. Sam Hunting Wolf stopped. His heart raced with love for that small white boy, a boy who could see what he should not see. The white man was lost only because he chose to be. The boy would be trained to be blind soon enough, to believe his TV more than his eyes and heart.

'There's no one there, sweetheart. Come on, get in.'

Sam's shoulders tightened. He turned away and, without looking back, walked on. Which is why he never saw the child wave happily at him from the back of the car as he slipped round the corner and walked boldly up his street.

57

Constable Jarvis Strang was playing with the tuning fork that lived in the car glovebox for testing the radar.

'Okay, Eddie. Listen.'

He banged it hard on the dash and put it right up close to his companion's ear, making him whip his head away in irritation. Jarvis chuckled like a kid as Eddie put a finger in his ear and waggled it about.

'Quit that, you asshole!'

Jarvis sighed and stared out the snowy windscreen again at the press cars that sat in Oriole Drive. The occupants would be as bored as they were. Except folk kept bringing them stuff, like coffee and french fries. No one brought the cops anything.

Jarvis sighed again, banged the tuning fork and hummed a harmony to it. The radio crackled. Eddie punched his colleague in the shoulder to shut him up.

'Detachment Two Alpha Eight.'

Eddie pressed *talk*.

'Two Alpha Eight.'

'Can you get Staff Sergeant McGee out of there and back to the detachment? Over.'

'Sure. Now? Over.'

'Yeah. Soon as you can. Over.'

'Will do. Over.'

Eddie reached over to the dash and grabbed his hat. Jarvis opened his door.

'This don't take two of us Jarvis. I'm only going to ring the fucking doorbell.'

'Need the air. My ass is numb.'

The two men got out of the car and crossed the road to the house. In front of the peeling blue door, the shaman, Hunting Wolf, stood watching them as they approached. The men walked either side of him, instinctively giving that three square feet of seemingly empty snow a wide berth, although neither would have noticed that they did or be able to say why. They stamped their feet on the step and rang the bell.

Sam watched them as if in a dream. Policemen, ringing his doorbell again. His state of purity was so intact, he felt no fear standing here beside them. As they waited, both men could smell delicious things. The smell of sweet grass, the delicate scent of wild roses blowing and clover trembling beneath a dew. Spring smells, that had no business wafting on the snow filled air of winter. Neither mentioned it. It was crazy.

There was no reply. While Sam watched, Jarvis rang again, and blew a low meaningful whistle at his partner. 'Looks like Mrs Hunt's being pretty helpful with old Craig's enquiries. Huh?'

Eddie gave a short snort of a laugh. 'Blame him? You seen her?'

Jarvis rang again and this time put his face against the door and hollered. 'Mrs Hunt! Police here. Not the press. Please open the door.'

Eddie smiled at his partner, and said in a stage whisper, 'And do up the buttons on your pants first, Craig.'

They sniggered, stopping abruptly when the door was opened by Katie.

And as they explained their quest, no one noticed the shaman walk up the steps between them and into the house.

She shut the door on the men and turned around. Sam's heart beat in his throat. That face. She had been crying, but the puffiness around her eyes just made her more beautiful, made him want to grab her face and kiss away the redness, to hold her and feel the warmth of her sweet, earnest face against his chest.

Those men, they had done something to his state of purity when they had laughed like that. Sam was confused. He felt his power diminished. What was it? Doubt? How could he doubt Katie, with her messy blonde hair and brilliant blue eyes, and those lips, pink and slightly ragged from the cold. He wanted to kiss them so badly. Katie raised her head slightly, as if she could smell something on the air. She looked around the lobby, her eyes lighting up with love as though she had glimpsed something precious. For a moment, Sam very nearly spoke her name.

But he had a task. And as she stood with her back to the front door, Sam moved towards the stairs. He stopped at the bottom as he saw Craig McGee come out of the lounge. Katie's expression of dreamy ecstasy faded. 'They need you back at the detachment.'

He nodded, putting his hat on and making for the door. Katie looked at his face and put a hand out to his arm as he reached for the handle behind her. 'Are you okay, Craig?'

Sam held his breath. Craig? Since when was his wife calling this policeman by his first name?

McGee looked at his feet and shrugged. His face had lost all colour. It was the grey mask of an ill man. Haunted, tired and fighting an internal battle for his reason. He looked up at her and tried to smile. 'Guess so.'

Katie kept her hand on his arm, and for a moment she knew how sore his heart must be. How lonely and sad and lost he was. She leaned across and kissed him. Craig McGee looked at her without expression, opened the door and left.

The feeling was like a numb leg coming back to life. Sam felt his blood return to his nerves, and the heady concentration that was keeping the prayer alive, keeping the pulse of his spirit pure, drained from him like it was being sucked by a pump. A woman and a man could do to the shaman what the Trickster with all his grisly visions could not.

They had broken his faith in himself. Broken the prayer with their betrayal.

Katie raised her head, looked across at the stair and her mouth made an O. She pressed herself back against the closed door again, this time with her arms across her chest.

'Sam.'

He looked at her coldly, turned and walked up the stairs.

It was under the bed where he'd left it. Nothing more than a piece of circular bone on a leather thong. Sam picked it up and held it in his palm for a moment, his eyes closed against the pain of what he had seen. There was no time for this. He must return. Must regain his cleanliness. The squalid stench of betrayal and vengeance would taint him as much as the guilt he had harboured for twenty years.

Calvin had removed that guilt and made him pure again, made him an Indian once more. This new nightmare must not pull him back into the material, spiritual desert of the white man. There, he would be powerless. In that place he was no more than a poor Indian who shovelled snow. Not a shaman who could command it.

He slipped the amulet over his head and walked quickly out of the room into Jess's bedroom. He had to see his children. Maybe for the last time.

Her head was on its side in her cot, the mouth open and her closed eyes almost hidden by a mop of black hair. Sam bent and kissed her fat cheek, paused to look at the tiny face for a moment, then left the room. Katie was on the landing, staring up at him.

She was so beautiful, and her face was so confused and wounded, he struggled to curb his longing for her. He looked away and stepped into Billy's room, closing the door behind him like a statement.

The boy's eyes glittered in the dark. Sam put a hand out and switched on the lamp.

'Dad.'

He ran forward and wrapped himself round Sam's sore body, his head buried in the torn plaid jacket, the arms circling his father so tightly Sam had to fight for breath.

Sam unravelled him, bent down to take his son's face in his hands and kissed him slowly on the forehead.

'I felt you coming.'

Sam nodded.

'I felt you watching.'

'Are you going away again?'

Sam nodded again. Billy looked serious, and Sam raised an eyebrow at the old expression that came into his son's eyes. Suddenly there was an adult in there.

'There's two cops out there at the back. Behind the log pile. I'll get them to come round the front when you're ready.'

Sam held the boy close again. 'I love you Billy. I love you all.'

'I know, dad.' The boy pulled out of his father's arms and crossed to his bedside cabinet. He opened the door, fished something out and brought it back across the room. 'This is for you.'

Sam opened his big palm and watched as Billy dropped a flat saucer of shiny metal into it.

'Queen of Queens. The biggest ever. Remember when we did it?'

Sam nodded, swallowing. He looked back up from the flat dollar into the jewels of his son's eyes.

'You must take care of them both. You understand?'

Billy nodded, that grown-up in his eyes returning. Sam slipped the dollar into his pocket and stood up. Billy pulled on his sneakers and looked across at his dad once more.

'Mom still loves you. I told her everything.'

Sam looked at him and lowered his head. Billy looked uncomprehendingly at the sorrow on his father's face for a moment, then opened the door and left. Sam heard him thump down the stairs past Katie with a few boyish words of explanation, then watched as her figure slid into view, standing in the doorframe.

'Sam. Speak to me.'

She breathed rather than spoke his name, and he stood by the window gazing at her, longing to speak to her and hold her. But he could not risk the questions he might ask, nor bear the answers if they were not the ones he had to hear. His power was his purity of heart, and already he had broken his prayer to go unseen. He would have to return to Calvin by his wits, not with the powers of a shaman. There was no time to pray again, to chant and prepare. She had broken him. For now.

He looked at her for a long time, and when the screaming that Billy started at the front of the house sent the two cops at the back running round to assist, Sam lifted the window and flung his legs over the sill. He looked back at his wife, frozen in the doorway as if she were in a dream.

'I love you more than my life,' he said, dropped ten feet into the thick snow, and slipped away into the night.

Craig McGee blinked at the windscreen, trying to keep his aching eyes open as he turned out of Oriole and into Lynx. Everything would change, he had said to Katie. It had. Except that he knew somewhere deep in his heart, that it had always been like this. Nothing had changed at all. The only change was that he was admitting it was true.

He had thought when that first shard of belief wedged in his soul that the policeman in him died. But it hadn't. The reverse was true. It was the policeman who listened to what Billy had told Katie and knew that there were too many answers to the impossible questions in that tale to be ignored. Bizarre answers, but answers nevertheless. Everything the boy said had a kind of deadly logic. It was the police-man in him who knew that Sam hadn't killed his dog. The boy's outrageous explanation of what happened answered the riddle so neatly, linking those animals at the murders in the way he knew something would, only a fool would refuse to give it brain-time.

And yet . . .

Where did it get him? Fast lane to the nut house? What now? Was he driving back to the detachment to tell Becker that they should be hunting down a malicious spirit as old as the earth? One that was going to destroy them all unless Sam Hunt sacrificed himself?

He stopped the car, watching the snowflakes settle on the glass between the intermittent wiper sweep.

What was his part in all this madness? He leaned his head forward and touched the wheel with a hot forehead.

Sylvia. The fucking thing had abused the memory of Sylvia. He hated it then, a hatred deeper than his grief. He pulled his head up and concentrated on that hate, pushing his fear aside with the intensity of the emotion. Because under all this stuff there was a pit of fear so profound he dared not peer over into its abyss.

The wiper-blades swept an arc across the snow-dusted windscreen, and in that two-second gap, Craig McGee saw him.

Sam Hunt. Running across Lynx Drive and heading for the railroad.

The tracks were easy to follow. Sam was a big guy. He left big, deep footprints. As soon as the tracks hit the railroad line, Craig hardly needed to look at his feet. The footprints ran straight up the centre of the rails, heading for the Corkscrew Tunnel. Craig slowed his pace, panting with the effort of wading through deep snow. He wasn't going to lose Sam now. The dark holes in the snow his boots had left would take hours to fill up again, even in this storm. Craig hung back and took his time.

So he'd been hiding in the tunnel? Neat idea. Hardly any freight came through at night. Anyone in Silver knew that. Knew that the trains mostly stopped at the bunkhouse in Stoke first, then pulled out at dawn. Smart.

The perfect refuge from Becker and his useless posse.

But the thought of that tunnel made Craig's spine crawl. That thing again. The thing in his brain he'd spent a lifetime ignoring. It had gone off like an alarm last week when they'd gone to collect the bits of the ski patrol boys who blew themselves up above the tunnels. Craig had walked down to where the landslide had partially blocked the entrance, just out of curiosity and to get a breather from the carnage, and he'd wanted to run. Very fast and very far away.

The tunnel was like a mouth. A great yawning, hungry mouth. Craig had stared up at the icicles hanging from the roughly-hewn arch and been repulsed by how much they looked like teeth. He had shivered and returned to his men, leaving the tunnel to drip and echo on its own.

Now Sam Hunt was running towards it. Craig sat on his fear again and walked slowly and silently between the tracks.

Twenty feet behind him a tiny chipmunk, torn violently from its winter slumber, walked equally slowly and even more silently.

He could feel the bone circle pressing against his collarbone. His sweat was making it slide around just as it always had, and Sam clenched his fists, resisting the urge to put his hand in his jacket and rip it from his neck. What if Calvin had gone? What then?

He staggered on through the snow. Headlights lit the sky and he fell to his face between the rails, waiting for the car or truck, or whatever it was crawling through the snow along the Trans-Canada, to roll past and leave him alone. He lay with his face against the stinging cold of the snow and, for a moment, opened his mind again and let the peace that was in those tiny crystals seep into his sore heart. They were part of him, those intricately designed flakes with their points and stars and diamonds. And he was part of them, his spirit remembering that the moisture that made up most of his flesh might once have fallen as a snowflake, perhaps right here or far away in a different part of the world. Maybe the flake that was once flesh had moved in a great ocean, just as the substance of his bones was once the earth the pines grew from. There was purity in that knowledge, and it had kept the Kinchuinicks strong and pious and full of magic for centuries, until the white man came with his corruption and blindness.

He felt the light from the road sweep over him and he stayed on the ground for a few moments, listening to the imagined voices of the snowflakes as he lay there. His prayer was short and fast but it thanked them for their beauty and their coldness and promised them life when it was their turn again to be part of an animal with warm blood and a beating heart. An old Kinchuinick prayer.

He lifted his head and got to his feet, sweeping the snow from his jacket. There was a figure up ahead. Something writhing on the tracks only yards ahead.

Sam swallowed, bracing himself, and walked on.

No. Not a figure. Two figures. Two naked figures having vigorous sex. Sam's throat was dry as he approached what he knew would be Katie, lying on her back in the snow grunting in pleasure as the man on top drove into her.

They both looked up at him as he passed. Craig McGee had something bloody in his mouth, and he spat it out to speak to Sam.

'Goes up her ass after we've done here, pal.'

Sam tried not to look, but it was impossible to avert his eyes from the horror, and in the half-light that a hidden moon behind storm clouds afforded he could see everything. Katie's chest was ripped open, and the beating heart that had been in McGee's mouth pulsed in the snow beside them. She threw her head back and laughed.

'At least he's white, you Indian shit. He fucks like a man!'

Sam panted through clenched teeth for a moment, willing himself to walk on, then he put his head back and bellowed. He closed his eyes and punched the air. 'You bastard! You evil fucking bastard!'

He gasped for a moment, swallowing back the bile that had risen in his throat, and when he opened his eyes there was nothing in the snow at all. Sam spun round to see if there was more. New tableaux for his amusement. Nothing.

But a voice in his head said quietly and seductively,

'Then destroy me, scum.'

Sam dug his nails into the palms of his hands and walked on, fighting back his rage, while far behind him Craig McGee heard the shout in the muffled night air and quickened his pace.

The tunnel mouth was ahead. The steep bank that ran up to its right was black with pines, darkening the white strip of track with their gloomy bulk. Sam staggered on towards that deep black arch.

'Calvin?'

His shout was sucked into the night and ignored. Sam's breath clouded out in front of him, and his heart became so heavy he felt it beating in his stomach.

'CALVIN!'

Nothing.

Sam took a few more faltering steps toward the archway. His foot kicked something in the snow. He stooped and dug into the soft white blanket. His hand met cold, hard leather and he closed his fingers round the object and lifted it. Calvin's medicine bundle.

The young shaman dropped to his knees with the pouch held out in front of him like an offering. His voice was a croak.

'God. No. No.'

That would be too much. To lose someone, find them again, then have them taken away once more. The bitter cold of loneliness blew in his soul and he bent his head to weep, and the snow he had prayed for fell on his head like a betrayal.

Then a noise made him look up. There was a small staccato crack from the tunnel mouth. Sam held his breath and struggled to his feet. With that breath still held prisoner in bursting lungs he walked a few more paces forward until he could see the arch full-on. There was a faint orange glow from that black hole. A fire. A fire cracking with life in the heart of the blackness. Sam let go a huge gasp of air, nearly laughing in his joy. He ran forward, slipping and stumbling as he went, and skidded into the tunnel mouth.

Behind the flames, against the wall, the old shaman sat staring into the fire, not looking up when Sam made his boisterous entrance. Sam cared little about the coolness of his reception. Calvin was here. Alive.

The old man spoke quietly, in ancient Cree.

'You fetched the Isksaksin?'

Sam fought to regain his breath, holding his hands to the flames. 'Yes.'

'Then let us use it. Now.'

Sam spoke in Cree too. This time as a mark of respect as much as anything. 'But I must prepare. I am not pure yet.'

The figure on the other side of the flames lowered his head further. 'You are pure.'

Sam wiped his eyes with a hand. He was so very tired. 'No, Calvin. I am still full of hate.'

The old man shifted on his crossed legs, bowing his head wearily to the flames. 'This is what you must understand, Sam. The hate in your breast does not kill your purity. It is a righteous hate. There was treachery waiting for you at home was there not?'

Sam closed his eyes and remained silent. 'Then you must give that hatred life. Think of it. Feel it. Make yourself pure by remembering the corruption of it. That is what will make you strong to fight this monster.'

Sam opened his eyes, confused and aching from the memory of seeing his family. 'I understand nothing, Calvin. The years you taught me, I learned nothing. I believed my purity would be an absence of hate, a love of myself and all living things.' He rubbed his aching eyes again and bowed his head in a gesture that was almost defeat. 'You confuse me, Soaring Eagle.'

The old man's voice grew urgent, almost angry. 'I came to give you the truth, Hunting Wolf, and that truth is that you must hate the Trickster as you hate yourself. And hate yourself, you must. You killed your father. What man could love himself who has taken the life of the one who gave him life? And you should hate your wife. She has stolen your love. Hate hate hate. That is the trick. Now use the Isksaksin. Quickly. Do not prepare.'

The flames between them flared, almost as if they echoed Calvin's sudden anger. Sam wrestled with the old man's ugly words, words that sounded so alien on the shaman's tongue. Calvin's power was of love. Now he was here to help Sam hate. He reeled from it, as he sat staring into the orange dancing flames.

The flames that were so bright.

The flames that were giving no heat at all.

His eyes slowly lifted to the figure opposite and as he did so the heatless flames seemed to grow higher, stopping him from seeing Calvin's face. Sam eyes's travelled down the old shaman's body. The wool jacket, the cord trousers, the Timberland boots. Calvin's jacket was open, just as it was when he went to fetch wood, and from the thick leather belt around his waist, Sam could see the medicine bundle hanging. The image of this same bundle that he held in his hand now, on the other side of this pretence of a fire.

He wailed and leapt to his feet, and the height let him look directly down into the face that had been talking to him. Whorls of blackness curled behind the image of that brown lined face, and the darkness behind the eyes was deeper and more profane than any it had revealed before. It started to laugh. That filthy noise again, touching the inside of his head like a rapist stroking a tethered thigh.

Sam gaped for a moment, defiled and violated by its trickery, then ran from the tunnel, gasping in the freezing air, his eyes swivelling in the dimly snow-lit night, searching in between those dark tree-trunks for what he dared not see.

And there it was, between the trees. No more than a dark man-sized mound on the light snow that had dusted the areas under the lodgepole pines.

Sam walked forward and stepped from the white track into the gloom of the trees. Calvin's face was twisted and grotesque, frozen in a contortion of agony, and the bloody penis that hung from his dead lips was almost comical, like a joke cigar. Sam turned away, the blood draining from his head threatening to make him swoon.

He had slept.

Sam had slept by the fire and now Calvin was dead.

He knelt down by the mutilated corpse and touched the old shaman's face lightly.

'Fly in the sunlight Soaring Eagle. The Grandfathers await you.'

Sam unfurled Calvin's good hand, clenched in a claw of pain, and placed the medicine bundle there. He bent and kissed the tortured face of his shaman tutor, then stood and walked towards the tunnel to make his preparations. It would take many hours. He must begin.

As Sam entered the dark arch, the snow outside stopped for a moment as a high wind blew a small parting in the clouds. For half a minute the moon shone onto the snow-covered landscape, bathing it in blue light like the ghost of daylight. Then the clouds reunited and the flakes began to spill again.

In amongst them, unseen by any living thing, riding the air with the same delicate grace as its white companions, a small eagle feather fell to earth like a tear.

58

'Margaret?'

The voice on the end of line confirmed it was indeed Margaret.

'I need your help. I know you've just opened up, but can I bring Jess into the museum for a few hours, ask you to look after her?'

Katie was twisting the flex of the phone round her wrist, in a unconscious physical imitation of the twisting stress that was winding round her guts. She nodded at whatever the voice was saying, and then replied.

'Yeah. There is something wrong. Billy's gone.'

She pulled the door closed behind her with a foot hooked round the edge. Both arms were occupied holding Jess and everything Jess would need. The hounds were on her before she got to the bottom step.

'Mrs Hunt. How do you feel about the police looking for your husband . . .'

'Mrs Hunt . . . over here please . . .'

The whirr of cameras.

'Mrs Hunt. Has your husband been in touch at all . . .'

The two cops who'd watched with their big arms folded over their big chests stepped forward at last. 'Okay, guys. Let the lady through. You can't obstruct the highway.'

She hurried to the car, fumbling for her keys. The cop strolled behind and stood beside her. 'We have to know where you're going, Mrs Hunt.'

She looked at him with distaste, Jess copying her mother but stretching a chubby fist out to the man as though she held something in her fingers he might want.

'Am I under arrest?'

'Well . . . no, but . . .'

'Then if you want to know where I'm going, earn your pay. Follow me.'

Mercifully, she located the car keys, opened the creaky old door of the Toyota and bundled Jess in. As Katie drove off, the blue car that sat outside all night stayed where it was, and a patrol car waiting round the block did as she suggested, earning their pay.

'Well, are we ready to shred?'

Pasqual made a camp-leader punching movement in the air with both fists and looked at Del Parkinson for response. He was sitting at the table by the window, still eating his hash browns and eggs. The weather was so bad that the lake in front of the Chateau was barely visible in the thick sheet of snow. Still, Del Parkinson wasn't that keen to get out of his robe, change into a dumb ski-suit and go ski with morons. Things were looking up since Pasqual had knocked on his room door.

'Have some toast. Come on. Sit down.'

'Hey, I'd kill for breakfast, but I got nearly a hundred people out there waiting for me to tell them when to eat, shit and breathe.' She shrugged, as if the power was a burden she accepted like a duty. Del looked at her and opened his legs a little, letting the white towelling robe slip back from his thighs. His thin legs were loose-skinned and baggy, but still brown from a ten-day commercial shoot in Miami.

Pasqual noted the action and felt uncomfortable. Her voice was half a pitch higher when she spoke. 'And boy are they all keen to see you down there.'

He looked out of the window again. 'Any of the news boys going to be there today?'

'I guess. I guess.' She nodded vigorously. 'But I think they're staking out Sam Hunt's house right now, pretty much. You know, waiting for the big arrest.'

In other words, no. This whole fucking trip was a waste of time. Who cared about the fucking useless cripples or whatever it was this shit was in aid of. He needed publicity, and it didn't look like he was going to get it. Del decided to get the next best thing.

'Then I think you and I should just relax for a while. Get a bit more friendly.'

She looked at him coldly, the camp leader gone. 'Come on Del. Play the game.'

'Sure. I'll come downstairs and play any game you want. You just need to play some with me. How's that sound?'

It sounded nightmarish. She looked at this horrible old man, a brown stick-figure in his expensive hotel robe, and thought fast. Was he useful? Yeah, he was really useful. He was famous for Christ's sake, what could be more useful than that?

Would it be so terrible? No. She'd done worse for less reason. Would she make him pay for it? Yeah. And some. The possibilities for emotional, and possibly even some career-orientated manipulation, were endless and juicy.

Pasqual Weaver looked at him some more, then walked to the bed, sat down and took off her boots.

'Oooh. My poppet! Come here and let your Auntie Margaret eat you up!'

Jess did that oscillation in the air with her arms and legs that meant she was pretty pleased about a whole lot of stuff. Margaret took her in her arms and looked at Katie.

'You told the police?'

Katie shook her head.

'Why?'

'I want to find him myself. I don't need any more press guys chasing my tail, looking for headlines.'

Jess wriggled and moaned.

'Come on then poppet. Let's go look at the train. Huh? You like that?'

Margaret looked at the mother of her burden. 'She loves that train. Will we take her upstairs?'

'Sure.'

The women and the baby climbed the creaking wooden stairs to the balcony, Katie lost in her white-hot thoughts, searching through endless mental files to imagine where her son might have run to.

Margaret chatted, grinning at Jess as if the words were meant for her.

'I only opened because of the Celebrity Ski you know. Remember how many we got last time? Dozens. That's how many. Even sold nine copies of *Indian Tribes of the Rockies*.'

They stopped by the glass cased model of the Corkscrew Tunnel and Margaret leaned forward to the big red button. 'Okay, sweetheart. Do you want to press the button for Auntie Margaret and make the train go?'

Jess looked down at the model that without fail had always made her scream with delight, then looked silently and solemnly up at her mother. She opened her little mouth into a great big mouth and started to bawl.

Margaret made a mock face of friendly surprise and, holding Jess close, looked over the little girl's shoulder at Katie. Her boss looked crumpled, defeated, old. Margaret hitched the wailing Jess higher in her arms and spoke in that kind, soft voice she used for children, this time for Katie.

'Let me take her down to the office and give her some toasty fingers. You need some space.'

Katie didn't respond, but watched gratefully as Margaret walked carefully down the stairs again with the screaming child and disappeared into the back room where she kept her cherished kettle and toaster.

Nothing was the same. Even Jess didn't like the train any more. Katie was too tired for tears.

She knew Billy had gone after Sam, but where was Sam?

Katie crouched down beside the model and pushed the red button absent-mindedly. The tiny train started its shuddering journey over the spiralling track, in and out of the hollows cut in the papier-mâché mountain. There was the front of the train pushing its way out of the upper tunnel, and there was the end of the train looking like it was going the other way.

She thought of Billy and his dollars, that dumb game he and Sam played every minute they had, dogging off domestic chores to spend hours sitting by that railroad.

She would have given anything in the world at that point just to see the two of them again, stepping into the kitchen, ruddy-cheeked and guilty, those big shiny saucers in their hands like trophies. Anything. Just to have things the way they were.

The train came round one more time and stopped. Katie punched the button again, and watched it make the same journey in reverse, shaking up towards those ludicrously long tunnels that so fascinated her husband and son, and until today at least, her daughter.

The tunnels.

Long dark tunnels.

Tunnels that could shelter and hide someone.

By the time the model had completed its second journey of the day, and came to a halt at the top of the papier-mâché mountain, there was no one there to clap their hands in delight and press the button to make it do it again. Because there was no one there at all.

59

Dawn brought sanity. Or was it madness? Craig wasn't sure any more. He was frozen and numb, but his vigil outside that yawning mouth of darkness had been impossible to break. Sam's chanting had been going on for hours. Stopping sporadically, and just when Craig thought about stepping through that black mouth and checking his quarry hadn't fled through the tunnel and off into the night, it would start again. So he'd sat and waited, listening and watching.

And of course Sylvia had come back.

It was getting easier to bear. The trick was to look as if you hadn't seen. That seemed to make it angry, and for that small victory he was grateful. After the fourth or fifth time, he forgot which, he didn't look, respond or reply. He just let the thing do its sick and perverted business with the image of his dead wife, while he bit the insides of his cheeks until they became ulcerated and bloody.

And then there was dawn, that thin grey light that started to sketch in detail where there had been only rough form. He thought at first that it was another trick, but he was intrigued at its change of plan. The mound was obviously a body, but it didn't look as if it was going to be Sylvia's.

Craig McGee had walked very slowly over to the trees and waited to see if the horror would rise up to greet him. But there was no black thing moving behind this mound of dead flesh. No clouds of oily depravity. This was what it seemed to be. A dead man, an Indian, mutilated in a way he was nauseatingly familiar with.

Craig looked away, out over the tops of the pines, to where he knew the mountains were hiding behind the misty snow clouds, and he felt his reason cracking down the middle like ice.

Sam Hunt. One call on the radio he carried but had switched off and they would be here. They would come and they would have all the goddamn proof they needed to lock away Mr Sam Hunting Wolf, the most notorious serial-killer Canada had ever boasted.

Here was the body. There was the killer. Here was the policeman.

So why was he standing alone outside this tunnel, listening to a crazy man chanting his dirge?

Craig turned and walked towards the tunnel mouth, his fear a hard, hot nugget in his chest. He stopped at the entrance, looking up at those teeth of ice that hung like threats from the rock. He should end this. The knowledge could be locked away again. He could become a sane man, searching for ski-thieves and drunks, drinking coffee with hotel managers and having dinner with tour operators. He was in Hell, but he had the power in that black radio to get himself back to Purgatory at least. Craig put a hand to his shoulder and touched the black plastic box. He fingered the switch and looked deep into the blackness.

There was a singing noise. High and sweet, the metal tracks vibrating with it. And the chanting had stopped. He stared into the gloom and when the single round light that had begun as a small thing became a big thing, his body took the initiative from his dazed mind, and sprinted out of the way.

The train took a long long time to pass, and while it did Craig McGee waited dumbly, hugging his resolve to his breast, waiting to call his men and end this insanity.

It was the only way. He was mad. Mad to see what he was seeing, to believe what he believed. He knew that now. He would simply keep that madness a secret, the way he had always kept it a secret.

The train was ninety-seven boxes long, and when it had snaked away, leaving Craig in a snowy silence, the radio also remained silent.

Because as the last car of coal swept away, in its wake the mangled body of Sylvia McGee twisted and tumbled on the tracks, making the snow bloody with the progress of her tattered remains.

Getting past those cops had been easy. Billy had slipped out of the bathroom window and scrambled along the porch roof. No one could see you up there, and better, you could reach the drooping mid-branches of the big pine that hung over the wood-pile. Billy had grabbed hold of one and swung himself over the fence, dropping softly down into the neighbours' yard, followed only by a quiet thump of shaken snow as the branch bounced back up. Piece of cake. He was off through the back yards of Oriole and out into the next street without anyone seeing a thing.

Although he had been scared, he had also been exhilarated. The wolf hadn't told him his dad was heading back to the Corkscrew Tunnel. He just kind of knew it when he'd put that coin into his hand.

At that moment in the bedroom, he'd suddenly smelled diesel fumes and that metallic musty smell that wafts out of a tunnel after a train has just passed through. He knew his dad was thinking about where he had to go back to. So Billy was going too.

He knew the way by road. Sort of. Mom had driven him and Jess up there to the viewing platform plenty of times in the summer. But it was miles and miles by road. It would be quicker just following the rail tracks out of town. That way you went right through the middle of the forest instead of skirting way round it.

But now in the middle of that dark black forest, with the dawn just creeping into the snow laden sky, all the exhilaration was gone. Billy was just scared.

There were animals or birds rustling from time to time in the thick deadfall and he knew he was being watched by eyes that were not human. But it was something worse than that. He could feel the dark thing near by. It felt different though. Almost like it was just a bit of the dark thing, instead of the whole monstrous mass he'd seen inside his father that night. It was as if the dark thing had split into bits, like it needed to be in lots of places at once.

The bit that was near him felt much weaker, much smaller, than when it was one thing. But it was still frightening him.

And as the light grew stronger and his fear increased, it did what he feared the most.

The air around his head seemed to shift, as though a door in a room had been opened, and as Billy stopped walking, staring into the gloom with glistening unblinking eyes, something in front of him on the tracks started to appear.

Like mist rising off the river, it was spiralling up from the snow. But it was black filthy mist, and it seemed like it was trying to look like his father. Billy's heart stood still as the curls of black badness tried to cover themselves with a layer of flesh. Trying to look like a human. It was horrible. Bits of a face floated over the clouds of moving blackness, then arms tried to appear, the hand reaching threateningly for Billy. His father's face very nearly came together in one tiny glimpse, mouthing something angrily at him, but it broke up again, the way smoke parts and regroups when a fast car drives through.

He had closed his eyes then and remembered what Eagle Robe told him.

I see nothing because you are nothing, he'd said in a shaky voice. And when his eyes opened again there was only the faintest trace of badness left, wisping between the snowflakes like smoke.

Billy exhaled through his teeth and pulled his fleece jacket tighter around him. He'd been roasting in it only minutes ago from the march along these endless tracks, even though its bobbly fleece was coated in a thick layer of sticky snow. Now, he was freezing.

Still, it hadn't been as bad as Eagle Robe had said. He had said it would look like his worst dreams come true and he might be fooled. Who would be fooled by that black misty thing?

Maybe, he mused, it was making someone, somewhere else, believe in it. Showing someone else their worst dreams come true. Billy closed his eyes for a second and prayed with all his heart that the someone would know it wasn't real.

He took a deep breath, opened his eyes and ploughed on through the snow towards his dad.

60

Alberta 1907
Siding Twenty-three

She walked slowly between the deep ruts in the snow that the dragged poles were making. The horse that pulled their belongings, a few pots and skins cradled in the stretched tipi hides, left piles of orange-brown droppings in its wake that steamed gently in the cold air.

Singing Tree stepped carefully over one then looked up at the jagged peaks that were searingly white against the blue sky.

The snow had stopped. It fell in great heavy thumps from the branches as the silent line of Kinchuinicks passed, loosened from its hold by the sun, and brought down finally by the brush of a shoulder against a low branch or a hoof snapping a concealed dry root.

Singing Tree could see an eagle circling below one of the peaks. It was a dark shape from below, its wingtips open like the fingers of a hand. But when it turned and caught the air again to soar its feathers glinted in the brilliant sunshine like a fish in a river flipping over with a silver wink.

Was it him? She stopped for a second and watched the bird, until it disappeared behind a tower of rock. She lowered her head and walked on.

Singing Tree thought then that perhaps the Great Spirit had created love as a punishment. The pain that it could inflict was unrivalled by any other. He was gone, and her heart felt as if it had grown claws and was tearing its way out of her breast.

Claws.

Tearing their way . . .

She flinched, longing to dampen her thoughts as she dampened the fire.

But it should be remembered. The worst of it. It had to be. If they were to forget, to keep the darkness of the events in a silent place in their hearts, then they would forget for the future too. Her face became hard and old, as she squinted into the middle distance. Remembering.

The white men. How they shouted and gestured and wanted her husband's blood. But they would not go into the hole they had made in the mountain. They stood instead at a distance from the entrance while the chief of them spoke and made wide sweeping movements with his hands. She had held Walks Alone tightly to her breast, for she had been afraid for him as much as for Hunting Wolf.

And then there had been the first scream. They had backed away like children from a wild dog, looking at the tunnel in the rock as though it were a mouth that would devour them.

He had broken free from her. A slippery weasel writhing from her grasp.

Of course she had run after him.

Her son had disappeared into the hole in the rock without any of the white men stopping him, even though she screamed at them to hold him. They knew the sense of the words she screamed: it was not that they did not know her tongue, it was that they despised it, as they despised her and her boy along with it. She could see it on their faces, as they stood aside and let a mere boy of nine summers run to the scream as though he were pulled on a string.

So she had followed him. And she had seen it. Seen it all.

What had her beloved become? It was impossible to reason at such a sight, and even though she had given herself up to remembrance, it was already dream-like.

The battle had been so awesome, so repugnant and sickening in its violence that she could barely remain conscious. But through the unimaginable horror, the mother in her had seen the more immediate danger. The rock was alive. It was quaking and it was falling and Walks Alone was running towards that sight that she could not behold. He would surely die under that rock, but she was too far to stop him.

And then the miracle.

The man Henderson.

A movement from a pile of rubble had alerted her to the injured man.

It had looked as though he had been stabbed in the chest and his broken frame was a hideous sight. He had raised his head and opened a mouth that was dribbling blood as a baby dribbles saliva. But he was alive. The action she saw was so slow, so elegant in its execution, that she had been frozen to the ground, an intruder spectating on another's nightmare.

Walks Alone was running to the thing. The thing that was so terrible and yet seemed to be familiar.

And the rock was falling in huge boulders. A thin white arm shot out like a lizard's tongue and grabbed the boy by the ankle. He had fallen forward, so slowly it seemed to Singing Tree, his hands above his head, and as he did so Walks Alone had opened the mouth that had been empty of sound and screamed, 'FATHER!'

She had watched in horror as his head hit the ground and he had lain still. Her feet that had grown roots had been released and she ran to him like a cougar would run to its young.

As she had cradled his bleeding head, the rock in this white man's cave was falling on the things that could not be beheld, and the fearsome noise had seemed to her as if all the world was ending. She had bent her head in stark terror, praying to the Thunder Spirit to deliver them from this dark chaos, when the man Henderson had started to crawl towards the mayhem. He had gasped through gritted teeth at the effort of moving, blood oozing through the fingers of the hand that clutched at his blackened breast.

She had not stopped him. The shame was still a hot iron in her. She was cradling her son, and she did not stop the man who had saved him.

She had looked up only in time to see his fate. The thing that was a claw, ripping and tearing and rending his flesh. And the screaming, that hungry venomous wailing that chilled the heart enough to make it stop. No animal had ever made such a noise. She had not known whether it came from man or beast.

Then the rock had fallen. It fell on the abomination, and the man Henderson had made a lunge towards something in the chaos before throwing his torn body back away from the avalanche of stone.

Singing Tree had howled from the torment of that noise and the screaming of the things that were trapped.

The dust had been thick, like smoke. She had coughed and spat, cradling Walks Alone to her body to keep him from inhaling the thick, acrid dust. And when she had been able to see and breathe again, both of the nightmares were gone. Lost beneath the mountain that had closed on its secrets again. But the white man's upper body had been still visible, his lower half buried beneath the rock. His hand was clenched tightly, and from a ripped and mutilated face he had been croaking at her.

Singing Tree had stared like a simpleton for what seemed an age, then gently laid her unconscious son's head down and stepped cautiously through the rubble towards the dying man.

She had knelt at his head and gently placed the bloody mess on her leg. Singing Tree had bathed his face before. Now there was no face to bathe. Part of a nose and a mouth, but hardly a face.

He had been trying to speak. She had bent her head to hear.

Her tongue. A dying man speaking in her tongue.

He had tried to smile with the words, not seeing, as both eyes were hanging and torn on the things that had been cheeks.

'James . . . Jamesss . . .'

She had held his head more gently, listening.

'James goes Eden. Eden. Begin again, like Adam.'

She had tried to soothe him, made noises as she would to a baby. He died with his last word as though it were a prayer.

'Eden.'

Then she had let down his head and stood up. His fist had been clenched and from it there had peeked a piece of leather thong. She had bent down again and opened his fingers.

It was Hunting Wolf's amulet.

But the thing . . .

The thing he had lunged at . . .

She had picked it up and held the bloody circle to her heart. Then she had walked to her son, lifted him in her arms and gone outside.

Singing Tree shivered as she walked in silence. The sun was not warming her. Since they had broken camp at dawn this morning, she had looked constantly behind her, waiting for the men who would run behind and bring them down with guns.

But they would not come after them now. Even with so many dead white men. What she had seen outside the tunnel had been just as beyond explanation as what she had seen inside. The Kinchuinicks would go back to the reserve and they would not follow. She felt it.

The white man needed things he could see and touch to deliver his justice, and what could they see or touch to make sense of the things that happened to their kind in that hole in the mountain?

She walked on with her head higher, but her heart still aching from his loss. If only he had known that she believed in him. That she was shamed by her betrayal.

Then he ran to her. Eden James Hunting Wolf.

'I saw an eagle, mother.'

She nodded, reaching out for him.

It was right to rename him. He was new. Saved by the thin white man who had tried to save her husband too. He spoke again. And he would be the keeper. Eden James wore his father's Isksaksin.

Singing Tree wrapped the boy in her arms and put her face in his hair. They held each other for a moment then walked on with the solemn party of their people.

The eagle they had seen flew high above them, watching the dark line of figures and horses moving east, as closely as it watched the hare hopping in the blue-shadowed snow.

61

'WHY?'

Fists clenched, head thrown back on his neck, eyes rolled inside his skull. Sam Hunting Wolf was naked, on his knees in the gravel of the tunnel, and as the agony of his shout returned to him, bouncing off the rock like a taunt, the clouds of vapour from his mouth died on the freezing air.

Feathers brushed his sweating brow. The soft feathers of a forgiving eagle guide. One that had been denied for more than two decades, and even now was still being resisted. He unclenched the fingers of his hands and clawed wildly at the empty air as if to ward off an insect, then fell forward with a grunt, his rigid arms holding him off the rocky tunnel floor.

He vomited once again as he crouched and remained still, panting, waiting for the nausea to pass.

'Lap up your hot sick, Kinchuinick. Fitting food for a pig.'

He stayed still, his eyes open now, staring at the undulations of the gloomy floor described by the daylight from the arched entrance. Gruffly into the rock-strewn ground, Sam spoke a question to himself.

'What did we do to make you hate like this?'

The laugh again, then a music-hall imitation of Sam's own voice. 'You breathed in and out.'

The laugh became manic in its filthy raucous rasping, and bile rose in Sam's throat again. He closed his eyes, fought it off, and pulled himself upright. He turned and slumped against the tunnel wall, oblivious to the sharp rock grazing his naked body, and as his eyes rolled back in a fevered head once more, Eden was back with him.

It was a state of bliss. Sam sought it and opposed it at the same

547

time. It was not a place he wanted to be, this land of spirits, that was reached only when the mind was clear and pure and the soul was that of a shaman. And yet who could resist this velvety, seductive haven?

They were together in a sweet meadow, as they had been a few moments ago before Sam had cried out in anger at the eagle's demands. He was young and straight and handsome, this Eden. Dressed in his robes with the sun glinting behind his head.

'He hates because he is hate. Do not converse with him.'

Sam felt the warm sun heat his frozen body. The sun darkened for a second as the great bird circled again, throwing its majestic shadow over Sam's upturned face.

He squinted up at the sky then back at the shining figure of Eden. 'If I cannot converse how can I understand his nature to battle with him. To trick him as you say I must?'

Eden tilted his head slightly. 'Tell me, Hunting Wolf. Tell me who you are.'

Sam frowned. 'I am Sam Hunting Wolf.'

'Your happiness lies where?'

Sam frowned again. 'In my wife and my children.'

'As it should. But in your ancestors, your elders? In your blood?'

'No. Not there.'

'Why not, my grandson?'

Sam moved his warm shoulders and felt the grass at his ankles stroke the skin of his legs. When he spoke in this place it was as though his words were spun from his mouth like strands of sugar. The speaker could see them, watch them form, and yet he knew somehow that there was no sound. It was easy for those words to come directly, being spoken before they were censored. Here, there could be no duplicity. No lies. Here the truth was that which was written on the heart.

'I despise it. White men are right to despise us. Look at the legacy you've left, Grandfather.'

Eden did not reply. There was a flap of wings above from the great bird.

'Are you proud of a people who sit on their tiny pockets of token land, laughed at and reviled by the men who took the great plains and the mountains from them? Killing themselves and dooming their sad children to a life of despair. Why did you not fight? You and all

your elders? Were you so foolish you couldn't see that the concessions
you won were in fact victories for the white man? He loves the Indian
dying on his reserve, a rural prison where the Indian is his own jailer,
a prison that keeps the white man's child from playing with the Indian
child. A sweetly wicked device to keep the Indian away from the
things that could be his, and should be his. To make him think he's
different, that he wants a cabin instead of a home, a horse instead of
a truck, a drink instead of a job.

'I believe the Trickster, Grandfather. It is not he who is nothing.
It is we who are nothing.'

The sun darkened again. The eagle circled as though it had been
listening, and then soared. Eden lifted his face to the bird and then
looked back at Sam.

'Then we are truly lost.'

Sam bent his head, ashamed. His heart was heavy with sorrow.
Eden stretched out his hand and lifted his grandson's chin. The touch
was like a feather brushing lightly against skin.

'That is the hurt child who spoke is it not, Hunting Wolf?'

Sam blinked at him.

'Now let me speak to the man.'

'You're speaking to the man.'

'No. The child is the one full of dark anger. Of hate for himself
and his people. But the man is a pure thing. The man has led his life
in the light. We have watched him, and he is strong and pure and
good. And his life is full of love where there was none for the child.
He has patched the holes in his heart where many would have made
them bigger. This love is your inheritance, Sam Hunting Wolf. It is
what you pass to your children and it is more precious and lasting
than any land or horse or house.

'We have kept what the white man could not take from us. We
know how the earth lives. They tell us with science what the raindrop
is made of. We know in the hearts of our shamans what the raindrop
knows, where it has been and where its spirit lies when it twinkles in
the sun and harbours its rainbow.

'To forget our knowledge, to lose that great love of all that is alive
is when we become nothing. Now look at me, Grandson and tell me
that you have forgotten your shaman's knowledge.'

Sam's eyes were moist. He looked into the face of his grandfather's
spirit and swallowed.

'I have not forgotten.'

'What does the raindrop know?'

Sam looked up at the black, circling silhouette of his rejected guide and swallowed. 'That it falls from a sky it is part of, onto a flower that it is part of, into the ground it is part of, to feed the fruit it is part of, that feeds the man it was part of long ago before it fell.'

'And?'

'It knows it will be a raindrop again as a man knows he will be a man again.'

'And are your children, your wife, as nothing, like the Trickster says?'

'No. They are everything.'

'And you?'

'I see my face in the raindrop. I am something.'

Eden sighed. There was a flap of wings. The eagle Sam could never quite see was so close.

'Listen now, my grandson. For you can stay no longer. You know I have nothing to tell you of the Isksaksin other than that you must have a pure heart to use it or you will be devoured. I know only what I saw, and that is not enough to know what the truth may be. For the truth is different for each shaman who becomes the boundary line. He calls only that which his heart can bear. But I may tell you of the Trickster.'

The sun was growing cooler. Eden was right. He knew this state would not last for long. Sam listened to Eden's beautiful voice, although the words made no sound that ears would recognize.

'He once had a face that he saw in the raindrop too. He was cunning and vain but he ran on the earth and moved in the heavens with other spirits of his kind before men came, before the mountains were finished and the seas had gone from the plains.

'And when man first came he played with them as a child would play with a new-born kitten. Sometimes roughly, cruelly, sometimes with affection, but always with curiosity and astonishment. But then the kitten became a cat and man grew wise to his games. He was played with by them. They knew him and they delighted in using his other-world skills for their own amusement. The shamans amongst them learned to shape-shift from him. They learned to move things with their mind and transport themselves to the moon and the stars with their spirits as he could. They could see what he could see, both into the future and into the past, and he grew more vindictive and more angry as they toyed with his powers and tricked him for their amusement.

'And his anger grew until he became a thing of great evil. Then men died trying to curb his dark, vengeful violence. Until Pitah Annes, the greatest of all shamans called him and tricked him into telling of the others that walked the earth with him before man came. The others that were more powerful, darker, less interested in man and his company, except as lowly conductors of dark forces. And Pitah Annes heard in the Trickster's heart that he was as afraid of these dark ones as man had become afraid of the Trickster.

'That is the lesson of life. The trick. Do you hear it? The others. The darker ones.'

Sam nodded, though uncomprehending. Eden continued, his voice growing urgent as though time were running out.

'The Isksaksin is from the skull of Pitah Annes, the shaman who tricked him away into his dark prison. But the Trickster has waited an eternity to realize his ambition. He wishes the earth to be free of men again. To be empty and violent with molten mountains, and storms that shake the earth, and floods that cover those boiling mountains. So that when the Great Spirit weeps for his creations, and makes man again as he must, the Trickster will not be fooled again. He will not let his kitten become a cat a second time. He means to destroy everything.

'You, my grandson, are the descendant of Pitah Annes, as am I, as was your father, as is your son. The Trickster hates you, and all of mankind more than he loves himself. Man has copied that hatred, too, without knowing it. Man does his will without the knowledge of it.'

Sam was panting now, sweating, as he realized he was losing a grip on this world of sweet grass and sunshine. He reached out to Eden.

'What is it I call with the Isksaksin? Eden! What do I call?'

The image of his grandfather was fading, and the sun was losing its warmth. He was beginning to see his breath once more and the light was turning to dark.

'Eden!'

Sam's head snapped back, bashing his skull against the rock and drawing blood beneath his matted hair.

Back in the tunnel.

The daylight was bright now. It had been many hours since dawn and there was no more time. He stood up and stroked the rock that had struck his head with affectionate hands.

A trickle of blood ran down the back of Sam's neck as he walked to the centre of the rail tracks, put the Isksaksin between his teeth, closed his eyes and raised his powerful arms above his head.

'Okay everyone. The course this morning is giant slalom.'

Baz used his best instructor's voice for this crowd of rich bozos, raising it above the clanking of the old Wolf chairlift that was moving slowly along above them on its frozen cable.

This was a dumb place to have a race, this little-used trail, but the weather had made them retreat round to this side of the mountain where there was at least no chance of avalanche. Desperate measures, and he could see Eric Sindon was as unhappy as he was.

He hated celebrity skis. Always an accident as some asshole tried to ski close to the celebs, and he always scraped it up.

The patrol had been working since just after dawn to try and make the area safer, fencing off anything that could lead to these jerks disappearing into litigation valley.

'You have to keep inside those orange snow-fences whatever happens. If you don't, you're gonna end up sliding down there, over some rocks you can't see from here, right down onto the railroad line. And who wants to come home from a ski trip with a leg broken by a freight train, huh? Tell that to your boss back in the office.'

A sour bald man looked at him. 'We are the bosses, kid. Get on with the bullshit.'

Baz bit his bottom lip briefly, managed a weak smile and continued.

From the trestle table where the contestants were bibbing up, Pasqual shifted uneasily. She was sore. He was a fucking disgusting animal. But he would pay. Oh shit, he would pay.

She'd laid famous guys before and enjoyed the kudos the gossiping ski bums gave her by spreading it round town. But this was ugly. This time it had grossed her out.

She watched Del putting his bib on with a comic flapping of his arms while the rich old gekkos crowded round him trying to help him out, and she hated him.

Enjoy, she thought. I'll get you back, buster. In ways you couldn't even imagine.

* * *

She drove carefully away from the museum letting the Crown Vic follow all the way to the busy junction of Campbell and Hector Avenue. Then she did that thing that she'd seen in a movie once. She sat at a green with cars pumping their horns, and when it changed to red she shot the light and sped off down Hector towards the four-way junction, leaving the squad car to negotiate the confusion of angry oncoming traffic. They'd be after her now for sure. But she'd lost them. Katie drove the Toyota into the cul de sac behind the lumber yard, where big trees and a high brick wall hid all the parking as if they were designed to. She got out without even taking the keys and abandoned it. No one would see it from the street and unless the cops suddenly needed masonry paint or loft insulation they weren't going to find it in a hurry.

It was only one block to Gerry and Anne's and she walked it in case anyone checked out she was running.

Saturday. Thank God it was Saturday. Anne opened the door still wearing her robe.

'Don't ask anything. Just lend me your car. Please.'

Without speaking Anne disappeared inside and brought out the keys. She handed them to Katie, and as her hand touched her friend's, she held it. 'You want help?'

Katie shook her head. She blinked back a tear, retrieved her hand and kissed Anne on the cheek. 'This is help. You haven't seen me.'

Anne nodded, and stood watching in the cold doorway right up until Katie threw the GMC Jimmy into drive and was way out of view. She passed a patrol car on the edge of town, but the driver didn't give her a glance. He was talking into the radio. Talking, she guessed, about an eight-year-old beat-up blue Toyota.

The viewing platform. That was the best place to get down to the tunnels. You could climb over the fence, scramble through the trees and get onto the track. But there were two tunnels. Long and dark. Katie would face that when she got there, right now she had to drive.

There had been no fear like it in his life. Not even at the hospital, seeing Sylvia the way he had. Once, a guy they'd cornered had levelled a shotgun at him and stroked his finger on the trigger. The thing that had happened in his guts then, that metallic taste of adrenalin in his mouth, the tightening of his neck, none of it was like this. It had taken him hours to find the courage, and now, at the moment he'd decided to step into the tunnel mouth, he knew what fear really was.

He could hear Hunt, but he couldn't see him yet. The curve on the tunnel meant there was only ever light from one end at a time. Craig McGee had now walked away from that light. It was a cave, a long, dark, dripping, terrifying cave. And above the eerie noise of Sam Hunt's nasal chanting, that echoed like a priest's droning in a cathedral, there was that moving air that was soundless and yet screamingly, terrifyingly loud at the same time.

Craig stood inside the entrance, waiting for his eyes to adjust, and when they did, he was sorry to have been blessed with sight.

They were words that had been stored in his heart. They were chiselled into his brain, and to read them was like running a finger over braille. Solid words. Words that had dimension as well as sound. Words that were not of this time or any time man should know. They were more than vowels and consonants, pauses and breaths. They flitted like scurrying things from his tongue and the earth shifted as they tumbled out.

And Sam knew. He knew so much as he spoke them. The Isksaksin had to be held between the teeth to pronounce these living words. They were not sounds the human mouth made in its normal function. Gritted teeth, aching jaw. It was all part of the knowledge that Pitah Annes had learned. He had spoken the words but knew that his descendants would lose the skill. It was he who decreed they should fashion the bone from his skull into this tool for talking when he breathed no more to make the sounds. It was he who carved these words onto the hearts of his descendants.

But he was not able to tell those descendants what these words would bring. Sam Hunt paused before the last word and hissed a breath through his gritted teeth. Then he spoke it.

It fell from his parted lips like a gravestone toppling.

The shaman opened his eyes and looked ahead. The Trickster was in his blond-trapper skin, smiling, ice-blue eyes full of that dark, swirling anticipation.

Waiting.

Waiting to give solidity to its unclean, corrupt hate.

And Sam Hunting Wolf waited, his heart a machine that was going to burst its casing.

Then he felt it coming.

From the pit of his stomach he felt a growth. It was a rapid sensation of being coated from the inside with something so thick and dark and hot that by the time he opened his mouth to scream, letting the amulet drop to his chest, it was growing in his head and had silenced his mouth with its searing viscous presence.

Then the darkness came upon him and he felt that hiss of ecstasy from the Trickster when it knew its power was returning, its fuel from the spirit of this shaman: the power to grow into its hideous and unholy self. The power to slash and rip and kill.

But as the darkness took him and the power flowed from his mind towards the thing that was already changing before him, Sam realized that this time he was still conscious. Still able to see and hear. The thing that was him, Sam Hunting Wolf, his spirit, his spark of life, was aware and alive in a bubble of thought within his own soul.

He felt calm and at peace as the fuel that the monster needed seeped from him.

And then, in that peace, he saw what was coming. Felt what was happening to this body he had all but departed.

The Trickster was growing in size, its form defining itself. That swirling darkness was becoming brittle and solid, forming itself into the grotesque, deformed killer that it had decided to be so many centuries before. Gaping black jaws slavered a sticky bile from beneath a snarling snout that was pitted and diseased with crawling black vermin. Its body was almost formless, a hunched mass of shining black segments, shifting and oozing as they moved with the power of the dark, angry motor that drove them.

All the demons that man had drawn and painted and feared were found in this form. It was a composite of terror, a patchwork of fear. A totem that was alive.

Its huge razor-talons sliced into its own dark flesh as it flexed them, and a black and green slime trickled from the wounds, followed by glistening worms that fell onto the rocky floor and writhed with life of their own, opening and closing round mouths that were dark circles of needle-sharp teeth.

The Trickster stretched and arched in its pleasure at finding form, and an icy sheath that was growing over the black, putrid skin crackled as it moved.

But Sam felt that other thing coming. It was splitting his body. The cells that made up his tight brown flesh were rebelling, both

555

against their owner and nature itself. For he was changing in size. He saw it in minute detail, each precious cell bursting and growing, doubling and doubling again, until the thing that was Sam Hunting Wolf was nothing like Sam Hunting Wolf. Nothing like a man at all.

But in this place, this bubble whose membrane was no more than his concentration, he could see things, understand things. Was this the pure place that he had worked so hard to make?

For he saw now what was coming, and it was something so dark and so ancient that it could have no name in the tongue of man. Its fuel was not from Sam. He knew that. And he understood why Moses had perished. It had fed on his father, for its fuel was the evil of man.

It was the darkness in all men's hearts made flesh, and it was feeding now. The Trickster was writhing, waiting for it to feed on its host. But its tendrils were stretching out around it.

Above the tunnel, only a few hundred metres from the source of this great darkness, was all the fuel it needed.

It pulled that black energy towards it, sucking it in, making the earth tremble as its power grew with each dark force it sucked from a mortal.

There was the thought from Pasqual Weaver's head. It was murderous. It was cutting a man's penis off, making him scream, suffer, watching the agony on his face. The fantasy of the thick blood, the stench of his death. It sucked the thought in and grew.

There was the man she was dreaming of, thinking about how he would like to come in a dead woman's anus. How would that feel? The pleasure. The dark, delicious evil of it. Make the bitch suffer first. Make her know it was going to happen. Watch her.

Growing. Growing.

The man just there was cradling the thought of torturing his wife with the knowledge of how he would hurt their son. How he made the terrified young man take his punches, made him bleed in front of her, her precious faggot boy, make him beg for his money and his mercy. Tell the cow exactly why her son wasn't ever coming home if he left. Make her weep. How the money he gave the wretch, the money that paid for their pool and their ski trips and their third house in France, came from selling arms, so that Arabs could blast the balls off each other's stinking asses.

Sucked it in. Growing ever bigger.

That woman. Here came her thought about the cripples she was skiing for. How she hated them. She wanted them killed. She was repulsed by their twisted limbs and their ugly faces, and she wanted them crushed and pulverized so they would never get in her face again. Some had children. It was too much.

Tear their babies from their wombs, these ugly monsters. She would ski until she dropped if only she could stop them living, stop them breeding. Kill kill kill them all.

Such a delicious, nourishing thought. Fuelling the darkness like gas on a barbecue.

And as the thing that was Sam grew with every thought, the energy was making the body strong. It was growing its own talons, its own huge jaws, a body that was so distorted a thing as to be almost a molten liquid. And Sam knew that the thing he had become was bigger, stronger, darker and more malevolent than the Trickster. It was an evil without purpose. Elemental and wild. No vengeance, no motive or malicious intention. A deviant purity that was so deep and black it bordered on white.

The Trickster was afraid. Sam could sense it. There was a vapour of fear from its foul bulk, and the essence of Sam Hunting Wolf rejoiced in the creature's uncertainty. It writhed and crackled in discomfort before the darker force, but it was not about to flee. It waited.

And Sam knew what it was waiting for, and he prayed inside his bubble of a soul. Prayed for the strength that would stop its trick.

It started with a tremble, and then Baz saw that it was more. The snow was undulating. Like a white sheet with snakes trapped below it, it was moving and writhing and squirming up the slope towards the crowd at a speed he could barely follow.

He stood like a fool, unable to shout or speak or move.

But what could he have shouted? There were no words to describe what he was seeing. His brain tried to understand, but it was beyond a ski-patroller.

And even before his instinct kicked in, the shapes in the ground had reached them, and the earth was beginning to shake like a gold-prospector's sieve.

The screaming started at once. From the pylon icicles began to fall and as he watched a woman looking up at the shaking wire was speared through the eye, falling to the ground as a jet of blood spurted from the burst white globe.

The snow was opening below them like mouths. But this was no quake. There were forms in the snow. Snaking forms that were ripping the earth open and shaking the rock to the core. The chairs on the cable were starting to bounce and swing and as he stood immobile with terror in the chaos, a pylon creaked and fell in a lazy arc like a pine being felled.

Four people took it, splitting the head of one man like a soft fruit, the other three crushed in a tangle of limbs and metal resembling a child's puzzle. But the chairs that held screaming passengers plummeted to the ground in a less complex mess of broken limbs and smashed bodies. It was easy to tell human from steel. Bones protruded from the shiny material of cheerful ski-suits, and the snow was host to the blackness of their occupants' blood.

From the snaking white ground a boulder burst through and split like a loaf, its huge weight dragging across the bodies of two fallen figures as gravity tried to pull it back into the splitting earth. Baz could just make out the ripped, screaming face of Del Parkinson as it was pounded and mashed by the rock. Rock that seemed to have more life than the momentum of a quake would grant.

It was almost comical the way the ground was swallowing up the skiers. Arms held high as they fell in to the crack made by . . . those snaking things. What the fuck were those snaking things?

He was a spectator. Pasqual moved almost in slow motion, but then everything had slowed down to dream-pace to Baz, and he watched his screaming boss turn and try and run uphill. The shapes beneath the ground heaved and twisted and she stumbled, panting into a crevice. The gap opened and closed like a mouth and her leg was snapped from its thigh with a thick sound.

As she screamed, a deep and bellowing wail that was from the pit of her stomach rather than her throat, Baz opened his mouth and vomited. He straightened up, and without a command from his conscious mind his skis started off to the left of the moving earth, crashing him through the orange barricade to the safety of the unpisted slopes.

It hissed through those ice teeth and knew its tricks had arrived. They were here, standing there in the tunnel mouth, just as his audience had been the last time. How easy man was to play. Then it hesitated for a moment. What had happened the last time?

The diseased mind struggled to recall the failure.

It had failed. But why? Why? The shits, the stinking shits and the whore were here. They were always here. It was all in place. The swirl of malice cancelled its own doubt and began its campaign.

Sam was a sack of sorrow in his bubble. His soul shed tears for the evil that was flooding into the space he had made with his magic. But he was strong. He was pure. There was only love in his heart.

And then it spoke to him.

'Your new family are here, Kinchuinick. See? The white man gets everything the white man wants.'

The words came from the depth of the thing's filthy black body. The thing that was no longer Sam halted its feeding as if it had been given a signal. He looked with the eyes of his spirit to the place the monster was indicating with its thoughts and he saw them.

Standing in the tunnel mouth, the light making them silhouettes against the frenzied snow.

Katie. Billy. The policeman. The white policeman.

He was holding Sam's wife by the shoulders and the boy was between them.

There was a sickly, torturous twist in a part of him he had been unaware of. Like the deep internal agony of a cancer. Impossible to locate, impossible to escape from its searing agony. It was his thick bubble starting to tear. He felt a dark shard of hate enter his world of love. It was cutting at him, slicing at him, making that space in his soul the thing he had become needed.

And he wanted to die then. To let go of this tenuous life and float away into oblivion where this stench of horror would be powerless to sicken him further.

The voice of the Trickster was a knife turning in his pain.

'Her house, not your house. Her son, now his son. You, who are nothing and nobody. A stinking shit of an Indian who kills like a madman and whom she hates as an enemy. She fucks him. And she fucks him and thinks of how she would like to see you die.'

The spiritual membrane that was holding the shaman in his body was tearing again. Sam wailed in his agony and spun in a dark circle of failure. It was over. There was no trick to be played on this nightmare. The trick was on him. He was a human sacrifice. That was the reason that no Kinchuinick knew the secret of the Isksaksin. Who would be the keeper in the knowledge that to be called upon meant certain death?

559

The line. The boundary. He was the line the Trickster needed to cross into this world. He knew what he had done. The thing that he had called. It had opened him like a box, made that space ready to occupy. That bubble. That was where the Trickster needed to be. In his soul. It meant to possess him. And then . . . then the world would see what vengeance meant when the hatred of centuries found flesh.

And the hatred was eating his soul.

He stretched his soul and moved the body that was now his. It lashed out at the monster before him, flaying the black flesh of the Trickster with a ragged claw. Pus and bile flowed from the wound, but the abomination opened its slavering jaws and laughed.

He shifted his great flanks and slashed at it again. More laughter.

And then the holes in his great shining scaly head that passed for ears heard the voice. His son's voice. The tiny figure stumbling blindly towards the two foul creatures that filled the tunnel. That voice. He could hear it the way one tasted something delicate, something exquisite.

'Dad. Listen to the eagle! The eagle!'

A voice from a dream. Then the talons of the Trickster flexed open with a pleasurable crackling and readied themselves to slash at that young, pure flesh.

Craig McGee acted faster than he had ever acted in his life. He threw himself after the boy, and as his hand connected with the back of Billy's jacket, the whole weight of the man came down on the boy's tiny frame.

From the tunnel mouth, Katie Hunting Wolf let go the howl that had been frozen in her throat since she saw the things her eyes would not relay to her screaming brain.

The eagle. Listen to the eagle.

Sam shifted in his torn bubble of self, and listened.

The beating of wings. A wind of truth blowing into his mind. There was only love there in the tunnel mouth where the Trickster saw hate. He was flying. He was a bird and he could see from a great height.

It was simple. He was a shaman. He could fly with the eagle. And those who flew with the eagle could see not just the mice in the fields, but the secrets of the human heart. Billy knew. He ran with his spirit, saw what it would have him see. Now Sam must look with his bird's eye. He was above them, and he could see their hearts.

Katie was faithful. Her soul was crying for her husband, for the doubts she had had, for the man she wanted so badly, whom she loved over all things. Craig McGee was tortured and honourable, a man with love that had no place to settle, a white shaman who denied his power, who struggled to be blind, to shut out his light. And Billy. Billy was his saviour. Billy was a Kinchuinick Indian.

And with his wings outstretched, Sam saw the trick.

The rock was trembling. The whole tunnel shaking and rumbling. McGee scooped the boy up and ran for the entrance.

The shaman faced the Trickster as his descendants had and knew there was a way. Had they been short of that love? Had they been full of doubt when they faced this thing? That was why they had been sacrificed. They had been abandoned by those they loved, and he had not. Love was the saviour. Love made the man pure. Gentleness made him stronger than a fiend. Absence of guilt made him impenetrable.

Slowly he looked into that demon face and started to open the bubble of his soul. The Trickster hissed and shifted and Sam felt its unclean blackness swirl towards him in triumph. Entering him. Eating into him. It licked around the edges of his mind, savouring the humanity it was flowing into. And Sam felt giddy in his spirit state as the rush of dark increased.

It was talking now. To itself. Not to him. He, after all, was almost it. 'Yes. Yes. The Trickster has tricked man again. I am Sitconski. I am Inktomni, I am Inktumni, I am Inktomi, I am who I wish to be.'

Sam waited, enduring the violation for a moment more.

'They will see. They will see what becomes of them.'

Now!

The shaman drew all his energy and love and shifted in his soul, moving the dark powerful being he had called. He spoke with the last shreds of his power that were fading from him as the Trickster gained more and more of his substance.

'We are no one now. You and I.'

It shuddered. There was hesitation in its motion.

'I am Sitconski.'

'No. You are no one. For I am no one. I leave, and I leave behind nothing.'

There was a sharp lance of rancour in the stream of corruption, and the dark swirled in fury.

Sam's mind was clouding. He must retain the power of prayer.

Must keep conscious in this unreal state of unconsciousness.

'You die, vermin. I become someone. I become you.'

'And when I die I leave you nothing. Except that which I have called. This is what I am. Will you become that? Will it welcome you? Allow you to command it? When I depart, it commands. It has beaten you to my soul, you nothing, you nobody. You cannot even possess that which you are invited into.'

There was a roar and a screaming, and the black fury that was the Trickster spiralled in its confusion. The darker thing that was in Sam moved in its own foul excitement, ready to take what the Trickster was hesitating to control.

As the two fiendish powers struggled with the morsel of this man's soul, one aching for the flesh to control, the other merely for the flesh and soul to devour, Sam Hunting Wolf found the last of his energy to speak his final prayer.

The core that contained his soul closed and expelled the fiend from him like a bullet. And as the shrieking and roaring of the foiled beast filled the tunnel, Sam spoke the rest of the prayer to expel that which he had called. It bellowed in agony as it struggled to retain a hold on its host. And in its frenzy it reached out to take more fuel.

The trick. The big trick.

The shaman would not be the meal.

There was so much fuel. A great dark well of evil from which it could drink. The Trickster was an endless feast of dark energy. It screamed as Sam's prayer continued to shrug it from him, screamed as its cells began to revert to the cells of a man, and the darker more powerful thing that was losing its host lashed out its tendrils and drew its sustenance from the Trickster before it.

It could have no hold on the earth. The man was too powerful. The walls tumbled around them as it began to enter, to devour its weaker dark cousin.

The Trickster screamed. More in fury than in pain. And as a numb Craig McGee watched, hiding the faces of his two companions against his breast, the thing that Sam Hunt had become shimmered and moved and glided like mist into the body of the demonic form that cowered against the shaking wall.

Sam Hunting Wolf stood naked in front of the horror, unable to move, his regained body a slashed and ruined mess.

He was still muttering the prayer, the simple one Calvin had taught him, though never knowing its purpose. It was the most simple prayer he ever taught Sam: a small prayer of thanks for the wind and the sun and the earth and the flower. It was a prayer that sealed his place on earth by rejoicing in it in all its forms, making him impenetrable and strong again with love. It was the prayer that would condemn this nightmare to a fight for its own soul with the dark one Sam had called, until the greater darkness sucked it dry and left it cancelled and powerless beneath the rock. Powerless until it could grow again. For grow again it would.

But then.

Then they would be ready once more.

A boulder the size of a car tumbled from the breaking walls and fell feet from the shaman. He continued to mouth the words.

Two huge cracks appeared above the writhing black beast.

McGee let go his two cowering charges and ran for the man. He stumbled and fell, picking himself up and scrambling along the rubble towards him. Rocks fell on him and he shielded his head with an arm.

'Sam!'

The shaman muttered on.

He lunged forward and grabbed the Kinchuinick by the wrist. With all his strength McGee pulled at the big man and wrestled him backwards towards the light. The tunnel was caving in with increasing force. As Craig pulled the muttering man free into the light, only he and Sam saw the huge section of wall fall that split the misshapen head of that bellowing horror and buried its screaming blackness beneath a mountain of living rock.

The naked man collapsed in his arms, and as Craig held him, with Katie and Billy sobbing at his back, the tunnel closed like a mouth and swallowed up its secret.

She held him, three coats wrapped around his bleeding body, and her head was bent, sobbing into the thick fleece of Billy's jacket that was lovingly, if ineffectively, laid over Sam's chest.

It was Craig who noticed it: their breath swirling around their faces, invisible breath turned to visible mist by the magician cold, was being expelled by only three mouths.

'Katie. Lay him flat. Quick.'

*   *   *

High. So incredibly high. From here he could see the whole Wolf River Valley. The snow was stopping. The last lonely flakes were leaving their mother cloud and spiralling down to earth.

He watched them fall towards the flashing blue-and-red lights that were moving along the highway. He watched them fall around the blades of the choppers that were hovering like bugs over the tunnel.

And he saw them fall on the four tiny figures, huddled in the centre of those straight, black lines that cut through the white snow so far below on the earth.

It was so very far away. Up here, where the sun was emerging from behind the retreating storm clouds, it was warm and fresh and beautiful. The peaks of the Rockies were endless. They stretched before him like waves on a stormy lake, their white and blue points casting shadows and painting gullies. Rivers and lakes sparkled in the light, and the world lay beneath him like an offering created for his approval, poured into a mould and made anew for his eyes. His eagle eyes.

Hunting Wolf.

Eden's voice. From somewhere. Somewhere in the sun, too bright for him to see.

Hunting Wolf. Hear me.

Sam stretched a mind that was already lazy with the warmth, dazzled by the light. He tipped his wings and circled, trying to see Eden. The sun blazed at him and he failed. His world was growing brighter, the details of the beautiful earth below him becoming more difficult to see.

Eden. I hear you. He spoke in his mind, knowing the voice that addressed him was also not one that had sound.

You part from the earth, my grandson. Is that what you wish?

The sun. So warm. So bright.

Do I Eden? Where am I going?

There was a breath of wind in his wings. It lifted him like a hand below his breast.

When we leave this earth, leave behind this fragile living dream from which we strive never to awake, neither you or I can know where we head.

Sam blinked in the light, his heart growing suddenly heavy at his grandfather's words.

Am I dying Grandfather?

There was another gust beneath his feathers, colder this time. He became aware that his body had weight.

Eden's voice was distant now, and it sighed on the air like the breeze, making Sam cock his feathered head to catch his words.

You were born Indian. You will die Indian.

Sam breathed in the cold air, now losing its warmth as he circled faster and faster, though he could not tell if he flew towards the sun or towards the earth.

It was so bright. There were faces in the sunlight. The face of a woman, her eyes full of love, and two children laughing and smiling.

There was a beating on his chest. A punching. Something so heavy, so hard striking him on his heart. Again and again and again.

Born Indian. He would die Indian. Yes he would.

He would die Indian.

The eagle, its wings burning in the sun, tipped its great span and dived.

62

'Four minutes. I guess four minutes.'

The man looked towards the distant tunnel. A neat concrete arch.

The small head had bobbed up from the rail to which its ear had been applied, and the child ran back to its father with rosy cheeks and swinging black hair.

The trains' new route made them appear faster than they had in the past, cutting a minute or so off their entrance into Silver from the time they first entered the re-designed upper tunnels.

'Get back then.'

The child obeyed and they waited until the singing rails gave way to the thudding of an engine and hundreds of tons of metal rolled slowly over two dollars.

It took longer than they thought, and the man sat with his big hands dangling over his knees while the train got on with its unpatriotic job of vandalizing coins. This was a big train. But the man and child could wait. They liked to wait.

Billy Hunting Wolf turned the flat shiny saucer over in his gloved hand. It caught the sunlight and lit his face from below.

He looked down at his daughter marvelling at her trophy.

'Do I win, sweetheart?'

The child looked up at her father with an unusually solemn expression, eyes black coals of serious love. 'I guess so.'

'Then I give you mine. You win it for knowing more about trains.' He held out his coin.

Her brown, oval face lit up and she threw herself at him and wrapped her arms round his big neck. When she spoke, it was rapidly, in a high, excited voice, as if there was little time to speak.

'Can I show it to Granddad and Grandmom when we get to the reserve and say it was mine?'

Billy nodded.

'Sure. Of course it's yours. Doesn't matter who put it on the rail, does it?'

She shook her head in glee, then thanked him solemnly in Siouan and ran off towards the truck.

He loved Smiles At Life so much that sometimes he wanted just to sit and look at her, watch her elegant movements and childlike concentration unobserved. But when he and his wife travelled to Redhorn to see Sam and Katie tonight, he was going to have to fight for her attention. They would be waiting on the porch soon as they heard the truck struggle up that snow-clogged dirt track. Probably before they heard it. The Long Bull family in the cabin right at the edge of the Redhorn reserve who waved at Billy, Lou and Smiles At Life every time they came or went, must phone Sam and Katie to tell them they had company. At least that's what Billy figured. The Hunting Wolfs sure knew when their family were approaching anyhow. And the moment they pulled up and that tiny girl ran to her grandparents it would all be over for Billy and Lou. There would be no competition. Sam would scoop her up and that would be it.

Billy stood up and brushed the snow from his trousers, and a sudden wind coming from the mountains assisted, chilling him as it whipped round him.

He looked towards the mountain above the darkening tunnel mouth, its violet peak cutting the sky like a broken blade, and shivered in the message of its wind.

Billy closed his eyes and spoke the prayer in Cree that his father had taught him.

'Great Spirit, I thank you for this wind on my face. The wind that was once upon the sea, that was once the rain, that once watered the flower, that was once the soil, that was once the earth that nourished me. I see you in the sky and in my child and I pray you keep my heart as pure as your love of me.'

He opened eyes that were brimming with tears, looked once more towards Wolf Mountain, and with a slow tread walked back to the pick-up truck and started the engine.